OTTOMAN

'Think, in this batter'd Caravanserai
Whose Portals are alternate Night and Day,
How Sultan after Sultan with his Pomp
Abode his destin'd Hour, and went his way.'
        Omar Khayyam
        (translated by Edward Fitzgerald)

OTTOMAN

Alan Savage

Macdonald

A *Macdonald* Book

First published in Great Britain in 1990 by
Macdonald & Co (Publishers) Ltd
London & Sydney
Copyright © Alan Savage, 1990

Reproduced, printed and bound in Great Britain by
BPCC Hazell Books
Aylesbury, Bucks, England
Member of BPCC Ltd.

British Library Cataloguing in Publication Data
Savage, Alan
  Ottoman.
  I. Title.
  823.914
ISBN 0 356 19125 7

Macdonald & Co (Publishers) Ltd
Orbit House
1 New Fetter Lane
London EC4A 1AR

A member of Maxwell Macmillan Pergamon Publishing Corporation

CONTENTS

BOOK THE FOURTH   THE FULL CIRCLE

The Hawkwood Family

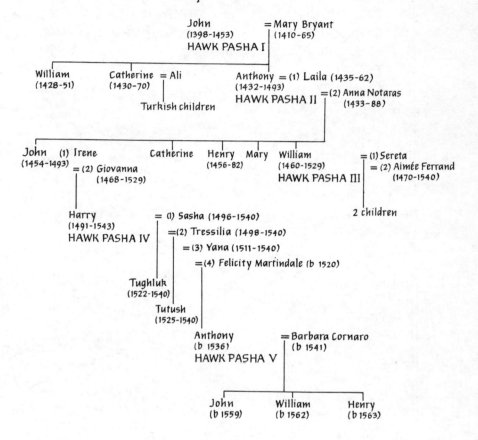

John (1398-1453) HAWK PASHA I = Mary Bryant (1410-65)

William (1428-51)

Catherine (1430-70) = Ali
Turkish children

Anthony (1432-1493) HAWK PASHA II = (1) Laila (1435-62)
= (2) Anna Notaras (1433-88)

John (1454-1493) (1) Irene
= (2) Giovanna (1468-1529)

Catherine

Henry (1456-82)

Mary

William (1460-1529) HAWK PASHA III
= (1) Sereta
= (2) Aimée Ferrand (1470-1540)

2 children

Harry (1491-1543) HAWK PASHA IV
= (1) Sasha (1496-1540)
= (2) Tressilia (1498-1540)
= (3) Yana (1511-1540)
= (4) Felicity Martindale (b 1520)

Tughluk (1522-1540)

Tutush (1525-1540)

Anthony (b 1536) HAWK PASHA V = Barbara Cornaro (b 1541)

John (b 1559)

William (b 1562)

Henry (b 1563)

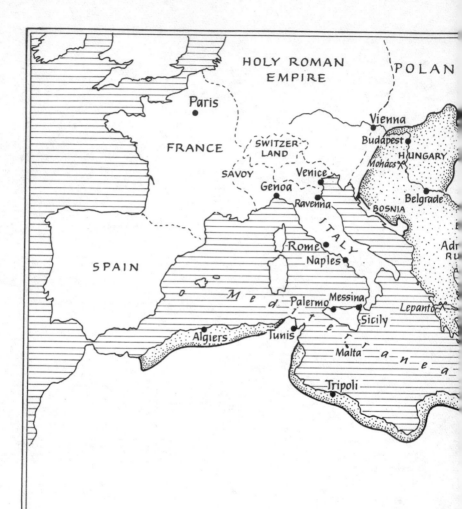

The Ottoman Empire of Suleiman the Magnificent
(1520 - 1566)

RUSSIA

MOLDAVIA

TRANSYLVANIA

WALLACHIA

Danube

BULGARIA

ople

IA

Crimea

Black Sea

Constantinople
(Istanbul)

Sea of Marmara

Bursa

ANATOLIA

Trebizond

Erzerum

Taurus Mts.

Euphrates

Tigris

Caspian Sea

Rhodes

rete

Cyprus

S - e - a

Damascus

Baghdad

PERSIA

Jerusalem

Cairo

Nile

Red Sea

Mecca

BOOK THE FIRST

The Capital of the World

"The spider's curtain hangs before the portal of Caesar's palace;
And the owl stands sentinel on the watch-tower of Afrasiab.

FIRDUSI"

Words spoken by Mahomet II on 1 June 1453, as he gazed at
the ruins of Constantinople.

1

THE GOLDEN HORN

Mail-clad soldiers stood on the outer wall of the city, by the Gate of St Romanus, and looked down on the cavalcade winding its way towards them.

The wall, made of cemented stone and brick, furnished with watchtowers from which pennants drifted in the breeze, rose twenty-five feet above a breastwork, which itself rose out of a ditch sixty feet broad and fifteen deep. Beyond the ditch were open fields, with not a tree to block the horizon or offer concealment to an approaching foe. These fields were mostly under cultivation, or used for pasture; the cattle-herders and farmers, roughly-dressed men whose backs were bent with toil, also ceased work to gaze in mingled alarm and disgust at the flowing, multi-coloured silk robes of the approaching horsemen, and then back at the walls of their city.

Constantinople made a reassuring sight. If the watchers from the fields could see the sun glinting on the spears and helmets of the soldiers, they could also see that behind the guards lay some sixty feet of open ground before the inner main wall was reached. This rose forty feet, and had one hundred and twelve towers, each sixty feet high. Defended by such a massive fortification, surely the people of the Byzantine empire could dwell in peace and security these walls, built by the Emperor Theodosius II in the sixth century, had never been breached.

But like the farmers, the soldiers muttered anxiously and pulled their beards as the embassy approached. For the horsemen rode beneath a fluttering green flag bearing the golden crescent insignia of the Ottoman Turks.

The gate was opened, and the embassy entered the narrow streets of the city, hooves striking sparks from the cobbles. The Greeks hurried from their homes and shops to gaze at the brown faces with the fiercely hooked noses and long moustaches, the

3

heavy beards and the rich silk robes, the domed helmets and chain-mail breastplates, the magnificent Asian horses and the gleaming spears and scimitars of the people they both hated and feared.

Once upon a time, a thousand years into history, the Byzantine Empire had stretched from the Taurus Mountains to the Pyrenees, from the Arabian desert to the Danube. Now it had shrunk to a single city, and where the mailed cataphracts had once rode in glory, the land now lay beneath the rule of the Turkish sipahis.

The word that an Ottoman embassy had arrived rapidly spread through the city. More and more people abandoned work to throng the streets, forming a crowd behind the Turks, which moved towards the old inner city of Byzantium and the royal palace.

For months they had been awaiting news of the great army commanded by the famous soldier. Janos Hunyadi, marching east from Hungary at the behest of the Pope himself. For years they had dreamed of succour from the West, as previous armies had sought out the descendants of Othman. But no previous army had been led by Hunyadi. Now the news had surely come.

But the men bringing it were not western knights, nor did they ride like defeated men.

In the Imperial Palace, beyond the white gate and inside the inner city of old Byzantium, Zagan Pasha was conducted into the great reception hall of the emperors. In the huge, pillared doorway he paused; he had not been here before.

It was not the business of an ambassador of the Emir Murad ever to show appreciation, much less awe, at foreign surroundings, but Zagan could not help but be impressed. He had never seen a room so long or so wide, a ceiling so high supporting pillars as thick and symmetrical. But then, he had never seen such exquisitely inlaid marbled tiles as those on the floor, such bright geometric designs as covered the roof. Only when he glanced left and right did he experience disapproval: the walls were covered in paintings, mostly of a woman and her child. No Muslim could accept such reproduction of the human form as being less than an affront to the teachings of the Prophet.

Also there were women present, a cluster of tall hats and heavy brocaded gowns on the far side of the room. The presence of women at a place where men would discuss business was frivolous.

4

Zagan marched forward, his soft boots making little sound on the floor; his aides marched at his back. He approached the throne, which was on a stepped dais at the rear of the room. It was the only chair in the hall. At the foot of the steps he bowed low before the Emperor John VIII Paleologus, as if he was still the most powerful monarch in the world, then straightened and looked at the men grouped behind the throne. These included the emperor's brother, Constantine Dragases; Grand Duke Lukas Notaras, the most powerful lord in the city; princes of the blood such as Theophilus Paleologus and Andronicus Cantacuzene; nobles such as the Bocchiardi brothers and Theodore of Karystos; and the patriarch Gennadius. Like the soldiers on the walls, these rich and famous men stroked their beards, pulled their moustaches, smoothed their fine robes, the crimsons and blues laced with gold and silver thread, and whispered at each other as the Turks approached.

Perhaps Zagan Pasha smiled; it was difficult to be sure as he also stroked his moustache, and in any event his face was immediately controlled. . o.

"There has been a great battle, Your Excellency."

John Paleologus leaned forward, lined face twisting with anxiety. He was still a handsome man, despite his age and permanent depression. His moustache was clipped short, his beard carefully pointed to give his features the appearance of strength. He wore a purple tunic with a stiff collar and a high-domed felt hat with a pronounced peak. He waited.

"At Kossovo," the envoy said, "twenty-five thousand armoured men marched behind Hunyadi's standard. They were armed with handguns."

A ripple of whispers swept through the Byzantine courtiers. Handguns were hardly more than a rumour to most people.

"The Emir met them," the envoy said, "with a hundred thousand men. The Janissaries had but bows and arrows."

"They were defeated?" John whispered, scarce daring to hope. "The Janissaries were defeated?"

Now Zagan Pasha did smile, openly. "For two days did the battle rage. The soldiers of both sides erected palisades in front of them as they faced each other at barely a hundred feet distance. The handguns did terrible execution. It is said there were counted thirty thousand Janissaries dead upon the field. The field is now

5

called 'the Field of the Blackbirds', from the crows which came to feast."

John sighed. Thirty thousand Turks. "And the Christians?" he asked.

Zagan Pasha bowed again; he had carefully saved the best for last. "The Christian army is no more, Your Excellency."

John stared at him and sat straight. His courtiers rattled their swords.

"You lie," growled Lukas Notaras.

Zagan Pasha bowed, and snapped his fingers. One of the men standing behind him stepped forward with a small bag. The envoy offered it to the Emperor.

John blanched, and would not touch it. Notaras himself came round the throne, took the bag, released the string and emptied its contents into the palm of his hand. It was a single object, a withered piece of flesh. Notaras shuddered, and let it fall to the floor.

On the far side of the reception hall the group of watching women whispered excitedly.

Zagan Pasha bowed again. "You will observe, Your Excellency, that it is uncircumcised. It was cut from the still-living body of a Hungarian knight but three days ago."

"It cannot be," Notaras muttered, still looking at the severed penis.

"Hunyadi was ill-served, Your Excellency. Prince Drakul of Wallachia deserted him during the fight, and Prince George Brankovich of Serbia followed."

"What else could you expect?" snorted the Patriarch. "The man's sister is in the Emir's harem."

Zagan Pasha bowed. Mara Brankovich was indeed reputed to be Murad's favourite wife.

"And Hunyadi?" the Emperor asked.

"The warrior escaped, with the remnants of his force. The Emir bade me bring you this news, Your Excellency. Truly, he grieves for you, and wishes you good counsel."

Again his gaze swept over the princes of the Empire.

"Hang the dog," Notaras said. "Hang him by the balls until they tear away. His insolence is intolerable."

"He is an envoy," John said wearily. He looked old, tired, and defeated. And ill. He was all of those. Janos Hunyadi had been the third general to lead an army against the Turks in the last thirty years; he was also the third to see his followers annihilated. There would be no more. But the Emperor could not allow the Turk to see his despair. "Thank your master, my cousin the lord Murad," he said. "Congratulate him on his victory, and tell him I shall pray for the souls of the gallant men who have died. Tell him I shall indeed seek wise counsel."

Zagan Pasha bowed, looked round at the princes a last time, and backed from the throne room.

"Take that thing away," the Emperor muttered, and a page hurried forward.

"Insolent dog," Notaras said again, staring after the retreating Turk. "You are too soft with these people, Your Grace."

"They are strong, we are weak," the Emperor observed. "To amuse ourselves by executing one Turk would do nothing to improve our position. I fear now that it can never be improved. We lie like a babe in the arms of a hungry giant, waiting to be consumed. What is the date?"

"It is the twentieth of October, Your Grace," said Gennadius.

"A black day: 20 October 1448. Remember it, my lords. A black day. It heralds the doom of Constantinople."

"Constantinople has never fallen to assault," Constantine Dragases declared, concerned at his brother's pessimism. "When the Franks gained the city in 1204, it was only by treachery. And it will not fall to assault now. There is no force on earth that can breach these walls, or climb them."

"True, had we the men to defend them," Notaras sneered. "You will hold thirteen miles of wall with five thousand men? These spineless rats will muster no more."

"There will be men," Constantine declared. "My mission to the courts of the Franks aroused great enthusiasm. There are men coming from everywhere, from Italy and France, Spain and Genoa."

"And from Venice?" the Grand Duke inquired.

Constantine flushed. "Not from Venice. They are the friends of the Turk. But," he added eagerly, "there are even men coming from England. Men who fought beneath the English king, the great Harry. Men who were at Agincourt."

"You mean you have recruited a lot of papists," Gennadius said disparagingly. "We want none of them here. I tell you frankly, I

7

would rather see Murad himself worshipping in our cathedral than any cardinal."

"They are men who will fight for us," Constantine insisted, and half turned his head to listen. Even as he spoke, the great bells of St Sophia were beginning a mournful dirge. The news had already reached the priests and was now about to be told to the populace. Hunyadi had been defeated.

The Genoese carrack made but minimal way against the fast-flowing current. There was a fair breeze and every sail was set, but the round ship, for all her three masts and varnished topsides, sailed like the tub she resembled. Her bottom was foul; long strings of weed trailed away from the carvel-built hull, but she was capable of little speed even when scraped clean.

"It is a slow business." The master agreed with John Hawkwood's unspoken impatience. "The current is very strong. The Black Sea, beyond that land you can see, is fed constantly by the great rivers. It is relatively fresh, and seeks an outlet. The Mediterranean is salt and evaporates. Thus the Black Sea flows constantly south through the Bosphorus and then the Dardanelles to join the Aegean. Between the two straits is this Marmara, the White Sea, constantly replenished. And debouching from those narrows at such speed ..." He shrugged.

John Hawkwood knew the man was speaking the truth. Three days ago they had clawed their way up that very narrow passage called the Dardanelles, which was hardly a mile wide, he estimated. The land on either side was dead: brown, hilly, uncultivated, deserted. Then he had seen a castle on the Asiatic shore, as brown and forbidding as the land out of which it rose, but it was towered, castellated, and occupied. There were flags streaming in the wind and he caught the glint of armour.

"Is that Greek or Turkish?" he had asked. He spoke Italian slowly, but well enough to make himself understood.

"It is Turkish," the Genoese captain had told him. "Whatever you see is Turkish. From the Taurus to the Danube, the Ottomans rule. Constantinople is but a jewel, floating in the midst of a hostile sea."

Hawkwood scratched his beard as he studied the shore. "And these Turks do not dispute this passage?"

The captain smiled. "They have tried to do so from time to time. My ship is heavily armed." He pointed at the swivel guns mounted on the lower deck, designed to sweep an approaching enemy with nails and pieces of scrap-iron as well as lead bullets. "They have but galleys."

"Were there cannon on that headland, they would render these narrow straits impassable."

"Cannon? What do you know of cannon, Englishman?"

"Something," Hawkwood said.

The captain smiled again. "The Turks know nothing of such things. They fight with bows and arrows."

"And yet conquer the world."

The smile faded. "There are great numbers of them," he muttered.

Hawkwood went down the ladder from the poop to the waist, to join his family and tell them that their journey would last a few hours longer.

Once they had left the Dardanelles behind, the carrack's progress had improved on the broad waters of the Sea of Marmara, yet it had taken two days to traverse the last ninety miles. Now they were again closing the land. Beyond lay the strait known as the Bosphorus, out of which, as the captain had explained, the waters of the Black Sea came eternally pumping.

Hawkwood's family had also seen the land, and were gathered to stare at it. They stood out from amongst the Genoese seamen by virtue of their size and colouring. John Hawkwood was proud of his sons. At twenty, William was two inches over six feet, the same height as his father, and he had the same curling red hair and ruddy complexion; the same heavy muscles, too, to accompany the bold, confident features.

Anthony, four years younger, was cast in the same mould, and would probably grow even bigger than his brother, even if he as yet lacked hair on his chin. Catherine, who was eighteen, matched them perfectly, not as tall, but with equally glowing hair and complexion. She would never be beautiful: her features were too strong — but what man could resist the swell at breast and buttock, and the suggestion of long legs beneath her green cote-hardie? She was wearing her best for their arrival in Constantinople.

John Hawkwood stood beside his wife, shorter than her children, a surprisingly slight mother for such a brood of lions. Now she

9

shuddered. "It is a dead country," she said. "There is no green."

"It is a heathen land," he offered by way of explanation. "We will be at the Golden Horn by nightfall."

There she would find beauty, he trusted. There they would find everything they sought. They had to, or he would have made a catastrophic decision. But the very name, the Golden Horn, promised wealth and fortune to a man bold enough to pluck it. John Hawkwood had never lacked confidence.

He was fifty years old in this Year of Our Lord 1448. From his earliest youth he had followed the profession of arms. Although descended from a tanner, his was now a martial family; his grandfather's brother, also named John, had been knighted on the field of Crécy by King Edward III of England, and had then gone to Italy to become a leader of mercenaries — a *condottiere*. The first John Hawkwood had married the daughter — illegitimate to be sure — of the Duke of Milan, and had risen to the rank of Captain General of Florence before his death, only four years before the birth of his grandnephew.

John Hawkwood the younger saw no reason why he should not emulate his famous namesake, save perhaps in the matter of marriage — he already had a wife. But as a leader of men he could go further. He was a specialist, as his father and grandfather had been before him. He was an artillerist.

Unfortunately the term was as yet hardly understood, even by armies. John Hawkwood's grandfather had fought beside his brother at Crécy. William Hawkwood the elder had been only a boy, but even then he had helped to serve the guns. They had not been needed; the Welsh archers had been sufficient to destroy the French. Sixty-nine years later, as a boy of seventeen, John Hawkwood the younger had followed Great Harry to Agincourt, marching with his father beside the guns. Then, too, the archers had done the work.

Few soldiers, even military geniuses like Henry V or his brother the Duke of Bedford, understood about guns. They thought of them as huge, unwieldy, expensive, noisy, smelly and immobile encumbrances. In particular the nobles who commanded the armies disliked them. A knight in armour expected to be faced by another knight in armour, lance or sword in hand, with victory going to the one with greater strength and skill. And when that victory was assured, he expected the certainty of a rich ransom from the vanquished foe. No knight would kill a wealthy opponent if it could be avoided, and no knight, in all the glory of mounted panoply, could be brought down by a peasant with a spear, if he knew his business. On those simple premises had an entire aristocracy been created.

In England the knights had even opposed the use of the longbow, until they had discovered it would enable them to win battles at great odds and earn them the reputation of being the most formidable soldiers in Europe. They had reconciled themselves to the change in their status; the longbow meant that the charging knight was no longer indestructible, but could be picked out of his saddle like a ripe apple from a low branch. Expert use of the new weapon demanded hours, years, of practice, and it was an art confined to the English and Welsh yeomen, who at least knew their place and touched their caps to their betters.

Artillerists might be yeomen, but their weapon was hardly skilled. It killed, blindly and indiscriminately, hurling huge stone balls through the air with utter carelessness. It was a weapon of the devil.

John Hawkwood was not enough of a theologian to argue the last point. But as he had been born into a profession, however unpopular, he had made the best of it. He was that type of man, and had brought up his sons and daughter to hold the same points of view. He had an inquiring mind. His father had been a Lollard, a follower of John Wycliffe, who held that God belonged to humanity and not merely to a handful of priests. Anthony Hawkwood the elder had had the sense to keep his opinions to himself; heresy could take a man to the stake and several minutes of agony before death. But he had bequeathed many of his views to his son, less on religion than on learning. John Hawkwood could read and write, Latin as well as English. This art, too, he had imparted to his sons, with the result that they had found it easy enough to learn passable Italian during the long voyage through the Mediterranean.

But, above all, John Hawkwood had thought about his profession and the tools of his trade. Cannon were everything that outraged nobility claimed ... at the moment. But they also encompassed the most destructive power ever to appear on earth. If that power could be harnessed, aimed, and made more mobile, then the general that commanded it would rule the earth.

He had sought, as a young man, to convince his superiors, but the time had not been right. Indeed, the time could never have been more wrong. For Great Harry had died in 1422, followed only a few years later by his equally talented brother, John of Bedford. England had been given over to the rule of a sickly babe and a quarrelling regency. The army which had terrorised France had begun to lose battles, even when faced by a peasant girl called Joan of Arc. Defeated and disgruntled, it had been withdrawn to England save for a few garrisons. The martial age was over. No doubt Edward III, and his son the Black Prince, and Great Harry himself were turning in their graves. Their veterans found themselves starving. For the archer or the man-at-arms employment was still available, in the private armies that were springing up like mushrooms as the country degenerated into anarchy. But no private lord could afford artillery, or would have known what to do with it if he could.

For John Hawkwood the end of his dreams had been shattering. He was not of noble birth, yet he had no profession save that of arms. For an artillerist to arm himself with breastplate and pike and trudge with the common herd was an insult to his forebears. Yet with three small children and a wife to support, he had had no choice. For nearly twenty years he had served and suffered, and watched his beloved England drifting ever nearer to civil war, until it was beloved no longer. Then, in his despair, he had heard a rumour, drifting across the Channel. A man, a prince, was come from the East, the cradle of civilisation, where great things were afoot, seeking soldiers.

John Hawkwood had, of course, heard of Constantinople — it was the capital of the once-great Byzantine Empire, and it remained the greatest city in the world. But it was a world apart. Four hundred years before, the Pope in Rome and the Patriarch in Constantinople had differed on various points of dogma, and the Christian church had been split down the middle. Indeed, in 1204 the Pope had even diverted a crusade to the capture of the city rather than send the crusaders against the Saracens. Then for fifty years a Latin Patriarch had sat upon the throne of the emperors.

That horrifying event was ancient history, but Constantinople had never recovered. How low it had sunk no man was prepared to believe. But this prince, this Constantine Dragases Paleologus, was touring the West, seeking fighting men to aid his brother the Emperor to resist a horde which had come out of Asia and was, he

12

claimed, threatening Europe itself.

What he was seeking had sounded very much like a latterday crusade, and John Hawkwood had felt in the mood for a crusade. When one of these Byzantines had come to England, Hawkwood had gone to listen, and been intrigued. "We need fighting men," the Greek had said. "Men of courage and resolution. To them we will open all the splendours of the Golden Horn. Come to Constant-inople and fight with us, and we will give you a home, money, fame and fortune."

These were words which John Hawkwood had not heard for a long time, but there was more yet to tempt him.

"Particularly we need artillerists," the envoy had said. "Men who know guns. We have guns in Constantinople — we need the men to fire them."

John Hawkwood the younger had promptly offered his skills.

"It is my great opportunity," he had explained. "This is my destiny."

His wife Mary had been horrorstruck. "You will go off to the ends of the earth and leave me here to starve with the children?"

"No," John said, "I will take you with me. The Greeks have given me sufficient money for us all." He did not immediately tell his wife he had also promised the envoy that he could supply two sturdy sons for the cause.

Mary had seemed even more alarmed. "You wish me to accom-pany you to a heretic and heathen land?"

"Their heresy is a matter of doctrine," John said. "But, if it will relieve your mind, I can tell you that His Holiness the Pope has given his special blessing to any man who joins the Byzantine army. I am no knight-errant, my sweet; it is simply a matter of necessity. Here is a chance to make my name and earn the keep of my old age. I cannot leave you here; your parents are dead, your brother is a rascal. You will come with me because you must."

"And the children?"

"They, too, of course. William and Anthony will help serve the guns. It is an honourable profession."

"And Catherine, poor girl?"

John kissed his wife. "Catherine, I have no doubt, will marry a Greek prince."

And now they were here. Anthony Hawkwood could hardly

13

believe it. But then, he had hardly been able to believe any of it. He had been born in Lord Monteagle's barracks; had grown up there. He had been taught the use of the pike and the sword by his father, as well as the pen. Father had also talked about bombards, and what they could do, but Anthony had never seen one. His future had seemed assured. He would march behind Lord Monteagle's banner, and, if need be, he would die beneath it. Hopefully, on that so-narrow journey through life, he would experience the comfort of a woman's arms and the joy of gazing at his own son. But he had counted on nothing more ... until Father had so suddenly led them away from the lord's castle.

They had sailed from Southampton, out of the calm Solent and into the turbulent waters of the English Channel, every man on deck searching for sight of a sail which might mean the French privateers were out of Dunkirk or St Malo. They had seen nothing hostile, and had found themselves plunging across the Bay of Biscay in an easterly gale. Cape Finisterre had loomed, huge and threatening, half-lost in low cloud, as they had scudded down the Portuguese coast, the distant land disappearing every few minutes as the carrack slid down the big Atlantic swell. But the wind had abated and their first port of call, Lisbon, had brought them their first taste of the climes for which they were heading. Anchored in Cascais Roads, sheltered by headland and sandbank from the ocean, the sun had shone; it had been hot enough to cause the tar to bubble in the decks. And they had seen their first palm tree.

From Lisbon they had rounded Cape St Vincent for Cadiz, a rocky promontory in a wind-torn gulf, and thence to Cartagena, tucked away behind its myriad headlands. With the whole of the Iberian peninsula reclaimed for Christianity — save for the tiny Moorish kingdom of Granada in the south of Spain — the voyage till then had been a safe one, apart from the weather. But Anthony had not even been seasick, so consumed had he been with wonder at what was unfolding before his eyes, at the skill of the Spanish sailors, the most experienced and daring seamen in the world.

From Cartagena they had coasted to Alicante, nestling beneath its huge castle of St Barbara, and thence crossed the broad Mediterranean to Genoa, a city of splendid palaces and hardly less famous seamen; the Genoese were the only nation of Western Europe bold enough to continue direct trading with Byzantium, braving the wrath of the Turks. In Genoa the Hawkwood family had embarked upon the last leg of their journey, under the flag of the famous republic.

The voyage had taken several months. It had ben an education even for John Hawkwood himself, Anthony knew, and he had campaigned the length and breadth of France. For his children it had been an exploration of a world they had not suspected to exist: lands where it was always at least warm, more often than not hot; seas which were calm for days on end and yet could be torn apart by fierce winds arising from a cloudless sky; mountains reaching upwards until they seemed to touch the firmament; men with black hair and beards and flashing dark eyes; women with unimaginable grace, whose eyes flashed even more alluringly: Anthony was already a man. John Hawkwood had been more afraid for Catherine, and had kept her close by his side whenever they were ashore.

They had seen men fighting bulls to the death, palaces which made the best manor house in England look like a hovel, clothes which had a brightness, quality and a freedom entirely lacking in the chilly north. This brightness extended to the way of life in the Mediterranean, where whole communities would down tools for days on end to enjoy a fiesta, drinking and laughing and loving — often illicitly — and parading in the name of some friendly saint.

"It is a paradise," William had declared.

"There are serpents, even in paradise," his father had warned him. For he could discern that, beneath the excellent manners and the unremitting gaiety, there were rivers of deep and unforgiving pride.

All the time Anthony had stared at it all open-mouthed.

From Genoa the new ship had taken them to Naples and Otranto, and then the Piraeus, before sail had been set for the Dardanelles.

Anthony would never forget Naples. The weather had been bad, and they had lain for a week alongside the Mole, where the Neapolitans paraded in their finery, and from where it was possible to look up at the forbidding walls of the Castel Nuovo, for so long the home of the foreign Angevin kings and queens who had brought so much misery to this sunny land.

Like the Genoese or the Spaniards, the Neapolitans had laughed and enjoyed their fiestas, but they too had dark streaks behind their smiles, a combination of pride and eroticism which was as fascinating as it was dangerous. Naples in September was the hottest place Anthony had ever known.

Confinement on board the ship in such conditions was impossible. When Catherine had wanted to stretch her legs, Anthony had been deputed to act as her bodyguard.

He had felt suitably proud to walk beside so striking a woman, even if she was his sister. They had always been close; she had mothered him from an early age. Now she tucked her arm through his as if they had been lovers.

They attracted attention, of course, both by virtue of their size and colouring and by their clothes, which were shabby and poor compared with the brilliance around them. Anthony would have cared nothing for that, but Catherine was embarrassed, and suddenly decided to return to the ship, preferring a side street to the main thoroughfare where she felt they had been laughed at. He willingly agreed, and they had sought the shadows — to find themselves surrounded by several young men with evilly smiling faces, hardly older than Anthony himself but dressed in a finery he had seldom seen.

They pointed at the strange pair, and came closer. Anthony and his sister were still in the process of learning Italian and could make little of what was said, but the little they understood was insulting even if it was rudely complimentary to Catherine's figure.

"Begone with you," Anthony had said, waving his arm, and had then found himself standing against a wall with the point of a sword at his throat, while the other men held Catherine's arms. One had released the strings at her bodice to expose her breasts. There was beauty which had taken their breaths away — even Anthony's. Now one of the wretches was actually fondling the glowing white flesh, while another clutched the girl's throat to prevent her from screaming, pushing her hard against the wall. A third now gathered her skirts and raised them round her waist, exposing not only her splendid legs but her every feminine secret; and he was clearly about to enjoy these himself as he fumbled at his hose.

Anthony's anger suddenly exploded. The sword confining him was so thin it might have been a reed. A sweep of his gloved hand had turned it aside, and in a moment his own weapon was drawn from its scabbard. Anthony Hawkwood wore no rapier, but rather a broadsword which had been his grandfather's. The would-be rapists stared at the huge, vengeful, red-haired apparition in dismay. One boldly presented his rapier — and had the blade cut in half by a two-handed sweep. In a flash they had all taken to their heels.

With remarkable composure Catherine straightened her skirts and re-tied her bodice. "We'll not tell Father of this adventure," she said, and squeezed her brother's hand. "But I could have asked for no better protector. You are my very own perfect knight, dear Anthony."

He treasured these words more than the easy victory. But he also treasured what had happened. He had not suspected his sister to be so beautiful ... or so calm. If he had loved her before, now he worshipped her.

But all of those experiences had been as if a prologue, before being allowed to enjoy the play itself. For now they were at last rounding the promontory, and could see the beginning of the narrow passage beyond the Bosphorus. John Hawkwood's heartbeat quickened. But as he waited for his first sight of the legendary city he heard a sound: the dismal tolling of a bell.

"What a dirge," his wife Mary commented.

Hawkwood looked up at the captain, who was standing above them at the break of the poop.

"That is the bell of St Sophia," the captain remarked, and crossed himself. "There has been some catastrophe."

The Hawkwoods continued to crowd the bulwark as the carrack swept slowly round the headland. Then they caught their breaths. On their right the coast of Asia was suddenly again close at hand, tall cypresses lining the cliff tops. They also beheld another castle, much larger and stouter in appearance than that which had aroused their earlier interest. It too flew the green flag of the Turks. But to their left, on the European shore — and straight ahead, as the ship turned to the north-east — they gazed at Constantinople itself. And they were prepared, at first sight, to concede that here was indeed the greatest city in the world.

Walls surrounded it on every side, even where they overlooked the water;high and thick, crenellated and forbidding, they were the strongest fortifications John Hawkwood had ever seen. Beyond rose the rooftops of houses and palaces. Above these again rose the campaniles of innumerable churches, and above them all towered the spires of the huge cathedral whence the mournful dirge was sounding.

But it was not so much the houses, the architecture, the defences that took the breath away, as the sheer size of the city. John Hawkwood's practised eye, used to judging distances, realised that the city could hardly be less than three miles across. Three miles enclosed within one set of walls! And it was at least as broad again, at its landward end.

"How many people might live within those fortifications?" he wondered aloud.

"Not less than a hundred thousand," the captain informed him.

Hawkwood stroked his beard; once he had thought London teeming. But if he could not yet see inside the city's walls, there was life enough down on the water, where a fleet of small boats cast their nets. Others, having identified her flags, surrounded the carrack with shouts of greeting.

As the carrack proceeded on its way, and the Hawkwoods gaped at the churches and palaces on the acropolis of the city — the north-eastern corner spreading over the seven hills which had encouraged Constantine the Great to make ancient Byzantium the site of his new Rome — the harbour slowly came into view: a wide inlet which formed the northern border of the city. Hawkwood gazed in wonder at a huge iron chain which stretched all across the mouth of the channel, just short of half a mile in width.

The captain pointed. "The Golden Horn."

"Why so called?"

The captain shrugged. "It has been so called for centuries. Because it is shaped like the horn of a ram ... and because to it come all the riches of the earth."

Beyond the boom chain rose the masts of many ships, while to the right of the harbour rose another walled town, only a fraction the size of the main city, but nonetheless clearly a bustling place.

"Galata," the captain explained. "Our Genoese colony here in the east. That is our destination."

Men on the Galata side of the entrance strained at the spokes of a giant capstan wheel to which the thick rope end of the chain was attached, and a portion of the boom was laboriously lowered. The carrack entered the harbour under shortened sail, to be immediately surrounded by small boats to take her lines and carry them ashore, so that the big ship could be slowly winched alongside one of the quays. The Hawkwoods hurriedly repaired to the cabin to assemble their scanty luggage; they were the only passengers to have come this far, and had had the afterquarters mostly to themselves in the fortnight since leaving Piraeus.

They found themselves the centre of interest as they stepped ashore, their legs uncertain on firm ground after so many weeks at sea. It was by now late evening, but people crowded to stare at their red hair and admire the splendid physiques of the new arrivals. "They are Vikings," someone remarked in Italian.

Oh, indeed, Anthony Hawkwood thought; we are Vikings, come to save you from the forces of evil. He felt the blood pounding in his arteries; if Galata was no more than a typical seaport, with its large warehouses and mean houses, brusque men and sideways-glancing women, he had fallen in love with the city across the harbour at first sight, even without having yet set foot in it.

They were given accommodation for that night in the inn where the captain himself lodged, all five of them huddled in one bed — and surprised to find the night air so cool. They had earlier found it difficult to digest the strange meal placed before them, in which meat and vegetables were combined to make a kind of dry stew, to which were added various unfamiliar spices; while instead of ale or the soft Italian vintages they had become used to on board ship, they were given Byzantine wine which was sharp on the palate and made them shudder.

"Is there no wholesome food and drink in this place?" Mary complained.

"You will cook what you wish when we have a house of our own," John promised her.

"And when will that be?" she inquired.

"Why, as soon as I have been interviewed by this Prince Constantine, tomorrow."

"May we come with you, Father?" Anthony asked eagerly.

John Hawkwood considered, then shook his head. "It is best I went alone." He smiled at the boy's obvious disappointment. "For tomorrow you can explore Galata — and mind you stay out of mischief."

He had been warned by the Genoese sea-captain of the hostility he, a Catholic, could expect from the Byzantines, so John was in no hurry to expose his family to possible insult in the city. Indeed, he was himself somewhat apprehensive as he took the ferry across the harbour the next morning.

If the huge harbour seemed oddly desolate with only the fishing fleet on the move — although he noticed some twenty war galleys moored further up the curving gulf — the city itself appeared even more awe-inspiring at close hand. As John climbed the stone steps from the ferry to enter by one of the water gates, he gazed up at the immense walls, higher and thicker than he had previously estimated. His soldier's eye immediately discerned that the defences were in need of repair in many places, the stonework beginning to crumble. There was also scarcely a handful of men in sight — but no doubt the embrasures would fill up rapidly enough, were a Turkish army to appear in sight.

Once within the walls, he looked around and found himself in a cauldron of noise and hustle and heat, even if it was late October. He gazed at narrow cobbled streets, teeming with humanity and domestic animals, with all their odours and bristling cacophony. He looked around at the close-packed houses, which varied capriciously from huts hardly better than hovels to porticoed palaces rising high above his head. He inhaled the scents of perfume and slops, roasting lamb and cooling retsina. John Hawkwood had visited London more than once, and had believed that one big city was much like another; but here, instead of claustrophobia, there was an odd sensation of freedom in the warm sunshine, the gentle breeze, and in the scanty clothing all around him. In his tunic and jerkin he felt quite overdressed.

The people themselves appeared to be of every size and colour, race and creed. They varied from fair-haired Macedonians to black-skinned Africans, though his was the only red hair to be seen. They spoke in a wide variety of languages, and Hawkwood was relieved to hear the occasional word of Italian; but there was no English.

The officer inside the water gate, resplendent in mail cap and corselet, examined his credentials: a piece of parchment given him by the Byzantine envoy who had enlisted him, and written in Greek. Hawkwood had no idea what it said, but it must convey not only that he was a volunteer come to serve the Emperor, but also the fact that he could speak only Latin, because the officer, having looked him up and down, summoned one of his subordinates and gave him instructions.

The man nodded. "You will accompany me," he addressed Hawkwood in Italian.

"Willingly," Hawkwood agreed. "But will you tell me where we are going?"

"I am to present you to the Prince. Your passport speaks of others?" the sergeant observed.

"My family waits for me in Galata."

During this time the captain's face never relaxed its severity. But soon the sergeant was leading the way through the crowd, Hawkwood attracting curious glances.

"Your captain is a stern man," Hawkwood commented.

"He hates all Azymites," the sergeant replied enigmatically.

"And he thinks that I am one?"

"If you are of the Roman communion, you are an Azymite," the sergeant declared.

Their route led them through a white gateway set in an inner, lower wall which enclosed the original city of Byzantium. In contrast to the human ant-heap outside, this central area contained only palaces and cathedrals separated by some attractively wooded parks; and at the southern end, up against the wall itself, lay a huge oval amphitheatre.

"The hippodrome," the sergeant explained, "where the circus is held. Do you have such things where you come from, Englishman?"

"No," Hawkwood said.

"You must tell me of England." The sergeant smiled. "My name is Panadou."

Perhaps he does not detest Azymites quite as much as his captain, Hawkwood thought. He gazed at the huge, curving bulk of the Cathedral of St Sophia, lost in wonder at so great an edifice, at the richness of the stained glass windows, the gold inlays in the corbels catching brilliant reflections of light. He did not suppose there could be another building like it in the world.

John Hawkwood was kept waiting in an antechamber for some time, before being admitted to the presence of Prince Constantine. The sergeant, Panadou, having delivered him to the Prince's major-domo, had bidden him farewell.

"No doubt we will meet again," Hawkwood suggested. The sooner he could make some friends here, the better.

"No doubt," Panadou said briefly, and left.

The major-domo did not speak any Latin, but there could be no doubt that *he* also hated Azymites. The same undoubtedly went for the many others waiting in the antechamber; without exception they stared at the big red-haired Englishman with undisguised hostility. Hawkwood tried to ignore them by studying his splendid surroundings. Inlaid mosaic tiles covered the floors and the ceiling; ikons bearing representations of the Virgin and Child were fixed on the walls. The red robes of the major-domo would have done justice to a noble earl in England. In fact Hawkwood became increasingly aware of his own shabby tunic and patched hose, both in their workmanlike shade of brown. Only his white shirt was fresh and crisp — kept especially for this occasion.

The Prince was a thin man of no more than medium height, with a straggly beard. He wore a round hat with a high crown and was notably more richly dressed than his major-domo, his fingers covered with valuable rings. But he carried his finery with an abstracted air, and his manner was courteous. Greeting Hawkwood in Latin, he extended his knuckles to be kissed. John was taken aback at this, but decided it must be the fashion and knelt. When he was standing upright again, Prince Constantine looked into his face and eyes.

"John Hawkwood," he said, "from England. You bear a famous name."

"I had a famous great-uncle, my lord."

"Then are we blessed. Are there many as large as you in that far-off land?"

"Many, sire."

The Prince sighed. "Oh, to have a few hundred such men at my back." He tapped the passport. "You are an artillerist?"

"That is my profession."

"Then are you doubly welcome. Cannon are our only hope now, had we sufficient of them. And sufficient gunners." He tapped the passport again. "But this speaks of sons."

"I have two sons, who have accompanied me."

"And are they fighting men?"

"They have come here to fight, my lord."

"It is a start — and there will be others. My agents report there are men coming to us from all over Europe." He glanced at Hawkwood. "Our people in Constantinople have lived in peace for too long."

Hawkwood made no reply to that. He had already commenced to wonder why, with such a large population, the Byzantines needed outside help to fill up the ranks of their army. Instead he asked, "How long will it be before the Turkish assault?"

The Prince's face grimaced and he sat down, motioning Hawkwood to a chair. John hesitated, he had never been invited to sit in the presence of royalty before. As he sat down, the hovering major-domo looked scandalised.

"There is no war at present between us and the Ottomans," the Prince continued. "Indeed, there is a treaty of peace between our two nations. Yet we know they do intend to stamp us from existence. Do you know much of them?"

"A little only, sire."

"Then listen, for they are formidable. Two hundred years ago no one had ever heard of the Ottomans. They are a race of hardy people who emerged from the depths of Asia, led by one Ertughril. They made their home in Anatolia, and troubled no one. It was Ertughril's son Osman, known to us as Othman, who began to lead his people to war. It is from him they call themselves Osmanlis, or Ottomans. Do you know what the name means in Turkish, Hawkwood?"

John shook his head.

"It means 'leg-breaker' — an apt description. Othman, as I say, led his people to war; and it was his fortune to do so when our city was just recovering from the sack by the crusaders in 1204. You will have heard of that?"

John nodded.

"It is not easily forgotten. If many of our people still hate the Franks, it is through tales of that act of treachery, as handed down from generation to generation. You are a Frank, of course ..."

"My lord, I am English. The French are my hereditary enemies."

"All Westerners are Franks to the people of Constantinople. Remember that, Hawkwood."

"You expect me to fight for a people who hate me?"

"You came here to fight the Turks. And if they are not checked soon, they will conquer all Europe — even England."

Hawkwood stroked his beard.

23

"You think I am being fanciful?" the Prince continued. "Then listen. Othman prospered because of our weakness. His son, Orkhan, prospered even more. He led his armies across the Bosphorus and into the Balkans. He so frightened the then emperor, John Cantacuzene, that a Byzantine princess was granted to the Turk as a wife. Can you imagine, a Christian lady enduring the horrors of the harem? It is unthinkable. And yet George Brankovich has done the same." He brooded for several minutes. "Thus Byzantium became virtually a fief of the infidel. Yet these were mere raiders from Asia. They could gain no lasting victories, it was supposed. The Turk is a nomad from the steppes, for all his fine airs, and he lacks discipline. He is a magnificent horseman, and when assembled they provide a general with the best light cavalry in the world. But the day of cavalry is past, as you well know. Without disciplined heavy infantry, true success in warfare is impossible."

You are wrong in that, Hawkwood thought. It is the possession of artillery that matters now. But he did not interrupt.

"It was Orkhan's son, Murad I, who realised he could never lead mere cavalry against the armies of the West with any hope of success. So he hit upon a plan, a devilish plan. He began to kidnap Christian children and educate them in the ways of the Crescent rather than the Cross. He instilled in them strict discipline and created, in effect, an army of military monks. Have you heard of these Janissaries?"

"I have heard of them."

"They are the most formidable soldiers in the world."

Hawkwood again stroked his beard; he himself had fought beside Great Harry.

Constantine observed his scepticism. "You will find out, before long."

"When did this Murad rule, sire?" Hawkwood asked.

"Sixty years ago."

"And Constantinople still stands."

Constantine gave a twisted smile. "A peculiar blessing of God, perhaps. Murad led his Janissaries into Europe, and defeated the Serbs at the Battle of Kossovo." He sighed. "The first battle of Kossovo. That was in 1389. After the battle, Murad himself was assassinated by a Serbian nobleman who had been taken prisoner, but his son Bayazid took immediate command of the army and the empire. Bayazid who called himself 'the Thunderer'. He was the second greatest warrior of the age. You have heard of the first?"

Hawkwood considered: 1389 was too early for Great Harry, too late for the Black Prince. "Bertrand du Guesclin?" He hated to praise a Frenchman, but was an honest man.

"Du Guesclin," Constantine snorted with contempt. "Have you never heard of Timur the Mongol? Timur they called 'the Lame'?"

Hawkwood frowned. He had indeed heard the name, but had always supposed it some legend from the East.

"Constantinople then lay at Bayazid's mercy," Constantine said. "My grandfather knew his hour had struck — but we were saved, by a miracle."

"By an infidel Mongol," Hawkwood suggested.

"God moves in a mysterious way, Englishman, but saved we were. Bayazid's sipahis, his Janissaries, his generals, he himself for all his reputation, were as nothing before Timur. They were trodden into the dust, and Bayazid the Thunderer was imprisoned in an iron cage and exposed to the multitude, to die of shame."

"And Constantinople then lay at Timur's mercy?" Hawkwood observed. "Yet it still stands."

"Timur had no interest in Europe. He sought to destroy Bayazid only because Bayazid was a rival in Asia. After that he marched away into China, his true goal, and died there. Thus we were saved. It was then we should have reasserted our greatness — while Bayazid's sons fought for the succession. Indeed we appealed to the West for armies to aid us in ridding the world of the leg-breakers. There were, we were told, great soldiers in the West. There was one in particular, who ruled your England: Great Harry. Did you know of him?"

"I fought beneath him at Agincourt, against the French," Hawkwood said proudly.

"Against the French," Constantine repeated sadly. "Brother against brother, Frank against Frank. *There* was our ruination, Englishman. Had that same battle been fought on the shores of the Dardanelles, and your mighty warrior opposed his strength to the Janissaries, then might Europe have been saved."

Hawkwood could think of no reply to make.

"Since then the Turks have rebuilt their strength," the Prince continued. "Out of the civil wars that followed Bayazid's death,

Mahomet I became Emir. The Ottomans call him 'the Restorer'. We called him 'the Gentleman', because he confined himself to righting matters within his father's domains, and treated us with dignity and peace. His son Murad II is a different man, a warrior with blood in his mind as well as in his heart. He besieged us briefly in 1422, but he could make no impression on our walls, and he went away again to extend his dominions to the west. Against him the Pope mounted a crusade, five years ago."

"I have heard of that, sire," Hawkwood interposed.

"Then you will know how the army commanded by Ladislas of Hungary was destroyed, the king with it. Only the great war-captain Janos Hunyadi escaped. Now this year Hunyadi raised another army. Four days ago it too was destroyed, once again at Kossovo." He uttered another sigh. "The Field of the Blackbirds."

"I knew there had been a defeat, from the tolling of the bell," Hawkwood said.

Constantine straightened up suddenly. "Englishman, there will be no more crusades, no more Papal armies. If Constantinople is to survive, it can only be through our own efforts now."

"Your walls have never been breached," Hawkwood observed.

"There is our strength — that and our cannon. But we have weaknesses enough. My brother the Emperor is a sick man. I doubt he will survive the year. Our people are torn by faction, and they are careless. Because Constantinople has never been taken by assault, they think it never *can* be taken. I can muster less than five thousand men-at-arms to guard our walls, yet I need men of courage. With them at my back, I could withstand the Turk — even Murad, who treats us with insolent contempt. But that is the Turkish way: he feels that whenever he snaps his fingers, this great city will be his. For the moment he is content that we retain some independence."

"But I would say this city is rich, my lord, although I do not altogether understand how."

"We are rich because we are the market of the world — the crossroads of the world. People come to us from every country known to man, to trade in freedom and safety. Even the Turks — for they wish to enjoy the fruits of other men's labour. Thus they now leave us in peace, while heaping insults upon us. But one day the Janissaries will march against our walls."

"Which will defeat them," Hawkwood said, "if adequately

26

manned, and defended by cannon. I am told the Ottomans do not have cannon?"

"They are nomads from the steppes. What do they know of cannon?" Constantine smiled. "Now you know the truth of us, Englishman. I would have no man fight for a cause he cannot make his own. Will you stay and fight with us?"

"I will stay and fight your guns for you, as long as you wish me to."

"Well said. Can you doubt I will ever choose otherwise?"

Hawkwood rose and bowed. "If my lord speaks for his people," he said, "I am content."

2

THE BYZANTINE

John VIII died before the end of the year, and Constantine succeeded as Emperor. Immediately all Constantinople became aware of the surge of new energy and optimism emanating from the throne. Some laughed, more grumbled ... a few responded.

News from the Turks indicated that the Emir Murad was concentrating all his energies on defeating the Albanian patriot, George Castriota, known as Scanderbeg. Thus the city was left in peace.

The Byzantines cared nothing for what might be happening in Albania, or for the steadily spreading Turkish envelopment of south-eastern Europe. Life was there to be lived: they drank and they ate, they traded and grew rich, they quarrelled, and from time to time they rioted at some real or imagined distress.

But most of all they played.

"The Green!" screamed Catherine Hawkwood. "The Green!"

"The Blue," screamed a nearby throng. "The Blue!"

But others in the crowd also cheered for the green colours, as the chariots tore round the hippodrome, four-horse teams panting and spitting, drivers straining over the reins, dust flying from hooves and churning wheels.

All Constantinople ceased work on circus days, and when there was a cause for celebration, as now, the entire population seemed to gather inside the walls of old Byzantium to enjoy the sport — and the rivalry, which too often degenerated into angry strife.

On days such as this, the hippodrome became more than a circus; it became the heartbeat of a nation.

From long before dawn men had toiled at sweeping the sand of the track smooth, making sure there were no impediments for the galloping horses; others swabbed and mopped the tiers of white stone seats that entirely surrounded the arena. These were hard to

28

sit upon for any length of time; the wise and the wealthy would bring their own cushions ... which could be used as missiles should their side lose.

The pie-sellers and the vendors of sweetmeats were early in place, followed closely by the dispensers of the favours, green or blue, that would denote one's allegiance on this day.

By mid-morning the flags and banners had climbed to the tops of their poles, and were surely visible on the far side of the Bosphorus, a swirling forest of colour to denote that the Byzantines were *en fête*. By now, too, the teams and the chariots had arrived, for inspection by their owners and trainers, and their drivers, famous men whose talents were disputed in the taverns. They wore leather caps and leather shields at knee, elbow and shoulder, leather codpieces to protect their genitals and leather masks for their faces. When a chariot went down in a flurry of breaking wood and thundering hooves, a man would count himself fortunate to survive with just bruises.

And then came the crowds. Most wanted to get to the circus early in order to secure their favourite seats. They jostled and bantered, in good humour, when they arrived; the extremes of exultation or anger would come later. And the throng stood to cheer the Emperor as he entered the royal box through its special corridor, clad all in purple and accompanied by his retinue. Bowing and smiling to the populace, he first had the owners and drivers presented to him, before giving the signal which had the trumpets blaring to announce the beginning of the games.

John Hawkwood hated the hippodrome and attended it as little as possible. But not to have come today would have aroused anger in his neighbours, and during the two and a half years he had spent in Constantinople he had learned to behave like a proper citizen of the greatest city in the world, even if he could never really become one.

For two days previously news had arrived of the death of the Emir Murad II, lord of the Ottomans. Constantinople had immediately been thrown into a frenzy of vicious joy. The devil was dead. As had previously happened on nearly every occasion when an emir died, there would surely be fratricidal strife amongst Murad's sons, perhaps years of civil war during which the Byzantines could continue to enjoy themselves.

The Emperor had proclaimed a holiday. In this, Constantine XI

29

was doing nothing more than was expected; his people preferred holidays to workdays. And Constantine was all too aware that he was not as popular as his late brother — for one very simple reason: he had wooed the West. Worse still, he had been received in audience by the Pope, in his anxiety to obtain additional troops to man his walls. To most of the Byzantines, this seemed worse than if he had crawled on his knees before the Turkish Emir.

But today he was acclaimed. He sat in splendour in the purple-swathed imperial box with his wife, Magdalena Tocco, and surrounded by his children, his sisters, and his younger brothers, Theodore and Andronicus, Demetrius and Thomas, his nieces and nephews ... and also by those who regarded themselves as the true upholders of the Byzantine tradition, men like Lukas Notaras and the Patriarch Gennadius, men to whom Turk and Roman were equally obnoxious.

John Hawkwood marked them well, as he had learned to on many occasions during the past two and a half years. If his dislike of them had been fuelled by theirs of him, by the many insults to which he had had to bow his head in subjection, it had a sound and justifiable basis.The walls of Constantinople were undoubtedly enormously strong, but the city could never be impregnable until every able-bodied man made its defence his common purpose. Yet the faction that threatened irretrievable ruin had been allowed to smoulder through the weakness of the emperors, and every so often, as today, was fanned into flame by the games. For if the Emperor cheered for the Blue, Notaras shouted for the Green, and the populace shrieked in their support for one or the other. These were not really games, Hawkwood thought; they were political gatherings of the deepest and most sinister importance.

Did he now regret his decision to leave England and seek his fortune in a foreign land? Sometimes, indeed, when he looked at his children. He hated to see Catherine wearing a Byzantine robe which flopped away from her shoulder to reveal her breasts or swirled away from her hips to expose a sliver of white leg; he hated to see her parted lips and flailing hair as she became as carried away as any Greek, her cheeks mottled red and white, teeth gleaming and seething with false passion. Catherine was now twenty-one, and a woman of striking loveliness. Had he remained in England and she not yet been married, he would have been disturbed, but in Constantinople he counted every day she remained a virgin a blessing.

Was he condemning his only daughter to spinsterhood? He could not be sure. There were suitors enough. Or were they suitors? Loose-lipped and seductive-eyed young men who came calling, hands sliding over each other's robes, arms round each other's waists, often to be found hand in hand, discussing poetry. Many possessed sound financial credentials, and parents apparently anxious to marry their sons to the daughter of a man who might be a heretic but enjoyed the favour of the Emperor himself. But marry his Catherine to one of those? Have her sucked into the Orthodox Church, and made the plaything of a Greek catamite?

Yet he was aware that the decision was hardly his. Catherine was a woman of character. Since coming to Constantinople that character seemed to have degenerated, and now she appeared determined to be more Byzantine than any Greek. Should she decide to wed, it would take a more brutal man than himself to forbid it. He could only pray that she would choose wisely when the time came, and that, until that day arrived, she would act wisely as well ... He disapproved of most of her current friends, especially the Notaras family.

His close guardianship of his daughter had done nothing to aid his popularity. But he worried hardly less about his sons — or Anthony, at least. William, he reflected with satisfaction, was a worthy Hawkwood. He was already an accomplished soldier and gunner, and was giving every evidence of developing into a sober, sensible man. He cheered for neither Blue nor Green, disliking the hippodrome as much as did his parents.

Perhaps Anthony, too, would develop satisfactorily. Perhaps nineteen was too young an age on which to form judgements, just as sixteen may have been too young an age to uproot the boy and carry him so far from his home. Now he looked quite as excited as Catherine did, screaming himself hoarse as the horses swept round the final bend ... and always glancing over to the royal box to smile and wave at that Notaras girl, Anna.

That was a more serious cause for concern, for both Catherine and Anthony had struck up friendships with the sons and daughter of the Grand Duke. Socially the Hawkwoods were in an anomalous position. As regards religion, for instance, since Mary flatly refused to worship in St Sophia, nor would she allow her children to attend, so every Sunday they took the ferry across to Galata to

31

attend the Genoan church. And though in receipt of imperial
favour, they were not of noble birth, while the Byzantine nobility
was perhaps the most stiff-necked in the world. Yet John
Hawkwood had come here as a master gunner, and the Emperor
had placed him in command of all the Byzantine artillery, with the
rank of general. Therefore he had stepped into the best circles, and
carried his family with him. Since young Basil Notaras aspired to
be a gunner himself, it was natural that the boy should have come
into contact with the young Hawkwoods — and fallen entirely
under the spell of Catherine's red-haired beauty.

Equally it was natural that the young man should have introduced the girl to his half-brother and his younger sister, and that
Anthony should have gone along as chaperon. John Hawkwood
didn't know if Anna Notaras had fallen equally for his red-haired
giant of a boy, but no-one looking at Anthony could doubt that he
was in love with her. They were very young, but John did not care
to imagine the Grand Duke's reaction should their relationship
become more serious — Anna Notaras was undoubtedly destined
for the bed of some Byzantine grandee. At the moment, his
concerns were more with Catherine, who had clearly fallen for
Basil Notaras. And although Basil might be only the bastard son of
the Grand Duke, Hawkwood could never see him being allowed to
marry a foreigner and an apostate. And the Notaras family needed
no favours from the Emperor. John had attempted to convey a
warning to the girl, and been impaled upon that imperious stare of
hers, so could do nothing more than pray that she would retain the
good sense and propriety to which she had been educated.

There were pitfalls to either side of the path he had chosen, but
there were pitfalls enough in England. And in Constantinople he
had at least been able to introduce his family to a luxury they had
never previously known, his yearly salary as general-in-command
of the artillery being more than he had earned in his entire life.
Long discarded were the short tunic and jerkin of an honest
English yeoman; the tunic he wore today all but brushed the
ground, and was of gold and black brocade. His chaperon and
liripipe were black, while his dark green undertunic was velvet,
and allowed to show at neck and sleeve. His long pointed shoes
were also black.

Mary was no less transformed in her patterned houppeland, her
jewelled girdle and her heart-shaped headdress with its jewelled

caul. But she was transformed in more than merely her appearance: the timorous, unhappy woman who had sailed up the Bosphorus had become submerged in the confident wife of a successful man. No doubt she was well aware how unpopular they were, as Catholics, but her house was filled with fine things and her husband was the friend of the Emperor. No doubt she, too, observed the dangers that surrounded her children — but she seemed confident they would overcome them. Indeed, confidence surrounded her like an aura; she had never believed her husband could achieve so much.

Even the meanest Byzantine enjoyed a luxury unknown to the average English lord. When John remembered the effort needed back home to fill a tub to bathe in — a single tub in which each member of the family must take his turn ... Here in Constantinople one merely turned on a tap; and in the better class houses one could have hot or cold water as one chose, supplied from the immense reservoirs that extended beneath the city.

Equally he could compare the tough and stringy English meat, so tasteless one could have been eating shoe leather, with the delicious Byzantine lamb dressed with spices he had only ever heard of before; or the rough English ale in contrast with the delicate red and white wines served here with every meal. Or, indeed, the rain of an English spring and the chill of an English winter against the perpetual summer of the Byzantine year. When the north wind blew off the Black Sea, and the locals shivered and grumbled, he felt tempted to suggest they should thank God they had never experienced a north-easterly gale coming off the North Sea on a January day in Suffolk.

Most important of all, he could contrast his humble standing in England with the eminence that had been thrust on him in Constantinople. He had an interview with the Emperor perhaps every week. That a man who ruled hardly more than a city should be so titled might seem a joke to many, but Constantine XI was heir to an imperial tradition which stretched back to the Caesars. And he had the character to support such a burden; more often melancholy than smiling, as he looked around himself at the immensity of the task he had inherited, he never doubted for a moment that the city could stand against the worst the Turks could do, or that he would personally conduct its defence.

The task was indeed immense. As the Emperor had once

explained to Hawkwood, the people of Constantinople had lost the martial vigour which had characterised their ancestors. It was not, John supposed, that they were cowardly; it was simply that they could not conceive of any force on earth interrupting their carefree existence. And if Constantinople had fallen to an assault once before, that was all but two and a half centuries ago. And if the week-long orgy of rape and pillage that had scarred the city forever was still remembered, it was also remembered that the hated Franks had been admitted by treachery; they had not stormed the city walls.

Thus, out of a population of some hundred thousand souls, less than five thousand were prepared to don armour in their own defence. This was far too few to adequately protect such an enormous circuit of walls. And Constantine's dream of an army of Western soldiers of fortune coming to his aid had long dwindled. There had been constant promises, but few volunteers had as yet followed John Hawkwood to the East.

So the city's defence rested on those five thousand — and it also rested with the artillery. But the artillery itself was not of the best. The iron pieces had been cast at least a generation before, and Hawkwood was not at all sure how they would stand up to continuous firing. He was not even allowed to practise with them often, because the citizens complained at the noise they made, and the Emperor worried that the walls would crumble under their vibration. So John had had to content himself with re-siting the cannon in what he considered were the most vital positions; a task accomplished with much grumbling by the soldiers required to drag the huge pieces of metal, and observed with an equal amount of contempt by those like the Grand Duke Notaras who felt that all Constantine's defensive efforts were bound to be futile, in view of the enormous strength commanded by the Ottomans, and that their only hope was to come to an accommodation with them — to pay them tribute and be left in peace.

"They want us here," the Grand Duke would insist. "We are their window on the world. Why should they seek to destroy us?"

John Hawkwood had no time for such defeatist talk. Constantinople *could* be held, even by the handful of men at their disposal. The Ottomans were no seamen, therefore the three miles of wall that stretched from the Golden Gate in the south to the Acropolis in the north-east, fronting throughout that distance the Sea of

Marmara, needed no more than regular patrols. Since there was no way the few galleys possessed by the Turks could hope to break the boom guarding the Golden Horn, as long as the Genoese held Galata on its north bank there was no possibility of attack from that direction either. This left the land wall of Theodosius, a long three miles, but, with the ditch and the double wall in front of them, four thousand resolute men supported by artillery could hold five thousand yards. Not even the Turks had the men to assault the entire wall at once.

"Constantinople will hold, Your Grace," he had assured the Emperor after his latest tour of inspection.

And now perhaps, he thought, as the steaming horses were brought to rest, and the winning Blues cheered themselves hoarse while the defeated Greens relapsed into sullen silence, these walls will not even be assaulted — at least for the foreseeable future. He wished he could catch just a glimpse of what was going on across the Bosphorus, in the seraglio of the dead Emir.

The crowd erupted from the hippodrome to make their way back into the city. It was early evening, and few people intended to sleep much that night. They thronged together in their factions, seeking the wineshops. And the more cautious householders began shuttering their windows; though it was a chill February night, no one could doubt there would be several violent riots before dawn, as the Blues and the Greens exchanged points of view.

"I believe our driver was bribed," Basil Notaras complained, white silk robe billowing as he strode in front of his half-brother and half-sister, his eyes searching the crowd. "The fellow should be whipped."

"He should be whipped in any event," Alexius agreed. "Look, there is your quarry, brother."

In front of them, Catherine Hawkwood's glowing head rose above the hurrying throng; she wore the fashionable *hennin*, the conical tall hat which added as much as two feet to a woman's height, and she stood out like a beacon.

"Damnation, her parents are with her," Basil muttered.

"Then we must coax her away," Alexius said. He was well aware of his brother's passion, and of Basil's determination to consummate it — this very night if possible. It was an occasion when normal guards would be lowered.

Basil increased speed, gripping his sister Anna by the hand as he forced his way through the throng without the slightest regard for whom he was pushing to left and right. People cursed, and more than once hands reached for daggers, but the weapons were always hastily released, for the people of Constantinople feared the anger of the Grand Duke far more than that of the Emperor — his arrogant sons had to be endured.

"Anthony!" Alexius called out, and Anthony Hawkwood turned his head, halting as he saw Anna Notaras panting at her brother's side.

"We are the losers," Alexius said, "so will you not drown your sorrows with us?"

"Why ... it would be a pleasure," Anthony agreed. Like all his family, he had learned fluent Greek since taking up residence in the city.

He smiled shyly at the girl. Anna Notaras was sixteen, tall for her age but very slender. Her features were as aquiline as those of her brothers, but softened into attractive contours; her chief beauty came from her eyes, huge and black and luminous. Her hair, as midnight dark as her eyes, was gathered in an enormous chignon, exposing the whiteness of her neck; above it rose a gold-coloured *hennin*. This was kept in place by a wide black band over her forehead and down to her shoulders, and matched the black girdle around the waist of her pale pink silk gown. On her right shoulder she wore a green rosette.

She was quite the loveliest thing Anthony had ever seen, as he thought every time he saw her.

He had raised his grey felt hat. He, too, was dressed in the height of fashion, in a brown and gold patterned jacket which ended at his thighs; his hose was grey, so snug-fitting as to outline at once buttocks and crotch — no woman in Constantinople could have any doubt about the endowments of the man she fancied, save that there were rascals who used outsize codpieces to disguise their shortcomings.

Anthony Hawkwood never wore a codpiece. But he, too, wore a green rosette.

"And you, William?" Alexius invited.

"You'll forgive me, sir, but I have things to do."

"Work, always work," Alexius smiled. "But you'll permit the lady Catherine to join us — in your brother's care."

36

William hesitated and glanced at his parents, who had stopped to overhear the conversation.

"We shall not be an hour," Anthony promised them. "And you are attending the Emperor's reception."

It sounded less a reminder than an accusation.

John Hawkwood looked at his wife. Mary's face was tight with disapproval, but she would not contest his prerogative as a father in public. Then he looked at his daughter, who returned his gaze. She allowed no change of expression, but it was clear she wished to accept the invitation. Her eyes were still dancing with the excitement of the race.

He felt a sudden spasm of apprehension clutch at his heart, but he would not risk a scene before the Notaras brothers.

"Be sure it is no longer than an hour," John Hawkwood said at last. "And stay well away from any brawls."

"Of course, Your Excellency," Alexius promised, making a leg and doffing his cap to Mary. "An hour, and they shall be returned safe to your house. You have my word."

He seized Anthony's arm. "We shall hide ourselves in my father's palace."

"Will he not object?"

"He is also attending the reception at the Imperial Palace — but why should my father object to your presence in our home? Are you not in Constantinople to defend us?"

Anthony was never certain how to take Alexius Notaras. Was he poking fun or paying a genuine compliment? But it would certainly be churlish to take offence at this moment, and besides he was being promised an hour in the company of the lovely Anna.

That a girl at once so beautiful and so well-born could ever smile upon such as him remained a source of total amazement. It had begun two years earlier, at the Emperor's coronation — the first time Anthony had ever entered the Cathedral, to gaze in wonder at the marble-faced walls into which were set magnificent mosaics, at the huge windowed vault of the roof, the private chapels, the gold embossed pulpit, the immense golden statue of the Virgin, the even more resplendent statue of Christ, the tall-hatted, black-robed priests ... and then at a girl standing quite close to him. Anna had been only fourteen years old, yet already she was, to his eyes, the most beautiful object of all in that mighty church. And she had smiled at him then, too.

Over the following two years they had exchanged further smiles and glances at the balls, regattas and fiestas that made up so great a part of Byzantine life. Exchanging words was a recent step, occurring only since Basil's so obvious infatuation with Catherine had led him to make advances to the Hawkwood family.

Anthony was not sure what Catherine really felt about Basil Notaras. He and his sister remained the closest of confidantes, and he shared her delight in the flowing febrile life of Constantinople, so different to their memories of England ... but on the subject of the young man, she had withdrawn into herself. She was undoubtedly very fond of his attentions, his continuous compliments, however, and she clearly found him attractive as a man, but she must be well aware that any ideas of a match would be frowned upon by both sets of parents.

But Anthony had no doubts as to what he himself wanted. And being masculine and totally confident, he desired nothing less.

Allowing his sister to be escorted by the two young noblemen, he dropped behind to walk beside Anna.

"I am sad when we lose," she said seriously. She was a true Byzantine from the top of her tall hat to the tip of the shapely little toes protruding from her sandals: the hippodrome was the most important thing in life for her.

"We shall win another day," Anthony promised.

"Another day is not good enough," she reproved him. "And to think of those awful Blues lording it over us ..."

As if she had given a cue, they heard the approaching chant: "Blue, Blue, Blue-Blue-Blue-Blue!"

"Quickly," Alexius called. "Down this alley."

Individuals might be afraid to cross swords with the sons of Lukas Notaras, but an excited mob was a different matter, and the five young people were still wearing their Green colours.

The brothers had already hurried Catherine towards safety; and Anthony felt emboldened to grasp Anna's arm to follow. It was the first time he had ever touched her, and felt shivers running up and down his spine. But before they could disappear into the gloom of the alley, there rose a shout.

"Greens! Stone the scum!"

Pebbles flew through the air, one striking Anna on the shoulder. She gave a little shriek, and appeared to faint into Anthony's arms. He was totally confused by this, uncertain whether to lift her on to

38

his shoulder, which was unthinkable — or indeed what to do.

The mob was now upon them, some twenty youths wearing the Blue colours.

"A girl," they hooted. "We'll paint her tits for her. We'll paint her blue."

"To me!" Anthony bawled desperately. "To me!"

But Alexius and Basil seemed to be out of earshot.

There was nothing else for it — and an alleyway in Constantinople was not very different from an alleyway in Naples. Anthony drew his sword and presented it to them. Though he dressed in the height of local fashion, he had refused to succumb to Byzantine custom in the manner of weapons, and this was his trusty broadsword. No matter that it would need two hands to swing properly, it yet gave the hooting mob pause for thought. But as he slowly retreated into the narrow alleyway, conscious of Anna weighing on his left arm, her scent clouding into his nostrils, he felt her stir.

"Anna," he said urgently. "Anna!"

She straightened, and seemed to realise where she was. His arm was around her waist, encompassing a great deal of unsuspected softness and she hastily stepped away from him. "My God!" she muttered.

"Make off," he urged her. "See if you can find your brothers, but make off."

"Her tits!" the youths howled. "We'll paint them blue. And her arse."

"Hurry," Anthony begged.

She fled.

"She's getting away." the mob hooted.

They surged forward, but Anthony now had both hands round the hilt of his sword, and he advanced towards them. They checked as he swung the great weapon, left and then right, performing the perfect figure-of-eight his father had taught him and which would mow down any living creature in front of him.

The mob hastily retired. Several had drawn their own small swords, but there was no possibility of getting close enough to use one without having his head cut from his shoulders. They retreated further.

Anthony completed their discomfiture by another advance. As long as he remained within the narrow alley — barely four feet wide — they could not surround him; indeed could only come at him two at a time.

They began hurling stones again, but half-heartedly now; they had sought a bit of fun, not a genuine set-to. And their prey had clearly made good her escape. Anthony retreated once more into the alley, and this time the mob did not attempt to follow. But he kept his sword at the ready until he had reached the other end, emerging into a broader but empty thoroughfare.

He looked left and right, but could see neither his sister nor his friends.

"Anthony! Hsst!"

He spun round and spotted Anna standing in the shadow of a wall. "Thank God, you are safe."

"I knew I would be safe with you." She trembled.

He put a comforting arm round her shoulders; it seemed the most natural thing to do. "Where are your brothers?"

"I haven't seen them."

Catherine left alone with the two Notaras brothers, when he had been detailed to chaperon her? Of all the misfortunes to occur, when he was so suddenly and strangely alone with the girl of his dreams.

She seemed to understand his anxiety. "My father's palace is in the next street," she said breathlessly. "They will have retired there."

"Yes," he agreed. "We must hurry."

She held his hand and led him on, while he gratefully sheathed his sword.

"Such a weapon," she remarked enigmatically.

At the portico of the Grand Duke's palace there were always two armed guards on duty.

"Have you seen my brothers?" she asked them.

"No, my lady," they answered without hesitation, staring at Anthony curiously.

"Master Hawkwood has saved me from violence at the hands of the Blues," she explained. Still clutching Anthony's hand, she drew him into the portico itself. Its roof rose a full thirty feet above his head, supported by splendidly carved stone pillars.

Inside the building, he blinked at the richness of the drapes and furnishings, the marvellous polish of the floors, the obsequiousness of the servants who bowed to their young mistress. Though John

Hawkwood's house was, by courtesy, referred to as a palace, this indeed *was* a palace.

Suddenly he inhaled a scent which was all too familiar. Catherine had been in this hall, and very recently.

Which meant she was still inside the palace.

"Master Hawkwood and I will have sherbet," Anna commanded, and the servants hurried off, save for one senior man, who continued to stare at Anthony. He was an elderly fellow, with grim features and a discerning eye; his tunic was rich enough in gold braid to indicate some authority in the Notaras household.

"Anna," Anthony said, "those guards outside were lying. I know my sister is here. I must find her immediately."

Anna frowned and turned to the major-domo.

"Have my brothers returned yet, Michael?"

"No, my lady."

"Are you sure of that?"

"Of course, my lady."

"Ah! But they told us to meet them here," Anna said. "Come, Anthony, you must be mistaken. We will await them on the terrace."

"She is here," Anthony insisted. "This fellow is but obeying someone's orders. Anna, I will see Catherine now."

"Are you accusing him of lying?" Anna demanded, her eyes suddenly cold. "My father's steward? Why ..." She gazed open-mouthed at the staircase, down which Alexius Notaras was at that moment descending.

"I heard your voices," he said. "You had no trouble with the mob, I trust."

"No thanks to you," Anthony snapped. He was now as angry as he was alarmed. "Where is my sister?"

"My brother is showing her round our house," Alexius said.

Anthony knew he must not quarrel if he could avoid it. "Then I also would like to see the house," he said. "Will you take me to them?"

"Why, I will not," Alexius declared. "I thank you for returning my sister to us, but now you had best take yourself off."

"But Catherine?" Anthony demanded. "She must come with me."

"We will escort her home when she is ready to return."

"Do you suppose I can permit that?" Anthony's anger at last

overcame his caution as his imagination roamed over what might be possibly happening upstairs to his sister, his darling Catherine. "You are a wretch, Alexius. Aye, you and your knavish brother. I will have my sister brought to me now, and if she has been harmed ..."

"By God, but you go too far, you Azymite scoundrel. Steward! Have this fellow thrown out."

The major-domo immediately clapped his hands.

Anna had watched the exchange in open-mouthed consternation. "Do not be hard on him, Alexius," she begged. "He saved me from the mob."

"Then let him play the gentleman and withdraw," Alexius snapped. "In my opinion he is a most importunate scoundrel."

Men armed with staves hurried into the hall — just as a servant carrying a tray of sherbet also appeared, and stopped to stare at the scene before him.

Without further consideration Anthony drew his sword, as he had done once before in defence of Catherine's honour.

"Strike him down!" Alexius shouted. "He means mischief."

"Stop him!" Anna screamed, her earlier gratitude changing into alarm. "He will kill us all."

"I will have my sister," Anthony yelled, and ran at Alexius, who promptly leapt behind his major-domo. Anthony ignored him and headed for the stairs. "Catherine!" he shouted. "Catherine, come to me!"

He took a few steps upwards, then checked. The landing above him had filled with women. Most of them were domestics, but they were dominated by Catherine, standing among them.

Basil Notaras was nowhere to be seen, but he could not be far away.

Catherine had removed her *hennin*, and her cotehardie was in disarray. Her cheeks were flushed and her eyes sparkling, although at this moment with disapproval.

"Anthony!" she called down. "You are causing a brawl. Please allow me to manage my own affairs."

He gasped in disbelief. "You ..."

"Anthony!" she screamed. "Look to yourself."

He heard a movement behind him, and hastily turned, but too late. There was a blinding flash before his eyes and he lost consciousness.

42

Moments later he came to his senses, stretched out on the marble floor with men and women all around him.

"Is he hurt?" his sister was asking anxiously.

"A thick-headed papist? We have not broken his skull."

"He deserves to have been killed," Anna said, her voice shrill. "He attacked my brother."

"Aye," Alexius said.

"I pray you, do not harm him," Catherine begged. "He behaved as no more than a brother would."

"And a hero." Alexius sneered. "Go upstairs, all of you. I will not harm him. You have my word."

Catherine hesitated, then hurried up the stairs.

Anna followed.

Alexius glared down at Anthony. "A hero," he scoffed.

"What is to be done with him, sir?" the steward Michael asked.

"Take him out on to the street," Notaras said, "and there beat him until he cannot walk. Then throw him into the gutter. And "— he flung out his hand to point at the broadsword — "break that into four pieces."

John Hawkwood stared at his younger son in consternation.

The elder Hawkwoods had earlier returned from the Emperor's reception to find William in a state of some alarm; Catherine and Anthony had now been absent for three hours.

"There is considerable rioting in the streets," John commented. "Your mother and I were nearly set upon."

"My God, if Catherine has become involved in a brawl ..." Mary's voice was tight with concern.

"She had three young men with her," John growled. And then they all heard the stumbling steps in the entrance hall.

Anthony's fine clothes were torn, he moved groggily, there was blood on his face, and he was without his sword.

Mary screamed, rushing to him.

William assisted his brother to a seat. "What happened?"

Anthony shook his head in misery.

"Where's your sister?" John Hawkwood demanded.

Anthony sighed. "She went ... She went off with Basil and Alexius Notaras. It was because of the mob, you see. And then ... at the Notaras' palace ..." His voice tailed away.

"Tell me what happened. Straight now, boy!"

Anthony obliged him — but he did not dare tell them that Catherine had wanted to stay there, had even allowed him, her own brother, to be beaten by servants. He did not suppose he would ever be able to comprehend that. He felt as if she had trodden on his very heart. But it would have to remain their personal secret, or he would never be able to look his father and mother in the face again.

His parents and brother listened in silence until he was finished.

"Those scoundrels," John growled. "They have had their way with her."

"She did not come when her own brother called," Mary snapped, seizing on Anthony's lie as the significant part of the tale. "She did not even answer him."

"I'll not condemn her unheard," John snapped in reply.

"They broke my sword," Anthony said in utter despair.

"Which you had used in the defence of their sister," William agreed.

John broke in, "Well, it is done. And you are all but done. Get you to bed, boy."

Anthony hesitated, then staggered from the room.

"You will not avenge him?" William demanded.

"And what of your daughter?" Mary inquired coldly; at that moment she was clearly not considering Catherine to be *her* daughter.

John Hawkwood buckled on the sword he had just discarded. "I must go to fetch her back. And, if necessary, I will avenge her."

"As will I," William agreed, and picked up his weapon, too.

"Ah, General," remarked the Grand Duke. "It is a late hour, but nonetheless you are welcome."

John Hawkwood's gaze took in the huge room into which they had been shown. It was hardly smaller than a baronial hall, although ikons rather than shields decorated the walls. But there was no furniture beyond a large wooden table and several chairs, and it was overlooked by a gallery. Hawkwood saw men up there, and he did not doubt they were armed, as were the Grand Duke himself and his two sons, standing in front of the huge table. To one side there were several servants carrying staves, which would prove formidable enough at close quarters.

But Hawkwood had faced greater odds than these, and at this

44

moment he had a total contempt for the Byzantines; also he knew that William, as tall and strong as himself, was standing at his side.

"I have come to escort my daughter home, my lord," he said carefully.

"It is your daughter that I wish to speak to you about," Notaras said. "Catherine elected to spend the night here, General. The streets are not safe for women, and there have been cases of assault.

"Your own daughter was saved from one such assault by my brother," William growled. "In gratitude for which your people broke his head."

"I apologise. There was a misunderstanding. But the boy is hot-headed. He drew on my servants, and they had to defend themselves.

"He drew in defence of his sister," William said.

"Be quiet, boy," John Hawkwood snapped. "My lord, I have come for my daughter. I will have her brought to me now. And I will tell you straight, I intend to seek satisfaction should any harm have befallen her."

Notaras snorted. "Do you suppose you can give orders in my house, General?"

"Catherine came here of her own will," Alexius Notaras said slyly.

"She is now with my sister," Basil told them. "They are friends. She can come to no harm."

"I will have her *now*," John Hawkwood repeated. "Or I will break down your house."

The Grand Duke stared at him from under frowning brows. Then he pointed. "Throw this carrion out," he commanded.

The servants advanced and John drew his sword. Behind him he heard the rasp of William doing likewise.

"The lads," John said in a low voice. "We'll take one of them. That'll settle the matter."

Shoulder to shoulder they charged the servants, who promptly turned and fled as they discovered themselves opposed by English steel, and knew that this time they were not faced by a boy but by two experienced soldiers.

"Cut them down!" Notaras bellowed, sword drawn, but retreating with his sons towards the inner doorway.

John heard the sound of men jumping down from the gallery,

but he knew he could leave his back to William, who without bidding swung to face this new assault. He hurled himself forward, but before he could reach the doorway the Grand Duke and his sons were through it, and it had been closed and the bolt shot home. John heard the clash of steel behind him and turned, to see William performing a two-handed sweep which sent one of the Byzantines sprawling with blood pouring from his shoulder into which the broadsword had bitten. The rest had retreated against the far wall.

"Bows," Notaras shrieked, emerging on to the gallery above them. "Shoot them down!"

Two of the men hurried from the room.

"Father, we do no good here," William said urgently. "If we both die, it will not help Catherine. This is a matter for the Emperor."

John Hawkwood hesitated, but he knew his son was right.

"Then let us charge those servants," he said. "And escape while we can."

The Emperor Constantine sighed and threw the piece of parchment to the floor. "You stand accused," he said.

"Of behaving as a father should?" John Hawkwood demanded.

"Of causing an affray. Of threatening behaviour. Of destruction to property."

"It was my intention to regain my daughter, Your Grace." John allowed his gaze to play across the faces behind the throne, his lip curling as he saw Notaras standing half-behind the Patriarch.

"And your son is accused of murder," Constantine said wearily.

"My son defended himself against armed men."

"But one of them died."

"That was likely to happen, Your Grace."

"The Frank has killed a Greek," growled Gennadius.

"My daughter had ben raped," John shouted. "The boy's sister had been raped. She is still held captive in the palace of the Grand Duke."

"I deny that," Notaras said. "She came to my house of her own free will. What took place between her and my son occurred also of her own free will."

"But lacking her parents' permission," the Emperor snapped in obvious displeasure.

Notaras drew a long breath. "My son will marry the girl."

Heads turned in astonishment. That the haughty Grand Duke was willing to let even his bastard marry an Azymite was virtually a confession of guilt.

Notaras pointed at William Hawkwood, standing at his father's shoulder. "In return, that scoundrel must die."

"He has murdered a Greek," the Patriarch repeated. "His life is forfeit."

Constantine gazed sadly at John — and John realised with horror that the Emperor did not feel strong enough to protect him.

"I protest, Your Grace," he said. "Had we not defended ourselves, we would have been cut down." He pointed in turn. "That man commanded it."

"But you are alive, and one of my subjects is dead," the Emperor said. "Your son must pay the forfeit."

"And do you suppose my daughter will wish to legalise her union with Basil Notaras if her brother is executed?"

"They will be married," Notaras asserted. "I will see to it."

John wondered if Catherine had any idea of the catastrophe she had caused by her careless, wicked behaviour. But he also realised that if he was to save William's life he had to play his trump card — and let his daughter go to the devil. "If my son is condemned," he declared, "then I can no longer remain in Constantinople."

As the Emperor stared at him, John could see that his friend was close to tears. But he slowly understood, and the sinking feeling in his stomach grew, that Constantine was not even prepared to defend his general of artillery if it meant antagonising the powerful Grand Duke.

"Yes," the Emperor said at last. "There is a Genoese carrack leaving Galata tonight. Be on it, with your wife and your younger son. No one will molest you before then."

John's head came up. "And my elder son?"

"His life is forfeit."

William gasped and glanced left and right; but they were not allowed to wear arms in the Imperial presence, and besides they were surrounded by guards.

"Your Grace, you cannot do this!" John shouted.

"I am giving you your life. I can do no more."

Still John could not believe his ears. "Your Grace," he said in a lower tone. "You are committing an outrage."

"Treason!" the Grand Duke shouted, and the cry was taken up.

"Silence!" the Emperor commanded. "I have given my judgement, John Hawkwood. Now leave my presence. If you or your son are found in Constantinople when the cock crows tomorrow, you will be executed. Get you gone, man, while there is still time."

"Look lively now," commanded the Genoese captain. He was a different one, of course, from the man who had brought the Hawkwoods to Constantinople more than two years before, yet might it have been no more than twenty-four hours between the two. "There's half a northerly gale blowing. We'll be out of the Bosphorus like a pip squeezed out of an orange."

John Hawkwood made no reply as he helped his wife up the gangplank and into the cabin. Anthony gloomily followed with the few bundles they had put together in the little time available to them.

They had simply walked away from their fine house — and from the life they had built for themselves. Mary had been too thunderstruck by the sudden change in their fortunes even for tears. After enjoying for two years such luxury as she had never known before, she did not seem able to grasp yet that her family had just been sliced in half and her prosperity trampled underfoot.

Anthony could understand her bewilderment. He was not at all sure how it had happened. Why it had happened, he certainly realised. His instincts were to feel himself guilty ... but once Catherine had made up her mind to commit an act of criminal folly, what had followed had been almost inevitable. That she had sent no word of excuse, much less sympathy, for the disaster she had inflicted on her family, was even more heartbreaking.

That the tantalising Anna Notaras had also clearly turned against him was but one of the many pains he now had to bear. But it was his pride that had suffered most. Even with constant twinges from his battered body, his cut face and hands, he still could hardly accept the reality that he had been punched and kicked time and again, rolled along the road like a barrel, and all the time helpless with his hands tied behind his back.

He could not really believe that they had broken his sword, or that the following morning they would garrotte his brother.

He placed the few bundles in the cabin and returned on deck. He did not wish to look at his parents' faces.

It was just dusk, and lights were glowing both in Galata and in the city across the water. After the excesses of the previous night, most of Constantinople would no doubt be early to bed. But William Hawkwood would be standing at his cell window, staring out at the night for the last time; he was to be executed at dawn.

And Catherine Hawkwood? What would she be staring at? What would she be thinking?

He was aware of a sudden, consuming anger. Worse than Catherine's behaviour, his own humiliation or William's condemnation was the terrible realisation that his father had accepted these catastrophes. It was easy to say he had had no choice. But Father, who had always faced up to his enemies, be they weather, pestilence or human foes, with his sword in his hand ... Father had accepted this total defeat, and was now fleeing Constantinople like a thief in the night, while the Grand Duke and his sons no doubt were laughing over their wine at the abject figure the great *condottiere* had suddenly become.

In a matter of hours, Father seemed to have been reduced from a demi-god to a very humble man. Anthony could not imagine where he could go from here — where any of them could go. Mother was shattered; since last night she had changed from a confident, attractive, middle-aged woman into a stricken old hag. Father's dreams were ended. He could do nothing more than crawl back to England and seek employment as a man-at-arms. But would he ever truly have the courage again to look an enemy in the face?

And he himself? They had broken his sword. They had taken his brother to strangle, and they had seduced his sister and turned her into a whore.

He stared back at the city as the brisk wind, even inside the Golden Horn, took them over the dropped boom and out into the Bosphorus. Now they were rounding the Acropolis, where the Emperor was no doubt dining at that moment.

"I hate you!" Anthony shouted, his words winging on the wind. "I hate you all. One day I will come back and destroy you. One day ..." The wind tore his sentence to pieces — but it had already ended. Tears were streaming down his face.

The wind freshened. Anthony had remained all the while on deck; he had no wish to be closeted below with his parents. Now he felt the storm tearing at his clothes and his hair, driving the moisture from his eyes, for as the carrack left the comparative shelter of the narrow strait and entered the Sea of Marmara the waves became huge, roaring up astern and yet sending spray flying over the decks. The very elements were sharing in his despair.

"It is too much," said the mate. "We must turn back."

"Turn back?" bellowed the captain. "What good would that do? Against both the current and a gale? We would sail backwards. God curse you for a poltroon. If the wind frightens you, shorten sail."

The mate gladly gave the commands, and men went aloft to reduce the canvas. It made little difference; the carrack still plunged along at ten knots, about double her designed speed. The lights of Constantinople remained abeam for no more than a few minutes, then fell astern. To starboard there were other lights, those on the Turkish side of the channel. But they, too, quickly fell behind.

"It will be better when we leave the land," the captain said. "You'll see."

"I cannot hold her," the helmsman gasped. "The wind has shifted."

The captain gazed aloft. Now they were well clear of the narrows, the wind had indeed backed to the west, and was blowing them off course. Hurriedly he gave orders to change the set of the sails, then himself went to the wheel to assist.

Anthony clung to the taffrail and stared back at the dwindling lights, at the white-capped seas which battered at the stern, throwing the ship from side to side, causing her to yaw dangerously even with two men on the helm. The last light vanished, and the night was black. Farewell, Constantinople, he thought. Farewell, William. Farewell, Catherine. And farewell, Anna Notaras. The tears started to his eyes again. He would never return. He would never be, or do, anything, now. He would never . . . There were shouts from the watch, and he turned to look forward, at an even darker blackness than the night. Before he could grasp what it was there was a terrifying jar, and the ship turned broadside to the waves. Anthony lost his grasp on the rail and was thrown headlong to the deck. He was brought up against the mizzen mast, just as the mast itself went by the board, snapping off only a few feet above his head and crashing over the side with a fearsome rending sound.

The other masts had also gone, and the ship itself was on her

50

beam ends, grinding and rising and falling with shattering crashes as the waves pounded her.

"Abandon ship," the captain was shouting. "Abandon ship!"

Father and Mother! Anthony clawed himself up from the sloping deck, gained the companion ladder in the midst of several other bodies, throwing them left and right. Out of the darkness and the noise he heard his father's voice calling to him, and a moment later he grasped John Hawkwood's hand. John in turn held tight to Mary, apparently paralysed by this sudden extra misfortune which had overtaken them.

"What has happened?" John gasped.

"We have been driven on to a sandbank," Anthony answered.

"The boat," John said. "We must make the boat."

Amidship, sailors were launching the boat, and Anthony led his parents towards it, struggling to keep his footing on the steeply sloping deck, constantly swept by the waves and flying spray which hit the now helpless hulk. He gazed at the land, that deeper darkness he had noticed just before the ship had struck, which now lay very close: a beach backed by low cliffs. He had no idea what land it was.

The boat was in the water, for the moment sheltered from the full force of the storm by the wrecked carrack, bobbing on the waves, held to the ship by two lines.

"Make room," Anthony shouted. "Make room."

They were allowed on board, grudgingly, and the captain gave the word to cast off. Anthony looked back at the wreck as the oars were thrust into the waves. There lay even the few pitiable belongings they had been able to take from Constantinople. Now they were truly destitute.

He had not long to grieve. The boat was picked up by a wave as soon as it left the shelter of the ship's side, and it was hurled forward. The stern went up, and men fell out of their seats. Oars flew through the air. So did Anthony, for the second time that night. This time he found himself in the water, went under, and touched ground. When he thrust his head up into air again, he was still standing.

He groped around and found his mother, hauled her up the beach, while waves broke against his back and made him stagger. "Father!" he gasped. "Father!" he shouted.

"Here, boy. Here!"

51

Still alive! Anthony waded out of the water, and placed his mother on the sand. She gasped and groaned, but she was safe. Then he helped his father and the captain from the shallows.

"That was a miracle," John Hawkwood panted. "I had supposed us lost."

"Lost," the captain said. "Oh, aye, we are lost."

"We are alive, man," John told him.

"But yet lost." The captain pointed at the horsemen who were guiding their mounts down a steep incline from the cliffs towards the beach. Anthony had a quick impression of flowing robes and superb horsemanship,

"Lost," the captain moaned again. "Those are Ottomans!"

3

HUNKAR

The captain was soon proved right. The survivors of the shipwreck, some fifteen men and Mary Hawkwood, were quickly roped together and driven from the beach and up the incline to the cliff-top, encouraged by the whips of the horsemen. When Anthony tried to save his mother from being manhandled, he received several cracks across the head which stretched him all but sense-less on the beach. It was the second time in two days he had suffered a beating, and he could now do no more than stagger in the gloom behind the sailor to whom he was tied.

"Merciful God!" John Hawkwood begged. "What have we done to deserve this?"

Mary could not even speak, but large tears rolled down her face.

They reached the cliff-top panting, and were then force-marched to an encampment a hundred yards away, its tents hardly visible in the darkness. There they were belaboured into a group, and left to themselves, although surrounded by Turks on all sides.

"Lost," the captain moaned. "Lost."

"Do you not know their language?" John demanded.

"I speak some words of it. That is why I say we are lost."

"Can you not ask for water? Without it, we shall be dead by dawn."

"We *shall* be dead by dawn," the captain agreed. "Or soon after."

His pessimism was most depressing, but John quickly under-stood his reluctance to beg for water. When one of the other seamen rashly did so, he was promptly beaten about the head and shoulders with a cane.

The night drifted slowly by, and while their thirst, hunger and discomfort of their bonds grew more taxing, the wind slowly began to abate. Had they delayed their departure from Galata by only a few hours they might have avoided the worst of the storm, and thus the shipwreck. It seemed as if a malignant fate was haunting

53

their every movement, determined to bring them to destruction.

This came closer at daybreak, which was heralded by the cry of a muezzin summoning the faithful to prayer. The call was swiftly obeyed by every man in the camp, who knelt facing to the south — the direction of Mecca.

Now the captives could look around them at the elaborate tents above which green flags floated in the dawn breeze. Each skin hut was large enough to contain several men, but equally capable of being quickly dismantled, and a rapid glance around informed John Hawkwood that this was very much the temporary encampment of a patrol. That the carrack should have been cast away at the sipahis' very feet was another example of the bad luck that seemed to have been following his family for some time.

The surrounding country was brown and arid, with nothing better than a few stunted trees to break the horizon, save to the south-west, where the waters of the Sea of Marmara moved restlessly.

John then studied the Ottoman soldiers who, having finished their devotions, ate and drank with great gusto, ignoring their captives' misery. Despite his fears and his physical discomfort, John Hawkwood's practised eye could not help but admire his captors for their sense of martial spirit and their confident demeanour, but also for the quality of their equipment. Each man wore voluminous blue breeches tucked into soft kid boots beneath a long-sleeved white tunic. Their headdress was a round steel helmet with a steel spike to turn aside a blow, and over the tunic they wore a loose chain-mail cuirass which fell to the thighs; the garments beneath were of thick felt, and would prove difficult to penetrate by any but the sharpest sword. The sipahis' own swords certainly looked as sharp as razors, and were curved; these were soldiers who slashed rather than thrust. They were also armed with lances and with bows and arrows, and in every way bore out the Emperor Constantine's description of them as being the best light cavalry in the world.

But there was no evidence of any firearms; so even these fine soldiers would be unable to stand up to cannon fire.

There was a sudden drumming of hooves as some more men rode into camp, escorting a splendid figure. Like the sipahis, he wore a chain-mail cuirass and a domed steel helmet, but his white tunic was heavily embroidered with cloth of gold, and he carried a horsetail wand with a single knot tied in it.

"Their pasha," the captain muttered dolefully.

The new arrival dismounted and strode across to gaze at them, while his officers stood to either side, grinning and making comments. Their fierce eyes, strong features and curling moustaches gave no indication of the least pity for the plight of the people they had dragged from the beach.

The pasha was a man of harshly aquiline features, only half concealed by his beard and moustache. He gave an order, and his men strode amongst the prisoners, swinging their canes and whips. Still bound together, and suffering from cramp as well as exhaustion and hunger, there was no possibility of the Christians offering any resistance, and they allowed themselves to be formed into a rough line, whereupon they were stripped of their clothing, the offending cloth being cut away where necessary.

"By God!" John growled. "What devilry is this?"

"They but wish to ascertain whether any of us are worth saving," the captain said.

To John's relief the assault did not include his wife, who was quite ignored. But the men's genitals were now examined by eager fingers. He could not bring himself to look at Anthony, who was clearly as dumbfounded as himself.

"If you were circumcised," the captain said, "you would have a chance of survival."

"By God!" John muttered again. It had never occurred to him that life or death could depend on a sliver of skin.

While the examination was going on, the pasha walked slowly up the line of prisoners, and now he arrived in front of the two Hawkwoods, frowning at them as he took in their great height and red hair. Then he turned his head and barked a command.

The soldiers parted to make way for another man, much older than themselves, who carried a staff rather than a scimitar, and wore a round white felt cap rather than a helmet. His equally white beard reached to his waist.

The pasha addressed him, and he in turn looked at John and Anthony. Then he spoke in Greek. "Halim Pasha asks you this," he said to John, his voice high and inclined to quaver. "Are you the man called Hawk, who serves the Byzantines?"

John hesitated, surprised by the Turkish knowledge of what went on inside the city. Presumably the Ottomans would regard a

Byzantine general as even more of an enemy than a Genoese sailor. But according to the captain they would be killed anyway.

"I am John Hawkwood," he replied. "But I have left the service of the Emperor."

The mufti translated for the pasha, who was stroking his beard.

"And this is your son?" the mufti asked.

"And my wife," John said.

"She is of no account," the mufti said.

"On the contrary," John said wearily, "she is of every account to me."

The mufti gazed at him for several seconds, then nodded, turning to confer with the pasha. The pasha also considered for a few moments, while Anthony found himself holding his breath — was there a chance of reprieve or merely an agonising death?

Suddenly the pasha gave an order, and the ropes binding the three Hawkwoods to the other sailors were cut. Other bonds were immediately attached to them, and they were led away from the Genoese seamen.

"Farewell," the captain called to them.

"What is to become of us?" John asked.

"I do not know, my friend. I do not know."

John addressed the mufti. "I beg of you, sir, my wife can hardly stand. A cup of water ..."

The mufti gave orders, and to their amazement food and water were immediately produced. The food was very dry, some kind of cereal in which a few pieces of stringy meat were buried, and they had to eat it with their dirty fingers, but it was none the less like a feast to them. None was offered to the Genoese sailors. That would have been a waste.

For the pasha had remounted his horse, and so had his soldiers. Now the sipahis began to gallop around the group of seamen. Taking their bows from their shoulders and drawing arrows from their quivers, they began firing into the throng of naked men. The first arrow struck home, and a sailor screamed and fell, pulling one of his comrades with him. The victim did not die immediately, but continued to scream and writhe. His fellows insensibly turned away from the horsemen to form a huddle, and a larger target. Uttering cries of pleasure, the horsemen drew further arrows from their quivers and fired into the mass of maked flesh now presented to them. They needed little accuracy; every shaft struck home.

Blood spattered and pooled on the ground as the Genoese shrieked their agony and begged for mercy. The huddle soon collapsed to its knees, several already dead, and then subsided further until it was merely a sprawl of dead and dying humanity. And still the sipahis fired, until there was no movement at all.

The Hawkwoods watched the destruction of their companions in horror, Anthony vainly tugging at the ropes on his wrists.

"My God, but what manner of men are these?" he gasped.

"They are certainly devils," John Hawkwood said in awe.

But superb horsemen and superb archers as well, he realised. The massacre of the Genoese had taken only a few minutes, so accurate was their shooting. Now the sipahis had dismounted and were stamping about amongst the dead to reclaim their arrows.

"Then what is to become of *us*?" Anthony asked.

"As that poor captain said, who knows? You'll die like a man when the time comes, Anthony."

When the time comes, Anthony thought. Alas, I am but nineteen years old. But, then, William was only twenty-one. And he would have been dying about the same time as these sailors ...

But perhaps they had been the lucky ones. For now the sipahis were mounted again, each with a full quiver again, and whips were snatching at the prisoners' shoulders as the end of the rope binding them was tied to the saddle of one of the horsemen. The pasha was soon leading his men away from the camp and over the stony countryside — and behind him the Hawkwoods stumbled, naked and bleeding.

In the heat and misery Anthony lost track of time. The sun burned his shoulders, arms and back; the stones cut his feet, his knees and belly when he tripped and fell, dragged onwards by the relentless movement of the sipahi's horse, trying desperately to protect his genitals from permanent injury.

But he worried more for his parents, who were so much older than he. Mary kept stumbling also, but always jerked back to her feet by the cruel rope dragging on her wrists, while her clothes were slowly torn to ribbons. Her head drooped and he knew she was all but unconscious, even though she kept moving.

John Hawkwood's head also drooped, but Anthony sensed it was more from despair and horror than from exhaustion.

The day grew hotter, until at last the cavalcade stopped in the shade of a clump of trees. Once again the Hawkwoods were fed and given more water to drink; their tongues were so swollen it was painful to swallow.

"At least they seemed determined to keep us alive," Anthony ventured.

"Where are you taking us?" John asked the mufti when at last the holy lawyer came to inspect them.

"To the Emir," the mufti replied curtly.

"But the Emir is dead," John said without thinking.

"The Emir is never dead," the mufti told him. "He is eager for information concerning Constantinople. You will please him if you talk straight to him."

"And will he spare our lives?"

"The Emir obeys the law," the mufti said enigmatically, and walked away.

"How far away, do you think, is this Emir?" Anthony asked.

"God knows, boy." But John was thinking. News of Murad's death had arrived in Constantinople only a few days ago. But already it appeared that there was a new Emir, and already he was close to the Bosphorus. Something remarkable must have happened within the Ottoman enclaves, and very suddenly.

All afternoon the sun remained breath-searingly hot, but the country through which they stumbled improved: from stones and dust to cultivated fields; then trees, mainly cypresses, became more common. Men were working in the fields, together with veiled women, who were totally concealed behind their haiks and yashmaks so that only their foreheads, eyes and feet were visible. They ceased their labour to stare at the two big naked white men, and clapped their hands with pleasure.

But the Hawkwoods were past caring.

Dusk brought the cavalcade to the castle of Anatolia-Hissar, which the prisoners had first beheld on their voyage up the Bosphorus two and a half years earlier, and from where the lights of Constantinople could clearly be seen scarcely a mile away across the strait. So, Anthony thought, they were going to die within sight of that accursed city after all.

But here there was nothing less than an army. For, stretching away from the castle on the landward side, could be made out, even in the darkness, an immense encampment of tents glowing with light within and without, as the Ottoman troops cooked their evening meal.

The castle itself, with its inner and outer walls, its crenellations, dry moat, keep, high towers, approach ramps which could be commanded by a handful of men, and its portcullis in the gateway, was clearly modelled on those built by the crusaders in the Holy Land three centuries before, many of which, John Hawkwood knew, were still standing. He found the design fascinating, as indicating that, far from being a savage horde from Central Asia, as they were generally regarded by the Byzantines, the Ottomans were clearly willing to learn from their enemies.

By the time they arrived before the open gates, even the two men could hardly stand. Mary had collapsed more than an hour earlier, and had been since carried by her husband, a double burden because of the rope constantly biting into his wrists. Now he and Anthony were cut free of her, and she was left to lie in the courtyard of the castle, while they were driven forward by the whips of their captors. Even in their distraught condition, they could not help but look right and left at the men who crowded forward to peer at them. These were garishly uniformed in dark blue cloaks over red tunics; their pantaloons were red, and over them they wore heavily embroidered white skirts. Their caps were yellow with white horsehair plumes. Their appearance might even have seemed effeminate, but both Hawkwoods knew that they were now in the presence of the most feared soldiers in the world: the Ottoman Janissaries.

Given some water to drink, they were then thrust up stone steps and into a large chamber on the first floor of the castle. Here were drapes and carpets of the richest design and material, luxuriously soft divans and low tables decorated with inlaid designs. The cool splendour of the apartment left the Hawkwoods breathless, even as they realised that their true ordeal might be only beginning.

For here, too, were a good score of men staring at the two naked, dust-covered, sun-burned and blood-stained captives. John and Anthony had been thrust through the doorway with such force that they fell to the floor, and were for some moments unable to regain their feet. But their guards were also prostrating themselves before the men who sat at the far end of the room.

Slowly Anthony raised his head, and his eyes met those of the man seated on the divan exactly opposite him. He was somewhat old — older than Father, Anthony thought — but dressed with extravagant richness, his green tunic laced with gold and his pantaloons clearly made of silk.

Their captor, Halim Pasha, was now kneeling beside this resplendent individual, whom Anthony assumed had to be the new Emir, speaking very rapidly to him. The man's gaze drifted over the pair of them. His eyes were black, deep and fathomless, his expression almost mild. Was this truly the lord of all the Ottomans?

Anthony endeavoured to look away, and his gaze moved upwards. High on the wall of the chamber there was a gallery, but entirely closed off from the lower floor by an intricate trellis-work screen through which anyone standing there could look down into the room without being seen.

And someone did stand there, he was certain. He caught the merest flutter of material as it pressed too close to the trellis.

Halim Pasha had now finished his explanation, and was bending low. Anthony looked past the Emir to the men around him. Those seated on the divans to either side were imams and muftis, he estimated; their dress resembled that of the mufti who had first interrogated them. Behind these were grouped several soldiers, clearly of high rank; their tunics were laced with gold thread and their helmets were worked with the most intricate designs.

The man in the green tunic spoke up in Greek. "You are the one called Hawk?"

Anthony swallowed, and he half-turned his head.

"I am Hawkwood," John said, rising to his feet boldly.

The man looked at him in surprise, and Anthony suppressed a shiver. But John Hawkwood remained standing, foursquare to the Ottoman.

The lips parted in a gentle smile. "You are a fighting man, Hawk, so I have heard. Now I see this with my own eyes. Why were you leaving Constantinople?"

John Hawkwood hesitated only briefly. "I have been dismissed."

The man raised his eyebrows. "Constantine is so rich in soldiers?"

"There was a quarrel, between myself and the Grand Duke Notaras."

"I have heard of him," the man said.

"He has executed my brother, and ravished my sister," Anthony blurted, instinctively feeling that they might have discovered an ally here.

The man gazed at them for several seconds more. "Then he is indeed your enemy," he remarked. "You are from the West. Are you Franks?"

"We are English, my lord."

"English?" interrupted a quiet voice, and both the Hawkwoods turned their heads sharply. Anthony found himself looking at a man seated on a divan to the left of the room, so far removed from their interrogator and his counsellors as to have escaped notice to this moment. He was a distinctly handsome man, of no more than middle height, but with a long aquiline nose which overhung thick red lips partly hidden by drooping moustaches, while his thrusting chin was also partly concealed by the merest down of a beard. The most amazing thing about this man, Anthony realised, was his obvious youth; he did not think there was much difference in their ages. He wore the plainest of white silk robes, and a plain white cap on his head; but for the silk, he could have been another mufti.

And this boy had interrupted the Emir? Or had Anthony entirely mistaken the situation from the start? And as the older man in green now remained silent, he realised that he was at last truly looking at the new ruler of the Ottoman Turks.

The young Emir's right hand drooped beside the divan on which he sat; his horsehair switch contained five knots. This he now flicked as he stood, and the pasha who had first interrogated the Hawkwoods rose from the central divan and stood behind it, allowing his youthful master to take his place.

The Emir seated himself before them and spoke, to Anthony's amazement, in Latin. "The English are famous warriors. You know, of course, of Great Harry?"

John Hawkwood had also realised the young man's identity. Now his chest swelled. "I served under Great Harry, my lord, at Agincourt."

"Agincourt," the Emir said. "I have hard much of this. And now you stand before me — that is a pleasure. But if you are English, you must be of the Roman persuasion."

"Aye, my lord."

"And the Byzantines are of the Greek faith. How can you love such men?"

"There is no love, my lord," John Hawkwood said. "I hate them for their perfidy." At that moment he even hated Constantine.

"And now you are here before me," the Emir mused. "Would you live, Englishman who has fought with Great Harry?"

John could guess what would follow; but he owed Constantine nothing now. "I would live, my lord. If my wife and son may also live."

The Emir shifted his gaze to Anthony, who underwent a most unusual experience. He felt almost caressed by the Ottoman's eyes, which were, surprisingly, ice-blue. Then the Emir turned his head to the right, to glance through the window of the room. This looked out on to the Bosphorus, and across it at the twinkling lights of Constantinople.

"Constantinople," he said softly. "How have I dreamed of thee. How have my father and my ancestors dreamed of thee. You are my destiny. Now, perhaps, my destiny will be realised sooner than I had anticipated." He turned back towards the room. "If you would live, Hawk, and your son" — again his gaze drifted over Anthony — "and your wife, you will speak to me of Constantinople tomorrow." He nodded to signify that the audience was at an end.

The two Hawkwoods were marched out of the chamber, but this time there were no kicks or slashes with whips. Nor were they thrown back into the courtyard, but instead taken along a stone corridor and down a flight of steps.

"There will be a dungeon," John Hawkwood muttered. "Courage, boy."

To their surprise, however, they found themselves in a bathing chamber. The floor sloped away from them in four levels, and there were huge tubs of steaming water at hand. There were also four black men — if they were men? They wore loin cloths and nothing else, and their faces and chests were quite hairless.

"Truly we have fallen upon strange people," John muttered, turning to the captain of their escort, who had already indicated that he spoke Greek. "What has happened to my wife?" The thought of Mary at the mercy of such strange men was alarming.

"Your lady has been taken to the harem," the captain told him.

"The harem?" Anthony repeated in dismay. In Constantinople,

the word was redolent of seductive sin.

"She will be cared for," the captain assured him.

"And what is to happen to us?" John demanded.

"You also, will be well cared for," the captain said. "It is the will of the Emir Mahomet."

"Mahomet," John muttered. "so that's the fellow's name."

"We would like food, water, and some wine," Anthony said eagerly.

"Wine is an abomination in the sight of the Prophet," the captain said severely. "The others you will have. But first you must bathe."

John Hawkwood had found the people of Constantinople far more concerned with cleanliness than those of England; now he and Anthony discovered that the Byzantines were positively filthy compared with the Turks. The bath took more than an hour, in which time they were required to do nothing but stand on the uppermost level, while the eunuchs ministered to them. Water, alternately cold and hot, was emptied over them, trickling away from level to level to exit through a huge gutter let into the lower wall. Their skins were massaged with sweet-smelling substances, the gentle black fingers seeking every crevice, their hair shampooed and combed. All the while, the eunuchs chattered amongst themselves, their voices unpleasantly high and harsh — but clearly they were delighted with the size and strength of their victims.

"By God," John observed at last. "How many times a year must a man undergo this treatment?" he asked the captain.

The captain looked astounded. "Except on a campaign, Hawk, a man is bathed every day."

John was left speechless.

By the time the bath was completed, both men were nearly asleep on their feet, but then they were escorted up other flights of stairs and into a bedchamber, sumptuously furnished, with two soft divan beds and a carpet on the floor. Here waited a pile of Turkish clothes and, better yet, a meal of lamb, couscous and water. If they required further stimulation, there was a drink called coffee, unknown in England but which they had already sampled in Constantinople, although hardly made as strong and sweet as this.

They ate and drank because they were hungry, and then collapsed on to the divans.

"Father," Anthony said, "have we been saved?"

"I don't know, boy. This Emir, Mahomet, may wish us to take arms with him against the Byzantines. Are you ready for that?"

"Yes," Anthony said without hesitation. "I hate them now. And how else can we avenge William? Or rescue Catherine?"

"It is a terrible thing to have to take up arms against fellow Christians under a heathen banner."

"Are these people any more heathen than the Byzantines?" Anthony asked.

"Sleep, boy. We may have much to undergo tomorrow."

Exhausted as he was, Anthony took some time to fall asleep. His body still ached from the enforced march, his sun-burned skin began to hurt again once the balm of the bath wore off, he was still stiff from the beatings he had received earlier, but his brain was suddenly active. He found himself thinking of the Emir, the boy named after the Prophet — and the way the Emir had lookd at him. Then he was alseep — but later woke with a start.

A figure stood in the doorway of the room, gazing down at him.

Anthony sat up and glanced at his father. John Hawkwood was still fast asleep, and snoring. There were no weapons in the room.

"Dress yourself, young Hawk," the man said, his voice high and harsh, even when whispering. "And come with me quickly. But quiet — do not wake your father."

Slowly Anthony got up. He wondered whether he should indeed wake his father.

The eunuch might have read his thoughts. "It will be to your great advantage to do as I say."

Anthony hesitated a last time, but reflected that no harm could befall him unless it was ordered by the Emir. And if the Emir wished to harm him, he certainly did not need to arrange it clandestinely in the middle of the night. So Anthony pulled on the loose pantaloons, so different to the tight-fitting hose he was used to, and then the embroidered shirt he had selected as his own the previous night. He thrust his feet into the soft boots, also close fitting but capable of expanding, and stepped outside the room.

"Wear this, too," the eunuch commanded, and gave him an outer robe made of some coarse material, which completely covered him from the shoulders down, with a hood to conceal his head.

"Now come," the eunuch said.

Anthony followed him, feeling very strange but aware that he must look like a Turk, even if an unusually tall one. "Who are you?" he asked.

"I am the Kislar Agha," the black man answered. "I am lord of everything that matters. You may call me Chelebi."

"Is that your name; Chelebi?"

"Chelebi is a title, young Hawk. It means 'lord'."

They had now descended the stairs and were in the presence of the night guard; these came to attention as the Kislar Agha passed them. They did not glance at Anthony at all, nor did they question what the black man might be up to.

So perhaps he was a lord, Anthony thought. But how did he relate to the Emir?

They crossed the courtyard to the opened gates.

"Where are we going?" Anthony asked.

"There is one who would speak with you," the eunuch told him.

Could it be Mother, Anthony wondered. They were now outside the castle and approaching the encampment, which he realised was even larger than it had appeared at a quick, exhausted glance the previous evening. Now, in the pale light thrown by the moon across the darkness, chased by the chill dawn wind off Marmara, he looked at an enormous number and variety of tents arranged in orderly rows. Within the outer rows the horses were tethered, and then there was a large open space before they reached the centre group. But these could hardly be described as tents; rather they were movable canvas houses of considerable size, and clearly containing several chambers from the varied heights of the roofs.

This "inner city" was patrolled by armed guards, but, as within the castle itself, no one questioned the Kislar Agha as he walked straight through the cordon, with Anthony at his heels. They made for the second largest of the tents, and stepped through a flap into a small chamber.

"Wait in here," the black man said, and opened another, inner flap and ushered him through.

Anthony looked around. There had been a light glowing beyond the inner door, but there was none here. In the gloom it was difficult to make out much of his surroundings, but he was alone.

Before he could deduce where he was, the Agha had returned. "Take off the cloak," he commanded.

Anthony obeyed, his powers of decision suspended by the sheer strangeness of everything that was happening to him.

"Now bow your head," the Agha commanded.

Anthony obeyed, the Agha passed a thick bandage round his head to cover his eyes, securing it from behind.

"As you value your life, do not shift the blindfold," the Agha said. "Now come."

He took Anthony's hand, and led him through an inner doorway. Even through the blindfold Anthony was aware of the lamps which surrounded him, and of the soft rugs into which his feet sank. He was led forward and through another doorway — his head brushing against the canvas lintel. Now the scents which had titillated his nostrils since first entering the vast tent became almost overpowering.

"Kneel," the Agha whispered.

Anthony obeyed, and heard the Agha speaking, presumably in Turkish.

When he had finished, a voice replied, and Anthony could not stop his head from jerking up. It was the voice of a woman, soft and musical, yet with currents of strength rippling through it.

The Agha spoke again, more vehemently.

My God, Anthony thought, what are they discussing?

The woman replied, and this time was undoubtedly giving a command. The Agha's acknowledgement was brief, and there was a rustle of movement.

Anthony waited, still kneeling on the rug.

"Remove your blindfold, young Hawk," the woman said.

"I have been warned not to do this ... my lady," Anthony instinctively added. "On pain of my life."

"Your life is mine," the woman said. "Remove the blindfold."

Anthony no longer hesitated but reached behind his head and unfastened the knot. As the cloth fell on to his lap, he blinked, slowly becoming accustomed to the light. His first impression was colour: there was colour everywhere, from the greys and blues of the rugs to the pinks and pale greens of the cushions on the divan before which he knelt. Even the lanterns gave off coloured light.

The woman, too, was colourful. She wore a voluminous, deep red, divided skirt which was caught in at each ankle, so that it was really a pair of silk pantaloons; her close-fitting tunic was a paler red; her skin was very white, her hair as red as his own and lay loose on her shoulders beneath a small jewelled crimson cap. There were jewelled rings on her fingers as well. But the glittering stones paled into insignificance when set against the woman herself.

She was fairly tall, Anthony estimated; she sat on the divan, one leg curled beneath her, but the other touched the floor; the silk of the pantaloons was sheer and she did not appear to be wearing anything beneath. It was a very well-formed leg indeed, with flawless bare toes. The upper half of her body was better concealed, but suggested a mature splendour. And then the face! The first impression was one of utter calmness, because her features were so perfectly relaxed. But they were also perfect features in their own right, moulded into the shape of a heart, within which lay a wide, full mouth, a small nose, and wide-set green eyes. Even this perfection had been assisted: her eyebrows and eyelids had ben painted with kohl, a dark dye made from lemons and plumbago; and her fingernails tinted a reddish brown colour with henna. Anthony soon realised that her hair had also been dyed in henna.

She was the most beautiful woman he had ever seen. And yet, for all the smoothness of her complexion, the grace with which she sat, even so inelegantly, he realised that she was at least as old as his own mother ... which would make her very nearly fifty!

She smiled. "You are handsome yourself, young Hawk," she said. "The Emir spoke to me of you last night, and he is a man of judgement. Do your knees not hurt? Why not sit."

Anthony slid over into a sitting position; his knees were indeed aching, while his brain was spinning. He discovered, to his relief, that the Kislar Agha had left them alone.

"My name is Mara Brankovich," the woman said. "Or it was, once upon a time. My nephew is Prince George of Serbia."

Anthony gasped. Everyone in Constantinople knew of Mara Brankovich, the Serbian princess who had been sent to the seraglio of the Ottoman Emir Murad, when just a girl. Just as everyone in Constantinople reviled the name of George Brankovich: his desertion of Hunyadi at Kossovo, three years before, had certainly helped bring about the defeat of the Christian army.

"My husband died but a fortnight ago," Mara Brankovich went on. "It has been a busy time for me — and for Mahomet."

"The Emir is your son, Highness?" Anthony asked, unable to control his curiosity.

Mara Brankovich smiled. "No," she said. "I was never able to bear Murad a son. And yet I was his favourite wife. No other woman gave him so much pleasure." She spoke with quiet arrogance. "Mahomet's mother was an Albanian slave girl." Now her tone was faintly tinged with contempt. "But she is dead." She paused to stare at him, and he realised that this beautiful woman was probably as cold-hearted towards a possible rival as any man could be. "Thus I am the Emir Valideh; that means, young Hawk, 'the Mother of the Emir'. Mahomet would have it no other way."

"As you have said, Highness, the Emir is a man of judgement," Anthony ventured.

The boldness of his reply took her aback. She gazed at him for several seconds, and then smiled. "You may go far, young Hawk," she told him. "My son is ... interested in you. He is very young, but he is yet a man. He is also an Osmanli. Do not ever forget that."

"A breaker of legs," Anthony murmured, remembering what his father had told him.

"Of more than legs, young Hawk," Mara commented. "Do you know what the Janissaries already call him? They call him Hunkar. Do you know what that means?"

"No, Highness."

"It means 'Drinker of Blood'. You would do well to remember this at all times."

"But he is also very talented, Highness," Anthony suggested, practising the most blatant flattery. "He speaks Latin like an Italian."

"But of course. As his mother died ... young," Mara said, "and as there was no older son of the great Murad, I saw to Mahomet's education myself. My adopted son speaks not only Latin, but Greek, Arabic, Chaldean, Persian and Slavonic. More, he can read and write in all those languages. I taught him these skills."

She paused so that he could appreciate that she must therefore know them all herself, which would make her just about the most accomplished woman in the world, he felt. "His father Murad taught him the art of war. To this end he has studied the lives of Cyrus, Alexander, Julius Caesar, Octavian, Constantine, and Theodosius. He is ... he will be the conqueror of the world. You can share in all this, young Hawk, if you have the wit and the courage."

Anthony supposed he might be dreaming to be holding such a conversation with such a woman on such topics. But he was determined to play his part. "For your son to conquer the world, Highness, he must first conquer Christendom," he suggested. "Are you yourself not a Christian?"

"A Christian indeed," she said contemptuously. "As are you, young Hawk. But what do we see when we look at Christendom?"

She rose from her divan and moved to and fro in front of him, a swirl of red silk and glowing flesh. "England and France locked in warfare. The Pope and the Emperor locked in enmity. And these bastard Byzantines preying upon the world like the veriest mantis. I did not tell the truth just now. My son did indeed speak to me of you, but only after I had spoken of you to him. I stood in the gallery above the audience chamber of the castle, and looked down upon you both."

The cloth behind the trellis, Anthony thought. This woman had looked upon his naked body.

"I realised then that God, whose aim is always unity rather than discord, had sent you to us. My son has dreamed, since birth, of conquering Constantinople. But how may Constantinople be conquered? Its walls seem impregnable. Now you will show us how."

"Highness?" Anthony asked uneasily.

Mara Brankovich paused in front of him. Through her transparent skirt he could see her groin, and he realised with consternation that it was shaven. He had no idea what he should have expected, never having seen a naked woman, but what was exposed seemed irresistible.

"Or you die," she said. Then she did an amazing thing. She dropped to her knees before him. "But live, and scale the veriest heights."

She stood again quickly, with hardly a flexing of muscle.

"Do you know how I am called?"

"The ... Emir Valideh," he said.

"That is nothing. It means Queen Mother. To the women of the harem I am Queen of the Crowned Heads. Not even Mahomet may take a woman to his bed unless I have first approved the girl." She stared at Anthony. "Nor a handsome boy."

Anthony gulped. "Highness ..."

"You are from England, where such relationships are frowned

upon. Here in the East they are commonplace. A woman is for comfort and children — so long as she provides them." Mara's lips twisted. "A handsome boy is for companionship and true enjoyment."

"Highness ..."

"Would you resist my son? He could have you stretched on your belly and opened to him by snapping his fingers. If you would not accommodate him, you must use art, subterfuge; illusion even."

Anthony frowned. "Do you wish this, Highness, that I should be all things to your son?"

Mara knelt again before him. "I wish my son to rule the world. In Constantinople they call me whore and succubus. I wish them to wallow in their own blood. But when the world is his, I wish him to be a second Caesar, a second Alexander. I too am read in these matters, young Hawk. A conqueror needs an aide ever at his shoulder, and not one appointed by law or religion or custom. The mufti are bound by the Anyi, the ancient law of the Ottomans, handed down from generation to generation. These are laws no man may break, not even the Emir. The imams are bound by the law of the Koran, which is even more sacred than the Anyi. The viziers are bound by their own interests. The very Janissaries are bound by their desire for plunder. You can be Mahomet's guide and friend. It is more important to be a friend — so you do not wish him to enter you. I will assist you in resisting his advances, because I too wish him to seek only women. The other way lies corrupt influence, and too often disaster. By remaining a friend rather than a lover, you can lead my son to strength and yourself to prosperity."

"You make me dizzy, Highness."

"I will make you more dizzy yet, young Hawk. You must persuade your father to lend his skills to the Emir's cause. Then there is no star in the firmament which lies beyond his reach. But you yourself will remain loyal only to me ... and to my son." She smiled and took his hands between hers. Her bodice had somehow opened, and his hands were placed on her naked breasts. They were as firm as a young girl's, but with nipples which seemed to fill his palms. "I have told you, I looked upon you in my son's audience chamber, last night, naked and filthy, and knew what I wanted, and how much I could do with a man such as you." And,

70

with another twitch of her lips, "I am a woman who makes decisions. I am also a widow — and the Emir Valideh. Since a fortnight ago, I own no master save my passions. But I will own you, young Hawk, and between us maybe we will own the world." She stood up, and his hands slipped down her thighs. But as they did so, her pantaloons slipped with them. Anthony stared in awe at her naked flesh, his aches and pains disappearing as if by magic.

The Emir Valideh gave a throaty laugh at his stunned expression. "Have you never been with a woman?"

Anthony shook his head.

Mara took his hands from her thighs and gestured him to his feet. "Then will you be even more truly mine," she said, "because, as long as you live, you will know no other woman to compare with me." She released his trousers and allowed them to fall to his knees. "How long have I waited for one such as now," she murmured. She stared into his eyes. "But this love is a secret one, young Hawk. Disclose any of this to your father, even to your mirror, and I will myself flay the skin from your living flesh."

Anthony licked his lips. "But the Kislar Agha ..."

"Like you, he will never betray me." She held him between both her hands; even her threat had been unable to stop him hardening.

"Now come to me," she said softly, "and I will teach you of love."

The Emir Mahomet II stood on the battlements of Anatolia-Hissar and gazed across the Bosphorus towards Constantinople. Around him were gathered his pashas and his advisors: Halil, the Grand Vizier, whom the Hawkwoods had mistaken for the Emir himself the previous night; Zagan, inferior only to him; Caraja the Anatolian; Isaac the Jew; Baltoglu the Bulgarian renegade, who was admiral of the Ottoman fleet; Hamoud, his deputy; and the others. Standing with them were John and Anthony Hawkwood.

Below them, drawn up on the cliff-top, as if about to launch an assault across the water, was a brigade of Janissaries, their brilliant uniforms glowing in the morning sunlight. And below them, moored along the beach, were the seventy-odd galleys of the Turkish fleet; not yet on a scale to match the ambitions of this young prince, John Hawkwood thought. But the Ottomans knew little of the sea.

"Constantinople," mused the Emir. "Tell me this, Hawk. My

sipahis water their horses in the Danube. My ancestors are buried in the shadow of the Taurus Mountains. Yet this one city, in the very centre of my dominions, still resists me. How can that be? Are those walls truly impregnable?"

"To the assault of flesh and blood, O Padishah," John replied, having been advised of the correct way to address his new master, "I believe they are, if resolutely defended."

"And are there sufficient resolute men within those walls?"

"The Emperor commands less than five thousand men."

"Less than five thousand? I command many times that."

"Five thousand are sufficient to defend the walls, and they will be resolutely led."

Mahomet frowned at him. "Are you telling me the city cannot be taken?"

"It would doubtless fall to a siege, O Padishah," suggested Halil.

"You are a frightened old man," Mahomet declared scornfully. "A siege? Has not Constantinople been besieged before? Did not the Arabs lay siege to those walls for two years, without success? I cannot wait two years for failure. My Janissaries wait for me to lead them to victory. If they have not yet overturned their kettles, it is because I have been Emir for scarce a week. But I must prove myself no less a leader than my father. And it must be done soon." He glanced at the Hawkwoods. "Know you the story of the Janissaries, Hawk?"

"I know of their reputation."

"They are our strength," Mahomet said. "And our weakness. When my great ancestor, Othman, rode out of the east, he led only Turks. Our cavalry was the finest in the world. It is, still. Othman had no need of foot soldiers. It was his son, Orkhan, who discovered that horsemen cannot capture walled towns. Thus Orkhan founded an infantry corps, which was called simply *yaya*, or foot soldiers. They were professionals, and were paid a silver coin a day. But they were useless. My people are like the wind. They cannot be tamed, only joined in their endeavours. The wind cannot take a walled town either. So the great Orkhan cast about him, and determined to create an army which knew nothing but war and obedience. Those men down there were all born Christians, but taken from their families in childhood, to be brought up in the Muslim way."

His gaze drifted over Anthony, standing at his father's side, and Anthony's heartbeat quickened. But this boy knew nothing. None of these men, even his father, knew anything of the true meaning of life. Because none of these men had ever knelt between the pulsing thighs of the most beautiful woman in the world and heard her moan in ecstasy.

"These levies were known as *tsheries*, or troops, and *jani*, or new, hence their name," Mahomet continued. "They were, and are, brought up in the strictest discipline and seclusion, and taught loyalty only to the Emir. And how may a man's loyalty be fully secured? Through his stomach. The Janissaries are fed as I myself am fed. Their very general is known as the *tshorbadji*, the soup-maker. Their colonels are the *ashdijbashis*, or chief cooks; and their adjutants the *sakabashis*, or water-carriers. If their blood-red banner, which you see yonder, bears the sign of the crescent and the two-edged sword of Omar, the regimental totem is the meat kettle.

"Their foundation was many years ago. Now they are, as you have truly said, a force to be feared throughout the world. And they are aware of it. They know their power. They know the tremor which runs through the veins of my people when the Janissaries overturn their meat kettles in discontent. They have not done so yet in my reign. They wait to be led against their enemies. But that must happen soon."

The Emir's fingers twitched. Anthony wondered at what might be the dreams of a man so apparently powerful, yet so aware that his power rested on the uncertain, seething heat of a volcano or, as he had himself put it, a whirlwind, upon whose terrifying might he must ride throughout his life.

John Hawkwood was no less aware of the Emir's agitation, and had already made his decision. This boy was his and his family's only hope of survival. But more: in his ignorance and uncertainty he was more of a ladder to be climbed to power and prosperity than ever Constantine the Emperor had been. And what did he still owe Constantine, who for all his desire to be loyal to his friends had lacked the strength to save William? Now they could only be avenged.

"I can show you how to take Constantinople, O Padishah," he said at last.

There was a rustle amongst the men surrounding the Emir, all of whom spoke at least a smattering of Latin.

"Speak," Mahomet commanded sharply.

"There are several things that need to be done. Mere numbers of men will not avail, by themselves. You need more than men. In the first place, you need ships: many more ships than you now possess."

Mahomet glanced at Baltoglu, and the admiral nodded vigorously.

"Then we will have ships," Mahomet said. "They will commence building tomorrow. You think ships will take Constantinople, Hawk?"

"Not by themselves. But ships will prevent men and food from reaching the city to relieve it. The next thing you need are handguns for your Janissaries.The defenders of Constantinople are already equipped with handguns."

Mahomet looked questioningly at Zagan.

"I have already said this, O Padishah," Zagan agreed. "At Kossovo the gaiours were armed with such handguns, and they did mighty execution in our ranks. I spoke of this to the great Murad, and he swore to consider it. But he was a sick man even then."

"Handguns," Mahomet mused. "Then we shall purchase handguns. And you maintain that handguns will capture Constantinople, Hawk? Handguns and ships?"

"Sufficient ships and handguns will enable your Janissaries to fight against the Christians on equal terms, but they will not cause the walls of Constantinople to crumble before your attack. Only cannon will do that."

"Cannon!" Mahomet exclaimed, and again his generals rustled. "My people know nothing of cannon."

"I know of cannon, O Padishah."

Mahomet was again staring longingly at the city across the water. Now he turned his head. "Is this true?"

"I am a master gunner," John Hawkwood declared proudly. "I served the guns for Great Harry."

Mahomet stroked his beard.

"Where are these cannon to be obtained?" Halil asked contemptuously. "Not even the Venetians will sell us cannon."

"I will build your cannon for you," Hawkwood declared. "But first give me a forge, and iron, and labour."

Mahomet continued to tug at his beard. "Will these cannon be as large as those on the walls of Constantinople?"

"I will build you the largest cannon ever seen on earth, O Padishah. The walls will tremble to its very report."

"By Allah," Mahomet said. "Do that, Hawk, and I will make you rich beyond your dreams. How long will it take you to build this machine?"

John hesitated. He had never actually made a cannon in his life, though he did know all the theory of it. "To cast a cannon capable of breaching the walls of Constantinople might take a year."

"A year?" The Emir's voice showed his dismay.

"You will need at least a year to build your fleet and to equip your Janissaries with handguns. It will be a year in which your people will clearly see what you are preparing, and will understand that you are but ensuring their victory."

"And a year in which Constantinople can be made ever stronger," Halil growled.

"Not so, Great Vizier," John insisted. "Constantinople lives in hopes and dreams. The Byzantines dream that with the death of Murad their troubles are over for several years. Assure them of this, O Padishah — convince them that you are a man of peace and they will believe you, even while you are preparing for war."

Mahomet smiled, and his white teeth gleamed. "Truly you are a man of distinction, Hawk," he said. "I believe you have been sent to me by Allah. Yes ..." He paused and looked over the battlements at a squadron of sipahis who had just galloped into the encampment in a cloud of dust. There was now a great deal of excited clamour from down there. "Mansur," he muttered. "Can it be?"

"It must be, O Padishah," Halil said, and hurried from the Emir's presence.

Mahomet followed more slowly, accompanied by the remainder of his entourage.

"Father," Anthony muttered, "do you know what you are doing?"

"Our choice is between death and life, boy. But life with fame and fortune, perhaps. I thought you supported me, in that."

"As regards Constantinople, willingly. But this Emir seeks the conquest of the world, Father. Give him cannon and he may well achieve that."

"Bah," John Hawkwood snorted. "He is but an inexperienced boy. He will follow the advice of his generals, of whom I shall be among the foremost once Constantinople falls. Then our family will be avenged, son. Remember that."

Anthony made no reply, remembering what the Emir Valideh had told him. But remembering that clouded his mind with too many other memories, too. Never had he known such satin skin, such unbridled passion. In a woman old enough to be his mother! Would she send for him again? If she did not, he believed he might die . . .

When they reached the courtyard where the sipahis had dismounted, they found, on the ground before them, two men bound hand and foot, writhing in the dust, choking and gasping. As they came closer, Anthony could see that both were very young — younger indeed than himself.

Mahomet stood before the two prisoners and addressed them in Turkish. Though Anthony could not understand what was said, one of the men, the more richly dressed of the pair, argued back with great vehemence, despite his discomfort.

Mahomet listened to him in silence, his face as softly impassive as ever. Then he replied, quietly but firmly. Two of the Janissaries had moved forward to stand at his shoulder. Now, without hesitation, they stooped beside the young man, a bow-string in their hands. He tried to protest, but the string was coiled round his neck, and quickly tightened by powerful fingers. The young man's eyes seemed to swell from his head, and his tongue from his gaping mouth. There came a dreadful gurgling noise from the back of his throat, and the veins seemed about to force their way from his temples . . . Then he died.

Anthony swallowed, in shock — and then again, as he discovered the Emir was gazing straight at him. He licked his lips nervously, and Mahomet smiled. "You should praise God that you are but the son of a soldier, young Hawk," he said, "and not the son of a prince."

For a moment Anthony could not speak. My God, he thought in panic, if this man ever discovers what has passed between me and his mother . . .

"What was that man's crime, O Padishah?" he asked in awe.

Mahomet's features twisted. "He was my brother."

"Your . . . brother?"

76

"He is the last of them," Mahomet said with some satisfaction, gazing at the distorted features of the dead youth. "I had almost thought he had escaped — but Mansur has done well."

"You have murdered all of your brothers?" Anthony gabbled in consternation, forgetting his place.

A brief frown crossed Mahomet's brow, but then he smiled. "It is not done so in the West — but the West is weak, and in great confusion. Here I am strong, and I am not confused. Does not the Koran itself say: discord is worse than murder? There will be no discord in the House of Othman."

Anthony was speechless. Beside him, John Hawkwood was also struck dumb.

"As for the other," Mahomet said, turning to look down at the second young man, whose eyeballs gaped white with fear. "He is guilty of helping my brother in his escape."

"Was he not obeying orders, O Padishah?" John Hawkwood asked at last.

"Orders which do not lead to success cause much misery to those who obey them," Mahomet agreed. "For this creature, I have in mind much misery."

The Hawkwoods exchanged glances.

"What will be his punishment?" John asked.

"He will be impaled," Mahomet said, "as a warning to others." He turned to Anthony. "You will watch this, young Hawk. It is a salutary experience."

4

THE FAVOURITE

When the man on the ground was told what was going to happen to him, he gave a scream of the purest agony and began to writhe and plead.

Mahomet regarded him contemptuously, and snapped out another order. Clearly the sentence was to be carried out immediately.

"By God," John Hawkwood muttered in English. "I should not like to fall foul of this young fellow. Nor should you, boy."

"What is impalement, Father?" Anthony asked in awe.

"A most terrible form of execution, boy. Brace yourself."

Already the preparations were in hand. Several of the Janissaries were digging a hole in the earth before the castle. Others had dragged the victim to his feet and were now stripping him of his clothing, mocking him as they did so, while tears ran down his face and his eyes rolled wildly as he continued to beg for mercy.

When he was totally naked, his wrists were bound together in front of him, and then attached to a rope so that he could be led off by the Janissaries to make the rounds of the camp. Everywhere men came out of their tents to jeer at him, and Anthony could not doubt that the women were also watching and laughing from inside, even if they did not show themselves. Was Mara also gazing at the stricken man, anticipating the horror that was to come?

By now the Janissaries had completed digging their hole, some four feet deep. In this they fixed the shaft of a wooden lance, some eight feet long, and bedded it so firmly and deep that only the top four feet protruded.Anthony gazed at it in horror. It was nowhere thicker than four inches in diameter, and the steel tip had been removed. But, in its place, the tip of the wood itself had been carved into a sharp point.

Anthony swallowed, his throat dry. He dared not even look at his father.

By now the condemned man had been brought back. Through exhaustion he had ceased weeping and begging, but when he saw the stake his face began to work in horrible contortions.

The Janissaries looked at their Emir — and Mahomet nodded.

As the naked man was hustled forward, he again began to scream in a high-pitched wail. His wrists were now bound behind his back, and then he was lifted high by four of the Janissaries. Though frenziedly kicking his legs, he was helpless against so much combined strength. Slowly the Janissaries placed him over the stake, taking great care to insert the sharpened tip directly into his anus. They held him aloft for a few seconds, laughing and abusing him, then they released him and stepped away.

The man's legs suddenly dropped to either side of the stake, just unable to reach the ground – and the most unearthly shriek broke from his lips. His body writhed as blood dripped down the lance, and he heaved desperately, attempting to throw himself clear of the stake — but it was already too deeply embedded in him. Anthony tried to look away, but discovered the Emir standing beside him.

"The more he writhes, the quicker the stake penetrates," Mahomet observed, turning to study Anthony's reaction.

Anthony forced himself to continue watching the dying wretch, forced himself to keep his face impassive. The victim's feet could now reach the earth, so deeply and quickly had the stake entered, but now there was no strength left in them to raise him up. Mercifully it was over quickly, but still the man hung there. To his horror, Anthony saw the tip of the stake begin to emerge through the flesh of his breast.

Suddenly Mahomet gave another order. The Janissaries dug out the stake and raised it above them, beginning yet another march round the camp, with their grisly trophy.

Mahomet smiled at him. "Men do not easily forget an impalement," he said. "Now come, we have much to do."

It was time to break camp. Mahomet had accomplished the essentials of succession: destroying all possible rivals. Now it was time to mourn the dead Emir, so the Ottomans were, for the moment, turning their backs on the Bosphorus and the new Emir's future ambitions.

Their destination was the city of Brusa, ancient burial place of the Ottoman emirs, where Murad was to be interred in great state. The Hawkwoods were amazed to learn that the embalmed body of the dead Emir was actually still in the camp with them.

Anthony was even more amazed and shocked to realise that Mara Brankovich had taken him into her bed with her husband's corpse lying only a few feet away. At such a time her thoughts had already been ranging into the future.

The army and the harem took the coast road by way of Nicomedia and Sakarya, thence along the valley of the Gok, before climbing into the foothills of Mount Ulu. Here, in the northern foothills of the seven-thousand-foot peak, stood the sacred city of Brusa.

Their route took them through stark and forbidding country which rose from the coast to a level of some three thousand feet, and this high tableland was punctuated by mountain ranges which rose far higher still. The terrain was intersected by ravines and river valleys which had to be laboriously negotiated, while every so often an earth tremor brought the army to a standstill as boulders came crashing down from the heights above.

Such terrifying phenomena were apparently common enough in this strange land, but intensely disturbing to the Hawkwoods.

The vegetation matched the terrain, being no more than scrub in the valleys, but noble yet sinister pine forests grew on the mountain slopes. Wolves and hyenas, foxes and wildcats prowled around the encampment at night, and made it hideous with their howling, and more than once the Hawkwoods caught glimpses of large bears prowling among the trees. There was even talk of lion on the plateau, but none were seen.

Mahomet proceeded in the very centre of a vast accumulation of his people, a throwback to the past when the Ottomans had been a nomadic tribe wandering across central Asia.

The core of this moving nation was the army, composed of four elements. First marched a vast horde of bashi-bazouks, the ir-regulars, hardly more than brigands. They wore neither armour nor uniforms, but each man dressed and armed himself according to his means — using tulwars and spears, bows and axes indiscrimin-ately; and where some wore silk, others were in homespun. Anthony gathered that they were paid no more than a pittance, and fought simply for the plunder they hoped to gain. They were thus even more restless in times of peace than the Janissaries, but

they also had homes to go to. On this occasion they had accumulated simply on the news of the great Murad's death, and would
disperse to their farms once the mourning period was over — to be
recalled to the Emir's standard when next he chose to go to war.
As soldiers, Anthony considered them worth only the uncertain
force of large numbers and a great deal of alarming noise.

Behind the bashi-bazouks came the Anatolians, the true Turks,
organised in infantry regiments, but still hardly more than irregular
troops because of the inability of the Turks to accept the necessary
discipline. Still, the Anatolians wore uniforms of a sort, thick green
felt tunics which provided some protection; and if they were not
fully armoured, they were equipped with a round shield to go with
their spear and sword. Equally, as upholders of the Ottoman name
and tradition, they were a more formidable proposition than the
preceding bashi-bazouks.

Behind the Anatolians came the sipahis, the elite cavalry, in all
the glory of their steel helmets and mail tunics, their baggy breeches
and their flowing capes. They gloried in their name and tradition,
and as mounted men came from the better class of people, fulfilling the only function acceptable to these born horsemen; for it was
written in the annals of their race. "If a Turk dismounts from his
horse to sit on a carpet, he becomes nothing."

The sipahis did more than provide an escort for the Emir and his
court. They ranged far and wide, sometimes riding with the bashi-
bazouks, sometimes even farther, continually scouting, checking,
warning ... and ensuring that the enormous amount of food and
grazing required by the army would always be available.

Behind the sipahis, and directly surrounding the harem and the
person of the Emir, came the Janissaries, the ultimate power
behind the Ottoman triumphs. Ten thousand strong, their gaudy
blue and red uniforms stood out even amongst the bright colours
of the Emir's entourage, they marched with strict discipline — any
man who disobeyed an order immediately suffered the bastinado
— an excruciating caning on the soles of his feet — while the
ultimate disgrace that could befall a Janissary was to be dismissed
from the service and sent home. Their weapons, which — like the
sipahis' — consisted of spear, sword and bow, were always at the
ready. They were a magnificent body of men, John Hawkwood
conceded, as good as any foot soldiers he had ever seen. If, as
Mahomet had explained, theirs was an inward-turned, intensely

private community which centred upon their precious food kettles, they were also a potentially irresistible weapon, if properly used.

The truly amazing aspect of this vast concourse of men, women and animals was its cleanliness. Any European army, even a fraction the size of this Ottoman force, encamped thus in one place for upwards of a week, would have turned the entire area into a vast, foetid cesspit, with all the consequent risk of disease, and the stench would have accompanied it on its march. But personal discipline was strict in the Turkish camp, and every man was required to dig his own latrine, and fill it up with earth afterwards.

In the very heart of this great army was the Emir himself, with his viziers and generals, his harem — even on the march concealed in curtained litters — and his adoptive mother. Also his two newest recruits. Often Mahomet would send for one or other of the Hawkwoods to ride beside him. With John he spoke of cannon and armaments, and the walls of Constantinople. With Anthony he spoke of other things.

"Your kings in England do not march like this?" he observed.

"They make processions around the country from time to time," Anthony explained, "but never on this scale. England is not so large a realm as your dominions."

"I know too little of my dominions," Mahomet observed, "and this I must correct." He sighed. "There is so much to do, and so little time. I know that this moving of every worldly possession, whenever the Emir must leave one place for another, is wasteful of time no less than resources. Yet it is the custom of my people, and of all the peoples in the world there can be none so ruled by custom as the Turks. We have a saying that perhaps you have not heard, young Hawk. It goes like this:

To hold a land you need armed men.
To keep armed men you share out property,
To have property you need rich folk,
Only by laws can you make folk rich—
If one of these lacks, all four will lack.
Where all four lack, the land is lost.

Do you agree with that saying, young Hawk?"

"I would say it is very true."

"But it is the law which is the foundation of everything. To be

able to change the law, I must accomplish something very great."
His expression grew solemn and his fingers curled into a fist. "I
must take Constantinople."

Was this thoughtful, ambitious, cautious young man the same
who had recently strangled his own brother, and commanded a
dutiful underling to be impaled.?

But, despite what Mara had told him of the Emir's rigorous
upbringing, Anthony found Mahomet more surprising yet in his
knowledge of history and politics, of the ancient Greeks and
Romans and of their writings, and above all of poetry.

"The Muslim world has been rich in poets," he told Anthony.
"Have you not heard of Omar Khayyam?"

"No, O Padishah."

"Then your education has been neglected, and must be
improved. Omar was a Persian, and is not perhaps the best guide
and mentor for a young man: he was overfond of wine, and thus
he broke the law. But his use of words is exquisite, and he is not
without philosophical value. I will give you a book of his work
when we reach Brusa."

Anthony could only bow his head, while the nearby viziers
pulled their beards; it was obvious they did not approve of the
favour being shown to the red-headed youth.

He saw and heard nothing more of the Emir Valideh during the
journey, which took several weeks, and he could not make up his
mind whether to be glad or sorry about this. Perhaps she had
sated herself with him, and had now forgotten him. He still
remembered the feel, the scent, and allure of her — as she had
promised he would do, to the end of his days. But the thought that,
if ever discovered in her tent, he might face impalement was
blood-chilling.

Equally terrifying was the realisation that if Mara Brankovich
ever sent for him and he did not obey her summons, he might be
flayed alive.

Brusa was like stumbling across an oasis in the middle of a desert.
Surrounded by orchards, and watered by several rushing streams
that cascaded down the side of the mountain, it was a town of
brightly coloured houses built on narrow, winding streets, their
gardens dotted with fountains in every possible design. There were
several thermal baths, fed by mountain springs, which were in

constant use, at least by the men of the city. If the Hawkwoods had been taken aback at the luxury of life in Constantinople, as compared with their native England, it was even more surprising to observe the comfort and cleanliness that every Turk seemed to regard as his right.

But Brusa was also the burial place of the emirs. On a terrace above the town were to be seen the tombs of both Othman and Orkhan. The Emir Mahomet I was buried inside the city itself, and work had already commenced on building a mausoleum, in the sacred colour of green, over his grave. Immediately on arrival in the town, the official interment of Murad began as well as the official mourning period, and plans were put in hand to erect another huge mausoleum over his grave, too, to be called the Muradiye Cami. All ordinary work was suspended until the full mourning was complete — even the local manufacture of silk textiles, which occupied most of the men not in the army. Every day the blowing of doleful whistles, the clashing of cymbals, and the slow and steady beating of drums filled the air.

The Hawkwoods were left very much to themselves during this period, but to their great joy Mary was released from the harem and allowed to join them in the house placed at their disposal. She looked in good health again, and had been given a deal of sumptuous clothing to wear; but she also seemed different somehow. In the privacy of their bedchamber, John discovered immediately that she had been shaved. She was embarrassed about this, but also defiant, explaining that all Turkish women were thus shaved, and that she had had no choice. Perhaps, he reflected, all her other slight changes stemmed from such simple cultural readjustments.

"Do the women shave each other?" he asked, intrigued despite himself.

"No," Mary replied, blushing.

"You mean you must do it to yourself?"

"No," Mary repeated, her colour deepening.

"Then who ... by God!" John said.

Mary rested her hand on his arm. "They are not men."

"Indeed? They are alive, therefore they eat and drink. Therefore they feel."

She sighed. "I cannot answer that. It is the custom." Suddenly she was anxious. "You will not tell the boy of it?"

"He has eyes in his head, and he must eventually discover how Turkish women behave. But I will not tell him."

It was a relief to see that she had regained a great deal of her confidence — even while being shaved by blackamoors! And what else had she experienced during her weeks in the harem? In Constantinople he had heard tales enough of the unnatural lusts enjoyed by women cooped up together away from all male company save that of their single lord.

Yet that thought too was strangely titillating, and besides, he had some confessing of his own to do, about enlisting with the Turks against Constantinople.

She gazed at him, blankly.

"I did it to save all our lives, for there was no other way to accomplish that. But equally do I still seek revenge upon those who have wronged us."

After a moment Mary smiled. "I love you now more than ever for behaving like a man instead of a whipped cur, husband. My heard bled for you when you were forced to creep away from Constantinople into the darkness. But if these people will give you a sword and armour, then I shall be proud of you again."

John Hawkwood's answering smile was grim. "They have promised me more than that, Mary. They have promised me steel, and a forge, and the men to make my cannon for me."

As soon as the official mourning period was over, John Hawkwood set to work casting the iron for his bombards, beating the leather to bind the barrels, designing the carriages, and calculating the charges. And also to put into practice one or two other ideas he had developed over the years of studying his profession.

He had no false optimism regarding the task he had been set. He knew, as he had helped maintain them, the sheer strength of the walls of Constantinople. He knew the sea-facing walls were indeed impregnable. Supposing the increased Ottoman fleet — the building of additional ships had already been put in hand — did manage to break the boom and occupy the Golden Horn, his task would then be simplified; but he did not know for sure they would be able to do that. And if the Janissaries could be armed with handguns, they would afford his artillerymen better protection than with bows and arrows ... but to approach too close to the walls would still be a most costly and dangerous business. Therefore, merely to build cannon similar in size to those mounted in Constantinople — and they were the largest he had ever used — would be a waste of time. At least one of his guns had to outrange those mounted on the walls.

They would also need to hurl their stone balls with sufficient velocity to smash a breech large enough to admit the Turkish army. Hawkwood was a professional soldier: he knew all about siegecraft. He knew that determined defenders could often repair in a night the damage done by besiegers during the day; just as he knew that a wall which collapsed in a pile of rubble could often be made even more easily defensible than one which stood upright, waiting to be undermined.

He needed exceptional guns — and he needed to design them himself. He must be certain, too, that the amount of powder used to achieve the results he sought would not simply blow his iron cylinders apart.

And he needed something even more than that — but he had a secret plan locked away in his mind.

John had never lacked confidence. And now he had a dream of building the ultimate cannon: a bombard so huge and destructive that it would bestow the mastery of the world on its possessor. The Emir Mahomet had just given him the opportunity to make that dream come true.

Anthony was delighted to see his parents enjoying a second childhood of love, even if his mother occasionally found it difficult to adapt to her new life. She was still afflicted by the catastrophes which had overcome her eldest son and her wilful daughter, but she never once reproached her husband for having launched them all on this unending adventure.

Now that she was restored to freedom, she longed to revert to normal western ways, but that was *im*possible. If she considered her Turkish clothes — pantaloons and bolero — to be obscene, nevertheless she had no choice but to wear them, and being wrapped in a haïk when going out gave her total anonymity. But when she ventured forth to the souk on their second day together in Brusa, she found herself the only woman without a yashmak, and fled back to the house in confusion.

Even more embarrassing were the servants the Emir presented to his commander of artillery, for these were eunuchs. But John gently persuaded her to accept them, as he himself was prepared to accept everything about their strange new life. Soon Mary was making her own couscous, and enjoying other Turkish culinary delights. The most popular vegetable was the aubergine, which was served by itself sliced, or stuffed with minced lamb and peppers, or in a variety of other ways. None of the Hawkwoods, however, could accustom themselves to the Turkish habit of eating just about every part of the lamb or goat, from the eyeballs to the testicles.

And Mary could not but be delighted with her new house and garden, not so large or well situated as in Constantinople, but of a totally different style in which soft archways replaced internal doors and gave access to paved central courtyards, each of which contained an elaborately carved stone fountain. This open building was full of light and air and the sound of rushing water, and if, in the winter months, a cold breeze from time to time swept down from the mountains, this made the warmth of the divan with its sheepskin blanket the more delightful.

Before long she even learned not to jump and scream at the almost daily earth tremors.

Only in matters of religion did she remain ill at ease. The Muslims neither criticised the Hawkwoods for not attending the mosque or obeying the thrice-daily call to prayers, nor did they attempt to coerce them into conforming. But there was no Christian church at all, and even more than in Constantinople Mary became aware of existing in the midst of a heathen community — and one in which the Christian virtues of charity and mildness — seldom observed in the West to be sure — were conspicuously absent.

John Hawkwood was certainly happy in his new life. There seemed a total absence of the overt hostility that had followed himself and his family everywhere in Constantinople: the Turks might pity someone who had not the sense to recognise the Prophet Mahomet as the final and only true messenger of God, but they did not hate him for revering instead the earlier prophet, Jesus Christ. In Brusa, too, everything he required was given to him, including the men to labour for him, and to be trained as gunners, so he immediately began forming his own company of soldiers who would obey his orders in the field. Anthony was of great assistance here, and was able to drill these men, resplendent in his new uniform of green tunic and white breeches, helmet and breastplate.

More and more Anthony found himself summoned to the presence of the Emir: to converse, to play chess or backgammon, or merely to stand at his side.

"He is powerfully fond of you," John Hawkwood remarked.

"*He will seek to make you his,*" the Emir Valideh had earlier warned. "*Between us we will resist him.*"

But the Emir Valideh had disappeared into the recesses of the palace in Brusa, although Anthony did not doubt that she watched all that was happening through her trelliswork screens.

A crisis occurred for Anthony on a morning soon after the ending of Ramadan — the holy month in which the entire community did nothing but fast and pray. As he was being bathed, the doors were suddenly thrown open by two Janissaries. The Emir himself entered the bath chamber, and stood gazing at Anthony's naked body.

Anthony instantly dropped to his knees and gestured the eunuch attending him to fetch his robe. Since Anthony had naturally applied himself to learning Turkish, he was now dumbfounded to overhear Mahomet instructing one of his retinue to commence a painting of the naked body in front of him.

The artist thus addressed was positively trembling. "It cannot be, O Padishah. Is it not written that eternal hell awaits him who reproduces the human form?"

"There is no such law in the Anyi," Mahomet retorted.

"That is true," intervened the Grand Mufti, "but it is the law of the Prophet, and is found in the Koran."

"The Law of the Prophet applies to true believers," Mahomet pointed out, clearly incensed by this unexpected opposition. "It has no relation to gaiours. Young Hawk is an infidel. He can be reproduced. I will have him painted."

The eunuch, also listening to the altercation, remained standing some distance away, holding the robe. Anthony dared not move, however hard his heart was pounding.

The painter had fallen to his knees. "Know that I will always carry out your bidding, O Padishah, but ... here I am not competent. I know nothing of the human body."

Mahomet pointed. "Have you no eyes? Paint what you see?"

The man was now grasping at straws to avoid having to commit what he clearly supposed was a mortal sin. "It is not so simple. To paint such a body I must need to know how it works, how the muscles and the tendons are connected, where one begins and the other ends. O Padishah, believe me ..."

Mahomet lost his temper. "You are a prevaricating rogue," he shouted, arm outstretched, finger pointing. "You seek to defy your Emir. Be careful I do not have you flayed. Then we will see how your muscles work, eh? You wish to discover these things? Then you shall." His pointing finger swung and settled on one of his black pageboys. "He will suffice. You and you," he shouted at his appalled guards, "take that boy. Slit him from neck to crotch. Lay him out before this coward and let him study how his muscles and tendons are joined." His finger swung back to the painter. "Then paint me that picture."

The entire entourage seemed unable to move for a moment, then the soldiers ran forward to carry out their master's command. The pageboy screamed, but was stripped and dead in an instant, his blood and entrails splattered across the floor, his muscles certainly exposed as they quivered for the last time. Anthony opened his mouth to scream as well — some kind of protest — but the Emir had already stalked from the bathing chamber ... and the dissection of the still bleeding corpse proceeded.

"Stay," Halil warned him, "and be painted. There are times when our master will not be crossed."

There were times, Anthony supposed, when Mahomet was not quite sane. But that very evening he found himself playing chess with the Emir in the Ottoman palace, in a small room off the main council chamber, where there were but two divans and utter privacy. He sipped at a sherbet while his master mused.

"It was not until I spoke the words that I became aware of their true import," he said. "Do you know I love thee, young Hawk?"

"I am the most honoured of men, O Padishah," Anthony said cautiously.

"And yet you are indeed an infidel. This makes me unhappy."

"A man who would change his religion is surely not worth the handful of earth on which he stands." Anthony said, feeling the hairs at the nape of his neck rising.

"You are right," Mahomet said, to both Anthony's surprise and relief. "And besides, I have important duties in store for you, which

I believe you will best carry out as a gaiour. I would not importune you to change your religion, young Hawk. But it offends me that your body should remain that of a beardless youth, not yet grown to manhood. I consider it time for you to take a woman. But how can I expose you to her contempt? Besides, how may a man enter heaven in such a state? It is not possible. I would have you be as one of us. You will not refuse me this."

Anthony swallowed. As if he could refuse such a request! "I am yours to command," he said.

Mahomet smiled. "I will speak to your father, of course. But I shall myself sponsor you."

That night, for the first time in four months, Anthony was summoned by the Kislar Agha, to meet him at midnight in an alleyway outside his father's house.

This time it was a matter of secret corridors and whispered voices, as he was taken, again totally concealed in a jibbah and this time with his face covered as well, into the presence of the Emir Valideh.

Tonight she wore pale blue, and was more beautiful even than he remembered her.

"You prosper, young Hawk," she said.

"I am in daily fear," he confessed.

She smiled. "I doubt that. You are apprehensive of being made a catamite. It will never happen to you, my Hawk, even if my son forces you to submit to his caresses. You are too much your own man."

"He wishes me circumcised, Highness."

Mara inclined her head. "So I am informed."

Anthony wondered which — or indeed how many — of the men and eunuchs who surrounded the Emir were her spies.

"Are you afraid?" the Emir Valideh asked. "It has the merit of improving cleanliness. Nor does it dull sensation; indeed it improves it." She loosed his pants and put her hands inside. "I may regret it, because you are strange to me. But I doubt not that you will perform as well when pulled back. As for the pain, you are not a coward, my Hawk, and it is a trifling thing in any event." She smiled. "I do not, of course, speak from personal experience. Do you then feel shame at such a public operation? It befalls all men, at least in the East."

"Perhaps I feel all of those things, Highness."

She laughed. "Yet are you twitching at the thought. Come, young Hawk, let us enjoy him for the last time, in his present state."

She was as irresistible as he remembered. Yet the thought of what lay before him hung at the back of his mind. He had no sooner climaxed than it occupied him fully again. He raised himself on his elbow and looked down at the lovely face below him, more serene than ever as Mara's eyes were closed and her own passion spent.

"The operation is performed in public, Highness?"

Mara's eyes opened slowly and languorously, and she stretched her body beneath his. "Oh yes," she said. "Even the ladies of the harem are present." Her smile became a laugh. "Behind a trellis, of course."

"What must be, must be," John Hawkwood decided grimly. "We must face it boldly. Only in that way lies survival."

Mary was prostrate with anxiety, and Anthony was increasingly terrified himself, although he refused to admit it to his father. He was not sure where his fear really lay. A cut with the knife he supposed he could stand. What then? Only the childish fear of total exposure, perhaps.

The Emir declared an "evening of joy" the day before the ceremony, culminating in a great feast in the palace, when Anthony was ritually presented with a suit of new clothes, both tunic and breeches of soft white silk decorated with gold thread.

Wearing these, he was next morning led in procession around the town, to be applauded by men and women alike. He could not help but recall the parading of that unfortunate man immediately before his impalement.

Having been shown to the people, he was led into the council chamber which was absolutely crowded with officers and muftis and imams; it was not every day that the Emir himself presided at a circumcision. Anthony looked up quickly at the trellis-work high on the wall. It remained as dark and impenetrable as that in the castle on the Bosphorus, yet he could make out a fluttering of colours. The entire harem, no doubt. As if it mattered. He would never see any of them, except the Emir Valideh.

Anthony was escorted by his father and Halil. In the chamber

91

itself, three cushions had been placed upon the very centre of the floor, and standing before them waited the Emir and the Grand Mufti, together with the two surgeons. Anthony was led up to them and officially given into their keeping, John Hawkwood having been carefully rehearsed for his part in the proceedings.

Anthony then sat on the middle cushion, while Mahomet sat on this right, and the chief surgeon on his left. For this occasion he was wearing special trousers, secured with a string which could be easily released.

The assistant surgeon now laid on the floor before them a silver bowl, in which was a knife which somewhat resembled a razor — and presumably as sharp — a little cap of white paper shaped like a hood, and another paper filled with a red powder. To these was added a small silver instrument with a cleft in it, as well as several linen bandages.

Meanwhile one of the imams was burning incense in a censer, and soon the pungent odour filled even the large room.

The Mufti stood before them and recited several appropriate verses of the Koran, then indicated that the ceremony could begin. Anthony was not supposed to move at all, but keeping still was intensely difficult when Mahomet knelt before him and unfastened the trousers, then caressed him.

"It is best when stiffened," he explained.

Anthony could not avoid staring into Mahomet's eyes, but as soon as the Emir resumed his seat, he raised his head to gaze at the trellis-work. If she was there, he wished to gaze at her during this vital moment.

The silver instrument was now used by the chief surgeon, kneeling before him, to gather up as much of the prepuce as possible. Once this was done he cut it away, sawing rather than slicing. The pain was sudden, but also brief. Anthony started, and felt Mahomet's hand on his arm, holding him still. To cry out, or even to move, would be a sign of weakness. He continued staring at the trellis as, to his consternation, the surgeon lay down to take the bleeding penis into his mouth and suck it clean; the blood he spat into a basin held by his assistant.

Next he rolled the prepuce back as far as he could, leaving a dreadfully raw section of flesh. This he now smothered in the red powder, which he then covered with the paper cap, before binding the wound in the linen.

The Grand Mufti was reading more verses from the Koran while Anthony was assisted to his feet. His legs felt weak, but Mahomet was there to guide him forward to some clean cushions, where again he sat, this time facing back into the room towards the assembly. Mahomet clapped his hands and everyone sat down, while eunuchs hurried forward with the bowls of food. The feast commenced.

"I feel about to faint, O Padishah," Anthony muttered.

"You will not faint; you are a man," Mahomet urged him.

"Certainly I cannot eat," Anthony protested, as couscous was placed in front of him.

"You must eat," Mahomet told him. "No one else may until you have taken a mouthful."

Anthony hesitated, then pushed his sleeve back and thrust his hand into the pot. He located a piece of meat, rolled it in the semolina, and conveyed it to his mouth. It was hot and tasty, and suddenly he was hungry.

Mahomet smiled. "It is good," he said. "Within a few hours the pain will have stopped. Within three days you will be strong again. And then ... I will give you a wife."

Mahmun Pasha bowed low. "Her name is Laila, O Padishah." He trembled from the honour of having the Emir inside his house. This day might make his fortune.

"Bring her to us," Mahomet commanded.

Mahmun Pasha bowed again, and signalled to the eunuchs guarding the door of the chamber. This was a small, private room, the *mabeyin*, which connected Mahmun's harem with the *selamlik*, the larger part of the house reserved for men. Only the Emir and Anthony were present, but now into the room there came two young men, brothers of the girl, walking on either side of a white-clad, heavily veiled figure.

"Her age?" Mahomet asked.

"She is sixteen, O Padishah."

Mahomet nodded, and glanced at Anthony. "Is she too old?"

Anthony gulped. They were speaking Turkish, and the girl would know what was being said. "By no means."

"Sixteen is old," Mahomet said. "Is there not a saying that there are but three things in life a man must do quickly? Those are to bury the dead, serve a guest, and marry off a marriageable daughter. You have been remiss, Mahmun. Uncover yourself, girl."

The girl turned her head to look at her father, and received a quick nod. Her brothers stepped away from her.

The girl took the veil from her head, slowly and with some coquetry. It had completely encased her hair as well. Now the hair, long and black, fell about her shoulders, and Anthony gazed above the yashmak at the high white forehead, the luminous dark eyes.

"Why was she not presented to the Emir Valideh two years ago?" Mahomet asked.

"She was presented, O Padishah, but the Emir Valideh refused her."

"Has she some blemish?"

"None, save ..." Mahmun hesitated.

"Speak."

"The Emir Valideh was displeased with her answer to a question, O Padishah. She commanded my daughter to be whipped for levity."

Mahomet smiled. "I had heard of that, but I did not know it was this girl." He glanced at Anthony. "Does this displease you, young Hawk? You can always whip her."

"It does not displease me," Anthony said. "If she can please me in other ways."

His heart was beginning to pound. If he was going to be a Muslim, in all but actual belief, then he must live as one. And they took their pleasures as men who were lords of all they beheld ... saving only that their own lives were at the mercy of the man who beheld them in turn. But he was close to that fount of power ... and this looked like a very pretty girl. He did not suppose she could ever replace Mara Brankovich in his memory, but this girl he would possess. If there was a certain air of the slave market about this transaction, that made him even more eager.

"Well said, young Hawk," Mahomet agreed, and looked at Mahmun Pasha. "Tell her to remove the yashmak."

The pasha looked astounded, the brothers angry.

"She is to marry a man from the West," Mahomet told them. "He would look upon her face. This is his will. And mine."

"But if he then refuses her ..."

"It will be because she is unmarriageable. She is all but un-marriageable now. She is too old."

Mahmun Pasha gulped and looked at his sons.

"And would you, also, look upon another man's wife, O Padishah?" the girl suddenly asked in a low voice.

Mahomet's head jerked, as he gazed at her. She did not lower her eyes.

Mahomet gave a shout of laughter. "I can see how easily you angered my mother, Laila," he said. "No, I would not look upon another man's wife. Unveil yourself to young Hawk alone."

He turned his back on her.

Anthony could not help holding his breath as the girl looked towards him. Then she reached up and unfastened one side of her veil, allowing it to fall beside her cheek.

He found himself staring at pert, pretty features, softly rounded and yet possessing a determined little chin.

The lips were parted and were moist, as she had deliberately licked them immediately before. The nose was a shade too large for her face, but was not unattractive. And the eyes beckoned him down endless corridors of pleasure.

"Am I displeasing to you, my lord Hawk?" she asked.

Anthony had to lick his own lips.

"No," he said. "No, you are very pleasing."

Laila refastened her veil.

"I am pleased, too," Mahomet said, turning round again. "You understand, lord Mahmun, that this irregular proceeding was necessary. But since young Hawk is pleased, you will benefit greatly."

"I understand, O Padishah." The pasha was now beaming.

"The ceremony will take place one week from today. I wish you joy, Laila."

"I anticipate it, O Padishah," the girl replied, and bowed, firstly to the Emir and then to her father, and was led from the room.

Mahomet snapped his fingers and gave a roar of laughter. "No wonder my mother had her whipped instead of sending her to my harem," he said.

"Do you have the choice of every girl in your kingdom, O Padishah?" Anthony asked.

"A selection is made every year," Mahomet explained, "of the most beautiful as well as the most talented. They are presented to the Emir Valideh, and she selects those she feels are suitable for the seraglio. These girls are the *guizde*; that means, literally, 'in the eye'. But they are in my mother's eye, of course. I have no choice at all, alas. The Emir Valideh is my mother in all things."

He stared fixedly at Anthony, and Anthony felt a chill run down his back into his legs. Did he know? Could he know? But surely if he did, Anthony thought, I would already be done for?

"She even chooses who I will sleep with each night," Mahomet went on. "These then become *ikbal*, or the favoured ones. But it is right that she should decide. There are so many — I could not possibly sleep with them all. There are women in my harem on whom I have never even set eyes — nor will I. Yet they are still either wives or concubines, and must be cared for." He brooded. "It is a great expense to me."

"Do you ever sleep with one girl more than once?" Anthony asked, agog.

Mahomet laughed. "Of course I have my favourites. I convey such thoughts to my mother, and the chosen girl becomes an odalisk. There is only one higher rank in the harem. The girl who first presents me with a son will have great honour heaped upon her, because she will one day be Emir Valideh herself."

"Unless she dies," Anthony said without thinking — and wanted to bite his tongue.

But Mahomet did not seem to notice his careless indication of knowledge of harem politics. "That is true. My own mother died too early. But in her place I have a better. She will be amused to know that you are married to one such as this Laila. The Emir Valideh is much interested in you, and your father."

Anthony swallowed nervously, but Mahomet remained smiling.

"Be sure you whip your wife regularly. Women should be seen and not heard. Or is this not so in England?"

"It is not so in England, O Padishah."

"A strange land," Mahomet said, and linked his arm through Anthony's. "Tell me more about English women, young Hawk. It may be that one day I shall possess one."

"It is not right," Mary Hawkwood declared. Now that she had regained her confidence and felt that she had a settled role to play in the community of Brusa, she was prepared to resume being a proper mother to her one remaining son. Besides, she could now speak some Turkish, and had even made friends amongst her female neighbours, spending long mornings in their principal relaxation of drinking coffee and gossiping. Her new acquaintances had not been slow to point out that the whole proceedings surrounding young Hawk's betrothal had been highly irregular — or to remind her that the bride would become head of the household should John Hawkwood die.

"Some chit of a heathen girl," she complained. "Why have we not been introduced to the parents?"

"In normal circumstances," Anthony explained patiently, "the girl *would* have been your choice, Mother. But the Emir wished this arranged differently. He seeks, I think, to change the law in many ways. He moves through life to a definite pattern, but with caution. I can promise you that she is very charming."

"A heathen Turk," Mary grumbled. "She will not lord it over me, Anthony. Not a sixteen-year-old girl."

"She will not expect to, Mother," Anthony said. "She will expect you to lord it over her."

But his mother's reactions were not those he truly feared. And, sure enough, the Kislar Agha came for him again that evening.

This night the Emir Valideh was veiled, and her eyes glittered like flint.

"You have betrayed me," she said.

As he had not yet been bidden to stand, Anthony remained kneeling at her feet. "I, Highness?"

"Who is this girl you have chosen? A girl who talks too much. One whom I have rejected, too. It is the gossip of the palace."

"I did not choose the girl, Highness. Surely, as you know all things, you know that also. She was offered for my acceptance by the Emir — I could do nothing else." Which was the truth, he reflected, though he had a notion he would never have rejected Laila, no matter who had presented her to him.

The Emir Valideh gazed at him for several seconds, then her yashmak inflated as she breathed out against it.

"Yes," she said, "I do understand."

Anthony wished that he did, himself.

"I had in mind to command you to forswear this girl," Mara continued.

"Highness?" Anthony was aghast. To do that would be to make her brothers sworn blood enemies of him and his.

Mara smiled. "Yes, I had it in mind, but I will not do so. We shall let Mahomet play his little games. But be sure you whip her often.

97

Be sure, too, you make her bring forth fine sons for you, young Hawk." She released her yashmak. "But tonight *I* will exhaust you."

"For the last time, Highness?" he asked, sadly.

Mara gazed at him. "Who can say?" she asked in turn. "Are not our lives and our lusts at the whim of God?"

The ceremony was a simple one, much less elaborate, than that of the circumcision. The two families sat and drank coffee together in Mahmun Pasha's house, the elder Hawkwoods meeting, on this first and last occasion, Laila's parents and family. The Turkish ladies were heavily veiled, but Mary refused to cover her face inside the house; as if she was determined to show her disapproval of the whole proceedings. There was a mufti who read from the Koran, while Laila sat alone, cross-legged on a cushion, shrouded in a variety of haiks and veils.

Then they ate sweetmeats, and Mahmun Pasha handed over gifts of cloth to Mary and weapons to John and Anthony, as well as the bag of golden coins which comprised Laila's dowry.

Two notaries knelt between the families and counted the coins, and John Hawkwood pronounced himself satisfied. Then he produced his own gifts for Mahmun and his family, but these did not include money.

Laila was then led away by the female members of her family, and Mary was asked to accompany them. As the men waited, they drank more coffee.

When Mary returned, her cheeks were pink and she breathed heavily.

"Is the girl to your satisfaction, mother of young Hawk?" asked the mufti.

Mary swallowed. "She is to my satisfaction," she said.

"And a virgin?"

"Yes, she is a virgin," Mary snapped.

"Then do you accept her as your son's wife?"

"I accept her," Mary said resentfully.

The mufti bowed and clapped his hands. Mahmun's womenfolk returned to the room.

"It is usual for the bride to be carried to her home by the brothers of her husband," the mufti explained. "This is an ancient custom, and commemorates the days of our people when a bride could only be taken by force." He smiled deprecatingly, to indicate that such things were far in the past. "But you have no brothers, young Hawk."

"I will carry my bride," Anthony said.

The mufti looked at Mahmun Pasha, who nodded his agreement.

"Then is the Lady Laila awaiting you, young Hawk," the mufti said.

Laila stood in the antechamber by the door, still totally invisible beneath layers of clothing.

Anthony went up to her, and lifted her into his arms. "You are my wife," he reminded her.

"Yes, Chelebi," she agreed.

She called him lord. He was her lord. It was a strange feeling.

The family bowed as Anthony carried his bride out on to the street and set her on the saddle of his waiting horse. It was just past dusk, for only at sunset may a bride be taken to her new home. The Hawkwood house was not far, but there was quite a crowd of people to be negotiated, all clapping and shouting, while small boys ran beside the horse trying to steal the sandals from Laila's feet.

Leading the horse by its bridle, Anthony looked over his shoulder at her and felt a tremendous, unexpected stirring of sexual desire.

Because for the first time in his life he possessed a woman.

The Hawkwood eunuchs opened the doors for them, and Anthony lifted Laila from the saddle and carried her inside, the noise of the crowd subsiding behind them. He carried Laila up the stairs and into his bedchamber, which had been refurnished for this occasion, the principal innovation being a huge double divan. On this he placed her gently, then sat down beside her to lift the first of her veils.

Promptly she sat up. "I must pay my respects to your mother."

"I doubt she has returned yet."

"It is the law," Laila insisted.

She very definitely had a mind of her own, and had no doubt been warned that this gaiour who was now her husband knew nothing of Turkish custom. Anthony had no wish to upset her on their first night together; besides, he could hear the sounds of voices downstairs. "Then go to her," he said.

"You must be present," Laila advised him, adjusting her yashmak.

Docilely Anthony followed her down the stairs to where his father and mother were being welcomed by the servants.

"My mother," Laila said, and sank to her knees.

Mary Hawkwood looked dumbfounded.

"I think you need to accept her as your daughter," Anthony suggested.

Mary hesitated, then placed both her hands on the girl's head. "Welcome to our house, child," she said. "I desire only that you make my son happy."

"Your wish is my command, Mother," Laila replied.

Anthony took her hand to raise her to her feet. "You'll excuse us," he said to his parents.

His desire was growing by the minute. Laila was clearly startled by his wish to undress her himself, but she submitted, and within minutes she lay naked on the divan. Here was no irresistible ripe beauty like that of the Emir Valideh, but the girl was compelling enough in her immaturity, in the slimness of her hips and the small mounds of her breasts. Her legs and arms were straight and strong, and her shaven pubes drew him to her in more haste than he had ever known. He was anxious because his penis was but recently healed, and he felt unsure of himself. Thus he made love to her as a Christian rather than as Mara had taught him, which appeared to surprise her, as no doubt her mother had prepared her for something quite different. But again she made no protest: he was her Chelebi.

Afterwards he lay on his back with his eyes closed. "I was too hasty," he said. "Next time will be better."

He knew he must have hurt her, but she had neither cried out nor winced. Now, to his surprise, he discovered she had left his bed.

He sat up, and saw her carefully examining his clothing — going through his pockets, removing the few silver coins she found there.

"What are you doing?" he asked, amazed.

She turned to face him without embarrassment, the coins clutched in her small fist. "I am taking my money."

"Your money?"

"Of course," she said. "When a woman lies with a man, she is entitled to whatever money he may have in his pockets."

"Laila," he said, "you are my wife, not a whore."

"It is a wife's privilege also," she explained patiently. "It is written."

"Splendid, splendid," the Emir Mahomet commented as he inspected the twelve bombards, each several feet of iron cylinder, blocked at one end to retain the force of the explosion which would fire it, bound in leather strips for additional strength, and resting in chocks on a wooden carriage. "You have done great work, Hawk. And you are certain these cannon will knock down the walls of Constantinople?"

"They will certainly breach the walls," John Hawkwood said, "if they can be placed close enough.

Mahomet frowned. "How close do you require?"

"Within a mile."

"Will that not expose us to the fire of their guns, in return?"

"That is so, O Padishah. As for the smaller guns" — he indicated the batteries of light cannon, man-killers more than wall-breachers — "they will only play their part should the Byzantines sortie against us."

Mahomet stroked his beard. "This task grows mightier with every day," he grumbled.

"That is why I have recommended using the fleet and arming the Janissaries with handguns. The artillery must be protected. But ... I have also another solution."

Mahomet gazed at him. "I am negotiating with Venice for the delivery of the handguns, and the new fleet is well in hand. So tell me of this other solution."

"If you would come with me ..."

Mahomet glanced at Anthony who was, as ever, in attendance upon his father, then followed the elder Hawkwood into the large wooden hut. The gate was guarded by two of John's gunners, who stood to attention as their Emir approached.

As Mahomet stepped through the doorway — a diminutive figure between the two huge Englishmen — he stopped in consternation as he stared at the enormous weapon before him, twice as long as any outside, and twice as thick.

"By the beard of the Prophet," he muttered.

"It has long been my dream," John Hawkwood said, "to build such a gun."

Mahomet went forward to stroke the iron monster. Its length was twice his own height, and when he stopped to peer into the barrel his head disappeared.

"That is twelve hands' breadth in circumference," Hawkwood said proudly.

Mahomet's head re-emerged. "And what will it fire?"

Hawkwood indicated the rounded stone shot which lay beside the gun. "Four men are needed to lift that."

Mahomet gazed at it. "What range?"

"It has not yet been tested." Hawkwood thrust his fingers into the touchhole where the powder would be poured before lighting. It absorbed two of his stout digits. "It is a matter of very careful calculation and some experimentation. But I believe it will achieve more than a mile."

"It will hurl that huge stone so far?"

"We will know when it is fired, O Padishah."

"Then haste, Hawk. Haste!"

John Hawkwood bowed. "You understand that it will take many men to manoeuvre this gun? Many men and oxen."

"You will have all the men and the oxen you require, Hawk."

John Hawkwood drew in a long breath. "And all the iron, Padishah?"

"You wish to make another such as this?"

"One will suffice. I wish to cast a shot."

Mahomet's frown was back. "In iron?"

"Padishah, this stone ball — and it is my intention to make a number of them — could well breach the wall of Constantinople. Yet it will be stone meeting stone. If we could hurl an iron ball as heavy as that stone one, I do not think there is any wall in the world which could withstand it."

"By Allah!" Mahomet cried. "You are a man amongst men! Cast me that iron ball and I will make you a pasha."

"I will need more than one."

"Then cast as many as you wish. I give you the right to requisition iron wherever it can be found. Keep me informed. Young Hawk, you will accompany me."

They mounted their horses and, surrounded by their escort of sipahis, rode back through the streets of the town to the Emir's palace. People stopped to watch them pass, and some applauded;

Mahomet was a popular ruler, and they were used to seeing him as he went about every day, inspecting his troops, visiting the mosques, consulting with the muftis and imams. He had now been master of the Ottomans for over a year, and it had been a year of peace. This satisfied the wives and mothers — and the Janissaries were still happy to wait for the order to march: they were well aware of the enormous preparations taking place throughout the Turkish empire.

"But it is time to begin our campaign," Mahomet told Anthony, as they sat together and sipped sherbet. He spoke Latin, which was known to few of his pashas. "Your father is doing wonders. I meant what I said: I will honour him above all other men."

Providing that huge bombard does not explode the first time it is fired, Anthony thought.

"Now it is time for you to play your part," Mahomet said.

Anthony felt his muscles tensing. He had seen somewhat less of the Emir since his marriage, and that had to be Mahomet's will, since he could send for his English protégé whenever he chose. There had not been any apparent loss of favour, however, and Anthony had been very content to be one step removed from the exhilarating but dangerous proximity of the Emir, and to carry out his duties as his father's aide-de-camp. Now he was not sure what to expect.

Mahomet had observed this slight shudder of apprehension, and smiled. "You have now been married six months. Is your wife not swollen?"

"Alas, I am not so blessed."

Mahomet sighed. "Neither am I truly blessed. My son Bayazid does nothing but sleep. At four years old I was already playing with a sword, but not he. Yet he is my only son. And I have more material with which to work. These women are lazy. You should beat your wife — and take another. I will give you another."

"As you wish," Anthony agreed, although he was not sure what he would do with another woman. Laila might not yet have been able to conceive — indeed the fault might be entirely his — but she remained a most satisfying sexual partner, while even his mother had warmed to the girl's strictly no-nonsense approach to life and her invariable good humour — although she also possessed a caustic wit she was not afraid to use. More surprising was the way she had adapted to her new surroundings. In the beginning she had been scandalised to discover that the Hawkwoods did not honour at least the *fedjeur*, the dawn hour of prayer, that their house contained no harem, and that she was expected to take her meals with both her husband and her father-in-law, and unveil before them both as well. Equally she had been amazed that Anthony intended to sleep with her every night, whether they had sex or not, and that he did not lock her away during her menstrual periods, when all Turkish women were regarded as dangerously unclean. But having discovered how the Franks lived, she had also discovered that it was infinitely preferable to anything she had expected, certainly from the point of view of a woman. He would hate to upset her new-found happiness by introducing another woman to the house — but if it was the will of the Emir ...

"As soon as you return from your mission," Mahomet said.

"My mission, O Padishah?"

"It is time for me to prepare my stroke against Constantinople. I can be under no illusions, young Hawk. Those walls have stood a thousand years; they have resisted a thousand attacks. Constantine's small army has undoubtedly grown. Your father may be right, and my fleet may be able to take the Golden Horn, to permit me to attack the city from every direction, yet it will be the greatest undertaking in history. And were I to be defeated ..." He brooded for several seconds. "This cannot happen, so there are other steps which must be taken before I ever launch my assault. I am telling you my own most secret thoughts, young Hawk, because I know you will never betray me."

Anthony bowed his head. He could never betray the Emir now, he knew, without sacrificing both his mother and father, and no doubt Laila as well. But he doubted he would, anyway, even if those three could somehow miraculously be transported to safety. Mahomet might be as cold-blooded as any snake, as bloodthirsty as any hungry tiger, but he was no more than a typical representative of his people. And he had the aura of greatness about him. Besides, he was going to take Constantinople.

"To give the guns your father is making for me the maximum support he needs," Mahomet said, "I must establish a base on the European side of the Bosphorus."

"But you already have vast territories in Europe, O Padishah," Anthony ventured.

"Territories which are vulnerable to sudden attacks by the

Christian princes of Serbia and Transylvania, should I ever become fully committed to a siege of Constantinople. That is one of the matters I wish to discuss with you ... But the vulnerability will remain: all Christians are treacherous, when it comes to dealing with us. All they require is some priest to tell them that a treaty with a Muslim has no importance in the sight of God, and they will break it. I must therefore look to myself, and myself alone, for security. And that means Anatolia. But to attempt to sustain my armies from Anatolia would be too dangerous. I am doubling the size of my fleet, but my people are not sailors by instinct; they are horsemen. I know that should a Genoese fleet arrive in these waters, and there are constant rumours of them sending one, my communications would be cut in an hour."

"Can you not obtain a fleet of practised seamen from Venice? They would be happy to fight against the Genoese, who are their deadly rivals in trade, and they are also the sworn enemies of Byzantium."

"Are not the Venetians also Christian? Will they not promise aid at one moment, and prevaricate at the next? Allah knows they have been delaying the delivery of those handguns which your father considers essential to the success of our enterprise. No, while I will endeavour to set all of these things in motion, my ultimate strength can only derive from myself. I need to create a castle, a fortified post, on the European shore of the Bosphorus. This I will do, north of Constantinople. But the moment I start this, Constantine will suspect my purpose. None of my ancestors has ever done such a thing before. He may well have it in his power to rush out and destroy my works before they are sufficiently advanced to repel him. So this must be prevented."

Anthony waited, his heart pounding. The Emir would not be confiding in him without a purpose.

"I must allay all suspicions on the part of the Byzantines," Mahomet said. "I wish you to do this for me, young Hawk."

"I, O Padishah?"

"You know them. You have learned their tongue. You have lived amongst them. So far, Constantine and I have done nothing more than exchange courtesies. Now you will go to him as my ambassador, and convince him that I and my people wish only peace with him and his; that building a castle on the European shores of the Bosphorus is for our mutual protection against the ambitions of

Prince Drakul of Transylvania. You have heard of the man?"

"Only the name."

"Well, I hear he is a ferocious monster." Mahomet paused, and Anthony wondered if he was considering how any man could be more ferocious than himself.

"May I remind you, O Padishah," he said, "that I was expelled from Constantinople on pain of death."

Mahomet gazed at him. "Are you afraid to go back as my ambassador? You will travel under my protection. Should a hair of your head be harmed, I will impale a hundred children for each one. Tell them that. But succeed in your mission, and aid me to take that accursed city, and I will tell you this: you may ask of me anything found within those walls, and it shall be yours."

Anthony swallowed. To imagine anything or, more important, anyone in Constantinople being his to seize was a delicious thought — but it would be dangerous to let his dreams run ahead of reality. "I will undertake your mission."

"Which begins at Constantinople. From there you will go to Prince George Brankovich of Serbia." He paused, his gaze on Anthony. "You have heard of him too?"

Anthony licked his lips. Not for the first time he had the uneasy feeling that Mahomet was aware of his liaison with the Emir Valideh; in the six months he had been married to Laila he had been summoned to Mara's bedchamber on six occasions, and fallen more deeply in love than ever. "I have heard of him, O Padishah."

"You will visit him also as my ambassador. I need his assurance that no Serbian armies will be raised against me in the course of this great undertaking, and that no armies from the West will be permitted to pass through his territories."

"I understand," Anthony said, his brain spinning at the concept that one so young could place so much of Europe within his undertaking.

"From the Serb I would have you seek a conference with John Hunyadi himself."

"Hunyadi?" Anthony frowned. "He is our enemy. All Hungary is our enemy."

"He is old, young Hawk. He has fought against the sons of Othman for too long. You will offer him peace, in my name, between our peoples. He will accept my offer."

Anthony bowed his head. He had to assume the Emir was right.

"There is yet a third prince you must visit on my behalf, young Hawk," Mahomet said. "Drakul."

Anthony's head came up sharply.

"He guards the approaches from the north, through the Transylvanian passes. He too must assure me of his neutrality. Young Hawk, that is a dangerous man. I sent him an embassy but six months ago, and still no man of it has returned. I do not even know if my people reached the prince. But you must reach him and convince him of my greatness, of the power of my people. You can do this, where my pashas may fail. You speak the languages of these people."

"Of Transylvania?"

"Drakul will speak Latin. You will converse with him, and tell him of me. Not of my plans — only that I demand his neutrality, or else my Janissaries will storm through his kingdom one of these days and hurl him captive at my feet." Mahomet smiled. "They will do so anyway, once Constantinople is mine. But you need not tell him that."

"I understand, O Padishah."

"You will be accompanied by two of my pashas, Halim and Mahmun." Mahomet smiled. "You do not mind travelling with your father-in-law?"

"I will enjoy it."

"You will command the embassy. They will accept this, though you are very young, young Hawk. What was your age on your last birthday?"

"Twenty, O Padishah."

"I was but a year older when, last year, I had to grasp my inheritance. You will grasp this opportunity to serve me, and rise to greatness."

"I will endeavour to do so." Anthony bowed.

5

CONSTANTINOPLE

Byzantine guards stood to attention; the cannon fired a salute of blank shot. Beneath the helmets and the flowing robes it was not possible for any man on the wall to discern that the entire embassy was not composed solely of Ottomans.

It was an imposing embassy. Sixty horsement walked their mounts over the flat countryside, their green and crimson banners with the insignia of the crescent fluttering in the breeze. Above them the walls and their towers reached upwards. They too were marked by fluttering banners.

Once Anthony had looked on those flags as symbols beneath which he would fight. Now they were symbols he would destroy. Nearly two years ago he had crept away from this city in the dead of night, with despair in his heart. Now he was returned to betray it.

He felt no remorse. Somewhere inside those walls were the bones of his brother.

Equally, somewhere within those walls were the living bones of his sister. He hoped and prayed.

John Hawkwood and Mary had been appalled at the mission he had been given.

"Notaras will take one look at you and demand your execution," John had warned.

"Not if I travel as the Emir's ambassador," Anthony assured him with more confidence than he actually felt. "He would not dare."

"You are our last remaining child," Mary had sobbed.

"No, Mother. You have another child — and I will bring you news of her," Anthony promised.

I may even bring her back to you, he thought. That was his dream. In the Ottoman empire all things were possible, providing one had the favour of the Emir. What he really wanted to do was return to Constantinople in triumph, and reveal that triumph to his once-loved sister.

And to the Notaras family. Every one of them.

Laila could not understand his parents' remonstrances, as they had been conducted in English. Neither could she understand why her husband would not travel, as a true Muslim lord, complete with harem — nor permit his two associates to take a vast retinue of camp followers.

"We have a long and dangerous journey ahead of us," he insisted. "We will take only our bodyguard of sipahis."

Laila was nonetheless proud. "You are employed upon the Emir's business, husband," she said. "You will become a pasha, like my father. With him at your side, you cannot fail."

The Emir Valideh had also been upset, when she summoned Anthony to her the night before he left. "It is his power to use men," she observed. "Now he sends you from my side."

"Sometimes I feel he knows about us, Mara."

Mara gazed at him in thought for several seconds. Then she smiled. "That is impossible, young Hawk. Or you would no longer retain a head, much less a penis. But I would have you come back to me. Be sure of that."

"When I come back, Mara, I must go to war. Along with the Emir."

"I know. But I will see you nevertheless before you go." She pressed an emerald ring into his hand. "That is my favourite stone — as is well known. Place it in the hand of my nephew, and tell him of me." Another roguish smile. "And of my power here."

But now the time for dreams and fears was past. The members of the embassy were walking their horses through the streets of the great city, and the crowds were out to gaze at them. Nothing much had changed there, so far as Anthony could discern. He studied everything with the greatest attention. The walls stood as strong as ever; the cannon were placed as his father had left them. The great chain still barred the entrance of the Golden Horn to all except peaceful ships.

And the people seemed just the same: brilliantly dressed and noisy, ill-disciplined and clamorous. No doubt there had been many a chariot race, and many an evening riot, since the one that had brought him and his family to disaster.

Anthony had never before entered the reception hall of the Imperial Palace. Now he strode up its centre aisle, hand resting on the hilt of his scimitar, green silk cape floating from his shoulders, as light drifted through the stained-glass windows to reflect from his cuirass and the steel of his helmet. Halim Pasha and Mahmun Pasha walked on either side, but slightly behind him. Though each was old enough to be his father, neither man had shown the least resentment at being placed in an inferior position to a gaiour and a boy.

Hawkwood had never stood face to face with the Emperor either; nor, as he bowed, had he time to scan the faces of the men behind the throne.

"My lord," he began, "the Emir Mahomet, the second of that immortal name, Lord of Sivas and Karaman, Anatolia and Jandar, Roumelia and Greece, sends greetings to His Most Serene Highness, Constantine, the eleventh of that name, Emperor of Byzantium."

"Your Emir's greeting has been long delayed," Constantine remarked mildly. "All we hear from Brusa and Ankara is talk of arms and armour, of vast armies being raised against us."

Anthony straightened. "Not against you, I assure Your Grace. But the Emir has many enemies in Europe as well as Asia. He has much to defend."

Constantine was frowning at him in puzzlement. Though Anthony's hair was concealed beneath his helmet, there was no disguising either his height or his ruddy complexion, through the overlay of sunburn.

"By God!" suddenly shouted the Grand Duke Lukas Notaras, standing as ever behind the throne. "That is Hawkwood's son."

Anthony bowed. "I have that privilege, my lord."

"Seize the fellow," Notaras bellowed. "He is a proscribed traitor!"

Guards hurried forward, and the Ottomans reached for their scimitars.

Anthony did not flinch. "I am sent as ambassador from the Emir, Your Grace," he reminded Constantine.

The Emperor hastily gestured his soldiers to fall back. "Then you are doubly traitor," he growled.

"How so, Your Grace? My father came here loyally determined to serve Your Grace's cause. But we were expelled, and my brother murdered ... But I did not come here to speak of things past." He raised his voice as the Byzantine nobles began to chatter amongst themselves. "What is done is done. Instead I come as an emissary for my new master, the Emir Mahomet, lord of all the Ottomans."

The muttering slowly died.

"And I come in peace," Anthony continued in a lower voice. "The Emir Mahomet seeks only peace with Byzantium. He has sent me here to tell you this. Moreover, he has sent me here to convey to you his plans, so that you may understand them. The Emir has information that Prince Drakul of Wallachia plans a campaign towards the south ..."

"I have heard of this man," Constantine muttered. "His deeds make even the veriest heathen seem like a saint."

"Then you will understand that the Emir must protect his territories against these savages."

"The Emir's territories south of the Danube are extensive," Constantine remarked.

"But scantily held with men, Your Grace. The Emir plans to build a great castle on the shores of the Bosphorus, some miles north of Galata."

There was a fresh outbreak of muttered comment.

"Such a castle would protect Constantinople equally with the Emir's possessions," Anthony said loudly.

"Or could equally be used against Constantinople," Notaras broke in.

"Why should our Emir seek to destroy Constantinople?" Anthony asked. "The castle will be built to restrain the ambitions of this Drakul. That is the word of the Emir Mahomet. Therefore the Emir extends the hand of friendship to the Byzantines, and invites them to join with him in a pact of peace between our two peoples."

"To such a pact would we happily adhere," Constantine agreed thoughtfully. "You have risen far in the service of your new master, Hawkwood, to have been entrusted with such a valuable mission."

"I am fortunate, Your Grace," Anthony acknowledged.

"You will dine with me, and tell me more of this Emir of yours," Constantine commanded.

Halim was jubilant. "They are fools who accepted your every word, young Hawk," he said. "They are like lambs ripe for slaughter. Our master will be pleased."

111

"It is sad," Mahmun commented, "for an emissary of the Emir thus to lie."

Halim snapped his fingers. "But that is why a gaiour was chosen, Mahmun. Can you not understand that? Lying is second nature to the Franks. Or to the Byzantines," he added.

Anthony decided not to take offence. The three of them had a long way to travel together. Besides, was the man not right? He had lied more convincingly than he had ever supposed he could. And Constantine had clearly believed him.

"Tell me of your father," the Emperor began, as Anthony sat beside him in the Imperial banqueting hall, looking in awe across the table at the assembled Byzantine nobility.

Anthony thought: did I ever expect to be seated here at the right hand of Constantine Paleologus? ... to be drinking wine — for the first time in over a year — from a golden goblet, and eating from a golden plate, and being served by these obsequious Greek flunkey? There was no such wealth in Mahomet's palace.

He wondered what the Emir's reactions would be to such unbridled splendour.

"My father is well," he answered the Emperor. "And he prospers."

"That is good. He was done a great injustice, perhaps." Constantine glanced at him. "You understand that I would have saved your brother's life if only I could."

"I believe that, Your Grace."

"I certainly did not intend that you or your father should take service with the Ottoman," Constantine said somewhat ingenuously. "Tell me this: does Hawkwood teach the Turks the arts of gunnery?"

"The Turks are nomads from the steppes of Asia. For all their successes and their fine airs, they remain nothing more. How may nomads understand gunnery?"

Constantine stared at him so hard that Anthony blurted out the truth. Then the Emperor sighed. "I believe you, young Hawkwood, because I must. Your master can march against the walls of my city whenever he chooses. But tell him this: Constantinople will be defended, and will survive."

"My master has no doubt of that, Your Grace. Which is why he wishes to live in peace with you. Have we not agreed a pact of friendship?"

Constantine stared into his empty wine glass, as if hoping to see the future. Once again Anthony's heart went out to him. When he had fled this city, he had hated everything Byzantine, and the Emperor as much as anyone. But this man deserved better than the fate hanging over him ...

Finally the Emperor smiled sadly. "You and your family were wronged here in my city. I acknowledge it freely. I am glad that you have prospered, though it saddens my heart to see you in Ottoman robes. Now I am in your debt. Ask of me what you wish and I will grant it, save only that it does not betray my city or my people."

"I would speak with my sister, Your Grace."

The Emperor frowned. "You know that she is married to Basil Notaras?"

"Yes, I know that."

"But she is still your sister — I understand that. I will convey your message to her. But you understand ... I cannot force her to see you."

"My sister will surely wish it, Your Grace."

"Very well. I will inform her of your desire. But that is a very small request, young Hawkwood. Is there no other?"

"Am I allowed to inquire after the health of the lady Anna Notaras?"

Constantine inclined his head. "I trust you will not wish to see her also. Anna Notaras is married to Count Drakontes. It would be very unwise for you to attempt to see her ... But I will endeavour to send your sister to you. More than that I cannot do. You are aware of the faction within this city — and now you are not only a Roman Catholic but you serve a Muslim prince." His lips twisted. "There are many who would like nothing better than to cut you down. And what would Mahomet do then, do you suppose? Guard your back, young Hawkwood, and do nothing rash. I will send your sister to you."

But the Emperor could not even accomplish that. As Anthony paced his apartment the following day, he received only a messenger with a letter.

'You are evil,' Catherine Notaras had written coldly. 'You serve the devil — you and my father. You are apostates. Judas Iscariot

113

was a saint compared with you. Get you gone from Constantinople. I do not wish to see your face again.'

"Well, young Hawk," Mahmun asked, as Anthony crumpled the letter in his fist. "How much longer do we remain in this accursed city?"

"We leave today," Anthony told him grimly. "Have we not accomplished everything we set out to do?"

They rode west, across the great plain to Adrianople, the capital of the beylerbey of Roumelia, as the Emir's dominions in Europe were known. This was a journey of over a hundred miles. It took them a week, for once they left the walls of the city behind them they were in Ottoman territory, and at every stop they were greeted and fêted by the local commander, who wished to feast them and present them with beautiful girls or handsome boys, at least for the duration of each visit.

They rode through a fertile valley watered by the river Ergene, which they had to ford several times. To the north they saw the low hills of the Istranca Daglari, but in the valley it was warm, and there were continuous olive groves around them. They passed little villages sheltering around Christian churches, for the Turks never interfered with local custom or religion as long as all taxes were promptly paid. Yet they were the lords of this land, who expected headmen and peasants to bow low as they approached, and were quick to react to any insolence, real or imagined, with a flick of their whips. Equally they were feared for their peremptory recruitment of young boys for the Janissary corps, and more than once Anthony saw mothers hurrying their sons indoors as the cavalcade approached — as if that could have saved them, had they really been out on a recruiting expedition.

Adrianople itself was a sprawling town at the junction of the Tunca and Maritza rivers, and had been famous as a stronghold since Roman times. Now it was the largest city in the Ottoman Empire; indeed the late Emir Murad, Mahomet's father, in the course of his endless wars of conquest in Europe had made Adrianople his capital.

Here they were treated to several days of feasting, and encouraged to sample the famous *peynir*, a white cheese of the district. Piri Pasha, the beylerbey, had heard of the red-haired gaiours who were serving the new Emir, and he was eager to look upon one of them. Every possible entertainment was provided for the delectation of his guests, while Piri's sipahis and Janissaries displayed their military skill in gymkhanas and archery contests.

Anthony looked on it all with cold eyes. After his sympathetic interview with Constantine, he had almost thought of trying to persuade Mahomet to leave Constantinople alone, and let it continue to exist, as it had existed for more than a thousand years, a relic of a glorious past which could not possibly interfere with Turkish aspirations. But he had left the city in a mood of simmering anger. His own sister had been turned against him — the only woman he had ever really loved, before the Emir Valideh. Well, then, let those arrogant tricksters experience whatever was now being prepared against them, and survive it if they could.

And when Piri Pasha insisted he sample the delights of a Greek virgin, selected especially for the Emir's ambassador, he used the girl harshly and left her weeping. In her slender form he tried to expiate his anger against all her people.

After leaving Adrianople they made their way up the valley of the Maritza River to Philippopolis, the ancient Roman capital of Thrace, but more famous for its conquest much earlier, by Philip of Macedon, who had renamed the then city of Pulpudeva after himself. There was no trace of the great Macedonian to be found, although the Roman ruins remained. Dominating them all, however, were the walls of Tsar Ivan Assen's fortress, for more recently the city had been the capital of the great Bulgarian military state which, under rulers such as Khan Krum, had posed such a threat to the then powerful Byzantine Empire. It had been Emperor Basil II who had finally crushed the Bulgars, earning thus the soubriquet of *Bulgaroktonos*, 'the Bulgar-Slayer'. When he had forced the Bulgarian army to surrender at Balathista in 1014, he blinded all fifteen thousand, leaving a single eye to every tenth man to guide the survivors home. Legend had it that when the Tsar, Samuel, saw these, the shattered remains of his military power, he dropped down dead.

Now it was just sad to see how degenerate these once proud fighting men had become, as they bowed low before their Turkish masters.

Yet they remained brigands at heart. On the embassy's second night in the city there was an alarm. Anthony threw aside his blanket, and the Bulgar girl who was warming him, seized up his sword and dashed outside to join the mêlée. Their camp had been invaded by several small boys in search of whatever they could find to steal. Five of them had been taken.

"Ha, ha," Mahmun said. "We will take a leaf from Basil's book and blind them. All except one, eh, to lead them home. Prepare a hot iron," he ordered his servants.

The girl, who had emerged from Anthony's tent, fell to her knees weeping. It appeared that one of the boys was her brother.

"Then she should be blinded, too," Mahmun declared, "since she undoubtedly guided them in."

I have no anger for these people, Anthony thought; they are not Byzantines. "No," he insisted. "There will be no blinding. Have them all soundly flogged." He pointed to the weeping girl. "And begin with her."

After Philippopolis, they climbed into the Balkan mountains, making for Sofia, which they reached a month later. Now they had left the warmth and the olives behind, and were entering a rugged terrain more reminiscent of Anatolia. The city, which nestled in a basin in the mountains, was remarkable for its symmetry, for every street ran either north–south or east–west, while its water supply all but equalled that of Constantinople.

Like Adrianople, Sofia was the capital of a Roumelian province, and here again the beyleybey, Ahmad Pasha, lavishly entertained the youthful ambassador, proudly showing him Buyuk Dzhamiya mosque with its imposing minaret, and forcing upon him, as gifts, examples of the local goldsmith industry as well as ornamental table pottery.

After another month's weary travel in the mountains, often swept by icy blasts which had them cowering in their tents at night, although it was only October, they came to Nish on the borders of Serbia, famous as the birthplace of Constantine the Great. Messengers had been sent ahead, and in a village perched like an eagle's nest halfway to the sky, with pine-clad peaks above and below, they were finally met by Prince George Brankovich.

For him Anthony had the same message as for Constantine.

"The Padishah is determined to settle once and for all the insolence of Drakul of Transylvania, Your Excellency," he explained. "For this purpose he is mustering a great army, and intends to build a castle on the European shores of the Bosphorus, as a depot for his men."

George Brankovich stroked his beard. Wrapped in furs and wearing somewhat decrepit armour, so that he looked as much like a bandit as any Bulgar, he had none of the beauty of his famous aunt, and his eyes were shifty — where one of Mara's glories was the steadfastness of her gaze. "What do the Greeks say to this?" he said at last.

"They understand the requirements of the Emir, Excellency."

Brankovich grinned. "Then must I also. His requirement is that I prevent Hunyadi from taking the field against the Ottomans while the Janissaries are committed in the north."

"The Emir's requirement is that you prevent Hunyadi from taking the field," Anthony explained, "wherever the necessities of his campaign may take the Emir."

Brankovich studied him for several seconds. Then he grinned again. "I am not a fool, young Hawkwood. Nor is Mahomet, it appears. I will do as he requires. Now tell me, you must be very close to the Emir to be given such authority at so young an age."

"I am blessed with good fortune," Anthony said piously.

"Yet since you are close to the Emir, have you no other word for me?"

Anthony gazed at him. "A word to be conveyed in private, Excellency."

The room was quickly cleared, much to the resentment of Mahmun and Halim.

"Well?" Brankovich demanded.

Anthony took out his purse, and from it removed the emerald ring, placing it on the table between them.

Brankovich stared at it. "Who gave you this?"

"Someone who wished me to present it to you as a gift."

Brankovich frowned. "You have seen my aunt? But that is impossible."

"The Emir Valideh has ways of making her wishes known, Your Excellency."

"The Emir Valideh," Brankovich mused. "She has risen so far? And you have seen her?" he said again.

But to Anthony lying was now second nature. "As you have said, that is impossible. Yet your aunt did know of my mission, and sent word to command me to give you that ring, so that you might believe the message I also bring from her."

The prince picked up the ring, looked at it carefully, then pocketed it. "Tell me the message."

"The Emir Valideh wishes you to know that she is all-powerful in the court of the Emir, and that she wishes him success in all things."

"Then must I labour to please my aunt," said the prince.

From Nish it was but a short journey to Belgrade, known as the White City from the colour of its houses. It stood on the borders of Hungary, and now for the first time they were venturing beyond Turkish territory, for the city had been besieged in 1440 and the Ottomans had suffered one of their few reverses before its walls. Yet the Hungarians were anxious to remain on good terms with the threatening cloud to the south-east — at least until they had recouped the immense losses they had suffered on the Field of the Blackbirds three years earlier — and the ambassadors were entertained in some style before being ferried across the Danube to the Hungarian shore. This was the first time Anthony had beheld the mighty, slow-moving river which was the main artery of Europe.

Waiting for them on the far bank was Janos Hunyadi himself.

Anthony had been looking forward to meeting this famous general, probably Europe's greatest soldier since the death of Great Harry. Nor was he disappointed.

Hunyadi was now over sixty years old, and had been campaigning for more than forty of them. If he had been defeated at Kossovo, that could well be attributed to Serbian treachery, and he had beaten the Ottomans often enough on other fields to earn their respect.

Anthony gazed at a man of medium height, clean-shaven save for a long moustache, with a strong mouth and chin and high cheekbones. He wore full armour, even a gorgette, and a curious peaked cap, also made of steel.

But his greeting was friendly enough. "Hawkwood," he said. "I have heard of your father — and of your troubles in Constantinople. Surely the Greeks heap perils on their own heads! And now you serve the Emir. Tell me of him."

"He is a mighty warrior, Your Excellency."

Hunyadi gave a cold smile. "A boy of twenty-two who has not yet led a campaign?"

"He will soon lead a campaign, Excellency. It is preparing now. It will be the greatest campaign since Timur the Lame marched on Turkey."

Hunyadi's smile faded into a frown. "Against whom will this campaign be mounted?"

Anthony gazed into the Hungarian hero's eyes. "Drakul of Wallachia, who no longer admits Ottoman overlordship."

"That will be the greatest campaign of the century."

"It would be wise for you to believe it, sir. The Emir wishes you to understand this, and wishes to be sure of your neutrality in the conflict."

"I have no friendship with Drakul," Hunyadi observed.

"Other factors may arise. The Emir offers a three-year pact of friendship between the Ottomans and the Hungarians. I am empowered to conclude such a pact."

"It will take three years for the Emir to defeat Drakul?"

"I have said other factors may arise, Excellency."

"Three years," Hunyadi said thoughtfully, "in which I will not war upon the Ottomans. And I will not lead an army to the succour of Constantinople, should that factor arise. Am I not right, boy?"

"You will not make war on the Ottomans, so long as they do not war on you," Anthony said carefully.

Hunyadi considered some more. Then he said, "I do not know if your Emir is truly a great warrior, young Hawkwood, but I understand that he is a careful man, who prepares his way. This is certainly admirable. I have no love for the Greeks: they always expect others to do their fighting for them. Tell your Emir that I will adhere to this three-year truce, and that I wish him well in his campaign ... against Drakul of Wallachia."

"I find it hard to believe," Anthony confessed to Halim and Mahmun, "that these leaders abandon each other so willingly to their fate, when if they would but combine against us our master's plans might be unachievable."

"But that is the Christian way," Halim explained. "They have always preferred to fight each other than contend with either the Arabs in the old days, or Genghis Khan, or ourselves. Do not the Franks fight each other constantly? You are a Frank, yet your father has told us how he fought against his fellows."

"My father is English," Anthony said, "as am I. The Franks are a different people, and our enemies."

"How can that be?" Halim inquired. "You are all Christians, and you all obey the Pope. How can you be enemies? I will tell you how," he went on to answer his own question: "It is because you are infidels, and lack the grace of God."

Anthony was not prepared to answer that. He was indeed appalled by the way the various Christian princes, even the great Hunyadi, were prepared to abandon Constantinople to its fate — although none of them seemed to have the slightest doubt as to Mahomet's true intentions. So perhaps Halim was right.

Now began the difficult and truly dangerous part of their journey, as they turned their horses to the east, for Wallachia. Mahomet's dominions were bounded by the Danube, although they could cut off the great bend of the river by traversing the mountains; this undoubtedly saved a great deal of time. But for the next month the going was harder than ever, as they made their way through the high passes, often along tracks wide enough to permit the passage only of a horse and its rider, with sheer drops of several hundred feet to one side; sometimes in blinding rainstorms which turned tracks into torrents, or snow flurries which had them shivering and unable to see more than a few feet in front of them.

They moved from one Turkish garrison town to the next, not only to rest, recuperate and change their horses, but also to ensure protection from the bands of fighting men not yet reconciled to Ottoman overlordship. These were hardly more than brigands, and generally not disposed to attack a well-armed party of sixty men. But as the embassy descended once more towards the river, they found themselves early one morning facing a track barricaded with tree trunks, and defended by a large body of men.

It was a carefully chosen spot, for the next Turkish garrison lay twenty miles in front of them, and the last fifty miles behind. There could be no question of going back.

"We must charge them," Halim declared. He was a commander of sipahis, and believed in straightforward assault.

"We will lose too many men," Mahmun objected. "Let us nego-tiate. If necessary, let us buy our way through."

They both looked at Anthony, although this was surely a business of which they knew much more than he.

He studied the situation as best he could. In the gloom of the winter's morning it was difficult to estimate anything clearly. But even if their enemies had been tracking the Ottoman party on the previous day, before setting up this ambush, it would have been difficult for them to determine the exact composition of the caravan.

On the other hand, an ambush presumed there were also men concealed in the trees to either side of them, awaiting a signal to attack. These would have to be drawn out before any real advance was possible.

He could feel the hair on his neck prickling. But he was the commander of these men, and he needed to make a decision. "How well are those people armed, do you suppose?" he asked.

"Oh, they'll be poorly armed, young Hawk," Halim said contemptuously. "Sticks and staves, some axes, rough pikes, perhaps a few swords. They do not even know the use of the bow in these mountains."

"And are your sipahis as expert as their forefathers?" He remembered Halim's men riding round the hapless Genoese sailors, destroying them with their arrows; he also remembered what Mahomet had told him of how the Turkish forebears had fought on the Asian steppes.

"They are better," Halim boasted proudly.

"Then listen closely to what I have to say. Because if we attempt my strategem and fail, we are destroyed."

Mahmun tugged at his beard as Anthony outlined his plan — but Halim was delighted.

"Truly the Emir will be proud to hear of this," he said.

"Only if it works," Anthony reminded him. "So let's get to it."

The Ottoman party approached closer to the barricade, from behind which a great shouting arose. Halim walked his horse forward, as if to inspect the enemy, then returned to the main body and gave his orders.

These had already been explained to the sipahis, so he merely went through the motions, with much gesticulating. The horsemen formed up, all forty of them, leaving the servants with Hawkwood and Mahmun to form a rearguard. Then, at the signal from Halim, they charged the barricade with their lances raised.

Instantly some hundred men rose up and began to hurl stones at them, while others emerged from the trees, as Anthony had expected.

The sipahis swiftly reined back their horses in apparent dismay, then turned and fled before the mob could reach them. It was the same strategy used by Genghis Khan two hundred years earlier and by William the Conqueror against the Anglo-Saxons at Hastings some two hundred years before that, and indeed by the Parthians against the legions of Crassus before the birth of Christ. But the Croatian bandits could hardly know of such military precedents. Whooping and screaming, they left their protected position, and ran along the road, brandishing their primitive weapons, while more and more men, and even women, emerged from the trees.

The sipahis galloped back to where Hawkwood waited, and there jostled about as if in great terror.

Anthony calculated that almost all of their opponents had by now left concealment.

"Now, Halim," he shouted. "Now!"

"Now!" Halim roared.

The sipahis turned their horses again. Their lances were back in their rests, and in their place each man held a bow with an arrow already on its string. Now they began to walk their horses back towards the advancing mob, which could not number less than three hundred.

The Croats checked as they observed this sudden volte-face of the cavalry ... and the sipahis urged their mounts into a trot, followed by Hawkwood, Mahmun and the servants, with swords drawn. Before the Croats could understand what was happening, the cavalry was within range, and the first flight of arrows was hissing through the air.

A great wail of dismay arose from the mob as some twenty of them sprawled on the ground, shrieking in agony. Before they could think what to do, a second flight tore into them — and then a third. As they began to fall back, the impact of the fourth flight sent them running helter-skelter along the track and into the trees, leaving some seventy men and women scattered on the ground.

Hawkwood raised his sword. "Charge them!" he shouted. "All together now."

The servants closed up behind the sipahis. The bows were slung and the lances again taken from their rests, then the entire Ottoman party surged forward. The wounded Croats screamed as they were trampled by flying hooves; those who had been slow taking to the trees screamed even louder as they were sought out by the couched lances. Then the Ottomans were through, and careering down the track, their horses snorting and panting.

"A splendid victory," Halim shouted. "Truly you are worthy of the Emir's esteem, young Hawk."

They were now sure of a welcome whenever they approached a town or encampment. The population was sparse and, apart from the garrisons, entirely Slav and Christian. As such they might have been expected to hate their conquerors even more than did the Greeks or the Bulgars. Or the Croats.

But the townspeople were mainly second- and third-generation Turkish subjects, who on the whole had learned to accept the whims of their masters, and to benefit from the rule of law which various emirs had firmly established, and which they carried out ruthlessly. There was some unrest amongst the Janissary commanders, however, as they asked when the new Emir, whom they had never seen, was going to lead his armies to war.

"There will be war soon enough," Hawkwood promised them; "war such as you have never seen. War to satisfy the most blood-thirsty man on earth."

"That is surely Drakul of Wallachia," said the commander of the border guard as he and Anthony stood on the banks of the broad-flowing river and gazed at the forest on the northern side. The embassy had been looking at Wallachian territory for some days now, but Drakul's capital, Bukres, lay well to the east, and Anthony was not anxious to enter Wallachia until he needed to. According to his map, this frontier post was actually the nearest to the city.

"Has there been no word at all of the last embassy sent there?"

"None. We see little of what happens yonder. But the Walla-chians are watching us all the time. You take your life in your hands, young Hawk."

"We are on a mission for the Emir," Anthony said severely.

But he could not help feeling sombre the next day, as the embassy was slowly ferried across the river by raft, along with their horses and equipment.

"I shall await your return with interest," the captain remarked.

Once they entered the forest, they were almost immediately out of sight of the river. Soon it began to rain, and the teeming downpour helped limit visibility but surrounded them with an eerie rustling noise amid the clustering trees.

"A dank and terrible place." Mahmun shuddered.

"You are an old woman," Halim sneered. "Are we not Ottomans? These savages are destined to serve us. They must never think they can aspire to anything better."

Anthony let them wrangle. He would decide how to handle the Wallachians when he needed to ... because he certainly intended to return alive.

They had progressed for a full three days before the trees began to thin, and they were stopped by Wallachian horseguards. They had known that they were being overlooked ever since leaving the river; more than once they had heard the clink of harness beyond the screening trees. Hawkwood had told his people to ignore such sounds; the Wallachians would show themselves when they were ready, and they themselves were not here to fight but to treat.

Now he faced several hundred mounted warriors wearing rudimentary armour — some had helmets, some cuirasses, and others shields, but none a complete équipage — and armed with spears and bows as well as swords. He did not reckon them very disciplined; a regiment of Janissaries would very soon have routed them, he had no doubt. But they certainly outnumbered the Turkish party.

He rode forward with his hand held high, and after a moment the commander of the Wallachian horse left his ranks to approach him.

"I am ambassador from the Emir Mahomet II," Hawkwood said in Greek.

"We recognise no Turkish emirs," the captain replied in kind.

"You will recognise this one, friend," Anthony promised him. "I have come to speak with your prince. So take me to him."

Drakul's capital city of Bukres was only a few days away, but it was an unpleasant journey for the Ottomans. They were surrounded by ever more Wallachian soldiers, both on horse and foot, as well as a growing band of camp followers. And although no violence was offered, they were very aware of being like prisoners.

124

On the fifth day they reached the city. It turned out to be nothing more than an accumulation of wooden huts, seeming even more desolate through the constant drizzle. Before the outlying houses, however, stood what appeared to be a grove of bare trees. It was not until they drew near that the startled Turks could discern that this was actually a grove of impaled men, long since rotted to skeletons, but still thrust skywards by the tall poles which had penetrated their vitals.

"By the beard of the Prophet," Mahmun muttered. "That is what happened to our people."

Anthony swallowed anxiously. As Mahomet had once said, an impalement once witnessed can never be forgotten — and here were the corpses of more than a hundred men. Wallachian children now played at the foot of these grisly totems with shrill, happy cries; no doubt they had uttered the very same cries while those men had been writhing and dying in agony.

"Courage," Halim growled. "We are Ottomans." He sat his horse with exaggerated stiffness.

The embassy proceeded further between the squalid houses, hooves squelching in the mud, while dogs barked and filthy children ran beside them. The palace of the prince turned out to be a much larger hut set within a wooden palisade. After the embassy was allowed into this enclosure, the gates were closed firmly behind them.

"These people are savages," Mahmun commented, looking around with visible distaste.

In silence the three envoys were escorted up some wooden steps and into a wooden porch, their wet clothes steaming in the sudden warmth. Here stood more guards and a couple of major-domos. Obviously news of their coming had been sent ahead.

"Uncover," ordered one of these officials in Latin. He wore a tabard of some value, but over mean clothes, and he did not appear to have washed in some time.

"Uncover?" Halim demanded.

"No man may remain covered in the presence of the prince," the major-domo announced haughtily.

Halim gazed at Mahmun in consternation.

"We are here on a peaceful mission, my friends," Hawkwood said. "It will pay us to humour this prince." He took off his helmet, and handed it to his servant.

The major-domo stared at him in amazement. "You are an Ottoman?"

"No," Anthony told him. "But I serve the Emir."

The man was still gaping at his red hair, when Halim announced loudly, "An Ottoman uncovers for no man. We do not even uncover for the Emir."

"Then you may not enter the presence of the prince," the major-domo repeated.

"I will see this prince," Halim declared. "I am an envoy of the Emir."

Mahmun stroked his beard.

"It really would be best to humour him," Anthony suggested again.

"Bah," Halim said, "you are a gaiour, young Hawk. You do not understand these things. Come, Mahmun, let us see this so-called prince.

The guards made to check them as the two Turks marched forward, but the major-domo shook his head, and they were admitted.

Hawkwood followed more slowly, into a smoke-filled room, for a huge log fire blazed in an open grate to one side. There were several men in the room and also, he realised with surprise, several women clustered on the far side, away from the fire, whispering amongst themselves and clicking their fans.

They were no more prepossessing than their menfolk, but were positive beauties when compared with the man who sat on the chair which faced the door. He was hunched over, which made him seem almost dwarfish, and his bare head was covered with shaggy black hair which mingled in with his moustache and beard, without any gaps. His hooked nose seemed to hang right over this thin lips, while snakelike green eyes peered out from beneath his low brows.

"Who are these people?" he demanded, his voice sibilant.

Obviously he already knew, but was ready to take offence at the Ottomans' lack of courtesy.

Anthony stepped forward. "I come from the Emir Mahomet, the second of that immortal name. My master is Lord of Karaman and Sivas, Anatolia and Jandar, Greece and Roumelia, and is paid tribute by the men of Serbia and of ..." he drew a long breath, "Wallachia."

Drakul's brows seemed to draw closer together. "You are no Turk!"

"I have the honour to be English, Prince. My name is Anthony Hawkwood."

"And you serve the Turk?"

"It pleases the Emir to employ me, yes."

"You are a renegade."

"I am a man who knows where his future lies; where all of our futures lie." Hawkwood gazed straight into the prince's eyes. "You would do well to know this."

They stared at each other for several seconds, then Drakul asked, "And these?"

"My associates here are Halim Pasha and Mahmun Pasha."

"Turks," Drakul said contemptuously. "They anger me."

"It is not their custom to uncover, even before their own Emir."

"What do I care for Turkish customs?" Drakul asked. "What has this Emir to say to me?"

"Firstly, he wishes to known for what reason you have put to death so many of his people."

"They angered me."

"I will return that answer to my master," Hawkwood said, firmly. "That will anger *him*."

"You are a bold rascal," Drakul commented, "but you have not come all this way to inquire after a few Turks?"

"No, Prince. My master tells me your father swore allegiance to the Emir's father, the great Murad."

"My father was a fool."

"I will relate that also to my master. But my master now wishes to know whether you intend peace or war with the empire of the crescent?"

"I will tell him when I have decided on that," Drakul said.

Anthony bowed. "My master has ordered me to tell you this. He is embarked upon a great enterprise. Those princes who give him their blessing will be honoured and rewarded when the enterprise is completed. Those who withhold such blessing will be regarded as enemies and driven to the ends of the earth."

Drakul gazed at him. "The Emir means to attack Constantinople," he remarked.

"He is embarked upon a great enterprise, Prince."

"He must take me for a fool. As he is a fool himself. A mere boy

127

pitting himself against Constantinople!"

"He asks your blessing."

Drakul considered for several seconds. "I give it to him," he said at last. "Constantinople is a den of apostates. It should be destroyed. My soldiers will not cross the river."

Anthony bowed, a surge of relief rushing through him. "I will convey that answer too to my master," he said. "He will be pleased."

"Then tell him so. Go now ... but not those," Drakul snapped as Halim and Mahmun made to move backwards.

"Prince?" Anthony asked.

"They have angered me," Drakul repeated.

"As I have explained, Prince, it is not the custom ..."

"I heard your words, English renegade. It is not their custom to uncover before anyone, even their Emir. Well then ..." Drakul smiled the most evil smile Anthony had ever seen. "Who am I to make a man break his custom? They do not uncover. Well, then, they will never uncover again." He signalled hs guards. "Seize those men and nail their helmets to their skulls." His grin turned to a bellow of laughter. "That will be sport for the ladies."

"Drakul did that?" Mahomet gazed at Anthony in astonishment. "And after impaling my previous ambassadors?" He gave a shout of laughter. "What a man!" he cried.

"Halim Pasha and Mahmun Pasha must be avenged, O Padishah," Hawkwood said. "Halim was a fool, but Mahmun was innocent — and my father-in-law. How can I face my wife with such a tale?"

"Oh, they will be avenged," Mahomet promised. "But that will have to wait. And it will be difficult. How do you destroy a man who acts in such a grand manner?" He grew serious. "But he let you return to me."

"Perhaps because I am a coward, O Padishah. I did not defy him."

"Because you are a wise man, young Hawk, and a trustworthy servant. It is not an ambassador's business to defy those he is sent to. You have faithfully carried out my instructions, and you have learned much on your mission."

"I have learned that the world is larger and more forbidding than I had supposed."

"That is knowledge worth having. I am pleased with you, young Hawk. Now ... now, we commence our campaign."

It was a sorry homecoming. The Emir might be pleased and amused, Anthony thought, but he himself had been bitterly humiliated at being forced to watch his two associates die in so terrible a fashion.

Then there was Laila to face. She beat her breast and tore her hair in her grief — all the greater because her father's body had not been returned. Anthony knew she blamed him for the catastrophe. He had been in charge of the embassy.

His parents were overjoyed to have him back after more than six months — but their joy was overshadowed by the news he brought them of their daughter Catherine, and by their realisation that the great campaign was at last about to begin.

"My family is all but destroyed," Mary Hawkwood said sadly. "Only you remain, Anthony. And now you, too, must go to war."

His father was more cheerful: the great bombard had been completed, and fired.

"It has done everything I had hoped," John Hawkwood boasted. "It has hurled a huge stone ball upwards of a mile. It is the most devastating weapon ever made."

"Have you fired an iron ball yet?" Anthony asked eagerly.

John shook his head. "I have been able to cast only six, for there is not much iron in Anatolia. They are not to be wasted in advance. But the Emir is pleased."

On his long, weary, dispiriting return from Wallachia Anthony had often dreamed of the arms of the Emir Valideh. But there came no summons. He sought out the Kislar Agha.

"The Emir Valideh is ill," he was told. "You would do best to forget she ever lived, young Hawk."

Anthony felt a chill run up his spine. For if the Emir Valideh was to die, he would be at the mercy of this eunuch.

There was little time for reflection on the precariousness of his existence, however, for Mahomet began his campaign at once. That very month, March 1452, he visited the mausoleum of Othman, and there, before the muftis and the commanders of the Janissaries, he affixed round his waist the sword of Othman, the traditional symbol that the Emir was going to war. The Janissaries raised a mighty shout of joy.

Then Mahomet took personal command of a force of workmen on the European shore of the Bosphorus, together with a protecting army of five thousand men, and began the building of Roumelia-Hissar.

Anthony soon realised that this was to be an immensely strong fortification. Even the Castel Nuovo in Naples paled into insignificance as the massive inner keep took shape, dominated by its high tower and surrounded by curtain walls which divided the bailey into a series of smaller sections which were easily defendable, should an enemy ever manage to enter it. But that was unlikely, since the outer walls rose twenty feet out of the rock. These were also twenty feet wide, and there was a thirty-foot-high watchtower set at every hundred feet. The outer walls ran right down to the sea, to enclose a spacious harbour into which the galleys from the Asian shore could discharge their cargoes of men and grain.

If Roumelia-Hissar was perhaps not as powerful as Constantinople itself, there was no prospect of it falling to an assault while the Ottoman sipahis and Janissaries dominated the surrounding country.

The Byzantines sent envoys to inspect the works; they were clearly impressed. They called it Cut-Throat Castle.

But Byzantium and the Ottoman Empire had just signed a peace treaty, so the envoys went away again, unprotesting.

The great castle took several months to build. Meanwhile the Ottoman army slowly began to cross the strait, in all its ponderous majesty. First the bashi-bazouks swarmed over the countryside; then the Anatolians; then came the Janissaries and the sipahis.

Last of all came the artillery. Anthony had returned to Brusa to assist his father in this gigantic logistical exercise. All the cannon were difficult to move, but the giant bombard required sixty oxen to drag it, two hundred men to march beside it and keep it in position, and another two hundred men to smooth down the ground over which it had to pass. Almost an entire year was needed to transport it to the Bosphorus, and then came the most difficult task of all: loading it on board a galley for transportation to the European shore. Mahomet himself rode down to the beach to watch, chewing his lip in anxiety as reinforced ramps were run out from the ship — creaking and groaning and threatening to crack beneath such enormous weight. As men shrieked orders and ran about in the shallow water, Anthony himself sweated with apprehension. But even though never trained as an engineer, John Hawkwood had worked out the stresses to be surmounted; and slowly — the muscles of the slaves attached to the ropes bulging with effort, the seamen turning the windlasses with sweat pouring down their bodies — the monstrosity was dragged on board. This caused the galley to tilt dangerously, and water rushed in at the lower oar ports. John Hawkwood shouted rapid commands, and every available man ran to the far side of the ship to counteract the huge weight. The cannon was gradually dragged amidships, and the ship cast off. The oars dipped into the water, and the slow passage began. On the European side, the unloading offered the same chances of catastrophe, but John Hawkwood remained in total control, and the cannon was landed safely.

The Byzantines were fully aware of the enormous force being gathered on their very doorstep, but they had to believe this Turkish armament was directed towards the Danube, and Drakul of Wallachia.

That was until the castle was completed. For then Mahomet took his personal guard of Janissaries and his sipahis — some fifteen thousand men — and with all his pashas, including the Hawkwoods, rode slowly along the land walls of the city, at a distance of some three miles. The Ottoman army presented a splendid array, the reds and blues of the Janissaries vying with the white and steel of the sipahis, while Mahomet himself, wearing golden armour and riding a pure white stallion, stood out gloriously at their head.

Certainly the sheer noise of their progress — the shouting of the Turks amplified by the beating of their drums, called the tabalcans, the clashing of their cymbals, and the blaring of their bugles — attracted a good deal of nervous attention. Anthony watched the walls of the mighty city slowly fill with its inhabitants. Perhaps Anna and Catherine were standing there, he mused. He wondered what they were now thinking. Because no sane man could now doubt that Mahomet was about to attack Constantinople itself.

But there remained a great deal of preparations to be made. The huge army was still accumulating from all over the empire, and it

131

had to be fed. Turkish galleys sped constantly back and forth to lands around the Black Sea to bring in the necessary corn.

The artillery had still to be augmented, because despite all his new bombards, Mahomet intended to use also the old-fashioned slinging weapons — mangonels and trebuchets — which had served besieging armies for so many centuries.

The Emir's headquarters had been established at Adrianople. From there he persisted in sending envoys to Constantinople, assuring the Emperor of his continuing friendship, and that his preparations were indeed directed against Drakul of Wallachia. It was his way to attempt to deceive until the last possible moment.

John Hawkwood had a heavy task in preparing his gunners for their supreme test. If he had calculated the rewards of success, by now he knew his master well enough to understand the certain penalty of failure.

Anthony worked with him twelve hours in every day, but was happy to do so. It seemed as if all normal life must come to a halt until Constantinople was taken.

In Adrianople, Mahomet had established his harem as well as his court, and he encouraged his pashas and chief officers to do likewise. Thus the provincial capital swelled into a huge city, and Piri Pasha was beside himself with excitement and worry.

Anthony and John duly brought along their own small household, but there was little joy in it for them. Mary was too worried by the impending conflict, and Laila still grieved for her father.

"You should beat her," Mahomet recommended impatiently.

"I cannot blame her."

Mahomet regarded him for a moment. "You will have another wife when the city is ours," he promised.

And what then? Anthony wondered. There was no word of the Emir Valideh, nor dare he ask again. He had always felt that Mara had promoted his career with the Emir. What would happen when she died?

The ever more obvious Turkish preparations for besieging the city provoked increasing reactions in the West. George Brankovich, Janos Hunyadi and even Drakul kept to their promises, and barred any intervention by land. But the Pope, at last deciding to do some service for his fellow Christians, despatched a legate, one Isidore, former Metropolitan of Kiev, in Russia, with two hundred soldiers.

He arrived in the city in November.

Mahomet was amused. "Two hundred men," he scoffed. "And I have heard there has already been a riot."

This was true. When Isodore attempted to hold a service in St Sophia, to celebrate the union of the two churches — as agreed between the Pope and Constantine — the Byzantines broke out in virtual revolt, and the cardinal had to be protected from mob violence.

His arrival might have caused amusement in the Turkish camp, but the next news was no laughing matter.

In January 1453, two huge Genoese carracks entered the Golden Horn. On board was one of the foremost soldiers of the age, Giovanni Giustiniani, and with him were seven hundred armoured fighting men, and a German artillerist, Johann Grant.

John Hawkwood had at last been replaced in the city.

"By Allah," Mahomet said, "the infidels are gathering. It is time to move against them before they grow too strong."

He commenced action against the Byzantine outposts. The small fortresses of Therapia and Studium on the Bosphorus were surrounded and summoned to surrender.

This the garrisons did readily enough, when confronted with such overwhelming force. But then Mahomet commanded that every man of them be impaled within sight of the main city.

"But they surrendered voluntarily, O Padishah," Anthony protested in great distress.

"They will serve as a warning to the Byzantines," Mahomet replied darkly.

Next the castle on the island of Prinkopo was reduced by the use of burning sulphur, to gas out the garrison. They too died to a man.

"He is a monster," John Hawkwood commented gloomily.

A monster who is going to take Constantinople, Anthony thought. Mara had called him Hunkar: "Drinker of Blood". He would have a lot of blood to drink when the city finally fell.

The following week Hawkwood received the command to advance his artillery. Surrounded by the entire Turkish army, some hundred and fifty thousand men, the cannon slowly rolled forward, as yet hidden from the watchers on the walls.

These rapidly grew in numbers as the Ottoman host

approached. If they had been alarmed at the sight of fifteen thousand men the previous autumn, Anthony wondered what they felt as they saw the entire plain before them covered with men and horses and flags. And they did not know the worst yet.

Slowly, and still concealing the guns, the army took up its allotted positions.

Zagan Pasha's corps moved to the north, to guard against any counter-attack across the Golden Horn from Galata. Zagan's men immediately commenced building a bridge across the inner harbour, watched helplessly by the small Byzantine fleet.

Caraja Pasha's corps took its place next to Zagan's, opposite the Xylo Porta and the Adrianople Gate.

Isaac Pasha marched his corps to the south, and deployed it facing the wall from the St Romanus Gate to the sea.

And in the centre, where the Lycus river flowed beneath the walls of the city, Halil Pasha drew up the main Turkish body.

To leave no one in any doubt that this was where he intended to launch his main assault, Mahomet had his own red and gold headquarters tent pitched immediately to the rear of Halil's men.

Offshore the Turkish fleet, now numbering a hundred and fifty galleys, waited in the harbour of Prinkopo to prevent any seaborne reinforcements from reaching the city. With the Byzantines' corn supply now cut off by the Turkish control of the Bosphorus, Constantinople was entirely beleaguered.

At dawn, on 12 April 1453, the muezzins, who were mounted on specially constructed towers in front of each section of the huge army, called the faithful to prayer. Anthony had heard the words often during the preceding two years, but today they seemed more meaningful than ever before:

> Allah is most great.
> Allah is most great.
> Allah is most great.
> Allah is most great.
> I testify there is no god but Allah.
> I testify there is no god but Allah.
> I testify that Mahomet is the Prophet of Allah.
> I testify that Mahomet is the Prophet of Allah.
> Come to prayer.

I have no power or strength but from Allah most High and
    Great.
Come to prayer.
I have no power nor strength but from Allah most High and
    Great.
Come to salvation.
Allah willeth what will be: What He willeth not will not be.
Come to salvation.
What Allah willeth will be: What He willeth not will not be.
Allah is most Great.
Allah is most Great.
There is no god but Allah.

When the prayers ended, the army gave a huge shout which
could be heard fifty miles away. Then the screen of cavalry moved
to either side, and the watchers on the wall gazed for the first time
at the giant bombard.

"Is your cannon loaded, Hawkwood?" asked Mohamet.

"It is loaded and ready, O Padishah," John said.

Mahomet pointed his horsetail wand at the city.

"Let the siege begin," he said.

John put his match to the touchhole, the army held its breath ...
the great bombard roared, and hurled the first shot of the battle at
the Wall of Theodosius.

6

HAWK PASHA

The huge stone ball flew through the air. It was so accurately ranged that it struck the base of the upper wall, before disintegrating into a thousand splinters, but also opening a crack in the structure.

The Ottomans gave a tremendous yell, while the Byzantines replied by shrieking their defiance.

Mahomet slapped his thigh in glee. "That was good shooting, Hawkwood," he shouted. "Smite them again."

"We need to elevate the cannon," John decided, and gave the orders. Then the bombard began to be loaded, and this took all of two hours. Meanwhile Mahomet walked his horse impatiently to and fro, giving orders for the smaller cannon and the trebuchets to be advanced to within firing distance of the walls. But this took them within range of the Byzantine guns, and soon an artillery duel raged the entire length of the land wall.

It was an impressive sight. Even the smaller cannon, on each side, took some time to load, and they were seldom ready to fire together. Minutes of silence would be followed by a sudden explosion and a cloud of smoke. As the stone balls struck walls or earth, they flew apart; the splinters, inches in length, were highly dangerous to anyone standing close by; Anthony saw several Ottomans struck down, with blood erupting from shattered limbs.

Every second hour the huge bombard itself spoke, its tone deeper and more resonant than any of the others, its effect far more devastating as well.

By evening — by which time the great cannon had only been fired seven times — cracks in the walls were becoming more obvious, and there was evidence, too, of subsidence.

Mahomet was now in high good humour, and entertained both the Hawkwoods to dinner in his tent. "A week," he said enthusiastically. "Only a week and the city will be ours." He turned to

John. "As of this moment you are Hawk Pasha, General of Artillery."

John bowed in gratification as he accepted the ceremonial horse-tail wand with its two knots.

But the next morning there was no clear evidence of damage at all; the Byzantines had worked all night to repair the cracks.

"By Allah!" Mahomet shouted. "How can this be?"

"We will need more than a week," John advised.

"If I may be so bold, O Padishah," Anthony ventured, "our cannon are each firing at a different section of wall, each causing some damage, but not enough that it cannot be repaired. If we directed our entire artillery at one spot, we might inflict so much harm in a single day as to force a breach."

"You are right, young Hawk. I should have thought of that."

Orders were given, and the bombards were all collected in the Lycus valley, in front of the St Romanus Gate. Now it was necessary to protect them with a large force of Janissaries, because their new position might attract a sortie from the city.

The plan worked so well that the damage done to the gate was considerably greater by that night.

"One more day, and we will have a breach," Mahomet declared.

But next morning most of the cracks had again been sealed.

"This is Giustiniani's work," John growled. "He knows siegecraft."

"What is to be done?" Mahomet demanded.

"We will keep firing," John said. "We will wear them down."

"Why do you not use your iron shot?" the Emir wanted to know. "Will that not breach the wall more quickly?"

"I have but six, O Padishah. It is best to keep them to make the breach only when the wall has been sufficiently weakened."

"And when will that be? Next year?"

He was now in a very bad humour, especially since the shouts of defiance from Constantinople grew ever more contemptuous as the defenders' confidence returned.

"He has no experience of warfare," John confided in his son. "He supposes a siege like this can be settled like a joust between two knights, in a matter of a few blows."

"He will learn patience, Father," Anthony promised.

But Mahomet's anger grew and, six days after the cannon had first begun to roar, he ordered a general assault.

*

"On unbroken walls, Padishah?" John asked. "It will not succeed."

"Bah! It will succeed because I have willed it," the Emir snapped.

The entire army was ordered into action, and the fleet was commanded to force the boom guarding the Golden Horn.

At dawn on 18 April, after every man had knelt towards Mecca in prayer, the signal was given. The cannon fell silent, and the bashi-bazouks were launched forward, swinging their tulwars, and screaming "*Yagma! Yagma!* — To the sack! To the sack!"

They swarmed across the once-tilled fields, now trampled into mud, and approached the ditch and the outer wall like a huge, roaring, mult-coloured wave, directing their main effort at the St Romanus Gate.

Behind them advanced the Anatolians, with more measured tread, kept in rough lines by their chaouches, or sergeants, their banners flying and their spearheads glinting in the sun.

Behind the Anatolians the Janissaries formed a compact red and blue mass, white plumes nodding as they waited their turn. For the first time they were carrying their handguns into battle and excitement ran high, but their time was not yet.

These were the very latest design in firearms, procured by the Venetians and sold to the Turks. When handguns had first been invented a hundred years earlier, they had been simple iron tubes, with one end blocked. Into the tube was poured a ration of powder and then a ball, and both well rammed home. Within the blocked end of the tube was a tiny touchhole, and this too was filled with powder. The gunner then applied a match to the touchhole, and theoretically the powder in the tube would explode and propel the ball for some hundred yards. But it took two men to load and fire each gun, and thus for a generation handguns had been an expensive foible. It was the Spaniards who had made a decisive advance, only a few years past. In place of the haphazard match, they had invented the 'serpentine', a long coil of oil-impregnated cloth which, once lit, would burn for a considerable time. With great ingeniousness, they had fitted this serpentine into the barrel, causing it to be withdrawn, fraction by fraction and still alight, through the movement of a lever attached to the top of the gun, and activated by a trigger. This meant that the marksman could concentrate fully on his target, certain that when he pulled the

138

trigger, the glowing serpentine would ignite the powder and explode the charge. To assist him further the gun had been fitted with a curved stock which could be placed against his shoulder to aid in his control.

But each piece still retained a range of only a hundred yards, and it needed a stake to steady it, and it still took several minutes to re-load. When Anthony recalled the long-ranged, accurate, quick-firing volleys of arrows delivered by his sipahis on the road to Wallachia, he could not help but suppose that the best feature of the handgun was the alarming noise it made when fired.

The Byzantines opened fire as soon as the bashi-bazouks came within range, their pieces braced in the embrasures of the walls, and soon the plain was dotted with writhing figures. Dull explosions mingled with the shouts of both attackers and defenders, the screaming of women inside the city, and the clanging of bells — for it seemed every church was endeavouring to encourage the inhabitants. Above the combatants, clouds of smoke rose so thickly that it was impossible to see exactly what was happening from the gun emplacements.

The bashi-bazouks swarmed into the ditch and began to erect their ladders, but Giustiniani, in personal command above the St Romanus Gate, now opened fire with everything his soldiers possessed: handguns, wall guns, bows, crossbows and catapults fired their missiles into the ditch. Ladders were erected and then thrown down again. The bashi-bazouks trampled on one another in their endeavours to gain a lodgement, but were repulsed time and again. The Anatolians went to their aid and were similarly struck down.

The Janissaries had now advanced within range, and began a steady firing which seemed to have no effect on the defenders. They were not launched into the assault itself, as there was no point in adding more men to the squirming, screaming mass in the ditch.

John and Anthony looked at each other glumly. The Emir was sacrificing his men unnecessarily: this assault was clearly not going to succeed. But Mahomet continued to sit his horse and watch the fighting before him.

Then an aide-de-camp came galloping up from Zagan's headquarters, on the Golden Horn.

"O Padishah!" he cried, "Admiral Baltoglu has been repulsed

from the great boom. The Grand Duke Notaras himself commands there, and our ships have been defeated."

"Strike off that man's head!" Mahomet screamed.

Four Janissaries hauled the aide-de-camp from his saddle.

"With respect, O Padishah," John protested rashly, "he is but a messenger."

Mahomet glared at him — then waved his hand. "Spare the dog." Then he growled. "Damn Notaras — I will have him flayed."

"We will not win today," Anthony said.

Mahomet glared at him, too, but then gave the signal for the tabalcans to sound the retreat.

The rumble of the drums spread across the morning and slowly the message reached the fighting men. Sullenly and angrily the Turks withdrew, pursued by the arrows and derisive jeers of the exultant Byzantines.

Mahomet rode forward towards the walls, although out of range. All around him the bashi-bazouks were dragging away their dead comrades, and they did not even look at the Emir.

"We have been defeated," Mahomet said. "The Ottomans have been defeated. How can that be?"

"The only defeat or victory in a siege is the final outcome of that siege," John told him. "The Byzantines are defending themselves with desperate valour, but we will yet triumph."

"They have killed so many of our men," Halil Pasha sighed, watching the growing pile of dead.

"We are many, they are few. If but one Byzantine fell today for every ten Turks, they are more grievously harmed than ourselves," John insisted.

"Ha!" Mahomet shouted. "You are right, of course. They have to bury their dead in there. Well, we shall give them more work to do." He pointed at the corpses of his own men. "Send these carrion to our trebuchets, that they may be tossed into the city. Let us see what they make of that."

Halil looked at his master in consternation, and then at John.

"With respect, Padishah," John protested, "to do that would turn Constantinople into a pesthole."

"Even a bashi-bazouk needs a decent burial," Halil ventured.

"Bah!" Mahomet said. "Do you suppose I care for the soul of a bashi-bazouk? Or whether the Byzantines die of the plague?"

"Indeed," John agreed tactfully, "it is nothing more than they deserve. But do you not intend to take the city as your own? If plague once enters, it will not be habitable for years."

Mahomet stared at him for some seconds. "What are you become? My conscience?" he asked at last. He turned his horse. "Very well. Have them buried."

The bells of St Sophia tolled a *Te Deum* in thanksgiving for the repulse of the Turks; the Emperor led the service, flanked by Lukas Notaras and Giovanni Giustiniani. The population prayed and sang with sincere fervour; they had been in a state of terror since the siege had commenced with the reverberations of the great cannon which had sent them shrieking into the streets.

But the cannon had not yet breached the walls, and the assault had been repulsed. A return of some of the old Byzantine arrogance could almost be felt.

Catherine Notaras and Anna Drakontes knelt and prayed together. They were now the closest of friends. After the service, they sought out their husbands at the Notaras palace.

"Have we really won?" Anna asked, anxiously.

Count Drakontes looked at Basil Notaras.

"We have won only a battle," Basil declared. "But we *shall* win, eventually. There is nothing more they can do. Not even your father's great cannon has been able to destroy us."

Catherine kept silent. Though she and her sister-in-law had drawn closer together, she and her husband had drifted apart. He was as handsome and compelling as ever, but he was bored with his foreign wife, regretting the sexual rapture that had led him into marrying her. He seldom came to her bed, and now was more likely to taunt than tempt her.

And for that she had wrecked her own family, with the youthful arrogance that was so much a part of her nature. She had cause to hate it in herself.

"But if they sit there and starve us out . . ." Anna probed.

"It is not the Turkish way to sit and besiege," Basil said. "If they do not soon gain a lodgement, they will melt away — as has always happened before. In any event, my father tells me there is a Genoese fleet on its way to our succour."

Catherine rose and went out onto the terrace. The sun was setting and the city was bathed in golden light. The Turkish lines, usually so exuberant, were silent.

Soon Anna joined her. "What did you feel when you saw your father and brother out there, riding behind the Emir?"

Catherine looked down at her; she was a head taller than the Greek girl.

"I wished that God could send down a thunderbolt and strike them dead," she said.

Anna could make no reply at first. She was a Notaras; and her love, her very life, centred on her family, her father and mother, her two brothers. Having come to accept Catherine almost as a sister, she could only feel sorry for her.

At last she remarked, "It must be a terrible thing to hate so much one's own relatives."

Catherine snapped, "What else can I do now but hate them?"

Anna lifted her head in consternation. For the first time that she could remember, Catherine Notaras was weeping. Huge tears rolled down those soft cheeks.

"If it is a judgement of God that has sent them against me, for what I did to them," Catherine continued, her voice quivering, "then either they or I must die."

Anna shuddered. "If it is God's judgement that they should not die, then we are all the victims of the devil."

All the pashas were assembled in the headquarters tent that evening to discuss the situation.

"The key lies where I have always known it to be," John Hawkwood advised them. "Constantine may have only a few thousand fighting men, but he is able to concentrate virtually all of them into a limited space: the land wall. While we, for all our numbers, can only launch the same number against him at one time. If we are going to succeed quickly, we need to be able to attack another part of the wall in strength, to divert his forces."

"And how may that happen?" Zagan Pasha demanded. "We have no means of gaining the sea walls. And today has proved that our galleys have not the strength to break the boom across the Golden Horn."

"There is nowhere else," Halil said miserably.

Mahomet looked from face to face, his eyes dull.

Anthony snapped his fingers and every head turned.

"With respect, my lords, the only way we can divert the Byzantines from the land wall is by attacking from the Golden Horn."

"But that we cannot do, young Hawk."

"We cannot force the boom, but can we not outflank it?"

"Explain."

"Marching round the boom will accomplish nothing," Zagan interrupted. "It is ships we need in the harbour, not men on the north bank."

"I am speaking of ships, Zagan Pasha," Anthony said. He prodded the map spread on the floor between them. "Here is Galata, on the north bank, held by the Genoese. But the garrison of Galata is not interfering with us; they know we could take them by assault any time we wish, and they desire only to be left in peace. North of Galata the land is low, and at sea level. And less than a mile inland from the sea is the river they call 'The Springs'. If we could transport our galleys across that strip of land, we could launch them on to the Springs and row them down to the harbour. We would then appear in the Golden Horn *behind* the Grand Duke and his defenders."

"Transport ships across land?" Halil asked incredulously.

"It can be done," Anthony said. "I am sure of it."

"How?" Mahomet asked, intrigued.

Anthony had not truly thought it out, but now he had an inspiration. "We will make a wooden roadway, Padishah, which we will grease with cattle fat, and over this we will drag our ships."

"It could be done," Mahomet agreed, his face glowing. "It will be done."

"There is one point you have overlooked." John Hawkwood turned to his son. "Our galleys may indeed be carried overland to the stream, but they can descend the stream only one at a time. What if Notaras concentrates where the stream debouches into the harbour, and so destroys our fleet piecemeal?"

"Notaras has but a score of ships, Father. Of course he can concentrate them at the exit of the stream, but to do that he must abandon the defence of the boom. If half of our ships were retained there, we should then advance wherever he weakened himself."

"A worthy concept," Mahomet said. "I am proud of you, young Hawk. Let the work be put in hand. And you will be in command."

Baltoglu was not pleased to discover he was about to share his command with an untried foreigner of barely twenty-one, but the

143

Emir would not be gainsaid. Next morning Anthony commenced his task, requisitioning thousands of workmen and all the wood that could be found, to build his trackway.

Meanwhile the cannon resumed their slow, inexorable bombardment.

The following day Mahomet rode over to see how work was progressing. The slipway had already been commenced.

"You are a man of genius, young Hawk," the Emir pronounced with pleasure.

He was at once distracted by a messenger with news that four large Genoese carracks had been sighted on Marmara, clearly making for the Bosphorus.

"They must be bringing reinforcements, and perhaps grain," remarked Baltoglu. "I will destroy them."

"A victory," Mahomet said. "At last! You *will* seize those ships, Baltoglu Pasha."

The Bulgarian bowed. "It will be my honour, Padishah."

"Wait! Listen to me," Mahomet said. "Allow them to enter the narrows. That way they will not be able to escape you. And that way, too, their destruction will be evident to the Byzantines."

Baltoglu galloped off to be ferried out to his waiting ships.

"This will be sport," Mahomet said.

After they had lunched, they rode down on to the beach itself to oversee the coming engagement.

The masts of the carracks, urged on by a fresh southerly breeze, could now clearly be seen. Their sails, emblazoned with the cross and various other devices, billowed towards the Bosphorus, and above them flew long red and blue and gold pennants. But the flags began to droop as the ships slowed on entering the narrows and came against the current. The walls of Constantinople were lined with people cheering as they saw this relief close at hand. Surely these were the advance guard of the fleet they had expected for so long? Flags were flown and trumpets blown to encourage the arriving seamen.

Out of the Prinkopo harbour the Turkish galleys began to creep like an army of beetles: one hundred and forty-five of them, an immense array of oars striking the surface in unison, while their drummers kept up a steady rhythm.

They were soon spotted by the watchers on the walls, and their

144

cheers changed to a great moan. No one could doubt that the Genoese would be destroyed by such overwhelming force.

The Turkish seamen, however, uttered a tremendous shriek of anticipated victory, with a beating of drums and clashing of tambourines, as they rowed straight for their enemies.

Mahomet rode his horse up and down in the shallow water, snapping his fingers as if to urge his men on.

The galleys swarmed towards the Genoese carracks. But the carracks were still impelled by the breeze, and their reinforced prows smashed into the first Turkish vessels to reach them. Sides were staved in and entire banks of oars sheered away as the huge ships forged steadily onwards, leaving their first assailants sinking — with men swimming for the shore, and the chained galley slaves screaming as the waters closed above them.

"Devils!" Mahomet shrieked, raising clenched fists. "They are devils. Why cannot they be stopped?"

"It is the wind," Anthony told them. "It gives them too much power. But look there!"

The ships had now reached the shelter of the Acropolis, where the wind was dropping; the carracks scarcely seemed to move.

"Now," Mahomet yelled. "Now we have them."

As the galleys entirely surrounded the four ships, grappling-irons were thrown. Men attempted to swarm up the high bulwarks of the carracks, but were driven back. The Genoese fought with desperation, panache and superior armament. On to the heads of their attackers they hurled rocks, pots of Greek fire, darts and javelins, while handguns and swivel guns mounted on the bulwarks continually swept the galleys with shot. Those few Turks who did reach the decks were soon cut down with axes.

This battle raged for two hours, and the longer it continued the more agitated Mahomet became. Waving his fists and shrieking encouragement to his men, he urged his horse up and down the beach — and into the sea.

After two hours the four Genoese ships were still untaken — and then the breeze returned.

Now the carracks forged ahead again. Galleys fell away to either side, their oars sliced off, and the ships were through. The boom was dropped, and the Genoese squadron safely entered the Golden Horn.

*

Mahomet said nothing as he rode back to his encampment, but he was clearly in the grip of a powerful emotion; his shoulders were hunched.

The pashas had all gathered there, but none dared speak. It seemed the most humiliating defeat ever suffered by Ottoman arms.

Baltoglu approached and bowed low. "They were too strong for us, O Padishah."

"Too strong?" Mahomet's voice was menacingly quiet. "Four ships were too strong for a hundred and forty-five?"

"They were large and well-defended ..."

"You lie!" Suddenly Mahomet was screaming. "You are a traitor. You have betrayed me."

"I, Padishah?" Baltoglu placed his hand over his heart. "I am the most faithful of men. Have I not proved this time and again?"

"You betrayed me today," Mahomet shrieked. He gestured to his guards. Baltoglu's arms were grasped. "Padishah!" the admiral cried in dismay. "I did my best."

"Prepare a lance," Mahomet ordered, "and thrust it up his arse. Stand him by the shore so that he may look at the scene of his disgrace, while he dies."

"Padishah!" Baltoglu screamed in terror, as the Janissaries would have hurried him off.

"Padishah," Halil protested, "you cannot do this."

"Halil Pasha is right, Padishah," John Hawkwood agreed. "Baltoglu did his best."

Mahomet glared at them both, and then at the other pashas. He could see agreement in their faces, as well. If they were each to be impaled every time some attack failed, they would never dare attack again.

The Janissaries had halted, a weeping Baltoglu in their clutches.

"He can have his life," Mahomet growled at last. "But he is dismissed my service — and he will be punished. Strip him naked and stretch him on the ground."

Mahomet snatched up a heavy cane, while his pashas looked at each other in amazement. When Baltoglu was stripped and stretched face-down on the earth, Mahomet began to beat him, blow after blow. The admiral howled in pain as his buttocks began to bleed, but Mahomet did not let up until he was exhausted. Then he threw down the cane.

"Drive him from the camp!" He stalked off towards his tent.

Yet that night he seemed as charming as he could be. However, the other pashas were in sombre mood, each counting the risk of personal failure.

"What are four ships and a few hundred men," the Emir said jovially. "It is *your* scheme which will bring about the fall of the city, young Hawk. I put my trust in you."

Anthony got back to work early the next morning; and from then on he kept his men at it sixteen hours a day — till the slipway was completed and the portage of the galleys began.

The Byzantines were undoubtedly aware of exactly what was happening, but there was nothing they could do about it. They lacked the men to make a sortie north of the harbour.

Hamoud now commanded the fleet, but was willing to let Anthony take over half of it. So seventy galleys were transported to the Springs, and floated down the river, while another seventy watched the boom. The Byzantine fleet did not move from its position; while the Genoese carracks were not manoeuvrable inside the narrow confines of the harbour, and could only wait and watch.

However, they remained formidable floating castles and, although Anthony's squadron gained the harbour without mishap, Mahomet refused to permit him to lead an assault on the boom from the rear.

"It will not do for us to be defeated again, young Hawk." he said. "It encourages the Byzantines too much. Your fleet will be a useful distraction. It will be needed when we decide to launch our great assault."

It was now 6 May, and all this while the bombards had been booming at the walls around the St Romanus Gate.

"I believe the wall is now weak enough for us to try our iron shot," John Hawkwood announced.

"Then let it be done," Mahomet commanded. "And let us have done with this place. News has reached me that a Papal fleet is sailing to relieve the city."

"That is but rumour, Padishah."

"Who can tell?" Mahomet said. "I am also informed that Constantine has despatched a brigantine in search of this fleet, to urge it to make haste. So *he* must believe this rumour. Should it appear on the Bosphorus we are defeated."

Anthony knew that the arrival of a Papal fleet of any size would indeed be a serious matter, if only because, should it defeat the Ottoman navy — as seemed possible — it would then be able to cut the Turks off from their homeland across the strait.

Next morning the entire army was assembled ready to launch an assault the moment the breach was made.

Before dawn John Hawkwood had loaded with a stone shot, and this was fired at first light. It smashed into the wall beside the gate with unerring accuracy, but roused nothing more than the usual shouts of derision from the defenders. They had become too used to the bombardment.

But next the bombard was loaded with one of the huge iron balls. Mahomet himself stood by to watch.

"We are making history, Padishah," Hawkwood told him. "Stand clear."

Everyone retreated as John himself applied the match.

The bombard roared, belching smoke. As the watchers gazed at the walls, they saw the iron ball smash into the stone like an axe-head into soft wood. Splinters cascaded, and this time the cries of the defenders were ones of dismay.

"We have them," Mahomet shouted. "We have them. One more ball, Hawk Pasha, and the gate is broken."

Feverishly the gunners reloaded the cannon — but with great care. In record time the ball and its wadding were rammed down the barrel, and powder added to the touchhole. Instead of two hours, the bombard was ready in an hour and a half. Mahomet and his staff rode some distance away, the better to oversee the effects of this second shot.

It was now nearly noon, and the sun hung in a cloudless sky, beating down on both the plain and the city — and the thousands of men accumulated there. Constantinople was silent as the Byzantines watched these preparations in consternation. No one could doubt that this might indeed knock down their gate ... and no one in the city had any idea how many of these iron balls the Turks possessed.

The glowing match in his hand, John Hawkwood looked at the

Emir. "To your victory!" he shouted, and applied the flame to the touchhole.

There was a huge explosion. Pieces of wood and iron, and pieces of men as well were hurled into the air amidst a cloud of smoke.

For several minutes there was complete silence in both armies, then, as the smoke cleared, the extent of the catastrophe became obvious. The great bombard had all but disappeared: its carriage had disintegrated. And so had the gun crew.

And John Hawkwood.

Anthony dismounted from his panic-stricken horse and ran forward. He saw only boots and blood, and a shattered sword. He stared at them in horror.

Mahomet rode up beside him. "What can have happened?"

Anthony sobbed, "Too much powder, perhaps. Or too much haste."

Shattered, Anthony returned to Adrianople to break the news to his mother. His father had been the rock on which his life was founded. Now, of the five of them who had set out from Southampton so confidently five years before, only his mother and himself were left.

"It is a judgement of God," Mary wailed. "Your father turned his back on God, when he left England to fight for the apostates. Then he leagued himself with the devil. This is the judgement of God."

"It was a cannon loaded in haste, Mother," Anthony insisted. "Nothing more and nothing less."

"A judgement of God," she repeated. "You alone remain, Anthony. And are you not about to die, also? What will become of me then?"

He hurried from her presence. Because he was more than half afraid that she might be right.

Laila attempted to comfort him. "Your father has now gone to join mine," she said. "My heart bleeds for you."

That night she made love to him with more warmth than on any occasion since his return from Wallachia.

Upon his return to the Turkish camp, Anthony was hailed as the new Hawk Pasha and presented with the horsetail wand.

149

"This is fitting," Mahomet told him. "You will be a more illustrious man than even your father."

Soon he was preparing yet another assault — but this too was repulsed. There was now an air of desperation in the Turkish camp. The cannon continued to boom, but the smaller bombards could not do sufficient damage. Next a resort was made to mining, and huge shafts were driven beneath the city walls. But the German engineer, Johann Grant, counter-mined, and grim battles were fought under the earth, invariably to the Turks' disadvantage.

Next Mahomet constructed a *helepolis*, or city-taker, an immense wooden tower able to hold a hundred men, which could be pushed up against the walls, whereupon a drawbridge would be lowered across the battlements, and the Turks could rush across. But Giustiniani destroyed it by rolling barrels of gunpowder down the slope of the fosse against it, and blowing it too to smithereens.

Mahomet stared at the city in a mixture of dismay and admiration. "How they fight," he growled. "What I would give to have that man Giustiniani on my side."

Turkish prospects were now becoming truly serious. If there was still no sign of the Papal fleet, rumours began to circulate that Hunyadi was contemplating breaking the treaty he had agreed the previous year, and would descend upon the Bosphorus with an army; the Christians would never have a better opportunity to deal the Ottomans a deathblow, while they were so heavily committed ... and while their morale was so low.

More important was the logistical position. Mahomet had steadfastly replaced even his enormous losses by sending for yet more levies of men from Asia, and these duly arrived. But, as May drew to a close, Halil had to inform his master that there was not sufficient food to supply the army for more than another week.

"How can this be?" Mahomet demanded angrily.

"Padishah, when we commenced this campaign I ordered food for one hundred and fifty thousand men to last for two months. I could not conceive that the siege would take longer, and I assumed that our numbers would be diminished as the weeks went by. But the siege has now lasted two months, and our numbers are undiminished. I have sent to the Black Sea for more corn, but the weather has been unfavourable ..."

"It was my intention to starve the Byzantines, if need be," Mahomet grumbled, "not to starve myself. Then are you saying we are defeated, old man?"

Halil Pasha bowed his shoulders in shame. The Emir looked around the faces of his other pashas, and saw defeat there, too.

"We are defeated," he said.

"With respect, Padishah," Anthony began.

"Ever faithful, Hawk Pasha. Speak."

"We have now besieged Constantinople for two months. In that time we have suffered grievous casualties; we have expended nearly all our ammunition; we have eaten up nearly all our food; and we are truly dispirited. We can, if you wish it, now cease this siege and return to our homes, and plan to come again when our strength is renewed. But should we not look at the situation through Byzantine eyes? For nearly two months they have been besieged; in all that time only four ships have got through to them. There is no certain word of any others coming. In that time, have they not also suffered grievous casualties? Have they not also expended nearly all their ammunition? Have they not also eaten up nearly all their food? And, unlike us, they cannot say 'Enough', and ride away. They must stay there at our discretion. So is their morale not bound to be even lower than our own?"

"What of Hunyadi? What of the Papal fleet?"

"These are but rumours, O Padishah. Rumours do not fill an empty belly or an empty quiver."

"By Allah, but the boy is right!" shouted Zagan Pasha. "Padishah, you remember Alexander the Macedonian, whom we call the Great. He conquered the known world with an army but a fifth the size of yours, overcoming every hardship. Will you let one city stand in your way? Order a general assault, Padishah, and order too that it will not cease until the city is ours. Let us give you victory, or let us die. For we are men — and we are Ottomans!"

Mahomet's enthusiasm then returned. He commanded every man in the camp to make preparation for a decisive assault. For the next two days and nights, while the cannon continued to boom, the Ottomans worked in light and in darkness; no less than two thousand scaling ladders were prepared, as well as iron hooks to pull down the barricades which had been erected on the walls, and fascines to fill the ditch.

151

During these two days Constantinople seemed surrounded continually by a ring of glowing fire.

On the second evening after the work had commenced, on 31 May 1453, Mahomet summoned Anthony to join him, and rode away from the camp to where the guns were for the moment silent.

The wind was in the east, and towards them from the city drifted the sound of bells, and music, and the voices of people singing.

"Are they mad?" Mahomet asked. "They are celebrating their doom?"

"No," Anthony said, recognising the music. "They are holding a *Te Deum*. They are singing the praises of God, that they may either conquer or die tomorrow."

"Tomorrow," Mahomet said. "Tomorrow will be the greatest day of my life, Hawk Pasha."

"And mine, Padishah. I would beg to be allowed to take part in the assault."

"And be killed?"

"I have my father to avenge. And my brother."

"That is your duty." Mahomet said. "I would not have you die. But ..." He glanced at Anthony again. "I have received sad news today also. My mother, the Emir Valideh, is close to death. It is said I will not see her again. It should be my duty to return to her side, but she has bidden me not to return without victory."

Anthony said nothing.

"Is that not strange, Hawk Pasha? As she is a Christian herself."

"The Emir Valideh has identified herself with your cause, and thus you, Padishah."

"Yes," Mahomet mused. "She is an exceptional woman, would you not agree?"

"I? How may *I* offer an opinion on the Emir Valideh?"

Mahomet smiled. "My mother and I have no secrets from each other, Hawk Pasha."

Anthony felt his stomach muscles tighten.

"She saw you the first night you were brought before me," Mahomet said. "My father had been dead but two weeks. But she is a woman! That night she told me, 'He is mine, my son'." Mahomet smiled. "I would have claimed you for my own, but I could not gainsay my mother. I envied you your joy, and begged her for discretion. This she has kept, as have you. If one word of your visits to the seraglio had ever escaped, I would have been obliged to have you flayed alive."

"I do not doubt it, Padishah," Anthony said, surprised to be able to speak.

"But you have played well the part she chose for you. And I believe you have given much pleasure to her declining years. Yes, I envy you. But you will not see her again. Will you weep?"

"Yes, Padishah."

"All the more reason for us to conquer here tomorrow, in her name. The Byzantines call her harlot, and more besides. Think of that when you assault these walls, Hawk Pasha." Mahomet turned his head. "You will sit at my right hand, always. Have I not said this? I desire your mind and your support more than your body. But ..." he leaned across and kissed Anthony on the mouth. "What lovers we could have been, my Englishman."

It began to drizzle as they returned to camp. The time was midnight.

"All is ready, Padishah," Halil said.

"Then have the fires doused, and tell the men to sleep," Mahomet said. "You also, Hawk Pasha."

"Where do I fight tomorrow, my lord?"

"Do you not wish to command the squadron in the Golden Horn?"

"They can but fire at the defenders. I wish to take part in the main assault."

Mahomet considered for some seconds. "Then you will fight with Zagan." he said at last. "You will lead the assault on the Xylo Porta. But, Hawk ... make sure you return to me."

"I will do that, Padishah," Anthony promised.

He rode off into the darkness. As the orders were circulated, all the Ottoman camp fires were being extinguished, and the plain was shrouded only in the rain.

To the east, Constantinople still glowed with light. No one was sleeping there tonight.

His mother had said that her husband John Hawkwood had sold his soul to the Devil. How much more had he himself done that. Mahomet was a devil, but a victorious one. And having chosen the side of the Devil, no man could afford to look over his shoulder. He would also be a devil, and prosper. The name of Hawk Pasha would reverberate through the world, and strike terror into the hearts of those who would oppose him.

Beginning with tomorrow, when he led his men into the city.

Everything would depend upon tomorrow. But tomorrow was now today.

This time, as Zagan had recommended, the assault was to be carried through without respite until victory was achieved. The main attack was to be launched again along the valley of the Lycus, at the St Romanus Gate. This was intended to draw all the Byzantine defenders to that place, and thus deplete the walls elsewhere for the rest of the Turkish forces. Then the ships in the Golden Horn were required to play their part.

This time there was no awaiting the hour of prayer. It was still dark when the drums began to sound and the trumpets to blow. As the Turkish camps came alive, men began to shout.

The rain had stopped but the ground was soggy, as in the gloom the bashi-bazouks moved forward against the St Romanus Gate.

They were met with the same resolute return fire, and they lacked the courage of previous assaults; too many of their comrades had died. Soon they sought to retreat, but were driven back to the contest by their chaoushes, who ranged up and down the ranks armed with iron maces and chain-whips.

Thus coerced, they returned to the assault, but after a while Mahomet signalled for them to be withdrawn, and sent in the Anatolian levies instead.

Watching from their position to the north, where no attack had yet been launched, Zagan Pasha and Hawk Pasha observed the Anatolians actually climb over the outer rim of the defences, to reach the area running between the inner and outer walls — the *peribolos*.

"You were right, Hawk Pasha," Zagan said, "The defence is weakening."

But the Anatolians were soon driven out by the desperate resistance of the Genoese who defended that portion of the wall. However, Anthony, studying the wall by the Xylo Porta, could see more and more men hurrying from there towards the defence of St Romanus.

Mahomet observed this as well. Again the drums sounded. The Anatolians retired, and now the Janissaries commenced their advance, racing at the walls with loud cries.

"Now," Anthony bellowed.

He dismounted and placed himself at the head of Zagan's Janissaries, and they too advanced. Waving his scimitar, Anthony was surrounded by shrieks and yells, by flying lead and flying steel.

The defences around the Xylo Porta had been so weakened that the ladders were soon set in place, and the assault on the outer wall commenced. Climbing up the nearest ladder behind two Janissaries, Anthony gained the battlements and was amazed to find no resistance there at all. The defenders had been withdrawn to the inner, higher wall, whence they were shooting at the intruders.

"On!" Anthony shouted, and jumped down into the *peribolos*, followed by his men, who were dragging their ladders with them. All the time the Byzantines continued pouring arrows and rocks and boiling oil upon them. Anthony was ordering the ladders to be set up again, when one of the Janissaries seized his arm and pointed.

He could hardly believe his eyes. A small door in the wall stood open!

Pointing with his scimitar, he ran for it, his men at his heels. They burst through the doorway and found themselves in a street of the city. A group of people stared at them in horror, mostly women and children passing food and munitions up to the soldiers on the wall above.

"To the St Romanus Gate," Anthony yelled. "We can take them in the rear."

Some fifty men had come through the gate with him, but even such a small body could produce a decisive effect in the right place.

Behind them, Byzantine soldiers hurried down the steps to close and bar the gate they had so carelessly left open. Then Anthony changed his mind: instead of attempting to force his way through the crowded streets to the St Romanus Gate, he would lead his small band up the same steps on to the wall, and rush the nearest tower. Here they found but a handful of Byzantines, who were quickly despatched.

Above them the Byzantine flag swirled in the morning breeze. It was the work of a moment to haul it down, and replace it with the green flag of the Ottomans. Instantly there arose a tremendous cheer from the Ottomans outside, and a howl of despair from the Byzantines within.

Armed men surged on to the wall to attack the tower. Shoulder to shoulder with his Janissaries, Anthony repulsed them once, then twice, his sword dripping blood, his voice hoarse from yelling orders. The fight continued ...

Then a whisper had rippled along the wall. "Giustiniani is wounded," it said. "Giustiniani has abandoned the defence." The Byzantines hesitated, looking over their shoulders. Anthony knew now was the moment for action, but he and his men were exhausted; there were only thirty of them left.

Then there came another whisper: "The Emperor is dead. Constantine is no more."

Suddenly the Byzantines turned and fled for the false security of the inner city.

Constantinople had fallen.

Catherine Notaras raised her head. The noise had changed.

In place of the shouts of anger and defiance, now there were cries of fear, shrieks of anticipation.

Had the unthinkable happened?

With every day that passed, the prospects of maintaining the siege until succour arrived had seemed to grow. The day her father had been blown to pieces by his own monstrosity had appeared to set the seal on their security. And, since then, every Turkish assault had been repulsed — as they would always be repulsed, surely? As one day a Genoese fleet would come sailing up the Bosphorus, surely?

When it became obvious, three days before, that the Ottomans were preparing for a yet more desperate assault, there had been an air of calm determination in the capital. The Emperor had called the faithful to church to reaffirm their confidence in the future of their city.

The great cathedral had been packed to the doors, and vast crowds had gathered outside. It was as if the people of Constantinople had at last thrown aside their contemptible divisions and petty squabbles, their naïve belief that their city was inviolable

156

simply because of the will of God, and had come together as a united nation determined to fight for their right to survive.

Catherine had gone to bed last night in a mood of defiant optimism. No matter that conditions within the city were desperate, that the dead lay unburied in the streets, that a loaf of bread was almost unobtainable ... Thanks to its enormous reservoirs Constantinople had all the water it needed, and if the Turks had opted for one last great assault, then the people of Byzantium were confident that they could be repelled.

She had lain in her room since the attack had begun before dawn, her pillows over her ears, trying to shut out the noise of combat, awaiting only the moment that someone should come to tell her the Turks were again defeated, and retiring.

But now ...

She left her bed, pulled her dressing-robe round her shoulders, and gazed at her husband standing in the doorway. Basil Notaras' armour was smeared with blood, he had lost his helmet and his hair was wild. He could only stare at her.

"Basil?" she whispered. "What has happened?"

"We are lost."

"Lost?" Her voice rose an octave. "How can that be?"

His shoulders sagged. "Giustiniani was wounded, and his men insisted upon carrying him to the rear. The Emperor begged him to stay on the wall: even wounded, he would have been worth something. It was at this juncture that some Turks gained access to the city by an unguarded postern. There were not many of them, but they seized a tower and hoisted the Ottoman flag. When he saw that, and with Giustiniani gone, the Emperor leapt from the wall into the midst of Janissaries, and laid about him until he was struck down." He sobbed. "I saw it all happen."

Catherine listened. The noise of fear was overlaid with yet another sound: a swelling paean of triumphant lust. She found both hands clutching her breast; she felt a very real pain there.

"Quickly," Basil said. "My father will be here shortly. He says that we are to withdraw to the cellars, and hide there for the first excesses to be exhausted. Then we will declare ourselves for ransom. It is the only way."

"What of Anna? We must bring her here."

"She must find her own salvation. Make haste and dress yourself."

157

Catherine dropped her dressing-gown on the floor and reached for her clothing, wondering what had happened to her maids. All fled, no doubt. But where could they flee to, in this shattered city?

"You cannot just abandon your sister," she protested.

"It is up to her husband to save her. For God's sake, hasten."

She ran behind him down the stairs, pausing only to look through a window. Smoke already rose above the city, where it had been fired. Crowds of people ran to and fro in the streets, screaming in terror and misery. Some were attempting to shift valuables from their houses, as if they had anywhere to take them. While above them all rose that dreadful howl of bloodthirsty triumph. She looked down the stairs at the drapes and the ikons, the luxurious appointments of the ducal palace. What was about to happen to them? What was about to happen to her?

They reached the lower hall, and found Michael the major-domo standing there, like some immovable statue. With him was the Grand Duchess, weeping and wringing her hands.

Basil Notaras turned to face the doors, which stood ajar. The servants had fled, but at least the gates were closed. Now they trembled to the force of many shoulders.

"Oh my God!" The Grand Duchess fell to her knees and began to pray.

"Mama!" Anna Drakontes ran in from the back of the house. Her hair was loose, the splendid braids a thing of the past. Her face was a white mask of terror.

"Mama!" she screamed. "The Turks are in the city. They are everywhere. Mama, they are killing all the men ..." She paused, staring at the trembling gates.

"The cellar!" Basil cried. "The cellar."

Catherine went to her sister-in-law and put her arm round her shoulders. Already it was too late: the gates were giving way, and men were swarming over the walls.

She had never seen a Turk close to. Now she gazed in awe at their long moustaches, hooked noses and the fiercest visages she had ever known.

Her muscles seemed to freeze, as the intruders ran up the steps towards them, waving their blood-stained scimitars. One even carried a lance thrust through the body of a small child, brandishing the corpse like a banner above his head.

They brought with them the stench of men who had fought, and been afraid, and now had triumphed.

Behind them rose the stench of burning houses, and burning flesh.

Michael stepped forward with upraised hands, as if to halt them. A scimitar flashed, and the major-domo toppled down the steps, his head all but severed from his neck. He had uttered not a sound.

The Turks surged past him, and Catherine closed her eyes. She felt Anna's body tensing against hers, Anna's breasts swelling against her arm as the younger girl began to scream.

Suddenly she was torn from Catherine's arms.

Basil fell to his knees. "Spare us," he shouted. "We are nobles! We are for ransom!"

Catherine was surrounded by excited, obscene laughter. She had experienced nothing like this since Naples — when Anthony had defended her.

But Anthony would not defend her now.

It seemed the Turks took notice of what Basil had to say; the richness of their surroundings suggested this indeed was a wealthy family. As hands seized her arms, Catherine opened her eyes to see her husband being stripped of his clothing and bound.

But that did not mean the victors would not first have their sport with them.

The Grand Duchess was already lying naked on the floor. She was a plump, comfortable woman, and the Turks chattered their approbation as they clambered over her.

Anna was also on the floor; she too had been stripped. Her slender body writhed, her legs kicking feebly, as a man knelt between them. Her hair flailed to left and right and thin screams issued from her lips.

Catherine was hurled on the floor too, her head aching where it struck the marble.

She gazed at faces leering down at her, heard the ripping of cloth and felt a sudden chill on her belly. She wanted to scream, but could not. As men closed in about her, she could see others climbing on each other's shoulders to tear down the ikons; others running here and there with priceless ornaments. Everywhere yelling and shouting.

A man was kneeling between her legs, and she looked down in panic at the whiteness of her naked limbs against the green of the Anatolian's tunic as he grasped her buttocks and raised her from the floor, the better to thrust himself into her.

Another crouched beside her, pawing her breasts. As soon as the first man had expended his lust, he pushed him aside and took his place.

Why do I not die? she wondered. Why do not the heavens open and blast down thunderbolts upon this stricken city?

Catherine Hawkwood finally wept as the second man rolled off her, and she was turned over on to her face.

The sun was high over the city, which reeked of blood and fear and smoke, and the flames began to spread.

As Mahomet II walked his horse through the St Romanus Gate, the animal picked its way delicately through mounds of dead bodies. Mahomet gazed around at his Turkish soldiers intent on emptying the houses of everything movable; on raping women and children — or from time to time murdering them, heedless of pitiful pleas for mercy; on dragging Turkish corpses to one side, Byzantine to the other. They castrated the Christians so that their severed genitals could be counted to assess the casualties; it made no difference whether the Christians were dead or merely wounded — they would soon be dead in any event. The morning was filled with shrieks of terror, yells of passion, moans of agony, wails of despair, barking dogs, collapsing timbers.

The soldiers scarcely paused in their bloody work to salute their Emir.

Waiting for Mahomet inside the gate were Halil Pasha and Hawk Pasha.

"I hear it was you who raised the flag," Mahomet said. "Blessed is the day you came to me, young Hawk."

They rode on through the streets, now filled with rampaging bashi-bazouks and Anatolians and Janissaries. At one point they watched a young girl dragged from her house, screaming in terror, to be raped at the roadside by half a dozen men in turn, clawing at her white body in their lust.

"Can you not stop this, Padishah?" Anthony asked, sickened at the sight.

"My men have fought long and well, and have suffered grievous casualties. It is right to allow them some pleasure now," Mahomet said firmly.

They rode on through the White Gate and into old Byzantium.

160

By then Anthony had seen so much horror it no longer made sense to him. The Janissaries were everywhere inside the old city, looting and raping and burning. A pall of smoke began to drift across the splendid palaces, to match that already shrouding the outer city.

"The city will be destroyed if you do not stop them," Anthony ventured.

Mahomet nodded, and turned to Halil. "Have the men brought under control. They may retain any booty or women they have seized, but the fires must be extinguished."

Halil bowed.

Mahomet directed his horse towards the portico of the Imperial Palace. "Constantine at least died like a man," he said, "but not all of his people had his courage." The Emir urged his mount up the steps and into the throne-room, its hooves echoing on polished marble. As he looked around him, he said, "The spider's curtain hangs before the portal of Caesar's palace, and the owl stands sentinel on the watch-tower of Afrasiab."

Anthony dismounted and held his master's bridle.

Mahomet climbed down and began to pace through the palace rooms, his bodyguard hurrying behind him. They came upon terrified women and weeping children.

"Who are these?" Mahomet asked. "Are these Constantine's women?"

"No, Padishah," one of the captains answered. "They are merely servants."

"Take them outside and share them," Mahomet said. He entered the banqueting hall and sat down in the huge imperial chair.

"I wish food," he told one of his aides. "Byzantine food. Have them bring me what Constantine ate." He smiled. "If there is anything left here."

An aide hurried off.

"Come sit at my right hand, Hawk Pasha," Mahomet ordered. "You and your father are the architects of my victory, and I am sorry he did not live to share our triumph." He beckoned to one of his captains. "I wish all the prisoners of noble birth brought before me."

Food was placed on the table, and Mahomet ate hungrily. He offered some to Anthony, but Anthony could hardly swallow. He realised that the tragedy of Constantinople had hardly begun.

Suddenly two men were dragged in by the Janissaries, both bruised and wounded. "Their names are Bocchiardi, O Padishah," said the captain.

Anthony recognised them, as they undoubtedly recognised him.

Mahomet gazed at them, while they endeavoured to face him out.

"Behead them," Mahomet commanded curtly.

"Can you not save us, Monsignore Hawkwood?" one of the brothers asked.

Anthony made no reply.

"Courage," said the other brother.

They were thrown to the floor, and the scimitars flashed. Blood spilled across the marble floor.

"Place their heads on the table before me," Mahomet said, continuing to eat.

Anthony gazed at the gaping mouths and sightless eyes. I have sold my soul to the very devil, he thought in horror.

Three women were then brought in, their fine clothes torn and dishevelled, their hair loose and tumbling past their shoulders. Anthony's heart surged, but they were not those he sought.

"They say they are Paleologi, Padishah," the captain said.

"Throw them to my Janissaries," Mahomet said.

The women stared at him in horror. "Kind sir," one ventured.

"Take them out," Mahomet said. "And when my men are weary of them, strike off their heads."

There was a reason for this terrible vengeance, Anthony realised: Mahomet was purposely inscribing the terror of his name on history for all eternity.

So the grim work went on, and the line of dripping heads on the table grew. Mahomet continued his meal.

Two hours later there was a row of twenty heads on the table. It was then that Hawkwood caught his breath as one particular group of captives was driven into the room.

Anthony started to rise, but forced himself back into his seat. His mind had become so attuned to horror that he had not immediately recognised them. The men and the women had been stripped naked, and had been thus marched through the streets for all to see. One was a tall and auburn-haired woman, with a magnificently full figure and tear-stained cheeks: he had never seen his sister naked before. The second was slender and dark beside her, small breasts trembling as she looked from left to right in terror. The third, short and plump, had once been the wife of the most powerful subject in the empire.

With the women stood four men. Anthony now recognised the Grand Duke and Basil and Alexius. The fourth man he did not know, but he guessed him to be Count Drakontes.

As they stared at the heads on the table, the blood on the floor, the women shuddered and held each other close.

The Grand Duke stepped forward. "I am the Grand Duke Lukas Notaras," he said as boldly as he could. "My wealth is beyond measure. I will ransom myself and my family, Emir."

Mahomet stared at him. "Notaras," he said. "Yes, I have heard of you."

Notaras endeavoured to meet his steady gaze but could not.

"Behead him," Mahomet commanded abruptly.

Anthony gasped.

Notaras stared at the Emir in terror.

"No!" shrieked the Grand Duchess, and fell to her knees. "For the sake of Heaven ..."

The Janissaries seized the Grand Duke and threw him to his knees.

The Grand Duchess screamed again, and fell to the floor in a swoon as the head of her husband rolled across the floor. The heads of the other three men followed immediately.

Anna and Catherine had also fallen to their knees, still holding each other close.

Anthony rose to his feet, staring at them.

As did Mahomet. "By the beard of the prophet," he said, "Is that your sister, young Hawk?"

"Yes, Padishah," Anthony said.

Hawkwood gazed at Catherine, who seemed to have only just recognised him.

"Anthony?" she whispered. "Oh my God, Anthony? You have murdered our husbands."

Anthony could not reply to this.

"Stand, woman," Mahomet said.

Catherine hesitated, then rose to her feet. Anna Notaras rose with her, afraid to let her go.

Mahomet stroked his beard as he appraised her. "Truly you are Hawk Pasha's sister," he said. "Had you not already been married

163

... but no matter. I give her to you, young Hawk. Take her home to her mother, and let them both grieve for her father and yours."

"I would rather die," Catherine cried. "You are heartless murderers, devils from hell both of you. I would rather die!"

"And be sure you whip her soundly," Mahomet said. "She is in sore need of it." He turned to the captain, who was arranging the bloodied heads of the Grand Duke, his sons and Count Drakontes on the table. "Give the other women to my soldiers."

The Grand Duchess moaned from the floor. Anna clung even more tightly to Catherine.

"I know it is what they deserve, O Padishah," Anthony began. "And you have been more than generous in the matter of my sister. But this is a woman whom I once wished to love ..."

Mahomet raised his head. "Indeed? Come closer, girl."

Anna shrank away from him, but was seized and thrust forward by one of the Janissaries. She stumbled to her knees before the table, staring in horror at her father's head immediately before her.

"You wish her as well?" Mahomet asked.

"Padishah ..."

Mahomet gave a shout of laughter. "You are all but overcome, young Hawk. Well, I promised you a second woman. Take this creature if she pleases you. She can even become your wife, since she is now a widow."

"Never," Anna moaned.

Mahomet looked at her darkly. "Would you rather be stretched on your back in the public street for the sport of all of my warriors?" he hissed. "I have given you to Hawk Pasha. And you, Hawk Pasha," he added, "service her well. If she does not bear your child within a year of this day, I will take her from you and give her to my Janissaries. Now go. Take your women and go." Mahomet laughed again, pointing at the Grand Duchess. "Take her as well if she will amuse you. She will hardly amuse anyone else."

Anthony vaulted the table and went towards them.

"You have sold your soul to the devil," Anna sobbed at him. "We can never forgive you."

"Well, so be it then," Hawkwood growled.

BOOK THE SECOND
The Seraglio

"Ah Love! could thou and I with Fate conspire
To grasp this sorry Scheme of Things entire,
Would not we shatter it to bits — and then
Re-mould it nearer to the Heart's Desire!"

OMAR KHAYYAM

7

THE BROTHERS

"There! There!

The tabalcans sounded, the trumpets blew, and the beaters raised their shrill shriek.

From the pine trees broke a huge yellow-brown beast, bounding stiff-legged as only a cat can, over the open ground towards the next wooded copse.

"A beauty!" shouted Prince Djem. "A beauty! Haste, Hawk, haste! We will claim him together."

William Hawkwood spurred this horse beside that of the prince, and the two men galloped away from their escorts, bows already unslung and grasped in their right hands, minds for the moment entirely consumed with the excitement of the chase, and the possible reward at the end of it. Once this high plateau of central Anatolia had abounded in lion; in this year of 1481 the mighty beasts were all but extinct. Thus it was that the very moment Prince Djem, in his city of Brusa, had heard there was such a creature loose on the Ulu Dag, he had commanded an expedition to be made ready.

Now the moment of fulfilment was near.

The two young men — Djem but twenty-two years old, and William Hawkwood a year younger — made a strong contrast as they chased behind their quarry. The Ottoman prince was small and compact. His body was muscular enough but tending to plumpness. His nose was long and curved, to overhang his lips, where his moustache was just beginning to sprout; in this he resembled his father, the Sultan Mahomet II.

He resembled his father in more than features. His eyes, a deep blue, could turn colder than ice, suggesting the facets of the mind that lay behind them.

William Hawkwood was two inches taller than six feet. His complexion was ruddy, his hair a glowing red. His features were large and bold, in keeping with his body and the reputation of his family — he had not yet had the chance to prove himself in the field to be a worthy son of Hawk Pasha.

But as Hawk Pasha's son, William had lived his entire life close to the side of the Sultan, and the Sultan's sons. Prince Djem knew he had no more faithful follower than the youngest of the Hawk-woods.

The lion reached the fringe of trees and there hesitated, perhaps winded because of the altitude — hunters and quarry were some three thousand feet above sea level — and turning to snarl at his pursuers. He made a splendid picture, mane bristling, tail swirling, features contorted as he drew back lips in an angry snarl to reveal his gleaming teeth.

Djem — allowed by a respectful William Hawkwood to draw in front — pulled hard on his rein. The horse panted to a halt, and the lion changed his snarl into an imperious roar, lowering his haunches as he prepared to charge.

"To me!" Djem shouted, his voice high with fear.

"I am with you, my lord," William replied; he had swerved his horse to one side, also drawing rein so as to whip an arrow from his quiver.

Behind them the earth still drummed as their escorts strove to catch up.

"Shoot, shoot!" Djem screamed. In his excitement he dropped his first arrow, and all but dropped his bow as well when he sought to retrieve it.

The lion swished its tail to and fro a last time, and bounded forward.

William released his string. Almost before the arrow had commenced its flight he was drawing and sighting a second. Like any Turkish noblemen, he had been taught horsemanship, and the art of fighting from horseback, from the moment he had been old enough to stand upright.

His first missile had already struck home. The lion was arrested in mid-stride, falling again to its haunches, stroking at its shoulder with a huge paw to remove the barb, and turning its head to snarl at this second antagonist. The doomed beast was so noble that William hesitated an instant in admiration, before loosing the second shaft.

Djem had now recovered himself, and fired at last. But his shot was wide — and the lion turned back to him.

"Shoot!" the prince begged. "Shoot!"

William's second arrow also struck home, and the lion fell on its side, blood dripping down its tawny flanks. It was ready for the *coup de grâce*, and William had a third arrow on his string. But he knew better than to fire it. The kill must belong to the prince.

Djem had now got both his mount and himself under control, and he took careful aim. As the lion raised its head to utter a last defiant roar, the prince's shaft struck it in the throat. The roar became a gurgle, and the beast fell over.

"A superb shot!" William cried. His upbringing had also taught him that a prince must always be congratulated.

"Is the beast dead?" Djem cautiously walked his horse forward.

"It is most certainly dying, my lord."

"Ha!" Djem dismounted and drew his sword. On foot he approached the quivering, groaning prey even more cautiously. Then he swung the scimitar, and hacked into its head. The lion growled, and rolled over. Djem leapt backwards, then moved forward again to strike at the unprotected belly of the beast. Blood spurted as the lion collapsed, all its great muscles seeming to lose their strength at the same moment.

William had also dismounted. "Bravo, my lord! You have despatched him."

"Ha!" Djem cried again, and started to hack at the body with all his force.

William could only wait until he was exhausted, as did the escort gathered at a respectful distance.

"Foul thing!" Djem panted, swinging his sword. "Didst thou think thou could match strength with a prince of the House of Othman?"

At last he stopped, sweat pouring down his face and soaking his silk tunic. "I have killed a monster," he said. "My father will be proud of this."

"No, my lord," William said. "You have killed a monarch."

Djem shot him a glance.

"Your father will be even prouder of that," William added.

"Ha!" Djem shouted. "Ha ha! You are right, young Hawk." He swung into the saddle. "Fetch home that carrion," he commanded his guards.

"You are a mighty hunter," Sereta said, and kissed her husband, while the two little boys scrabbled at his boots.

"Hush," William said. "It was the prince who slew the lion." He placed his finger on her lips, as she tried to protest. "The prince slew the lion, wife. There is an end to the matter."

Black-haired and black-eyed, softly plump of body, Sereta pouted and threw herself on to a divan. She was nineteen years of age, and had been William's wife for four of them.

The Sultan himself had chosen her with the agreement of Anthony Hawkwood, Hawk Pasha, his dearest friend, the moment William had been circumcised and become a man. Sereta was the daughter of an army commander, and had brought with her a large dowry and a determined sense of loyalty to her new husband.

After the dream in which every virgin in the empire was supposed to indulge, that of succeeding in one of the annual selections for the Sultan's harem, the next best thing was surely to aspire to the House of Hawkwood. Sometimes it was whispered that this order was reversed in the hearts and minds of many. To be selected for the Sultan was not necessarily to attain power or happiness; more often than not it entailed a lifetime of sexual and social neglect — except where relief could be found amongst the other hapless inmates of the seraglio ... or from a helpful eunuch.

But marriage to a Hawk, it was known, introduced a girl to an unimaginable world: where there were no other wives; where the yashmak was not worn, even in the company of male relatives and guests; where the wife was allowed to remain at her husband's side, at least while indoors. Laila, daughter of Mahmun Pasha, had been the first to sample such strange delights, when the Emir — as the Sultan was then known — had given her in marriage to Anthony Hawkwood. But Laila had been a sad choice. However much she might have enjoyed her illustrious position, she had proved barren. She had died relatively young, many said of grief.

Anthony Hawkwood had by then taken another wife, the proud Greek lady, Anna Notaras, whom he had plucked from the burning ruin of Constantinople. Rumour had it that his physical relations with his second wife had at first resembled repeated rape: that the most heart-rending screams had been heard in his palace during the early days of their marriage.

However true that might be, Anna Notaras had yet borne three sons and two daughters for her renegade English husband. And

Anthony Hawkwood had not found it necessary to marry again.

William knew all the rumours. He granted some truth in them, because in his own youth he had observed his mother watching his father always with a peculiar apprehension. Beautiful in an aquiline fashion, and still haughty when the occasion permitted it, she had somehow reminded him of a proud mare who has been broken by the horsetamer.

William and his mother had never been close. Like his two older brothers he had been educated with men, sent to the school of the Janissaries before he was ten years old, learned to kill before he had learned to love. Thus he had never learned to love: Sereta and her children were possessions, symbols of his wealth and his manhood. Perhaps love would come in time.

The Sultan, although he insisted upon certain essential rites such as circumcision, had never sought to force the Hawkwoods to Mahommedanism; he understood that part of their value to him lay in their being gaiours who, when necessary, could be used to deal diplomatically with other infidels. More important he knew that, as Christians, their place and power within the Ottoman structure depended on him and him alone. No other family could he allow himself to trust so completely.

Thus it was that he had brought up William Hawkwood and his own youngest son, Djem — also his favourite, it was said — almost as brothers. But William was not summoned to prayer, and it was understood that his sons would be Christian, whoever their mother. And if, like his father, he chose to live in the Frankish fashion, with a single woman, that was his own business.

William Hawkwood quarrelled with none of this — concerned only with acting the part given him by fate: that of being Hawk Pasha's youngest son. He had known virtually from birth that his was a renegade family, destined not only to live but also to earn fame and fortune in a heathen land — and more often than not to lead the Turks in battle against Christians. He had also understood from childhood that it was his destiny to be a soldier: a commander of artillery like his famous forebears. Though he himself he had never actually fired a shot in anger, he knew that his father had been a formidable soldier, and this was a cause for pride. And if he had been told often enough that the Sultan's nickname, as a young man, had been Hunkar, 'Drinker of Blood' — nowadays Mahomet preferred to be known as 'the Conqueror' — yet he did not fear him; because he himself was the son of Hawk Pasha. Rather was he proud, too, to serve the greatest monarch in the world!

William Hawkwood had also long been aware that the favourite prince with whom he was so closely associated was a coward — and a vicious one at that. This was a penance to be borne by those who served. Djem certainly relied on his English friend, and more so with every passing year, it seemed. When he had been given command of the garrison of Brusa, it was natural that William would accompany him as his captain of artillery. Anthony Hawkwood was the greatest artillerist in the world; his sons could only succeed him.

That way lay advancement, even if a certain amount of sycophancy was needed — that too was a requirement for those who served. William could at least be sure that Djem would never be Sultan, at least as long as his elder brother Bayazid lived. But even Bayazid's inheritance of the sword of Othman was surely many years in the future: the Sultan was hardly fifty, and as powerfully strong, in both mind and body, as ever.

Meanwhile there were the perquisites of independence to be enjoyed. Nestling at the foot of Mount Ulu, Brusa was one of the most delightful places on earth, where the only sound competing with the sighing of the wind was the even more restful ripple of flowing water.

Though cold in winter, it was never uncomfortable. Even when it snowed the sun was soon out to create a vista of breathtaking beauty, while in the summer the climate was perfect. The high Anatolian plateau behind the city provided not only an ample playground for hunting, but also ideal territory for William and Djem to exercise their troops, which included a regiment of Janissaries.

The city itself was the focal point of the entire Ottoman state. Constantinople might have risen from its ashes of 1453 to become the supreme city it had previously been, but Brusa contained the tombs of Djem's ancestors. And it would no doubt contain his tomb as well, in the course of time.

It was a place far removed from the constantly warring boundaries of the empire, or the intrigues of the Porte — as the Ottoman court had come to be known, from the Sultan's habit of receiving foreign ambassadors in the porch of his palace. It was a place where the Turks practised the arts of peace; working at ceramics, or at their silk embroidery which was already world famous. It was a place in which to be happy and grow fat, to hunt and to play, to make love to one's willing wife, and watch the growing strength and vigour of one's children.

So long as nothing changed.

The horseman's face was grey with fatigue, and fear, as he galloped his exhausted mount over the cobbles, striking sparks to left and right. People hurried from their houses and employments to gaze at him, and discuss what news he might have brought. Terrible news, to be sure: his haste and his demeanour indicated that.

"There has been some calamity," the onlookers whispered.

"The Janissaries have been defeated!"

Unimaginable thought.

No one was capable of imagining the news the messenger actually did bring.

Prince Djem stared at him in consternation. "The Conqueror is dead?" he whispered. "How can this be?"

"Poison," growled Omar Pasha, the commander of the garrison.

"Was it poison?" William Hawkwood asked.

"It is not supposed so, my lord," the messenger said. "The Padishah suddenly collapsed, complaining of great pain, and then died. My lord prince, your brother the Sultan Bayazid, commands your presence in Constantinople."

"Strike off that man's head," Djem commanded.

"My lord prince!" William protested.

"His head," Djem shouted. "Take his head."

The messenger was hurried from the chamber. He did not protest; he could have hoped for little else.

"The Sultan Bayazid," Djem growled, sagging back on to the divan from which he had risen on hearing the news. "By what right does he claim the sultanate?"

"By right of birth," William ventured. "He is the eldest son."

"I would have been my father's choice, had he lived," Djem said.

"I have no doubt of it, my lord. But who can gainsay the will of Allah?"

"Ha! I do not accept that. And Bayazid must take me for a fool. Go to Constantinople? I might as well cut my own throat."

"But you have been summoned by the Sultan," Omar protested.

"I have been summoned by my brother, who now claims to be the Sultan," Djem declared. "He summons me to execution."

"You do not know this," William said.

"Did not my father murder every one of his brothers? Did he not set the precedent, and justify it by quoting the Koran? And Bayazid hates me for being my father's favourite. I will not tamely go to be slaughtered like a sheep."

"But if you defy the Sultan, my lord," Omar said, "you will be regarded as a rebel."

"The Padishah will most certainly send an army against you," William said.

"And do we not have soldiers of our own? Have I not two proven generals?" He looked from face to face. "Besides, I have a plan which will weaken Bayazid's resolve; he has never had much stomach for war. I will offer to divide the empire with him. He can have Europe, and even Constantinople. I will keep Asia, and Brusa." He leaned back with a smile.

Omar and William gazed at each other. To suppose that any Ottoman sultan would agree to dividing his empire was equivalent to supposing that one day the skies might fall. And to rebel against the Sultan could lead only to death. William's predicament was even worse than Omar's.

"With humble respect, my lord prince," he said, "if Bayazid declines your offer and sends an army against you, it will most certainly be commanded by my father, who will have my brothers at his side. I would therefore beg you to permit me to withdraw."

"I will not permit you to withdraw, young Hawk. I need you to command my artillery."

"But, my lord ..."

"As to opposing one's relatives, if Bayazid is foolish enough to refuse my offer, will I not be opposing my own brother?"

William opened his mouth and then closed it again. That was Djem's own choice. Perhaps it was his only choice. But it was not William Hawkwood's only choice.

Djem frowned at him, and pointed. "You will serve my guns, young Hawk. Put any thought of treason towards me from your mind. You will serve my guns, or you will watch your wife and children die. Think on that at all times."

*

The Golden Horn and the Bosphorus were shrouded in doleful sounds.

Anthony Hawkwood remembered how, when he had first come to Constantinople, as a boy of sixteen following his father's dream of military renown, he had listened to the tolling of the bells of St Sophia as the Genoese carrack had slowly breasted the current pouring out of the Black Sea into Marmara, telling the whole world that the Christian host commanded by Janos Hunyadi had been annihilated.

Those bells had long been silent; St Sophia had been converted, by command of the Sultan, into a mosque.

Bells were not the Muslim way. This day the air was filled with the sound of cymbals and tambourines, tabalcans and kettle drums, each giving forth a steady, mournful cadence — as they had done for the last month. No doubt any ship approaching the city by way of Marmara would be similarly forewarned of disaster.

The Sultan was dead! It was difficult for anyone in Constantinople, anyone in all the domains ruled by the Ottomans to understand the true enormity of what had happened.

No doubt, in Rome, His Holiness the Pope, Sixtus IV, would hold a *Te Deum* and celebrate the death of the devil.

For Anthony Hawkwood it was more difficult to believe than for most. He sometimes thought that his life had only truly begun when he had stood before that slight, boyish figure thirty years before. Mahomet II had been his destiny in every possible way. The Sultan had stood sponsor for his circumcision, had presented him with both his wives, had given him high command in the army.

Together they had assaulted the world. The taking of Constantinople had been no more than a first step. With Hawk Pasha to command his guns, Mahomet had then embarked upon that career which had truly earned him the soubriquet of "Conqueror". Only Belgrade, valiantly relieved by the ageing Hunyadi, and the island of Rhodes, equally valiantly defended by the Knights of St John, had withstood his arms. All of Serbia except the White City had fallen beneath the Ottoman yoke, the Morea had been overrun, the Black Sea coast and the Empire of Trebizond had been absorbed, Bosnia and Herzegovina had collapsed.

175

The price of these unceasing conquests had been the enmity of Venice, whose benevolent neutrality had been so helpful in the campaign against Constantinople. The Venetians had grown anxious at the spread of Turkish power, and angry at Turkish interference in their lucrative Levant trade.

The Venetians never did things by halves. It was their ambition to destroy the Ottomans once and for all time. They enlisted the support of the Pope to preach a crusade against the anti-Christ, the Drinker of Blood, and they even sent emissaries into far-off Persia to summon to arms Uzun Hasan, ruler of the Akkoyunlu, who as Shi'ites abhorred the more orthodox Muslim Sunnites such as the Turks, the followers of the traditional way.

Mahomet had defeated them all. The so-called crusade had been scattered; the Venetians, attacked by a Turkish fleet in their very lagoon, had been reduced to paying tribute; and only two years ago Hasan's great army had been shattered at the battle of Otluk-Beli, on the Upper Euphrates.

Mahomet had stood astride the world from Italy to the Taurus, master of all he surveyed.

And surely with many more years of conquest ahead of him, as he was in no more than early middle age. Only a month before, he had sent his heralds to summon his Janissaries, his Anatolians, his sipahis and his bashi-bazouks to arms, to launch another campaign against the Shi'ite Persians and crush the heretics forever.

Two days later the Sultan was dead.

Anthony Hawkwood had been one of those kneeling by Mahomet's side when he died. This was fitting, as he was perhaps the dead Sultan's closest friend. Now he took the ferry across the Golden Horn from his home in the suburb of Galeta to attend the person of the new Sultan, Bayazid.

Like his father, Bayazid was the second of his name. His previous namesake had called himself "the Thunderer", and pretended to be the greatest soldier in the world; but he had been crushed out of existence by Timur the Mongol. For those who prospered by the greatness of the Ottomans, as did Anthony Hawkwood, it was fervently to be hoped that this young man of thirty-four would prove himself to be the true son of his father rather than a replica of the first Bayazid. Mahomet had called himself nothing — he had left the nicknames to those who feared him — yet had indeed proved himself the greatest warrior of his time.

Bayazid had much to live up to — more than just his father's conquests. Mahomet had been the first Emir of the Ottomans to call himself Sultan. The title had been used in the Koran to denote a person of moral or religious authority. In this form it had, some centuries later, been adopted by political leaders as well, to suggest that their authority was both physical and approved by God; the first so to use the title in this sense had been Mahmud Ghazni, greatest soldier of the eleventh Christian century.

The caliphs of Baghdad had taken up bestowing the title on certain other prominent Muslim rulers, seeking to bolster their own declining authority with the distribution of honours. The forerunners of the Ottomans, their kindred people the Seljuks, who had first waged successful war on the Byzantines, had had their sultans. But it was not the Caliph who had granted this title to the Emir Mahomet II: he had claimed it himself, and by his victories had forced the world to recognise it and do homage to it.

Now, only by right of inheritance, it belonged to his son.

Mahomet had been more than a mere soldier. No doubt he had spent too much of his time campaigning to properly achieve everything else he had wished to achieve; but, then, he had not expected to die so soon. Perhaps he had left too much to be accomplished in his declining years, when campaigning could be left to others.

He had sought to rebuild Constantinople, without much success. As Anthony Hawkwood and his sons disembarked from the ferry and entered the water gate, though the walls to either side had been largely repaired from the battering they had received from the Ottoman artillery twenty-eight years before, they could see that great portions of the city were still tangled ruins.

Out of the desolation the monument to Constantine the Great still poked skywards as a last reminder of Christian defiance. Mahomet revered the memories of famous men, and had resisted the importunities of his imams to have the statue destroyed.

Where he had built, the Sultan had built well. The palace of the Paleologi had been transformed from a gloomy edifice of sharp angles and dark rooms into a magnificent mansion of airy apartments and flowing curves, with the constant, soothing trickle of running water everywhere to be heard. Gone were the no-less gloomy ikons which had hung from every wall; not only was any reproduction of the human form against the Muslim law, it was also repulsive to their sense of beauty. In the place of the Virgin and child were silken drapes in the softest of colours.

Mahomet's pashas had emulated their master, and Hawkwood's own palace, in Galata suburb, was a smaller reflection of the Seraglio, as the Sultan's palace was known.

There was one custom Mahomet had perpetuated, a part of the Muslim tradition; a man's wealth and power was indicated by the reputed beauty of his wives and the number of his concubines. In this alone was Anthony Hawkwood not pre-eminent.

Mahomet had dreamed of turning Constantinople into a purely Muslim city. But the Turks were not city-dwellers by nature or habit. While Mahomet's pashas had somewhat unwillingly followed him behind the walls of Theodosius, and endeavoured to make their homes there, the rank and file had preferred to return to their farms. Nor were the Turks clerks or merchants; they were horsemen from the steppes, who held that a man's true place was in the saddle.

Mahomet would thus have found himself in possession of a ghost city, save for the thousands of Greeks, Genoese and Christians of varying denominations who had been gathered into the market places to await either execution or sale as slaves.

But the Conqueror was nothing if not a pragmatist. He had no intention of seeing this pearl he had plucked from Christendom die. Constantinople needed people. It needed clerks and merchants, entrepreneurs and tradesmen, if it was to preserve its place as the greatest city in the world. All of these people were to hand. What matter if they were gaiours who up till a few short months before had been his bitter enemies?

He had offered his captives their freedom if they would continue living and trading in Constantinople. More, he had found their patriarch, Gennadius, hiding in a monastery, and had reinstated him. The Conqueror had no wish to forcibly convert the Greeks to the one true religion; he preferred that they should remain inferior in every way. But he recognised that every man needed a religion; Gennadius was therefore told to preach to the people and accept their penance, as he had done for so long under the Paleologi.

Gennadius was no less a pragmatist than his new master. He could see no point in playing the martyr when he had been given a Christian duty to perform, albeit at the bidding of a heathen. Close one's eyes to the banners of the crescent, the measured tread of the Janissaries, the brilliant flowing robes of the sipahis, and Constantinople was again a Byzantine city.

Only St Sophia had been barred to the Greeks for ever.

The transition had not been easy. Hawkwood could still remember the look of shocked horror on the Patriarch's face when he found himself standing side by side with his bitter enemy, Hawk Pasha, before the divan of the Conqueror. The Greeks, the most turbulent of people, had needed to learn that they were not actually free, and that to strike a Turk meant instant death. Yet Constantinople had been reborn, and beneath the aegis of the crescent was now more prosperous than it had been for five hundred years.

Mahomet had then had to learn how to cope with the administration of so vast a source of wealth. Again, the Turks had no knowledge of — or use for — money; their lives had been governed by barter or plunder. But in dealing with the West, with the bankers of Hamburg and Florence — who would negotiate even with the anti-Christ were he prepared to pay their interest — and indeed, with the everyday taxation of his subject peoples, Mahomet had been forced to accept ledgers and accounts. There was no profit in demanding payment in kind from a Greek merchant on the waterfront of the Golden Horn — but there was a great deal in demanding a tithe of his earnings in gold coin.

Here again it had been necessary to employ Greeks. But the Greeks had their own traditions, their own concept of how things should be done. The Byzantine Empire had been accumulating traditions a thousand years before the first Ottoman had raised his horsehair wand and led his sipahis out of the steppes.

Imperial accountants needed names. The Ottomans had always been nothing more than a huge clan. The Emir had had his viziers who conducted his day-to-day business to save him having to do it for himself; he had had his pashas to command his men and his ships into battles; he had had his beylerbeys to govern the various provinces of the empire. Below them had been little order; each vizier, each pasha, each beylerbey conducted his affairs as he thought best, only always aware that to displease the Emir or misinterpret his will might mean a swift and sudden death.

The Sultan retained all of these, but to them had been added a host of other officials. For the Turks, no less than the Byzantines, had discovered that a title adds to a man's stature, however falsely. To gain entrance to the divan, even Hawk Pasha must pass scrutiny by the Keeper of the Gate, and then the Keeper of the Door, and then the Captain of the Guard, and then the Keeper of the Inner Chamber, every one dressed in the most resplendent robes, and every one wearing, round his steel helmet, a swathe of cloth.

Thus slavishly did the Ottomans imitate the habits of their master. It had been Mahomet, on his campaigns in the east, who had first wound a strip of cloth round his helmet in order to counter the heat of the sun on exposed metal. Soon every man in his army had adopted the fashion. Now this was regarded as an essential article of dress. Like everyone else, Anthony Hawkwood and his sons also wore the turban.

As he proceeded towards the huge arch which gave access to the divan, guarded by eunuchs armed with the scimitar, Hawkwood could look to his right into another large room, where the Greek scribes laboured at their desks, attempting to keep the financial affairs of the empire up to date. They too had little titles: Keeper of the Books, Keeper of the Accounts, Keeper of the Records.

If he chose to look to his left, through the arched windows, into the Sultan's gardens, he would see the Head Gardener speaking with the Head Under-Gardener amidst the magnificent, multi-coloured blooms, from jacarandas to roses, which grew in profusion in this perfect climate and which had been the Sultan's pride and joy.

All of these positions were not only well paid but had already become hereditary. The wild horsemen who had first followed Ertughril out of the steppes must be turning in their graves, Hawkwood thought, to see their descendants so cosseted and debased.

But was he not himself General of the Artillery? And would not his eldest son John succeed him?

Mahomet had allowed these trappings of civilisation to grow because he understood their power to bind men to him. He had always regarded them with cynicism, though; he had not altered his own habits, but had still gone abroad as and when he chose, shown himself readily to his people and even stopped to speak with them. If, as was the Ottoman way, he had allowed his viziers to conduct the business of the divan, he had always been present to one side of the room, ready to interfere as necessary. And he had always ridden at the head of his own armies.

The new Sultan had not been seen in public since his father's death — and seldom before then, either. It was difficult to imagine him in the saddle, scimitar in hand. Bayazid was no taller than Mahomet had been, but at the age of thirty-four he was already fat. Though he had his father's cold eyes and cruel lips, his face lacked purpose. In place of determination there were merely sensuality; it was said that he already possessed a harem equal in number to that of his father.

This Hawkwood could believe. He had watched the doleful procession of veiled women, with their attendant eunuchs, filing out of the Seraglio in which most of them had lived since girlhood — now destined for a convent where they would spend the remainder of their lives in cloistered secrecy. In their place had been the procession of Bayazid's women entering the palace, joyous in their new elevation above the common herd.

Only the Sultan Valideh, the mother of the ruler, spanned the two groups. The mother of the younger prince, Djem, had been dismissed with all the others. But this new Sultan Valideh could be no more than a pale replica of Mara Brankovich, Anthony felt sure. Naturally he had never laid eyes on her.

Djem was the burning question of the moment. Anthony Hawkwood could still remember the brother of Mahomet being strangled by a bowstring held by two Janissaries. All Mahomet's brothers had perished in the same way. When reproached about this, he had quoted from the Koran: God hates discord worse than murder. Yet to kill one's own brothers seemed abhorrent to one brought up as a Christian. Thus Anthony had beseeched Bayazid, in the first hours of his succession, to spare the prince's life.

"Djem is still but a boy, twelve years younger than yourself, O Padishah," he had said. "Confine him by all means, but do not stain your hands with his blood."

Bayazid had seemed to agree. "Just let the boy come to me, and accept me as his lord and master," he had said.

Hawkwood had been forced to accept that decision, even if he knew that were Bayazid truly the son of Mahomet, Djem's death had already been decided. He could only hope to intervene again when the boy reached the city.

But this urgent summons ... Hawkwood studied Bayazid's face, as he approached the divan, his soft kid boots making no sound upon the polished marble floor. The younger man did not entirely lack virtue. He was a collector of books and, even more than his father, a composer of verses. He showed a lively interest in the intellectual lives of other countries, even Christian countries. Yet he had been brought up too much in the consciousness of his greatness. He conducted his own divan, so jealous was he of his new prerogative; and he was not surrounded by armed pashas, as Mahomet had always been.

Anthony now gazed at the Chief Armourer, who bore the Sultan's scimitar in its velvet case; the Chief Huntsman wearing a horn-shaped cap made of cloth of gold; the Overseer of the Sultan's Perfumes; the Chief Keeper of the Nightingales; and the Custodian of the Heron's Plumes. Each official's clothes were studded with precious stones and laced with gold thread; they almost rivalled their master in magnificence. None of them seemed happy to gaze upon the huge, battle-scarred figure of the empire's most famous living soldier.

"Have you not heard, Hawk Pasha," demanded the Vizier, "the news from Brusa?"

"Not yet," Anthony replied.

"We are defied," said the Chief Armourer. "The Prince Djem refuses to attend our presence in Constantinople."

"He disputes our master's claim," said the Custodian of the Heron's Plumes.

Anthony looked at the Sultan.

"It was on your advice that I sought to treat fairly with my brother," Bayazid said. He spoke very softly, in hardly more than a whisper; Hawkwood had never heard him raise his voice. "And this is his reply. He declares that it is only just that the empire should be divided between us. He lays claim to all Asia. He declares his intention of fortifying Brusa and defending it to the last. How may I bury my father if I can gain no access to the Holy City? How may I call myself Sultan while this canker exists in the bowels of my empire?"

"He is a foolish young man, and afraid," Anthony said.

"Yet he commands an army."

"A small one, Padishah. And one in which the commanders are no rebels. I chose them myself. Omar Pasha will never take up arms against the Sultan. And William Hawkwood is my very own son. I will send a messenger to Brusa and endeavour to make the prince see sense."

"Who will you send?" Bayazid asked.

Anthony hesitated a moment, and then half turned his head; his son Henry stood to his left.

"I will send Henry Hawkwood here. He can speak with his brother and with Omar, and they will bring the prince before you."

"See that it is done," the Sultan said.

Prince Djem stood on the hills above Brusa and surveyed the approaching horsemen.

"There are no more than sixty of them," he remarked.

"Your regiment of sipahis will make short work of them, Omar Pasha. Do so now."

"With respect, my lord prince," Omar said. "It is undoubtedly an embassy from your brother. It can do no harm for us to hear what he has to say."

He looked at William Hawkwood for support. Once recovered from their dismay at Djem's decision, and his manner of implementing it, the two commanders had had several private discussions during the last month. They had even contemplated binding Djem and delivering him to Constantinople themselves. But that way lay grave risks. No one could tell what the Sultan truly had in mind.

Furthermore, they could not be sure whether their men would follow them. Whatever his private faults, Djem was a popular prince. He had taken care to make himself so since his arrival in Brusa. There was little doubt that his army would fight for him, if he offered them sufficient rewards.

From William Hawkwood's point of view, the idea of opposition to the prince was nearly impossible. Sereta and his sons had been taken into the prince's own harem, out of reach of all save the prince's eunuchs.

"Your family will be safe with mine," Djem had said, "until we have gained our victory."

To abandon his family was unthinkable, but to fight against his

183

family was equally unthinkable. William was uncomfortably aware of his youth and his inability to make a decision. He could not overcome the feeling that his father would never have submitted to such a humiliation, would have reacted violently, and either triumphed or died. And sacrificed his family in doing so, if necessary.

Did he, then, lack the stomach to be a Hawkwood?

But ... perhaps the crucial moment was now approaching. William's eyes narrowed as the cavalcade drew closer: a bright picture of flashing lance-heads and floating pennons, of multi-coloured silk cloaks and burnished, cloth-wrapped helmets, of small and powerful horses.

But the man in front was larger than the rest, and rode a larger horse in a distinctive manner.

William's heart swelled. "The ambassador is my brother Henry, my lord prince," he said. "Now we shall discover truly what is in your brother's mind."

Henry Hawkwood stood before the prince's divan.

"My lord and yours, the Sultan Bayazid, sends greetings, lord prince, and wishes to inquire why you have refused his invitation to Constantinople?".

"Does he take me for a fool?" Djem demanded.

"My lord the Sultan has requested me to inform Your Highness that he cannot accede to your desire to divide his empire. He says that such a procedure has never been undertaken in the history of our people, that it is against the anyi, and that the Grand Mufti can find no excuse for it. But my lord the Sultan has commanded me to say this to you: that he wishes only to honour you, and to preserve your life. To this end, he has instructed me to assure your highness that he has issued a safe conduct which will ensure your journey is not interfered with."

"And when I reach Constantinople?"

"He is preparing a palace for Your Highness. It will be close to the Seraglio. My lord the Sultan wishes to have his brother ever at his right hand."

"He takes me for a fool," Djem said again.

Henry looked at his brother William. "Our father has asked me to enlist your help in persuading his highness to do nothing rash."

"Willingly," William replied. "I am certain that Bayazid means what he says, my lord prince. He would never break his word, given so publicly."

"Young Hawk is right, lord prince," Omar said. "The way of prudence is here the way of justice and fortune."

Djem turned his head to glare at them each in turn. Then he looked back at Henry Hawkwood. "And if I refuse to act the fool?"

"My lord, if you do not return with me to Constantinople, the Sultan will declare you a rebel and hurl all the armed forces of the empire against you."

Djem stroked his beard. "And who do you suppose will command this host?"

"Alas, my lord prince, the command will undoubtedly be exercised by Hawk Pasha."

"Then let him have a care. He will war upon his own family."

Henry gulped, and looked at William for guidance.

William could do nothing more than raise his eyebrows, hoping for a private conference later to explain the situation.

Henry faced Djem again. "Is this the answer I must carry back to the Sultan, my lord prince?"

"No," Djem said. "You will carry nothing back." He looked at the man standing by Henry's shoulder. "How are you called?"

"I am Enver Pasha, lord prince."

"Then do you take this message back to my brother Bayazid. Tell him he is a usurper. Tell him that my father had long ago selected me as his successor. Tell him that I declare myself to be Sultan of the Ottoman Empire, and that I will defend my prerogatives to the death. Tell him that in the course of time I will assert those prerogatives in Constantinople itself. And tell Hawk Pasha that if he marches against me, he marches also against his sons." He pointed then at Henry Hawkwood. "Seize that man!"

Guards ran forward. Henry's hand had dropped to his scimitar, but he did not draw; he knew he was outnumbered.

William made to move, but was restrained by Omar's hand on his arm. The general had no wish to lose his artillery commander before the first shot was fired.

"Do not harm the young Hawk," Djem instructed the captain of the guard. "But place him in secure confinement until I have further need of him."

He pointed at the thunderstruck Enver Pasha. "You had best now make haste to my brother and tell him my words."

185

*

"You have fathered a brood of vipers, Hawk Pasha," Bayazid said, speaking as softly as ever.

"Not so, Padishah. We have Enver Pasha's evidence that my son is under restraint."

"And your other son?"

"It is Enver's opinion that he too is acting under duress."

"I care not," Bayazid said. "They are in my brother's camp. And my brother has now defied me to the death. He threatens my power. He is hateful to me. He is declared outlaw and rebel. How long will it take you to mobilise my armies?"

The lead in Hawkwood's stomach grew heavier; the one thing he and every pasha had feared was civil war on the death of the sultan, such as had blighted the beginning of too many Ottoman emirates in the past. And to have his own sons involved, however inadvertently ...

"They were already summoned by your father for his coming campaign. They will be fully mobilised within three months."

"You will ride to meet them, Hawk Pasha. You will assume command, and you will lead my army against Brusa."

"With respect, Padishah, three months from now will see the leaves falling. It is not less than a month's march to Brusa; within another month there will be snow on the high ground. Your father did not intend to begin his Persian campaign until next spring. It would be wisest for us to do the same, even against Brusa."

"And let the usurper enjoy a winter pretending to be sultan, raising armies, seeking allies? Hawk Pasha, you will march on Brusa as soon as your men are levied. I do not care if you have to wade through snow as deep as your waist. You will bring this brother of mine, and all the vipers who support him, before me here so that I may judge them. Carry out my command, or yield your wand to another."

Hawkwood hesitated but a moment. If anyone was to destroy Djem's army it had to be himself; that was the only way he had any hope of saving the lives of his two sons.

"I will deliver the rebels before you, Padishah," he said. "My son John will ride at my side."

Bayazid's eyes glowered at him. "As you wish, Hawk Pasha.

186

Your wife and daughters will remain in Constantinople, anticipating your return."

"You will lead an army against your own sons?" Anna Notaras stood before her husband, her body quivering. Only two years younger than Anthony, she was now forty-seven, but in many ways remained the girl of fourteen he had first seen and loved and then hated for her betrayal of him.

She remained, equally, the girl and then woman after whom he had lusted. On the day Constantinople had fallen he had led her away, with her mother and with his sister Catherine. The other women had been confined; Anna Notaras he had bidden his servants to strip again, so he might gaze upon that slender, white-skinned dream.

Anna had understood that her only choice lay between submitting to him or being thrown to the Janissaries. He was in a dark and unpredictable mood, and she knew that he was strong enough to break her arm with a twist of his fingers, or else could summon his servants to hold her down while he raped her.

Yet although she had lain down for him without protest, in her mind it had still been rape. She had wept and called him every name she could think of, while still unresisting. In his anger he had beaten her until her buttocks were raw, and she had not resisted him, save with her mouth.

He had often been in despair at her intransigence, and his hopeless passion for her. His sister Catherine, hating no less the brother who fought for the anti-Christ, had been no more amenable, and she had joined her curses to those of her sister-in-law. Sometimes he had contemplated putting them both in a sack and throwing it into the Bosphorus. When, to remove the constant hostile nagging of the sister he had once so loved, Anthony had given her in marriage to a Turkish pasha, Catherine had gone off without demur, and no doubt Ziglal had also had to beat her. In his harem she had died only recently, and he hoped she had found some happiness in the end.

Anna had refused to soften. He had indulged himself on her in every aspect of physical love which he had learned at the hands of the Emir Valideh. He had mounted her as a Turk and as a Christian. On occasion he had refused to mount her at all, and instead had stimulated her with his hands. He had gained a triumph there. Not even Anna Notaras, hating him with every fibre of her being, had been able to withstand the art of a man taught by Mara Brankovich.

But it had been a barren victory. She still hated him and every-thing about him. She hated being the inferior wife to Laila, she hated the Turkish way of life. She hated the fact that her husband was an apostate, and she would chant her own Orthodox rituals by the hour in the hopes of angering him.

Small wonder that he had willingly ridden away to war, had fought with a desperate and careless courage which earned the plaudits even of the Janissaries. He had no happiness to go home to. But his obsession with her prevented him disowning her.

Then she had become pregnant. Her obvious pleasure at the birth of her son John had pleased him, and taught him the way to continue. He had kept her pregnant for the next ten years. Some had died in childbirth, some of fever in infancy. But five had survived; three strong boys and two sturdy girls.

Inevitably she had found fresh causes for hatred, in his deter-mination to teach his children English and Latin, but not Greek, and in his even greater determination that they should be brought up in the Roman rather than the Orthodox faith. But by the time these new hatreds surfaced, they no longer mattered: he had gradually ceased lusting after her. If his Christian upbringing deterred him from taking a second wife after Laila's untimely death — dearest Laila who had been his constant solace amidst the discord in his home — he had instead added concubines to his household, and ultimately left his wife in peace.

By then too he had almost forgotten his mother — who had not long survived the fall of Constantinople — and even his father. But he had named his sons dutifully: the eldest after his father, the second after his grandfather, and the youngest after the brother whose execution by the Byzantines had turned Anthony into the man he was.

But they were Ottomans now. If he did not kneel to Mecca, still less did he consider attending Gennadius's masses, or even those held in the Genoese church according to the Communion of Rome. He had become the renegade of all renegades. He had become the servant of the anti-Christ.

His children, born of a Greek woman and an English father, looked and acted like Franks. But he did not expect the Hawkwoods to survive another generation, so had married them all to Turks — a fresh cause of misery to Anna. He did not even suppose that any of his grandchildren would be taught English in their turn.

Even more than his father, he had sold his soul to the devil, glorying in the devil's progress and in his own success as his henchman.

He had no other happiness.

But even devils die. And now his sins were coming home to roost. If he could not love his wife, and had long since lost any contact with his daughters after he had sent them into harems, still he had loved his sons. Now he must lead one to war, and perhaps destroy the other two in the process.

Only two months ago the world had lain at his feet.

"Yes, Anna," he said. "I will lead an army against my sons. And, if they have betrayed the Sultanate, I will deliver their heads to Bayazid. If they have not, then I will deliver them to you, safe and sound."

He left her weeping.

8

THE ENVOY

"There are so many," growled Prince Djem, pulling at his scanty beard.

With his officers he stood on a high bluff overlooking the road that followed the winding valley of the Gok. It was early in the morning, and the sun, just risen above the mountains in the east, played over the valley like a huge lamp. That tree-lined road, winding to and fro alongside the river between the steeply rising cliffs to each side, came from Sakarya in the north. Along it, for as far as the eye could see, were stretched the various detachments of the Ottoman army.

Standing next to the prince, William Hawkwood could make out the advance guard of sipahis, the conglomerate mass of the bashi-bazouks, the green tunics of the Anatolian infantry and, at the rear, the red and blue uniforms of the Janissaries, their white horsehair plumes nodding as they marched.

Back there, too, would be the pashas commanding the Sultan's men. Back there would be his father.

And behind the Janissaries and the pashas, escorted by another squadron of sipahis, rumbled the guns. These were vastly different from the bombards his grandfather had built for the Conqueror to knock down the walls of Constantinople. These were guns developed by his father, and were for use in the field. They were smaller, more manoeuvrable, and fired a lighter missile. And well handled, they could destroy an opposing army.

William Hawkwood knew they would be well handled.

Behind the guns, and again guarded by sipahis, came the baggage-wagons, the commissariat, the remounts, and the servants and harems of the pashas; a Turkish army on the march was a moving nation.

More than once in his life William had stood and cheered as the Ottoman horde had marched away to war, to bring death and destruction wherever it was pointed. He had never suspected that one day he would watch that horde marching on him, equally determined to deal in death and destruction.

"I would estimate that army to number sixty thousand men," Omar Pasha remarked.

William looked over his shoulder, to some miles behind their vantage point, where, also in the valley of the Gok but as yet out of sight of the approaching force, Djem's army was encamped close to the village of Yeni-Shehr, from which it presently drew its sustenance.

It was quite an imposing force, for in the desperate summer months since Djem had thrown down the gauntlet to his brother he and his officers had recruited far and wide. There were some forty thousand men encamped down there. Only the pashas knew how uncertain was their fighting quality. There was one regiment of Janissaries, who had agreed to follow the prince because of the lavish donation he had given every man — but would they truly stand and fight against their brothers-in-arms?

There were several squadrons of sipahis who, William thought, could be relied on; they had been raised by the prince himself. But, these apart, the rest of the rebel army consisted of hastily-raised foot soldiers. Djem called them his Anatolians, but they were more like bashi-bazouks, good for irregular warfare, but not certain to hold their place in a line of battle.

And there were the four cannon which he commanded. Cannon were the decisive arm in modern warfare; the side which possessed artillery, with resources large enough to permit the building and transportation of these iron monsters, was invariably victorious.

But here each side possessed artillery. And the Sultan's was commanded by perhaps the greatest gunner in the world.

"We must meet them on the road," the prince decided.

William looked at Omar.

"With respect, O Padishah," the general addressed him, for Djem had insisted upon all the trappings of the sultanate, "it would be better to retire upon Brusa, and make them attack us there."

Brusa was only twenty miles to their rear.

"Brusa is not a fortress," Djem pointed out.

"It can nonetheless be defended. Its natural position on the side of the mountain means that it cannot be surrounded, and can only

191

be assaulted up a steep slope. Also your men will be heartened, despite the numbers against them, by the knowledge that they are fighting beneath the tombs of your ancestors."

"Then there will be a siege," Djem grumbled. "How may we withstand a siege?"

"We would not have to for very long, Padishah." Omar pointed at the sky, which was darkening with cloud. Despite the sun, the breeze coming down the mountain was chill enough to have them all wrapped in their cloaks.

"October is late for campaigning," Omar said. "I see the hand of your brother in this; he is impatient. Had the decision been left to Hawk Pasha, that army would not have approached you before next spring. In this your brother has erred. Within a month the winter rains will have started, and then the winter frosts. Even Hawk Pasha will then have to raise the siege. He will be hoping that you attempt to meet him in the open field, so that he may settle the matter quickly. It would be best not to oblige him."

Djem glanced at William. "What is your opinion?"

"I agree with Omar Pasha, O Padishah."

"Ha! You would. You are afraid of facing your father in the field," he sneered. "But remember your brother. Remember your wife and children."

"I do remember them," William said quietly. "I will fight for you. I have said this. But it makes sense to fight where we have the greatest chance of success. Once you force my father to retreat, you will be able to claim a great victory. Men will flock to your standard from all Anatolia. Next year we may be able to meet your brother's army in the field on equal terms."

Djem stared at him, then down at the advancing horde again. His fingers twitched, and despite the chill wind he sweated. Like his brother, he was too unsure of himself to wish to prolong this trial of strength a moment longer than was necessary. He would, as William realised, stake everything on a gambler's throw.

"I say we fight now," he declared. "Do you suppose that rabble down there will stay with me a moment longer if I order a retreat? If I withdrew to Brusa, my brother will label me a coward."

And would he not be right? William wondered.

Djem pointed to where the road debouched from a defile through the hills, about two miles east of the village. "We will advance and deploy beyond there. It is a strong position. Hawk

192

Pasha will only be able to come at us in small detachments. See to it."

He touched his horse with his heel and galloped off, followed by his officers.

"What do you think?" William asked Omar.

They stood their horses on the roadway about four hundred yards west of the pass. It actually was a well-chosen position, for the road dipped behind them into a shallow valley before rising again to Yeni-Shehr; and in addition it was well wooded, so their army as deployed was invisible from the pass itself.

Omar had divided his bashi-bazouks into two contingents, and placed one on each side of the road in the valley, sheltering behind the pines. Immediately at the lip of the valley the cannon were emplaced, but had been concealed as best possible by gathered brush. Behind them, in the dip, were the Janissaries. And behind the Janissaries were the sipahis, the *coup de grâce* to the opposing army should it begin to break.

There too was Prince Djem. He had pitched his black and gold tent where the ground rose again, but it was concealed from the pass itself by the wood, and, as he had brought with him from Brusa several of his concubines, he could be expected to remain there.

"We can do no better," the general said. "And it is possible that we may succeed. Our success depends upon your cannon and the swiftness of our manoeuvres, young Hawk. Remember, do not fire until at least a third of your father's army is through the pass. Then commence firing and maintain your rate as fast as you can. With fortune, the suddenness of our attack will scatter our opponents. At which time I will loose the bashis at them. Then, again with fortune, the enemy will flee in terror back to the pass. There they will encumber the rest of the army attempting to advance. There will be much confusion. If I can then attack with my Janissaries and sipahis, the day may well be ours.'

"With fortune," William said grimly.

Omar's smile was equally grim. "Without fortune, young Hawk, every one of our men is doomed."

He rode off to join the Janissaries, and William walked his horse back to the artillery battery and there dismounted. His men welcomed him warmly. He had selected and trained every one of them, and they would fight for him against their own fathers.

William knew the power of artillery, and this strategy of massing the guns instead of having them widely spread — as was the usual custom — had been invented by his own father. Anthony Hawkwood would also be intending to mass his guns, once he was through the pass. Therefore he must not be allowed through the pass.

But what a terrible prospect, to be planning the defeat of his own father! He had always held him in the highest respect, even if Anthony's grim figure had never encouraged love. And to do so for a man he loathed and despised!

If only it were possible to speak with Hawk Pasha for a moment, to explain his situation ... but would not Hawk Pasha realise the situation, since his other son had not returned? He could hardly suppose they had both turned traitor. But Hawk Pasha believed only in duty to his acknowledged lord. He would slay his own sons without compunction, were he to suspect them for a moment of treason.

William sighed as he walked up and down, settling his helmet more comfortably on his head, feeling the sun's rays heating the chain-mail breastplate beneath his cloak. The rainclouds had gathered around the mountains behind him. Every few seconds he gazed up at the hills, where a party of sipahis oversaw the approach of the Sultan's army. How slowly time seemed to pass. But as he and his men ate their midday meal, the quiet of the morning slowly dissipated into a distant rumbling, like the sound of a river in full spate. The Sultan's army was approaching.

Hooves drummed and Prince Djem galloped up to the artillery.

"Do you hear them?" he panted.

"I hear them," Anthony said.

"Are your guns loaded?"

"My guns are loaded, Padishah."

Djem shaded his eyes to stare up at the hills. "Why do not those rascals signal?"

"They will do so when the moment is right."

And, indeed, only a few minutes later there came a flash of light from the hillside.

"The enemy is entering the defile," Djem muttered.

"Will you withdraw, Padishah?" William inquired.

"No, I will stay here with you." He gazed at William, and actually flushed.

He still distrusts me, William thought. Does he not realise that by staying here he may place himself in my power?

If only he knew what orders Djem had left at Brusa regarding the disposal of the other Hawkwoods.

"There!" Djem pointed.

The first squadron of sipahis was emerging from the pass. They rode slowly, looking from left to right, blinking in the light of the sun, which was now settling into their eyes. They had no knowledge of where the rebel army was, but they knew they were in Djem's territory; and they had surely seen the flashes of light from the hillside. Thus they must expect to encounter their enemies at any moment.

"Kill them!" Djem shouted, in his excitement riding his horse up the slope on to the road, in full view of the sipahis. "Open fire."

William rode behind him. "With respect, that is but the advance guard. We do not want to reveal our position until more of the army is through."

The enemy sipahis had checked their advance at the sight of the two men, but they would hardly retire on that account.

"We must get out of sight, Padishah," William said urgently.

The sipahis gave a shout and began to canter forward, anxious to take them prisoner and obtain information about the rebel dispositions. Seizling Djem's bridle, William led the horse down the incline, but Djem wrenched himself free.

"Traitor!" he screamed. "I knew you would not fire upon your father's people." His face contorted. "Seize him!" he shrieked. "Seize him!"

The gunners stared at him in dismay as Djem called out to his escort.

"Seize him!" he bellowed.

William hesitated, uncertain what to do. To ride for the approaching sipahis was to die; their arrows would bring him down long before he could identify himself.

It would also mean the death of his wife and brother, and his young sons. But were they not now doomed in any event?

Roughly his arms were seized and he was dragged from the saddle.

"Pinion him," Djem commanded. "I will execute him and his father together, when we have gained the day. You ..." he gestured to the horrified gunners. "Open fire! Open fire, I say!"

The enemy sipahis had drawn rein again as the group of horsemen disappeared down the slope, suspecting that they were about
to ride into an ambush. Behind them more of the cavalry were
emerging from the pass, but there was no sign of the bashi-
bazouks as yet. Now the cannon roared. The stone balls careered
through the air, and several of the advance guard were struck
down. The rest promptly wheeled and galloped back to the pass.

"Load!" Djem screamed. "Load, and fire again."

Still being dragged to the rear by four of Djem's guards, William
looked back to see Omar spurring his horse towards the battery to
discover why his instructions had been so catastrophically disobeyed. He had no idea what was then discussed between prince
and general, but Djem was apparently not to be gainsaid, for the
cannon fired another futile round as soon as they were reloaded
about half an hour later. This time the shots bounced off empty
rock. The sipahis had withdrawn.

"He is delighted," Omar said gloomily. "He thinks we have
gained a victory."

"What is the Sultan's army doing?" William asked.

His arms had been unbound to enable him to eat supper, and
Omar had come to share it with him. It was dark now as they sat
together, surrounded by the Janissaries, some quarter a mile
behind the cannon and half a mile from the pass itself.

The darkness had not brought silence, however. All around
them was the din of men and horses, shutting out the shrilling of
cicadas and the cries of owls, the distant howling of a wolf. And
over all played the night wind, cold as it soughed through the pines.

"They are encamped beyond the pass," Omar told him. "Our
chance of gaining a quick victory is gone. Now we can only hope
that your father will attempt to force the pass tomorrow."

"Will he?"

"Hawk Pasha is not so stupid," Omar said.

"What is his alternative?"

"To flank-march us to the north; he will hardly try to march
south round the Ulu Dag. But to flank us will take several days,
even weeks. Perhaps it will all work out for the best. If your father
attempts to flank us, we will have to fall back on Brusa in any
event, which is our best chance. But you, young Hawk, I fear for
you."

196

"The prince lost his head."

"And will do so again. I have spoken with him, told him you were but obeying my command in not opening fire so soon. He seemd to understand, but he has given no order for your release."

"Then I must be patient." William rested his hand on the general's arm. "I thank you for your friendship, Omar Pasha."

Omar grinned. "I must speak with the prince again. Should we have to fight a battle tomorrow, I wish you in command of the guns. Not him."

William slept fitfully and awoke with a start at the blast of a trumpet and a great commotion.

Father is attacking through the pass, he thought, throwing off the blanket and reaching for his sword — before remembering that he was still under arrest.

But his guards were also on their feet, and staring towards the hills. It was just dawn, and the valley was shrouded in mist. And there was no alarm from the pass, where Omar had stationed a squadron of sipahis to give him early warning of any move by the loyal army. Instead men were pointing at the hills, which were now emerging from the mist, and from which the sipahis were signalling with desperate haste.

William frowned and looked from left to right. There was no sign of the enemy, no way they could have debouched on to the plain ... yet something catastrophic had clearly happened.

The whole rebel army was astir now, and someone was pointing to the north and shouting in a loud voice.

William looked to the hills which guarded the north side of the valley, at the same moment as the sun rose out of the hills before him. As he stared, narrowing his eyes in a frown, he discerned men toiling up a narrow mountain track, many men, straining and tugging at ropes — and behind them was a cannon.

His stomach heaved, even as his heart swelled with pride. They had thought Hawk Pasha possessed only two alternatives: either attempt to force the pass, or flank the rebel position. But Anthony Hawkwood was not called the greatest soldier in the empire for nothing. He had devised a third way of dislodging the rebels.

William did not care to think how many men his father must have employed, how many must have fallen to their deaths in the darkness, or slipped and savagely injured themselves. He had made his men labour all night, and now the gun was almost ready to be emplaced, on a vantage point where it could command the entire rebel position.

Djem came galloping down from his tent, screaming orders. Omar had already despatched a regiment of the Anatolians to climb the steep slope and seize the gun. But, anticipating that, Hawk Pasha had not merely sent his gunners into the hills. As the Anatolians began to scramble up the slope towards the cannon, the ledge above them was suddenly lined with blue-coated Janissaries armed with handguns. These rippled smoke into the morning air to mingle with the mist, and the rebel infantry fell back, leaving several of their number scattered on the slopes.

The rest hurried back to the main force, and would not return, no matter how much Omar rode amongst them, ordering and then imploring. The rebel army rippled with apprehension and could only watch as the sun rose further and the gun was slowly emplaced.

William saw Djem come galloping back from the cannon. Without even halting, he made off down the road towards Yeni-Shehr and then, no doubt, Brusa. His attendants hastily packed up their tents and made to follow. The women screamed in dismay as they were roughly bundled on to their horses in a kaleidoscope of haiks and yashmaks.

The guards looked in puzzlement at William, and he looked back. They had been given no orders as to his disposal. But now the whole rebel army was disintegrating: the bashi-bazouks were moving towards the road, as were the Anatolians. Only the artillery and the Janissaries held their positions.

And then the cannon exploded. The shot screamed out of the hillside, and with deadly accuracy struck the ground immediately behind the rebel guns. Earth and stone and human bodies flew into the air. There was no chance of responding; the rebel artillery could not be sufficiently elevated to return fire.

A great moan rose from the rebel ranks, and the bashi-bazouks took to their heels.

Omar galloped up. "Release that man!" he commanded, and William's bonds were struck from his arms.

"The day is lost," Omar said. "As our noble master has fled the field, we must retreat as best we can, and hope that we will yet muster sufficient men to defend Brusa."

"I must save the guns, if I can," William said.

"You must save yourself and your family," Omar told him. "I will bring the guns. You must ride for Brusa. Take my own escort; they are men you can trust." He grinned. "If you can overtake our master, so much the better. Then we will have to make what terms we can with your father."

William leapt into the saddle, and Omar's guard of sipahis fell in behind him.

He led them at a gallop along the road to Brusa. Behind him he heard the sounds of the cannon on the hill exploding again, and looking over his shoulder saw the loyalist army debouching through the now undefended pass. He knew that he was playing no heroic part this day, but there were too many differing hopes and fears tugging at his heartstrings. Though he could do nothing to help his comrades; he could at least hope to save his brother and his family ... and present the wretched Djem bound to his father.

They galloped into Yeni-Shehr, now a huge throng of confused and frightened people, the fleeing soldiers mingling with excited villagers. Here the harem was also bogged down, and the women cried out to William to save them. But he had no time for that. He and the sipahis had to fight their way through the mob, shouting and cursing, but at last they found themselves on the road beyond. This was also full of fleeing bashi-bazouks, but now the horsemen could urge their mounts into a gallop.

It wanted some twenty miles to Brusa, and the horses were blown long before the city was reached. It was necessary to slow down to a walk, and even dismount for a while and lead the animals on foot. William understood he might need their strength at his destination, for Djem had a long start.

Now the mountain loomed above them, and at last they saw the domes of the mauseoleums where the Ottoman chieftains were laid to rest, rising above the white walls of the houses.

A handful of Janissaries, members of Djem's personal guard, barred the road.

"Has the Padishah been this way?" William asked.

"He has commanded that no one is to follow, young Hawk," the captain said.

"Stand aside," William said, "or we will charge you."

Gazing at the sipahis, the Janissaries were outnumbered and confused; and like everyone else they were aware that their prince had fled the battlefield.

"We yield to your superior force," their captain said at last.

William raised his arm, and led his men through. They urged their still weary mounts up the steeply sloping streets, past gaping women and children and old men.

"What has happened?" they cried.

"We have been defeated," the sipahis told them. "Stay inside your homes."

The prince's palace was in a state of utter confusion. Guards and clerks milled about in the courtyard, chattering excitedly at each other; eunuchs hurried here and there; from the harem came shouts and shrieks.

William dismounted and ran into the midst of the excited people. "Where is Prince Djem?" he demanded.

"He was here but an hour ago, young Hawk," they told him. "He paused but a moment to gather some money and then left again. But he will soon be back."

"What makes you think that?" William asked.

"He has taken none of his women, nor any attendants, save only two. How may a prince go far without women and attendants?"

He could be making for the south coast and a ship, William knew, hoping to escape the vengeance of his brother. He did not suppose the prince would ultimately succeed; the Ottoman tentacles could reach into almost every city of the world.

But he himself had more important business, and he ran across the courtyard, through the reception halls with their brightly painted mosaic tiles, and up the stairs to the harem.

Here the Kislar Agha barred his way. "Are you mad, young Hawk?"

"Stand aside," William said, "or die."

The huge black man hesitated, gazing at the drawn scimitar, the determination in the face of the Englishman, the big shoulders, his red hair tumbling from beneath the helmet. Then he stood aside.

William burst through the curtained doorway, hesitated, surrounded by strange sounds and stranger odours. He had never entered a harem in his life, as he did not own one himself. A chorus of screams broke out, and he realised that although he stood in an apparently empty corridor, he was being watched through the trellis-work walls to either side.

Not all the screams arose out of fear. Physically, William Hawkwood was a far more attractive man than Prince Djem.

Seeing a door in the trellis a few feet down the corridor, he ran for it, hurling it open and facing the women inside. All were scantily clad, but not all hastened to cover themselves.

William seized one of the older women by the shoulder, brandishing his scimitar. "I am Hawkwood," he said. "My wife and sons were brought here. Take me to them."

The woman merely goggled at him.

"Quickly," he said. "Or I will cut your throat."

She gasped. "The eunuchs took them, my lord. The eunuchs came ..."

William released her and ran back into the corridor. Several eunuchs had gathered there, but they scattered when he approached them. He caught hold of one of them, however, striking him on the back of the head with the hilt of his sword, so that the frightened Negro fell to his knees.

"The wife of young Hawk," he snarled. "Take me to her."

The eunuch shivered with fear. "It was the orders of the Sultan, young Hawk ..."

"Take me," William commanded again, though he felt a black cloud descending on his brain.

The eunuch scrambled to his feet and led William along a corridor towards a locked door.

"Break it down," William commanded.

The eunuch summoned some of his fellows and they broke open the lock. As the door swung wide, William stepped inside, nostrils flaring at the odours within, and his heart sagging at the sight before him.

There were four in the cell: Sereta, the two young boys, and Henry Hawkwood. Each had their hands tied behind their backs, and the bowstrung coiled round each neck was deeply embedded in the flesh. All of them were dead.

"Rebels!" said the Sultan, surveying the men grouped before him. Bound and ragged, many of them were frost-bitten after their forced march through the mountains to the Bosphorus in the dead of winter. "Traitors. Scum of the earth."

The captives were all of higher rank. Hawk Pasha had executed a few of the common soldiers, primarily as a warning to the others.

The officers he had then brought to the vengeance of the Sultan. Now he stood beside them like a huge avenging angel. Yet he had a life to save, if he could.

The prisoners retained little of their finery. They had been dragged behind the tails of the sipahis' horses, all the way from Brusa, mile after weary mile, day after endless day. Their armour had been torn away, their tunics were in rags, their faces and knees and legs bled from where they had fallen, their shoulders and backs from where they had been beaten.

They had paid for the price of failure.

And they knew that nothing they had suffered so far could be as terrible as the manner in which they were about to suffer now.

In some, their eyes were dull, as if their brains had collapsed under the strain of their ordeal; they were the lucky ones. Others even tried to muster the courage to gaze at the Sultan. But most stood with bowed heads, staring at the floor. All were trembling.

Omar Pasha's head was high, and he stared straight ahead. William Hawkwood stared at his father.

"Impale them," Bayazid said. "Impale them all" — he gestured towards them — "as common criminals."

There was a gasp from the pashas standing around the throne. Impalement at all was as horrible an execution as man had been able to devise, — but at least when inflicted upon enemies taken in battle it left the victim some little last dignity. Common criminals were denied even that. Instead of being made to sit upon sharp wooden poles, the condemned man was held over a high curved saddle, then a stake, perhaps four feet long, was driven into his anus with strokes of wooden mallet until it re-emerged from his body somewhere above the waist. The execution was performed in a public square, and it was at the discretion of the executioner how quickly or slowly he swung his mallet.

Even Omar's face blenched. From the moment Hawk Pasha had refused to discuss terms, he had known that he was bound to die, and painfully. But this ...

"You have no right, O Padishah," he protested. "I am a pasha, and I was taken with arms in my hands."

"You are a rebel against the law of the Sultan," Bayazid spat at him. "Keep him to the last," he ordered. "And be sure the strokes are slow."

The guards began to march the prisoners away.

Only one remained: William Hawkwood, bound and filthy like the others but separated from them by Hawk Pasha's orders.

"I can make no exceptions, Hawk Pasha," Bayazid said, "great as have been your services to me. All rebellion must be stamped out."

"With respect, Padishah," Anthony said, "my son was no rebel. He was constrained to take the field with the traitor because his wife and family were in custody. As was my other son. He refused to fire the cannon upon your army, Padishah, and was arrested for it. Djem did not murder him then because he wished us to die together after his hoped-for victory. When my son followed the fleeing traitor in an effort to capture him, he found his wife and brother and his sons all murdered. My son now hates the traitor more than any man on earth. It is a hatred I share."

Bayazid stroked his beard as he stared at his commander. Then he turned his gaze on William.

"You did not overtake my brother," he said. "That is a pity. As long as he lives, he will be as a knife embedded in my side. Your father claims that you hate your one-time friend. Is that true, young Hawk?"

"Padishah, my soul cries out for vengeance against him. Were he to appear now at your side I would strangle him with my bare hands."

"Well said," Bayazid acknowledged. "Very well then, young Hawk, I will give you that opportunity. I have received information that Djem, after taking ship from Smyrna to Egypt, has fled to Rhodes, to the protection of the Knights of St John. I have sent ambassadors to the Knights, warning them that he must be surrendered or I shall raise an armament against them such as no man has ever seen — an armament greater even than that commanded by my father. And this time I shall not raise the siege."

"The Knights will not surrender Prince Djem," Anthony said.

"This I know. But I also know that they will not give me cause for war. They will send my brother away. Who can say where they will send him? Back to Egypt? To Italy? France? The ends of the earth?" He threw out his arm, his finger pointing at William Hawkwood. "I make this your commission, young Hawk. Go, and fetch me back my brother. Or slay him with your own hands and bring me proof of it. Follow him down to hell if necessary, but bring me his living body or proof of his death."

"Gladly, O Padishah," William cried. What else did he have to live for now?

Bayazid smiled. "You have a year, from this day, to accomplish your mission. Remember that. A year from today. If you do not return with my brother, or my brother's head, within that time, then ..." his gaze swept to Anthony Hawkwood who, as always, had his son John at his shoulder. "Then your other brother will die."

There was a moment's silence, then a gasp from the viziers. Anthony Hawkwood stiffened with anger. He was the personal friend of the late Sultan, the greatest soldier in the empire. And his eldest son had ridden beside him in defeating the rebellion. Could he possibly be treated now as a slave by this cur who would not even accompany his army to battle?

Bayazid continued to smile. "Remember my words, young Hawk. Now go — and return with my brother's head."

"He is not a reincarnation of Mahomet, or even of the first Bayazid," Anthony Hawkwood observed, "yet is he our master. You must never forget that."

"I will not forget it, Father," William said.

He stood in the *selamlik*, the private chamber of his father's house. The palace of Hawk Pasha overlooked the Golden Horn itself, and the crowded shipping at anchor there. Vessels came from all over the world, for as long as their countries were at peace with the Sultan, and paid him tribute where it was due, all merchants were welcome in Constantinople. Venetians rubbed shoulders with Frenchmen, Italians with Germans, Ethiopians with Indians, in the market places of the city. There were also slant-eyed yellow men from the farthest reaches of Asia where, they claimed, there was an empire even greater than that of the Ottomans.

There were even, on occasion, Englishmen among the throng.

The wealth they brought in their search for the fine silks, the damascened swords, the soft linens, the magnificent horses, and, above all, the mouth-watering spices which found their way to Constantinople from the East, had made the empire the richest ever seen.

It was from this wealth that the Conqueror and his pashas had been able to build their palaces. William Hawkwood stood on a marble floor, beneath a marble roof, sustained by huge marble pillars carved after the Greek style known as Corinthian. The windows were shrouded by velvet drapes, and the arches to the inner courtyard of the house by floating, pink-dyed gauze. The house was filled with soft air and distant sound.

Not being a Muslim, Anthony Hawkwood even had pictures on his walls: a representation of the Virgin and Child, and an ikon with the same theme.

Only twenty years ago, the site where this palace now stood had been empty ground on the shores of the harbour.

William had spent too little time here to call it home. Now he must leave it again. For how long?

"Here is your passport," his father said, holding out the rolled document. "It describes you as Ambassador for the Porte. It will be honoured in all countries which trade with us, on pain of reprisal. Only in lands ruled by Castile and Aragon, or by the Emperor, will you be treated as an enemy. Avoid them."

"Yes, Father."

"As to your situation when you overtake the fleeing prince, that I cannot foresee. I must leave that to your own good sense and courage."

"Yes, Father."

"You will not fail. You are a Hawkwood. You must not fail. Not merely because of your brother John, but because your future is here. Remember my words, and come back safe to me."

"I will return."

"Return," Anthony Hawkwood said, gazing at him, "because you are my son." His voice was almost soft.

"I grieve for my brother Harry."

"So do I, boy. To die in battle is an honourable end. But to be strangled ... Avenge him."

"I will."

"I have decided, in view of your purpose, that it is best that you travel light. You will be accompanied by one servant only: Hussain. He will care for your every want. He can be trusted with your life — so do not sacrifice him unless you have to. For your other needs, here is a bag of gold coin. Use it well."

William took the bag; it was very heavy.

"Now say farewell to your mother," Anthony Hawkwood commanded.

William went into the women's quarter of the palace, and knelt before Anna's chair.

"I ask your blessing, Mother," he said.

"My blessing," Anne said contemptuously. "This business has already cost me a son. Now it will cost me another. Go! I doubt I will see you again."

William stood up, disappointed, yet there were tears in his mother's eyes. He kissed her hand.

Few Turks knew much of what lay beyond the Danube or the Black Sea. Men like Anthony Hawkwood had led embassies north of the great river, sea captains had taken their ships into the harbours of the Crimean peninsula; they were unanimous in their opinions that while here was a vast granary, fields of waving wheat for as far as the eye could see, it was a country with little to recommend it, entirely lacking in cities, populated by wild and uncultured people, and gripped for six months in every year by blood-chilling cold.

Anthony Hawkwood could remember England and the coasts of Spain and Italy. Especially he remembered Naples. He could speak of busy seaports and hot-blooded, passionate men and women. The Turks, the most hot-blooded people on earth, smiled at his reminiscences. But even Anthony Hawkwood knew only hearsay about the heart of Europe.

Those Turkish sea captains who traded with Venice spoke of the wealth and luxury of the great island republic. They spoke too of the land beyond, where mountains far higher than the Taurus rose straight to the sky. Around these mountains were lands even more fertile than the steppes of Russia, so they had been told, marked by large towns of incredible prosperity. They told tales themselves of huge fairs to which people came from miles around, of knights in plate armour, unveiled women in swirling skirts, rich merchants in fine brocades. It was a mouth-watering prospect to a bashi-bazouk who knew only of Constantinople, Adrianople, Brusa and the high Anatolian plateau.

And of all these towns, with their quaint names such as Munich and Strasbourg, Augsburg and Mainz, Milan and Florence, the greatest, they said, lay far to the west, and it was called Paris.

William Hawkwood had been taught that his grandfather, serving with Great Harry at Agincourt and after, had visited Paris with that King in his quest for the hand of the daughter of the Dauphin.

How strange, he thought, that sixty years later I should tred the same path, but with no romantic notions in my head.

He was ever conscious of haste, for his year of grace was well advanced, and Djem remained beyond his reach.

As Bayazid had predicted, the Knights of St John, while it was against their principles to surrender a fugitive, had not felt able to contemplate a fresh war with the Ottoman empire, or a fresh siege as damaging as the last. Djem had been hurried on his way as soon as Bayazid's envoys had delivered their ultimatum.

He had taken ship, in the first instance, for Venice — hoping to rouse those erstwhile rulers of the eastern Mediterranean once again to arms. William Hawkwood had followed him there.

Like the Knights, the Doge was not yet prepared to resume opposition to the Ottomans, and Djem had again been sent on his travels, this time to France. William had arrived in Venice a month behind him, somewhat apprehensively. But the Doge had extended the hand of welcome to a young man who travelled as the Sultan's ambassador, and had entertained him in the official palace.

Despite her recent defeats, Venice was yet a flourishing, febrile community. Arriving at the beginning of February, after a stormy voyage up the Adriatic Sea, William had found himself required to remain for the great carnival which marked the beginning of the Christian festival of Lent.

Although not a Muslim, William was hardly a regular Christian. He could remember in his extreme youth his mother attempting to teach him certain dogmas and litanies, but these had quickly been interrupted by his father, as being of the Greek instead of the Roman persuasion. Between these two widely differing interpretations of God's law, William and his brothers had fallen adrift, unable to make much of either. They had been taken into the Church in Galata to attend mass as very young boys; but once their military training had commenced, this was no longer regarded as necessary. They had, in fact, often enough knelt in prayer towards Mecca, simply because it was in youth's nature to fit in with the customs of one's comrades.

Living in a Muslim country they had, of course, been subject to the rigorous abstinence of Ramadan, the month when all true believers spend most of their daylight hours in prayer and fasting, and when it is decreed by the law that so long as a black thread can be distinguished from a grey one, no food may pass the lips. Thus William recognised that Lent was a similar festival, although not so strict.

What he could not understand were the two days of mayhem permitted before the official commencement of the fasting period.

"It is good for our people," the Doge explained, "to be allowed a brief period of licence." His wrinkled features broke into a cold smile. "It takes them most of the remainder of the year to recover."

For two days and nights, then, Venice was given over to every conceivable form of vice and merrymaking. William was astonished to discover that even grave counsellors, members of the Council of Ten, could cast aside their reservations and their morals and sally forth to drink themselves insensible, but not before they had bedded every available woman, married or single. And all the women of Venice seemed to be available during those two days and nights.

William looked upon it all with sombre eyes. He was not in a mood to enjoy himself; still less was he in the mood to hold a woman in his arms. He had never supposed he had really loved Sereta, and he had not been sure even of his love for his sons — under Sereta's guidance he knew they were innately different to himself — but they *had* been all he possessed in the world, and to see them so cruelly strangled was as if a knife had been driven through his heart.

There were other reasons for his refusal to participate in the general licence. Venice was the first non-Turkish city he had ever visited, and he was shocked by it. The buildings had a beauty not even Constantinople could equal, the canals were romantic ... but the place itself was filthy, and so were the people. When, at his lodgings, he requested a bath, he was stared at in amazement. Nobody bathed in February.

"Truly are we among strangers, young Hawk," Hussain remarked.

A man in his early forties, tall for a Turk, and pot-bellied, Hussain was an ideal companion. For all his ungainliness, he knew the use of weapons. But he, too, was shocked by Western habits. Particularly they were shocked by the way the women of the city walked the streets unveiled and unescorted, their shoulders and breasts often exposed, talking and flirting with whoever they chose. Though the Greek women in Constantinople were not veiled, they dressed and behaved with the utmost circumspection when in public, for fear of a whipping.

"This is an ungodly place," Hussain observed.

Having done his best to persuade this Turkish envoy to enjoy himself, the Doge then abandoned him to his own devices, regarding him as a dull fellow. Afterwards, William was happy to shake the dust of Venice from his feet.

From there it was necessary to proceed overland, and with caution. As Anthony Hawkwood had warned him, most of the Christian states had been forced to accept the expanding empire of the Conqueror as a reality against which they could achieve little or nothing. The great exception was the house of Habsburg, who ruled the Holy Roman Empire, and the united dynasty of Castile and Aragon, whose mastery — with their ally the republic of Genoa, equally hostile to the Porte — of the western Mediterranean made travel by sea to France an impossibility for any Ottoman ambassador.

William had thus had to follow Djem's route through Switzerland and Savoy, and into France — even the fleeing prince had known better than to entrust himself to the mercy of Ferdinand and Isabella of Spain.

This was another severe journey, especially as winter was not yet over. William Hawkwood spent days at a time snowed in at remote hill villages. There he was welcome enough, thanks to his satchel of gold coin, but he constantly chafed at the thought that each day's delay brought close the end of his year of grace.

The country through which he passed, when conditions permitted, was breathtakingly beautiful. Snow-covered mountains reared against the sky, and lakes of unimaginable depth filled the valleys between with a perfect blue.

The people were unlike any he had known before. No more hygienic or modest in their habits than the Venetians, they were far more hardy, as they clearly had to be, for they prospered despite the appalling weather. They lived together in a loose confederation of districts called cantons, ruled by an even looser federal law which allowed each canton to operate very much as it pleased.

Such a lax situation suggested to William they would be an easy prey to any covetous neighbour, and indeed the Swiss cantons had until quite recently been subject to Austrian rule. But the development of their young manhood into the most famous infantry in Christian Europe, allied with the difficulties of mounting a major campaign in their mountainous country, had allowed them to gain their freedom, and this they were determined to preserve.

William could not but wonder how the redoubtable Swiss pikemen would fare against the Janissaries.

From Switzerland, travelling as fast as the snowbound passes would permit, Willian and Hussain made their way into Savoy, and from there into France at the beginning of spring, informed as always that Prince Djem was but a few weeks ahead of them.

Here was a green and pleasant land basking in sunshine, and enjoying an early growth of trees, fruit and vegetables. William knew of course that France had been a battleground for more than a hundred years, while successive English kings had sought to make good their claims to the French throne. But most of the fighting that had repeatedly devastated the country had occurred in the south and west; so the east had been relatively untroubled. Thus his journey was a pleasant one, until he neared the environs of Paris itself. There he found numerous once-substantial buildings reduced to ruin.

But Paris drew him on like a magnet. The city surprised and disappointed him. Certainly it possessed a splendid cathedral surrounded by substantial buildings, and it looked easily defensible, since it clung to a small island in the centre of the river Seine. But the small extent of the island meant that its buildings were crowded together on either side of the meanest and narrowest of streets, and even if the growing population had overflowed beyond the bridges, to surround the city with a variety of suburbs, these were no less dank and gloomy.

The filth was indescribable for a man who had lived for the past several years in Brusa, the cleanest and sweetest of cities. It was far worse even than in Venice. Also it rained constantly, and then the streets became open sewers, down which flowed waste matter of every description and every possible odour. Beggars abounded; so did dogs, some of them vicious. Well, there were sufficient beggars in Constantinople, too, but there they were treated with respect, since the giving of alms was a sacred Muslim duty.

Dogs, however, were regarded as lower than snakes in Turkey, and were regularly kicked out of the way. In Paris one apparently kicked the beggars out of the road, and endeavoured not to antagonise the savage dogs.

The inhabitants varied from the very poor to those who at least appeared to be very rich. If William had been amazed at the immodesty of dress and behaviour in Venice, here the upper classes — most particularly when gathered together in the ante-chamber of the royal palace, in a vast crowd of both sexes chatting animatedly together — were throwbacks to a past only vaguely remembered from his father's reminiscences. There were men in hose so tight their every particular was revealed — their tunics scarcely reached their thighs — and wearing a variety of hats decorated with plumes or hanging tassels. And women in richly embroidered velvet gowns which they constantly swept from the floor to reveal their no-less-attractive underskirts, and with neck-lines only barely more decent than those of Venice — due more to the cooler climate, William suspected, than to any modesty.

The rich women were surrounded by a great variety of veils; some, called butterflies, extended to each side of the head on wire frames, while others descended down the back almost to the floor, so that every time one of these replendent ladies moved, anyone standing close by was liable to become entangled in yards of white gauze.

These exquisite creatures, male and female, looked askance at the tall, red-haired man with the sun-burned features, wearing the loose trousers and tunic, the flowing caps and the spiked steel helmet of a Turk. William had even retained a turban to add to his distinction. But he understood that it was the custom in France to uncover when presented to the sovereign, so this he proceeded to do when he was called forward.

The crowd rustled in curious hostility, but William was concentrating only on the King as he was escorted forward.

"I am informed you speak no French," said a quiet voice in Latin.

William straightened and found himself gazing at a somewhat short and distinctly fat man. He knew that Louis XI was by no means aged — he was fifty-eight — but he looked much older and his movements were slow and painful, as if he suffered badly from rheumatism.

William had also learned that this unprepossessing man with

211

the poor complexion, the big nose and the protruding lips was known throughout Europe as the Universal Spider because of the way he dabbled in every court and every plot.

"That is my misfortune, Your Grace," he replied.

"But no doubt you speak English," the King suggested.

William was taken aback; he did not know what to say.

The King smiled. "Fear not, Monsieur Hawkwood. Your King Edward and I are friends nowadays. Our people have fought each other long enough."

"With respect, Your Grace, the King of England is not my ruler," William said.

Louis stared at him. "So I have heard," he said. "You claim allegiance to a mightier power."

William bowed.

Louis waved his hand. "Send this herd away," he told his chamberlain. "And you, boy, sit here at my feet and tell me of these Ottomans."

Hardly daring to believe his good fortune, William hastened to obey, and for the next hour answered every question Louis cared to put to him — about Bayazid, his armies, his people, and his intentions.

"All you have told me concurs with other information I have gathered," Louis mused. "I find it interesting that your master and I should rule at opposite ends of the continent; it seems to me that we have therefore much in common."

For the life of him William could think of nothing that Bayazid could possibly have in common with this man, but he sensed immediately what was in the Frenchman's mind.

"I have no doubt my master feels the same way, Your Highness," he said.

"Why, that is good. I suspect that recent events have worked well for my people and myself, surrounded as we are by enemies. Monsieur Hawkwood, would I be right in assuming that your Sultan regards Ferdinand the Catholic as his most bitter enemy?"

"You would surely be right, Your Grace."

"Well, I can tell you that the Spanish are mine also. So there is a bond, is there not? And I will also tell you that they are a far greater danger to me than to Constantinople, as their power lies to my south and now, through connections of marriage, to my east and north. It is an intolerable situation."

"I have no doubt my master will well understand your difficulties," William said, cautiously.

"Why, this is splendid," Louis declared. "Then I would have you explain them to him immediately. An understanding between our peoples, an exchange of ambassadors ... perhaps an alliance, would profoundly affect us for the better. Will you undertake this task for me, Monsieur Hawkwood?"

"Willingly, Your Grace. But I fear that for me to return to Constantinople without him whom I seek would anger the Sultan, and negate all our efforts."

Louis gave him a long stare. "As I was unaware of your coming, Monsieur Hawkwood, and as Prince Djem gave me to understand that he is the lawful heir to the throne of Mahomet, I offered him asylum. You would not have me break my word?"

William endeavoured to prevent any trace of his desperation appearing in his face. "Then, Your Grace, I fear your hopes of an understanding with my master will be stillborn."

Louis considered him again. "There is no mountain so high or so precipitous that it cannot be climbed," he said at last. "I can see, Monsieur Hawkwood, that we are both men of sense, and of business too. You will readily understand that pre-eminent in my mind is the good and safety of my kingdom and my people. A king, alas, must allow this overwhelming responsibility to override even his honour at times. But you will equally understand that for me to break my word to Prince Djem, and release him into your custody, without any assurance from your Sultan that he would be interested in my proposals — that would be an act of folly."

William bowed his head, but his spirits were soaring. He had no doubt now that Louis had discovered a solution to their problem.

"It is my opinion, therefore, that you should communicate with your master, setting out my proposals. I shall await his reply with pleasure. In the meantime, Prince Djem will remain in Paris as my guest. I give you my word that he will not be permitted to leave, and that should your master's response be favourable, it will place me in a position entirely to reassess my considerations *vis-à-vis* the prince."

William did some hasty calculation. It would take him not less than three months to regain the Porte ... Three months would be the end of August, and time was running out. While to return empty-handed, with only the French King's uncertain promises to

213

give to Bayazid, would be to invite disaster."

"Alas, Your Grace ..."

Louis smiled. "You fear for your family — and even for yourself."

"Your Grace?"

"I am informed of what takes place throughout Europe, Monsieur Hawkwood. Word has reached me that the great Hawk Pasha, commander of the Sultan's armies, is confined to his house and property until the return of yourself with Prince Djem."

William sighed, realising that dissembling to this man was a waste of time. "Alas, Your Grace, that is the absolute truth."

"Thus your evident anxiety. No doubt the Sultan has cause to view life with suspicion," Louis said. "I can tell you that the experiences of my own youth and my first years on the throne have not inspired me with any great faith in my fellow man. But I have a solution for that also, if you are willing to take a certain chance. You will not return to Constantinople, young Hawkwood. You will write a letter, which will accompany one of mine, setting out my proposals and your endorsement of them. We will be able to convey to the Sultan that should he wreak vengeance upon your family, it will be to no purpose, because in that case I may easily release Prince Djem to do his utmost, perhaps with you at his side. Whereas a little temperance and understanding will not only win him the prize he seeks, but will also enable him to retain the services of his greatest pasha. Surely only an imbecile would refuse such a fair and advantageous offer?"

"Your Grace, if I could believe that ..."

"You fear that your Sultan is an imbecile?" Louis gave a brief laugh. "Well, if he is, think on this: you at least will be safe here. I would have you talk to me again, Monsieur Hawkwood. I find your company refreshing. Besides, you may be able to teach my marshals something of artillery."

The letters were written, sealed by the King, and despatched by special envoy. After that there was nothing to do but wait, and pray. William realised that he would hardly receive a reply before the new year. If ever.

He also understood that he, no less than Djem, was the King's prisoner. Louis might consider an alliance with the Ottoman empire a useful counterpoise to Habsburg power but, separated by over a thousand miles from Constantinople, he had no reason to fear a quarrel with Bayazid.

There was nothing William could do about his situation. He was allowed to overlook Djem walking in one of the palace cloisters, closely attended by guards, to reassure himself that the prince was alive and well, but he was not allowed to approach or speak with him. He toyed with the idea of leaping down from the wall on which he stood and despatching the murderer of his family before being himself cut down by the guards. But that he *would* be cut down by those guards immediately afterwards was certain. Nor did he see how committing suicide would help his cause; it would be a very simple matter for Louis to conceal the fact of Djem's death from the outside world, and he would continue to conduct his negotiations while informing Bayazid that his ambassador had met an unfortunate accident.

If Bayazid was bent upon destroying the Hawkwoods, he would do so anyway. Thus the entire future of the family turned on whether or not, as Louis had said, the Sultan was a sensible man or an imbecile who would destroy his best general out of spite. And William was in the unhappy position of being unable to affect the situation either way. Thus he realised he might as well throw off his grief and his apprehensions, and sample life as much as was possible under the circumstances.

This was not difficult to do, for he enjoyed the favour of the King — though he realised this was like the infatuation of a child with a new toy. Not that Louis was a child: he was the most astute as well as the most ruthless man William had ever encountered. Louis' attention to detail was remarkable, and unbelievable in a monarch. He delved into the remotest aspect of his kingdom and the lives of his people, accumulating knowledge about them which was carefully recorded and kept in case of need; he boasted that he could arraign any one of his nobles for treason whenever he chose, even if the rash word or deed was an echo from twenty years in the past.

He was also incredibly parsimonious, and this too William found remarkable in a monarch, used as he was to the profligate habits of the sultans. But Louis would never send fifty archers to carry out a commission where forty-nine might suffice — he would save the pay of the extra man.

This did not mean that he disliked splendour and spectacle. Indeed he encouraged it, so long as the cost was borne by his courtiers. The men and women who thronged his court wore the finest silks and satins, as William had early observed; and the balls and pageants were of a splendour he found breathtaking.

For sport there was mainly the hunt, in which the entire court, ladies as well, would take horse and charge into the woods which lay to the north of the city. There were no lions or wolves to be discovered here, but deer — and sufficient wild boar to add to the spice. Dressed in newly purchased tight hose and tunic, and with a feather in his cap, William charged along with them.

But Louis was also a rapidly ageing man. He was aware that he was in the grip of a creeping malady which left him with only a short lifespan to enjoy. Already he could no longer ride to the hunt, even if he liked watching the sport, and often rode out with the cavalcade in a jolting, uncomfortable carriage.

His principal pleasure, however, was in surrounding himself with youth and strength and, where possible, beauty. During the ups and downs of his tortuous life — much spent in open rebellion against his father — he had either betrayed or been betrayed by almost every noble in the kingdom. Though, in the course of time, he had brought them all to heel, he knew just how many of them secretly hated and feared him, and this left him eternally suspicious of them.

His council was composed not of nobles, but of merchants and lawyers of Paris, men he knew he could trust, since their prosperity depended entirely on him.

Thus someone like William Hawkwood, tall, strong, and boldly handsome, an alien from another world and thus entirely dependent upon the King's favour, could have been designed by Providence to be a favourite. And William soon became aware that he was very much a favourite. Where Louis would never spend a sou upon clothes for himself, and indeed was the meanest-dressed person at court, his tailors bedecked his youthful visitor in the height of fashion — and at great expense to the King. William was given the finest horses to ride, the finest swords to handle, encouraged to dance with the finest ladies in the land ... once he had been taught the necessary steps, and sufficient French to carry on a flirtation.

This was heady stuff. William had never touched a woman in his life save for Sereta, for in the Muslim world a man dealt only with his wives and concubines. In Paris he was expected to hold the hand of his dancing partner, to smile into her eyes, to look, if he dared, down her décolletage — she would have been offended did he not — and even, on occasion, to hold her in his arms as they wheeled through a routine. And she was always either the wife of another man, or an unclaimed virgin.

He was popular with the ladies, especially as his French improved. He was distinctly unpopular with the men, at least the courtiers. Here was an upstart heathen Turk, for so they considered him, arriving in their midst and immediately becoming the King's boon companion. William soon realised that only the King's favour stood between him and a challenge, and much was made of the refusal of the King to allow him to enter the lists: tourneys where knights in full armour charged at each other behind couched lances.

The King's reason was obvious: William had no knowledge of such combats, and for a foreign ambassador to be hurt or perhaps killed on being unhorsed would be a sorry affair. William regretted that he was not allowed to chance his arm; he had no doubt he was a better horseman than any French knight, and would very soon master the art of wearing armour. Yet the idea of fighting in such weight and heat — the knights had to be hoisted from the ground on to their saddles by a crane, and if they were dismounted they could only lie on their backs like stranded whales, quite unable to move — was ludicrous, and a waste of time. There was no armour ever made would protect against a cannon ball.

This last was the ostensible reason for the King's friendship. William was shown what cannon the French army possessed, invited to lecture the gunners, and to recommend improvements. This he was quite prepared to do; like Louis, he regarded the possibility of a French army ever opposing an Ottoman in the field to be utterly remote. Equally, he was prepared to accept the King's claim that warfare between England and France was ended. Besides, the French cannon were greatly inferior to those his father commanded. Thus he readily instructed the gunners in tactics and manoeuvres, especially with regard to massing their pieces, for like all other European artillerists the French custom was to place one gun in front of each infantry brigade or tercio, rather than concentrating the fire at a given place, as Anthony Hawkwood had learned during the siege of Constantinople.

Needless to say, William's obvious expertise and the delight

217

King Louis revealed in his prowess endeared him even less to the French nobility, who did not approve of cannon anyway. Their antagonism was now headed by the King's eldest daughter, Anne of Beaujeu. Anne was one of the very few women at the French court who had not taken a liking to the man from the East, and she made that very plain. She could never of course succeed to the throne, because of the Salic Law, but it was disturbing to see how she influenced the Dauphin, Charles. Here was a sickly and slightly deformed young man of twelve years, of low intelligence and very easily swayed. He would most certainly be the next King of France, however, and his enmity was not to be taken lightly.

The royal family's disgust with the situation was increased when the King, feeling more ill than ever with the onset of winter, and growing bored with the life at court, retired to his country home of Plessis-les-Tours in the rolling green countryside of Touraine ... and took his favourite with him. But so long as the King lived, these were more remote fears than the anticipation of news from Constantinople. When Christmas arrived with no word, William was in despair: he had now been at the French court six months.

"Patience, my boy," King Louis said. "Patience. It is the greatest of virtues. News will come eventually. But if not ... why, here will be your home. Were you to make the decision in any event, I would be much pleased."

"Your Grace is too kind," William muttered somewhat apprehensively.

"You fear the future," Louis said. "Suppose I were to make it secure for you?"

"Sire?" William had no idea what he meant.

Louis merely smiled then, but a week later revealed his plan.

Although absent from Paris, the King was far from absent from his post as ruler of France. Despite the appalling weather, where often the snow lay several feet thick on the roads, relays of horsemen constantly arrived at the château, bringing all the information the King required. His principal ministers, also, were required to leave their shops and offices and journey down to see him with great regularity. Often they were accompanied by their families, as it was necessary for them to spend several days, or even weeks, if the weather was unusually severe, before they could return to their homes.

Their comings and goings were so continuous that their different faces were hardly noticeable. But on this day Louis drew William to a window overlooking the courtyard, and there showed him a group of men and women dismounting from their horses, their cheeks pink from the cold and their cloaks bespattered with the snow which was falling lightly.

"That is Jacques Ferrand and his family," Louis explained.

William had of course met Ferrand, who was a member of the King's Council. He was not aware that the merchant had any family, however; the wives and daughters of the middle classes were not received at court.

"Ferrand is, I should guess, the wealthiest man in my kingdom," Louis continued. "Perhaps even more so than myself."

William frowned.

"Now study the fourth figure from the right," Louis suggested.

William's frown deepened. The fourth figure from the right was extremely small, and suggested hardly more than a child.

"Aimée is twelve years old," Louis agreed. "But watch."

The party approached the steps leading up to the guest apartments. In doing so they came under the overhanging eaves, and threw back their hoods as they gained shelter. William had no eyes for either Ferrand or his wife, or the two smaller girls; he gazed at the one called Aimée, at a head of the most perfect pale gold hair, so pale indeed as to be almost white, at a complexion no less flawless, and features sculpted into a chiselled beauty, heart-shaped face, small retroussé nose, wide-set eyes, generous mouth, and pointed chin, such as he had never seen before.

"Is it not remarkable how to the wealthiest man in the kingdom is also given the most beautiful daughter in the kingdom?" Louis observed. "Aimée is Ferrand's senior heiress. To her beauty will be added untold wealth. The possessor of that need fear no man. It would of course be necessary for her husband to live in France." He glanced at a thunderstruck William. "But think on this, William: should your master be agreeable to my proposals, and Prince Djem be returned to Constantinople to receive his punishment, your family will be safe. But your wife and sons are dead. Is there really any reason for you to return to that heathen land, when honour and prosperity indicate that you should remain here?" He paused to let his words sink in, then said, "I have already spoken with old Jacques, and he is agreeable to my proposal." He gave a cynical smile. "Especially since I have offered to ennoble him. Now, come, would you care to meet your future bride?"

I should refuse, William thought. Because I am a heathen, and a man of strange customs and stranger configurations. Will this charming child not faint at the sight of such an alien? Will she not vow suicide rather than submit her body to the hands of a Turk?

But the glittering prospect was irresistible. He accompanied the King into the guest apartments and was there presented to Madame Ferrand, and then to the girl.

She gazed at him from sombre blue eyes, yet smiled as he kissed her hand.

"Papa has spoken to me of you, *monsieur*," she said.

In what respect? he wanted to ask.

"I am honoured to make your acquaintance, *mademoiselle*," he said.

Aimée Ferrand gave him a little curtsy. "The honour is mine, *monsieur*."

She and her sisters were removed by their mother, and William now faced Ferrand.

"Aimée is very young," Ferrand commented.

"Agreed," said the King, who stood between them. "But not too young to be betrothed. Is she at puberty?"

"Yes, sire, but still young. I would fear for her health, in childbirth."

"Of course. The betrothal will last for two years. The marriage will take place on Aimée's fourteenth birthday. Is that satisfactory to you, *monsieur*?"

Ferrand bowed.

"And to you, young Hawkwood?"

I am overwhelmed, William thought. And I should be suspicious and aware. This man is binding me to him for at least two years. But the picture of the girl — and her wealth — floated in front of him ...

William bowed.

Then it was truly just a matter of being patient, of waiting for Aimée to grow up and, even more important, of waiting for news from Constantinople.

He was allowed to visit the Ferrand mansion in Paris once a

month, when he would sit and sip wine with Madame Ferrand and Aimée, and play games with her two young sisters, and talk about this and that.

Aimée was a remarkably well educated girl. She could speak Latin fluently, and was well acquainted with the politics and the economics of western Europe. She had a lively mind as well as a happy one, and sought ever to broaden her horizons. Her immediate wish was to have him speak of Constantinople and the world of the East, but this he preferred to do only in the most general terms. For, as winter softened into spring, and spring reached into summer, and he had now been absent from his family for eighteen months, he had to assume them already dead and himself an utter outcast — save for this girl and the King. And if the one was his gaoler, he had absolutely no idea about the other's feelings.

Save in one respect. She looked at him, at his hose and his codpiece, with a frank interest which was perhaps indecent in a young girl but suggested an earthiness that promised the utmost delights. To imagine sharing with such beauty the pleasure he had shared with Sereta was to drive himself half mad with desire. But was he deluding himself? Did she not perhaps look at every man like that? Aimée always seemed pleased to receive him, but at no time did she ever indicate that she felt more for him than the respect due to the man she had been told would be her husband.

How could she feel otherwise, he asked himself, since she was but twelve years old.

His loneliness grew.

Until, one day, the messenger arrived. He had been forced to wait long in Constantinople for Bayazid's decision, and had been further delayed on his journey, but now he was here. And the news he brought was all that William could desire.

The Sultan was pleased to open negotiations for an alliance with the King of France, one of the conditions being the return of his brother. More, the Sultan was pleased to congratulate his ambassador, young Hawk, for having carried out his duties so effectively. Now the Sultan only waited to hear the King's concrete proposals, in order to substantiate his own thoughts.

These negotiations, William thought, could take several years. Years in which he would be married to Aimée, and enjoy the life of the French court. As for spending the rest of his life in France ... the rest of his life seemed a very long time.

221

Years in which the burden of worry would be lifted from his mind. For the messenger also brought a letter from Anthony Hawkwood, assuring William that they were all well, and greatly relieved at the news from France. Anthony had been restored to his military command, and John to his.

William decided he must be the happiest man in the world.

The King was also delighted with the news. Perhaps too much so, because only a month after the return of his messenger, he died on 30 August 1483 in his bed at Plessis.

9

THE CARDINAL

William had been in Paris, on a visit to the Ferrands, when the King died. He had spent the afternoon with the family except for Jacques, who was attending to his business, and had already returned to his lodgings when a messenger came hurrying for him, summoning him back to the Ferrand house.

He returned at once, to find the ladies in a state of great agitation as they listened to the news Jacques had brought them.

"It must mean a great change," he said gloomily. "The Lady of Beaujeu will hardly wish to perpetuate her father's men, and she has a most hearty dislike for me. I pray to God that I will be permitted to merely abandon politics and go about my business in peace."

"What of me?" William asked.

"I should think you will be perfectly safe. You are an accredited ambassador of a foreign power, and negotiations for an alliance between our two countries are under way."

"Should I call on the Lady?"

"I would wait a while," Ferrand said. "By French law, King Charles is of an age to govern, although he is only thirteen. As to whether he will wish to assert his prerogatives, or will be allowed to do so ... In any event, my young friend, I suggest that you practise some more patience, and wait until the Court is ready to do business again."

"And Aimée?"

"You are betrothed. She will be waiting for you." Ferrand smiled as he spoke, but it was an uneasy smile and William's heart gave a sudden lurch. It was impossible to suppose he had fallen in love with a girl barely half his age, with whom he had never spent a moment alone. Yet over the past six months he had grown very fond of her, had come almost to feel they were married already, with all the pleasure of it still to come. Young as she was, she had revealed to him a very lively mind gifted with both wit and imagination, while her already transcendent beauty seemed to grow with every day. And those inquiring eyes promised so much . . .

Or was it the thought of the wealth attached to her name?

But now he was suddenly conscious that it had all been part of a bargain; and the progenitor of that bargain, the man who would have raised Jacques Ferrand to the nobility, lived no more. Where was the value in a heathen ambassador now?

However unhappy he was about his new situation, there was nothing William could do save follow the merchant's advice. And for the next few months very little business was done by the French court, as the King was solemnly laid to rest and the entire country went into mourning.

This was terminated early in order that Christmas might be celebrated; William got the impression that the court was heartily glad to be rid of the Universal Spider, and had only been going through the rituals of mourning for appearance's sake. Christmas meant very little to William — he had never celebrated it in his youth — so he remained in his lodgings during the festivities. But he spent his time chafing, and immediately put forward his name for an audience with the new King. It was another several weeks before this was granted.

Equally disturbing was his inability to see Aimée. She had apparently come down with some kind of distemper, and had been forbidden by her doctor to receive even her betrothed. Greatly alarmed, William then tried to see Ferrand but was informed that the merchant had been called away on business.

The whole thing made him uneasy, and he was more uneasy still when finally he was ushered into the new King's presence and found the boy, sitting hunched and sullen on his throne, with his sister and her husband standing one to each side.

William bowed and offered his congratulations upon the accession. The boy merely stared at him, without replying.

"We are cognisant of your reasons for being here, Monsieur Hawkwood," the Lady of Beaujeu announced. "I must inform you that your passports await you with His Majesty's secretary."

William frowned at her. "Passports, Your Highness?"

"It is our assumption that you will now wish to return whence you came," the Lady told him. "We no longer have any desire to detain you here. No doubt you will inform your master of this decision."

William attempted to suppress the waves of panic crashing in his mind. "But there is a negotiation at present being conducted between the court of France and that of my sovereign. Surely it is my duty to remain here in Paris until this is brought to a successful conclusion?"

"His Majesty has summoned you here today, Monsieur Hawkwood, to inform you that these negotiations are terminated as of now. It cannot be the policy of a Christian monarch to form an alliance with a heathen. This decision you must communicate to your master."

William felt physically sick. "The Prince Djem ..." he stammered.

"The Prince Djem is no longer here. He has been sent to asylum elsewhere."

"Elsewhere, Your Highness?"

"The prince is now in Rome, where he is a guest of His Holiness the Pope."

William gasped. All without a word being said to him! That a Turkish prince should be offered asylum by Pope Sixtus VI seemed impossible to accept. Clearly Djem had been sold, in the coldest of blood, to the highest bidder — to one of the men most concerned to bring damnation to the Ottomans.

He managed a smile. "Then, Your Highness, as the welfare of Prince Djem is my particular responsibility, I must take myself to Rome. But as to the matter of my betrothal to Mademoiselle Ferrand ..."

"That also is terminated." The Lady of Beaujeu stared at him coldly. "It is equally against the principles of His Majesty to permit the marriage of one of his subjects to the servant of a heathen." She paused to let the words sink in. "You have fourteen days to find yourself beyond the boundaries of this kingdom, Monsieur Hawkwood. On pain of outlawry."

Totally stunned, William returned to his lodgings. That magnificent world which Louis XI had suggested might be his had now been crumpled up like a piece of paper; it had no more substance. Perhaps it had never had done. Obviously Aimée's supposed illness had been a ruse of the crown.

And he himself was helpless. Now he could only forget her and her money, and flee the country as rapidly as possible, his very life and those of his family forfeit.

There was but one saving grace: he had been ordered to communicate the termination of negotiations to his master personally. Thus if he did not do so immediately, it could be some considerable time before Bayazid learned of the true situation.

Unless the Pope immediately sought to make capital out of the possession of Prince Djem.

William needed to act with the greatest speed. Hastily he penned a letter to the Sultan, informing him that the situation remained unchanged despite the death of Louis, but that there would be inevitable delays in concluding the treaty, due to the accession of a new king. The letter was despatched at once, then William and Hussain rode off to the south-east as swiftly as they could.

It took some considerable time to reach Rome, for it was again winter, and necessary to retrace their steps through Savoy and Switzerland and Venice to avoid entering Habsburg or Genoese territory. Once again, however, William was assisted on his way by the Venetians, and since Venetian territory abutted the Papal States, he could assume his journey would be all but over by the spring of 1484.

This was far from being the case. The Doge was concerned at the modesty of his entourage, which was limited to Hussain, so hasty had been their departure from Paris.

"The roads are dangerous," Foscari pointed out, anxious that no harm should befall such a delicate mission within Venetian territories.

At last William accepted an escort of six lancers, since the Doge was determined to prove to Bayazid that he was a reliable ally. He also changed back into his Turkish cuirass and helmet, with his trusty bow and quiver as well as scimitar, and his men carried their lances at rest.

Their journey took them by ship to Ravenna, prior to making the long trek across the Appenines and into the valley of the Tiber.

Ravenna was reminiscent of Venice herself, and owed its erstwhile greatness to being situated among lagoons and marshes which in antiquity had made it difficult to assault. But unlike

Venice, its greatness was long past. The marshes were silting up, and the city was in utter decay.

From there they took the coast road to Rimini, the city held by the infamous Sigismondo Malatesta, who was reputed to have killed off two wives in succession to make way for the beautiful Isotta degli Atti. For this he had been placed under a papal interdict and forced into submission, but his illegitimate son Roberto, having slaughtered Sigismondo's legitimate heirs, had then become reconciled with the Pope.

All of this suggested that Italian politics were even more blood-stained than Turkish — or at least among the Malatesta. An ancestor, Gianciotto the Lame, had executed both his wife Francesca and her lover, his own brother Paolo, on discovering them *in flagrante delicto*.

After Rimini, their way lay south-west to Urbino, now enjoying a burst of splendour under the rule of the Montefeltro family; and thence to Assisi, basking in the glory of its local St Francis, recently canonised. In each of these places the passage of the Turkish envoy was an object of great curiosity and some alarm. But the presentation of his passports, from King of France and Doge of Venice, earned William and his men safe conduct.

Outside the towns, the hillsides and more lonely valleys were the haunts of some of the most desperate people William had ever encountered. He was told that they were relics of the dreadful plague known as the Black Death, which had ravaged Europe a hundred and fifty years before. William knew that it had reduced the population of England by a third, and the Greeks in Constantinople still shuddered at the thought of it.

Apparently in Italy it had waxed more virulent than anywhere else. Whole communities had been wiped out; others had been shut off from the outside world for many months. The unfortunate people had turned into human wolves: starving, angry and vicious. Their descendants had found no reason to return to an honest living of tilling the soil or manufacturing. Instead they prowled the forests, poorly armed yet dangerous through their numbers, their knowledge of the terrain and their stealth. Obviously eight well-armed men were less of an easy target than a caravan of fat priests, but even so the temptation proved too much for bandits on more than one occasion.

Once Hawkwood's camp fire was attacked by night, and the assailants driven off by a series of well-directed arrow volleys. On another occasion they found their path, through a narrow defile between steep cliffs, barred by some fifty ragged scoundrels, including women. Here was a chance for true Turkish horsemanship, in which the Venetians were happy to follow William's lead. As the eight charged the human wall in front of them, William and Hussain fired their arrows with deadly accuracy at the full gallop, then drawing their scimitars just before impact, the Venetian lances at their shoulders. The sheer impetuosity of their assault carried them through, but Hawkwood had to mourn the loss of one of his men — brought down by a swinging club and immediately torn to pieces by the hungry savages. They rode on in an increasingly sombre frame of mind.

Because of all these delays, it was mid-August before they reached Rome, to find the Eternal City in turmoil. The Pope was ill and not expected to survive.

William thanked and dismissed his Venetians, with a suitable donation for their services. Thanks to King Louis' generosity, he still possessed the larger part of his bag of gold. Then he sought lodgings for Hussain and himself — which was not difficult, even for heathens, so long as they were well supplied with gold. He then despatched another letter to Constantinople, again holding out promises. He was all too aware that he was working against time, and that his subterfuge would be revealed eventually, unless he could manage somehow to open negotiations with the Pope regarding Djem.

But he was allowed no admittance to the Vatican, despite presenting his credentials. For two weeks he laboured in vain, being met with polite but firm refusals by a certain Cardinal named Giuliano della Rovere, who seemed to act as the Pope's secretary. He even told William that His Holiness would have nothing to do with any Turk save at the end of a lance.

When William was bold enough to ask if the Pope was also dealing with Prince Djem at the end of a lance, the Cardinal merely stared at him and turned to leave the room.

Once again he all but despaired; and the riotous conditions obtaining in this capital of the Christian world seemed to mock his plight.

In Paris a man needed to carry a sword and have a faithful servant at his back, but the criminal faction had clung to the back

228

streets. Here in Rome there seemed even less respect for law than in the wild mountains. To go abroad without Hussain — and both of them heavily armed — was to risk being set upon by thugs at any hour of the day or night — the more so as he was obviously a foreigner.

The city was beautiful enough, with its myriad fountains and the ruins of the palaces and baths of the Caesars pushing their ancient stones up through tangled foliage which sprouted everywhere. By contrast Paris was crowded and mean and dirty, yet also vitally alive; while Rome presented an overwhelming aura of decay. Once-grand *palazzi* mouldered, the streets were unpaved and filthy, the surrounding countryside was crowded with half-starved beggars and bandits, and the streets of the city equally so. In the midst of which turmoil, the Roman nobility loved and laughed as if there was not a care in the world. While at the centre of all of it the Vatican still presumed to an external omnipotence of its own.

William had not yet determined how to breach that unassailable fortress, when the city was for the moment hushed by the news that the Pope was dead. But it reawakened into tumult the following week when the cardinals gathered to elect a new Pope.

Each reverent, scarlet-clad prince of the Church had to run the gauntlet of a seething mob yelling advice, threats and imprecations; and they only gained the sanctuary of the Vatican under the protection of the armed guards with which each was surrounded.

The mob then betook itself to the forecourt of St Peter's, where it screamed and yelled its approbation or revilement of the various candidates.

William moved among them, and on this occasion he left Hussain at home, deeming that the mob was for the moment more interested in politics than mayhem. With them he stared up at the Sacred College, and with them could not help but shout his satisfaction when a puff of white smoke issued from the chimney to inform all Rome that a new Pope had been chosen.

Almost immediately a crowd of cardinals appeared on the balcony high above the square, and announced to the anxious people that the new Pope was Cardinal Giovanni Battista Cibò, late Bishop of Savona, a Genoese who would take office under the name of Pope Innocent VIII.

This news was hailed with shrieks of execration by the mob,

and for moments it seemed there would be a riot. However the Papal guards, composed of those same redoubtable pikemen William had met in Switzerland, moved forward to send the crowd scattering down the side-streets.

William would have hurried with them, but he was suddenly checked by a tall and cadaverous figure wrapped in a cloak, who gripped him by the arm and drew him into an alleyway.

William's hand dropped to the hilt of his dagger.

"I mean you no harm," the stranger said. "Are you he called Hawkwood, from Constantinople?"

William frowned at him. "What is it to you?" he demanded, still clutching his dagger, and glancing to left and right lest the stranger had accomplices.

"If you are the man I seek, there is one who would speak with you, and it will be greatly to your advantage."

"Where is this man?"

"You will have to come with me."

William studied him. It was not beyond the bounds of possibility that Djem had sent an assassin after him. Yet was he forced to take the risk, for time was shorter than ever.

"The first sign of treachery, and you are a dead man," he growled.

The stranger smiled. "I obey my master, and my master has bid me bring you to him. There is your safe warrant, Signor Hawkwood."

William followed him round the side of the piazza, then down another side-street until they came to a postern gate set into a wall. This gate was locked, but his guide opened it with a key, and ushered him into an enclosed garden surrounded by high walls on three sides. On the fourth side was the *palazzo* itself; the place was thus utterly private.

Across this garden William followed, and through a doorway into the house. For all its decrepit exterior, as with most Roman houses, it was a place of some elegance within. And there was a figure seated in a chair.

"Your Eminence, this is the Turk, Hawkwood," the guide said.

William found himself gazing at a man of medium build, with heavy, stern features and a pronounced nose and chin. He was not very old, perhaps in his early fifties, and exuded an air of arrogance and command William had rarely confronted before. Then he realised that the man wore the red robes of a cardinal, yet a stranger cardinal could rarely have been seen, for leaning on the back of his chair was a singularly beautiful woman, whose long dark hair drooped on to his flat red hat; while at his feet sat two young children, a boy of about ten and a girl of perhaps five, both exquisitely lovely, and both leaning against him intimately.

The Cardinal extended his hand to be kissed.

William hesitated, glancing at his guide, who nodded. William kissed the ring.

"Signor Hawkwood." The voice was harsh. "I have heard much of you. But perhaps you have not heard much of me?"

William did not know what to reply to that.

The harsh features broke briefly into a smile. "I am Cardinal Rodrigo Borgia. The late Pope Calixtus was my uncle."

The Cardinal paused to let that sink in, but William had in fact never heard of Pope Calixtus.

"He summoned me to Rome while I was still a young man, and indeed raised me to my present eminence. He died some time ago, and no doubt is receiving his just reward in Heaven," the Cardinal said drily. "But until we, too, attain that state of grace, it is necessary to concern ourselves with the living. You are an ambassador from the Turkish Sultan?"

"I am, Your Eminence." Suddenly Hawkwood's spirits were lifting.

"And you are concerned with the whereabouts of Prince Djem."

"That is my appointed mission, Your Eminence: to return him to his family."

"So that he may be executed?"

William hesitated.

Again a brief smile crossed the Cardinal's face. "For rebellion against his rightful sovereign. That is indeed a crime worthy of death. I would have you know that Prince Djem is safe and well in the Vatican. He will remain there until I have decided what to do with him."

"You, sir?"

"Aye, me, boy. Me!" Suddenly the voice was strident. "It is my word that will rule here. Understand that and you may prosper."

His brows were close-knit, his eyes flashed fire. William was taken aback by the sudden change of personality.

"So tell me what your master will offer for possession of this

231

prince," the Cardinal continued in a lower tone.

"You have but to name your price, Your Eminence. An alliance with the Padishah ...?" he hesitated.

The Cardinal stared at him. "It would not be seemly for His Holiness to conclude an alliance with a Muslim. Rather he should preach a crusade against the fornicators and whoremongers who have stolen Constantinople from the Holy Church."

Once again William was surprised by the change of mood, the gleaming eyes, by the vulgarity of the language.

But he also knew that with any habitual bully subservience was a mistake.

"There have been crusades against them before, Your Eminence. There are fields in Serbia where the grass is still obscured by whitened bones — and still the Ottomans prosper."

Their eyes met, and suddenly the Cardinal was on his feet, glowering.

Anthony continued smoothly, "But my master has no need of further conquests, and he would live at peace with all the world. But make no mistake: he has the strength to oppose all the world and stamp it into the dust. Would it not be better to live at peace with such power?"

For several seconds longer the Cardinal glared at him, breathing heavily. Then, as suddenly as with all his moods, he sat down and smiled.

"You are a bold rascal, Signor Hawkwood, and we must talk again. Meanwhile you will write to your Sultan, and tell him you have had an audience with me. Tell him I may be prepared to deal with him, on behalf of His Holiness, if he so desires it. And perhaps we can agree upon a common point of view as regards Prince Djem." He extended his finger once more to be kissed.

William returned to his lodgings in a sorely puzzled frame of mind, but too relieved at the sudden upturn in his affairs to be concerned as to who actually controlled the Vatican, or with the morals of Cardinal Borgia.

He sat down and wrote to the Sultan immediately, this time setting forth everything that had happened, altering the dates to make it appear that all had transpired without his knowledge, and that his race from Paris to Rome had taken a much shorter period than in reality. He allowed himself to be bitterly vindictive against the machinations of the new French rulers, and advised Bayazid to have nothing more to do with them. He pointed out that any alliance with France would have advantages only for France, none for Turkey.

But the Pope was a different matter. As best he could, he suggested the great advantages to be gained were the Ottomans to gain the ear of His Holiness and come to an understanding with him, even if a formal alliance was out of the question. Certain that he had interpreted Cardinal Borgia's meaning correctly, he indicated that Djem was probably available for ransom, and he strongly recommended that a suitable amount be offered.

He could do no more, save send the letter off with Hussain himself. The Cardinal was helpful here, and provided an escort to Ravenna, whence Hussain could take a Venetian galley for Constantinople.

But the Cardinal was more helpful yet. No sooner had the letter been despatched than William found himself invited to dine with him — and was again utterly astounded.

The dinner took place in the same *palazzo* where they had first met and which he soon discovered belonged to the dark-haired woman, Vanozza Catanei. She was the mother of the two beautiful children and several more ... and was accepted by all as the Cardinal's mistress. Signora Catanei indeed presided over the banquet, at which several other ladies were present, all dressed in diaphanous gowns and revealing extreme décolletages; all drinking wine and exchanging bawdy stories with the men. Several of the latter were wearing clerical garb, albeit there were no other cardinals present.

The whole was presided over by Borgia himself, who smiled benignly on the gathering, and indulged with the best of them.

If William seemed to have fallen on his feet, it was an extremely uncertain footing which seemed to grow more treacherous as the weeks went by.

He at least discovered something of the intrigues and hostilities which bedevilled the Holy City and its rulers. Rodrigo Borgia, born a Spaniard, had been appointed Bishop of Valencia while still less than twenty years old, thanks to his all-powerful uncle. Then summoned to Rome, as Vice-Chancellor of the Church he was raised to greatness at a very youthful age by Pope Calixtus. In this capacity he had quickly amassed a great fortune, while astonishing even the Romans by the profligacy of his lifestyle. But he had been safe from criticism as long as his uncle reigned.

Borgia had, however, the sense to appreciate that Calixtus would not live for ever, and he had spent his money not only to enjoy himself but also to make himself secure. It was a simple task: he used his great wealth to buy cardinals, and soon had accumulated no fewer than twenty-four lords of the church who were bound to his person, or at least to his purse-strings. With such a considerable proportion of the Sacred College at his back, he could afford to ignore the criticisms of Calixtus' successors.

It early became apparent to William that Borgia's sights were set on the Papacy for himself, but actually getting the Fisherman's Ring on his finger was proving a long and difficult task. Only twenty-seven when his uncle had died in 1458, he had played the part of "kingmaker" to both Pius II — who, under his real name of Eneo Silvio Piccolomini had earned such a reputation as a skilful manipulator of foreign affairs on behalf of the Papacy that there really could be no other contender — and his successor Paul II, a nonentity named Pietro Barbo.

Barbo had died in 1471 and Borgia, then forty, had felt his moment was approaching. There was, however, another family which had the foresight to equip itself with a large block of captive votes in the Sacred College — the della Roveres. They had used this power, combined with a general revulsion at Borgia's blatant profligacy, to secure the Ring for one of their own. Francesco della Rovere had ascended the Papal throne as Sixtus IV, and it was his death which had coincided with William's arrival in Rome.

In these circumstances, it was surprising that the election had been effected so quickly, but Borgia had here revealed considerable statecraft. The ruling spirit behind the rival family was Cardinal Giuliano della Rovere, the same who had contemptuously turned William away from the Vatican (a man every bit as ambitious and forceful as Borgia himself — and destined to become famous as Pope Julius II). But in 1484, at just over forty, Giuliano della Rovere felt himself somewhat young to tilt for the supreme office. This did not mean that he was prepared to let the Papacy go to Borgia. Instead he sought out a suitable candidate among those cardinals in his pay: Giovanni Battista Cibò, who had duly taken the name of Innocent VIII.

Thus, it seemed, he had managed to exclude Borgia yet again, but he had made a grave mistake — as the Vice-Chancellor well knew. Cibò might have been in della Rovere's pay, but he was even more venal and corrupt than Borgia himself, and now he regarded the papacy as very much his oyster. To della Rovere's fury, he quickly began to show more regard for Borgia, a man who shared his tastes and cupidity, than for his erstwhile patron.

Soon Cibò was openly acknowledging both his mistress and his illegitimate children — the first pope ever to do so. In this he was but aping Borgia, as did his entertainments which never lacked half a dozen pretty women anxious to flirt with the Pontiff.

But, more than anything else, Innocent craved money. Thus it was that, by nipping in when della Rovere had wanted only to reject any kind of a deal with Constantinople, Borgia had scored a triumph. The Pope was in entire agreement with the Cardinal in judging that Djem was a man out of whom a great deal of profit could be made.

All depended upon Bayazid's reaction to these new circumstances.

For William Hawkwood it was again a matter of waiting. By the spring of 1485 he had been absent from Constantinople for three years, and the pain of his bereavement was beginning to fade. The memory of Aimée however remained as bright as ever — that triumph of beauty and wealth which had only narrowly escaped him, and was the more to be regretted for that. So much so that one night in his cups with Rodrigo Borgia, being unused to wine, he poured out to the Cardinal the story of his life and his misfortunes.

Borgia seemed to listen with sympathy. "My poor young friend," he said when William had finished. "How my heart bleeds for you. We shall have to see what can be done."

"I am afraid there is nothing that can be done, Your Eminence," William moaned. "She is a great heiress, and will by now have been betrothed to some French nobleman. Perhaps she is even married."

"There is always something that can be done," Borgia insisted. "You may leave that to me. We must at least endeavour to discover what has become of the girl ... But my heart bleeds even more to think of you living almost in chastity. Tell me about the harems, the seraglios, about the life those beautiful captive maidens enjoy."

235

William knew next to nothing about life in a harem, but he realised the Cardinal wanted to be entertained, so he garnished his account with every spicy anecdote he had ever picked up, true or false.

Borgia was delighted. "And have you yet sampled our Roman womanhood?" he inquired.

"I know nothing of them."

"And you a terrible Turk? This I propose to rectify at the very first instance. I am holding a gathering at my country house at Tivoli in a week's time. You must attend, and have no fear. I will send an escort for you and you will spend several days there. Tivoli is a delightful spot, and I will guarantee you delightful company."

Well, why not? William wondered. For three years he had been under the most extreme pressure — and for those three years he had lived like a monk. He would be a fool not to accept whatever choice morsel the Cardinal threw his way.

And by the following week he was in the right mood to enjoy himself, for Hussain had at last returned from Constantinople. All was well, for the Sultan seemed pleased at the doggedness with which William was following Djem around Europe.

"As to an understanding with His Holiness," wrote the Vizier, "the Padishah considers this to be in the best interests of us all. You are instructed to open negotiations on these lines, providing that it is understood that the surrender of Prince Djem into your custody is a prerequisite. The Padishah understands that some kind of ransom is appropriate, and authorises you to offer His Holiness the sum of five hundred thousand crowns upon delivery of the prince, or his body, into your keeping."

Here was a promise of instant success. So William took the road to Tivoli in the best of humours.

Set in the foothills of the Apennines, some twenty miles east of Rome, Tivoli was indeed a delightful spot. It had been chosen by wealthy Romans as an ideal place in which to take their leisure ever since the days of the Emperor Hadrian — the ruins of whose villa could still be visited by the curious.

Hadrian's villa was a place of cool ponds and running water, reminiscent of Brusa. But it paled into insignificance beside the villa of Rodrigo Borgia, some distance away, with its white marble floors and huge reception rooms hung with paintings by the Italian masters Botticelli and Perugino, and where the ceilings were decorated with frescos of naked nymphs and cupids frolicking, or worse.

Brought up in Muslim purity, William had been astonished in Venice and in Paris by such constant reproductions of the human form, but never had he seen such a display of indecency.

Greeted most warmly by Borgia, he was embraced on telling the Cardinal the good news from Constantinople. William was then ushered into guest apartments that were the last word in luxury. After the simple Turkish divans, he had been struck with wonder at the great tester beds with their cavernous soft mattresses, which were used by the Western aristocracy, but he had never come across anything quite so luxurious as here.

Anxious pageboys waited to attend him, and there was even a bevy of girls standing by his bath, simpering gracefully. These he dismissed, but his male attendants were embarrassing enough. When he had been bathed every day in Turkey, the eunuchs had kept their thoughts to themselves. But these boys constantly chattered about him in rapid Italian, so that he could gather only the gist of what they were saying. What he did hear made him feel distinctly uncomfortable.

Then he allowed them to dress him in the very finest silken hose and satin doublet, silver-hilted misericord at his belt, the drooping cap known as a chaperon on his head.

He thought he made a very handsome fellow, and so did Borgia and his guests, who applauded his entrance. Some of the men he had met before, but the women were entirely strange to him. Although expensively dressed, their flashing eyes and suggestive movements indicated that they were certainly not ladies.

Even more to his surprise, present at the dinner were the two lovely children he remembered from his first meeting with Borgia. The little girl offered him her hand to kiss, and said in a high voice, "You are a very handsome man, *signore.*"

"There," Borgia said. "Your future is assured. My dearest Lucrezia has given you her mark of approval."

The supper commenced about ten o'clock and lasted until two in the morning. Dish followed dish, and an enormous amount of wine was provided. Unused as he still was to drinking alcohol, Hawkwood's head soon began to spin, but it cleared soon enough when Borgia suddenly stood up and hurled a bag out into the middle of the floor beyond the dais. For the bag burst open and gold coins scattered in every direction.

The guests clapped their hands in anticipation, and several of the women stood up.

"No hands," the Cardinal declared. "And no clothes, either."

To William's amazement the female guests, without hesitation, began removing their clothing at a great rate. When they were entirely naked, they offered their wrists to the waiting servants, who tied each pair of hands behind the owner's shapely back with silken cords. The women then ran down into the main body of the hall, fell to their knees, and attempted to pick up coins with their teeth.

The entire room seemed to fill with surging buttocks, trembling breasts, flexing muscles in belly and thigh, flailing hair ... as well as occasional screams, for the women were not above biting one another to repel a rival for one particular coin.

William looked over at Borgia and found the Cardinal smiling, widely.

"They are all whores in any event."

As one of the girls succeeded in getting a coin between her teeth, she ran back to the table and spat the coin on to the cloth in front of William.

"I make you my keeper, *monsignore*," she said and darted back into the fray.

Borgia clapped his hands. "There! You have made another conquest. Margherita is a young woman of many parts."

William could not resist glancing at the little girl, to see her reactions to the obscenity in front of her. She was leaning forward, eyes glowing, her hands clapping together whenever some girl was successful.

Everyone else in the room was equally excited, each applauding his own particular favourite — for each girl had chosen a custodian for her wealth. His Margherita was indeed a great success, for she had deposited five gold coins in front of him before Borgia stood up and called a halt.

"Enough!" he shouted. "Let the jousting begin."

William had no idea what was to happen next, but now every man was on his feet, so he followed their example. Meanwhile servants moved amongst the girls, releasing their wrists. To his astonishment Margherita now ran back up towards him, her entire body a jiggle of pulsating flesh and streaming hair, leapt on to the table, scattering valuable plate and utensils, and before he could protest or defend himself she had mounted his shoulders, sitting with her legs in front and her ankles tightly crossed, her naked pubes pressed into the back of his neck.

"To the fray, *monsignore!*" she shouted. "To the fray!"

All the other men were by now mounted, saving only the Cardinal, who continued to laugh and clap his hands — as did his daughter. Having each secured a mount, the girls were urging them forward into the main hall, where a tremendous battle commenced, the object of each being to unseat every other girl.

As William caught hold of Margherita's thighs, the better to hold her in position, he came face to face with a red-faced priest while the two girls on their shoulders wrestled as if their lives depended on it. Being a head taller than the Italian, William found his own face repeatedly banging into the naked belly of the other's rider, which produced loud shrieks, whether of pleasure or pain he could not tell; until she gave a louder shriek still, and slipped backwards, losing her grip on her mount, and pulling him heavily to the floor.

"Next!" screamed Margherita in joy, flailing with sweat-moist arms and breasts, her thighs still tight around William's neck.

They engaged another — and then another. With William's size and Margherita's eagerness, none could stand before them long. Suddenly the bizarre tourney was over, and William alone stood upright in the midst of scattered, panting bodies. He felt more aroused than ever before in his life.

"The victor!" Borgia was on his feet. "To the victor the spoils!"

There was another bag of gold coin on the table, and this the Cardinal held out. Margherita hastily grabbed it and hugged it to her breasts. The girl still clinging to his shoulders, William was urged from the room.

"Your clothes!" he said, checking.

"I have no use for clothes, *monsignore,*" she laughed. "Not now, at least."

Still aflame, he carried her into his bedchamber and dismissed his servants. Then he laid her on the bed, where she immediately arranged herself with legs spread wide, her body aglow with sweat.

She was not strictly a beauty, but she was most attractive. And different for him, too. Like all Turkish women, Sereta had shaved her pubes. Now, as he looked at Margherita, William realised he had never supposed an untamed growth could be so luxuriant. He tore at his clothes, rolled down his hose and ran at her.

She gazed at him for a brief moment, then suddenly sat up with the most piercing shriek. "A Jew!" she screamed. "My God, a Jew!"

He reached for her, but she slipped under his arm and ran for the door.

"A Jew!" she screamed again. "I am beset by a Jew!"

Servants appeared in the corridor, but she burst through them into the dining hall, where Borgia and the other guests were still gathered.

"A Jew!" she shrieked. "Save me!"

William had set off in pursuit, but checked himself as he remembered his nudity. Instead he retreated into the bedroom in confusion. A minute later he gazed up at the Cardinal, who appeared at the door dragging Margherita by the wrist. The girl was attempting to hold back.

"What is all this?" Borgia demanded, staring at William. "By Our Lady ... *are* you a Jew? You gave me to understand you were a Christian."

"Of course I am not a Jew!" he almost howled.

"But you are circumcised!"

"It is the Turkish custom, Your Eminence."

"The devil! Well, then, you silly girl, there it is waiting for you. I'll wager you enjoy it." He pushed her towards the bed.

"You command me, my Lord Cardinal?" she asked.

"Indeed I do. Enjoy her, William. I am very glad that you are no Jew. Otherwise I would have had to burn you at the stake for contaminating a Christian woman."

William was sufficiently taken aback by this parting shot to lose a great deal of his ardour, but Margherita was now once again filled with energy and did not leave his bed until dawn, by which time they were both sated and exhausted.

She then departed with half the bag of gold, having spent perhaps the most profitable as well as the most enjoyable evening of her young life.

William would cheerfully have spent the remainder of the day in bed, for he now had a painful headache and an equally painful conscience. He could not imagine what his father would say were he to learn of the events of the previous night. But before long he was summoned to join the Cardinal, whom he found walking in his private garden, pausing now and then to sniff a bloom, and looking the most contented man in the world.

If cardinals have no consciences, why should I? William pondered.

"My dear boy," Borgia said. "How good to see you. I trust you did not sleep too soundly?"

"I do not think I slept at all, Your Eminence."

Borgia chuckled. "A lively girl, Margherita. But now is the time to put thoughts of the flesh from our minds. Come walk with me."

William fell into step beside the red-robed figure.

"We have not had an opportunity to discuss your master's response to my overtures," Borgia remarked.

"As I have told Your Eminence, the Padishah's response has been wholly favourable."

"Indeed, indeed," Borgia agreed. "I am most gratified. However ... there are problems."

William frowned and waited.

"As you are aware, I have a rival in my claims in the ear of His Holiness," Borgia said.

"Cardinal della Rovere."

"The same. Our new pontiff has made the mistake of mentioning our plans to della Rovere, who strongly opposes them. Indeed he is even attempting to persuade His Holiness to proclaim a crusade against the Turk. The idea offers a strong appeal, of course, since every crusader must contribute some of his wealth to the Holy See. It stands to reason, therefore, that della Rovere is totally against our releasing Prince Djem into your custody."

"Then we are entirely undone. My God, if a crusade is proclaimed against the Padishah ..."

"It would be meaningless, William. I give you my word on that. Tell your master so. That is the least of our problems. It is Djem in whom you are interested, and in whom I am interested on your behalf. I had assumed that the offer of five hundred thousand crowns would be sufficient to sway His Holiness. Alas, since he has been listening to the despicable fellow della Rovere, he has become full of pity and declares that it goes against his conscience to abandon a prince who approached him as a suppliant."

"I had the impression Prince Djem, far from being a suppliant, had been sold to the previous Pope by the French," William responded angrily, conceiving that once again all his card castles were crumbling to the ground.

"He is nonetheless a suppliant," Borgia pointed out. "I am afraid it will be necessary for us to pursue our plans with the utmost caution, remembering always that Innocent is an elderly fellow, and cannot be expected to live long. As I see the situation, he may indeed proclaim a crusade against the Turk — but I have promised that will amount to nought. He will also seek to retain Djem for his own ends, but at least you will be certain that the prince is securely incarcerated inside the Vatican. And I can give you my word that once I become Pope, Djem will be yours."

William sighed. "Then I must accept your advice, Your Eminence. I shall write to the Padishah as soon as I return to Rome, and put this new situation before him. I can only hope and pray that he will understand it."

"His chief desire is to prevent Djem ever returning to Turkey to dispute his inheritance. You and I are both working to make sure that he never does, so I cannot see that Bayazid will be aggrieved about this new situation."

"I am sure you are right, Your Eminence. But I think I had better go back to Rome and pen that letter immediately."

"Indeed. Before you go, however, there is the matter of the prince's income to be discussed."

William stared at him.

"Obviously the Sultan cannot expect the Vatican treasury to support his brother indefinitely," Borgia pointed out. "Without an adequate income, it may not be possible for us to properly guard the prince at all times. I am sure you will agree it would be a catastrophe were he ever to escape."

William goggled.

"I would estimate that the sum of one hundred thousand crowns would be acceptable, to be paid annually for as long as the prince is our guest."

"One hundred thousand crowns," William muttered in disbelief."

"It is surely a trifling sum for the Sultan. And there is also the matter of a gift."

"A gift?" William cried in alarm.

"The money is solely for the prince's upkeep," Borgia explained patiently. "It would assist me to gain the ear of His Holiness, were the Sultan to present His Holiness with a gift."

"A gift," William muttered. On top of one hundred thousand crowns a year?

"It would have to be something of unique value," Borgia went on.

William sighed as he was reminded of the saying that those who sup with the devil need a long spoon. "You will have to tell me what you have in mind."

"Well ..." Borgia appeared to consider. "I have heard it said that when the Conquerer took Jerusalem, he found there the Holy Lance, the spear thrust into the side of Our Lord at the crucifixion. Is that true?"

"Yes, Your Eminence," William gritted his teeth.

"Well, I think *that* would be a most appropriate gift. Your Sultan can hardly find anything of interest in a Christian relic. Such a gift would convince His Holiness that the Sultan truly wishes to be his friend. And once that also is received, I can give you my word there will be not the slightest risk of Djem ever escaping from the Vatican."

Once again William was obliged to write to Constantinople to explain the situation — and once again to wait in dread for a reply. Surely Bayazid's patience must be wearing thin?

But yet again a reassuring reply was received, agreeing to pay one hundred thousand crowns annually until Djem could be obtained, and sending the Holy Lance with every sentiment of esteem for the Pope.

Even more reassuring was a letter from Anthony Hawkwood, revealing that he and the Sultan were again on good terms. Turkey and Egypt were on the verge of war over long-standing disputes, and Bayazid needed his great pasha to command his army.

"We must accept the fact," Anthony wrote, "that our new master has little of Mahomet in his make-up. I think I am right in saying this will be the first time a Turkish army will take the field against a foreign foe without the Sultan at its head. But Bayazid prefers the company of musicians to soldiers, and enjoys the harem more than the divan. This is of course to our advantage, but is nonetheless disturbing in its implications for the future of our empire.

"As for yourself and your mission, the Sultan's indolence is even more to our advantage. I believe he does not actually wish Djem to be returned for execution. He is quite content that he should be imprisoned far away, forgotten by everyone and a nuisance to none."

Emboldened by this, and anxious to fight at his father's side in the coming war, William wrote back begging permission to return. He pointed out that both Cardinal Borgia and Pope Innocent, while undoubtedly two of the most treacherous men who ever lived, preferred money even to betrayal, and that as long as one hundred thousand crowns were regularly paid, they would most certainly keep Djem in custody.

But permission was refused. The Grand Vizier replied in turn, pointing out that Prince Djem remained William's responsibility; that it was his business to see the prince at regular intervals to ensure that he was indeed still in custody and the Papacy was not collecting money under false pretences.

Borgia readily agreed that once a month William be admitted into the Vatican and allowed to look down from a small window into the courtyard garden where Djem would take his daily constitutional.

William had once supposed that he hated the murderer of his wife and children more than any other human being on earth. But his adventures of the past few years had done much to soften the memory of those poor strangled bodies, and now he almost felt sorry for the unhappy prince condemned to a lifetime of imprisonment which could only end in death, whether from natural causes or the executioner's bowstring.

"But death is the ultimate fate of us all," Borgia would point out. "The important thing is to live while one can. Djem does not do too badly. He may pine and lose weight, but not for want of feeding. We have introduced him to the delights of the wine bottle, and he is now an accomplished toper. And once a week he is allowed the company of two whores for a whole night. After all, he is a Turk." He laughed.

It seemed that he had been exiled from Constantinople forever. Weeks became months, months became years, and the Eternal City pursued its merry way, with Pope Innocent enjoying the fruits of his power, and Giuliano della Rovere and Rodrigo Borgia each jockeying for position when the next election should be due.

Under della Rovere's influence, Innocent duly proclaimed a crusade against the Turks. This could have been a serious matter, as the news from the East indicated that the assault on Egypt had not proved the simple affair supposed by both Bayazid and Anthony Hawkwood. The Ottoman fleet and army were both totally tied up, and would remain so for some time yet.

But, as Borgia had predicted, the crusade turned out to be still-born. Perhaps the age of the crusades was long past, and men were more anxious to dabble in their own affairs than risk life and limb for a religious ideal.

So life went on. William had a pleasant house in Rome, procured for him by Borgia, where he and Hussain lived in great comfort, looked after by a bevy of servants. He had all the food and all the drink he could wish — and a regular income paid by the Sultan. He even had the use of Margherita whenever he wanted. The spritely courtesan satisfied all his wants, and he remained chary of the better-born Roman ladies who eyed him with interest.

And also he seemed to enjoy the devoted friendship of Rodrigo Borgia. William had come to understand his patron very well, and realised that the Cardinal did nothing in life without carefully calculating the possible benefits to himself. Therefore he must assume the friendship was as false as every other emotion Borgia pretended to. Nevertheless William Hawkwood was Bayazid's ambassador, and there could be no doubt that Borgia's great plans for his papacy, when that day arrived, included a close relationship with the Porte.

"I meant what I said when I explained that an alliance between the Vatican and the Porte would be impossible," he said, "for it would rend Christendom in two. But that is no reason why we should not have an understanding between us. We share a common enemy: the empire of the Habsburgs. It abuts your territories and hovers around mine like a greedy vampire bat, dreaming only of its own aggrandisement. If your master ever went to war against Vienna, it could prove greatly to both our advantages. I would have you put this to your master."

William did so willingly. Yet the more he saw of the Cardinal the more he distrusted the man. Borgia possessed every vice imaginable, and perhaps a few which were difficult to imagine. As an accepted visitor in the Cardinal's household, William spent many a tumultuous week at Tivoli. There he watched the Cardinal's five children growing up, and was amazed at the intimacy they shared with each other and with their father.

Arriving one day unexpectedly, he found the Cardinal and Vanozza romping in the garden with little Lucrezia. Neither female wore much in the way of clothing, and from their heated cheeks and embarrassed departures, he could not avoid the impression that the horseplay had been partly sexual. Well, true, Vanozza was Borgia's mistress. But Lucrezia was his own daughter! And she was only eight years old!

She remained a laughing, happy child, but the same could not be said of her favourite brother, Cesare. As he moved through his teens he became a most handsome boy, and most winning, too. He could be charm itself when he chose, but there were unguarded moments when William watched him regarding one or other of his father's guests with his eyes glittering like a snake's. No doubt he would grow up to be a true son of his father, William supposed.

William was present at supper one evening when one of a considerable party of guests was taken violently ill. Instantly all was confusion, the Cardinal shouting for servants and doctors, and giving a magnificent display of astounded grief that such misfortune should happen at his table.

Nothing could be done for the unhappy guest, who died after several hours of agony. As the party broke up in mutual melancholy, and the other guests found their way home, William lingered to offer his patron some condolences on the tragedy. He found Borgia standing in an antechamber to which the body had been removed, staring fixedly at the corpse. Its face was already beginning to blacken horribly, suggesting poison rather than death from natural causes.

The Cardinal was twisting his fingers together as if in mental anguish — playing with one particular ring of most unusual design. The expression of delight on his face was terrifying to behold, although it disappeared rapidly when he realised he had company.

"Poor Sacorro," he said. "His has been a most unhappy life. And he was one of the wealthiest men in Rome! Do you know he lost his wife but a few months ago, and before that his only son. In his despair he re-wrote his Will, leaving all his possessions to the Holy Church. And now he has gone to join his family. Ah, well, I have no doubt he will be much happier there than he ever was on earth."

"And his property is now yours," William observed.
"It belongs to the Church, William. To the Church."

Even if it was difficult to accept that this prospective pope had actually had a guest poisoned, his transparent delight in the death revealed him to be a devil. But a friendly devil at least as regarded those he considered could be of use to himself — and William ranked high there. He was also a devil with whom the world would soon to have to deal. For after a reign of some eight years, Pope Innocent VIII died. Whether he was helped on his way by the Cardinal, William had no means of knowing. Perhaps the Pope's overindulgence had helped him into his grave at the age of sixty.

Having long anticipated this event, both Cardinal Borgia and Cardinal della Rovere had marshalled their forces. It was supposed that the election of the new Pope would be a matter of lengthy discussion and debate, which would result in yet another nonentity controlled by one or other of the factions. To the amazement of all Rome, however, and the dismay of a good many, the election was settled in a single day, Rodrigo Borgia being chosen as Pope Alexander VI. He had clearly taken the precaution of bribing more cardinals than had his rival.

However sorry he might feel for Rome, and indeed for all Christendom, William was delighted. He had now been absent from his home for ten years. In that time his mother had died, no doubt cursing her fate to the end, and his father had victoriously concluded a long and bloody six years' war with Egypt. Now at last he would surely be able to complete his mission and return to Constantinople.

The new Pope was deeply immersed in the business of assuming all the prerogatives he had anticipated for so many years, and it was more than a week before he could spare the time to grant William Hawkwood an audience.

William had to admit that the new honour, the greatest to which any Christian could aspire, sat well upon Borgia's brow. His bearing was positively regal as he extended his finger for William to kiss, and then bade him sit nearby.

"You see a man who has at last achieved his just deserts," he said. "This will be the beginning of a new era — the greatest the Church has ever known. But I will not forget my friends, William. I have obtained for you the greatest gift in the world, as a mark of my approbation. Come."

He led a bemused William from the audience chamber and along a corridor to a window overlooking one of the many private courts of the Vatican.

My God, William thought: Djem has died.

"Look there, dear boy, and tell me what you see," the Pope invited.

Cautiously William stood against the window and looked down. And frowned in puzzlement. Instead of Djem's body he found himself looking at three nuns who walked in deep conversation. When they turned and faced the window, it was all he could do to prevent himself from crying out. The centre one of the three was Aimée Ferrand.

10

THE HAREM

Pope Alexander pulled William back from the window.

"I am bound to say she is a most entrancingly beautiful creature," he remarked.

Far more beautiful than he even remembered, William realised.

"I do not understand," he stammered.

"It is very simple — and very touching. Your Aimée loved you truly. At least, she certainly considered herself betrothed to you. Thus, when informed by her father that you were banished from France, and that she must now be betrothed to another, she utterly refused. Not even floggings, or weeks confined to her room, or an interview with the Lady of Beaujeu herself could change that staunch little mind. She was finally given the option of being married to a man of the Lady's choice or of taking the veil. Whichever way, others would take control of her fortune."

"Noble Aimée," William said. "But what is she doing here?"

"Having discovered her fate, it was a simple matter for me to discover her convent," the Pope explained. "It was not so simple to remove her from it. It caused me a great deal of bother."

"And you never confided in me?"

"I did not wish to raise your hopes, as I could not be sure of my influence with the French. However, that is behind us now. She has now been in Rome for some time, in a convent where the Mother Superior is beholden to me. She is unaware of your presence here, of course, or of her purpose in being here. Now that I have been elected to the Supreme Office, I have been able to bring her to the Vatican — and there she is." He peered at William. "You are sure you still love her? To enter the Church she had to renounce all her worldly goods, that is to say, her inheritance. From being one of the richest heiresses in France, she is now the poorest."

"Of course I still love her, Your Holiness," William protested —

249

and at that moment he had no doubt that he did. The sight of that utterly beautiful face ... "But of what significance is her presence here to me, since she has taken holy vows?"

"Tush," Alexander said. "That might have been a problem when I was a mere cardinal, but the Pope has the dispensatory power to let a nun abandon her vows."

"But will she?"

"Of course she will," the Pope declared. "I did not go to all this time and trouble to be gainsaid by the foolish whims of a young girl. No, she will be released from her vows, and I will marry the pair of you myself. Will that not be splendid? In return, you will continue to put my concrete proposals before your master."

"As I have already done, Holy Father."

Borgia smiled.

As always, William found himself carried along by the Pope's enthusiasm, and by his bland confidence that whatever he decreed should be done, must be done, and would be enjoyed by all concerned. But for all that he felt an unusual degree of nervousness when informed, a week later, that Alexander would receive him in the Vatican for supper, together with his prospective bride.

During that week he had refused to see Margherita, much to her annoyance. As a consequence of their lengthy relationship she had come to regard herself almost as a wife; notwithstanding that she insisted on being paid for her services, and that she continued to offer those services elsewhere when William did not require her. Thus he felt very much the chaste bridegroom as he entered the papal apartments to find Alexander waiting for him with his favourite son, Cesare, a tall, handsome youth of seventeen, now Bishop of Valencia. He could only be grateful that young Lucrezia was absent.

"I anticipate this evening with great pleasure," Alexander announced silkily, "because I am going to give great pleasure, and that always pleases me. Now, brace yourself. The Signorina Ferrand is still unaware of your presence, and the poor child is sufficiently confused already. Stand over there behind that curtain, and await my summons."

William obeyed anxiously, gazing through the folds at the inner doorway. A few moments later it opened to admit Aimée, alone.

She had discarded her nun's habit for the height of Roman fashion: a patterned gown with ermine trimming, which flowed to the floor; the skirt, raised in her left hand, exposed a dark green underskirt, which was also revealed at her bodice, for both gowns were cut in a square if modest décolletage. Her head was concealed beneath a black velvet hood which rested on her shoulders, and she wore jewelled lappets and a gold chain round her neck.

She was much taller than William remembered and her figure, perfectly delineated by the gown, had filled out elegantly. She was of course twenty-one years old — and the loveliest woman William had ever seen.

She looked around the room in some confusion, and then dropped to her knees to kiss the Pope's ring.

"My dear girl," Alexander spoke in Italian, a language she had obviously learned during her sojourn in a Roman convent. "My dear, dear girl."

He held her hands to raise her, and she curtsied to Cesare in turn.

Cesare's eyes devoured her.

"And now I have a great and welcome surprise for you," Alexander confided.

"Surprise?" Aimée breathed, also in Italian.

It was the first time in eight years that William had heard her speak, and he was taken aback by the way her voice had deepened and strengthened. "These last few days have been one long surprise, Holy Father. And I am so confused. Mother Superior has told me that I am absolved of my vows. How can that be? And now these clothes in which I have been instructed to dress ..."

Borgia took her hand and guided her to a waiting couch. "It is very simple really, my dear. You imagined that you had been called to the service of God. Well, so are we all. But we are each required to serve God in different ways. How would the world survive were all men priests, or even sailors or soldiers? Or if all women were nuns? That would not do. You were mistaken when you assumed God had called you to a life of chastity. It is my pleasure and duty to release you from that life."

Aimée stared at him and made an ineffectual tug at her hand, still imprisoned in his grasp.

"But I have taken sacred vows, Holy Father. No man can release me from those."

"No man may, to be sure. But the Vicar of Christ is no ordinary man."

Still Aimée stared at him, realising that he was too powerful an antagonist to risk an argument. "What do you wish of me, Holy Father?" she asked quietly.

"Why, my dear child, only that you be happy. Nothing more and nothing less. There is your happiness, awaiting you."

He beckoned, and William stepped from behind the curtain.

Aimée gaped at him. "My God!" she whispered.

"Is that all you can say?" Alexander demanded. "To your betrothed?"

Colour flared into her pale cheeks. "My betrothal was terminated."

"A betrothal is never terminated. It is virtually the same as a marriage. Only the consummation remains to be accomplished. Now, will you not greet your husband?"

She looked at William again, her mouth slightly open.

"Greet your wife, William," Alexander invited.

William stepped forward, took Aimée's other hand, and kissed the sweet-smelling palm. "I am overwhelmed," he confessed. "After so long, to be with you again, my dear Aimée."

It was a poor speech, and brought a snicker from Cesare Borgia, but he could do no better at that moment.

"You wish to marry me?" Aimée asked.

"You are already married in the eyes of God," Alexander explained. "It but remains to hold the ceremony, which I shall conduct myself. And then the consummation ... and then, why, a life of wedded bliss lies before you."

Aimée's self-control broke. "I am married to God!" she wailed. "No one can alter that."

"I have already done so," Alexander reminded her patiently.

"Can you permit this?" Aimée asked William. "Yes, I did conceive myself betrothed to you, as the Holy Father has said. But then I took a sacred oath. Signor Hawkwood, I beg of you ... It would be a mortal sin."

Her lips trembled, and she was clearly on the verge of tears. She was not a woman ever to be forced.

He looked at Alexander. "If the idea so repels her, Holy Father ..."

"What nonsense! I have never known a young woman not

252

terrified by the thought of losing her virginity. Nor one who could get enough of it afterwards. Come along, our guests are waiting. The marriage will be solemnised immediately. It is my will."

Aimée cried out, "It will be a crime against God!" She looked from one to the other, and William wished he were somewhere else.

"If you blaspheme again," the Pope snarled, "I will have you whipped. Come along."

Cesare was waiting by a door which he now threw open to reveal a huge inner chamber. There was a table laid for a good score of people, all of whom stood awaiting them. At the sight of the bridal party they began to clap.

"Take her hand, William," Alexander commanded, "and follow me."

William clasped her right hand. She gave it a little tug, then let it rest in his.

"I had supposed you a gentle man," she muttered.

He made no reply because he did not know what to say. His mind was spinning. It was his business to humour Alexander in everything, and here was something which had greatly appealed to him. He had dreamed often enough of possessing this girl. And there was clearly no alternative: he knew Alexander too well to suppose that he would ever be crossed. If he did not take Aimée for himself, she would undoubtedly be debauched by the Pope himself, or Cesare ... he had seen how they looked at her. For all his youth, and his recent appointment as a Cardinal, Rome abounded with the tales of Cesare's lusts and the total ruthlessness with which he pursued any woman with whom he became infatuated. There was still a rumour concerning a beautiful girl whose naked body, bound and gagged, was found floating in the Tiber three months after her fiancé had been murdered at her side and she abducted — to be the plaything of the Borgia until he tired of her.

Surely, when all things were explained to her, Aimée would accept her situation, and love him in return. She claimed to have done so once.

He heard little of the marriage service. He was too conscious of the girl standing beside him, of the feel of her hand in his. He remembered only that Alexander spoke sharply to her once when she would not respond, and then she repeated the words in a subdued voice.

The feast which followed seemed no less unreal. A great deal of wine was drunk, a great many toasts offered. He did his own share of drinking, seeking courage for what would come later, while he listened to the bawdy jokes ... and from time to time he glanced at his bride, who sat white-faced and tight-lipped, only allowing a goblet to brush her lips when required.

"She is impatient for her bed," the Pope declared. "Well, and should she not be, having waited eight years to be rammed?"

There was a gale of laughter.

"To bed," they chanted. "To bed!"

The ladies surrounded Aimée, pulled her to her feet, and marched her off. The men similarly escorted William from the room. The air was filled with jocular obscenity.

"Here, Holy Father?" William gasped. He had anticipated some privacy.

"For this night, you will sleep under the roof of the Vatican," Alexander declared. "There could be no more profound blessing upon a marriage than that."

William was stripped of his clothing and bundled into an embroidered nightshirt, then marched along the corridor to the bedchamber. This was already crowded with women, who in turn surrounded him, kissing his face, thrusting eager hands at his body, feeling for him through the thin linen. Their deft attentions had him hard as rock in a moment, and they screamed their delight.

On the bed Aimée sat, her back against the pillows. She wore a white linen nightgown and a white linen nightcap; no trace of her magnificent hair was to be seen. Her face was pale save for an angry flush in her cheeks.

Howling like a pack of mad dogs, the wedding guests escorted William to the bedside, and Cesare whipped back the sheet. Aimée sat with legs straight in front of her, the nightgown down to her ankles. She made no demur when Cesare pulled it up to her thighs, and only shuddered when two other men seized her ankles to draw her down flat on the bed, the nightdress rising higher until it was round her waist.

William had never hoped to see such beauty, and perhaps even the crowd agreed with him; there was a hush as they gazed at the narrow hips and perfectly formed legs, the pulsing belly ... but

254

then they were lifting him over her, and raising his nightshirt above his waist.

The shouts grew louder as his circumcision was revealed.

"A Turk!" the women screamed. "She is married to a Turk!"

He was laid upon her, her legs pulled apart to accommodate his.

"Decency! Decency!" declared the Pope. "Cover them up for the first thrust."

The sheet was thrown back over them, and William gazed down at that lovely, anguished face. He could feel the nipples of surprisingly large breasts through the thin material of her bodice.

Then the cap slipped from her head, and he jerked in dismay. Her scalp had recently been shaven, and in place of the magnificent ash-blond tresses there was only light down.

The crowd bayed their delight. "A nun!" they screamed. "The Turk is deflowering a nun."

"Her hair will grow more luxuriant than ever," Alexander said. "Now come, William, play the man. You have sixty seconds, or we will have at her ourselves, eh?"

Anything less like his first few moments with Sereta could not be imagined. He sought for her lips as he found his way into her, moving as gently as he could to avoid hurting her. She moaned and twisted her body, and tried to pull her legs together, but Cesare signalled to his friends and they caught hold of each knee to hold her helpless.

Her mouth flopped wildly as her head turned again. His mouth was next to her ear.

"Forgive me," he whispered. "I do what I must. But Aimée ... I do love thee so."

She gave a sudden gasp of horror and fear and pain — and he was surging back and forth inside her, exploding within seconds.

Then the sheet was jerked away, and he was rolled on his back, and Aimée's body pulled aside.

"There!" Cesare shouted, pointing at drops of blood on the under-sheet.

"A consummation!" they shrieked. "A consummation!"

"A noble effort," Alexander declared, and patted William on the head. "You are a worthy Turk. Now come along," he shouted above the racket. "Let us leave the happy couple to themselves."

Reluctantly the excited crowd left the room, Alexander waiting until last. At the door he made the sign of the cross, and then closed it upon himself.

"He is a devil," Aimée panted.

"Aye, he has his faults." William raised himself on his elbow. "You will understand, my dearest, that I did what I must. It will not be so again."

She half-turned her head to stare at him. There were tears on her cheeks. "You have violated a nun," she choked. "You are damned. I am damned. While that creature is Pope, we are all damned."

Was there ever a Hawkwood blessed with happiness, William wondered. Or was the entire race, as Aimée had said, damned?

His father no doubt would have gone at her again and again, raped her into subservience. In that, he was not his father's son. He remembered too well the bitterness of his father's house, the unending misery of his mother. Just as he remembered the pleasure with which Sereta and then Margherita, in so different ways, had come to his bed.

Therefore he must again practise patience. Not without hope, though. She had wept and she had pleaded, but she had not become hysterical. And he could swear that immediately after the first thrust her hands had closed on his shoulders, perhaps involuntarily, but nonetheless it had seemed a gesture of possession.

So when he told her, "I shall not lay a hand on you again unless you desire it," he meant what he said.

When next day he took her back to their lodgings, he gave her the use of the main bedroom to herself, and also hired her a maid.

Being a Turk, Hussain was little surprised at these arrangements; men only went to bed with a woman when they wanted sex. No doubt the other servants gossiped, but William cared nothing for that. Because he also believed that, with kindness and understanding, Aimée would grow to accept her situation, and might even turn to him from sheer loneliness.

He sat and explained to her again the story of his life, of what he had had to do. He told her of Constantinople where they would soon be returning, of the beauties he would show to her, of the house he would build her. But her face remained stony.

"If your fate distresses you," he said at last, "let us at least kneel together and pray for forgiveness."

"I can never pray again," she told him. "I am damned."

*

He was now anxious to leave Rome, and the following week he again attended the Pope — to receive the surprise of his life.

Alexander was not in a good mood. "How now, Signor Hawkwood," he began, "I have just received the following communication from your scurvy master. Here, read it for yourself."

William took the piece of parchment, recognising Khalid the Vizier's handwriting.

His eye skipped over the lengthy and flowery greetings until he found the crucial part of the text: "... Owing to the tranquillity and prosperity of his realms, the Sultan is pleased to inform His Holiness that the usurper and traitor known as Djem is no longer considered a threat to the peace and prosperity of the Empire. In these circumstances, the Sultan neither wishes the usurper and traitor known as Djem to be returned to Constantinople, nor is he concerned to have the said usurper and traitor confined at further expense. The Sultan therefore wishes to inform His Holiness that the subsidy of one hundred thousand pounds a year will no longer be paid ..."

The letter rambled on for some time, but William had stopped reading. He raised his head to stare at the Pope.

"Your master cheats me," Alexander growled.

"I am as surprised as you, Holy Father," William said, thinking, here have I wasted ten years of my life stalking the murderer of my wife and sons, and now ...

"What are you going to do?" Alexander inquired, ominously.

"Why ... there must also be a letter for me, with instructions."

"None came in this batch."

"Well, then ... with your leave, Holy Father, I would deem it my duty to return to Constantinople with all haste."

"Ha! And what of this useless burden I have in my possession?"

William hesitated. He knew Bayazid well enough to be certain that even if the Sultan decided Djem was no longer a threat to him, he would still not be pleased to have him let loose or returned. He could not guess what had caused Bayazid's change of heart.

"This man murdered your wife and children," Alexander reminded him. "Ha! But now you have no interest in him either. You are as shallow as your master."

"Not so, Holy Father ..."

"I am disappointed in you, Hawkwood. Leave me. I will have to consider what shall be done."

William returned to his lodging and gave his servants orders to pack up.

"We are going home, my sweet," he told Aimée. "We are going to Constantinople."

She sighed and made the sign of the cross. But this he found reassuring. She could not really believe she was eternally damned if she still performed this Christian gesture.

Three nights later, when everything was ready for his departure, he was summoned again to dine with the Pope.

"I must attend," he told his wife. "It will be in the nature of a farewell."

Alexander seemed in the best of humours, and greeted him affectionately.

"To lose the pleasure of your company will grieve me greatly, dear William," the Pope said. "But as you are resolved to leave me, I have determined that you shall have one last pleasant surprise."

As he was ushered into the same dining hall in which his wedding had been celebrated, William caught his breath in dismay.

Standing before him was Prince Djem.

This was the first time in more than eleven years that he had come face to face with the prince. Eleven years of captivity had played havoc with that once arrogant man. The prince had lost weight, yet his cheeks were puffy, and he had unwholesome jowls beneath his chin. His shoulders were hunched and, although only a year older than William, he looked an old man.

And also a frightened man, as he gazed at William, and took a step backwards. "You told me I was to be freed!" he gasped.

"And so you are, noble prince. You are free as of this moment," Alexander assured him slyly. "I but thought that you might first like to come face to face with your old adversary."

"He will murder me the moment I leave the Vatican," Djem declared.

"Have I not promised you a safe conduct out of my dominions? And Signor Hawkwood is of my mind in all things. Besides, he has quite forgotten the past. Have you not, dear William?"

"Indeed I am endeavouring to do so, Holy Father," William

replied in astonishment.

"Splendid!" the Pope declared. "It is my joy to bring peace and harmony to mankind. Shall we now dine together?"

William was placed on the Pope's left, Djem on his right. Cesare sat beside the prince, and his elder brother, the Duke of Gandia, sat on William's left. Only men were present.

The meal proved as luxurious as any other entertainment given by the Borgias, and when it was over there were scantily-clad dancing girls to entertain them.

"A touch of eastern promise," the Pope said. He was in the most genial of moods. "Some more wine."

Instantly their goblets were replenished.

"There is an old Papal custom," Alexander said, "of blessing the wine whenever an honoured guest is about to depart on a long journey. Will you permit me, both of you?"

He was already extending his hands over Djem's goblet, twisting the fingers together. "*Pax vobiscum!*"

He then turned to William's goblet, performing the same ceremony. William gazed at his hands and wondered where he had seen that unusual ring before.

"And now a toast," Alexander said, raising his own goblet. "To our Turkish friends who are leaving us, and whom we may never see again."

"To our Turkish friends," said the company, rising together.

As William brought his glass to his lips, he suddenly remembered where he had last seen that ring — on Borgia's finger when he had stood gloating over the dead body of the merchant Sacorro. He felt a tingling throughout his body. He knew he was about to die.

Or to live, if he had the courage of a true Hawk.

He lowered his goblet and stared at Djem. The prince had drunk deeply, draining the dregs. He now set down the crystal goblet with a sigh of satisfaction.

"You have not drunk the toast, dear William," the Pope observed.

"No, Holy Father. Forgive me, I am suddenly unwell. I would beg your permission to withdraw."

"Withdraw? But the night is young. No, no, sit down and drink some wine and you will feel better."

William had been studying his situation. Every guest at table

259

had a dagger hanging from his belt, but not one of them wore a sword, and there were no guards in the room. He would be taking a great risk, of course, but no greater than drinking the poisoned wine. It was a question of whom to take hostage. Alexander himself was the most obvious, but William distrusted the hot-headedness of Cesare, even with the life of his father at stake. Whereas Alexander loved his second son more than any other living creature, save Lucrezia.

"With respect, Holy Father, I must leave at once."

With tremendous speed, he tipped his chair backwards to the floor, stepped round and grasped Cesare's arm, jerking him to his feet. At the same time he drew his misericord and presented the point to the young man's throat.

"If any man of you moves, the Bishop of Valencia is dead," he growled.

Cesare made an abortive struggle to free himself, but was help-less against William's desperate strength.

"You are mad," Alexander gasped. "For this you will burn forever in the lowest pit of hell."

"No doubt I will have there a great deal of company," William snarled, pushing the helpless Cesare towards the door. The other men in the room remained spellbound, as if watching a huge snake in their midst.

All except Djem — who suddenly gave a heart-rending scream and fell forward across his plate.

"He has begun his journey," William said grimly, and tightened his grip so that Cesare gasped in pain. Some of the guests rose to their feet.

"The Bishop and I intend to make a small journey, too," he said. "You can all continue with your merry-making. And be sure that no one leaves this room for two hours — otherwise the Bishop will surely die. Tell them so, Holy Father."

Alexander seemed to have difficulty in speaking, but at last he urged them in a hoarse voice, "Stay here. Stay here!"

"You will burn," Cesare snarled. "You will burn!" But he had no intention of burning himself.

Hawkwood closed the doors of the dining chamber behind them, and escorted Cesare through the antechamber, walking arm in arm, with his dagger pressed into the Bishop's side, concealed by the lavish folds of his sleeve. As William was known to be a friend of the Pope, and a frequent visitor, no guard questioned them as together they left the Vatican and stole into Rome itself.

It was late at night and there were few passers-by. Soon they were at William's lodgings, where Aimée and Hussain stared at Cesare Borgia in consternation.

"My God!" Aimée gasped. "What have you done?"

William kept his dagger at Cesare's throat while the last of their belongings were packed up.

"You will not kill me," the young Bishop begged. "I have kept my part of the bargain." His terror was almost amusing.

"You may thoroughly deserve death, my lord," William told him. "But I need you to see us past the guard. This house is the first place your father will look."

"For that reason, I should remain," Hussain declared. "If the house is barricaded and defended, the Pope must assume his son is still within, and his people will consume valuable hours trying to gain entry. Hours in which you will be spending on your way."

"And when they gain entry they will kill you, old friend," William said. "I cannot permit that."

"With respect, young Hawk, I am not your servant. I am the servant of Hawk Pasha, sent to watch over you. I will have served him well if, in dying, I return his youngest son to him."

They gazed at each other, and William heard Aimée catch her breath.

"So go now, young Hawk. But speak of me to my master, and tell him I have served him dutifully. Go!"

There was no way he would be gainsaid. William understood the reasoning behind his decision: for his charge to be killed would bring eternal shame upon not only Hussain but on all his descendants. That was not something this servant could afford to risk.

Thus, much as he was tempted to stay and fight at Hussain's side, or at least take all the Borgias with him to hell, William rode out of Rome around three in the morning, accompanied only by Cesare, Aimée and her terrified maid. They were again unchecked by the guards as soon as the Bishop showed his face, and William kept them on the go until mid-morning. By then there was little advantage in retaining the Borgia, who could well prove a liability at the next town they entered, so Cesare was forced to dismount, and left to walk.

"I swear by God that you will suffer for this, Hawkwood."

"I have no doubt of it, but at least I shall be alive," William told him. "And you will have company for your walk." He made the maidservant climb down as well. She could most certainly prove a liability, as her loyalty was suspect, and now he gained two extra horses.

He turned to Aimée. "Now let us make haste."

Once they were safely across the Apennines, a week later, William altered his direction, as he had always intended to do. Instead of Venice, the natural refuge, he headed for Ravenna. This meant they remained in Papal territory, but his sole object was to board a boat at the earliest possible opportunity, and cross the Adriatic.

It took them two weeks to reach Ravenna, which was a good deal quicker than the earlier journey down. And William now knew where the hidden dangers lay for he remembered where there were likely to be ambuscades, and the signs that indicated *banditti*. As for the towns, he still possessed not only his passports but a safe conduct signed by Alexander himself some while ago. It was only necessary to change their horses occasionally, giving the reason that he was on an urgent mission for the Pope himself. He preferred that they should sleep in the solitude of an empty hillside or a forest, wrapped in their cloaks and ready at any moment to spring into the saddle.

His only concern was for Aimée, but if from time to time she was obviously exhausted, she kept up the pace very well. There was little opportunity for discussing what had happened, but after her initial dismay she had made no more demur.

At least they were two against the world, and now that her hair was starting to grow again she would soon be as beautiful as ever before.

For himself he still could not quite come to terms with what had happened. He had always recognised that Rodrigo Borgia was an irreligious man, but it horrified him that a man who had shown him such generosity and benevolence should decide to be rid of him forever just because he was of no more use to him. And that such a man was now the spiritual head of all Christendom!

His mind was bent entirely upon escape: to be captured by the Borgias did not bear consideration. He wasted no time in Ravenna, knowing all the while that he could be no more than a day ahead of the Papal pursuers. They went straight to the harbour and he hired a small boat to carry Aimée and himself across the Adriatic. He still retained a large proportion of his satchel-full of coin, but his forbidding figure and drawn scimitar discouraged others from any thought of murder, rape or robbery.

Fortunately the weather was good, and two days after leaving port they came to a Venetian town on the Dalmatian coast. There they purchased horses and headed out into the Turkish-ruled hinterland. Within a few hours, they were surrounded by a patrol of sipahis, and they were safe.

There was still a considerable journey ahead of them before reaching Constantinople, but now they could take time and draw breath.

William felt more optimistic once again: his mission had in every way been completed. But there remained the question of his relations with Aimée. He had kept to his vow not to attempt sexual relations with her until invited, but the necessary intimacy into which they had been thrown by their circumstances had been a joy. He had done a good deal of thinking about her as they had galloped through Italy. Her demeanour had altered since the night they had ridden out of Rome, and she remained deeply shocked by revelations of the true nature of the Borgian papacy. Her faith was shaken: all the tenets in which she had been educated torn asunder. But she also clearly understood that her husband, however much she might regret her forced marriage, was now the only friend she possessed in the world.

It was upon that friendship that he conceived her love for him might grow. It was on that friendship — however much the temptations of the flesh rose within him every time he looked at her — that he based all his hopes for their future.

Thus he acted more as a brother than a husband during their journey through the mountains. He showed her the important sights on their journey and explained their history; he introduced her to Muslim customs and Muslim food. He bought for her haiks and yashmaks, and taught her how to conceal herself.

She obviously found it all very interesting, and exciting.

"You do not have to wear the yaskmak inside our house, or even in public, unless you wish to," he told her. "We Hawkwoods maintain some pretence of still being Franks. We do not, for instance, maintain a harem."

"Would it not be better to do so?" Aimée asked. "Believe me, my lord, I can see the desire in your eyes every time you look at me. It grieves me to see you so beset."

"And can you never hope to gratify that desire, my dearest? That way lies the greatest happiness you can imagine."

She sighed and looked away. "I do not know. I do not know what is right and what is wrong any longer. I had conceived myself married to Christ, and was content in that role. Now ..."

"Christ will surely forgive you, Aimée. As He must know all things, He will also know that you were forced into what you did, and will forgive you that. But, of all things, I am sure He most abhors a wasted life. You are now a married woman, and you must remain one. Not to share in the joys of marriage, not to bear children to worship His name, will surely be a greater sin in His eyes than any you may have been forced to in the past. And surely God's judgement is based upon our acceptance of the cards we have been dealt in life, and our determination to do the best with them, for ourselves and for mankind?"

Aimée considered what he had said with her usual seriousness, and at last replied. "I have no doubt there is much in what you say, my lord. I can but ask you to give me time. I am sensible of your regard for me, and I have always held you in the highest esteem. There is no man in the world with whom I could live save you, and I am aware that there is no man in the world could have treated me with such gallantry. If you would allow me but a few weeks more to compose myself, and come to terms with this upheaval in my affairs ..."

He squeezed her hand. "Gladly, my dearest. My only wish is for your happiness. You will have all the time you wish."

He knew he was going to win when, only two weeks later, they arrived in Constantinople.

A messenger had been sent ahead to inform the Sultan of their approach. At Adrianople they were met by his brother John Hawkwood and his new wife.

William was considerably astonished at this. John, like himself, had been married to a Turkish girl while still a teenager, and had had several children by her.

But this woman, in her middle twenties, was no Turk. She was fairly tall, and olive-skinned, with boldly handsome features and a mane of tawny hair, which was her most attractive feature after her eyes, which were deep green and sensuous.

She wore the yaskmak, but like Aimée removed it when the four of them were alone together.

"Her name is Giovanna," John informed his brother.

"Italian?" William cried. "But how is that?"

Giovanna blushed. "The ship on which I was travelling was seized by Turkish corsairs. I was fortunate in being a virgin and, instead of being raped, I was confined and sold in the market place of Constantinople. There I was again fortunate, in that your brother saw me and bought me, instead of some Turkish pasha." She gave a little shiver. "He bought me as a slave, but made me his wife."

Both William and Aimée stared at her. So much was concealed beneath that simple explanation: the terrors of a pirate attack; the horror of being at the mercy of grasping fingers during the examination which had established her virginity; the misery of captivity; the shame and apprehension of standing on a public block to be examined for defects, not knowing which of the leering men around her would carry her off to a life of secluded slavery.

She could not have known what sort of a man John Hawkwood would prove to be. She could not have gone to his bed any more willingly than Aimée. She too must have wept and thought herself the most forlorn of women. Yet now she sat at his side with pride and dignity. Here surely was a lesson for Aimée.

But there was more. Giovanna was already the proud mother of a little boy, hardly a year old, whom they had named Harry.

Their conversation turned to recent news.

"You should know that Prince Djem is dead," William began.

"This we have heard. He choked on a fruit pip at dinner with the Pope."

"He was poisoned by that same Pope. But ... you already knew of his death?"

"Oh, indeed. Pope Alexander has sent to the Porte, demanding your head."

"And Bayazid's response?"

"He has made no response at all, since he had learned by then of your approach. He wishes to hear your account."

"But I am on trial?" William said, wondering if it would be better to flee while he had the chance. But flee where?

"Not necessarily. This Sultan of ours is a strange fellow, much given to moods. But he is even more given to debauchery, and spends more time in his harem than ever in his council. He leaves the management of his kingdom to his viziers and pashas. And of all the pashas, none is so great at present as Hawk Pasha. In that lies your safety. Our father has long been urging your recall, and there is much hostility still towards Rome. Your brush with the Pope may cause some amusement."

"And Father is well?" William inquired.

"You'd not believe he is past sixty," John told him. "I swear he could outride even you. But let us make haste now. Both he and the Padishah await you."

That night Aimée asked William to stay with her.

"Perhaps I understand more now than I did," she said. "Your sister-in-law is a woman of marvellous courage. I doubt I could have survived what she did."

"You do not lack courage, Aimée," he assured her.

"It is impossible to know until the moment of test. But I do now believe what you say, that when Fate deals us a hand we must play it to our best ability. You were chosen as my husband many years ago. I have always respected you. Now I would learn to love you."

Here was happiness. And more. Because, as he had suspected almost from their first meeting, Aimée was possessed of an earthy interest in all matters sexual which made her even more exciting than Margherita. He wanted to sing as they rode along the valley, and first saw the battlements of Constantinople in the distance. He wanted Aimée to be as proud of the life she would lead there as he was of her love.

Certainly there was much to admire in the first sight of the great walls rising sixty feet out of the plain, and the watch-towers rising higher yet, in the myriad banners which drifted in the breeze, in the obsequiousness of the soldiers who came out to greet the sons of Hawk Pasha.

The outer city could not match Rome or Paris for beauty of architecture, since too much of it bore witness to the sack of 1453, but it was a good deal cleaner and better ordered than any Western city, and the crowds who gathered to watch the arrival of the cavalcade were better behaved than any European rabble.

He knew she would be entranced by old Byzantium, now

known as Seraglio Point, and by the new palaces, the lovely gardens, the bustling population in the heart of this huge empire.

Just as he knew she must be impressed by the splendour of the Ottoman court. For all the fine clothes and elaborate manners of the French aristocracy, Paris had been a mean and dirty place, blighted by the parsimoniousness of its King, and more often than not shrouded in grey rain. Though the sun had shone in Rome, there the accent had been on crumbling decay.

The Hawkwood brothers were clearly expected. A regiment of red-and-blue-clad Janissaries was drawn up outside the palace, their white horsehair plumes fluttering in the breeze. Two squadrons of blue-and-white-uniformed sipahis were sitting motionless on their horses, also as still as ebony statues.

Heavily veiled, Aimée was led into the palace courtyard between bowing major-domos, and beheld there white-clad imams and muftis, those — a surprising number — who claimed descent from the Prophet wearing green turbans.

She gazed at marble walls and floors, stared at the eunuchs, craned her neck at the high ceilings and at drapes fluttering in the breeze which rippled in from the Bosphorus, and she instinctively clutched for the hand of Giovanna walking beside her.

She had not truly understood that her husband moved in such exalted society.

Aimée and Giovanna remained in the outer court while John escorted William inside the Porte itself, where Bayazid waited, together with his sons. There were three of these, all grown to manhood: Corcud, only a few years younger than William himself; then Ahmed; and the youngest, Selim, in his mid-thirties.

But William had no eyes for the princes, because, standing behind the Sultan and amid his viziers, was Hawk Pasha himself.

William bowed and made the obeisance: a quick movement of the hand from chest to mouth to forehead. Suddenly he felt somewhat uneasy. The Sultan had clearly put on much weight, and from a flabby countenance his eyes glittered like a snake's.

"You have been absent many years, young Hawk," Bayazid observed.

"Too many, O Padishah. I was but endeavouring to carry out your wishes."

"Did my wishes include the death of my brother?"

"That was my original mission, Padishah. But on receipt of your

267

last instructions, I abandoned my quest. The Pope, however, had already decided on the prince's death."

"You have no proof of what you say."

William looked him in the eye. "I am the son of Hawk Pasha, sire. And I do not lie."

"Ha!" Bayazid commented. "If your crimes are forgiven, it is only because this Pope has shown himself no friend of mine."

William bowed, feeling the tension melt away.

"But tell me this," Bayazid went on. "Did my instructions permit you to marry while on your mission?"

"In that I disobeyed you, Padishah. But my wife is a woman of wondrous beauty and intelligence. Were you to see her you would understand my failing."

"Then I would see her," Bayazid said. "I would look upon her face."

William stiffened again and looked at his father.

Hawk Pasha was frowning deeply.

"How can this be, sire?"

"Is the woman not a gaiour? Does she not go uncovered? Bring her before me."

Hawk Pasha gave a brief nod. John left his brother's side and went out into the courtyard, to return a moment later leading Aimée by the hand. If she was alarmed, she gave no sign of it.

"Uncover your face, woman," the Sultan ordered.

"With respect, Padishah," William protested.

Bayazid smiled. "You are a jealous husband."

"I am a husband." He gestured around at the fascinated throng.

"Ha! Then she shall do so in privacy." The Sultan rose slowly, owing to his bulk. "Bring her here." He went into the inner chamber.

"It were best to humour him," Anthony Hawkwood said in English. "His temper has grown uncertain."

"Nonetheless it is against the law and an insult to our family," John Hawkwood said.

"Humour him," Anthony commanded. "He is our lord. It is his misfortune that he is besotted by the thought of woman. Humour him, and be done with it."

William took Aimée's hand. "Courage," he said.

"I am not afraid of that fat old man," she said.

The pashas and viziers were now muttering amongst themselves. Certainly Bayazid was wantonly breaking the anyi by showing such interest in another man's wife.

William led Aimée into the private chamber, where Bayazid had already seated himself upon the divan, having sent his guards away.

"Reveal your face," William instructed.

Aimée hesitated but a moment, then unclipped the yashmak and let it fall.

Bayazid stared at her, with unconcealed lust.

"By Allah, she pleases me. Can there be a more beautiful face in all the world?"

"The Padishah is most kind," William said stiffly. "Will you permit us to withdraw?"

"But I have heard that her hair is even more beautiful than her face," Bayazid said.

Aimée reached up and slipped the haik from her head. Her ash-blond hair had regained some of its youthful length.

"By Allah," Bayazid said, "it is like spun gold."

The Sultan continued to stare at Aimée, his gaze drifting up and down the haik-shrouded body.

"You are to be congratulated, young Hawk," he said at last, as Aimée covered herself again and withdrew. "But now to your future. I am concerned to give you a position commensurate with your talents. I have decided you will take command of the garrison of Erzurum, with the rank of beylerbey."

William stared at him in delight mingled with consternation: Erzurum was a great command, but it was also the farthest outpost of empire, situated in the Taurus mountains at the very border of Ottoman rule, where Turk and Persian glowered at each other perennially. It was a post of honour which could bring either fame or disaster.

And it was several months' journey from Constantinople.

"It is a distant post," Bayazid continued, "and one which requires great ability. I know you possess that, young Hawk, but you are young. Therefore I will send your father and brother with you, with a force of sipahis and Janissaries so that the frontier will know my strength. When they have established you, they will return here, and you will be left in sole command."

"I am overwhelmed, O Padishah."

"Then see to it. You must leave soon."

*

"I do not like it," John Hawkwood declared.

The two brothers sat with their father on the porch of his house, and looked down upon the Golden Horn. Their women sat inside, gossiping. All Constantinople was gossiping about Bayazid's behaviour with the wife of the youngest Hawk.

"Nobody likes it," Anthony Hawkwood agreed. "The imams are deeply disturbed. But he is the Sultan, and there is an end to it. Is it not better for us to look on the bright side — on William's advancement?"

"I only fear for him. William, have you ever commanded an army?"

"No," William acknowledged.

"Yet you are suddenly appointed to a post of great military responsibility."

"The Sultan has an eye for talent," Anthony Hawkwood argued.

"No doubt. But the important thing is that we will be gone from Constantinople for a year, while our two wives remain here."

Anthony Hawkwood glanced at him and frowned. "You could hardly take them with you on a campaign."

"Agreed. Yet we are being sent on an unnecessary campaign, all within a week of William's return here ... with his wife. Perhaps the most beautiful woman the Sultan has ever seen."

"What you are suggesting is impossible," Anthony Hawkwood declared. "Not even Bayazid would dare to break the Anyi to that extent. Is not adultery the gravest sin a Muslim can commit?"

"Amongst Muslims," John pointed out. "Does the Anyi really apply to gaiours?"

"It could never happen," Anthony insisted, and got to his feet. "It is time we ate."

William held Aimée in his arms for a last time. His escort, including his father and his brother, awaited him, as did the galley that would ferry them across the Bosphorus. Parting from her was grieving; he had only so recently found her again. He was a man who had never loved until now. Now he loved in a fashion he would not have thought possible.

He fondly stroked her hair — like fine-spun gold, the Sultan had said.

"I will send for you the moment I have made the frontier safe," he said.

"I shall await your summons."

He stood away to look at her. "You will be happy here."

"I am sure I shall be, for Giovanna is a splendid companion. But I will be happier when I can come to you."

He kissed her a last time, before striding from the room.

It was not done for a Turkish soldier to display affection in public. Aimée therefore stood at the window to watch the horses disappear down the roadway to the harbour — a group of men dominated by the huge Hawkwoods.

She pondered the strangeness of her life. She had been brought up to the arrogance of great wealth; thus money and possessions had never meant much to her. She had accepted that she would probably be married to an impoverished nobleman who had been promised advancement by the King, and she had come to understand that her sons could well rise far above her own station.

As the daughter of a king's favourite minister, she had not feared the future, had indeed anticipated it. Her only impatience was to become a woman. With reason, for she had early been aware of her physical desires. Perhaps she was a born sinner. She dreamed strange dreams, and they always concerned men, and the bodies of men, even when she had no idea of what to expect. Only in marriage, and in the constant attentions of just one man, could she ever hope for salvation.

All those years ago, the King's choice had surprised and delighted her as much as it had horrified her parents. For here was a stranger from a heathen land who must be considered very much of a heathen himself. She had overheard her family speak of him in anxious tones, wondering how he would misuse her body, and to what unknown countries he would take her.

But William Hawkwood had been a young man — and a handsome one. And gentle, too. She had not feared him or anything he might do to her. Rather had she wanted to be his wife the moment it was possible, and so begin to live her real life.

The sudden termination of her betrothal had been a shock to her and a delight to her parents. They had been overjoyed to be able to reject the Turk, especially when the Dame de Beaujeu designated one of her political favourites as the future husband of this richest and most beautiful girl in France. But the princess's choice was a widower; to Aimée he seemed old and weakly, and her sexually romantic imagination had always craved good looks and sound health. A man such as William Hawkwood, in fact.

But rather than be debauched by a man who looked old enough to be her grandfather, she had doggedly affirmed that she would not marry at all. This had been totally perverse of her, and she knew it, even while suffering for her decision. Both her father and her mother had flogged her; the princess had lectured her. They had painted grim pictures of the dreadful existence she would endure as a nun, while if she married their choice, within a few years she would probably be a widow. But even this prognostication could not change her mind; the Count might live to be a hundred, or he might leave her encumbered with a dozen unwanted children.

Having made her decision to take the veil, she was determined to stand by it. Her inheritance, and the proposed marriage with it, befell the lot of her more biddable younger sister. And no doubt Aimée had been fortunate in her Mother Superior, who allowed her access to suitable books and in all ways acted with a kindness she had seldom received from her own mother. The convent had been a contented period of her life, if not a particularly fulfilling one. But she had become sincere in her devotions, had truly felt that she was now the bride of Christ, and in her new-found piety had suppressed her physical yearnings.

And then, without warning, her life had again been turned upside-down.

To be sent for by an eminent cardinal might have suggested unexpected advancement in her new calling, had not Mother Superior wept so bitterly as she set off for Rome. No doubt the good woman already had some idea of the character of her new patron. And yet the journey itself, the astonishing sights and sounds and smells, had provided the most exciting experience of her life ... until the sudden, terrible revelation.

She had been genuinely horrified at being told she was no longer to consider herself a nun, when with no more than a snap of the fingers her eight years of determined chastity was ended — though some devil within her had given her a sudden frisson of anticipation. And if she still shuddered when she considered the hereafter, it was easy to believe that her husband was right, and that she had been given this special path to tread by God. And if, in so doing, she found an unbelievable happiness, then she had best enjoy it while she could, for she would surely have to pay for it in the end.

Meanwhile she could dream of the great joy of motherhood. Surely it would happen the moment they were reunited.

"They are a noble family." Giovanna spoke at her shoulder. "Even if they do fight for the anti-Christ."

"They are a noble family," Aimée agreed, preferring to leave it at that.

She was anxious to explore this delightful palace, and to learn something of its management. Giovanna was very much the lady of her father-in-law's household; her forceful personality had led her to supplant John Hawkwood's servile Turkish wife, and even Anthony Hawkwood's two concubines bowed before her.

The palace was a treasure house of unusual objects and views and delights, but soon Aimée wanted also to explore Constantinople. She felt like a bird the door of whose cage has suddenly been allowed to swing open. All of her life she had been confined, first within the protective walls of her father's house, then within the walls of her convent. Now she was free. Perhaps more free than she would ever be again, with as yet no children to be responsible for.

Giovanna never ventured into the city unless accompanied by her husband; she had too many unpleasant memories of the slave market there. But she made no demur when Aimée wished to see it for herself, only insisting that she be accompanied by one of the female servants.

Several weeks after the departure of the three Hawkwoods, Aimée ventured out with Gislama the maid, both totally concealed beneath their haiks and yashmaks like any Turkish women, and took the ferry across the Golden Horn to wander about the old city and mingle with the crowds. Most of these were Greeks, the women unveiled and noisy, and all made way for the Turkish lady and her servant.

Aimée even went to the slave market, trying to imagine what Giovanna must have felt standing there, her body all exposed ... and experienced a curious weakness in her knees as she watched naked men and women being carefully examined and herded about as if they were prize cattle.

Instead she hurried off to visit the old hippodrome, which had been converted into a large garden, since the Turks had neither the time nor the taste for organised games.

They were on the point of leaving the hippodrome when Gislama muttered, "We must hurry, lady. We are being followed."

Aimée paused and looked behind her. There were three men walking behind them, and she thought she had seen them earlier outside the house in Galata, when they had been first setting off for their walk. They had clearly been followed ever since then. Thus these men must have been waiting, perhaps for days, for her to leave the safety of the house.

Then Gislama gasped. Turning round, Aimée saw there were also three men in front of them, barring their way. All were Negroes.

Aimée felt a lightness in her chest. There were other people about, but they were carefully moving away now from the little group in the gardens.

In panic she pointed to an alleyway, and hurried towards it. Then she realised her error; the alleyway was dark and deserted.

As she turned back again, the eunuchs were upon her, so suddenly that she did not even have time to cry out. A sack was thrown over her head, and fell below her waist. The mouth of the sack was corded, and before she could raise her arms, the cords had been pulled tight and secured, leaving her helpless, her hands constricted against her thighs.

Hands scrabbled for her legs, and she tried to kick, but that too was futile. With other hands gripping her shoulders, she was lifted bodily from the ground, and lowered into another sack. The neck of this was also secured, and, thus wrapped up helpless, she was hoisted on to someone's shoulders and carried away.

She had been abducted in broad daylight, in the middle of Constantinople, and no one had raised a finger to help her. But she was the daughter-in-law of the great Hawk Pasha. Who would dare commit such a crime?

Who, indeed? She was suddenly seized with a violent under-standing.

Her uncomfortable journey was fairly brief. In place of the sun's heat she felt shaded cool; in place of the city's noise there was silence. Then she was lifted down from the shoulder of her captor.

The sacks were torn away and she could breathe freely. She

sank to the stone floor on which she had been placed. When her breathing was back under control, she discovered herself surrounded by the eunuchs who had kidnapped her — and another. Her original abductors were richly dressed, but this creature was positively resplendent, his tunic decorated with gold thread. And his face wore the look of one used to authority.

"My lady will rise," he commanded harshly.

Aimée stared at him and did not move.

"My lady will rise," he repeated. "I am the Kislar Agha. My lady will obey, or she will be caned."

Realising he meant what he said, Aimée scrambled to her feet. But she knew she must not give way to the terror which was tearing at her mind now that she understood what was to be her fate. Besides, she told herself, what is there to be afraid of? This Bayazid may be fat and disgusting, but is reputed to be supremely sensuous.

What terrible thoughts for the wife of young Hawk!

And surely she would be avenged.

Certainly she had no intention of being frightened by these poor half-men: they could do not more than bruise her body. And that too would be avenged.

"Where is my servant?" she demanded as forcefully as she could manage.

"My lady has no more use for that servant." The Kislar Agha stepped forward and removed the yashmak from her face. She made herself keep still.

"My lady is indeed as beautiful as the moon," the Agha said.

Aimée tossed her head. "I am the wife of young Hawk," she said. "Do you not suppose Hawk Pasha will avenge me?"

"Hawk Pasha is far away," the Agha said. "My lady will accompany me now."

To another interview with the Sultan, no doubt. Could one refuse a sultan?

The antechamber in which she stood was devoid of windows or furnishings, and lit only by two torches in sconces on the wall. She had no real idea where she was, although she was sure it was somewhere within the royal palace.

The Agha had already opened an inner door, and this she stepped through to find herself in a corridor filled with a delightfully fragrant scent. This gave way to another chamber, where there were several divans, and a thick carpet on the floor.

By now Aimée was aware of feminine sounds from all around her. She must be in a harem.

"My lady will disrobe," the Agha said.

Aimée's head jerked up. "Are you mad?"

"You must disrobe to be examined," the Agha explained. "If my lady is blemished ..."

"I would be released?" She had been unable to resist the question.

"There is no release from the harem, save in death," the Agha said.

Aimée stared at him, fear again threatening to overwhelm her. This could not be true. Had she escaped the prison of the convent to be incarcerated in some sultan's palace for the rest of her life?

"My lady will disrobe," the Agha said again.

"Before you? Never."

"My lady," the Agha said patiently, "I have power of life and death here. My master desires you, but should you be damaged or tarnished in any way, he will not receive you. Then I must tie you in a sack and drop you into the Bosphorus. Now, obey me, or my people here will strip you. In doing so, they may well damage you."

To her consternation, Aimée found she was already tearing off her clothes. She could not doubt the truth of what he had said. Now the mixture of apprehension and excitement which had filled her mind since her abduction was replaced by real fear.

She gathered the haik and threw it on the floor. She wore only a linen tunic beneath, and this she threw after the haik.

The Agha's eyes seemed to devour her. As he came towards her, her knees seemed about to turn to water. If he touches me, she thought ...

But she stood quite still as he did touch her. He stroked the line of her jaw, her neck, then each breast in turn, cupping them from underneath as if weighing them.

That done, he made her turn round, to examine her shoulders and back. Then he knelt.

"My lady will spread her legs," he commanded.

No, she thought. No! she wanted to shout. But she dared not resist him.

Was this not her fate?

276

Aimée spread her legs and tensed her muscles as the Agha parted her buttocks to look between, and then moved round in front to do the same with her sex. She thought of the slave block: had Giovanna had to suffer this? My God, she thought, I am being examined like a slave. Because that is what I am now.

But she knew there was no use in calling on God. If He had not finally forsaken her, He would expect her to follow this road to the end. To the best of her ability, as William had said.

The eunuch stood. "My master will be pleased," he said. "You are very nearly perfect. Were you a virgin, he might have taken you to wife. As it is ... he is impatient."

She stared at him. Could he really have touched her, or any woman, so intimately, yet show no reaction at all?

The Agha walked away from her and opened yet another door. "My lady will enter."

Aimée started, as if waking from a deep sleep, and stooped to retrieve her haik.

"My lady does not require clothes," the Agha said.

Aimée straightened again and moved to the door. Calm, she told herself. Stay calm.

She followed him through, and paused in surprise. She stood in what was clearly a bathing chamber. The doorway led on to a slight dais, on which were several magnificently draped divans. A shallow flight of steps led down to a marble floor, in the centre of which was a large marble slab, rather like some sacrificial altar. Another three steps led down to a third level, again marble, although covered with wooden slats, and off which led several large drains. Onto each level opened a doorway, but the entire room was empty. It was lit by several huge skylights in the ceiling.

On the lowest level stood two large wooden tubs of water, one of them steaming. More surprisingly, set into the wall of the second level was a roaring fire, above which a spit was suspended on tripods. From this spit there hung an iron pot from which a most enticing aroma emanated.

Did they mean to feed her here? Or cook her?

To her dismay, all the eunuchs came into the chamber behind her. One of them closed and locked the door, and then, like the others, he began to undress.

They cannot be going to strip completely, she thought. Then I will surely faint.

But they stopped at their loincloths.

The Kislar Agha pointed to the marble slab. "My lady will lie down," he said.

To endure some obscene assault?

"Why?" she demanded.

"My lady's hair must be removed," he explained.

She stared at him open-mouthed, then at the eunuchs, who stood in a row looking at her face rather than her body. Somehow their impersonality was harder to bear than if they had showed some lustful reaction, just as the thought of being shaved actually seemed somehow worse than rape.

She turned away from them, descended the three steps, and lay down on the slab. The marble was cold and her flesh came up in goose pimples.

The Harem Agha came and stood beside her, raised her head and gathered out her hair, scooping it from beneath her so that it flowed over the edge of the altar.

One of the other eunuchs appeared on her other side, carrying a tray on which lay a curved knife some eight inches long.

The Kislar Agha now lifted her right arm, extending it above her head. "My lady must lie absolutely still," he said. "I am skilful, but even I may not be able to cope with a sudden movement."

Aimée sucked air into her lungs, as slowly as he began to hone the knife. Meanwhile another of the eunuchs was powdering her armpit, coating it thickly and pulling the hairs through it. Then the blade scraped with the utmost gentleness across her flesh.

Her left armpit was equally treated.

"Now, lady, spread your legs," the Agha commanded.

How strange, Aimée thought as she obeyed; I give not a thought to defying him, where only this morning such a suggestion coming from any man but my husband, much less a half-man of an alien race, would surely have sent me into a swoon.

She closed her eyes as the fingers began to rub the powder into her flesh. There was something gentle about the feel, yet it was all she could do to keep still. Once again the Kisler Agha was scraping away, his head bent over her groin.

"Those ladies who prove recalcitrant," he said conversationally, "are depilated by having the hairs plucked individually from their flesh. It is very painful, and can leave considerable inflammation for some time. You are wise to submit to the requirements of the harem, lady."

Aimée closed her eyes. The knife was now moving between her legs, guided by those so knowledgable and yet so disinterested fingers. It required all her willpower to lie still.

"My lady will stand," the Agha commanded.

Aimée opened her eyes, sat up and looked down at herself. She now realised that she had never before known what an adult woman truly looked like there. She felt heat again in her cheeks, and glanced anxiously from side to side as she swung her legs to the floor, but the eunuchs were busy peering into the iron pot, and two of them were stirring vigorously.

"This may feel hot to your flesh, lady," the Agha told her, "but it will only provide a temporary discomfort. Now kneel, and stretch your arms across the block."

Aimée obeyed, still wondering at her total subservience to this creature. In fact she was even curious to discover what next would be done to her. She watched as the heavy pot was carried across the room, and placed on the block, between her arms, then felt a mixture of fear and disgust as a giant ladle was dipped in and a molten brown mess lifted out. Some of this was dripped on to her left arm, producing a gasp of pain. It was extremely hot. Then fresh pain as some of the toffee-like mixture was dropped on her right arm. The eunuchs immediately smeared the mess over her skin, coating every inch of each arm from wrist to shoulder.

"It is a mixture of sugar and lemon," the Agha said. "Now you must lie absolutely still. What follows is a great test of skill. I cannot be responsible if you move. The slightest mistake in applying pressure will result in skin being removed."

He had gone round the block to face her, and now leaned on the marble surface holding a length of silken thread between both hands. This he placed on her shoulder, where it joined the upper arm. He pressed gently, until the thread dug into the brown substance coating her skin; then slowly and carefully, watched with intense interest by his subordinates, he drew the thread down the length of Aimée's arm, removing the bulk of the smothering mess as he did so — but also, she discovered to her fascination, every trace of hair. The golden down that normally covered her arm was entirely gone by the time he had reached her wrist, leaving her flesh absolutely white and clear.

Her arms completed, the Agha made her lie down again while her legs were attended to. Then she was made to kneel again while her back was coated and cleaned, and then she lay down yet again while her armpits received another scouring.

The Agha grinned at her. "Now is the truly difficult part, lady. I can only advise you again: lie still."

She closed her eyes. She could not bear to look at their faces, so close, so eager, although still without any hint of sexual interest. The mess was smeared over her breasts — she could not possibly have hair on her breasts, she thought desperately — coated on her stomach, reaching her groin and between her legs. How could they avoid harming her down there, she wondered in sudden desperation.

She gave an involuntary shudder and received an admonitory slap on the thigh.

"I am commencing now, lady."

Aimée attempted to hold her breath, then abandoned that in favour of slow and careful breathing. She felt the cord sliding over her skin, slipping between her breasts, and discovered that a subordinate had hold of each nipple, gently but firmly pulling the mounds apart to permit their master's thread to pass between.

Her breasts were released, then the cord passed over her stomach. She tensed her muscles and felt it coursing across her groin. She felt fingers once again on the inside of her thighs, stretching them so wide she thought she might be torn in two. She wanted to cry out in anticipated pain, but there was none — and suddenly she was released. She received another gentle pat, and looked up to see the Kislar Agha grinning at her.

"You are well disciplined, lady," he said. "Now, come, it is time for your bath."

Aimée sat up and slipped off the table. The eunuchs had already descended to the lowest level, where the huge tubs waited. They carried silver bowls in their hands.

She was first made to kneel while the Agha carefully soaked and then washed her hair, using a soap of remarkable fragrance. Her hair was then rinsed and tied on top of her head with a length of ribbon. Next she was made to stand on the wooden slat, and hot water was poured over her seven times. The water, she discovered, was already soapy.

"My lady will lie down."

280

Aimée obeyed, stretching herself out on the wet boards, and the eunuchs each armed himself with a loofah and massaged her from her neck to her toes. Her flesh was warmed, and the feeling of cleanliness and well-being was now overwhelming. She discovered she had quite lost both her horror of them as creatures and her embarrassment at being so intimately manhandled. There seemed to be nothing worse they could possibly do to her compared with what they had already done.

Besides, the strange excitement remained ... and was even growing.

The soaping process completed, she was made to stand and was rinsed seven times in cold water.

"Now, lady." The Kislar Agha wrapped her in a large towelled robe and released the ribbon holding her hair. He escorted her up the steps to the top level and sat her on a divan. She was amazed to discover just how exhausted she felt, and wondered for the first time how long she had been in the steamy confines of the bath-chamber.

Several hours, apparently, for no sooner had she sat down than the sounds of a gong reverberated through the palace and the eunuchs immediately prostrated themselves for the afternoon prayer, apparently knowing the direction of Mecca even in this enclosed room.

She closed her eyes and leaned against the wall. She wanted only to sleep.

But her toilette was far from completed. While she sat on the divan, feeling her body slowly drying, the eunuchs finished their prayers and continued to fuss about her, extending arms and legs, first to trim and then to paint her fingernails and her toenails with henna. Others with great care circled her eyes and coated the lids with kohl.

The Kislar Agha himself gently rubbed her hair dry, seeming to work from strand to strand.

"In most cases," he explained, "we henna the hair as well. But in your case, lady, it could do no more than detract from your beauty. The Padishah made particular reference to it." She supposed he was paying her a compliment.

Her nails were now finished, and a eunuch was offering her a cup of steaming black coffee, so strong it made her gasp, to be followed by a mouth-watering sherbet which seemed to trace its way down her throat like a cascading waterfall. She had eaten nothing since early morning, and she realised, looking up at the skylights, that it was all but dark.

Giovanna would be at her wits' end; her servants would be scouring the city. Would any of them dare grasp the truth?

She accepted another cup of coffee while the Kislar Agha continued to busy himself with her hair, brushing it and combing it, smoothing it with his fingers, endeavouring to remove the very last suspicion of a curl, to have it lie absolutely straight on her shoulders. And discovered that one of the eunuchs was standing before her, holding a tray on which lay a fearful mess: all the hair which had been removed from her body, sunk into the coagulated sugar and lemon mixture, together with all the parings from her nails.

"He wishes you firstly to confirm that there is none missing," the Agha explained. "And secondly to tell him your wishes as to their disposal."

"Should I be concerned with either?" She was coming to regard the Kislar Agha almost as an old friend. Certainly she had never spent so long naked in the company of anyone else — not even her husband!

"Of course, my lady. For if any is left about, to be secreted by some other *guizde*, you may be sure that one of your rivals will secure it and use it to cast an evil spell upon you. A sickness, perhaps, or a skin blemish."

She was to have rivals! She had not thought of that. "Then what do you suggest?"

"That these are cast into the flames, here and now."

"Very well," she agreed. "Will you instruct him?"

The Agha gave instructions in Turkish, and the contents of the tray were immediately tipped into the still smouldering fire, causing it to flare up and give off again that unusual smell.

The Agha then removed Aimée's robe and made her lie down on the divan, whereupon she was massaged by the four of them, front and back, with an unguent which gave off the same delicious fragrance as her hair, and left her smelling sweeter than she would have ever thought possible. It also sent her mind soaring into the most erotic of daydreams.

"And now, lady," the Agha said, "your toilette is complete. Will you dress?"

A eunuch waited with a fresh tray, on which lay a pair of silk trousers, a bolero jacket and a jewelled cap, together with a pair of felt slippers. The motif was crimson, with gold thread intertwined at the hem and through the shoulders. It felt extremely odd to be wearing clothes without a single undergarment, and she could not reconcile herself to the way the bolero failed to meet across her breast, so that whenever she moved, her nipples were exposed.

Then to her surprise the Agha adorned her with a clean white yashmak. He clapped his hands and one eunuch hastily produced a large mirror, which he held up for her inspection.

Aimée gazed at herself in growing wonder. The heat from the bath had introduced a faintly pinkish tinge to her flesh, which seemed to glow after its massage. The sheer crimson trousers outlined the shape of her limbs — another shock, as she had never exposed her legs in her life before. Her nipples peeped round the hem of the bolero, and she was delighted with the way her breasts seemed to rise up, without a trace of sagging.

And, to top it all, the half-concealed face, and the white-gold hair flowing out from beneath the crimson cap.

"Well, lady, are you satisfied?"

"I am amazed," she said. "How often is a woman required to suffer such a metamorphosis?"

"That depends on how you please the Padishah, my lady. As a *guizde*, why, not more than once a year, if at all. As an *ikbal*, why, perhaps once a week. But should you ever become an odalisk, then you will spend much of every day in this chamber, so as always to be ready for your master's summons. Although clearly future occasions will not require so much attention."

Will there be future occasions? she wondered. Especially when the Hawkwoods find out what has happened to me.

Instead she said, "I am glad to hear that. And now may I be shown to a bedchamber? I am extremely tired and wish only to go to sleep."

The Kislar Agha permitted himself a smile. "Sleep is not for you this night, lady. Come, it is time for you to visit the bedchamber of the Padishah."

11

THE DAY OF RECKONING

The mountains seemed to climb forever in every direction. Once William Hawkwood had thought the Ulu Dag high. And once he had stared up at the Matterhorn. He had never anticipated having to climb such heights.

Brusa was now eight hundred miles behind him as the crow flies. But it had not been possible to travel in a direct line.

The little army had been several months on the march. It had followed the coast as far as possible, and even that had proved hard going. But when they had turned inland, for the mountains, they had encountered terrain such as only Hawk Pasha and his veterans of the Persian war ever suspected to exist.

They had wintered in Trebizond, on the coast, where the Black Sea surged into a wide bay, forming over the centuries a triangle of tableland between two deep ravines, separated from the main part of the Anatolian plateau by the Pontic mountains.

Traditionally the place where Xenophon the Greek and his ten thousand had reached the sea after escaping from Persia, this seaport was a relatively recent acquisition of the Turks. Backed by those formidable mountains, it was difficult of access; here the Grand Comneni, descendants of the Byzantine emperors who had been ousted by the Frankish sack of 1204, had lived and ruled for two hundred years and more, describing their limited kingdom as the Empire of Trebizond. The ruins of their palace could still be seen. The walls erected by the Byzantines in those days of their glory still stood.

It had been Mahomet the Conqueror, with Hawk Pasha at his side, who had finally annexed Trebizond, soon after the fall of Constantinople.

The beylerbey, Mustafa Pasha, was an old friend of Anthony, and had made them welcome. But, with the first melting of the snows, Anthony had driven them onwards into the mountains.

Now they gazed at snow-covered peaks more than ten thousand feet high surrounding them on every side. Even in the passes the temperature plunged below zero every night, so that the men and horses huddled together for warmth.

"It is never hot in Erzurum," Hawk Pasha informed them. "It is six thousand feet above sea level."

William was glad to see the towers of the citadel emerging along the pass. It was not merely the length of time already spent on the road, or the lonely nights when he dreamed of Aimée and wondered how she and Giovanna were faring, he also feared for his father, Anthony Hawkwood, who was now sixty-four years old. True he had spent almost his entire life either campaigning or travelling, first for the Conqueror and now for Bayazid, but he was old to be climbing up and down mountains, and there were days when his face looked grey. But he would accept no concessions in his determination to cover a predetermined number of miles a day. Others might collapse with exhaustion, but Anthony drove himself onwards.

And, at last, Erzurum. It was a surprisingly large city, and an old one. Known as Theodosiopolis by the Romans, even in those antique times it had been a frontier fortress, guarding Anatolia against the men from the steppes and the even greater mountains of the Hindu Kush. More recently it had been the home of the Seljuks, who had called it Arzan-ar-Rum, or Land of the Romans, whence came its present name.

The Seljuks had been the first wave of Turks to come riding out of the steppes to challenge the might of the Byzantine empire — at a time when the Byzantines had still been thought to possess the greatest army in the world. The Seljuks had triumphed.

Several of their sultans were buried in Erzurum, their mausoleums, as with the Ottomans at Brusa, dominating the city, but overlooked by the dome of the Great Mosque.

More interesting to William were the high, strong walls and the central citadel.

Riders had been sent ahead to warn the garrison that a new commander was arriving, so the troops had turned out on parade. There were not many: one regiment of Janissaries and one of sipahis — the same size of force Djem had been given to garrison Brusa, before he had started recruiting.

There was no artillery.

"To bring cannon into these mountains would be an impossible task," Hawk Pasha growled.

"And the Persians have none," pointed out Walid, the acting commander of the garrison, a small, slight, dark man who looked more Arab than Turk. But he had fought under Hawk Pasha, and Anthony knew him to be a good man.

"Has there been much hostility?" William asked.

"Border raids. Those will never change." Walid pointed at the mountains which rose sheer in front of them at only perhaps ten miles' distance. "It is not possible to march an army of any size through those without hardship. Genghis Khan and Timur did it, but the Persians have sufficient problems at home."

"Are you pleased?" Anthony Hawkwood asked his son. "You are far removed from Constantinople and any interference, so up here you are very much the ruler of your own little kingdom."

"Remembering always that the Padishah is still your master," John Hawkwood advised.

"I am not likely to forget that," William said. "But I will be content here, and do my duty until I am called to better things. My only wish is to have my wife here with me."

"I shall attend to that as soon as I return," Anthony said, "now that we know all is peaceful. But it will be a long and difficult journey for her."

"She has made long journeys before, Father. But I fear it will be a long and difficult return journey for you."

"Nonsense. One would think I was a babe in arms the way you have been fussing over me."

"But you will rest before leaving," William insisted.

"I will remain here a week," Anthony agreed.

It was on the fourth day of that week that the messenger arrived. The Hawkwoods stared at each other in horror as they heard what he had to say.

"Can this be true?" Anthony demanded.

"I have told you what the lady Giovanna bade me say, my lord," the man repeated. He belonged to Anthony's own household.

"It has taken you this long to reach us?" John growled.

"It has been most difficult, my lord — and for the lady Giovanna, too. When the lady Aimée disappeared, it was said that she had been murdered by footpads, especially after the discovery of her maidservant, Gislama, floating in the Bosphorus. Her throat had been slit from ear to ear. My lords, the Sultan himself was most concerned. He gave orders that every itinerant in the city was to be arrested and tortured. But none confessed. The lady Giovanna did not know what to do. She sent a messenger immediately to inform you, my lord."

"We have received no messenger before you," Anthony Hawkwood said.

"Bayazid must have been watching," John said.

"Go on," William told the servant. His brain seemed frozen.

"This is what the lady Giovanna feared. It was not until several months had passed, my lords, that, as she had received no reply from you, she realised some mishap must have overtaken her messenger. It was at that time she heard a rumour of the white-haired woman in the Sultan's harem, who was kept in a separate apartment from the rest of the women. Only then did the lady Giovanna understand the truth, my lords. She was nearly prostrate with anxiety, grief and fear. But then she despatched me, secretly at night, to find you and tell you what she suspects. My lords, I have ridden day and night to bring you this news."

"You have done nobly," Anthony Hawkwood assured him. "Now go and rest, and be sure that you will be rewarded. But, Malik, no word of this must pass your lips again."

Malik bowed. "I understand, my lord." He left the room.

William was on his feet. "We will leave tomorrow."

Anthony Hawkwood looked at his youngest son. "With what in mind?"

"You cannot expect me just to accept this, Father."

"I expect you to act with common sense. A great crime has been committed. And the criminal is the Sultan, the all-powerful. His crime will be condemned by the imams and the muftis, when they know of it eventually. For you yourself to act rashly would enable to Sultan to strike you down without hesitation. And leaving a military command without his permission amounts to rebellion."

"My God, Father! You expect me to sit here while Aimée is forced to embrace that monster? You do not know her. She has spent all her adult life in a convent. She will die of shame."

"I grieve for you, but dying is no way to right a wrong. Leave it

287

with me. On my return to Constantinople I will consult the Grand Mufti, and together we will decide what is to be done. I promise you, not even the Sultan can thus break the law and hope to escape unpunished. At the very least he will be forced to let her go ... I will send you word. John, we leave tomorrow at dawn."

William knew his father's advice was sound; it was always sound. The moment he appeared in Constantinople without the permission of the Sultan, he would be outlawed and chased to the ends of the earth, as he himself had pursued Djem to destruction.

And Bayazid had broken the Anyi. He would suffer for it — by the will of the people. But until that, he would do with Aimée as he wished. That thought made William physically sick.

And, as had so often been his fate, there was nothing he could do save wait for fate itself.

He could, however, keep busy. And more: he could set about attaching at least this garrison, this city, to his own person. The soldiers, and Walid, were already devoted to the name of Hawk: the famous battleground of Otluk-Beli lay only a few miles to the south-west. They were pleased to have the youngest Hawk as their commander, however lacking in either years or experience. William set out to raise that respect and admiration for his famous name into respect and adoration for himself personally.

When, as the summer sun melted the snows, it was necessary to send patrols into the mountains as far as the Persian border, he led them himself. He even led raids across the border, bringing back booty and slaves that pleased the Janissaries. By exposing himself recklessly, he also earned their plaudits. Soon his name spread even into Persia.

He led raids to the north as well, over the mountains into Armenia and Georgia and Circassia. On the last of these raids, for the month was September, Walid appeared before his tent, dragging by the hair one of the captive women. She had been stripped of her clothing and her hands were tied behind her back.

"It is not good for a great soldier to live without women, my lord," Walid said gruffly. "I have heard how your wife was the most beautiful woman in the world; how her hair was like fine-spun gold. But she is dead, so will you not accept a substitute?"

Like everyone else in Erzurum, Walid had no inkling of the truth. She was Circassian, her skin pale and her eyes blue. Her hair, tumbling in wild disorder down her back, was brilliant gold. She was not pretty, but there was a symmetry about her features which was most attractive, and there could be no denying the voluptuousness of her figure.

And suddenly he wanted a woman with desperation, if only to work out some of the passion that was consuming his soul.

"Her name is Golkha," Walid told him. "I would recommend you leave her hands bound until you have tamed her."

There was no surrender in Golkha's hate-filled eyes.

Nor in her mouth. William had to gag her simply to avoid being bitten whenever he came too close to those snapping teeth.

He used her well, if roughly. She had breasts to be fondled, buttocks to be slapped, long, strong legs to be parted, and a great deal of warmth between them. He lay with her all night and sated himself time and again.

She would at least be his companion for the winter, because there was no hope of news from Constantinople until the spring. It began to snow before they had even regained Erzurum, and within a week of their return the city was entirely cut off from the outside world, surrounded by a glistening white wonderland which spelt death to anyone who wandered into it.

One could either sit and weep at one's misfortune, or one could take one's pleasure and look forward to better times.

Golkha gradually learned to speak Turkish, for she quickly realised that since this was her fate, she had better make the most of it. She ceased to snap and kick, and indeed began to love him with an earthy determination which was heart-rending because it reminded him so much of Aimée.

By the spring she was pregnant.

As soon as the roads were clear he sent down to Trebizond to discover if there was any word from Constantinople. The messengers returned empty-handed. As the weather warmed up, he and Walid could go hunting for bear, but his mind remained in turmoil. If he continued to lead his men in raids over the border, his heart was no longer in it. Eighteen months had passed since his father and brother had set out on their return journey. Eighteen months was too long.

He knew he could wait no longer to learn of their fate, yet there was the birth of his child to be anticipated, and the certainty that once he left Erzurum for Constantinople he was throwing down the

gauntlet. Would even his own men follow him on such a dangerous adventure, much as they now adored him?

But in the late summer, as the leaves began to fall, and before
he had made any decision other than to accept that he would now
have to wait for the following spring, three horsemen were seen
approaching — not from the north, and Trebizond, but from the
mountains of the south-west.

William and Walid stood together on the gate tower to inspect
these strangers.

"By Allah," Walid commented, eyes narrowed. "Is that not the
man Malik?"

"With two women," William said, and commanded the gate to
be opened for them.

He hurried into the courtyard to greet them. Giovanna almost
fell from the saddle into his arms. Her maidservant was carrying
John's little boy, Harry Hawkwood.

Giovanna's face was burned by sun and scorched by winter wind.
She would not appear in front of William before she had bathed
thoroughly.

Her travel clothes were in rags, but she had an extra gown in
her saddlebag, and this she donned to take dinner with him. It was
a black gown.

He already knew that she must be the bearer of terrible news.
Or she would not have risked coming virtually alone over the
mountains.

Understanding her distress, he must wait for her to tell him in
her own time. It was clearly what he had always feared. Now it
had happened, it remained to learn the details, and make his
plans.

She sipped heated goat's milk, and shivered. He had sent away
the servants, and they were alone.

"Tell me," he said at last.

She shivered again. "Your family is no more. My husband is
dead. Your family is no more."

"Tell me," he said again.

"I do not know how."

"Tell me from the beginning. My father and my brother left here
in the spring of last year. Tell me what happened in Constantinople."

Giovanna sighed. "They returned in the late summer. But your father was ill. When he arrived in Constantinople he could hardly sit upon a horse."

"He seemed ill when he left," William said, "but he *would* go."

"He had to take to his bed, and there was little we could do. When it was realised that he would not rise again, my husband felt it necessary to act on your behalf. He consulted the Grand Mufti about the abduction of your wife. The Mufti was shocked, and went to the Sultan. Bayazid denied any knowledge of your wife. He did what no Sultan has ever done before: he took the Mufti into his harem and let him study all the women. There was not one yellow-haired woman between them, save for a few who were obviously Circassians."

"Then he has put her to death."

"Nobody knows. But not even the Grand Mufti could call the Sultan a liar. He was forced to proclaim that John Hawkwood had falsely accused the Sultan." Another sob. "My husband was executed that same day in the palace. Strangled."

"And my father?"

"The executioners came for him too, but I begged the Vizier to intercede and spare the life of a great man and loyal servant who was in any event dying. This they agreed, with the proviso that none of us should ever leave the Hawk Palace again. I sat with your father until he died. I could not tell him of John's execution, but told him my husband had been sent on a military mission. His mind was wandering and he could not reason. He accepted my words."

"And died," William said sadly.

"His last words were of you," Giovanna said. "And my next thoughts were of you. I am no Turk: I have no affinity with them. And I was condemned to be a lifelong prisoner in my own home. Besides, I knew that Bayazid would seek to be rid of me before long. Thus I planned my escape with only my son and a single maidservant, and our faithful Malik.

"I was well supplied with money, but I knew the Sultan would send soldiers behind me the moment he learned I had left. Thus I did not dare take the coast road, so went into the mountains. I have been travelling a year to come to you, young Hawk." She paused, staring. "I had nowhere else to go."

William clasped her hand. "Here you will be safe." He gave a twisted smile. "For as long as I myself survive."

William got up, walked to the window, and gazed out at the mountains.

"Do you think Aimée is dead?" he inquired at last.

"I am sure of it. He had his way with her, and then ... no doubt a sack tossed into the Bosphorus. Is that not the way with unwanted concubines?"

"Yes," William said. All of that beauty and grace drowned in a sack. After being debauched in a manner even the Borgias would not have known existed. So much wasted. So much to be remembered — for as long as he lived. Because he *had* to live until he could settle his account.

"Then she must be avenged," he said, his voice icy calm. "As also my father and my brother. All of my family are laid at the door of this accursed Sultan, and his brother."

"Can you oppose his might?"

William remembered Djem, and Omar, and the encounter in the hills outside Brusa. He also remembered his father's advice: that he should use his head rather than lose it.

"No," he said. "I cannot lead an army sufficient to meet that which Bayazid could range against me. But I do not believe he can bring an army against me here so long as my men will support me. I have been forced to practise as great deal of patience in my life. A few more months, years even, will not hurt me. So I will wait, because in time Bayazid must fall. He is a man who makes more enemies than friends, and he earns contempt rather than respect. He must fall eventually."

"And will your men support you?"

William gave a grim smile. "That must be my first charge."

He assembled his men the next day and told them what had happened: how his wife had been abducted by the Sultan, and his father and brother executed.

The news that Hawk Pasha was dead brought a greater gasp of dismay than learning of the Sultan's sexual crime.

"Can we serve such a man?" William asked. "Need we fear him? If he comes at us in these mountains we will destroy him, and he knows that. And if he does not come, we may live our lives here without fear. I do not ask you to forswear the House of Othman, but there are good and bad in every family. This Bayazid is the false bearer of a famous name. Can he truly be the son of the Conqueror? Has he ever led an army into battle? He prefers to sit in his harem, but can such a man truly call himself the descendant of Othman, or the son of Mahomet the Conqueror?

"I promise you this. I will lead you, and we will prosper. We will take what we wish from the north and from the south, and we will grow rich. We will hold the border in the name of Othman, until the day a true member of that house sits upon the divan, and then resume our allegiance. That is all we can do, as we are honourable men."

There was a brief silence when he had finished, then Walid said, "Hawk Pasha is dead. But there is a new Hawk Pasha, chosen by ourselves." He drew his scimitar. "Hawk Pasha!" he shouted.

"Hawk Pasha!" the Janissaries and the sipahis shouted together.

Watching from the window of the governor's palace, Giovanna wept.

It was the following spring that the messengers arrived from Constantinople. They had travelled the usual route and wintered in Trebizond.

William received them in the doorway of the governor's palace.

"My master the Sultan," said Abdul Pasha, "sends greetings to young Hawk, beylerbey of Erzurum and the Taurus. He wishes to know if young Hawk has learned of the sad news of his father's death."

"I have learned of it," William said briefly.

"My master the Sultan grieves, and consoles you. Now he commands you to give up your post here and return with me to Constantinople, so that he may have you at his side."

How the years rolled away. It could have been Henry standing in front of him, in Brusa.

He took a long breath. "Return to your master the Sultan. Tell him that he is a murderer and adulterer and a stealer of men's wives. Tell him that we shall defend Erzurum to the death, and that we shall await the time when so false a Sultan will tumble from his divan, and grovel on the ground like the snake he is. Tell him these things, from Hawk Pasha."

Abdul Pasha stared at him in astonishment. He had known William Hawkwood since birth.

"You have just condemned yourself to death, young Hawk," he said.

293

"I have just condemned myself to life, Abdul Pasha. Go now and tell Bayazid what I have said."

He stood at the window and watched the embassy making its way back down the sloping road through the mountains.

"Those were brave words," Giovanna said, beside him.

He turned. She had spent the winter dressmaking and attending to her wardrobe. She now wore a western-style gown, and was filling out again; her cheeks were clear olive. Her hair was a great tawny mass clouding on her shoulder. She was a strong and handsome woman.

"Brave words cost nothing," he told her.

"But you will implement them with brave deeds, when the time comes," she insisted. "You are the strongest of the Hawks."

"I?" He gave a brief laugh. "Compared with my father and my brother, I am a weakling."

"Not so. For all their strength they were bound by their acceptance of the Sultan as omnipotent, all-powerful. Neither would have had the courage to defy him as you have done."

"It takes little courage to shout defiance, when the alternative is death."

"But you have done it," she repeated. "I am proud of you. I am proud that you will act as father to young Harry."

He gazed at her. She was a woman who had suffered much — as much, perhaps, as poor Aimée. Aimée had seemingly been born to suffer. If he could be grateful for anything, it should be for those two months they had spent together as man and wife, and for that brief joyful week when they had loved. It was the only true happiness he had ever known.

Golkha seemed totally ignorant of anything save the functioning of her body, and since the birth of her daughter she had developed an almost animal-like maternalism, grudging the time she spent with him when instead she could be with her child.

But Giovanna provided intelligent companionship.

"Much news reached Constantinople in your absence," she had told him. "Of how a Genoese in the service of Spain, one Columbus, has sailed across the great ocean and come to Asia. He has proved that the world is round. Is that not marvellous?"

"Yes," William agreed, intrigued.

"And from England, that the heir to the throne is dead. It is said that his younger brother will wed Prince Arthur's wife, the Princess of Aragon. It is even sanctioned by the Pope."

"By that wretch? He is a greater scoundrel than Bayazid."

"Nonetheless, the sanction is accepted." Giovanna came closer. "I do not ask to be your wife, William. I know I can never replace Aimée, nor would I seek to do so. But I cannot live an empty life."

No more can I, he thought. And we are the last relics of the Hawkwood family. Save only for little Harry.

It were best he had both a father and a mother.

William took her into his arms.

Giovanna made love almost with desperation. But then, so did William. Both had much to forget, and much to anticipate ... not all of it pleasant.

Aimée was dead. Once he had supposed her lost to him, while knowing that she still laughed and perhaps loved. That had been bitter gall to his spirit.

But now she was dead. Raped until she no longer pleased her master, and then tied up in a sack and drowned. Aimée was dead.

He would never love again. But he could make love.

And Giovanna was a woman born to be loved. She was a true Neapolitan, tempestuous and moody. There were days when she would speak to no one, days when she would break crockery, days when she looked sinister enough for murder. But there were also days, more numerous as time passed, when Giovanna laughed and sang, when she cooked exotic meals, when she played for hours with her son.

When she was happy. On those days William was happy too.

He expected her to become pregnant, but she preferred not to, by means of douches and various other remedies which she did not confide to him. He could not blame her. Their future was too uncertain, and Harry was sufficient for her to worry over.

But the boy was a joy. William very soon indeed came to regard him as his own, delighted in teaching him horsemanship and the use of weapons ... instilling in his mind a hatred of Bayazid.

Every summer, for the first few years following their declaration of revolt, both William and the garrison anticipated a punitive expedition. They did not greatly fear it, but they did not see how Bayazid could let them exist without at least an attempt to bring them down. Every spring William sent spies down to Trebizond, who brought back news of the outside world — but of no great summons to arms within the Ottoman dominions.

It seemed that Bayazid, lost in his pleasures, was content to forget about them. But also, it seemed, he remained securely upon his throne.

Thus one summer melted gently into another and William's pain began to subside. His anger never would. From the viewpoint of either Turk or Englishman the rape and death of Aimée was of less importance than the necessity to avenge his brother.

But the doing of it was going to take time.

It was time William used well. His mountain warfare against the Persians and the Circassians taught him the skill at arms he had hoped to learn from his father. Equally it kept his men honed to a hardness and keenness they had not known since the days of Mahomet.

Slowly, every year, he increased the size of his army. He remembered too well the hastily-raised and totally ineffective levées which had followed Djem to catastrophe. He could not increase the numbers of his Janissaries, because in the Taurus mountains there were no Christian children to be kidnapped, but he could recruit and train a hand-picked body of mountaineers, men who swore allegiance to him and in time would follow him anywhere.

He had not the handguns to arm them as well, but the mountain Turks were as deadly with their bows as the average musketeer, and once disciplined became a truly formidable fighting force.

They lived very much off their own, farming the fields in the summer and retreating into hibernation in the winter, complete with their cattle. They made their own clothes and their own bullets. And, as time passed without any move by Bayazid, they began to venture more often into Trebizond, where they were welcomed as friends. They beylerbey even entertained William in his own home.

Mustafa was gloomy. "I see the dissolution of our empire," he said. "You are not the only beylerbey who has virtually declared independence, Hawk Pasha. Even I no longer receive instructions from Constantinople. Though I at least still send tribute," he added morosely.

William marked him as a man who might possibly be useful when the day came.

His visits to Trebizond were most useful for discovering what was happening in the world beyond Constantinople. He learned how the boy king Charles VIII had invaded Italy and marched as far south as Naples; how Pope Alexander had formed a 'Holy League' to expel the invaders. But the French had only left Italy when disease had shattered their army.

He learned how Cesare Borgia had embarked on a career of conquest through central and northern Italy, earning for himself the title Duke of Romagna.

He learned of the spread of a dreadful sexual disease called syphilis from Naples, during its siege by the French. Surely, he thought, a judgement of God.

He learned of the early death of Charles VIII and the succession of Louis XII in France. And of the launching of a crusade by Alexander VI against the Turks; everyone had to pay a tithe of their wealth towards the raising of a vast army. But it was never raised.

He heard of the continuing explorations of the Genoese seaman, Christopher Columbus.

And then in 1503, ten years after he had left Constantinople, he heard that Pope Alexander VI was dead.

Four years later, forced to flee Italy, after the support of the Papacy had been withdrawn, Cesare Borgia was killed in a skirmish in eastern Spain.

Alexander's successor was, predictably, Cardinal Giuliano delle Rovere, who took the name Julius II. He was a bitter enemy of the Borgias all his life, and after an attempt on his life had even been forced to flee to the Emperor for protection. Now he was back, and the Papacy, which had been reduced to the level of a brothel by the Borgias, was due for an overhaul. It now ceased to present any threat to the Ottoman empire, which was apparently maintaining good relations with its immediate neighbours, happy to be relieved by Bayazid's indolence from the constant probings of the Conqueror.

Venice thus renewed her alliance with the Porte, and even proposed a joint Turkish-Venetian conquest of Egypt with a view to building a canal through to the Red Sea, shortening the trade route to India and the East. Venice was alarmed by the progress made by Spanish and Portuguese seamen. The Portuguese sailors, Vasco da Gama and Bartolomeu Diaz, going south instead of west, had rounded the Cape of Storms at the bottom of Africa. Portuguese carracks were appearing in the Arabian Sea, and Venice saw the approaching end of her carrying monopoly unless the intruders could be thwarted.

But Bayazid turned a deaf ear to the importunities of the Venetian ambassador. He did not care what happened beyond the walls of Constantinople.

It was in the late summer of 1509 that a messenger toiled up the road to Erzurum with the news that Constantinople had been devastated by an earthquake.

William Hawkwood and Walid gazed at each other in consternation. It was hard to imagine that mighty city laid low.

Equally it was hard to decide whether this was the act of God for which they had been waiting.

"The Sultan?" William asked.

"The Sultan is unharmed, great lord. The Seraglio is undamaged."

William snapped his fingers in dismay.

"But there is much unrest," the messenger continued. "It is said that the Janissaries have overturned their meat kettles. They are complaining that it is the duty of the Sultan to lead them to war, not to keep them sitting at home to be killed by falling walls."

"Now, that is good news," Walid said. "Which of the young princes will they follow, do you suppose?"

William knew none of the princes well enough; only that they had spent their entire lives submerged in the shadow of a debauched libertine.

"I doubt they will follow anyone," he said.

"Then, like Mustafa Bey, you foresee the break-up of the empire," Walid said sombrely.

To know what to do: it was not the first time in his life that William had been faced with this dilemma. And now he had no one to whom he could turn.

He was forty-nine years old; and the last fifteen had been by far the most contented of his life. Could he rid himself of the burden of guilt that he had not yet avenged his wife and his brother, he would indeed have been happy.

He could see Harry Hawkwood growing into a tall, strong youth. As he was tawny-haired Giovanna's son no less than John Hawkwood's, his hair was red and his shoulders broad. Already he rode at William's side on the summer campaigns. If he succeeded to nothing more than the city of Erzurum, and rule over the mountains, he would yet have a great inheritance.

The others had died so long ago. Yet they must be avenged.

"We will give the Janissaries a few more months to foster their discontent," he decided, "and meanwhile prepare ourselves for war."

That summer he took almost his entire army through the mountains, meaning to raid for a hundred miles along the west bank of the Tigris, as far as Mosul. There were the usual skirmishes with the locals, but no resistance to speak of until they had advanced some fifty miles, and were almost down into the plains. Then the advance guard of sipahis sent a messenger back to the main body, to announce that they had made contact with a large force of Persians who wished to hold a parley.

"What have we to say to the Persians?" Walid asked. "They are our enemies."

"It can harm no man to listen to what others have to say," William told him. "Even his enemies."

Not wishing to fall into any trap, he deployed his army carefully, keeping the Janissaries close to the river that guarded his left, marching his mountaineers on the right flank stretching into the desert, and covering the whole with a screen of sipahis. Then he rode forward, with Walid and his personal escort, to where the advance guard waited.

Before him was indeed a considerable force of both horse and foot, but encamped on the bank of the river, with banners flying and tabalcans sounding.

Between the encampment and his sipahis there waited a picquet of horsemen beneath a white flag.

Walid advanced to interrogate them, and then returned. "Someone who calls himself the Shah of all Persia wishes to speak with you, Hawk Pasha. His name is Ismail. We have heard of this man."

They had indeed. Part of the reason for their successful raids into Persia over the past fifteen years had arisen from the fact that the once-great Iranian kingdom had been split by faction and civil war. Recently, however, word had reached them that a single warlord had been slowly accumulating territory, bringing the rebellious khans to heel. The name they had heard was Ismail. He claimed to be the son of the Sheikh Haidar by a daughter of the same Uzun Hasan whom the Conqueror and Anthony Hawkwood had defeated thirty years before.

More important than that, his paternal grandfather, Sheikh Joneid, claimed descent from Ali, the fourth caliph. This made him a Shi'ite Muslim, as were the majority of the Persians; as Ali had been murdered, they claimed that all the caliphs since him had been usurpers.

And so William rode forward to greet the self-proclaimed Shah of Iran.

He saw a man of medium size, with a clean-shaven chin but upturned moustaches, dressed in a tunic of cloth of gold with tight white leggings beneath, and wearing a turban in which was set an ostrich plume secured with a sapphire brooch.

"You are Hawk Pasha, the rebel against the Sultan," Ismail declared.

"I am Hawk Pasha, defender of the true Ottoman cause," William replied.

"You are outlawed by the Sultan."

"Yet I am ruler of the Taurus, and all the lands close by. You must be aware of these things, my lord Shah."

Ismail stared at him, and then smiled.

"Come and sit with me."

They rode into the Persian encampment, and sat on a carpet in the golden tent of the Shah. Coffee was served.

"Your warriors worship a false principle," Ismail observed.

"They think that of you, my lord Shah," William replied. "But they are *my* warriors. Where I point my sword, they march."

"And you point your sword against my people. This is senseless, Hawk Pasha. Your sword should be pointed against Constantinople, against the false Sultan who has betrayed and humiliated you."

William bit his lip. Did all the world know of it?

"My sword will be pointed at Constantinople when the time is right."

"Is the time ever more right than now? Bayazid is discredited. His Janissaries overturn their meat kettles; his capital is in ruins. He has proved himself a coward. Can you await a better opportunity?"

William studied his face. "The Sultan yet commands mighty armies, and great soldiers to lead them. More important, he is the Sultan, and commands the allegiance of all men not already sentenced to death."

"A sultan who has broken the law of the Anyi is no sultan," Ismail declared. "If the imams and the muftis lack the courage to replace him, then the task must fall to abler hands."

"But those hands must belong to a member of the royal house," William said.

Ismail smiled. "You are right, Hawk Pasha. You understand the law." He clapped his hands, and the inner flap of the tent was lifted.

A man stood there. He was in his early forties, William estimated, dressed as a Turk, but richly. His features, the drooping upper lip and the cold eyes, denoted his family.

William was on his feet in an instant, making the obeisance. "My lord Prince Ahmed."

The Prince came into the room and took his hands.

"Hawk Pasha. My father has grievously wronged you."

"You do me great honour, my lord Prince."

"I am honoured to be in the company of so great a warrior, Hawk Pasha. And of so great a name."

"It is well," Ismail said impatiently. "Acquaint Hawk Pasha with your reasons for being here, my lord Prince."

Ahmed sat down, cross-legged, between them. William sat on his left.

"My father has sinned against you, Hawk Pasha," Prince Ahmed declared, "and against the Anyi. He had sinned also against his sons. My brothers are weak men, unable to determine what is best to do. I know what is to be done: my father must be deposed. I mean him no harm, but he has proved himself unworthy of ruling the Ottoman Turks. The Janissaries need but a sign. And who may better give them the sign than the pasha my father has wronged — and who will now march under a royal banner? My own."

William glanced at Ismail, and the Prince continued.

"The Shah, here, who seeks justice in all things, has promised us his support. He has promised money, guns and ammunition. More,

301

he has promised a contingent of his own men. He has promised forty thousand Persians to march beneath our banners."

William continued to gaze at Ismail for a confirming sign.

"I have indeed promised these things," Ismail said.

"You will be the commander of my army, Hawk Pasha," Ahmed announced.

"Shi'ites," Walid said. "That is not good. The people will not accept it. The Janissaries will not accept it."

"They *will* accept it," William said, "because I will explain it to them."

He assembled his men and spoke to them. He reminded them of the patient years they had waited to strike at Bayazid, to replace him with an Ottoman more worthy of the name. He told them that they would never have a better opportunity than now. And he reminded them that the Conqueror, in the furtherance of his plans, had made alliance with Greeks and Christians, infidels all, for as long as it suited him. There could be nothing wrong in a temporary alliance with heretics, if it gave them the victory.

The Janissaries seemed satisfied.

William was thoroughly aware of the enormous risk he was taking. He understood that Ahmed, however disparagingly he spoke of his brothers, was himself the true son of his father: Mahomet would have taken command of the army himself, not handed it over to another general while he lurked in safety.

He also understood that the Prince must have somehow sold himself to the Persians in order to gain their aid. He could not tell what promises had been made, but undoubtedly it involved some cession of territory — perhaps even a withdrawal of the Erzurum garrison and a yielding of the entire Taurus region to the Shah.

But those were things which could be settled after the victory — if there was one. He himself had not been a party to any agreements, therefore could not be bound by them. He was aware, too, that even with the assistance of forty thousand Persians he would command an army inferior to that which Bayazid could put into the field, if he chose. And that if he lost this time, he would surely be impaled. And this time no one would lift a finger to help him.

Yet he had no choice but to act ... or to admit that he was hardly better than the craven Sultan himself.

*

"So now you go to war," Giovanna said.

They had shared their bed for so long they seemed as married as two people could ever be. He never summoned Golkha nowadays; the Circassian had grown enormously fat and listless.

"It is what we have planned for fifteen years," he reminded her.

"They have been good years." But she knew better than to allow her sadness to interfere with masculine ambitions. "Bring my son back to me, William."

For Harry Hawkwood, now seventeen, would ride at his uncle's shoulder.

William went about his business as cautiously as ever. As always he hoisted the standard, not of Prince Ahmed, but of "the True Sultan", and under this, the following spring, he led his men down from the mountains to the Black Sea coast.

Mustafa Pasha of Trebizond surrendered without a fight. "I have long known this day must come," he said, "and I congratulate you. My men will ride beneath your banner."

But he frowned and tugged on his beard when he considered the Persians.

William now held the Taurus region and a Black Sea port, thus he also commanded a fleet of sorts. The ships he despatched to Caffa and Kerch, on the borders of the khanate of the Crimea. The Crimea had paid tribute since 1475. Now it paid tribute to the one True Sultan. With their corn William could feed his growing army, augmented as it was by the Trebizond garrison.

The following spring he marched through the mountains to Sivas. Capital of the province bearing its name, the city, although situated at more than four thousand feet above sea level, lay in the broad, fertile valley of the Kizil Irmak. A century earlier it had been reputed to contain a population of over a hundred and fifty thousand people, but it had never recovered from the frightful sack by Timur and his Mongols.

The city abounded with Seljuk relics, including a Great Mosque, and the mausoleum of its founder, Sultan Kay-Ka'us I.

More importantly, the valley of the Kizil Irmak stretched south almost to Kayseri, and then bent back to the north-west. By following this valley, assured always of food and water, an army could approach within a few miles of Ankara, and find itself in the very heartland of Anatolia — with the mountains behind it, and Brusa, the coast and Constantinople before.

In the past all invaders from the east had approached by way of Sivas and the Kizil Irmak.

William had expected to find the city barred to him, but the beylerbey, Ibrahim Pasha, willingly joined the rebel army, and another twenty thousand men enrolled beneath the green and crimson banners. William now commanded an army of a hundred thousand experienced soldiers.

Prince Ahmed came to review his army outside Sivas.

"When will you march?" he asked Hawk Pasha.

"In the spring, my lord Prince," William told him. "When will the cannon promised by the Shah arrive?"

"There are difficulties, but they will be here, Hawk Pasha."

William realised he would have to do whatever he could, without artillery. Which meant that he must draw Bayazid's army into the field and defeat it there; he had no means of assaulting walls.

Ahmed remained in Sivas over the winter. He had brought his harem with him, and made himself thoroughly comfortable.

William sent for Giovanna, and did likewise.

"Next year," he told her. "Next year will be one of the most important in the history of the Ottomans. Perhaps of the world."

"Next year you may well die," she brooded. "Then I must die also, for I have no one else to live for."

"You have Harry," he reminded her.

"When you die, Harry will surely die at your side," she said.

Next year! William was fifty when the snows melted and the army began to prepare for its advance on Ankara; he meant to be across the Bosphorus by the autumn. As he could not batter down the walls of Constantinople, he must campaign as the Ottomans had done before the coming of the Hawkwoods, and overrun the entire rest of the empire. That would surely draw Bayazid into the field: he was no Constantine XI.

But, before he had given the order to march, news came that an army was marching to meet him, flying the banners of the Sultan.

William could hardly believe his good fortune.

"Does the Padishah command in person?" he asked the messenger.

"No, my lord. The army is commanded by Prince Selim."

William looked at Ahmed.

"Bah, he is but a boy," Ahmed declared. "There is nought to fear."

"I did not suppose there was, my lord Prince." William turned back to the messenger. "Does the Sultan's army have artillery?"

"Yes, my lord. There are twelve guns."

"Two batteries," Ahmed muttered, his ashen face entirely belying his earlier words. "What will you do, Hawk Pasha? We have no artillery."

"Your ally has let us down, my lord Prince. But, no matter, we shall fight the decisive battle outside Sivas. Will you take command?"

"Me?" Ahmed looked startled. "No, no, I must return to Mosul and report the situation to the Shah. He will be interested. Send me word of your victory, Hawk Pasha, so that I may then return to you."

But not of my defeat, William thought. Because then you will stay in Persia, awaiting your father's bowstring.

"Why do we fight for such a creature?" Walid growled.

"Because he is the son of the Sultan."

"And another approaches," Walid reminded him.

But this one was prepared to fight in person.

William sent an advance guard of sipahis out to discover the whereabouts of the royal army, while he marched his own men out of the city and encamped them on his chosen site: an open area of some miles' breadth. It could be no part of his strategy merely to repel the Sultan's force; he had to defeat them decisively, despite their artillery.

The people of Sivas watched them go with grim faces. They knew that were this rebel army defeated, their city would again be sacked.

William rode amongst his men, speaking with every regiment, telling them that they *must* win this battle, or else they and their families would all perish. He promised them each a large donation when finally they marched into Constantinople.

He could not speak Iranian, so he had the Persian commander, Nadir Ali, translate for him.

Then he returned to his tent to wait.

305

He had sent Giovanna back to Erzurum. He could do nothing more for her. She, like everyone else, lived or died on the outcome of the coming battle.

He was conscious of a great sense of loneliness. When he had been young, he had relied on the support and advice of two strong brothers and a great and powerful father. Now they were all gone, with their talents and their knowledge. He was fifty, and he was the very last Hawkwood save for the boy who waited outside his tent.

For all his successes as a guerilla leader over the past fifteen years, he had never commanded an army in a pitched battle against an equal enemy. Much less one likely to be superior.

But then he remembered that Selim was ten years his junior and, owing to the weakness of his father, he too could never have commanded an army in battle.

Harry Hawkwood now stood at the doorway to the tent. "The Sultan's army approaches, Uncle," he said.

It was just dawn.

"Have the tabalcans and bugles sounded," William said. His servants came in to strap on his cuirass, hand him his helmet and wrap the turban round the steel. They buckled on his scimitar.

When he went outside, his stallion was waiting for him. His quiver hung down on his left-hand side, his bow on his right. He mounted and rode out to watch his troops deploying: Ibrahim Pasha commanded the men from Sivas and Trebizond on the right; Mustafa had been left to guard the coast road; the Persians were on the left. The Janissaries and the mountaineers, in the centre, he would command himself. The sipahis were stationed even more to the right than the Sivans, concealed in a wood. His victory depended on them, because success depended on eliminating the guns at the very outset. He planned to hold off the royal army with his infantry, and deliver a flank attack with his cavalry aimed at the artillery batteries.

It went against the rules of war to launch cavalry against unbroken troops. But they would be attacking from the flank, and the guns would be pointing straight ahead; they would not be turned in time, and an attempt to do so would surely disrupt the loyalist ranks.

He had nothing better.

"Remember," he told Walid, who commanded the horse. "Your

charge must succeed. We cannot stand a bombardment for long."

"It will succeed," Walid promised.

His dispositions made, William walked his horse out in front of his men, Harry and his bugler at either side. They watched the road where it followed the bend of the river, some three miles away. They could hear now the sounds of many marching feet and hooves — and the rumble of the gun carriages. He listened to the approach of such an army once before.

He glanced at Harry, and Harry grinned at him. The boy knew no fear.

A regiment of sipahis came into sight. They were followed by the bashi-bazouks, who took up their position exactly opposite the centre of William's army. The Anatolians debouched to left and right to form the two wings. Behind them were the Janissaries, several thousand of them, denoted by the white plumes in their helmets. When they halted at their appointed position, the plumes gave off a tremendous rustle. William could not see what they were doing, but he knew they were placing the rests for their arquebuses.

William could not see the cannon either, but he knew they would be in front of the Janissaries and behind the bashi-bazouks.

Behind the Janissaries was the main body of sipahis, and behind them again the baggage-train.

William estimated there were not less than a hundred and twenty thousand men opposed to him.

Slowly the royal army marched into position. Messengers rushed from one command to another, ordering, instructing, directing. But it was already approaching dusk. There would be no battle until tomorrow.

William frowned. Making their way through the ranks of the irregulars, and greeted by them with huzzas and the clashing of weapons, was a group of horsemen. They rode beneath the green flag of the Ottomans fluttering in the breeze, and there were personal pennants as well.

William narrowed his eyes still further, trying to identify some of the officers, but the distance was too great.

The officers reached the foremost rank of the bashis, who gave a great cheer. The rebels returned a loud shout, and then both armies fell silent, save for the stamping of horses' hooves, the shuffling of feet.

Two of the horsemen left the bashis and advanced into the open space between the armies. One carried a white flag.

This man left his companion in turn, and trotted forward. He advanced to within twenty yards of William, and called, "Are you he who calls himself Hawk Pasha?"

William was looking at a boy younger even than Harry. He had a long, thin face, as yet beardless, nor was there a moustache. The lips were firm, the forehead high. The face lacked the cruel cast of Mahomet and his immediate descendants, but possessed the boldness of his great-grandfather.

"I am he," William answered.

"My father, Prince Selim, would speak with you."

William realised that this must be Selim's only son, Prince Suleiman. He looked past the Prince at the lone horseman, who sat in his saddle, absolutely still.

"It may be a trap, Uncle," Harry muttered.

"I will speak with him," William decided, and urged his horse forward.

Suleiman rode in front of him until they came up to the Prince.

"Return to the ranks," Selim said to his son.

Suleiman cantered back to the bashis.

William gazed at Prince Selim and was suddenly conscious of apprehension where he had known little before.

Was this truly a son of Bayazid? William could hardly remember the Conqueror, but this trim, erect horseman, his cuirass inter-twined with gold thread, reminded him of everything he had heard of Mahomet. The thin lips, the slightly drooping nose, the moustache, were all reminiscent of his grandfather. No doubt his brothers and his father possessed the same characteristics.

But none of them had the firmness of expression, then steadi-ness of eye of this man.

William at once understood that here was the true Ottoman — the only true living Ottoman, save perhaps for the boy who had now regained the royal ranks.

For his part, Selim inspected William with no less interest.

"I last saw you seventeen years ago," he said. "When you stood before my father on your return from Italy."

"I remember, my lord Prince."

Selim studied him. "Before a great wrong was done you, Hawk Pasha."

William frowned. This was hardly the statement of an enemy.

He looked past the Prince at the royal army. "Your men are well disposed, my lord Prince."

"I was well taught, Hawk Pasha. I campaigned with your father."

"You are fortunate, my lord."

"Indeed. I would have you be fortunate also, Hawk Pasha. You have taken up arms against my father. That I can understand, because of the wrong done to you. But you fight for my brother, who is a fool and a coward. Do you not realise that?"

William made no reply, which was reply enough.

Selim pointed at the rebel left wing. "You also ally yourself with the Persians. Surely you know that they are our hereditary enemies, who seek only to create discord among us for their own benefit? Do you not also know that they are heretics who are an abomination in the sight of Allah?"

"A man must seek his allies where he can find them, my lord Prince. There are not sufficient men in these mountains to raise an army to oppose yours."

"Then why oppose mine, Hawk Pasha? Do you not realise that there are sufficient men in your army and mine to work our will upon the whole world?"

William gazed at him.

"I offer you a free pardon if you will march beneath my banner," Selim said. "More, I offer you the command of my army, beneath me. You bear a famous name in the history of my people. Do not now disgrace it and cast it in the dust."

"My lord, I am sworn to the cause of Prince Ahmed."

"Not so, Hawk Pasha. I have been told that you are sworn to the cause of the true Ottoman. Is that not so?"

William gazed at him.

"My brother's cause is a false cause, Hawk Pasha, and you know this. My brother is a vicious man. Once you have gained his victory for him, should fortune smile upon you, he will have your head because you will be grown too powerful."

"My lord . . ."

Selim gave a grim smile. "And would I not do the same? I do not fear you, Hawk Pasha, because I too am a soldier. More than that, I know I can trust you because your name is Hawk. I will honour you above all other men, as my grandfather honoured your father. I swear this, by the memory of Mahomet."

309

An oath he would certainly keep. And this was a man to be followed by one who had once determined to devote his life to the service of the Ottomans. He was the only one to follow.

"My lord Prince, I am outlawed by your father. Nor can I accept any forgiveness from him, for I have none for him."

"Hawk Pasha, Bayazid has sat upon the divan too long and to too little purpose. Unite your force with mine. As I have said, there is none can stand against us."

William stared at him. Does Bayazid have any idea, he wondered, how all his sons despise him?

Selim had noted the hesitation.

"When my father is deposed," he said, "he will be incarcerated in a special palace I shall have built. With him will go his favourite wives, concubines and eunuchs, to a certain number. All save one. She was obtained illegally, and has been used illegally ever since."

William's head jerked. "Surely my wife is dead?"

"Not so. She lives in my father's harem, Hawk Pasha. I know this, for he has boasted of it. I do not know what tenderness you can feel for your wife after so many years. Perhaps you wish only to strangle her; that will be your decision. But I will restore your wife to you."

William could hardly believe it: Aimée still alive!

What would she be like after eighteen years in Bayazid's harem? Would she be anything like the girl he had once loved? That was impossible. So, as Selim had suggested, perhaps all he would wish to do to her would be to wrap a bowstring round that marvellous neck and consign her to the Bosphorus.

But he knew that he had to see her again, no matter the pain involved.

"If we agree to march together, my lord Prince," he said. "What am I to tell my allies?"

Selim gave another grim smile. "The only good Shi'ite is a dead one."

"They are my allies," William protested.

"They are Shi'ites. Did you ask for their help, Hawk Pasha?"

"No, my lord."

"They were foisted upon you by my brother and his ally, the so-called Shah of Persia. You have no reason to support them."

"They are forty thousand men."

"Forty thousand Shi'ites, Hawk Pasha."

"Who have marched beneath my banner."

Selim's teeth gleamed through his beard. "You are an honourable man, Hawk Pasha; that I know. Send your Persian allies home. Tell them to inform their Shah that they are little men, and that if he does not send my brother Ahmed to me I will come to him, and destroy him and his puny people."

"My lord, that will mean war with the Shah."

"War is what I wish, Hawk Pasha. War is man's natural state. I wish war with all the world. If you would ride at my right hand, that must be your wish, too."

William remembered what he had told Giovanna: that this year would be the most momentous in Ottoman history. He had been right without understanding it.

Mahomet the Conqueror was reborn.

The Kislar Agha opened the door and gave a brief bow. "Ya Habibti, the Padishah comes."

Aimée had been reclining on one of the divans, playing with her lapdog. She sat bolt upright and stared at the eunuch.

"Here?"

For the Sultan to visit the private apartments of his concubines was unknown.

"He is much distressed," the Agha said warningly.

His name was Ali and he was a friend. She had known him for so very long: eighteen years. He had held the tray with her nail parings and her bodily hair for her inspection on that unforgettable day when she had first entered this palace. He had been a subordinate then, but had succeeded to his all-powerful post on the death of his predecessor seven years ago. She did not suppose there was a living creature on the face of the earth she knew so well, or who knew her so intimately.

Now he had come to prepare her ... for what?

It was difficult for Aimée to consider any change in her situation, after eighteen years, even if she knew that her life still hung on the whim of her master. No doubt the lives of everyone in the empire hung on that whim, but the inmates of the harem were more readily exposed to his uncertain temper.

Aimée remembered well how some of the other women had disappeared a few years before. No one had known where they had gone — and it was unthinkable to suppose they had been sent out of the Seraglio. As she had been told when she had first entered the palace, there was no escape save in death. Yet no sultan in history had murdered his concubines *en masse*.

But soon Constantinople had been rife with rumour, brought into the harem by the eunuchs, how a fishing boat had struck a rock and sunk off Seraglio Point, and, when the owner and his sons had dived to the wreck to see what they could salvage, they had come face-to-face with a score of drowned women, manacled together, waving to and fro on the tide.

They had been *guizdes*, the unwanted ones. Such a fate could never overtake an odalisk, much less the highest odalisk of them all.

Aimée could clearly remember what had happened to her that first day, when she had been taken to the bedchamber of the Sultan.

The Agha had remained to undress his master. Curious as she had been, Aimée had yet been revolted by the rolls of fat. She had begun to grow afraid again when the Kislar Agha had been dismissed. Amazing that she should find reassurance in the presence of a eunuch, who clearly regarded her as no more than a lump of meat.

She had then been stripped by Bayazid, to submit to his maulings and explorations, his entry and his mutterings. That was her fate and she must accept it.

He had been pleased.

"You are exquisite," he had told her when he had regained his breath after finally climaxing. "From now on your name will be Ya Habibti: My Darling."

As he had entered her from behind, his weight had caused her knees to collapse, but she had lain still beneath him, fighting for breath. She had been aiming only at her own survival.

Understanding had come later for Ya Habibti. She had been summoned to the Sultan's bed every night for a fortnight. During that time she had been secluded from the other women, served only by her eunuchs and her maids. They told her how it was rumoured that the Sultan was ill, because he called no other woman to his bed. They told her that she was the most privileged woman in the history of the world.

She had not thought so, then. The true horror of her situation had only slowly been dawning on her. To come face-to-face with the fact that she must spend the rest of her life within these four walls ... At times she had screamed uncontrollably for William, and had to be restrained in case she harmed herself.

Yet did she really wish William to return for her, when it would probably mean his death — and hers? But not to dream of him, to pray that he might somehow secrete her away from the harem, would be a betrayal of her love for him. That at least she could preserve, no matter what course her life took.

But even that became difficult after the first month. Because after a month she was pregnant.

Bayazid had been delighted. His sons were all grown men, and he had long deemed himself impotent.

Now there was even more reason now for secreting her in her own private apartments. The mothers of Corcud, and Ahmed, and Selim, would have given this rival short shrift.

With the birth of her first daughter, her husband William had seemed more remote. When she asked about him from the eunuchs, she was told that William had vanished into the mountains of the Taurus — officially dead. His name was never uttered at the divan.

So this was her Fate. If Bayazid was disappointed that she had produced only a daughter, he had still been proud of his prowess. Within a year she had again been a mother. This too was a girl, which she found reassuring. There was no risk of rivalry for the future sultanate, to threaten her child.

By then, too, the need for concealment was passed. She had retained her private apartments, but had been given the freedom of the harem. This proved a joy. She had now been surrounded by other women, and she had won the special friendship and protection of the Sultan Valideh, Gulbehar — the favourite wife of the Conqueror. Gulbehar had been only fourteen when she had given birth to Bayazid, so even when the Sultan reached the age of sixty she was still only seventy-four, a neat, trim little woman whose wrinkles could not conceal the beauty that had once turned the head of Mahomet.

No doubt, Aimée supposed, that was an age she would reach herself; at thirty-nine she was well over halfway. Would she also still reveal traces of her beauty?

Her life had slipped into a serenity she had never known in her

313

youth. Bayazid had aged and degenerated too rapidly to be a continuing nuisance. He had not succeeded in impregnating her again, and as time had passed he had sought variety. Nowadays she went to his bed not more than a dozen times a year, but even that was more regularly than any other inmate of the harem.

She knew him for a debauched and drunken roué. She knew him for a physical coward: his terror had been pitiful that day two years back when the earth had shaken and cracks had appeared in the palace walls. She knew him to be a mass killer and an utterly vicious creature. Yet, by sheer familiarity, he had become more like a husband to her than William had ever been.

And he was not entirely given to vice. Though his viziers might regard him with contempt because he preferred peace to war, he spent his time in filling the palace with books and art treasures gleaned from all over Europe, although he dared not display any paintings which depicted the human form.

He lavished presents upon her, of jewellery and fine stuffs. He clearly adored her daughters, who had now grown into lovely teenage girls.

Left to herself, Aimée could attend to their education. Left to herself she could form friendships within the harem, even if the Greek girls and the Bulgars, the Anatolians and the Circassians remained too childish and banal for her to ever seek intimacy with them. She preferred the company of her eunuchs, and in particular Ali.

There could be no true happiness in the harem. But there could be a great deal of contentment.

But now Bayazid was coming to see her in her own apartment — and in great distress. Something terrible must have happened.

The Sultan sank on to the divan, his fat dissolving into rolls of shivering jelly.

"I have been betrayed," he moaned. "I have been betrayed."

Aimée sat down beside him. "By whom, O Padishah?"

"Selim! The best of my sons. There was a rebellion in the Taurus, inspired by that fiend Ismail of Persia. I sent Selim against the rebels with an army. Now he and the rebel army march together on Constantinople. March on me! By Allah, I am forsaken; I have fathered a brood of vipers."

"Perhaps you frighten yourself without cause, Padishah," Aimée

314

said. "You sent your son to suppress a rebellion, and he has done so. If he has accomplished this without fighting, but has instead persuaded the rebels to return to their loyalty, is that not something for which to be thankful?"

"Bah! You know nothing, woman," Bayazid snapped. "Have you no idea who commanded these rebels?"

Aimée stared at him, a monstrous suspicion starting up in her mind.

"Aye," Bayazid said. "Young Hawk. Who now styles himself Hawk Pasha." He threw off her arm and strode to the window, which looked down on the courtyard of the harem. "Hawk Pasha! He is a nightmare risen from the grave to haunt me."

Aimée's hand flew to her throat. A Hawkwood marching in arms on Constantinople! William! After eighteen years!

Bayazid flung out his arm.

"He seeks my death, and somehow he has suborned my son. But I will tell you this: before he sets foot in this palace you will die. Ya Habibti. He will never recover you!"

He stamped from the room.

Aimée sat motionless for several seconds after he had left. She had never been more afraid in her life.

She was less afraid of anything Bayazid might do to her. He could not be serious; she was Ya Habibti. But the thought of having to face William again ... coming to avenge her after eighteen years.

She felt like a young girl. Her heart fluttered and her cheeks grew hot. William was coming.

She made herself think. If, after eighteen years, he wished to march on Constantinople, could it be her he sought? Yet he must know how she had spent those eighteen years. He knew, and yet he came.

She must be alive to receive him. It was her fate, her kismet. She had only survived by believing that utterly. God had led her a merry dance, but at last He was returning her to her rightful lord.

There was no need to be afraid. She was thirty-nine, and she had put on some weight, but not so much as most of the other older women. She was still Ya Habibti, the most beautiful woman in the harem. Her hair was still like fine-spun gold, her skin unblemished.

William would love her once again. Because he was coming for her.

More than ever she relied on Ali; he was her friend. News was of vital importance, and Ali knew as well as anyone what was happening in the outside world. She pressed him for further information.

"They call the Prince Selim the Grim," Ali told her. "He destroys every man, everything that stands in his way. And now he is past Brusa, and marching on the Bosphorus."

"Will the garrison here fight for the Sultan?" she asked.

"If he were to put himself at their head, perhaps," Ali said.

But Bayazid would never have the courage to do that.

"Is it true that Hawk Pasha marches with the Prince?" she persisted.

"It is true, lady."

"And what of the other princes?"

"They are fled. Ahmed is with the Persians. Corcud has gone to Venice. They are as nothing now, unless Selim dies."

But Selim could not die; he was bringing Hawk Pasha to her. She was so excited she thought she might die.

Constantinople waited.

"The Prince is at the Bosphorus, lady," Ali reported. "He has summoned his father to surrender."

Aimée could hardly breathe.

The women of the harem gathered whispering in groups, afraid to say out loud whether they feared or anticipated the deposition of their master. No doubt the people of Constantinople did the same. The night air was filled with sound: a gigantic whisper seeping through the darkness.

Aimée woke with a start, surprised to have fallen asleep. She sat up and gazed at the doorway of her apartment. It was opening.

But there were no lights.

"Who is there?" she demanded, anxiously.

"It is Ali, lady."

He was not alone. There were two other eunuchs with him.

"What is happening?" she asked.

"The army of Prince Selim is across the Bosphorus. Tomorrow it will enter the city," Ali told her. "The Janissaries of the garrison have declared for the Prince."

He had advanced until he stood by the bed. The others remained a little further away.

Aimée's eyes were accustomed to the darkness, and she gasped in horror at what she saw. The two eunuchs carried a sack, and Ali held a bowstring in his hands.

She propelled herself backwards with her heels and touched the wall.

"No," she said. "You cannot!"

"I am instructed by our master, lady."

"You cannot! You, Ali? You cannot."

"I must obey my master, lady. Come."

Aimée panted. "My daughters ..."

"They will not be harmed, lady. But my master has ordered that you must not fall into the hands of Hawk Pasha."

"Ali, please ..."

"It is better to die with dignity, lady, than to be dragged screaming to the sack."

He reached for her, and she kicked out at him. In the darkness neither could see the other properly, and her toes struck him in the chest. He grabbed at her ankle and held it for a moment, but she twisted free, and sprang for the end of the divan.

He reached for her again, but she slept naked and his fingers slipped on her sweat-coated flesh.

Though the other two also tried to stop her, she wriggled past them, through the open door, and she was in the corridor. Panting and gasping, she ran for the outer door, which she had never before been through. She knew it was guarded, but the suddenness of her appearance took the eunuchs there by surprise. They shouted in alarm but she was past them, into the main body of the palace.

She knew she was on an upper floor, but she also knew that this building stood against the outer walls of the city itself — the seaward walls where the Bosphorus flowed by Seraglio Point. She was intended for the Bosphorus anyway, but if she could reach there unbound ... Memory took her back all of twenty-seven years, to French summers when she and her mother and sisters had bathed in the Seine. She had swum in that wide river, flowing far more quickly than the Bosphorus. Twenty-seven years — but surely she would be able to swim again.

The palace was lit by torches set high in the walls, and Aimée ran straight for the windows at the far end of the upper gallery.

Guards appeared from archways to either side, and began to yell — but mainly at each other. A naked woman running through the corridors was not a sight any of them had expected to see in their wildest fantasies. Her pale skin and floating golden hair told them who she was: everyone had heard of Ya Habibti, even if no man save the Sultan had beheld her for eighteen years.

While they hesitated, Aimée reached the window.

Ali appeared at the far end of the hall. "Stop her!" he shrieked. "Seize her."

As the guards ran forward, Aimée looked at them in panic, then at the darkness outside. She had no idea what lay there: beneath her could be gentle water or hard rock.

But it would be better than the bowstring and the sack.

As the first guard reached out for her, she threw herself, out and away from the sill, into the darkness.

Once I hated this man, William Hawkwood thought, as he gazed at the one-time Sultan Bayazid II.

But how was it possible to hate such a bent, broken, shameful figure?

Mounds of fat at jowl and shoulder, chest and belly trembled with fear as Bayazid faced his son.

"Go with these men, Father," Selim commanded.

Bayazid shivered even more.

"You are not to die," Selim told him. "But the world will not look upon your face again. Go with these men."

Bayazid shambled forward between his guards. As he came level with William, he glanced at him and shuddered again. He now stood in the Porte and gazed at the ranks of the Janissaries drawn up there. His troops, at whose head he had never marched.

Now they belonged to his son, and for *him* they would march to the ends of the earth.

Selim the Grim! It was a name well earned, William thought. It would be a name to reckon with.

"I am sorry, Hawk Pasha," the new Sultan said, "but I am forced by circumstances to break my word to you. Your wife is dead." He gestured at the waiting eunuchs. "These tell me she threw herself from an upper window of the palace rather than be strangled at my father's command."

"No man may challenge kismet, Padishah," William said. "have I your permission to reclaim my house?"

Selim grasped his shoulder, the greatest mark of appreciation that can be shown by a Muslim.

"Reclaim your house, Hawk Pasha," he said. "But we then have much to do, you and I."

There were two brothers yet to be destroyed, the Shah to be defeated — and the world to be made aware that a new force had arisen in Constantinople.

"I am at your call, Padishah." William bowed.

He took the ferry to Galata, and entered his father's house, young Harry at his side. The servants bowed low to him; Anthony Hawkwood's concubines and John Hawkwood's Turkish wife stared at him curiously. They had lived alone here for seventeen years; as the wife and concubines of a dead pasha, they had been amply provided for. Now they had a new master.

"Peace be with you," he said, and went into his father's private apartments.

Harry hovered in the doorway.

"I will send for your mother immediately," William said. "We will make this place once more into a home. Now leave me."

The boy withdrew, and William stood at the window, looking down at the Golden Horn. He was home at last, after more than thirty years. He had been only nineteen when he had left here to ride to Brusa at Prince Djem's side; in the interim he had returned here but twice, for just a few days. Now he might stay hardly any longer, if the Sultan had need of him. But this was his home now: it belonged to Hawk Pasha.

Useless to look over his shoulder, to dwell on might-have-beens. He had known triumphs and he had known disasters; marching beside Selim there could only be triumphs in the future. Harry Hawkwood would be a fit bearer of his famous name.

He had known happiness and great sadness. He felt a great sadness now. But Giovanna was coming to him, and if she could never replace Aimée, she was still a source of great comfort.

So then ...

He heard a sound and turned — and gazed at a ghost.

319

Involuntarily he took a step forward.

"I had to see you again," Aimée said.

They stared at each other.

"I had to know," she continued, "if I can live again, and laugh again. And love again."

Still he stared at her in silence.

"Alas," she said, "it seems I should have stayed and accepted the bowstring."

William Hawkwood held out his hands to her.

BOOK THE THIRD

Lord of All

"One Moment in Annihilation's Waste,
One Moment, of the Well of Life to Taste,
The Stars are setting and the Caravan
Starts for the Dawn of Nothing — Oh, make haste!"

OMAR KHAYYAM

12

THE SULTAN

"Look there, young Hawk!" Diniz grasped his master's arm. "We must turn back."

Harry Hawkwood frowned across the water. On the northern horizon a few minutes ago there had been a dozen galleys creeping towards them, like huge beetles on the surface of the water.

They had not disturbed him; in the year 1525 AD, the Black Sea was very much a Turkish lake.

But now, suddenly, the galleys had disappeared beneath a wall of darkness which covered the surface of the sea and was advancing rapidly. The Black Sea was renowned for its sudden storms.

Harry glanced over his shoulder. The land, even the sun-glimmering domes of Constantinople, was lost to sight; in the pursuit of his hobby of sailing he had ventured even further afield than usual.

He looked forward. His craft had no oars. She had been designed for him by a Venetian; broader in the beam and deeper in the draft than any galley. She was propelled by a lateen sail, controlled by a boom almost as long as the thirty-foot hull. She was fast and handy, and in her he could escape the heat and the bustle of the greatest city in the world.

Now she would have to prove her seaworthiness beyond doubt; there was no time for him to regain the shelter of the Bosphorus.

But she was undecked, too, and could easily fill with water.

His men watched him anxiously. The six of them were devoted to the name of Hawk, and equally to this youngest member of the illustrious family. They had sailed with him for many years.

"We must ride it out," he said. "Take down that sail, double the lines, and pay it out over the bow."

They worked with a will.

323

"You break out every utensil that can be used for bailing, Diniz," Harry told his servant.

Diniz hurried about his duties.

Harry studied the horizon, now hardly more than a few miles distant and closing every second. He wondered how the galleys were faring: they were hardly better fitted to withstand a storm than this little yacht.

He had no sensation of fear. Harry Hawkwood had never known fear. When his father, John Hawkwood the Younger, had been murdered by the Sultan Bayazid, he had been but a babe in arms. As he had grown to manhood, he had ridden at the side of his uncle, William Hawkwood, and, after the deposition of Bayazid by his son, under the banner of the new Sultan Selim himself, that greatest of warriors.

Harry Hawkwood had known nothing but triumph throughout his life ... unlike, he would sometimes reflect, his famous forebears.

He was unlike them, too, in his love for the sea. William Hawkwood could not understand this passion; the Hawkwoods had always been artillerists, men with their feet firmly planted on the land. No Hawkwood before young Harry had ever dreamed of mounting a gun of any size on board a ship!

His mother, Giovanna, had an answer to his strange obsession: her father had been a Neapolitan sea captain, as had his father before him. Indeed, she had been sailing on one of her father's trading ships when it had been taken by a Turkish corsair and she was sold as a slave in the market at Constantinople.

That was long in the past. Under the aegis of the Hawkwoods she had regained her laughter and her confidence. But she was pleased that her only son took pleasure in the sea.

Not that she would be pleased, at this moment, to look from the window of the Hawk Palace outside Galata and watch the Black Sea swept by a summer storm.

It was nearly upon them. But Harry was as ready as he could be. The sail had been thrown over the bow, attached to the yacht by the strongest lines they possessed; it would act as an anchor and not only keep them up to the wind, and thus reduce the chance of their being swamped by the waves, but it would also slow their rate of drift and save them, he hoped, from being dashed ashore.

324

The crew meanwhile crouched in the bottom of the boat, armed with bailing cans.

Harry tied a rope round his waist and secured it to one of the exposed ribs; there was nowhere stronger. Then he wrapped both hands around the tiller, and uttered a great laugh as the first raindrops splattered across his face. Six feet three inches tall, with a mass of red-brown hair flying in the wind, his firm muscles exposed to the elements as he wore but a loincloth, he was in every way a Hawk and his men loved him for it.

The sky was now obliterated by the sweeping clouds. The rain teemed down and for the moment calmed the sea, but the wind was already tearing at the waves, causing spray to fly. The bailing cans got busy.

Harry Hawkwood strained on the tiller, face upturned to the driving wind and water, keeping the bows up to the seas. They were held there, anyway, by the waterlogged sail, but even so kept threatening to pay away, so great was the force exerted on them.

The day became dark as night, and the seas rose higher. Waves twelve, fifteen feet in height reared about the little ship; most broke on the bows and scattered away to either side, but enough came over the gunwales to leave several inches of water slopping to and fro in the bilges. As fast as this was emptied over the side, more came in.

Yet they were holding their own. Harry Hawkwood gave another shout of triumph, as if challenging the elements to do their worst.

Thunder rumbled and lightning bolts slashed at the sea to either side. The bailing was slackening as the men became exhausted. And still the storm raged.

There came a twang from forward, and one of the lines holding the sail parted, chafed through on the gunwale. There was still a second rope, but that too was chafing, seriously.

Harry realised that he might have laughed too soon. The wind was stronger and the waves higher than anything he had previously experienced. But there was nothing to be done save hang on and wait for the weather to improve.

As the second rope parted, the yacht immediately began to fall away. Harry knew that he could no longer keep her heading the wind — her safest position — and that his only hope was to bring her right round and try to run before the storm. The risk was that they would pile up on the rocks to the south, some twenty miles away.

But bringing her about without being swamped by waves was going to prove an enormous business; he had no means of gaining way to expedite the turn.

He drew a long breath.

"Cut the sail free," he bawled.

The canvas was still held by the other ends of the frayed warps.

Diniz scrambled forward, soaked by the water splashing over the bows as the boat began to roll. He drew his knife and cut the ropes with a single sweep.

"Bail!" Harry shouted, and thrust the helm hard over.

There was almost no response. The yacht fell away, but she was doing so anyway. The men shouted in alarm as they were picked up on a wave, hung there for a moment, and then went over. Harry was catapulted from the stern into the sea, still held by the rope round his waist. Water clogged his nostrils as he sank beneath the surface. Desperately he drew his own knife to cut himself free, then reached upwards and found the ship again.

She had capsized, but there was sufficient cordage surrounding her to be grabbed and clung to, while the waves broke right over the keel. She showed no signs of sinking, however; there was too much air trapped in the hull.

He twisted his head from side to side, peering through the teeming rain and the flying spray to discover which of his men had survived. Then he saw Diniz holding on to the upturned bowsprit, rising and falling in the huge swell; there were others, too, clinging on for dear life.

So much for pleasure sailing, Harry thought.

Harry had no idea how long they clung to the half-submerged hull. One of the men close to him released his grip and drifted away, to disappear under the waves. He encouraged the others as best he could by yelling out that the weather was abating, as indeed it was. The seas were going down and the rain had stopped. There was even a patch of blue sky above.

But the water was very cold. He summoned all his failing strength and, clinging by fingernails and toes, climbed up the overturned hull to sit on the keel, peering round him into the still lowering afternoon. And then he saw a dark shape not half a mile away.

Reaching down for his surviving crew members, he slowly pulled them up beside him, one after the other. When he had got Diniz up safe, there were six of them; two had drowned.

But it could easily have been all of them.

He set them then to shouting and waving, and gradually the dark shape approached, her oars striking the water rhythmically. Behind her came others; the galley squadron had survived unharmed.

And now Harry could make out the ensign flying above the lead ship.

"Halloo!" he shouted. "Halloo, Khair-ed-din! Halloo!"

The oars ceased to beat the water, and the galley came to a halt. A boat was put down from forward, and rowed rapidly towards the upturned hulk.

The shipwrecked men were transferred, and a few minutes later were climbing up the ladder let into the galley's bow. Harry was hurried along the gangway, between rows of oar-slaves already being whipped into action again, and on to the wide stern deck. Waiting for him was a heavily-built man whose rich dress was dominated by the full red beard that hung midway down his chest.

"Khair-ed-din." he said, seizing the older man's hands. "I think you have just saved my life."

Khair-ed-din grinned. "Young Hawk," he replied, "yours is a life worth saving."

Harry Hawkwood had known Khair-ed-din — and his younger brother Arouj — for years. They had always been unashamed pirates; even the Turks knew that.

The brothers' more normal haunt was the western Mediterranean — calm, sunlit waters that might have been designed by God especially for the use of galleys. Those were waters which did not interest the Ottoman empire. The sea itself hardly interested them; the Turks were horsemen, not sailors. That a war fleet was necessary to protect their far-flung dominions had been obvious even to the Conqueror, but the fleet's business was supporting and transporting armies. The Ottomans could not conceive of ships acting independently.

Khair-ed-din and Arouj were not true Ottomans. They were indeed Turks, but had been born and grown to manhood on the island of Lesbos in the Aegean Sea. They had been seamen almost

327

from the moment they could first walk. No one knew for certain when that had been; their father had been illiterate, and no record had been made of either of their birth dates. But Khair-ed-din was at least sixty years old.

For long he had been content to play the lieutenant to his younger, more brilliant brother. From fishermen they had became masters of a galley, and then a squadron of galleys. From the Aegean they had taken their ships west, to where the Mediterranean was virtually a Spanish-Italian lake. Spain was the greatest maritime power in the world. The discoveries of the Genoese seaman, Christopher Columbus, a generation ago, had given the spur to an already burgeoning national ambition, which had been set alight by the capture of Granada, the last Moorish kingdom in Spain, in January 1492.

Now tales were spreading of great ships ploughing their way across the Atlantic Ocean to the goldmines of the New World, to bring back to Cadiz and Barcelona, Seville and Cartagena more wealth than anyone had ever dreamed could exist.

Not even Arouj had ventured out into the Atlantic. He had known nothing of the currents and tides, the tremendous winds and the huge seas which lay beyond the Straits of Gibraltar; and what he had heard had dissuaded him from any suicidal adventures.

But the wealth of the Indies spilled over into the Mediterranean, as Spain expanded. In those calm waters even an ocean-going carrack might lie becalmed, helplessly vulnerable to attack from a quarter her guns could not reach. The Spanish and their Genoese allies also used galleys, but none were so fast or commanded with such desperate courage as those of Arouj.

That the brothers had not in the beginning sailed beneath the Ottoman flag, and indeed had scarcely recognised the Sultan as their overlord, meant nothing to the Spanish and Genoese. Suffice it that Arouj was a Turk. No nation in the world hated the Turks more than did the Genoese. A price had been put on Arouj's head, and in time been redeemed: he had fallen in battle. Spain had breathed a sigh of relief. But then Arouj's brother Khidr, for the first time calling himself Khair-ed-din, had taken command, and in him the dons had found an enemy more brilliant and more implacable even than the one they had slain.

But Khair-ed-din had been ambitious for more than the fame of being accounted the greatest pirate the world had yet seen. The Moorish principalities along the northern coast of Africa were in a state of disarray, fighting each other when they were not fighting the Spanish. Khair-ed-din dreamed of setting up his own kingdom there. To do this he needed powerful support, so he had taken himself to Constantinople, knelt before the Sultan, and put forward his plans.

Selim had been no more than vaguely interested. He, above all of the sultans, was a soldier rather than a sailor. He had granted Khair-ed-din the title of beylerbey, and told him to do what he wished, enlist such volunteers as he could find.

That had not been enough, and Khair-ed-din had appealed to Selim's general, Hawk Pasha, but William Hawkwood was even more land-bound than his master. So Khair-ed-din had gone back to piracy and dreams.

But he had taken to visiting Constantinople regularly; since he was now a beylerbey, he had to be treated with respect. He had also made friends there; one of them was young Hawk. Harry Hawkwood had already known the fascination of the sea, the envy of watching the galleys put forth, bound no man knew where, to encounter no man knew what. Harry had appealed to his uncle to allow him to volunteer for the pirate enterprise, but William Hawkwood had refused. Harry was already nearly thirty, a colonel in the Ottoman artillery, a man destined for greatness; and greatness was not to be found at sea.

So Harry had to content himself with sailing for a hobby. A hobby which had today turned out so catastrophically.

They sat in the richly-carpeted cabin of the galley and drank coffee. Heavy embroidered drapes swayed to and fro over the stern windows, and the door was closed to keep out most of the stench from the galley benches, although they could still hear the inescapable beat of the drum that regulated the strokes, the occasional crack of the whip when one of the boatswains felt a slave was not pulling his weight.

It was not a system Harry had ever considered deeply. Though brought up a Christian by both his mother and his uncles, he was a Turk by adoption in every way. And besides, the Christian powers who sailed the Mediterranean also employed galleys, and slaves to row them.

329

Now he was just content to let the warmth seep through his benumbed body, and to smile at his friend.

"What brings you north of the Dardanelles?" he asked his host.

Khair-ed-din grinned and tapped his nose. "Even a pirate must do some honest trading sometimes, young Hawk. I have had a prosperous voyage — until that storm tried to rob me of my profits."

"You mean that, together with your honest trading, you have found somewhere else to loot?"

"The Russians are always worth looting, young Hawk. Oh, they have nothing of their own worth taking. But their women ..." Khair-ed-din smacked his lips. "They are a perpetual delight."

Even for a Turk, Khair-ed-din's sexual capacity was reputed to be enormous. It was said that in the little harbour of Algiers, which he had made his western Mediterranean base, he kept a harem several hundred strong.

It was not a rumour that greatly interested Harry Hawkwood. He was a Turkish nobleman and at thirty-five years old, his life had not lacked women. He had been given his first concubine at the age of sixteen, and his first wife at the age of twenty. Now he possessed two wives and four concubines, and was the father of several children — the two youngest of which were the all-important boys.

He was fond of his family, but the relationship with his women was on a purely physical basis. For intellectual feminine company he sought out his mother and his aunt, and he envied his uncle the possession of two such supremely beautiful and intelligent wives.

Aimée Ferrand was now fifty-six. Her golden hair was streaked with grey; the pristine beauty of her face was beginning to crease. She was a women unique because of the years she had spent in the harem of Bayazid II. Her two daughters, married to Turkish pashas, were called aunt by the new Sultan. Yet her love had always been constant for William Hawkwood, and now in the twilight of her years she had found a very real happiness.

Partly because of the woman with whom she shared management of Hawk Palace, even as she shared the bed of Hawk Pasha himself, Giovanna's life had hardly been less tumultuous. She was more fortunate over the years in having been able to spend so much of it close to William Hawkwood, and had learned to love him even more than her first husband, who was Harry's father.

Harry Hawkwood had little hope of ever achieving such domestic triumph: no beautiful French or Italian captive had ever drifted into his orbit. Thus he had accepted the Turkish view that one's women were for pleasure and child-bearing. A man had more important things in his life to concern him.

Harry had always been a soldier. He had ridden at William Hawkwood's side from the age of sixteen, firstly as a rebel against Bayazid, and then as one of Selim's most faithful followers. When he had returned home from campaigning, there had been much business to deal with, which had limited his visits to the harem. And also, in the last three years of unbroken peace, there had been his little yacht. Now ... he would just have to build another one.

"I can see that you do not believe me, young Hawk," Khair-ed-din said. "Would you like to see some of the treasure I have brought out of Russia?"

"I would rather go to bed, old friend. That water still strikes a chill to my bones."

Khair-ed-din gave a bellow of laughter. "Why, so you shall go to bed, and be warmed. But first see what might warm you." He rang the golden bell which waited on the table, and the door was immediately opened by a bowing eunuch.

The still-fresh breeze seeped into the cabin, rustling the drapes, reminding Harry that they were still at sea.

"Fetch me the two pale women," Khair-ed-din said. "And that fellow Ivan."

The eunuch bowed again and left.

"Pale women?" Harry asked. "Circassians?"

For his uncle also possessed a Circassian concubine, a massive yellow-haired woman called Golkha. Golkha had no doubt warmed William Hawkwood once upon a time, but now she was an undulating mass of fat, although good-humoured enough.

"No, not Circassian — from further north. They are quite remarkable, and I would have your opinion."

The door flew open again as people were forced into the cabin. The two women, wrapped in voluminous if torn and threadbare cloaks, were each manhandled by a eunuch. Behind them came a thin man, also in a tattered cloak and with manacles on his wrists.

"This fellow speaks Greek," Khair-ed-din explained. "His name is Ivan."

Ivan bowed low before his captor.

331

Harry found himself staring at the women. For the moment all he could see were eyes gleaming at him.

"Tell them to disrobe, Ivan," Khair-ed-din commanded.

Ivan spoke in a quite unintelligible langauge.

"It is a barbaric tongue, eh?" Khair-ed-din commented.

One of the women replied in a low voice, while Ivan argued with her.

"Tell them that if they do not obey, I will have them stripped and given to the galley slaves," Khair-ed-din said. He winked at Harry. "I would not, of course; they are far too valuable. Watch, now."

The threat produced its effect. The two women shrugged their cloaks from their shoulders and let them fall to the ground.

Beneath they were naked, with strong, voluptuous, very pale bodies, and Harry did not suppose they were more than fifteen or sixteen years old. But entrancing as were the rounded breasts and smooth bellies, he was more taken with their hair. It was a wild yellow-brown mass of curls which tumbled down past their shoulders to the middle of their backs. Their faces were curiously strong, with high cheekbones and powerful jaw-lines yet remarkably attractive in conjunction with their straight noses and full lips and burning amber eyes.

"I would say there is Tartar blood there somewhere," Khair-ed-din remarked, "but it is well diluted. Are they not a handsome pair?"

"Indeed," Harry agreed.

"They are sisters, I believe. What are their names, Ivan?"

The Russian bowed again. "My lord, their names are Yana and Roxelana."

Khair-ed-din glanced at Harry slyly. "I can see you are interested. Would you like to take one of them?"

Harry stared at the girls — and they stared back. No doubt he was the most outstanding man in the cabin; if his hair and beard were almost as red as Khair-ed-din's, he was twenty-five years younger.

"One of these could warm your blood for you," Khair-ed-din suggested.

"If she did not scratch my eyes out first," Harry said. "How much?"

"For you, my friend?" Khair-ed-din shrugged. "Fifty dinars."

"Fifty dinars? That is a great deal of money for an unintelligible woman."

"But not unintelligent, young Hawk. That is the important factor. I took these from the tent of a chief. I killed him with my own hands. These girls are of the best stock, and they will learn. At fifty dinars, each is a snip."

As Harry surveyed the girls further, he realised that Khair-ed-din could be right. There was certainly intelligence in the eyes glaring back at him. Angry intelligence, to be sure: they had recently seen their father and, no doubt, their mother and their brothers murdered so that they could enter a Turkish harem. But a great many female slaves acquired in such unfortunate circumstances had yet proved the chief adornment of the harems in which they later found themselves.

"You are right," he agreed. "Very well, Khair-ed-din, I will take them both, since they are sisters."

"Well, now, you are a glutton," the pirate declared. "No, no — Only one of them."

"You do not think I can handle both?"

"My dear Hawk, I am sure of it. But one of these is a present for Ibrahim, which I promised him before I left Constantinople. Bring me a Russian, he commanded. I long to lie with a Russian." Khair-ed-din shrugged. "Who am I to gainsay the Grand Vizier? But I am now giving you first choice, because you are my friend."

Despite his name, Ibrahim was a Greek and few of the Turks actually liked him. He was an excellent man of business, and ran the empire effectively for his indolent master, Sultan Suleiman II — but he was nonetheless a Greek, and the conquering Turks resented having one of a conquered race set above them. Yet he was a friend of Hawk Pasha, who was also an infidel.

Harry Hawkwood carefully studied the girls. Although they were clearly sisters, he estimated that there was some considerable difference in their characters.

Roxelana stood absolutely straight, her high breasts heaving, as she breathed, her muscles twitching with suppressed energy, her eyes flashing fire. She would have to be conquered again and again, perhaps over some considerable time.

Yana projected much less aggression. She too breathed deeply, aware that her fate was being decided, but her her expression was more anxious than defiant. She was also, marginally, the more lovely of the two.

333

Harry Hawkwood was all for a quiet domestic life.

"I'll take Yana," he said finally.

Khair-ed-din's squadron was in the Golden Horn an hour later. There Harry was told by the captain of the port to report immediately to his father's house outside Galata. Everyone had supposed him drowned in the storm, and besides there were great deeds afoot. So the captain said.

Harry bade Diniz follow with his new purchase — he had given Khair-ed-din a promissory note for her — and hurried ahead, leaving the great walled city, huge and bustling, behind him. Here on the north bank of the famous harbour the suburbs extended further as the Ottoman wealth grew and grew, and as Constantinople expanded in worldwide importance.

The crowning achievement of the reign of Selim the Grim had been the capture of Baghdad and of the Caliph himself. Caliph Mutuwakkil had been brought to Constantinople a captive, and had died there. Selim had then announced that henceforth the Ottoman Sultan would be Caliph: the spiritual as well as military head of the entire Muslim world.

And there had been none to defy his word.

Of all the many palaces which adorned the Galata shore, none equalled that of Hawk Pasha. It had been built by Anthony Hawkwood in the days of his intimacy with Mahomet the Conqueror, and embellished by William Hawkwood in the days of his intimacy with Selim the Grim.

A horse had been provided by the captain of the port, and Harry spurred it up the road, his heart pounding with a thousand apprehensions. Slaves hurried forward to grasp his bridle and assist him to the ground, gaping at his seeming undress, for Khair-ed-din had lent him a kaftan many sizes too small.

Running into the marble hallway, he encountered Aimée. However much the Hawkwoods had adopted Turkish habits, there was yet no harem in William Hawkwood's palace: the women of the house were free to come and go as they pleased. He did not fear that any of them would try to escape.

"Harry!" she cried. "We have been so worried. Your mother is quite distraught."

Harry kissed her hand. "It was a sudden squall. I lost the boat and two good men."

334

"But not yourself." She squeezed his fingers.

Harry turned to greet Giovanna, hurrying from the centre court-yard. Two years older than Aimée, at fifty-eight Giovanna Hawk-wood was no less compelling in personality, even if she too revealed signs of age. Her once-tawny hair was now streaked with grey.

"Harry, my love, your uncle is in a rage, and wishes to see you on most urgent business."

Harry embraced his mother. "I shall go to him immediately. But I am safe, Mother. Does that not please you?"

Giovanna's eyes filled with tears. "Is there anything could please me more? Now haste, and beg Hawk Pasha's forgiveness."

Harry hurried to the door of his uncle's office, knocked and entered.

Seated at his desk, William Hawkwood looked up and frowned. Hawk Pasha was sixty-six years old now, and had travelled and campaigned almost every year of his adult life.

"Your mother supposed you dead," he remarked gruffly.

"Fortunately she was wrong, Uncle," Harry said, closing the door. He spoke in English, as William Hawkwood insisted when-ever they were alone together. As no one else in the house, indeed scarcely anyone in all Constantinople, knew the language, their conversations were thus ensured a most complete privacy.

"So I see. Sit down."

Harry lowered himself into the chair before the huge desk littered with maps and reports. He could tell that something signifi-cant was indeed afoot.

"That would have been a waste," Hawk Pasha remarked, "when there is so much to be done. The Pope has preached a crusade against us, and Louis of Hungary has raised an army. My reports say it numbers twenty thousand armoured knights, and God alone knows how many men in total."

"But there has been no declaration of war?"

"Does he need one? Whatever he does will have been sanc-tioned by the Pope." William hated the Papacy with good reason — even if Rodrigo Borgia was now only an infamous memory. "They will have been preparing this since the death of the Sultan."

Like many of his fellow pashas, William Hawkwood still referred to Selim as "the Sultan".

There was no man alive who could remember Mahomet the

335

Conqueror, though the fact that he had been rightfully named was in evidence every time any Ottoman stepped out on to the streets of Constantinople. But Mahomet had been a many-sided genius, a man for whom warfare and conquest had been a means to an end. A man who would as soon write a couplet of poetry and design a beautiful house as set loose an arrow.

There were too many men who remembered the indolent excesses of Mahomet's successor, Bayazid II, when the reputation of Turkish arms had sunk to its lowest ever level. Thus the glory of Selim's reign had also been an epoch to remember. Too short an epoch for the soldiers, to be sure. He had deposed his father in the year 1512, and he himself had died only eight years later. But what triumphs he had achieved in that short span!

He had begun by declaring war on Shah Ismail of Persia, ostensibly for supporting his brother Ahmed, but principally because the Persians were Shi'ites and Selim was a fanatical Sunnite. On 23 August 1515, the two armies had met at Chaldiran, and Ismail had been defeated in one of the bloodiest battles in history. A fortnight later Selim had taken the Persian capital of Tabriz. In the course of the campaign he had put forty thousand Persians to death — merely for being Shi'ites. Not for nothing was he called Selim the Grim.

Harry Hawkwood had marched with his army, and fought in that battle. The Sultan had then wanted to continue his advance, following the route of Alexander the Great into India. But his men, and principally his Turkish light cavalry, had refused to follow him on so unlikely an adventure. The Sultan had thus turned aside and conquered the middle Euphrates. It was on that same campaign that he had captured Baghdad and the Caliph.

Following this victory he had been attacked in the west by the Mameluke Sultan of Egypt, Kansu al-Gauri. Selim had never doubted that the Mamelukes would prove his most severe antagonists; for these had been precursors of the Janissaries — the word *mameluke* meaning owned men, or slaves — and they had first been raised by the immortal Saladin to become the most formidable fighting men in the Arab world. They had been the only military force ever to defeat Genghis Khan's Mongols. Themselves of Turkish origin, they had exercised control over the Arab countries, and even the Caliphate, electing and deposing caliphs and sultans as they chose.

Selim had advanced so rapidly into Syria that the famous Mameluke cavalry had been overwhelmed at Merj-Dabik, a battle fought and won in less than an hour. In that hour, however, Kansu had died and his army had been destroyed.

Selim had then invaded Egypt itself. At the battle of Ridanieh, on 22 January 1517, he had routed the army of Kansu's nephew and successor, Touman Bey, and subsequently executed him. By the end of that year the Ottomans had occupied Mecca and the Caliph had been transferred to Constantinople. When there were religious outbreaks against such sacrilege, Selim had put these down with a ruthless ferocity that had terrified both friend and foe.

On all of these campaigns, Hawk Pasha and his nephew had ridden at the Sultan's side; in one five-year period Harry had scarcely slept five nights in his own bedchamber. And the path of conquest had seemed never-ending. In 1520 Selim had begun to prepare an immense expedition against the island of Rhodes and its defenders, the Knights of St John. He had no Constantinople to set up as the ultimate target of his life. But Rhodes had been the one objective in which Mahomet the Conqueror had been defeated. Its capture would set the seal on Selim's own fame as the greatest of Ottoman soldiers.

By the end of the summer the expedition had been ready; it was just a matter of giving the word to sail. Harry had been convulsed with excitement; at last he was going to campaign across water. Out of the coming events he might influence Selim to undertake further naval expeditions — to the West.

But, on 22 September 1520, Selim the Grim had died.

The world had breathed a gentle sigh of relief, in every way. Because, unlike events following the sudden death of Mahomet, or preceding the deposition of Bayazid, there had been no clash at all, no civil war as the new Sultan had taken his place. For Selim had not spent enough time at home to father more than a single son.

Harry had first met Suleiman when he had been nineteen years old, and the prince two years younger — on the day William Hawkwood had abandoned his revolt and agreed to fight for Selim. For a brief while the two young men had become intimate friends while they campaigned with their illustrious fathers.

But since Selim's death they had drifted apart. This had been inevitable: it is easier to be friends with an heir apparent than with

337

a monarch. But there had been other reasons, particularly the striking differences in their characters. Where Harry regarded life as a series of challenges, to be met with brute force and cold steel, Suleiman increasingly revealed a reflective, even a studious cast of mind. This had aroused considerable alarm among his great pashas, who remembered too well the indolence and vices of Bayazid.

But they had soon realised that their fears were groundless. Suleiman was indeed studious, but he entirely lacked vice. If he preferred discussing the anyi with his imams and muftis to galloping into battle, his personality was if anything too gentle for the cruelty of uncertainty. If, by force of custom, he maintained a harem, it was well known that he habitually slept with just one girl. She had the same name, Gulbehar, as his own grandmother, and had already fulfilled her essential duty by bearing her master a son, Prince Mustafa.

Above all, he did not interfere with his late father's military plans. Indeed, he added some of his own; within a year of succeeding to the sultanate he sent a small army, commanded by Hawk Pasha, on a sudden campaign to the west, ostensibly at the invitation of certain Hungarian magnates discontented with the degeneracy of government since the death of Hunyadi. The principal achievement of this campaign had been the capture of Belgrade; so sudden had been the appearance of the Turks that the city had been hardly defended. The White City of the Serbs, it was another stronghold to have repulsed the Conqueror, as it had repulsed his father Murad. In fact Mahomet had not pressed the seige with any great vigour; Belgrade being on the very limits of his empire. Yet in capturing the town Hawk Pasha had made the name of the young Suleiman resound throughout the Western world.

Meanwhile Suleiman had carried forward his father's purpose against Rhodes. When Hawk Pasha and his subordinate commanders had landed on the island on 25 June 1522, the Ottoman force had numbered a hundred thousand men; in the course of the seige this number was doubled.

What followed had been an epic encounter reminiscent of the seige of Constantinople itself. The Knights of St John had numbered only seven hundred, supported by six thousand auxiliaries and several batteries of artillery. Their commander, the Grand Master Philippe

Villiers de l'Isle Adam, had refused to surrender and had fought for six months with a courage and determination even the Turks could admire. During that time every device known to warfare was employed, from bombardment to mining. Great breaches were smashed in the walls, and the Turks had swarmed to the attack, only to be repulsed time and again with enormous slaughter. As with Constantinople, the slightest effort on the part of the great nations of Christendom could have saved the day; surely the combined fleets of Spain and Genoa would have destroyed the Turkish galleys and left the Ottoman army stranded like cut flowers in a vase. But Charles V of Spain and the Empire were too busy fighting Francis I of France.

Suleiman himself had come to Rhodes in the autumn. His essentially sensitive nature was appalled at the apparently useless slaughter, and he had instructed Hawk Pasha, old and grizzled, and angry at the loss of men, though determined to push the siege to a victorious conclusion, to offer generous terms.

Negotiations were rapidly concluded. The Knights and their followers were allowed to march out unharmed and sail away, carrying all their possessions and their weapons; there were only a hundred and eighty Knights left, and fifteen hundred auxiliaries. No doubt suffering from his conscience for having done nothing to defend them, the Emperor Charles V had presented the Knights with first the seaport of Tripoli and then the island of Malta, in perpetuity.

The Turks had gained an enormous triumph, but the cost had been frightful; the official casualty figure was fifty thousand men. In private Hawk Pasha confided to Harry that it was in reality much nearer a hundred thousand. Since then it had not appeared as if Hawk Pasha would ever campaign again. Suleiman, horrified by the casualties, had decreed an end to expansion.

So Harry Hawkwood had once more to put an end to his dreams of an Ottoman navy carrying the crescent flag throughout the length of the Mediterranean, and instead content himself with sailing his little yacht.

But now at last they were being forced to action; the Hungarians had flung down the gauntlet, as they had done so often in the past.

And Suleiman had given Hawk Pasha the order to march.

"You will go to war," Giovanna said sadly. "I had supposed such things were at an end."

"Did not the great Selim tell us that war is a man's natural state, Mother?" Harry protested.

"The great Selim is dead," she pointed out. "I would like *you* to be alive when I die. Harry."

"Oh, I shall," he laughed. "If a storm sent by Allah could not kill me, how may a mere mortal? But, come, I have something to show you. Some one," he added archly.

He led her into his women's quarters, where Sasha and Tressilia stood regarding the new arrival with some uncertainty.

Sasha, his senior wife, was now thirty years old. The seductive curves she had brought to his bed as a fifteen-year-old were threatening to dissolve into fat, but she remained a loving and attentive wife, and a gentle mistress of the harem.

Tressilia, two years her junior, was more abrasive; she was from Constantinople, while Sasha had been born in Brusa. Where Sasha was pure Turk, Tressilia had Greek blood. But that had given her the long, straight nose and the high forehead that lent distinction to her face.

Each had presented her husband with a son, and if Sasha's Tugril would be the next Hawk — and the first ever to bear a Turkish name, so thoroughly had the family now been assimilated — both he and Tressilia's Tutush were so young, six and four respectively, that they and their mothers could remain the best of friends.

But, as it was a dozen years since young Hawk had added to his harem, neither woman was very happy with the idea of having this wild creature from the steppes introduced into their lives.

Yana, on her part, glared at them as if daring them to lay a finger on her; the eunuchs stood hesitantly by, since they had been given no orders as to her disposition.

Giovanna frowned. "Where did you get her?"

"I bought her from Khair-ed-din."

"That thug? How much did you pay?"

"Fifty dinars."

Giovanna raised her eyes to heaven. "I suppose there is no point in possessing wealth if you do not squander it from time to time." She went closer to the girl. "Where did Khair-ed-din find her?"

"Russia. But not Circassia. She speaks neither Latin nor Greek."

"Perhaps Golkha may be able to understand her."

"She'll learn our languages in due course." He grinned. "I may teach her English."

"That would be as senseless as any other." Giovanna looked the girl up and down. "She is well endowed: she must be quite old."

"Khair-ed-din swears she is but fifteen years old, and a virgin. And the daughter of a chieftain. She has a sister who is to go to Ibrahim."

Giovanna continued to stare into Yana's eyes. "I do not like the look of her, Harry. She will bring you great misfortune."

"Oh, Mother, I am not a boy to be influenced by a pair of lips."

Giovanna made a moue. "I suppose you are anxious to mount her."

"Yes," he said. "Yes, I am." Oddly, he suddenly realised he had never so wanted to mount any woman before.

"Then I will leave you to your enjoyment. But, remember ... there is something evil about her." She left the room.

The head eunuch bowed. "Is the lady to be prepared, my lord?"

Harry gazed into the amber eyes. She knew what was going to happen to her, and she knew he was going to be the man. She also knew her own helplessness. Her tongue stole out and circled her lips quickly.

He looked her up and down. Perhaps his sudden ardour was because she had come to him unprepared; his Turkish brides had been shaven from puberty. What was the point in sampling something new and undoubtedly strange if she was not to be *entirely* new and strange?

"Yes, Sayyid," he said. "I wish the lady bathed — but not shaven."

A twitch of the eyebrows was Sayyid's only comment on his master's whim. Sayyid was a devout Muslim; as his master remained a gaiour, if he chose to break with custom that was his business.

He seized Yana's wrist. "Come," he said.

Yana gave him a quick, outraged glance, and looked back at Harry.

Harry nodded, and the girl allowed herself to be led from the room.

"Your mother is right," Sasha said. "She is an evil thing."

Harry grinned, and ruffled her hair. "And you are jealous, my pet. I think this Russian girl will restore my vigour — so you can only benefit from that."

341

He attended the bathing chamber himself. This was again unusual, but he was still salty from his immersion in the Black Sea. Besides, suddenly he did not wish to allow Yana out of his sight.

His presence seemed to give her courage; she seemed to have accepted that she was his, no one else's. No doubt they had neither eunuchs nor bathing chambers in the Russian steppes, for she shrank away from the black men as they marched her down the steps and on to the wooden slats. But when he came too she recovered her confidence, and when he removed the kaftan she gazed at his body with a boldness that surprised him.

They faced each other as the warm water was poured over them, and as the slaves got to work with their loofahs. Again she seemed to shrink as they sought the most intimate crevices of her body, but regained her composure as she saw them do the same with him. He could not but wonder how her sister Roxelana might react to such treatment.

She shuddered when the cold water was poured over her, but so did he.

"The lady's hair, master?" inquired Sayyid.

Now it was damp, it had lost some of its curl, but he did not wish it elaborately dressed. He wanted the wildness of her without the anger of her sister.

"Leave it," he ordered.

It was a most unusual feeling: to wish to woo a woman rather than merely lie on his divan and know she would come to him because she must.

They were next wrapped in huge towels and patted dry. Sayyid now brought the customary clothes for Yana to wear.

She gazed in amazement at the silk pantaloons, so sheer they left nothing to the imagination, at the bolero jacket which did no more than brush the sides of her very full breasts, at the soft felt slippers in which her feet were encased, and at the jewelled fez which was set on her head. The entire ensemble was in pale green; Sayyid had a perfect sense of colour.

"Bring her a glass," Harry commanded.

One of the eunuches hurried forward with a mirror, which he held before the startled girl.

"You are a beauty," Harry told her.

She gave him an anxious glance, saw his smile, and smiled in return.

"*Beauty*," she said, hesitantly.

It was the first time he had heard her speak; it was only Roxelana who had spoken earlier. Her voice was just as low, and even more husky. It possessed an almost masculine quality.

Now wrapped in one of his own kaftans, Harry held out his hand. After the briefest hesitation she took it, and he led her towards the door, which was hastily opened for them.

Sasha and Tressilia stood there, looking behind him for the Russian girl.

"Off with you," Harry told them, "or I will have you caned."

They giggled, and scurried away.

He led her up the stairs and into his sleeping chamber. She gazed at the huge divan, at the carpets on the floor, the window drapes fluttering in the evening breeze.

Then she went over to the window and looked out, at the Golden Horn, and beyond, at the walls and towers and domes and minarets of Constantinople gleaming in the setting sun.

"Beauty," she said.

He stood behind her, put his arms round her waist and pulled her back against him. She half-turned her head, looking almost surprised. Perhaps she had expected no gentleness from a Turk.

He slipped his hands inside her bolero and caressed her breasts. She gave a little shiver, whether of pleasure or distaste he could not tell.

He turned her round and kissed her mouth. For a few seconds it remained closed, then it opened beneath the quest of his tongue, and he found hers. When he released her he was also gasping for breath.

Moving away from her, he took off his kaftan and lay down naked amidst the cushions. Still by the window, she continued to gaze at him for a minute, then appeared to come to a resolution.

She reached up and took the cap from her head, stepped out of the slippers. She shrugged the bolero from her shoulders, released the string tying the pantaloons, and let them slip down her hips.

Although he had already seen her naked, it was a most provocative strip-tease.

Slowly she moved towards the bed. As her knees touched it, she hesitated. When Harry held out his hand, she took it in her warm, dry fingers, allowing herself to the pulled forward, to kneel beside him.

Then he pulled her down on top of him and kissed her mouth, feeling her body warm on his. He rolled over on top of her, and was in her even before he intended.

Once there, he could not withdraw. Even as her eyes glazed with pain, her legs, long and strong and powerful, were wrapped about him and he was sucked into her, deeper and deeper. Images whirled through his mind, his mother's warning, the raging sea and, oddly, a vision of Roxelana.

But, as he surged to a climax, he could not doubt that he had made the right choice.

The Porte was crowded with imams and muftis and pashas, and with mere hangers-on anxious for the latest news. The empire was going to war for the first time in three years.

Ibrahim sidled through the throng and grasped Harry Hawk-wood's arm. "That pirate Khair-ed-din tells me we have twin sides of a purchase."

Harry grinned at him. Unlike many others in Constantinople, he was genuinely fond of Ibrahim. Tall, if not so tall as a Hawkwood, bold-featured and black-haired, the Greek Vizier was only a few years his elder. He exuded energy and purpose; no man could doubt his intelligence or his loyalty both to the Sultan and to the Ottomans. In the five years he had held charge of the empire's finances, taxes had been reduced for the first time in history.

Men complained that he was an infidel, which he was; they complained that he was a renegade, which he was. In these things he was much the same as the Hawkwoods.

They also said that he was too intimate with the Sultan, but the same might also be said of the Hawkwoods, considering William Hawkwood's relationship with Selim.

They also said that a good half of the money he was saving through his efficiency at trimming government waste was going into his own pocket. That was a more serious charge, but not one which could be levelled against any Hawkwood.

Yet Hawkwood wondered if it mattered. The efficiency was there, government was less wasteful, the empire thrived as never before. Did not the man who could perform such apparent miracles deserve an adequate reward?

No man could accuse the young Greek of being cold towards those who gave him friendship. Already his arm was around Harry's shoulder.

"Are you pleased with her?" Harry asked.

Ibrahim snorted. "I shall be pleased, no doubt, if I live to enjoy her. I have already had to tie her to my bed and cane her. And how of you?"

"No bonds and no canes." Harry smiled. "She seemed eager to please."

"And you had the pick! Well, mine is a tigress. But what glory to behold!"

"I prefer a quiet life at home," Harry said. "Time enough for excitement on campaign."

"Ah, yes." Ibrahim was suddenly serious. "And this will be an important campaign for us. It is said that King Louis commands an immense army."

"My uncle will match him."

"I have no doubt; but it will still be a clash of Titans. I intend to accompany you."

"You, Ibrahim?" Harry was amazed.

"I know you soldiers; you think of me as a clerk. But it is the Vizier's responsibility to command the Sultan's armies in battle, is it not?"

"Indeed — when the Sultan himself is not present."

"Small chance of that. No, no, I intend to take my rightful place against the Hungarians."

Harry frowned. "Does my uncle know of this?"

"Of course. Do not be alarmed, young Hawk. It is not my intention to interfere with your uncle's dispositions. Heaven forbid! I simply wish to witness a campaign" — his smile returned — "in comfort. I will take Roxelana with me."

It was Harry's turn to grin. "We had now best attend my father."

William Hawkwood was about to address the pashas.

"My messengers have already been despatched," he announced. "I am summoning levies from every available part of the empire. We shall muster ten thousand Janissaries, five thousand sipahis, ten thousand timariots, twenty-five thousand Anatolian foot, and fifty thousand bashi-bazouks: altogether one hundred thousand men. We shall be accompanied by one hundred cannon. It is time to settle this Hungarian business once and for all." He paused and looked over their faces. "I have also to tell you that the army will be accompanied by his eminence Ibrahim Pasha."

There was a rustle amongst the soldiers.

Ibrahim moved forward to stand beside William Hawkwood. "It is my duty to accompany the army of the Padishah into the field," he said. "And I shall not shirk my duty."

The muttering continued for a moment, and then abruptly stopped — in its place the silence of amazement. Then every man in the room made the obeisance.

From behind the screen on the far side of the room had stepped a man. He was slim, and not very tall, his features were aquiline, his moustache and beard thin. He wore a white silk kaftan with a cloth-of-gold belt, and a white turban in which cloth of gold thread had been worked.

What the people in the room were staring at, however, was the sword girded round his waist. It was the holy sword of Othman, founder of the greatness of the Ottoman house — and it was only worn when a sultan himself was going to war.

"With respect, Ibrahim Pasha," Suleiman announced in a quiet voice, "I will lead my armies against Hungary in person."

13

BARBAROSSA

The Porte fell silent for some seconds after the Sultan's announcement. Then Hawk Pasha bowed deeply.

"Now we know that victory must attend our arms, O Padishah," he said.

"Will he seek to interfere in the conduct of the campaign, do you suppose?" Harry asked when they had regained the privacy of the Hawk Palace.

"He never has before," William said, "save to command me to make peace with the Knights of St John. We must hope that he is less soft-hearted with the Hungarians; they are the hereditary enemies of the Turks. I think that he is aware of this, and feels his presence on so important a campaign is essential. At any rate, I hope that is the reason."

Harry knew his uncle was worried. To have the Grand Vizier accompanying his military expedition was bad enough; to have both Vizier and Sultan looking over his shoulder could not but be intensely inhibiting.

Yet William Hawkwood was recognised as the master soldier of the empire — even Suleiman knew that.

But also, no doubt, Suleiman realised that William Hawkwood's days on earth must now be numbered. Perhaps that was the true reason for his decision to campaign: the wish to discover a possible successor to Hawk Pasha.

It was a heady thought for Harry that the choice might one day fall upon himself. As yet he was still too young, he supposed. Besides, he would rather command a fleet than an army.

All through winter, and from all over the empire, soldiers marched towards Constantinople. The area outside the city became a huge encampment, and riding out to watch the sipahis and timariots

347

practising their manoeuvres or the Janissaries firing their arquebuses became a popular pastime for the people.

The officers worked harder than anyone, drilling their new
recruits, attempting to beat some order into the bashis, meting out
punishment when men, becoming bored as the months went by,
invaded the city and caused disturbances or raped local women.
But Ottoman discipline was strict in Ottoman lands; a few impale-
ments soon kept the men in hand.

Hard as this work was — there was no opportunity for sailing,
even had the winter weather been good enough; and Khair-ed-din
had meanwhile taken himself off to North Africa — Harry had time
to return to Hawk Palace nearly every night and seek the arms of
Yana. Sasha and Tressilia were disgruntled, of course, and he
realised the necessity of accommodating them both at least once a
week.

But Yana was the magnet that drew him again and again. He
had experienced nothing like this before — he was like a young
boy in his ardour, delighted yet dismayed. He could not really
suppose he had fallen in love with a Russian savage; they had
nothing in common save physical allure.

Yet an allure was there: he now thought only of Yana's body,
her lips, her hair. It was a preoccupation soon observed by his
mother and his aunt, and clearly it concerned them; they might be
gaiours, but they had lived most of their lives in the Ottoman world
and they understood as well as anyone that here a woman was
solely for pleasure and child-bearing. A man's major interests lay
elsewhere.

So perhaps they even welcomed the coming of spring, and the
orders for the army to march.

By then Harry had made a decision.

"We shall wait for news of you," Giovanna told him tearfully, as
he appeared before her wearing a chain-mail cuirass over his felt
tunic, carrying his steel helmet wrapped in its turban, with his
scimitar hanging at his side. "From Buda itself," she added.

"We shall get there without fail, Mother." He kissed her hands.

"And we shall keep your wild Russian safe for your return,"
Aimée added.

Harry grinned at them both. "You will not have to. She is to
accompany me."

He turned to the archway and pointed out Diniz waiting with a shrouded figure.

"You are taking Yana on the campaign?" Giovanna demanded.

"A man must have a woman. This campaign may last for more than a year."

"Then take one of your wives."

"I prefer Yana. Besides, the Vizier Ibrahim is taking her sister, so they will be company for each other."

He felt that his mother's continuing distrust of the Russian girl was absurd. Yana was merely his concubine, and there was no way she could have any influence over him or his career.

Of course, if she secretly hated him, as Giovanna seemed to suspect, then she could poison him or stab him as he slept ... but that would involve her in the most horrible death William Hawkwood could devise. The last concubine to kill her master had been tied in a sack with four cats and suspended from the upper windows of her late owner's palace until all five were dead — and Yana would know of that.

Besides, if she truly hated him, then she must be the best actress in the world.

Bands played and pennants flew as the Sultan rode out of Constantinople, accompanied by his staff. The army had started moving some hours before, the timariots forming an advanced screen, followed by the bashi-bazouks and the Anatolians, with the elite sipahis and Janissaries now waiting to be led by the Sultan and the Grand Vizier, and Hawk Pasha.

Harry Hawkwood could scarcely remember the number of times he had watched this army march forth — always to victory. But then it had been commanded by Selim the Grim. He wondered by what name the new Sultan would be remembered to posterity?

Suleiman made a diminutive, trim, erect figure in his cloth-of-gold tunic, riding a similarly caparisoned black stallion. He smiled all around at his people, and they cheered him. No sultan since the Conqueror had been so well known to them. Bayazid had lived in seclusion, Selim had spent hardly a year of his reign in Constantinople. Suleiman had been among them all the time — this was the first time he was leaving the city in three years. And if the growth of custom and protocol made it less easy for him to go personally amongst his people than did his great-grandfather, he still attended

349

the mosque regularly, surrounded by his pashas and viziers and guards to be sure, but nonetheless visible at a distance.

His youth also made him popular. At twenty-six he had been the youngest new sultan since Mahomet, and he was still only thirty-two; while his brief reign had been one of unbroken success.

Behind the pashas came their baggage-trains, and the harems comprising those of their women they had selected to accompany them on the campaign. Few had brought more than one or two favourites. It was noted that the Sultan did not bring a harem at all. Neither did Hawk Pasha.

The army had a long way to go, supposing that King Louis did not assume the offensive and risk an invasion of Ottoman territory. From Constantinople the mighty force took the road to Adrianople, so well known to both Hawkwoods, and thence into the mountains — towards Philippopolis and Sofia, Nish and Belgrade.

This route Anthony Hawkwood had ridden on an embassy for Mahomet the Conqueror, William Hawkwood had ridden the opposite way with his beautiful French bride, and William and his nephew had led this same army to the conquest of Belgrade.

It took the great army four months to reach Belgrade, but they were four boisterously happy months. The Turks, with their extreme concern for personal cleanliness, were able to avoid the diseases which would have decimated a Christian army over such a long period. They marched through lands which paid tribute, and which were obliged to support the army, and therefore they suffered no privations — however much the Greek, Bulgar and Serb communities starved as they were stripped bare by the passing horde.

Wherever they camped, they formed a tented city several miles square. Overnight the camps became huge markets, to which hawkers came from miles around to offer their wares to the soldiers. No doubt many of these were spies, but Hawk Pasha cared nothing for that; any information carried away by Hungarian agents could do nothing more than strike terror into Christian hearts.

Information about the Christian force was entirely lacking, however. Hawk Pasha did not suppose any would be gained before he debouched on to the Hungarian plain.

The pashas and viziers had each his own tent, varying in elaboration according to his desire for display and the size of the harem he had brought with him. They invited each other to meals and vied in the entertainments they could produce.

Suleiman often ate with the Hawkwoods and Ibrahim, as if these were his closest associates. None of them were Turks, of course, and this disturbed many of the other pashas. But Suleiman wished to discuss military matters, as this was his first major experience as commander, so he listened raptly to William Hawkwood's tales of past campaigns, imbibing the older man's expert knowledge.

Ibrahim preferred to tell jokes and speak of women. He never mentioned the finances of the empire, although Harry noted that in every village that they passed the Vizier would ride off to confer with the local garrison commander or headman about the efficient collection of taxes, seeing for himself where taxes could properly be increased. And he was as tireless in his pursuit of business during the day as his pursuit of pleasure during evening and night.

On one unusually warm July evening, when they were within a few marches of Belgrade, and the air was sultry with the promise of rain while thunder growled in the distance and lightning flickered over the mountains, it was Ibrahim who proposed to have the girls dance for them. Harry did not immediately understand which girls he meant, but Ibrahim was conferring with the Sultan.

"You have not seen these girls, O Padishah. They come from the Russian steppes and are creatures of wondrous beauty. At least, my Roxelana is." He glanced at Harry. "I have no doubt her sister is just as splendid."

"Russians, you say," Suleiman mused. He too glanced at Harry and could read the disapproval in his face. "But they are your women, Ibrahim. They should not be displayed."

"It is of no matter, Padishah. They are but slave girls."

Harry no longer regarded Yana as merely a slave, and he looked at his uncle for support. But Hawk Pasha's eyes were shut; he was finding the march fatiguing, although he refused on that account to slow the Turkish advance.

"Roxelana is an exquisite dancer," Ibrahim continued. "How about her sister, young Hawk?"

"I have never seen her dance," Harry confessed. It had not occurred to him to ask her to; just looking at her was titillating enough.

351

"It is in their blood." Ibrahim clapped his hands. "Bring the woman Roxelana to me," he ordered the eunuch, then glanced at Harry.

Harry sighed, but Suleiman was looking interested. The Sultan had been too long without women's company.

"Tell Diniz to have the woman Yana sent to me," Harry said resignedly.

"You will not forget these women, Padishah," Ibrahim promised.

The two girls were brought in, suitably shrouded in haiks and yashmaks. They had spent considerable time together on the march, often sharing the same pannier on the back of a mule. Harry wondered if it was time they spent swearing eternal hatred to their captors, or merely comparing the sexual attributes of their respective masters ...

Ibrahim had sent for musicians, and two came in to sit on the floor at the far side of the tent. One would blow a pipe; one would beat a tabalcan. A eunuch had blindfolded each of them.

"Play," Ibrahim commanded.

The somewhat plaintive music drifted across the tent, punctuated by the rhythmic thudding of the drum.

William Hawkwood stretched and opened his eyes.

"Dance!" Ibrahim said.

It was a word Roxelana understood. She murmured to her sister, and after a moment's hesitation herself began to move, slowly and sinuously, in time to the music, twisting her arms, posturing her shoulders, occasionally stamping her feet.

After a few moments Yana followed her example. Despite himself Harry was fascinated.

Roxelana was the leader in everything. After she had postured before the four men for perhaps sixty seconds, her haik began to slip. First one shoulder was revealed, then the other. Then the garment dropped lower. For a few seconds more it clung around her hips, exposing her white tunic, then it fell to her ankles and she stepped out of it. The tunic extended down to her thighs, so her legs were now revealed. She had also kicked off her sandals.

Yana eventually followed her example.

Now Suleiman was leaning forward with interest, and even Hawk Pasha was sitting up to stare.

Roxelana's movements quickened. When she turned, often on one leg, the tunic fluttered open to reveal traces of pale buttock.

Roxelana now gripped her tunic in both hands as she spun round and round; her hair flew straight out from her head as she exposed herself from the waist down, and then lifted the garment even higher to show her breasts. The tunic covered her face as she danced, and Harry Hawkwood heard the sharp intake of Suleiman's breath as he gazed at her.

Finally the tunic floated to the floor. Yana's soon followed, and for a few seconds the sisters danced naked save for their yashmaks. Then Roxelana stopped, and Yana beside her. Roxelana gazed at Ibrahim. He had certainly tamed her, Harry thought, and she had lived with Turkish custom long enough to await his command before unveiling herself.

"Show yourself," Ibrahim commanded with pride.

A quick movement and the yashmak was gone. She stared at the Sultan now, a woman less of beauty than sheer animal attraction as her nostrils dilated and her breasts and belly heaved.

"Will you not reveal yours, too, young Hawk?" Suleiman asked softly.

"Of course, Padishah."

Harry waved a hand and Yana removed her yashmak in turn.

"As you said, Ibrahim, they are rare gems," the Sultan commented.

"Does Roxelana please you, Padishah?"

"I would have to be a eunuch for her not to do so, Vizier."

"Then she is yours."

Suleiman frowned at him in surprise.

"She is my gift to you, Padishah. For how may any man campaign without a woman."

"And you?"

"I will find something worth buying in the market at Belgrade, I have no doubt, or amongst the Magyars. Why do you not take them both? I have no doubt young Hawk will be pleased to follow my example."

Suleiman looked from Roxelana to Yana, while Harry held his breath. There was no way he could refuse; but the thought of losing Yana was distressing.

But Suleiman shook his head. "No. I think one Russian at a time is all that I can manage. You are indeed generous, Ibrahim Pasha. I am in your debt."

He stood up, a sudden heat rising within him as he looked at the naked beauty before him. "I will retire now. Does she speak Turkish?"

"Alas no, Padishah, but I have taught her some words of Greek."

Suleiman nodded. "Have her washed clean and sent to me." He disappeared into the inner chamber of the tent.

"Ibrahim is a very smart fellow," William Hawkwood observed as they returned to their tents. "I imagine he had some such plan as this thought out. He seeks always the favour of his master, by whatever means."

"Do you suppose I should have insisted that he take Yana as well?" Harry asked.

"I am glad you did not. I would not have you go to such lengths to ingratiate yourself with the Sultan as to play the pimp. Besides, I have heard it said that you are inordinately fond of that little Russian."

"I have never met a woman who so pleases me, Uncle."

"Well, there is no harm is that," William said. And he should know, Harry thought, remembering how his uncle had kept his love for Aimée Ferrand alive over eighteen years of separation. "Provided, of course, that pleasure never interferes with your obligations as a man. Our business is fighting the Padishah's wars, Harry, and nothing else matters. And that is ultimately the surest way to the Sultan's esteem. We are only a few days from Belgrade, and thus from Hungary. We are on the path to glory, boy, so now is no time to think of women."

But Yana had never proved so loving as she was that night. Harry could not decide whether she was grateful for not being sent to the Sultan's bed, or merely excited by the evening and the presence of other men.

Belgrade was reached in the third week of August, and the army was immediately ferried across the Danube to assault the frontier fortress of Peterwardein. Now they had passed beyond the boundaries of the Ottoman empire, and were in Hungary.

Peterwardein fell without much delay, and every man of its garrison was beheaded. Hawk Pasha immediately sent out a screen of timariots, while the army slowly advanced northwestward, in the general direction of Buda.

Now they had left the high country behind and were marching on a great plain which stretched as far as the eye could see, and on which rustling wheatfields, only half-harvested because of the war, suggested unimaginable fertility. The weather was warm, the breezes balmy ... Harry had never known a campaign undertaken in such delightful surroundings.

They came across villages whose barns were bulging with corn, their byres filled with cattle. They killed all the men and older women, and took the younger women and children as slaves. They ate the cattle and the corn.

The timariots returned in great excitement. The Hungarian host had now been sighted; occupying a position on the plain known as Mohacs, in a huge bend of the Danube.

Hawk Pasha rode forward to see for himself. With him went the Sultan, Ibrahim, Harry and several pashas. They stood their horses on a shallow rise and looked out at a sea of waving banners and glinting armour. The Hungarian army was already drawn up in battle array, as if expecting an immediate assault.

"How many?" Suleiman inquired.

The distance was too great to attempt counting heads, but William used his years of campaigning experience to estimate the size of each of the contingents facing him. "I doubt there are more than twenty-five thousand, Padishah," he said.

"Are these all the men Europe can send against me?"

"No. But the Franks continue to be disunited. That is their curse and our advantage, Padishah. Every Frankish king thinks he alone can command an army, and is jealous of sharing his prerogatives; they will not wait for aid, even if it is on its way. This Louis of Hungary is a young man eager for glory."

"He will acquire the glory of the grave," Suleiman remarked. "Tell me what you deduce from his dispositions, Hawk Pasha."

"The King means to fight a defensive battle, Padishah." William pointed from place to place as he spoke. "You will see that his infantry are drawn up in three phalanxes; each must be about four thousand men."

"Are they all Hungarians?"

William studied them a few minutes longer. "Some are Germans, I would say, from their helmets. Many have arquebuses. The rest have pikes."

"He has squadrons of cavalry between each of the infantry

355 .

battles," Ibrahim observed.

"That is so. Why, I cannot imagine. They will do him no good there. But you will see, Padishah, that the main body of his cavalry is assembled behind the infantry, and that cavalry numbers at least half of his entire host. And you will also see that his cannon, it looks like a score of guns, are placed in front of his centre. He is thus established in a position which it will be hazardous to attack frontally without incurring severe casualties. You will further see that the Hungarian left flank rests on that marshy area where the Danube has broken its bank. Any troops advancing through that morass would have a hard time of it."

"But his right flank is exposed," Suleiman said.

"Indeed it is, Padishah. It is in the air. But the King has surely intended this."

"Why?"

"It will be his understanding that, as we cannot outflank him on his left, and to attack frontally will be too costly, in his estimation, we must outflank his right. Thus he is in possession, he assumes, of our strategy. He will be seeking to launch his cavalry on us when we are committed to that manoeuvre."

"We outnumber him four to one," Ibrahim said contemptuously, "and with the same ratio in cavalry. Do we have anything to fear?"

"See the sun glinting from those horsemen?" William asked. "That is plate armour. Those cavalry are far heavier than our timariots or sipahis. They are a formidable body of men, especially if their charge is well timed, and our people are strung out to any extent."

"What then is your plan, Hawk Pasha?" asked the Sultan.

"It is a very simple one, based upon my knowledge of these people. I have said that their kings are proud and foolish; their knights are hardly less so. We will order our army into three lines. The first line will be the bashi-bazouks, the second the Anatolians, the third the Janissaries. Then we will do what it is supposed we cannot do, and make a frontal attack with the bashis."

Suleiman waited, frowning.

"It will be repulsed, of course. And our people will fall back in great disarray. The *first* line of our people. It is my certain belief that when the Hungarian knights see that happen, they will not be able to resist the temptation to charge home and complete the victory they will feel they have gained."

"And suppose the bashi-bazouks break and flee?" Suleiman asked.

"They may well do so, Padishah. They may even affect the Anatolians. But I can vouch for your sipahis and Janissaries. They will fight to the end. I can also vouch for the artillery. These we will mass behind your attacking lines, and they will only be uncovered when those lines are opened. Our cannon will be chained together, so that there can be no question of any guns being carried or driven off, or even being ridden through. It will be a hard contest but one which will bring us certain victory."

"What of the cavalry?" Ibrahim asked. "As you have said, Hawk Pasha, more than half the Hungarian army seem to be cavalry. Will you not oppose them with our sipahis because of their armour?"

Again his tone held some contempt.

Hawk Pasha did not take offence. He had been winning campaigns when both these men were children.

"Cavalry are best used in the counter-attack, Ibrahim Pasha. Our cavalry, timariots and sipahis, will be held in reserve, to be launched when the enemy onslaught is broken."

Suleiman pulled his beard while he gazed at the Hungarian camp. "No victory is ever certain until it is gained," he remarked.

"That is true, Padishah. I can only offer my experience as a guide."

"Experience I value highly, Hawk Pasha. I have no doubt of your success. But is it not possible to make it even more certain than it now appears?"

It was William Hawkwood's turn to wait.

"Your strategy would be even more likely to succeed were we able to launch our counter-attack before the enemy has broken."

"Padishah?"

"You estimate that the knights will take advantage of our retreat in order to charge — supposing at the moment they did so they were struck in the rear, or at the side, by a body of horsemen. Would that not have a most powerful effect upon their morale?"

"Indeed it would, Padishah. But where would that body of horsemen come from?"

"We will arrange it now," Suleiman said. "How long would it take a division of our timariot cavalry to march ten miles to the west, then move to the north, and then swing round to come in

357

behind the Hungarian host — remembering that our enemies must know nothing of our manoeuvre."

"They would have to walk their horses for the first part, certainly," William said, pulling at his beard in turn. "I would say not less than twenty-four hours."

"Well, then, let us despatch them now and not engage until this time tomorrow. We shall fill the time with making our dispositions at apparent leisure."

"And if the Hungarians will not wait twenty-four hours?"

"If they attack us without our having attacked them, will we not have gained the first part of your strategy without the consequent loss of men?"

Hawk Pasha was silenced.

Suleiman looked left and right at his pashas, and then gestured towards Harry Hawkwood.

"Young Hawk. You will take command of ten regiments of timariots and carry out the manoeuvre I have outlined. Mark me well: you must be in a position to launch your assault by the fourth hour after sunrise tomorrow morning. Our attack will be made at the third."

Harry saluted. "I will leave within the hour, Padishah."

It was Harry's first entirely independent command. Never had he felt so exhilarated. His uncle rode with him to select the horsemen.

"This young master of ours has a touch of genius about him," William Hawkwood confessed. "Nevertheless, manoeuvres of this sort are always attended with risk of delays or mishaps. I do not believe it will affect the outcome of the battle, but it will certainly affect your reputation. Do not fail your name, boy."

Harry clasped his uncle's arm. "I will not fail either you or myself."

There was only time to give Yana a quick embrace, and gaze in surprise at her tears as she realised he was being sent on special and possibly dangerous duty, then he was hurrying away to join his men.

The timariots were pleased to have been selected for such a mission, even if they hardly understood what they were about. Harry marched them away from the camp, and behind the shelter of the hillock. There was no way he could prevent them sending up a cloud of dust in the August heat, even at a walk, so he took them even farther back than had been originally intended, as if on a search for forage.

Behind him the Ottoman army slowly took up its positions, watched closely by the Hungarians. But gradually the sound of their movements, the clank of weapons and the chatter of men died into the distance, submerged beneath the clip-clop of his own company's hooves.

He commanded six thousand men! His heart swelled as he looked back at them, strung out in column behind him.

They marched south-west for three hours, then turned due west. It was mid-afternoon when they at last turned north. At dusk Harry called a halt. He forbade fires, and made each man dine off biscuits and water. Harry made the rounds of the various regiments himself, accompanied only by Diniz, speaking to the ordinary soldiers as well as the officers, telling them at last what was intended, and what they must needs do on the following morning.

He allowed them six hours sleep and roused them at four in the morning, when it was already light. Now they moved rapidly, behind a screen of skirmishers. They rode through two villages, but the terrified inhabitants they ignored in their haste.

At six, as the sun began to rise out of the mountains to the east, Harry swung them south-east. Now they trotted more often than walked, but he made them halt for ten minutes in every hour to rest their horses.

He watched the glowing ball ahead of him, flooding light across the plain, and listened carefully.

Time seemed to pass so very slowly, and more than once he felt a sense of despair that he had taken the wrong way and was missing the battle altogether. Yet surely he would hear its clamour from some direction?

Then he heard it: the blowing of bugles and the beating of the tabalcans, the cries of many thousands of men preparing to die. It came from the south-east at the third hour of the day, almost at the moment his skirmishers rode back to tell him they had spotted the sun glinting off the armour of the Hungarian troops.

He halted to give the horses a last breather, and to order his men. He formed them into three lines of two thousand men each, all the while hearing the shouting and the clash of arms of the battle drifting towards him on the morning breeze.

Then he rose in his stirrups and pointed his sword towards the enemy. The timariots gave a great shout and trotted forward.

Minutes later he could see what was unfolding. The battle had followed exactly the pattern his uncle had predicted. The bashi-bazouks had charged, but were scattered and retreating in every direction, exposing the Anatolians. These were now under attack from the heavily armoured Hungarian and German infantry, advancing behind their fearsomely long pikes. Behind the Christian foot, the horsemen were surging forward, lances couched, ready for their own charge.

Harry raised his sword again, and the timariots began to canter.

The Anatolians broke before the impetus of the Christian charge, and then the Janissaries were exposed. Now the Christian infantry moved to either side, to allow their cavalry to pass to the front. The knights and their squires and men-at-arms — six men to each "lance" or platoon, each lance led by a knight in full plate armour — trotted forward, the earth shuddering beneath their hooves. As they did so, the Janissaries, beautifully disciplined, also moved to either side, white plumes nodding as they emplaced their stakes and levelled their arquebuses.

Exposed by their manoeuvre was the Ottoman artillery, which belched fire and smoke, sending men and horses tumbling to and fro.

The knights checked their advance for only an instant, then rode forward again at a canter.

Harry's force was now within half a mile of the battle. He raised his sword yet again.

"Sound the charge," he yelled to his bugler, and the notes swept across the morning.

The timariots screamed as they levelled their lances and surged forward.

Before them the cannon exploded again, and tore great gaps in the Hungarian cavalry. The horsemen halted briefly, and then advanced again; the cannon would take time to reload.

Now they were assailed by the bullets of the Janissaries, yet they rode right up to the guns, only to be checked there by the lengths of chain stretching from cannon to cannon, behind which the artillerymen were safe even from the long spears of the Christian cavalry.

While the knights were trying to devise a way though, the Janissaries dropped their muskets and ran forward with drawn swords, the sipahis charging from the other wing.

The Christian infantry, rallied by their commanders, were about to return to the fray when they were distracted by the drumming of hooves from behind them . . .

And beside them. King Louis had kept a division of his own horse in reserve, and these now charged from the flank. Just in time Harry realised his danger, and swung his entire force to meet the threat. The two divisions crashed into each other, the heavily armoured knights and men-at-arms bringing the timariot charge to a halt.

For a few moments it was a wild mêlée. Harry saw an armoured and visored man in front of him, swung with his scimitar, and felt a jar go up his arm as it struck steel. The man fell away before the impact, although Harry did not suppose he was seriously hurt. He had problems of his own, since the much larger Hungarian warhorse had struck his Arab on the shoulder, and the stallion then fell to its knees. This may indeed have saved Harry's life, as a lance passed immediately above his head, and another body cannoned into his. He thrust with his sword, aiming low, where the knight sat his saddle, and was rewarded with a scream of pain. Once again his Arab had been struck, and this time the gallant little horse all but rolled over, but recovered himself and rose again, Harry still firmly in the saddle.

There was no one in front of him. He wheeled his panting mount and found Diniz and his trumpeter still at his shoulder.

"Sound assembly," Harry bawled, his voice hoarse.

The notes rang out, and the timariots disengaged themselves, where they could, and clustered around him. They had suffered severe casualties but so had the knights. Fallen men and horses were scattered across the wheatfields.

But the battle had been decided: Hungarians and Germans were fleeing in every direction, since the armoured knights had broken before the impact of the Janissaries reinforced by the sipahis.

Harry immediately realised that the personal pleasure of engaging further knights must take second place to making sure the Christian army did not have a chance to recover. So he led his men amongst the fleeing foot soldiers, scimitars flashing in the sunlight. The Hungarians screamed and fell; the timariots beheaded each victim and attached the dripping mementos to their saddles.

When the remnants of the Christian cavalry saw what was

happening, they galloped off. There were not more than two thousand of them left. The army of Hungary had been destroyed.

When Harry reached the royal standard, the grim work of tallying the dead was in progress. It was not the Turkish custom to take prisoners when fresh slaves were not needed. Those Hungarians who had thrown down their arms were forced to kneel before Suleiman and his pashas, and one by one had their heads struck from their shoulders. The pile of heads grew and grew.

William Hawkwood, bloodstained and powder-stained, embraced his nephew.

"A great victory," he said. "The scribes say more than twenty thousand of the foe are dead."

"And our losses, Uncle?"

Hawk Pasha's face was grave. "Scarcely less, for the enemy fought like demons. But their king is amongst the fallen. There is not an organised force between us and Buda."

Harry bowed before the Sultan. "I fear my men played but small part in the battle, Padishah."

"Your manoeuvre was decisive, young Hawk," Suleiman said. "You ended any chance of a Christian rally."

"You have gained the greatest victory in the history of the Ottomans, O Padishah. The Hungarian army has been annihilated."

Suleiman's lips twisted. "I have the power to annihilate empires — and that is what we must now do."

Ten days later the Ottoman army was in Buda, and this after spending three days on the field of Mohacs to tend their wounded and bury their dead. The Christian dead were left to bleach their bones in the sun.

Outside Buda they were met by a small force of armoured knights under a flag of truce. Their commander, Count Janos Zapolya, was brought before the Sultan. He spoke in Latin.

"I advised the late King against so rash a venture," he said; "against opposing the might of the Ottomans at all. But he was a foolish man. I offer you now the keys of our city and the allegiance of my followers and myself."

"Do not trust this man, Padishah," Hawk Pasha said in Turkish. "He has betrayed his King and his own religion. Do you suppose he will not also betray you?"

"Perhaps he will dream of it, Hawk Pasha," the Sultan said, "but he could be of use to me." He changed to Latin. "If you would serve me, Count Zapolya, you and your men, and every man in Hungary capable of bearing arms must march beneath my banner. Do this and I will make you King of Hungary."

"You are too generous, my lord," Zapolya gushed. "You have but to tell us where to march, and we will follow."

"Bah," Ibrahim commented. "Making such a fellow a king!"

"It will ensure nothing but discord in central Europe for a generation," Suleiman said mildly. "Zapolya undoubtedly has supporters. And we know how the Christians are confounded by oaths. I will have Zapolya crowned by the Archbishop in Buda, then all the world will know he is the lawful king of Hungary. But most of the Christian world will hate him for it. Yet those who take the oath with him will be forced to defend him or break their vows." Suleiman smiled. "As you manage money, Ibrahim Pasha, so I must manage men."

"That boy grows on me," Hawk Pasha confessed. "He has more true knowledge of men than Selim, and is not greatly inferior as a soldier."

"Could he combine the two," Harry suggested, "he would be the greatest of all the sultans."

"Supposing a woman does not bring him down," William remarked.

For the pashas could not but observe how the Sultan no longer sat with them in the evenings for longer than etiquette demanded; he was invariably in a hurry to seek his divan, where Roxelana waited.

And they were further distressed when, with all of the central European plain at his mercy, the Sultan marched his armies back to the Bosphorus.

"The Hungarians are now our allies," he told his generals. "We have accomplished what we set out to do. There is work to be done at home."

Harry was happy to be going home, no matter what the pashas thought. He worried for his uncle, who had aged considerably during the rigours of the campaign; he had no desire to see

William Hawkwood exposed to a winter in the field.

And indeed winter came on them before they regained Constantinople; the army suffered as many casualties during the return march as during the battle itself. But Hawk Pasha, wrapped in his cloak and indomitably marshalling his men as usual, survived to regain the ministrations of Aimée and Giovanna, and Harry could seek those of his own women.

Yana's sexual attraction grew for him with every embrace, and Harry wondered if Suleiman felt the same about her sister Roxelana.

And what would Gulbehar, reputedly so sweet and gentle and loving, think of her latest rival? Or did Gulbehar feel secure in the certainty that, as mother of the Sultan's eldest son, she would eventually be Sultan Valideh and supreme ruler of the harem, and thus fear no rivals?

Events in Hungary turned out as Suleiman had predicted — up to a point. Half of the country accepted John Zapolya as king, the other half did not. The latter appealed to the Emperor, whose brother, Ferdinand of Habsburg, led an army into Hungary and defeated Zapolya at the battle of Tokay 1527. A month later, messengers arrived in Constantinople appealing for aid.

"Let him sink or swim," Ibrahim recommended.

"Then all my strategy is proved a mistaken one," Suleiman observed. "What do you recommend, Hawk Pasha?"

William Hawkwood stroked his beard, nowadays more white than red. "We will have to return, O Padishah. But this time let us make certain of the task we have undertaken. Hungary and Buda are but outposts on the European plain. The true limits of your empire should be Vienna, and then the Rhine."

"The Rhine?" Suleiman muttered.

"You speak of a campaign which will devastate our people," Ibrahim objected, "and consume our wealth."

Suleiman looked at William. "Can we do it, Hawk Pasha? Have we the men?"

"I believe it can be done. But with some diplomacy and much haste. Instead of summoning your levies from all over the empire, a gathering which would be readily apparent to the Europeans, let us march when we are ready, with whatever we have available in Constantinople and Europe."

"How many men would that be?"

"Perhaps fifty thousand."

"You would invade Austria with fifty thousand men?" Ibrahim snorted.

"We would pick up our garrisons as we advanced. I would say we should command eighty thousand by the time we reached Buda. They would be professional troops rather than bashis, and we would also have all our artillery."

"Eighty thousand men," Suleiman muttered. "Would that suffice? The Franks would no longer remain disunited once we threatened Vienna."

"It is our business to keep them disunited, Padishah. Many years ago, when I was a boy, your grandfather sent me on an embassy to the West. I went to Paris and there spoke with the King, Louis XI. He hated and feared the Habsburgs, and wished to make an alliance with the Sultan so that, from each end of Europe, between them they could constrain Habsburg ambitions.

"Then King Louis died, and the government of France fell into lesser hands. But their present King, Francis I, has spent his entire life fighting the Habsburgs. I believe he would welcome an alliance with us. Once we have achieved that, we may be sure that the Christian princes can never unite against us."

"*If* we could achieve that ... Who would we send as ambassador to the French court, Hawk Pasha?"

"Who could be more suitable than my nephew, O Padishah?"

Aimée was overwhelmed with joy at the thought that her nephew would be returning to her homeland, and only wished that she could accompany him. For many an hour she told him what and who to look for, and where to go.

William Hawkwood told him what to do and what to avoid.

In the event, none of their advice was of much value: the France of 1528 was considerably different from that of 1483.

Harry took the same route as his uncle had done forty-five years previously, to avoid falling into the hands of either the Habsburgs or the Pope. He reached Paris after a journey of three months. Like his uncle, he found himself welcomed and fêted; the French knew a great deal of what was going on in the Muslim world, and the name of Hawk Pasha was a famous one.

He was astounded at the gaiety and extravagance of the French court, so unlike the description of it offered by either his uncle or his aunt — and by the openness of Francis's personality, so unlike that of the Universal Spider.

Francis was handsome and courtly, a knight-errant at heart but embittered by a series of over-ambitious failures. Only a few years earlier his army had been shattered at Pavia, and he himself was taken prisoner by his arch-enemy, the Emperor Charles V, who was also King of Spain and the Indies, and rivalled the Sultan himself in the extent of his power.

To gain his freedom Francis had been forced to swear all manner of oaths, which he promptly broke on his return home, claiming that they had been extracted under duress.

The thought of Charles's brother holding sway in central Europe all but curdled his blood.

Nor did he have very much love for England. Henry VIII was Charles's kinsman by marriage, and a staunch supporter of Spain. He and Francis had met a few years previously outside the English enclave of Calais, for a conference designed to bury their differences. Instead it had multiplied them, for the assembly had evolved into escalating rivalry as to which monarch could put on the finer display of wealth and power and personal strength and vigour — a display of riches which had earned it the title of Field of the Cloth of Gold. And once again Francis had been bested.

"Had all the kings of Europe but a single head, I would strike it off," he now told Harry. "I hate them all. But your Sultan ... ah, let him march on Vienna and I will applaud him all the way."

So Harry had got what he wanted, and was in a hurry to get home. The acquaintances of whom Aimée had spoken were no more, or not to be found. The climate was damp and depressing. The women who wished to flirt with the handsome renegade Englishman — for such he was still regarded — lacked the cleanliness and the allure of his own Yana.

He returned to Constantinople in April 1529 with the news of the treaty. On 10 May, the Sultan Suleiman, without divulging his purpose to anyone — least of all the many ambassadors and Christian traders who thronged the city — marched out of Constantinople with eighty thousand men.

This time Ibrahim remained behind, to continue raising troops who would follow the main army. And this time there were no harems;

speed was the essence of Hawk Pasha's plan.

Harry once again had to big farewell to Yana and his wives, to his mother and his aunt, before he had even a chance to tell them about his experiences in Paris.

Speed! Hawk Pasha drove his men hard. As they were professional soldiers, they responded eagerly, but soon the weaker fell out. Harry continued to watch his uncle with considerable misgivings, but Hawk Pasha never faltered.

This time the border was reached in three months rather than four. The Hungarian army fell away before them, and Buda was besieged on 3 September. It fell five days later, and Suleiman ordered a general massacre of the garrison while turning the city over to his men for looting.

This was a deliberate act of policy by the Sultan and Hawk Pasha; both wished the terror of the Turkish name to be spread abroad. Harry was less certain of its effectiveness, since he felt it might merely stiffen Austrian resistance.

But Suleiman persisted with his policy. His timariots were sent ranging across the Austrian countryside, burning and beheading, raping and looting. All the country east of Vienna was turned into a smoking desert. The invaders prospered, for Hawk Pasha had planned this ultimate campaign with the greatest care, and was using the Danube itself as a highway. The galleys plying to and fro brought food from Hungary and Serbia for the marching troops; no less important, the armed ships on the river formed a permanently defended right wing for the army, and prevented any risk of sudden attacks from that quarter.

Not that there was any risk of that, for Hawk Pasha's entire manoeuvre had taken the Habsburgs by surprise, as he had intended. When, a fortnight after leaving burning Buda, the Sultan and his Pasha gazed at Vienna, and the Ottoman cavalry which entirely surrounded the city, they learned that there were no more than seventeen thousand men against them.

Surprised as they may have been, however, the commanders of the garrison, Philipp, Count Palatine of Austria, Nicolaus, Count of Salm, and Marshal Wilhelm von Roggendorf had placed the city in a state of defence with an efficiency as ruthless as that of the Turks themselves. The watchers could see that all the houses outside the walls had been levelled, to give a clear line of fire in every direction; additional gun emplacements had been built; and they could make out that any wooden roofs inside the city itself had been torn away so as to reduce the risk of fire from incendiary shells lobbed over the wall.

"These men mean to fight, Hawk Pasha," Suleiman observed.

"We shall see how well they fight when the siege artillery arrives," William said. For the Ottoman cavalry, with which rode the Sultan and his pashas, had far outstripped the infantry and the baggage train.

Harry Hawkwood looked at the sky, now a mass of dark cloud. If the siege artillery arrives at all, he brooded.

That night it began to rain. It rained steadily for a week. The river rose and the plain was turned into a morass. Yet the siege was pressed forward with all the vigour associated with the Otto-man name. The flotilla ascended the Danube above the be-leaguered city, and finally cut off the defenders from any hope of supplies. When the infantry arrived, tramping through the rain and the mud, Hawk Pasha launched one or two probing attacks against the walls. As he had expected, they were met with firm resistance.

Eventually the cannon arrived, the horse teams nearly dead with the exhaustion of pulling them through slushy ground. Emplacing them proved nearly impossible, as with each discharge the huge bombards sank further into the mud. Hawk Pasha called on all his own experience and on everything he had ever been told by his father Anthony about the siege of Constantinople. He had his men start to dig mines. Sometimes the walls caved in, and whole companies were engulfed in mud and suffocated. Others pressed on to reach beneath the walls, only to be met there by furious counter-attacks. So regularly was each Turkish tunnel met by counter-mining that William began to suspect some sort of treachery, although even the most determined investigations did not reveal how anyone in the Turkish ranks could communicate with the Viennese commanders. He never did discover the answer, but Harry in later years learned how the Viennese had placed bowls of water at regular intervals along their battlements, and whenever one of these bowls began to tremble they knew that men were digging underneath!

What William *did* understand was that he was making no progress, that the weather was getting steadily colder without the rain in any way abating, and that the Turkish habits of cleanliness and hygiene were of little avail in the midst of this sea of mud.

Men began to die of disease.

Then, on 10 October, a messenger rode into the encampment with news which shocked both Suleiman and his pasha: King Francis of France had concluded an alliance with Charles the Emperor.

"It has been arranged by their respective mothers," Suleiman added, reading the missive. "What influence women have in this world!"

"The Frenchman has betrayed us," William growled. "He has betrayed me. Padishah, I have failed you. You have the right to strike off my head."

"What, am I to strike off my right hand?" Suleiman inquired. "Tell me straight, Hawk Pasha, have we any hope of succeeding in this siege?"

William sighed, his shoulders hunched. "No, Padishah. In another month there will be snow on the ground. By next spring the Emperor will have concentrated all his resources in Austria, now that he no longer has to fear the French."

"Can we ever take Vienna?"

"I believe so, Padishah. But my strategy this time was faulty. Even with all the haste we put forward, we cannot move the army from Constantinople to Buda in under three months. That leaves us with too little time before winter comes in. Our plan must be to concentrate an army on the Hungarian border in one year, and launch our assault as soon as the weather improves in the next."

"But then all the world will know what we intend."

"That is inevitable, Padishah."

Suleiman nodded. "We will have to discuss this. But for the time being, Hawk Pasha, we have been defeated. Command the army to begin to withdraw. We must be away from here before the cold weather comes."

"We have been defeated," William Hawkwood said quietly as, wrapped in his cloak, he watched the Turks begin their retreat.

"It must happen sometimes," Harry said. "Even the Conqueror failed to take Rhodes."

"But I did take Rhodes," William replied. He had never lost a battle until now.

The Viennese raised a great shout of derision as they watched the Turks withdraw. But the shout changed to one of anger and dismay when Suleiman commanded all his male captives to be beheaded before the walls.

With the failure of his crowning project, William Hawkwood's mood seemed to deepen as the homeward march commenced, and daily it grew more destructive. By the end of the month the snow began, and the carts and wagons had to be abandoned; it became a matter of saving men rather than material.

Men and the guns. No descendant of the first John Hawkwood would ever risk losing a gun. As they could no longer be dragged over the soft ground, Hawk Pasha commanded them to be loaded on board the flotilla that still dominated the Danube. This was an immense task, carried out by exhausted and freezing men. But they endured it because of their devotion to Hawk Pasha.

Thus the guns were saved — but at the cost of many men. Amongst them was Hawk Pasha himself. Catching a cold from his incessant labour in the snow, he was determined to ignore it, but it soon developed into a fever. He was then forced to take to a litter, carried by his faithful artillerymen. Harry was riding beside Hawk Pasha when he died.

William Hawkwood was embalmed, and his body taken back to Constantinople, to be buried in the garden of his palace. Aimée, Giovanna and all their servants wept.

Afterwards the Sultan Suleiman sent for Harry.

"You are now Hawk Pasha," he declared, handing him the horsehair wand with two knots.

"I have done nothing worthy of the honour, Padishah," Harry protested.

"I have no doubt you will," Suleiman said firmly. "Now tell me where you seek employment."

"I will go wherever I am sent."

"We have suffered a grievous defeat," the Sultan remarked, "in the death of your uncle no less than in our repulse from Vienna. Now I return to news that the Persians are making war on my eastern provinces. This I cannot permit."

"We will campaign again next year?" Harry asked eagerly.

"I will have to do so. But the Christians will say that I have turned away from them because I have been defeated, and because I now fear them. That, too, is intolerable. Yet I have not the men to wage two great wars at once."

He paused, and Harry waited. He understood the Sultan's dilemma but had no idea how the resolving of it could involve himself. He was surely too young to be given command of a campaign against the Empire.

"We must make them aware that their respite is but a temporary one," Suleiman said at last. "That, when I have dealt with the more pressing matter of the Persians, I shall return and implement Hawk Pasha's plan to take Vienna. We must keep them in a constant state of agitation and alarm. Above all, we must make that treacherous Frenchman regret his betrayal of our alliance. You will undertake this task for me, Hawk Pasha."

"Willingly, Padishah, If you will tell me what force I will command, what strategy I must follow."

Suleiman gazed at him. "Khair-ed-din is in the Golden Horn."

Harry's heart gave a great bound.

"He speaks of great fleets raiding the commerce of the West. More, raiding the coastal cities themselves and driving terror into the hearts of the infidels. I have heard you speak of such things, Hawk Pasha."

Harry could now hardly contain his excitement.

"Khair-ed-din speaks of extending the Ottoman empire along the whole North African coast, and making it a base from which to attack the underbelly of Christendom. Do you believe that is practical, Hawk Pasha?"

"I believe it may well be, given sufficient resources."

"Every Janissary I possess must march with me to the Taurus. Your resources you must create for yourself, but you may recruit here in Constantinople, and you may draw upon the royal treasury and indeed the royal armoury for whatever you require. I am placing you in overall command. You are a friend of Khair-ed-din's. He is a great rogue, but a bold and resourceful man. He will command his own fleet of pirates, but you will command him in the name of the Sultan. I will make this clear to him, and you will remember it at all times."

"You have given me a post of great honour, Padishah, and great responsibility. Be sure I will use it to bring honour to your name."

"Make the infidels weep, Hawk Pasha. That is your business."

Ibrahim Pasha looked down the list of stores and money presented to him.

"Our master sometimes appears to believe that I snap my fingers and dinars appear, hanging from trees," he grumbled. "Cannon? You are going to take cannon to sea?"

"The Spaniards do so."

"Hardly in their galleys."

"If I am to attack their carracks, I need cannon."

"And you intend to attack their carracks?" Ibrahim remarked. "Well, who am I to say you nay, young Hawk? My apologies, I meant Hawk Pasha. Yours has been a sudden elevation. Believe me, I grieve for the death of your uncle."

"Thank you," Harry said.

"As I envy you your removal from Constantinople — and perhaps grieve that also. Tell me your opinion of our Sultan."

"It is not my business or yours to make an opinion about the Sultan."

"He is younger than you or I, Hawk Pasha, and now he lacks the guidance of the great Hawk on whom he leaned so heavily throughout his reign. There are troubled times in store until this Sultan finds his own feet."

"You are close to speaking treason, Ibrahim," Harry suggested.

"Only to you, Harry. And you will not betray me. But tell me this: how does your Russian charmer do? Does she speak Turkish yet?"

"A word or two."

"Her sister is fluent."

Harry frowned at him. "How do you know that?"

"Our master has told me. Our master is in love, Harry, with the cast-off concubine of another man. How can that be?"

"You should at least be pleased that the other man is you," Harry said. "How can you possibly determine that he is in love?"

"Because, when in private with me, he wishes to speak only of Roxelana, of what can be bought for her and given to her as presents, of the alterations and extensions she wishes made to her quarters. Her quarters, Harry, not the harem! She has apartments of her own."

Harry scratched his head. "What does Gulbehar think of this?"

"Whatever she thinks, she says nothing, so the eunuchs tell me. No doubt she hopes that Suleiman's passion for Roxelana is a passing fancy."

"And is that not likely so?"

"Not now," Ibrahim said thoughtfully. "The Padishah has just informed me that Roxelana is pregnant, and he is like a dog with two tails. You understand that all this is confidential. Should you repeat it, you might well lose your head."

"Then I shall not repeat it," Harry said, "I cannot understand your concern. Roxelana is a concubine. Furthermore, she is a slave. Slaves from time to time give birth; it is of no great importance."

"And suppose she gives birth to a boy?"

"Well, no doubt the Padishah will be very pleased. But Prince Mustafa is his first-born by several years, and Gulbehar will become Sultan Valideh in the course of time."

"I wish I could be certain of that," Ibrahim said. "I wish I could feel that I had not made a terrible mistake in sending Roxelana to the Padishah's bed. I wish I could feel that the entire empire, the world, might not one day regret that decision."

He appeared genuinely distressed.

Harry could only say, "I am sure you concern yourself needlessly."

Ibrahim gave one of his sudden attractive smiles. "No doubt you are right. But do not lose yourself away in the West, Hawk Pasha. Be sure to come back to us. We may well have need of you one of these fine days."

Ibrahim, being a Greek, was keenly aware of the insecurity of his position, knowing that he was hated by the Turkish pashas and that he remained in his exalted position entirely by the favour of the Sultan. But was he not certain of that favour? If only for having introduced Roxelana to the Padishah's bed?

Harry frowned. Or was he? He recalled Ibrahim boasting of how he had "broken" the girl. Suppose Roxelana really did gain some influence over Suleiman, might she not use it to bring down the proud Grand Vizier who had tormented her into subjection?

Ibrahim did indeed have something to worry about.

But the Greek had made his own bed, thanks to his overweening ambition, and must now lie on it.

While he, Harry, had nothing but bright prospects ahead of him, so far as he could see. Even if Roxelana were to become Sultan Valideh — which was an inconceivable thought — he would surely remain high in favour; for Yana was her sister. He had never ill-treated Yana and he was more certain now than ever that she loved him.

And he was now Hawk Pasha, and entrusted with a mission of the greatest importance.

Aimée and Giovanna were desolated to learn that Harry was to leave Constantinople for what might be a considerable time. Nor could he alleviate their grief by pointing out that even if he had not been given this command, he would be accompanying the army to Persia the following year.

Sasha, Tressilia and Yana were all delighted when told that they would accompany him. So were the boys, who had already dreamed of following their father on a campaign.

Khair-ed-din was even more pleased, and seemed not in the least disturbed at being placed under the command of a man thirty years his junior. His eyes gleamed as the cannon was brought on board, pushed and dragged up a ramp from the dock by slaves, to be placed on his foredeck.

"I have dreamed," he told Harry, "and despaired of my dreams ever coming true. Now they will do so. You and I will make them come true, Harry. Because we are two of a kind, eh?"

"We even look alike," Harry reminded him. He was in the best of humours.

Khair-ed-din looked from Harry's red beard to his own, and gave a shout of laughter.

"Oh yes," he cried. "Redbeard! They will know us as Redbeard. How will the Franks say Redbeard?"

"Ah ... I should think in Latin they would call us *Barbarossa*," Harry suggested.

"Now there is a name with which to conjure: Barbarossa. It sounds better than Redbeard — more formidable."

He gave the orders to cast off, and then went aft and stood on his poop deck, legs apart and hands on his hips. "Barbarossa!" he yelled. "Let the Franks beware!"

14

THE SPANIARDS

Khair-ed-din's squadron of six galleys drove through the calm
waters of the Mediterranean. Here, far to the south of Constantinople, south even of Peloponnesus in Greece, was a climate Harry
Hawkwood had not known since the Egyptian campaigns of Selim
the Grim. And he had never known it at sea.

The sky was a cloudless pale blue, the sea a ripple-less dark
blue. Dimly on the northern horizon there was a trace of purple:
the mountains where once the Spartans had been lords.

The galleys surged smoothly forward, all hundred and twenty
oar-blades of each ship — sixty to a side, arranged in three banks
of twenty — striking the water in unison. They were cruising, and
the slaves were not being extended.

The only sound above the swish of the water past the hull was
the regular beat of the drum; the drum major had a stick in each
hand and a drum on each side, which he crossed his arms to strike
— one surface every other second. He was relieved every hour; the
slaves would not know any relief until speed was reduced at dusk.
But Khair-ed-din kept going throughout the night — he knew these
waters so very well he did not fear shipwreck in the darkness —
and the slaves could only sleep in relays, every third oar shipped
for four hours ... unless they were fortunate and a breeze sprang
up.

The pirate captain had no doubt that his rowers could be
replaced as and when he chose. He did not regard them as human
beings; a man chained to his oar became lower than a beast of
burden. His only value was the strength in his arms and back.
Once that failed he was thrown over the side without the slightest
ceremony; there was always a couple of dozen relief oarsmen
confined forward, waiting to replace them.

They were nearly all Christians taken in battle, with just a
scattering of Africans. They sat on their benches naked, their

beards extending to their laps, their flesh whip-scarred and wind-burned, their backsides blistered and rotting from the constant friction, surrounded by their own odours and their own filth. Twice a day, at dawn and at dusk, the pumps were manned and canvas hoses were played over the benches, driving the sweat and urine and faeces into the bilges, whence some of the effluvium found its way over the sides. The hoses made very little difference to the stench which hung around the galleys like a vast miasma. But, as Khair-ed-din jovially remarked, "One soon gets used to the stink."

He no doubt knew that were he ever to be taken by the Spaniards or the Genoese, his fate would be even worse than that of a galley slave — if less prolonged.

Presumably, Harry Hawkwood reflected, as he stood at the break of the poop and looked down through the open deck at the straining bodies beneath, he himself now risked the same fate.

He wondered what he would feel like, to be chained to an oar, to know that he must row until he dropped, given the minimum of food and water to keep him alive, and then be thrown over the side? It was not a fate he had ever contemplated, for the Hawkwoods lived and fought as nobles ... and died as nobles too.

Hearing a rustle, he looked down at the woman now standing beside him, her small fingers clasped on the rail. She too watched the men, her lips slightly parted. Her head was bare; since Harry had given his women permission to abandon the yashmak if they chose. Sasha and Tressilia did not choose, of course, and in any event were still seasick.

But Yana had taken to the sea as if born on it. She had never cared for the yashmak, and now her golden-brown curls floated in the breeze as she stared at the men below. They had no galley slaves in Russia, because they had no galleys. Here were probably more naked men gathered in one place than she had ever seen before — though none of them was a particularly pleasing sight.

She felt her master's gaze on her, and flushed.

"I feel sorry for them," she murmured. She spoke perfect Greek now.

Her sympathy surprised him; but she was an altogether softer character than her sister.

"And what do you feel about your own position?"

"I am happy, master. I am happy on the sea — and with you."

Poor Ibrahim, Harry thought, to have thrown away this chance of bliss.

"I wish there was some better way of using so much strength," she said wistfully, again looking down at the labouring oarsmen.

"Yes," Harry said thoughtfully.

At dusk a breeze sprang up from the east. The oars were shipped and the sails were set.

Khair-ed-din entertained his guests to dinner on the afterdeck.

"An east wind is good," he said, "when one is heading west. It drives away the stink, eh?"

The old pirate could not stop himself from leering at the three women. He did not usually carry women on board his ships, unless as captured slaves.

"How long is the voyage to Algiers?" Yana asked, suddenly.

She had the confidence to engage men in conversation as an equal, where Sasha and Tressilia waited to be addressed.

"With this wind, another six days," Khair-ed-din told her. "And without this wind ... another six days." He gave a guffaw and poured her a goblet of wine. He paid no more than lip service to the rules of his religion, just as he paid no more than lip service to the rules of life itself.

"And will I like Algiers?"

"Oh, yes. It is a white place. The houses are white and beautiful. And the harbour is good. It is well sheltered; I have made it so. And now that it is to be ruled by a pasha it will become a true city, will it not, Hawk Pasha?"

"That is possible," Harry agreed.

"Ahoy the deck," came a cry from the masthead, where a lookout was maintained twenty-four hours a day.

Khair-ed-din was on his feet in an instant. "Report!"

"Lights on the starboard bow."

Khair-ed-din climbed into the rigging, his kaftan swinging to and fro, and Harry followed him. Shading their eyes, they could make out faint glimmers on the horizon.

"Land?" Harry asked.

"There is no land between us and Italy, and that is still a hundred miles away," Khair-ed-din said. He dropped back to the deck, where his officers had gathered. "Signal the squadron to douse all lights," he commanded.

377

"Do we row?"

"Not while the breeze remains fresh. We will need our fullest speed later on. Call me the moment it drops or changes."

He returned to the table, which was in darkness since the lanterns had been extinguished.

"Is there to be a battle?" Yana asked, excitedly.

"A battle?" Khair-ed-din guffawed. "No, no, my pretty little girl. A conquest, not a battle. But not until tomorrow. You may sleep sound."

This was a new experience for Harry. On land, when you sighted the enemy you saw at once his size and strength, and you knew battle would be joined in a matter of hours. At sea you chased an unknown quantity. Khair-ed-din told him that the lights were undoubtedly stern lanterns, and that therefore the ships in front of them were following the same course.

"That means they are out of Crete or some such place."

"If they are Venetian, they are our allies," Harry pointed out.

Khair-ed-din grinned. "At sea, who's to tell? But those are not Venetian."

"How can you tell?"

"Were they bound for Venice they would be steering further north, to pass up the Adriatic Sea. These are holding the same course as ourselves; they are steering for the toe of Italy and the Straits of Messina. Thus they are either Neapolitan, Genoese or Spanish."

"And you mean to have them," Harry observed.

"That is our duty to the Sultan," Khair-ed-din said. "Besides, it will be sport."

He retired to his divan, but Harry remained on deck. For almost the first time in life he was anxious about the approaching encounter.

Towards dawn he dozed, to awake with a start to the sound of barked commands. The breeze had dropped. Khair-ed-din was on deck again, the sails were coming down, and the oars were dipping into the water. The rowers had enjoyed the rare luxury of almost a full night's sleep, so the water was struck with vigour; the drumbeat had quickened.

Harry stood at the rail and peered forward. The lights were now much closer; clearly the ships had no idea they were being stalked. He looked to left and right, noting the tell-tale flurries of white as

378

the oars from the other galleys cut through the slight sea. But they would only be visible from close to.

The darkness began to fade to grey. Khair-ed-din joined him. The lights in front of them grew faint.

The daylight improved, and the sea itself was grey. To either side the galleys sliced through the water; each had a cannon mounted on its bow, the eager gunners bending over their pieces to sight them.

And there, in front of them, were three high-sided round tubs of merchantmen.

"Genoese carracks," Khair-ed-din growled. "How fortunate can we be?"

Harry chewed his lip. He remembered his uncle telling him of how his grandfather, Anthony, had spoken of the siege of Constantinople, and of how the Genoese warships had cut through the Turkish fleet on their way to the Golden Horn, their iron-shod prows splintering the oars as if they were straws.

But those had been smaller galleys then, manned by inexperienced crews. Khair-ed-din appeared to have no doubts. Besides, those were not warships.

The Genoese vessels continued sailing quietly for another half an hour while the galleys approached. The breeze had dropped almost to calm now, as it so often does at dawn.

The first glow of the rising sun was flickering across the morning before the watch on the carracks noticed what was behind them. By then the galleys were within a mile of their prey.

Instantly all was pandemonium. Harry could see men running to and fro, guns being loaded, boarding nets strung ...

"Can they escape us?" Yana asked at his shoulder.

"I doubt it. But you must go below," he told her.

She pouted, but obeyed him.

The corsairs were all on deck now, every man armed with a scimitar thrust through his belt, a boarding pike clutched in his hand.

"Fire!" Khair-ed-din bellowed, and the cannon roared. His shot was wide, but the other five galleys also fired as soon as their admiral did so, and two of the balls smashed into the sterns of the carracks, without doing appreciable damage.

The Genoese fired in turn, but their hastily aimed shots all plunged into the sea.

"Attack speed!" Khair-ed-din shouted, standing at the break of the poop, hands tight on the rail.

"Gags!" commanded the officer beneath him.

Every galley slave had, slung round his neck on a length of line, a wooden bolt about six inches long and two in diameter. These they now thrust between their teeth as the drumbeat quickened to a stroke a second, and the deckmasters strode to and fro, their whips flailing across naked backs.

"If they do not use these gags, they begin to scream and howl," Khair-ed-din explained. "No one would be able to hear my orders."

The galleys were now closing the distance at great speed; what wind there was did no more than flutter the carracks' sails. Their crews lined their decks and began firing with handguns, but again did almost no damage.

"They are merchant sailors," Khair-ed-din said contemptuously. "They know nothing of fighting."

Harry knew a curious sensation. If he had spent his entire adult life campaigning, it had always been against other soldiers. When civilians had been executed, it had been a deliberate act of policy, committed in cold blood away from the arena. Now he was about to fight against civilians for the first time.

"Come," Khair-ed-din said, and hurried forward. Harry followed him to where some fifty of the corsair's crew were gathered.

They were now within a hundred yards of the carrack they had chosen as their victim, and a second of the pirate galleys was close behind them; the squadron had broken into pairs, two to each of the Genoese.

Faces, some shouting, others grimly silent, appeared at the bulwark above them. Arquebuses exploded; boiling water was poured on to the heads of the Turks and rocks were thrown, taken from the ballast in the hold.

Nothing made any difference. As soon as the galley was close enough, grappling-irons were hurled, snaking through the air at the ends of their lines to lodge on the gunwales. Instantly the bow of the galley was pulled right under the stern of the carrack, and secured. The oars were shipped, and the corsairs went swarming up the ropes.

Frantically the Genoese slashed at the ropes with swords and axes. Several parted and the men on them fell into the sea with howls of rage, to clamber back over the galley's prow, dripping water. But inevitably some reached the deck, as more and more grapples were thrown. Others crashed in through the stern windows, scattering glass as they burst into the cabin.

Harry was one of these, swinging his scimitar from left to right; the deckhead was too low for an overhead blow.

People screamed and tumbled away from the flailing steel. These were not even sailors determined at least to fight for their lives. They were stout merchants and terrified women — another new experience, for Harry had never faced a woman in battle before.

The sensible ones threw themselves on to the swords; their blood splattered across deck and bulkhead. The faint-hearted allowed themselves to be corralled in a corner of the cabin, where fingers were already snatching away their jewellery and snatching, too, at bodice and crotch.

Harry smashed his way through the closed door and ran up the ladder to the deck. Here Khair-ed-din reigned, surrounded by his men. The fight for possession of the ship was already over. The dead and wounded Genoese were being thrown over the side, as were any of the surviving crew not immediately regarded as worth keeping. The younger, more handsome sailors and the boys were kept for rape.

The women were dragged on deck and there stripped to the lewd comments and the jeers of the pirates. They were thrown on their backs to be examined for their virginity — apparently each of the corsairs regarded himself as an expert on this subject. Those pronounced virgins were at least spared further torment for the moment; they would be put on the selling block in Algiers. Those whose chasteness was in doubt were immediately put beyond recall as they were mounted by their captors, one after another. The deck became a seething mass of naked flesh and gasps and moans ... and odours.

It was a bestial scene, far more so than after any land battle, and there was no escaping it. Harry was keenly aware that it was one his own mother Giovanna might so easily have endured. Sickened, he went aft, on to the high poop of the carrack, and looked down at the galleys trailing behind at the end of their warps. They, by contrast, were comparatively peaceful, with just a handful of Turks left gathered on the foredeck. But, despite his instructions, the women had come out of the cabin to see what was happening.

381

Khair-ed-din clapped him on the shoulder. "A first victory. Are you not pleased, Hawk Pasha?"

"Of course," Harry said.

"And they are rich prizes," Kahir-ed-din assured him. "You have not looked in the holds. We have wine, we have fine stuffs, we have gold, and we have slaves. A rich prizes."

"What will you do with the ships?" Harry asked.

Khair-ed-din grinned. "They are of no use to me. I will burn them. All save one. I will leave one, with a crew of ten men. These men will sail their ship back to Genoa, to tell them what we have done. To tell them they were taken by Barbarossa! That will strike terror into the hearts of the infidels. Barbarossa!" He went to the break of the poop. "Barbarossa!" he shouted.

The cry was repeated by all of the galley crews.

A new dimension had been added to Mediterranean warfare.

Algiers did indeed gleam white in the afternoon sun as the squadron approached it. At first sight, to the eye of an experienced soldier like Harry Hawkwood, it suggested little of defensive value. But as he got closer he realised that Khair-ed-din, or Barbarossa as he now insisted on being called, had created a very secure little port out of virtually nothing. From the apparently featureless coast two long, thick moles had been extended, one crossing the other, so that any fleet attempting to close the shore would have to alter course twice. And the space between the moles was narrow enough to ensure that speed would have to be reduced to a minimum, and the attacking fleet would have to be in single file. On each mole was mounted a battery of artillery.

Behind the moles and above the town rose a considerable fortress, also gleaming white in the sunlight, from the towers of which floated the green flag of the Ottomans.

A brief strip of low and fertile land backed the fortress, which provided the Algerians with most of their food supply. Then the land rose rapidly into hills and mountains. The mountains, as Khair-ed-din told Harry, were named after the mythological Greek giant Atlas who had supported the heavens on his shoulders, and they stretched for roughly a hundred miles inland — and for far more than that parallel to the coast — before descending into the desert.

"Fleets can approach by sea," Khair-ed-din said, "but no large force can cross that desert."

Algiers had been founded by the Phoenicians long before the births of either Christ or Mahomet; the Romans had known it as Icosium. Many subsequent invaders had destroyed the city and left it in ruins, but it had been refounded by the Berbers in the tenth century, and indeed was still ruled nominally by a Berber prince who was happy to have Khair-ed-din use it as a base. It not only provided protection for the prince and his people, but enabled him to collect in rent a tithe of all the loot and slaves brought back by the pirates.

It was actually a much larger city than Harry had anticipated, and his practised eye immediately saw where its defences could be strengthened.

Khair-ed-din certainly proceeded ashore like a beylerbey, even if he could not as yet use the title here. Bowing officials greeted him, and they bowed even deeper when he introduced Hawk Pasha, sent by the Sultan himself to "visit" their Dey.

Together he and Harry called at the Dey's palace, where Harry was introduced to Al-Rashid, a tight-faced little man who welcomed the ambassador of the Sultan. Clearly he had not the slightest suspicion that this might be the first step in his ultimate forced submission to the Porte.

Then Khair-ed-din and Harry climbed the steep, narrow streets, through the kasbah, to the open space above, where the fortress stood. Within it was Khair-ed-din's palace, which was indeed filled with beautiful young women, the pick of his female captives.

Harry was taken up the highest towers, to look down on the busy little port and the sparkling waters of the Mediterranean.

"Had you eyes capable of seeing two hundred miles," Barbarossa told him, "you would look upon the mountains of southern Spain. They rise between ourselves and Granada, which, Allah willing, will one day again belong to us."

Harry tugged his beard. "So close," he mused. "I wonder the Dons do not attempt to destroy you."

Barbarossa grinned. "The Emperor has more important things to do — or he thinks he does. Besides, he knows we would be a tough nut to crack here. We would see his fleet long before it got close to us, and we would be waiting for him."

"Suppose he timed his assault for when you are not here?"

"Who is to know when I am not here, Harry? Besides, he has

missed his chance. From now on one of us will always be here, will we not?"

A section of the palace was given over to Harry, and there he installed his wives, and concubine.

He was, however, more interested in the task ahead of him. Soon he accompanied Barbarossa on a raid to Sicily, where he was surprised at the ease with which the corsairs stole into a deserted bay, landed a formidable force, crept up the cliffs and overran a sizable village, holding it for two days while they totally ransacked it, carrying off some fifty girls and boys as slaves, as well as a huge accumulation of cattle and grain — and departing the moment a large body of troops was observed marching towards them.

"That is the secret of sea warfare, Harry," Barbarossa explained. "We can go anywhere, land anywhere. No coastline can be protected in its entirety. Therefore every coastline is vulnerable. Now, did we but possess Tunis as well ..."

Harry had never needed much influencing to concur that this was the way that wars should be fought. Eventually he took one of Barbarossa's small, fast galleys and returned to Constantinople. The Sultan was not there. He had left Ibrahim in command of the war against Persia, and had once again led an army into Austria. And once again he had been forced to withdraw from Vienna, this time opposed by a large Imperial army. At least he had not been defeated in a battle.

Harry spent a single day with his mother and aunt, reassuring them about his health, then set off to join the great army. He caught up with the Sultan at Belgrade, and was disturbed by what he found.

"It is good to see you, Hawk Pasha," Suleiman said, as Harry was shown into the private chamber by a heavily armed guard. "It is good to see a man I can trust."

"Padishah?" Harry would have supposed there was hardly a man in his empire this well-beloved Sultan could not trust.

"I am surrounded by dishonesty and treachery," Suleiman said, "and there is so much to be done. I must contend with Austrians, I must contend with the Persians, I must deal with all pressing matters of the law and religion back home ... and to whom may I delegate authority, and rely on for for complete understanding and loyalty?"

"Surely Ibrahim ..." Harry ventured.

"Ibrahim! Ha! That treacherous Greek. I raised him from the gutter. You know that, Harry — the three of us were young men together. You remember how my father frowned upon my friendship with the Greek. No doubt he was right."

Harry could not believe his ears. "Ibrahim has betrayed you?"

"Not yet. But there can be little doubt that he means to."

"You have proof of this?"

"Do I need proof? He commands in Anatolia. Oh, he has accomplished some fine things, and has repelled more than one Persian attack. He is proving himself a good general, but is that to my advantage? He keeps appealing for more troops. More troops! He says it is to drive back the Persians, but is it not to create a huge army with which to march on Constantinople and restore Greek rule?"

"O Padishah, I cannot believe it of Ibrahim. He is your most loyal servant. And lacking any proof of treachery on his part ..."

"There are those who know the Greek better than even you do, Harry."

Roxelana! Harry thought. Ibrahim was right; she means to poison the Sultan's mind against him.

"But that is not the least of my troubles," Suleiman growled. "There is treachery even within my own harem."

"Treachery, Padishah?"

"Oh, yes. Plots have been discovered. My own son, Mustafa, is being turned against me. Fortunately there is one I can trust ..." He sighed. "And I now have another son." Suddenly his face grew animated. "I have named him Selim — is that not appropriate?"

His child by a Russian slave named after the greatest of the Ottoman warriors? My God! Harry thought. How high does Roxelana's ambition soar?

"What do you mean to do, Padishah?" he asked.

"I mean to act! I must take my enemies one at a time. I am currently negotiating a peace settlement with this Ferdinand of Austria, to end the European war. Then I shall march to the east and Anatolia. I will take command there and settle with the Persians. I will also settle with Ibrahim."

Harry had no reply to make to that; there was nothing he could say.

"Now tell me what you have come to say," Suleiman invited.

385

Harry swallowed. "I also have come to ask for men, Padishah."

"Ha!" Suleiman exclaimed. "But you at least I know I can trust, Hawk Pasha."

Because of Roxelana's sister? Harry wondered.

"What do you need these men for?" Suleiman asked.

Harry outlined his plans. "But if you now seek peace with the Empire, Padishah, my plans are rendered empty."

Suleiman raised his finger. "Not so. I did not say I sought peace with the Empire, or with the Emperor. I am seeking peace with Archduke Ferdinand, who is but ruler of Austria. I seek no peace with his brother Charles, and neither with that perfidious Francis. What we shall have here is no more than a frontier truce. Oh, indeed, Hawk Pasha, the more you can consume Spanish energies and arouse Spanish fears, the better I shall like it. You will have your men, and I wish you every success."

Harry bowed in gratitude. "And may all go well with you, Padishah."

"It is my business to see that it does," Suleiman said grimly.

"I can only beg you not to act too hastily, or without proof."

"I shall act as I find," Suleiman told him.

Harry could do no more, however uneasy he might feel as to the possible course of events. He sailed from Constantinople with twelve galleys and a thousand soldiers, in addition to their crews, and reached Algiers a fortnight later. He saw more than one tempting prize on the way, but was not to be distracted from his purpose.

Al-Rashid pulled his beard at this unexpected influx of Ottoman power; nor was he reassured when Harry promised that the men were solely for a campaign against Tunis. Al-Rashid hated Mulai-Hassan, Dey of Tunis, but he also knew that, unlike himself, Mulai was on good terms with the Emperor — and so he feared repercussions.

"Will my ships and my men not be here to protect you?" Harry protested.

Barbarossa was delighted with the augmentation of his fleet, and Harry immediately set to work to reconnoitre Tunis from both sea and land, undertaking a long and dangerous five-hundred-mile trek along the mountains, accompanied only by Diniz and a guide. His mission, which took three months, convinced him that the

386

assault must take place from the landward side, not only because of the strength of the seaward defences of the city, but so that the Spaniards would be unaware of what was intended until it was too late. They regarded Barbarossa as nothing more than a pirate, even if he did choose to call himself beylerbey of Algiers in the name of the Sultan. But when he began to expand along the North African coast they would need to take him more seriously.

Meanwhile Barbarossa put to sea with his augmented fleet, and carried fire and sword right round the Spanish and Italian coasts, from Cartagena through Alicante and Valencia, Tarragona and Barcelona, Sete and Marseilles, Nice and even Civitavecchia, which was the port of Rome. Only Genoa, strongly defended by its own fleet, escaped this holocaust. Barbarossa's name was on everyone's lips, together with those of his most famous lieutenants, of whom Dragut was best known.

Harry did not spend all of his time planning the assault on Tunis. The sea remained his greatest interest — but no longer just the Mediterranean. From Spanish prisoners brought as slaves to Algiers he heard tales of the Atlantic, where there was always a wind and where great voyages were possible in the right ships.

But, for all their naval supremacy, did the Spanish have the right ships for the purposes he had in mind?

They were developing a new war vessel, he learned. The carracks and their smaller editions, caravels, which had dominated the oceans for more than two hundred years — the sort of ship in which Christopher Columbus had crossed the Atlantic and Vasco da Gama had rounded the Cape of Good Hope — were proving increasingly useless as ships-of-war. They could be built to huge sizes, some of a thousand tons burthen, and they could be powerfully armed and filled with fighting men, but their ponderously broad hulls left them totally unmanoeuvrable in anything but a fair wind. The greatest fleet of carracks in the world could sail up to an undefended seaport yet be left helpless if the wind was offshore.

The Spanish seamen were thus engaged upon changing hull and sail design, seeking to improve fighting qualities. They were increasing the length-to-beam ratio from two to three, or in cases even four, thus placing much more hull in the water for greater speed. They were reducing the huge bow and stern castles to nothing more than slightly raised observation decks, thus eliminating the enormous windage which made many a carrack sail faster sideways than forward. And they were improving their sail plans: in addition to long bowsprits to which could be carried several foresails or jibs, they were learning to pull the square yards as nearly as possible fore and aft, to enable their ships to work to windward. These new vessels were called galleons.

There was even talk about building a galleon which would have oars as well as sails. Such ships would be called galleasses, but as yet they remained as plans on the drawing-board.

There were, of course, drawbacks to the new vessels. Their low profile meant they were useless as carriers; there was simply not sufficient room. Intended for long voyages — crossing the Atlantic might take upwards of two months if the weather was bad — their lowest or orlop decks were crammed with water and food, and there was no space for cargo. There were also problems with the guns; in a fully-armed ship the lower gun-ports were very near to the water, and would be unusable in a rough sea, while their relatively narrow hulls made their captains reluctant to have guns of any size mounted on the main deck. But that they were formidable vessels could not be doubted.

Nor could Harry doubt that one day he would have to fight against such ships.

But they were quite useless for the piratical raids he wished to carry out into the Atlantic, along the coasts of Portugal, Spain and, above all, France. The main drawback was that they were too large and too unwieldy; they could still be rendered helpless by the weather, and there was no prospect of taking them into shallow estuaries.

But they were also designed to perform functions for which Harry had no use. He was not setting out to engage an enemy fleet, if he could avoid that, therefore cramming his ships with as many broadside cannon as possible was a waste of time; all he required was a powerful bow-chaser to bring down the mast of fleeing merchantman. What he did require was a large complement of men for the short raids he intended. Again, he never meant to be at sea for more than a few days at a time without being able to replenish both his food and water supplies, thus a deep hold in which to stow water casks and salted beef was unnecessary.

Above all, he wanted yet more windward ability.

His memory of sailing in the Bosphorus, Marmara and the Black Sea came back to him. A Venetian shipwright had built that little ship, which had done everything he had wanted of it, on a small scale. Why could the scale not be enlarged?

He put this to Khair-ed-din the next time the corsair fleet happened to be in port.

Barbarossa stroked his beard. "It is certainly possible, Harry, to build a larger version of your yacht, but I am not sure it will serve any useful purpose. You mean to take your ship through the Straits of Gibraltar and into the ocean? Have you any idea what you will find there? Do you remember what happened to your yacht in the Black Sea?"

"She wasn't decked, but these new ships *will* be decked. They will be able to ride out even an Atlantic storm. And are we going to admit that there is any sea we are afraid to sail on? Especially as the Spaniards already sail on it?"

Barbarossa grinned. "I am happy to admit there are things I do not wish to challenge or learn, at my age, Harry. The Mediterranean is my sea. Here I prosper. And it is about that I wish to speak. You have heard of Andrea Doria?"

"The Genoese admiral?"

"The same. But he is no longer merely an admiral; he is now dictator of the republic."

"Then he will have less time to chase about the sea behind you."

"Quite the reverse. My prisoners inform me that he intends to devote the entire resources of his nation to my destruction — and yours. He is apparently building ships at an unheard-of rate, heedless of whether he bankrupts his people or not. And he is constantly importuning the Emperor to join with him in an assault to destroy Algiers."

"Hm. Does Al-Rashid know of this?"

"No, and we are not going to tell him. He would have a nervous fit, and ask us to leave. But we cannot remain passively awaiting their attack. There are two things we must do."

"Yes?"

"The first is, the moment this new Genoese fleet puts to sea we must seek it out and destroy it. It will be manned by untested crews, and the ships themselves will be untested."

Harry nodded. "That makes sense. And the other?"

"We must take Tunis immediately, before the Genose fleet is

ready. That means within the next year: I do not think Doria will be able to have his ships at sea before the end of next summer. It is not merely that Tunis is an even stronger base than Algiers. It will give us a second fortress stronghold against the Spanish and Genoese positions. Should the Emperor Charles and Doria consider attacking one, they must also consider the possibility of being attacked from the other. This has now become a matter of great importance."

Harry agreed. Therefore he reported to Constantinople, preferring to send a messenger rather than go himself. He had no idea what situation he might find there, and he rather dreaded what news might come back.

But the news was all good. The Persian campaign had been brought to a successful conclusion, and Ibrahim had been awarded a triumph for his successes there. He was still Grand Vizier, and it was he in fact who replied to Harry's letter. So he and Suleiman must have become reconciled.

Additionally, Prince Mustafa was seen in public and was being given important commands by his father. Harry felt tremendous relief: Roxelana had clearly failed in her harem intrigues.

Best of all, the Sultan fully approved Hawk Pasha's plans to expand Ottoman rule in the western Mediterranean through the capture of Tunis.

Harry and Barbarossa got to work with a will. While Barbarossa made a showy demonstration of force off the coast, Harry marched his small army along the mountain route he had reconnoitred the previous year. Thus the somewhat sleepy city of Tunis was assaulted unexpectedly from the land side, and fell very easily. Only then did Barbarossa risk taking his galleys into the shallows.

For Tunis had never been fortified to resist an attack by land; it stood virtually on the site of ancient Carthage, with all the advantages enjoyed by that famous seaport. The city occupied a hummock of land jutting out from the mainland, protected on each side by an extensive salt lake. These were just deep enough to float the average galley, but they were surrounded by sandbanks and small islets, and the dredged passage through them into the main lakes was narrow and well protected by a fort.

Yet, had Mulai-Hasan ever troubled to look over his shoulder, he could have made his stronghold impregnable.

As they intended to make this city their headquarters, and needed the goodwill of its inhabitants. Harry refused to permit a sack; indeed, those of the existing garrison who wished to take service under him were welcomed. To his disappointment, however, the Dey Mulai-Hassan managed to escape, and all Hawkwood's efforts could not find him.

Later he discovered that Mulai-Hassan had made his way to Madrid and was there importuning Charles V to assist him in regaining his lost kingdom.

As Harry immediately set about strengthening the defences of the city, especially on the landward side, he transported his wives and family from Algiers to his new capital. Algiers was just too close to Spanish anger, and Tunis was definitely the stronger of the two ports.

Once Tunis was secure, early in 1534, he commenced his own private project. He built four ships, each only a hundred feet long and twenty-five wide; they were nearly as narrow as a galley. Each was fully decked, and flush-decked. Below was storage space for munitions and for captives and booty when taken. The crew, himself included, was expected to sleep on the deck.

For propulsion he used the lateen sail to which he had become accustomed in his yachting days. Experimenting, he found that he could sail within fifty points of the wind, which was superior to the performance of any galleon.

To his surprise and delight, Yana here put forward a suggestion.

"I understand it is your intention, my lord," she said, "to build ships more able to withstand the storms of the ocean than galleys can. But on the ocean, or near to shore, there will be times when there is no wind, or when you will wish to move your ships from place to place *against* the wind. My lord, we do not employ galleys in Russia, but on our rivers our boats are propelled with great sweeps."

"Sweeps?"

"These are long oars, perhaps one, perhaps two to a side, depending upon the size of the vessel and of the river it intends to use. Your ships could carry two a side. These oars are laid on the deck when not in use. When required, they are thrust over the side through rowlocks mounted on the gunwales. Some three men each are required to pull them. You will find that they will move your ships through the water at a good speed."

Harry realised she had made a brilliant suggestion, especially for the type of work he had in mind. Sweeps and rowlocks were put in hand immediately.

When he eventually called for volunteers to help take his little squadron to sea, he was surprised at the response. He allotted fifty men to each vessel and announced that he would command the expedition himself.

Barbarossa and Dragut were dumbfounded.

"What of Doria? they demanded.

"You have told me his fleet cannot be ready for sea before this autumn. I will be back by August — and certainly before the October gales."

"Supposing you come back at all," Barbarossa grunted.

Tughluk wished to accompany him; he was now eighteen years old and a capable seaman. Tutush, only two years his junior, was equally enthusiastic. But Harry could not bring himself to take his only two sons on what might prove a most dangerous adventure; from the Turkish point of view, he was challenging the unknown.

"You will remain here in my place, and sail with Barbarossa," he told Tughluk.

The boy was sufficiently well disciplined not to argue

Tutush he told to remain in the fortress, in charge of the palace.

He did not tell them that he had a private reason for commanding this expedition himself, and for separating himself from his family.

If he was going to raid France, why should be not visit England? It was now eighty-seven years since the Hawkwoods had left England to seek their fortunes in the East. But not one of them had ever been allowed to forget their heritage, and they had all been taught English as their first language.

To return there, however briefly, had become an ambition of his since he had first tasted the delights of sailing.

The little fleet left Tunis at the end of May, Harry having learned from his Spanish prisoners that the weather in the great bay lying to the north of Spain first improved about June.

It was already fine enough in the southern Mediterranean. They made their first stop at Algiers, and learned that there was no sign of any Spanish movement at sea. This suited Harry, well aware that his men were intensely nervous at the thought of facing the Atlantic. But, then, so was he.

Next day they put out, running before a light easterly breeze. Soon they sighted the huge rock of Gibraltar, beyond which was Algeciras bay, a large and sheltered anchorage. Here they made out some ships riding at anchor, but none showed any interest in the four dark shapes creeping along the far side of the eight-mile-wide channel.

Although the breeze had freshened somewhat, their speed dropped to a considerable extent, and the sea grew quite choppy; Harry soon realised that they were fighting a strong current. Indeed at one stage they remained motionless for several hours, only barely holding their own. Then the tide turned and the current weakened, but it still was not with them.

He deduced that, because of evaporation, the waters of the Atlantic must always flow into the Mediterranean, only slackening somewhat when the tide was on the ebb. Equally he deduced that for the tide even to match the current, it must be running at several knots. There was clearly a great deal to be learned about ocean sailing.

But at last they were through. The land dwindled away to either side, and they found themselves climbing great walls of slow-moving water, then shooting down the other side. The Turks were extremely alarmed at this first evidence of the immense power of the ocean, but after a few hours became used to the movement, especially when they discovered that these water walls, some thirty feet high, did not break.

But Harry understood that were the wind to freshen to any extent, they would indeed break — and would then become most formidable.

The little squadron steered steadily north-west, and they found themselves again closing the land. Two nights out from Gibraltar they sighted the lights of Sagres, on Cape St Vincent, where Harry knew that the Portuguese prince Henry the Navigator had in the previous century established an observatory to learn all that could be discovered about the sea, its tides and currents, and indeed about the weather.

He gave the Cape a wide berth, not wishing to have his presence reported; but once round it and sailing north, he kept within ten miles of the coast, closing it every dawn and dusk to ascertain if there was anything worth attacking. The weather remained entirely on his side, the breeze having shifted from east to south-west, so that once again he had a fair wind.

Two days later they came upon the rocky promontory of Cascais, guarding the river Tagus. Harry knew from his captured maps that a few miles up the Tagus lay the great city of Lisbon, capital of Portugal. To attack that was beyond his means, but on standing in to the anchorage at Cascais, he was amazed to find it crowded with shipping, some of a good size.

"Plump ducks," commented Diniz, who had been promoted to second-in-command of the admiral's ship.

"We must have one, at least," Harry decided, and studied the situation. It wanted but an hour to darkness. But he was more interested in the way the ships lay to anchor. When he had first sighted them, they had all been with their bows facing west towards the open sea. But, as his squadron approached, the ships drifted in various directions round their anchor chains, and now they were all swinging so that their bows pointed upstream towards Lisbon.

Clearly the tide had just turned, to the ebb. His observations had told him that each tide lasted approximately six hours, therefore it would flood again at about midnight, and begin to ebb about six the following morning. This was knowledge that could be put to his advantage.

He set his signal flags, and the squadron — which had aroused some interest on shore, judging by the activity in the fort — stood out again for the night. When they were hove-to Harry called his captains on board the flagship to give them their instructions. Shortly before dawn he led them back again, steering on the lights of the fortress and a much larger light displayed further up the estuary to mark a sandbank, and carried along by the last of the flood.

Silently the four little ships slipped through the dark water, Harry himself leaning on the steering oar of the lead vessel. During his brief reconnaissance of the previous evening he had marked the rocks tumbling down from the fortress, but had formed the impression that the bay itself was clear, from the way the ships were anchored. Thus he led his little squadron well past the fortress before turning back; with the wind in the south-west, this was not a difficult manoeuvre. The tide was now almost slack.

He was also waiting for first light, and it was at this moment that he approached the anchored vessels.

The previous evening he had marked his chosen victim, a large carrack on which he had observed a great deal of activity, as if she was ready for sea and awaiting only a fair wind. With the wind still westerly, or foul for her purpose, he estimated at least half of her crew would be ashore. He led his squadron straight through the many smaller vessels anchored outside the merchantman, still maintaining absolute silence.

Before anyone in the anchored fleet was aware of it the four corsairs were alongside the carrack; the sails were dropped and the grapples thrown. The Turks swarmed over the gunwales from both sides. The anchor watch were disposed of almost before they could shout, and the ship was taken but five minutes later. As Harry had guessed, many of the crew were ashore; those who could escape the flailing scimitars of the pirates leapt overboard. Several died.

The holds were a mass of fine stuffs, but Harry was principally interested in gold on this occasion — there was no time to take slaves, or to transport a great deal of booty into the waiting feluccas. Within fifteen minutes he was chasing his men back over the side, and had laid a powder trail from the deck to the carrack's magazine.

The grapples were freed, the sails were set and the corsairs surged away from the side of the doomed vessel. The wind was now foul for them as well, and it was impossible to sail directly out to the anchorage, but this was to the good. Harry directed his ships up the estuary, and away from the hubbub that had suddenly erupted as the people of Cascais realised what was happening.

The guns of the fort opened up and boats began to put out from the shore to regain control of the carrack. By now Harry's squadron was about a mile up the river, beyond cannon range. He came about and stood down the estuary; the tide had turned and the ebb enabled him to keep even closer to the wind than usual. He intended to pass outside the range of the fort on the outward journey as well.

But the fort was soon distracted. The men from the shore had just reached the carrack, when it blew up. Even the feluccas were rocked by the force of the explosion, which sent masts and guns

395

and pieces of timber flying skywards.

For several minutes afterwards there was silence, so shocked were the Portuguese by what had happened. In those minutes the pirate squadron made good its escape.

"What will they say of us now?" Diniz asked triumphantly.

But Harry knew that so far on their voyage they had had nothing but good fortune.

Their luck changed further north, soon after they had passed the grim promontory known as Finisterre. The cliffs there, several hundred feet high, were shrouded in low cloud, but next morning these cleared and the south-westerly wind which had been bowling them along in a most friendly fashion, increased to gale force and above.

Now the swell did begin to break, great ten-foot-high walls of water that came surging down on the little ships. This time Harry, after dropping the sails, elected to run before the storm under a bare pole. The other masters followed his example, but it was an anxious twenty-four hours as the feluccas hurtled into the Bay of Biscay, being constantly submerged beneath the foaming white. Their crews wailed their fear and begged Allah for mercy, and Harry clung grimly to his steering oar as he fought to keep the ship stern-on to the seas and avoid being rolled over.

Not all the masters were as expert. One lost control just after dawn. Harry could only watch in horror as the felucca turned broadside on, was picked up by a wave in that position, and then rolled down the slope in a slurry of wood and water and drowning men.

He looked back to see her floating upside-down, about to be smashed by another giant wave. There was nothing he could do to help her — or her people.

When the storm abated later that day, the three surviving ships could set their sails again.

"By Allah, does such a thing happen often in these waters?" Diniz asked fearfully.

"Too often," Harry told him.

The other two captains were all for turning back but Harry would not allow it. It was too soon yet: the Portuguese coast would be alive with men-of-war seeking the pirates. And, as far as he was concerned, the voyage had not yet properly begun. He held on into the bay in increasingly fine weather. They came across some scattered islands, and then a little river. This they followed, to appear suddenly before a sizable town guarded by a small fortress.

The French defenders were taken entirely by surprise as the corsairs, having dropped their sails and got out their sweeps, surged alongside the stone dock, leapt ashore and assaulted the fort. People fled screaming in every direction. Harry had his men manhandle two of the cannon standing on the battlements round to oversee the houses, then fired them. Walls came tumbling down and fires were started. People streamed into the fields and hillocks outside the town, but Harry despatched a body of his men to see what could be gained in the way of slaves. They returned with a good score of pretty girls.

Meanwhile the mayor of the town had hoisted a white flag and offered to parley. He nearly fainted when Harry ransomed the town itself at ten thousand gold pieces, and it took two days to raise the money by digging into the cellars of every local merchant.

By then Harry's scouts, proceeding further up the river in small boats, reported that one of the local lords was assembling a militia. Harry hastily re-embarked his men, with their slaves and their gold, with stocks of fresh food and the water casks refilled. Then he bade goodbye to the mayor and put to sea. Within an hour the shore was lost to sight.

The raid was repeated further along the coast, and when there was another gale, Harry kept his ships in a sheltered, deserted bay in complete safety. But here, if the storm did them no damage, they nearly met with disaster. They had dropped their anchors just before dusk, to awaken a few hours later to hear and feel their keeps grinding on the sand. A few hours later on three vessels were high and dry, lying on their sides.

The Turks were terrified, and assumed themselves lost, especially when daylight came to reveal the extent of their plight. Harry understood what had happened, and he could also see the tide slowly returning. But he realised too that if a body of French soldiers were to come upon them now, they were indeed lost. Fortunately none did, and in the middle of the morning they were floating again and able to put to sea, since the storm had abated.

But clearly there was still a great deal for him to learn.

By now it was the end of June, and the ships were nearly full of booty. But he had that last ambition to fulfil before sailing for home.

From the Brittany coast he led his three ships northward. amd after two days sighted hills which rose gently from the shore towards the interior.

He wondered at his emotion, or perhaps the lack of it, as at last he gazed at his homeland. It was probably the greenest land he had ever known; not even France could compare. And it looked so utterly peaceful.

When they passed a fishing boat a few miles from shore, its crew stood up to wave, even as they stared in amazement at the unusual craft and their even more unusual crews. Then they hastily set sail, away from the strangers.

The feluccas stood on, and sighted an empty beach in a shallow bay. The breeze was light, and the clouds not the least threatening; there was no evidence of any rocks encumbering the bay itself, although they clustered to either side. Harry put in and anchored, having carefully measured the depth of water by means of a heavy stone tied to a line, and decided that there would be sufficient to float his ships even at the bottom of the tide.

The small boat was launched and he was rowed ashore. He leapt from the bow on to the sand — the first Hawkwood to set foot on English soil in eighty-six years.

Diniz joined him. "Your ancestors were born here?"

"In this land, certainly. But far from here, on the eastern side of the country."

He climbed up the cliff-path, Diniz at his heels. They emerged into a large field stretching back towards a village dominated by a church. Beyond stood a rather large and splendid house.

"These people have never been to war," Diniz said. "They will provide easy plunder."

Certainly the peacefulness of the place was astounding, but he had not come here to make war ... until he heard shouts from below him, followed by shots.

Looking down, he spied a body of horsemen galloping along the beach. Clearly they came from some other town, and no doubt had been alerted by the fishermen. As they galloped they fired off pistols — a cluster of yeoman led by two or three brightly dressed gentlemen.

The corsairs were taken by surprise, and several had already fallen. The rest were hurriedly struggling to relaunch the boats. In this they succeeded, before they were surrounded by the horsemen, though they had no choice but to abandon their wounded, and also their pasha. The crews still on the ships were reluctant to open fire for fear of hitting their own comrades.

Harry and Diniz cautiously began their descent. As they watched the scene beneath them, they saw two of the captured sailors being dragged across the sand towards the stunted trees which grew at the bottom of the cliff. It all happened very quickly. A rope was thrown over the branch of one tree, a noose was looped round the neck of the first Turk; and a moment later he was dangling. One of the horsemen pulled hard on his thrashing feet in order to break his neck. Then the second Turk was hustled forward.

Harry was aware only of fury, that he had led his men to such an ignoble death. Standing up, he cupped his hands and bellowed, "Open fire!"

If his men were going to die, they should do so in conflict.

The Englishmen were taken by surprise in turn, looking left and right as they tried to discern where the voice had come from. Now the guns on the bows of the feluccas opened fire, and round shot ploughed into the hesitating group. Several men fell. Some of their compatriots ran to the foot of the path and began to clamber up, waving swords. Harry drew his scimitar and charged towards them, followed closely by Diniz. The first man fell to a sweeping blow, and the rest scurried back down the hill. Most of their comrades had already remounted, and were retreating along the beach, leaving their dead, and the two Turks dangling from the branch. The men who had confronted Harry leapt hastily into the saddle and followed them.

Harry cut down the hanged men with a slash of his scimitar, and soon found himself surrounded by his people, who came ashore. They were angry and wanted blood.

And did he not too? This pilgrimage back to his homeland had turned out badly. Well, if they wanted war, they would have war.

The horsemen were still watching them from about half a mile up the beach, so Harry put into practice the same strategy he had carried out successfully at Cascais. He and his men re-embarked with every evidence of haste, set their sails and put out to sea. He carefully took a compass bearing on the cove.

They sailed out of sight of the land, then dropped their sails and drifted. Towards noon the wind dropped, and it was a calm and lazy day. Harry kept lookouts active in case any ships approached them, but none did. Then, in the afternoon, his men got out the sweeps and began slowly to return to the shore.

Just before dusk they sighted the same beach, now deserted. Since they had seen no other boats, it seemed most likely the Englishmen assumed that they had indeed fled.

Although a breeze sprang up just after dusk Harry continued to use his sweep, and took his ships even closer in than the last time, having ascertained that there was deep water almost up the steeply shelving beach. He left ten men on each ship, and led the other hundred odd up the path to the clifftop. Every men was armed to the teeth, and eager to avenge the deaths of his comrades.

The night was already dark — the moon would not rise until after midnight — and quiet. No doubt the militia were celebrating their victory in the local inn.

The corsairs crept across the fields and were nearly at the houses before the first dog barked. Then a regular cacophony began, but it was already too late for the villagers.

Diniz led a third of the men along the main street, battering down doors and crashing inside to loot what they could and burn everything else. Harry led the main assault on the inn itself, which lay at the other end of the street and at some distance from the nearest houses.

By the time he got there, the whole village behind them was in flames; women were screaming, dogs were barking, and the church bell was tolling.

Drunkenly the men in the taproom reached for their weapons as the doors burst open. As they gazed astonished at the Turks and their huge, red-headed leader, a pistol exploded and the Turks surged forward, cutting and thrusting. Barmaids and whores screamed as they tried to escape by the rear, but were hauled tumbling back and stretched out on the floor, where beer and blood now mingled freely. In less than ten minutes the massacre was over, with none left alive save for the women being raped.

"Get our people out and fire the building," Harry ordered his captains, and went outside to find Diniz and his men waiting.

Behind them the village blazed in a huge conflagration that had to be visible for miles.

"There are other men approaching, my lord," Diniz warned.

"Call our people to arms," Harry snapped, and a bugle immediately blared into sound. The Turks poured from the inn, which was already burning.

Harry moved some distance away from them, along a lane leading inland from the village, and stared into the darkness beyond the flames. Out there were the lights of the large house, clearly that of the lord of the manor. The house and its garden were surrounded by woods, which in turn were encompassed by a wall. The wrought-iron gates stood open, and from them advanced perhaps a score of men, well-armed — from the gleam of steel — and accompanied by half a dozen large dogs, still leashed, which were baying angrily.

The party checked at the sight of the Turks so clearly visible in front of the burning houses.

"Fall back," someone yelled. "They are too many. To the house. Fall back."

Harry was the only one amongst the Turks who understood.

"Charge!" he yelled, and ran forward.

His men ran at his heels, with bloodcurdling shrieks.

Then the dogs were loosed, and came at them. They were magnificent beasts, but helpless against the razor-edged scimitars. Then their masters fired their pistols. A ball strick Harry on the helmet, but the range was too great to cause anything more than a jar. Then the defenders were running back for the house ... but not fast enough.

Their blood stirred by their activities in the village, the Turks raced after them. Round a bend in the wooded driveway stood the house itself, set on a terrace above wide steps. Here the Englishmen gathered for a last stand, but they were outnumbered by some four to one and the battle was brief. Harry burst through his assailants behind his swinging scimitar, blood splashing over his arms and face — and then he was up the steps and at the front door.

The door was closed and barred, as were the windows to either side, but the stout oak resisted only two charges before breaking inwards.

The Turks tumbled in, and gazed around at the high-ceilinged hall, with carved oak stairs leading up to one side, and richly furnished rooms beyond, at the paintings of austere men and women on the walls, the suits of armour, the long table laden with silver plate ... There was considerable wealth here, Harry realised.

But no people.

"Sack the place," he ordered, and himself took the stairs three at a time. Some of his men followed him; others scattered to left and right.

He reached a first-floor gallery, off which opened several more chambers and parlours, every one as richly furnished as the ones below. His men whooped as they began gathering up all the valuables they could carry.

Harry ranged through all the rooms, then took another flight of stairs to the second floor. Here he found bedrooms with cambric sheets and down pillows, and glowing candles — the family had clearly been about to retire.

He ran back down the stairs again, and entered the kitchens, where some of his men were feasting off the remains of a luxurious dinner. There he discovered what he sought: the stairs to the cellars.

He descended these, and found first a well-stocked wine cellar. Beyond was another stout wooden door, firmly closed and clearly barred on the inside.

"Break it down," he urged those who had followed him.

They charged the door with their shoulders. At the third attempt it creaked, at the fourth it cracked, at the fifth it burst open.

The Turks tumbled in, and remained on their knees as they gazed at the scene before them, illuminated by a singled guttering candle.

There were some fifteen women in the room. Most were clearly serving maids, but three were dressed as ladies of quality. All of them huddled together in terror.

As Harry stepped forward through his men, there was an explosion. The pistol ball passed so close to his head he could feel its passage. The flash of it left him half-blinded for a moment.

Two of his men uttered a roar and ran past him to seize the woman who had fired the shot. They dragged her forward.

Harry stared at her. She could hardly be more than fifteen, a wisp of a girl. She was clearly not a servant, for her gown was of the best brocade. Still narrow-shouldered and slim-hipped, her breasts no more than a swell at her bodice, it was her face and hair which gave her beauty. The hair was yellow, like Aimée's, but this girl's was a profusion of curls tumbling on to her shoulders and down her back.

Beneath it was a somewhat long face, a pale complexion high-lighted by the colour which had flooded into her cheeks as she realised her peril. High forehead, small nose and mouth, softly curved chin, and above all wide-set pale blue eyes were carefully combined to leave a quite delightful picture.

She now hung limp in her captor's hands, anticipating her fate; her tongue came out to give her lips a quick lick. Around her the Turks surged towards the other women, and the cellar became a place of screams and grunts.

While Harry stared at the girl, the bloodlust of vengeance in his brain suddenly seemed to cool, and he realised that here could be a prize indeed. "Do not harm these women," he told his men.

They stopped, hands already tearing at bodices, to stare at him in amazement.

"There are riches for everyone in this house," he told them. "Take what you wish. But make haste and let us be out of here before the whole county is raised."

They shouted their agreement and rushed back up the stairs to grab everything of the least value. A bellow of triumph from along the hall told Harry that someone had found the squire's treasure chest.

The women seemd to huddle even closer. Some had fainted, but most now stared at Harry as rabbits might stare at a snake.

The girl remained in front of him, gazing at him with her mouth slightly open.

All manner of thoughts rushed through his mind. He had come here wishing only to see the country of his ancestors. Now he was as much in contest with them as with any other Christian country, for to these people he was a Turkish corsair. And here in front of him was a woman to make any heartbeat quicken.

She was English, so was he — so their son would be the truest Hawkwood born in three generations. And his blood was aflame after the excitement of the assault.

As he reached out for her, she uttered a faint exclamation and tried to turn. He caught her arm, swung her round, and lifted her from the floor. Her head hung behind, with hair brushing the

403

ground. She pounded on his back with her fists, but he hardly felt her. He wrapped his left arm round her thighs to keep her in place, and strode back to the foot of the stairs.

"Scoundrel!" shouted one of the women, bolder than the rest. "Put her down, sir, Put her down!"

Harry ignored her, and a few moments later he led his loot-laden men back out of the manor house.

Regaining the beach and their ships, they were jubilant with the success they had achieved and the revenge they had inflicted. The village was still in flames, and the noise everywhere was tremendous. Undoubtedly the militia was alerted for miles around, but this time they would be too late.

The girl had ceased screaming, and he thought she might have fainted. He set her down, but her legs gave way and he caught her against him. Her eyes were open and her cheeks were stained with tears. She looked more appealing than ever.

He put her in a boat and sat close beside her as they were rowed back to the ships.

"Please, sir," she said, her voice trembling.

He didn't know whether she was begging for her life, her chastity, or just her freedom. She could have no idea that he understood English. When he put his arm round her shoulder and kissed her hard on the mouth, his men laughed. She gasped and shuddered as his tongue burst in upon hers, and she tried to push him off with her hands.

"She'll not be long intact for the market place," one of the Turks chortled.

"Unless the pasha tires of her soon," agreed another.

Harry took his mouth away and gazed into her eyes. I shall not do that in a hurry, he thought.

She was weeping again.

As they came alongside, he bundled her on board. "Take her aft," he told Diniz. "Stay with her and watch her at all times."

He did not wish to confine her in the hold with the captive Frenchwomen.

Harry watched the rest of his men come aboard, and he watched the shore too. Before the last Turk was safe the cliff was lined with people and shots were fired — but the range was too great.

The sails were set, the anchors taken up, and the feluccas made out of the bay. Horsemen thundered along the strand, but they were also too late. Within an hour the feluccas had lost sight of the land and its lights. It was still hardly midnight.

Harry went aft to inspect the girl. Diniz was on the steering oar only a few feet away, but most of the men were forward. They talked of the recent adventure and of their deeds of glory.

She sat leaning against the bulwark and stared at him as he knelt beside her. Her legs were drawn up beneath her voluminous skirt, and her face was pale in the darkness. A rope had been secured round her waist and thence to the gunwale, so that even if she did manage to throw herself overboard, she could easily he regained.

"Please, sir," she whispered again, her entire body trembling.

"How are you named?" he asked in English.

She stared at him in consternation.

"Oh, yes," he said. "I speak your language. I am English myself," he found himself adding.

She seemed to draw herself up. "But then ... you will save me?" As though forgetting it was he that had just abducted her.

"Why, yes, I will save you from a lot of terrible things."

She clutched at his hand. "My father, Squire Martindale, he is a wealthy man. He will ransom me, I know that, sir."

Obviously she was unaware that her father was probably dead.

"All the money in England could not ransom *you*," Harry told her. "What is your name?"

She licked her lips. "My name is Felicity Martindale."

"Felicity Martindale," Harry said. "It has a ring to it. You will be the mother of my son."

She gasped at him, then gave a convulsive start. She leapt to her feet, and ran for the side.

But Harry had firm hold of her skirt, and brought her back to the deck. She screamed and attempted to fight him off, panting and writhing as if expecting immediate rape.

He held her tight against him until she subsided.

"You will come with me to Tunis."

Next morning she had to be force-fed. But she was so very young that her powers of resistance were soon governed by her bodily needs and comforts. Before long she was violently seasick, and then grateful for the slightest amount of solicitude.

For the next few days they ran down the Channel and towards the Bay of Biscay. After three days Felicity appeared to feel better. When she attempted to sit up, Harry had had a blanket thrown over her to protect her marvellous pink and white complexion from the wind and the sun. Eventually he sat beside her and offered her food.

She stared at it, and then at him, and then began munching hungrily.

"Consider this," he coaxed. "It is probably your fate to be married to some man chosen by your parents — one you would never previously have seen. Can you not regard me as such?"

She swallowed, then whispered, "You are a pirate, a thief and murderer."

"Your people first killed some of my men."

"All French pirates are killed the moment they land," she said fiercely. "They raid our coasts constantly."

"Ah." He began to understand the instant hostility of the militia. "But I am not French."

"If you are English you are doubly damned. And those men there ..." She stared at the dark-visaged crew and shuddered.

"They are Turks, Felicity."

"Turks!" she gasped in horror. No doubt everyone in Europe had heard of the Turks.

"My master is the Sultan Suleiman ..."

"Suleiman," she whispered. "Suleiman the Magnificent!"

Harry raised his eyebrows. That should please the Sultan, he thought, to be known as such ... and at such a distance.

"I am taking you to a beautiful city where you will be very happy. I promise you that." He felt as if talking to a child.

"I can never be happy," she declared.

He grinned and ruffled her golden hair — the first time he had touched her since bringing her on board.

"You will, you know. And you will adore my Yana."

But he wondered what Yana would make of her.

For the next few days there was no time to talk further with his latest acquisition, for the weather changed. This time the wind blew from the north-west, and sent huge seas piling up against the

Spanish and Portuguese coasts. Harry took the decision to stand out to sea to prevent his small squadron being driven ashore. But he told himself that this storm was a blessing in disguise: it would drive any Portuguese ships out looking for him back into port.

But it was not a blessing for all of them. When finally the wind abated and the seas subsided, it was to find himself with two ships instead of three.

They were not short of food after all they had plundered from the English village, but their water casks were running low, and the French girls secured in the hold were suffering terribly. Harry had them brought up, stripped and doused in sea water. They shrieked and shuddered and pleaded, but undoubtedly it did them good.

Felicity, tied to her bulwark throughout the gale, and soaked time and again by spray, gazed at them with sombre eyes. Clearly she assumed they were all going to die.

Sometimes he suspected that himself, but he refused to be downhearted. As soon as they could, they stood in for the shore, and came upon a little village on the south coast of Portugal. This they pillaged, but only half-heartedly, for all they really needed was water, and to be safely home in Tunis. They passed through the Straits of Gibraltar four days later, aided now by the current, and at last debouched into the Mediterranean.

Instantly their spirits rose, and the men began to smile. The captive girls were allowed on deck for the first glimpse of the sunlit paradise that was to be their future home. It was late July and the sun was at its hottest.

Even Felicity shrugged away her blanket and turned up her face to the life-giving warmth, and the balmy breeze. Harry even released her from the rail, no longer fearing she would throw herself overboard.

They passed close by Algiers, but although there was only a little water remaining in their barrels, they preferred not to stop. Tunis was only a couple of days away. The fort above Algiers flew all manner of pennants, and Harry responded. They even fired cannon from the shore to attract his attention, but he merely saluted in return.

At dawn two days later the two ships crept round Cape Bon and into the Gulf of Tunis. Men scampered into the rigging for a first sight of their home — and stared in horror.

For Tunis burned.

15

ROXELANA

There was no sign of the Ottoman fleet, nor was the fort manned. Harry steered his ships with reduced sail up the narrow channel, gazing at the smoke still rising, the torched buildings now blackened ruins, and the scattered people signalling to him. He dropped his canvas altogether and went up to the docks under his sweeps.

"Hawk Pasha, you must leave this place," they told him, clustering around. "The Dey, Mulai-Hassan, marches upon us with a great army to regain his lands. A Spanish army."

Harry stared at them; few of them were Turks, and they were all old. "Who did this?"

"The Genoese fleet and their Spanish allies, great Pasha."

"But what of Barbarossa?"

"No one knows. There was a mighty battle within sight of our shores, but then the wind blew, and the seas grew rough. The galleys of the great Admiral were sore beset. The Genoese had galleons as well as galleys, and these rode the storm better. When the wind dropped, the Admiral and his ships had vanished."

Harry could not believe his ears. "Sunk, you mean?"

"We do not know, great Pasha. They have not been seen since. You must make haste to leave this place."

"I must go to my home."

"The Spanish sailors were put ashore to sack the town, before they went to sea again in search of Barbarossa. But we have lost our families and our possessions — and now we will be enslaved by Mulai-Hassan."

Harry strode through the smouldering streets. He could see that the enemy had done a thorough job; corpses lay scattered in the midst of the discarded booty. Dogs feasted, and snarled at the intruders.

Barbarossa defeated, perhaps dead? Harry found that impossible to accept. Because if Barbarossa was dead, then surely

Tughluk also had perished. His brain rejected what he knew he as going to find at the end of his quest.

His palace also had been burned; every possession he had ever prized was looted or destroyed.

Except for the possessions he had prized above all: those had been left for him to see. Out in the courtyard, where the flames had hardly reached, he found the bodies of his family. Tutush had been hanged, after castration. His sister had been spitted with a lance, which still protruded through her body. Tressilia had been beheaded. Sasha had been gutted. Yana's breasts had been cut off, leaving her to bleed to death. Undoubtedly they had first been raped, horribly.

Diniz had found his own family also murdered. He stood beside Harry, quivering. "Were these men?" he sobbed.

"Oh, indeed," Harry said. "Men who consider us as beasts. We must be sure to repay the compliment."

Diniz could discern the raging anger which seethed in his mind, in his very soul.

"What will we do first, master?" he asked.

"Build ourselves another fleet — in Constantinople."

They rekindled a fire and burned the tortured bodies of their loved ones. They refilled their water casks and took on board what food was available. Then they set sail that afternoon: two feluccas which were the sole remnants of the once-proud Ottoman fleet led by Barbarossa and Hawk Pasha.

But there would be another fleet, and then revenge.

From on board ship, Felicity Martindale could tell that something horrible had happened. She had stared at the burning city with appalled eyes. On the south coast of England they might have grown used to French pirates, but she had never seen a city burn.

She could not prevent herself feeling sorry for this tall red-bearded man who had snatched her away from all the happiness she had ever known. She could tell how he suffered by looking into his eyes. She shuddered and wrapped herself in her blanket, sitting in a corner of the deck.

It was a Saturday, the Muslim holy day which begins on Friday at dusk. Just after dawn, the two feluccas slipped quietly from the Sea of Marmara, round Seraglio Point, and into the Bosphorus.

Felicity stood on deck to gaze at this wondrous city of which she had heard so much, holding her blanket close against the dawn breeze sweeping out of the sea.

Beside her Harry leaned on the steering oar. He was pleased to hear the sudden intake of breath at his shoulder. They had scarcely spoken on the fortnight's voyage from Tunis. No man in the fleet had much to say; all had left wives and families dead behind them.

Yes, if Constantinople was to be Felicity's new home, she must learn to love it.

Right now she was absorbed by the sheer size of it — and its beauty. The city looked perhaps more beautiful at dawn than at any other time of day. The sun rising out of Anatolia to the east reflected from the burnished domes of mosques, highlighted waving banners above the walls, even reflected pinpoints of light from the helmets and spears of the guards.

Its very surroundings were also beautiful, thrusting as it did between Marmara and the Strait. As the little ship rounded the point, the Golden Horn came into sight as well as the red roofs of Galata. Rising high amongst these was the roof of the Hawk Palace.

"That will be your home," he told her.

Her mouth dropped open in awe.

As the two feluccas slipped alongside the dock, people came over to stare at them.

"Hawk Pasha," one whispered, almost in disbelief.

The cry was taken up. "Hawk Pasha! Hawk Pasha has returned."

"Did you suppose me dead?" he asked.

Apparently they had.

There was a great deal to be done, and Diniz was left in charge of unloading their booty and the captives. The poor French girls were more dead than alive, so he gave instructions for them to be taken to Hawk Palace and there tended carefully for a week or so, before they were placed on the auction block.

In the portico of the Hawk Mansion servants stared at Harry as if he were a ghost, then prostrated themselves before him.

Aimée stood at the head of the great staircase and gazed at him, looking as entrancing as always.

"Harry?" she whispered? "Oh, Harry!" she then screamed — and ran down to throw herself into his arms. "They said you were dead. Khair-ed-din said you were dead."

"Khair-ed-din is here?"

"He has been here nearly a month, replenishing his fleet. It was badly damaged in a storm."

Harry felt an overwhelming sense of relief. As long as Barbarossa lived, Tunis would be avenged.

"Then Tughluk is also here?" he said, scarce daring to hope.

"Tughluk?"

Harry stared at her, his heart seeming to slow. "Tughluk was with Barbarossa."

Aimée sank on to a divan. "I have not spoken with Barbarossa," she said. "I only know what is the rumour. He has not been to see me."

Harry frowned at her. "How long has he been back?"

She shrugged. "Two, three weeks. I did not know Tughluk was with him, or I would have sought him out ..."

"Does he know of Tunis?"

"Yes. All Constantinople knows of it. The Emperor has sent ambassadors to boast of the destruction of the pirates. I assumed Tughluk was there, or with you."

Aimée bit her lip — then looked past him at Felicity.

"Treat her kindly," Harry said. "She is very young and very afraid."

Aimée stood in front of the girl.

"She is also very lovely," she said, glancing at him. "Your mother would have approved."

"My mother?" For the second time in a few minutes Harry's heart seemed to constrict.

Aimée frowned, then turned quite pale. "My God! I sent the message to Tunis ..."

"Tell me now," he said.

"Dear Giovanna died in the spring. Her last words were of you, Harry."

Harry's shoulders sagged. "Where is she buried?"

"Beside your uncle and your father."

"I must go to her grave. Then I must also go to the Sultan. And to Barbarossa. There is a great deal to be done, Aunt, so I must leave my young wife in your care."

"Wife?" Aimée asked.

"That is my intention. She has much to replace."

411

Aimée nodded. "I will see that she is ready for you. It is a pity she does not speak French."

"I do speak some French, madam," Felicity intervened.

Aimée clapped her hands in pleasure.

"Then you understand this lady will take care of you until I return," Harry told her. He changed to Turkish. "I do not wish her shaved, Aunt."

Aimée inclined her head.

Tired as he was, Harry left the house as soon as he had been bathed and changed his clothing. When he took the ferry across the Golden Horn, local people greeted him to left and right as his tall, red-bearded figure was recognised. But he was in a hurry; it was the Sultan's custom on Saturdays to attend the new mosque he had built, the Mosque of Suleiman — greater and more splendid even than St Sophia — and Harry hoped to reach the palace before he set out.

But he was too late, and the processional route was already crowded, with armed Janissaries lining the way. Harry could only push his way to the front of the throng. Not even Hawk Pasha could disrupt the ceremonial procession of the Sultan.

The enforced delay gave him the opportunity to pause and put things in perspective.

He had almost felt his world had come to an end with the sack of Tunis, and the destruction of everything he had built up throughout his life. The death of his mother and now the almost certain death of his eldest son Tughluk were but extensions of that tragedy. Yet here, all around him, was a world of vibrancy beyond any other he had ever seen.

Not least was the architectural beauty by which he was surrounded — much of it so new he did not recognise it. He remembered tales of the smouldering ruin that had been this city after the sack of 1453, and of the slow and hesitant rebuilding undertaken by Mahomet the Conqueror. And Harry himself remembered the earthquake which had all but levelled the walls in 1508. Years ago, when he had ridden here with Selim the Grim, the scenes of devastation had still been widespread.

Selim had shown no interest in rebuilding cities; but Suleiman had turned Constantinople into the most beautiful city on earth, through the genius of his chief architect, Sinan. Hardly a trace of those earlier devastations remained in the area around old Byzantium.

More than ever Constantinople had become the meeting-place of the world, in which men of every race, colour and creed enjoyed peace and prosperity under the rule of the Ottomans. This too was largely Suleiman's doing. If Mahomet had permitted the conquered Greeks to reinhabit their city, and had thrown it open to all who sought to trade, under him and his two successors the only law obtainable in the empire had been that of the anyi, which catered solely for Turks. Suleiman had spent many hours with the muftis and the imams, and other experts in Islamic law, labouring on ways to broaden the laws to include even infidels, and so had drawn up his own elaborate code. Nowadays everyone was protected by the law, and for all his military achievements, Suleiman was better known as "the Lawgiver" by his subjects.

He was by far the most popular of the sultans, because he revealed himself to his people in a manner no sultan had done since the days of Mahomet. But, unlike the Conqueror, on such occasions he was attended by a pomp equalled by no sovereign on earth.

The procession was now approaching. First came the Janissaries, white horsehair plumes rippling as they marched, yellow boots clattering on the cobbles. Their eyes flashed to left and right, daring any man to challenge their prowess. Then followed the sipahis, sitting their magnificient horses with all the superb panache of which they were so proud.

After a space came the royal party, preceded by two officials in fur-trimmed robes who carried silver staffs with which they struck the ground as they advanced. Five yards behind them came Ibrahim, clad in cloth-of-gold and with a conical, gold-ringed turban of office on his head. Harry gave a sigh of relief to see that his friend remained in power.

Behind the Grand Vizier marched the lesser officials of the Sultan's court, from the Head Cook to the Head Gardener, every man in his best robes and wearing his official hat or carrying an official staff. Resplendent among them was the Kislar Agha of the Sultan's harem.

Suleiman himself was surrounded by the members of his divan, and they in turn were surrounded by the Sultan's personal guards, wearing huge feathered headdresses which half-hid their master from watching eyes.

Harry frowned at this. In the days of William Hawkwood, Suleiman had needed no such close protection.

The crowd grew excited as the procession came closer, people jostling Harry as they tried to obtain a better vantage point. He found himself shoulder to shoulder with someone he recognised as a Venetian.

"What did I tell you?" the Italian demanded. "Is it not the most splendid sight you ever saw?"

"It is indeed," acknowledged his companion. "Truly do they call him Suleiman the Magnificent."

When the procession had passed, Harry presented himself at the palace. He waited patiently in the Porte with several ambassadors from Western countries.

A eunuch approached him and bowed. "There is one would speak with you, great Pasha."

Harry frowned at him. "Who?"

"You must come with me."

Harry hesitated, then followed the African down a series of corridors until he entered a room reminiscent of an outsize Catholic confessional; one entire wall was composed of fine trelliswork.

The door closed behind him, and he was left alone, but not for long. From behind the trelliswork came a voice.

"Tell me of my sister, Hawk Pasha," Roxelana said.

"She is dead, alas."

"How did she die?"

"She was slain by the Spaniards when they captured Tunis."

There was a moment's silence, then she spoke again, her voice tinged with anger. "Then why are not you dead beside her?"

"I was not there."

"You stole away and left my sister to die?"

"No, I was absent on a raid when the assault took place. I knew nothing of it until too late."

"Nonetheless, you let my sister die. Will you avenge her?"

"That is my intention, if the Padishah will grant me the means."

"You will have the means. Avenge my sister, Hawk Pasha — die yourself."

414

He waited, gazing at the trellis for a few seconds, until he realised that she had left.

A Russian slave girl threatening a pasha of the Ottoman empire! But a Russian slave girl who held the Sultan in the palm of her hand.

"Hawk Pasha! Harry!" Suleiman held out his arms to embrace him as he entered the private chamber. "They told me you were lost at sea."

"I bring you no good news, Padishah."

"I have heard it all from that scoundrel who calls himself Barbarossa. He has lost me the western Mediterranean, after all his proud talk!"

"I am told that he has returned here?"

"Yes. I have placed him under arrest."

"For losing a battle, O Padishah? I understand that was due to the weather."

"Well ..." Suleiman stroked his beard. "I have a mind to let the rascal out again. Allah alone knows what he will do now."

"We will seek your permission to rebuild our fleet, so as to reconquer what we have lost. Algiers still holds out — and this time we will conquer."

Or die, Harry thought, remembering Roxelana's words.

"And suppose I need you here, Hawk Pasha? I am beset by enemies."

"You, Padishah? The Porte is crowded with ambassadors from every nation of Europe, seeking your alliance. They speak of you as Suleiman the Magnificent."

But the Sultan did not seem interested in what the Europeans called him. "I do not speak of infidels. Them I can chastise as is necessary. My enemies are here in Constantinople, in my very Seraglio ..."

My God, Harry thought: nothing has changed.

"Padishah," he said, "I am sure you concern yourself needlessly. Are you not happily reconciled with the Grand Vizier?"

"Do not speak to me of that man," Suleiman whispered.

"But I see him ..."

"Stepping forth at the head of my people with all the arrogance of a sultan himself? Indeed you have seen that, Hawk Pasha. That is no less than he considers himself. Do you know that he boasts

415

that he is wealthier than I? Do you know that he has built himself a palace, here in Istanbul, which is greater than the Seraglio? That he boasts it was his genius which won the war with Persia?"

"You went to Persia," Harry said, striving to understand.

"To settle with him, yes. And what did I find? That he had suborned more than half my army — that they looked to him rather than to me. I had no choice but to dissemble. We returned here together after the Persians sued for peace, and I awarded him such a triumph as has not been seen since the days of imperial Rome. But, even so, I became daily more aware of his threat to my position. I even sent messages to Tunis, for you and Khair-ed-din to return to my rescue. By the time they reached that unhappy city your fleet had already been defeated."

"Dispersed by a storm, Padishah," Harry corrected.

"It is no matter. Your fleet was no more. For all I knew, you were no more."

"But I am back now, Padishah."

"Yes. Now listen to me, Hawk Pasha. I will release Khair-ed-din from arrest, and between you both you will build another fleet, against the Genoese. You will recruit a vast force in men, too. But you will not leave Constantinople until I give the word. Is that understood?"

Harry understood too well. The Sultan planned civil war against his own Vizier. But he knew that Suleiman's suspicions were ill-founded — that they were inspired only by the ambitions of Roxelana.

There was much to be done. Harry went straight away to Khair-ed-din's palace and dismissed the royal guards.

"Harry!" Barbarossa embraced him. "I had heard you were returned, and I told myself: my next visitor will be either Harry Hawkwood or my executioner. Or have you come in both guises?"

"I have come to put you to work, old friend," Harry told him. "We have much to regain."

Barbarossa clapped him on the shoulder. "And we will, by Allah!" Then he grew serious. "I am sorry about your wives, about Yana."

"You lost yours, too. And your fleet — what happened?"

"I have never known weather like that, it was so unexpected. I have seen sudden storms in the Gulf of Lyons, those they call

416

mistrals, but not so far south. Next time I will know what to do."

"Tell me about Tughluk."

Barbarossa sighed. "He was talented, that boy. I had given him command of a galley. It just disappeared, Harry, with all its crew. Water must have entered the oar-ports. It was the most terrible storm I have ever known."

"Dragut?"

"He survived. He is here in Constantinople."

"That is something."

"But as for the women ... I doubt I loved any as well as you loved that Russian girl." He gave a great shout of laughter. "You should entreat your friend the Padishah to give you Roxelana in her place."

"Heaven forbid," Harry said.

He accompanied Barbarossa down to the shipyards and they began to consider plans for bigger and better galleys than any ever seen before, capable of riding the worst of Mediterranean storms as well as fighting Andrea Doria's ships.

"And of braving the Atlantic waves?" Barbarossa asked.

"That is something we will tackle when we have dealt with Doria," Harry promised him. "You have never seen such lands just waiting to be stripped bare."

He sent Diniz, whom he could trust absolutely, to arrange a private meeting with the Grand Vizier.

And then he returned to the Hawk Palace.

"You look a different man," Aimée said. "But you must be exhausted."

"I am exhausted," he acknowledged. "And perhaps I even feel a different man."

"The Sultan has forgiven your defeat?"

"It was no defeat, Aunt — but the Sultan has given me a new fleet."

She sighed. "When next you return, I shall be dead."

"It will take at least a year to build our new fleet — and besides you will live for ever. But now I have my bride to attend."

"Harry ..." She caught his hand. "She is only a child."

"Why, fifteen, surely. Tressilia was no older. Neither was Yana. And you have told me you yourself were to be married to my uncle when you were but fourteen."

Aimée bit her lip. "That was a long time ago. And, with respect, Harry, Tressilia was a half-Turk, Yana a savage. This is a young lady." She gave a wistful smile. "They are more sheltered in their upbringing than any you have known."

Harry frowned at her. "You have told her what is to happen to her?"

"Have you been gone six months? A year? What am I supposed to have said to her in just a few hours? I have told her that, no matter what happens, you are a kind and gentle man at heart."

"I shall endeavour to be so."

"Use her gently, I beg of you. You may find you have a treasure."

Harry strode up the stairs to his own chamber. He had not slept on this divan for two years. The last time had been with Yana in his arms.

The slave girls bowed before him as they opened the doors. Felicity stood before the open windows, looking down at the Golden Horn and the bustle of the shipping. Undoubtedly she had seen him returning from the ferry.

Now she turned. Aimée had dressed her in Turkish harem garb, and Harry caught his breath. Here was none of the voluptuousness of Yana which had been so irresistible; but in its place there was a virginal purity and a slenderness that was no less compelling.

The golden curls had been vigorously brushed, and tumbled in ordered confusion around her shoulders; a pale blue fez rested awkwardly on her crown. The pale blue bolero had been pulled across her naked breasts, as far as it would extend and was now held in position by both her hands, revealing only a sliver of white flesh between. There was more white flesh below: the flatness of her girl-belly. The pantaloons, also in pale blue, allowed no more than the outline of her legs to be seen. But there was a darkness at the groin: she was a woman.

They stared at each other, then he waved away the servants, who closed the doors behind them.

As he moved towards her she began to curtsy. The fez slipped from her head, and she could not resist a giggle as she attempted to straighten it.

"I have been practising," she gasped, her cheeks scarlet.

She then realised she had released the bolero, and hastily

grabbed for it again. But Harry's hands were there first, pushing the cloth right back to her shoulders.

Her breasts were those of a young girl, little pointed mounds, but the more delicious for that. He touched the nipples, and watched them stiffen as a shudder ran the whole length of her body.

How old are you?" he asked.

She licked her lips. "I am fifteen, master."

He took the bolero off to expose her glowing white skin. If the wind and the sun had darkened her face, there was no mark on the rest of her body.

He released the cord of her pantaloons and let them drop about her ankles. Again slenderness, hips as smooth as silk, buttocks firm as hillocks.

Be gentle with her, Aimée had begged; but it had also been a warning.

He put one arm round her shoulders, the other under her knees, and lifted her from the floor. She reached her arm round his neck, and with a wriggle of her feet, kicked off her shoes and the trailing pantaloons.

He wanted to shout for joy. She knew what was going to happen to her, and she was not afraid.

But he would have to use her as a Christian, he knew. This first time, at least.

He laid her on the bed and stretched out beside her, kissing her mouth for the first time since in that dramatic escape from England's shore. Her breath was sweet, her tongue surprised — and then eager.

As he played with her breasts again, her eyes grew wide. Then he stroked her between the legs, and she began to breathe deeply.

He dared not lie on top of so slender a form. Instead he knelt between her legs and lifted her small buttocks for the entry. Her gaze remained fixed on his, her mouth sagging. It closed with the gasp of pain as he thrust, then opened again. Her eyes did not close at all.

Still grasping her buttocks, he remained kneeling until his passion was spent. Then he let her slide down his thighs.

"I will teach you the art of love," he promised her.

She was still breathing deeply, her cheeks suffused with colour.

"I will be pleased to learn, master," she said quietly.

419

Book The Third

*

The meeting with Ibrahim appeared a normal procedure. Hawk-wood was obliged to visit the Grand Vizier to obtain his signature on the vast amount of money he proposed to spend.

Harry studied his friend. Ibrahim did not look as if he had anything on his mind.

Harry glanced left and right, to check there was no one within earshot. He spread his list on the table between them. "Pretend to study that, and listen very carefully."

Ibrahim raised his eyebrows, but did as Hawkwood asked.

"Do you remember what we discussed, oh, five or six years ago concerning Roxelana and her influence over the Sultan?"

"Yes. I was a trifle apprehensive then, I suppose."

"And now you are not?"

"That was some six years ago, and I am still Grand Vizier — still Suleiman's closest confidant."

"You are his deepest enemy, so far as he is concerned."

Ibrahim frowned at him.

But Harry continued, and told him of Suleiman's fears.

"But that is absurd," Ibrahim protested. "I could not stop the Janissaries coupling my name with his in Persia ... and, after all, I had won some victories before he appeared."

"That is the point. He envies your success, at every level. Even Suleiman, for all his splendour, is no more than a man. You should not splash your wealth and power around the way you do."

"Because I have built myself a couple of new palaces, am I a traitor? I tell you, Harry, I find this very difficult to believe."

"Disbelieve it at your peril."

"So what would you have me do? Lead a revolt and become the traitor Suleiman thinks I am? That would be a fine end to twenty years of intimacy."

"I would not have you lead a revolt," Harry said. "Indeed, if you did, I would oppose you myself. But, if I were you, I would beg to be relieved of the duty of Grand Vizier, and then retire."

"And would that not make the Sultan more suspicious than ever? No, no, I will start to look about me and listen more. I thank you for the warning. If it is Roxelana who truly seeks to bring me down, then forewarned is forearmed. She is merely a concubine. I am the Grand Vizier."

Harry sighed, but there was nothing more he could do.

420

*

The next few months proved happy ones. Harry sometimes wondered if the profession of shipwright was not the one for which he had truly been designed by kismet. He spent much of every day in the docks, watching his new ships come to life. Often Barbarossa and Dragut were with him, and the three discussed the strategy they would employ against the Genoese when at last ready to put to sea.

But he spent as much time as possible at home, for he now had an over-riding reason.

He not supposed he would ever be able to replace Yana, the Russian girl, but night by night Felicity became more and more important to him. Making love to her was a delight. She had to be taught everything, yet she learned with the utmost enthusiasm. He did not know if she mourned her life in England; if she did she gave no sign of it. She appeared to be totally happy, and he wished her to remain so. He watched her grow, mentally and physically day by day ... and then more quickly as she became pregnant.

"Sixteen is a trifle young to become a mother," Aimée said anxiously. She calculated that Felicity would give birth some time the following summer.

But the fleet was actually ready to sail by mid-March of 1536, and so Hawkwood reported to Suleiman.

"That is splendid news," the Sultan said. "I will hold a grand review of your troops so have them march up here to the palace. Bring with you Khair-ed-din and Dragut, and all your captains. All of your faithful captains."

Harry bowed in assent.

It was the end of the month when Suleiman and his pashas were ready to inspect the men of the new Ottoman navy. While Dragut led the parade, Barbarossa and Hawk Pasha accompanied the Sultan himself as he walked through the ranks of sailors and marines.

"You will now avenge Tunis," he told them. "You will bring great honour to your name and mine, to the names of Hawk Pasha and Khair-ed-din Pasha. And now you will feast at my expense."

The men, several thousand of them, gave a mighty cheer.

Harry walked beside Ibrahim as the pashas returned to the

Porte. There Suleiman seated himself on his divan, and looked around at his ministers and generals and admirals.

"It is good," he said. "But let me be more pleased, still."

Four eunuchs who had been waiting to one side stepped forward. Before any man in the room could move, two of them grasped Ibrahim's arms while the others wrapped a bowstring round his neck and pulled tight.

The Grand Vizier could do nothing more than gasp, and then he was dead.

16

THE ASSASSIN

Ibrahim lay on the floor of the Porte, his assassins kneeling beside him. For several seconds no one in the room moved. Harry could only gaze down at the lifeless body almost at his feet.

Suleiman stood up. "He was a traitor who sought to suborn my power. Announce his execution to the people. Tell them that the Grand Vizier's stolen wealth will be divided amongst them. Khair-ed-din, see to your men."

Khair-ed-din understood the situation perfectly. He hurried into the courtyard.

Suleiman gazed from face to face. "He was a Greek," he said. "It was my mistake to raise him so high. His successor will be a Turk, and I will announce his name shortly." He gazed at Harry. "Come with me, Hawk Pasha."

Slowly Harry moved forward. The eunuchs were dragging Ibrahim's corpse away.

Suleiman entered his private office and sat at his huge desk.

"I did what had to be done, Harry."

"With respect, O Padishah, did he not deserve at least a formal accusation? An opportunity to defend himself?"

"He has had that opportunity for the past five years, ever since I first began to suspect his treachery. He has never once approached me and sought to make his peace with me. He has treated me with contempt. Worse, he has divided my people. I must be seen to be Sultan, supreme above everyone within my domains. I meant what I said when I ordered his wealth to be divided amongst the poor. I have also ordered his family destroyed, as a warning to other would-be rivals to my power. Now, there is an end to it."

Do you really believe that? Harry wondered. Or is it all a matter of where Roxelana turns her Medusa-gaze next? He found his heartbeat quickening.

She had begun by eliminating the most powerful subject in the empire. Now surely she would seek out the next most obviously powerful man — and did she not also have a personal grudge against Harry, since he had been unable to save her sister from a horrible death?

And she had ordered Ibrahim's entire family to be destroyed.

"I understand your grief, Harry," Suleiman continued. "I also grieve. He was a friend to both of us, and a man of considerable talent — but no man is greater than the state. Harry ... there is no man I would rather have take Ibrahim's place than you."

"Padishah," Harry began uneasily.

"But it cannot be," Suleiman added.

Harry sighed with relief.

"I meant what I have said to my pashas: the new Grand Vizier must be one of them."

"That is as it should be, Padishah. Besides, I am a simple soldier and sailor. I crave only your permission to take my fleet to sea and seek out the Genoese."

Suleiman nodded. "I give you that permission — for one campaign. Restore the glory of my name in the Mediterranean, Hawk Pasha, and then return here. I will seat you on my right hand, as my general-in-chief of both land and sea. Together we will campaign — as my father did with yours — and together we will take Vienna."

Harry bowed.

He told Barbarossa to prepare the fleet for sea. The seamen had not after all been needed to overawe the Janissaries, who had accepted the death of the Grand Vizier with indifference. But Harry himself could have told the Sultan that would be the case; for the 'conspiracy' had all been in Suleiman's mind, planted there by that Russian witch from the steppes.

Now it was time for haste before she started plotting mischief again. He hurried home to Hawk Palace.

Aimée had already heard the news, and the official pronouncement that Ibrahim had been discovered plotting a rebellion.

"How incredibly foolish can one be?" she asked wonderingly. "He had everything — and just to throw it away."

As Harry told her the truth of the matter, she listened to him with an ashen face.

"If that is true," she said when he had finished, "then no man is safe here."

"And no woman, either, if she can be used to hit at the man. Aunt, my fleet sails within twenty-four hours. I wish you and Felicity to be on it."

"Go to sea after all these years? I doubt I can do that. And Felicity with your child in her belly? You cannot take the risk, Harry."

"Nor can I take the risk of leaving you here. I swear to you that where that woman sends her fingers seeking, all is lost. Ibrahim's entire household is now destroyed."

Aimée clasped her hands to her neck in dismay.

"Where can we go?"

"Algiers — or Tunis, after I have retaken it. Somewhere I alone command. In the name of the Padishah, to be sure, but where his executioners cannot reach me.

He acted with the greatest caution, concerned that were Suleiman to suspect his plan, he might force him to leave the women here as hostages. As long as his wife and child remained, he would eventually have to return to Constantinople.

But was he really planning to abandon the Sultan? He could never do that: his roots were too firmly planted in Turkish soil. He could only distance himself from the present danger until the situation changed — until Roxelana died or Suleiman ceased from his infatuation with her. Surely she would overreach herself in her ambition before long?

Aimée, Felicity and their immediate attendants boarded the fleet just half an hour before it was due to sail. Aimée was apprehensive, but Felicity was happy to be at sea again.

"Will we make our home there now?" she asked. "In Tunis?"

"Algiers for the beginning. About Tunis we will have to see."

Barbarossa was less ebullient. He had enjoyed his nine months in Constantinople. "I am getting old, Harry," he confessed. "I had forgotten how pleasant luxury can be."

Harry realised that the old pirate must now be well past seventy. He had recently spent a fortune in the slave market, filling his palace in Constantinople with every beautiful girl he could find.

"I should have brought some of them with me," he remarked,

"But we are here to fight, not make love."

"I am here to make a new home for myself," Harry reminded himself.

They traversed the Mediterranean without seeing more than the occasional sail. Harry gave all land a wide berth, since he wanted to reach Algiers without a fight.

They found the city basking peacefully beneath the summer sun. Al-Rashid told them that, although Spanish ships had been often sighted there had been no attacks on the port. The Emperor clearly considered that Turkish seapower had been shattered off Tunis.

Barbarossa brought all his ships inside the moles, and made them strike their masts so that no one at sea could even guess at the numbers he had at his command.

By now it was too late for a campaign; the winter gales would soon be upon them. So it was possible to spend an untroubled six months during which Felicity gave birth to a son, a lusty, pale-skinned, blue-eyed boy whom Harry named Anthony after the greatest of the Hawkwoods.

Felicity was delighted — and so was Aimée. Both women were also pleased with Algiers. If their residence was not so grand as that in Constantinople, the weather was so much better, especially in winter — and here Hawk Pasha ruled supreme.

He bought a young Arab girl named Ayesha, about the same age as Felicity, to help nurse the baby Anthony, and to be a loyal companion for her.

But Harry was also there to avenge what had happened at Tunis, so the following spring he and Barbarossa took their fleet to sea. They encountered no opposition, but by now there could be no doubt that the presence of such a large number of Turkish galleys in the western Mediterranean had been reported in Genoa and Madrid.

The following year, as they rounded the toe of Italy on one of their great sweeps, they learned the Genoese fleet had been seen patrolling these same waters only a week previously.

"They sailed north into the Adriatic," said the captain who had brought them the news.

"They will be raiding among the Ionian Islands," Barbarossa

suggested. "There we will bring them to battle."

They sailed in three columns, for Harry was determined not to let the enemy escape. Barbarossa commanded the centre, Harry the right, closest to the shore, and Dragut the left.

A week later they saw a cluster of ships emerging from behind the shelter of the islands that lined the west coast of mainland Greece. Instantly the battle flags were hoisted to Barbarossa's masthead, and the tabalcans began to beat.

Harry was conscious of a distinct quickening of the pulse. Although he had campaigned since the age of fifteen, this would be the first full-scale naval battle in which he had taken part.

Barbarossa's flagship was already increasing the stroke of its oars. Harry gave the orders for his own men to do likewise, and the great ship, two hundred feet in length from its protruding gilded beak to its castellated stern, began to hurtle through the smooth water. The slaves strained and sweated, chewing on their wooden gags.

The Genoese approached confidently beneath a multitude of floating flags and pennants, but that their admiral was surprised both by the numbers of the Turks and by the size of their ships was evident in a last-minute attempt to change his order of battle. Indeed, Harry got the impression that Doria would rather avoid battle, if he could on this occasion.

The Turks hurtled into their adversaries. The cannon on the foredecks exploded and round shot smashed into the opposing hulls, severing oars, causing the ships to veer about out of control. The Genoese replied, but less accurately.

Harry had ordered every Turkish vessel to reload with grape after the initial discharge, and this was now done, the round shot being replaced with the canisters of deadly iron balls. None was larger than an inch in diameter, but in a cloud they were capable of sweeping an enemy's deck clear of living men.

Now these exploded again, and the hail of small shot burst over the Genoese fleet. But the Genoese also had cannon, and Harry was aware of flying shot all around him. Some of the men on his foredeck were struck down, and then the two fleets met with a crash like opposing cavalry at the charge.

Harry's helm went over as a Genoese galley surged by, and his rowers hastily shipped their oars, dragging them inboard as far as they could. The Genoese were slower, and several of their blades were sheered off. Both ships slewed sideways, exchanging a hail of missiles that even included pots of burning oil hurled by small trebuchets. Before Harry's galley was back under control he had rammed a second Genoese, but now with full force. Men scrambled over his bows, firing their pistols before coming to close quarters.

He drew his scimitar and let his marines forward, and for a few moments there was a fierce mêlée until the Genoese were all killed or forced to jump into the sea; their own vessel had drifted away.

The din of battle was now tremendous as some three hundred ships engaged. Harry saw Turkish vessels to every side and realised, as he had earlier suspected, that the Genoese were endeavouring merely to fight their way through their adversaries so as to escape into the open sea. He had his cannon reloaded and fired again, as quickly as could be managed, and then hoisted the signal for pursuit as the enemy made off to the south, out of the Adriatic and into the Mediterranean.

Diniz touched his arm. "The order is countermanded, Hawk Pasha."

Harry turned towards the flagship and saw Barbarossa's flags signalling the fleet to reform. He looked left and right. There were perhaps a dozen galleys in the process of sinking, their crews swimming frantically and their chained slaves screaming as they drowned. Of these, eight were Genoese and four Turkish. Another dozen galleys lay dead in the water, their oars sheered off. These were more evenly divided: six from each side. The Genoese ships were now being boarded by Turkish crews, and would be made prisoner.

Presumably it was a victory, but hardly a decisive one – and certainly not yet any adequate revenge for the sack of Tunis. And the Genoese fleet was now nearly out of sight.

Harry had a boat put down, and was rowed across to the flagship. There he found Barbarossa sitting in a chair on the afterdeck, his arm being bandaged by his surgeon.

"Are you badly wounded?" he asked.

"A sword slice. It is painful, but it is clean."

"We should be pursuing those fellows."

"I know — but I am tired. I am too old to fight these battles. Still, we have won a victory." He pointed at the distant land. "Over there is the town of Prevesa. We will call this the victory of Prevesa."

"Hardly one to shout about."

"Do you not think so? Our men would not agree with you."

From all around them there came the blowing of bugles and loud cheering as the Turks decided they had gained the day.

"A victory is what Suleiman wanted, and a victory is what he has got," Barbarossa said. "A victory is what I needed to complete my career, and a victory is what I have achieved. I am now going back to Constantinople."

"But why? We will have to fight Doria again — and the Spaniards."

"Young man's work," Barbarossa said. "I will soon be eighty; it is time I enjoyed life." He pointed at Dragut's ship approaching. "There is your fleet commander, Hawk Pasha. He is hardly less talented than I. Meanwhile I will report your victory to the Porte."

He would not be dissuaded, nor did Harry feel he could press the matter. His friend was undoubtedly old and very tired.

They embraced, and the admiral's galley began to row for home. Harry and Dragut steered west, but there was little chance now of overtaking the Genoese.

"What are your orders, Hawk Pasha?" Dragut asked.

"Algiers first, to refit. And then Tunis."

Barbarossa played his part well, and the entire Mediterranean soon resounded to the news that the great Andrea Doria had been defeated. As the old pirate had said, this set the seal on his career, and left himself a legend that would alarm men for years to come.

That Doria — and his master the Emperor — would now be planning a counter-stroke could hardly be doubted. But Harry was determined to keep the initiative he had seized. In Algiers he strengthened the defences; he resolved to leave half his fleet there to defend the town. For him Algiers was more than simply the Ottoman bastion in the western Mediterranean; he had no intention of losing yet another family.

The child, Anthony, was now a year old, and showing every sign of becoming a typical Hawkwood, at least in size.

But Harry's main preoccupation remained Tunis. It could be rendered more secure than Algiers — and he wanted it for personal reasons.

As all the world supposed, with Barbarossa retired, that the

Turks no longer posed an immediate threat, he determined on surprise. The following spring he and Dragut crept out of Algiers at dusk with fifty galleys. Two days later they were off the salt lakes and feeling their way through the narrow channel, before the Tunisians and their Spanish officers, as somnolent as ever, even realised what was happening.

The outer fort hardly fired a single shot before it was over-whelmed by the marines Dragut had sent against it.

In the city itself alarm bells rang, bugles blew, drums were beaten. Mulai-Hassan's men swarmed to the walls.

Each Turkish galley was loaded with soldiers and siege material; Harry had even shipped a regiment of sipahis and their horses. These were now landed and started their operations, Harry going along to oversee them. Meanwhile Dragut lined up his ships in the salt lakes and commenced a bombardment of the walls. The garrison replied vigorously, but their aim was not so accurate as that of the Ottomans.

Meanwhile Harry sent his detachment of sipahis inland of the city to cut it off from the hinterland, and he formally summoned Mulai-Hassan to surrender. The Dey refused.

Harry then began mining, and the digging of parallels to advance his siegeworks against the walls. Dragut landed artillery and these were dragged into position.

The siege was proceeding exactly to plan, and Harry had no doubt at all that Tunis would fall within another month ... until he was shaken awake one morning by Dragut himself.

"What is the matter?" He sat up in surprise.

"We have been caught napping," Dragut said, his face the picture of dismay.

Harry ran out of his tent on the shore, to gaze at the harbour. The Turkish fleet was drawn up as before — but outside the entrance channel was another fleet, flying the gold and red colours of Spain. There were ocean-going galleons as well as galleys; a quick count estimated some ninety ships, nearly twice as many as the Turks possessed. And they now commanded the narrow entrance, from which the Turks could emerge only one at a time.

"Did you not have guard ships out at sea?" Harry demanded.

"I did, Hawk Pasha. They must have somehow been surprised."

Bugles were blowing from the ramparts; the Tunisians had also seen the Spanish ships. Now the situation was reversed: the besiegers were themselves besieged, caught between the city and the enemy galleons. Dragut called a conference of his captains.

"There is nothing else for it," one of these said. "We must disembark our crews, burn our galleys, and march back to Algiers."

"March several hundred miles across the desert?"

"To stay here is to starve. We cannot fight them."

Dragut pulled his beard and looked at Hawkwood.

"There would seem to be no alternative, Hawk Pasha," he muttered.

Harry glanced at him and then stared across at the Spaniards again. So once again he would be defeated, outwitted by the Dons. He would crawl away form them across the desert like a whipped cur.

Immediately he felt tears of anger and frustration seeping into his eyes. The margin was so very small. The sandbanks which enclosed the salt lakes were nowhere more than a few feet above water level, and nowhere more than a few yards wide. Were there tides, such as he had seen on the French and English coasts, it would be possible to send the whole fleet out, at once, at the top of the flood, and thus fight their way to freedom. But there were no tides, and therefore ... He frowned as he studied the sandbanks.

"Will you give the order, Hawk Pasha?" Dragut asked.

Harry stood up. "I will give the order to engage the Spaniards at dawn tomorrow morning."

The captains looked alarmed. Had their Pasha gone mad at this juncture?

"We can hardly issue forth one at a time, Hawk Pasha," Dragut protested. "They will merely sink us one by one."

"Were you ever told about the capture of Constantinople?" Harry asked.

"Every Turkish warrior knows of that, Hawk Pasha."

"Then think how the Turkish galleys were introduced into the Golden Horn."

Dragut gave a yell. "By Allah! They were dragged across the land."

"It was my grandfather's scheme," Harry said.

"But he built a wooden roadway, and greased it with fat," said one of the captains. "We have no wood, and we have no fat. And the Byzantines were unable to interfere with your grandfather's plans because they lacked the men. Here the Spaniards not only

431

overlook our every move but outnumber us."

"I realise it is not practical for us to build a railway for our galleys," Harry said. "But it should be practical for us to dig a canal deep enough for us to get our ships to sea."

The captains looked at one another in thought.

"It can be done," Dragut agreed.

"But the enemy will still see what we are about," the pessimistic captain objected, "and block that route as well."

"Then we must accomplish our task before the Spaniards can see what we are doing," Harry said. "We muster seven thousand galley slaves, five thousand seamen, and four thousand soldiers. You will find the best place for a channel to be cut, Dragut, and then our men will get to work at dusk. We will have to dig ourselves a channel in one night."

"That is an immense proposition, Hawk Pasha," the captain said.

"So is death or captivity, Baspar. Which would you rather contemplate?"

It was essential to give the enemy — either in the city or on the ships — no inkling of what was intended. All that day the siege-works were carried forward, and Dragut sent one or two of his ships down the channel to exchange shots with the nearest Spaniards — only to come limping back as though thoroughly disheartened.

That afternoon Dragut took a bow and arrow and had himself rowed into the marshes on the northern side of the salt lake, as if hunting the wildfowl which abounded. There he carefully sought the best place for their canal.

Meanwhile the captains released the galley slaves from their benches and marched them ashore, allowing them to bathe in the shallows. This would make sense to the watching Spaniards, for it was obvious the Turkish galleys were now quite cooped up. The slaves were kept ashore until dusk, and then put to work. They were guarded by sailors with drawn swords and orders to cut down without hesitation any who made a noise.

On shore, Harry withdrew all of his men save a few marksmen who had orders to keep firing at the walls and so occupy the minds of the defenders. With his people he then descended into the lake, and they also commenced the work of cutting into the sand.

It was an immense undertaking to be completed in a single night, but Harry was determined that it would be done. He and Dragut ranged up and down the huge throng of labouring men, some digging and others carting the sand away. They watched and listened too, because it was impossible to achieve their task in complete silence. As an immense rustle spread across the evening, it was fortunate there was a land breeze out of the desert to blow the sound away from Tunis.

Thus, it was blowing towards the Spaniards, but there was no sign of alarm in the enemy fleet. Undoubtedly they had no idea what the Turks were up to.

The night drifted by far too quickly. Men cursed and swore, and slipped and fell. Several even drowned, trampled on by their fellows in the shallow water. But progress was made.

An hour after midnight, Harry had the galley slaves assembled and returned to their benches. It would take time to lock all the chains.

His soldiers and sailors continued working, now often waist-deep as the channel was hacked through the sandbank and the waters of the Mediterranean began to flow in.

When there were only a few yards to go, Harry sent the sailors back to prepare their vessels, but kept the soldiers working. By the time the last barrier was removed, the first galley was already in the channel. And the breeze was turning chill with the hint of dawn.

Hastily the soldiers began to scramble on board. Hawkwood sent messengers to summon his skeleton force from the trenches. The sipahis had already been recalled and were now on board.

The darkness was beginning to fade as Harry stood beside Dragut on the lead galley and gave the signal to row.

The galley moved forward slowly. The channel was only just wide enough for the ship and its oars. But it was only a hundred yards long, and although they touched the sides once or twice, and the oars struck the sand to send men tumbling, they were through in ten minutes, and surging out into the blue water.

Behind them came another, and then another. And still there was no sound from the Spanish fleet. It was a watcher on the walls of Tunis who first discovered that the Turkish anchorage was deserted, and then gaped around to find them.

A bugle blew and there was instantly a terrific rumpus on the battlements. This aroused the Spaniards, who commenced to fire minute guns.

But by then all but ten of the Turkish ships were free of the land, and the rest were emerging every minute, bow to stern.

"Your orders, Hawk Pasha?" Dragut inquired.

"We'll not sail off without giving them a taste of our metal," Harry growled.

Dragut smiled. "Signal attack!" he yelled at his officers.

It was not yet light enough for signal flags to be discerned, but the Turkish commanders could have no doubt about their admiral's intentions. As the drumbeats sounded through the morning, the already exhausted galley slaves were driven to yet further effort.

The bow gun was loaded, but Harry held fire until they were right up to the first galleon, which was only just raising its anchor and setting its sail. The cannon exploded, and the shot smashed into the stern gallery. Dragut put his bows up to the broken timbers and his men swarmed aboard.

The fight was brief, for the Spaniards were taken almost by surprise. Then it was a matter of tossing them overboard, dead or alive, and of setting fire to the looted ship. And then of sounding and signalling recall.

Not all the Turkish attacks had been as successful, but Harry could look back on half a dozen burning ships, and he had no doubt that a great number of dead Spanish were littering the bay. Of his own fleet only two ships had been lost, and the rest were surging away from their victory, now clearly lit by the rays of the rising sun.

Yana, Sasha, Tressilia and the children had all been avenged.

Tunis remained untaken, of course, which was something Harry had much on his mind. But he realised that he could not achieve that without first utterly defeating the Spanish fleet. So he hastened back to Algiers to mobilise the rest of his command.

There he found Aimée and Felicity beside themselves with worry; they had seen the Spanish ships making east. Now they were overjoyed at his success.

Harry despatched a galley to Constantinople with the news of his victory, and promised Suleiman that there would soon be news of an even greater victory. "I shall yet turn the Mediterranean into a

Turkish lake," he wrote, "for the greater glory of your name, O Padishah."

Then he took his ships to sea. But the Spanish fleet had disappeared, scuttling back to Barcelona. Campaigning was over for the year.

Hawkwood spent the winter repairing his ships and building new ones. He had every intention of having an even greater fleet at sea in the following spring.

It was a happy winter. There was some rain, which was unusual enough, and the countryside around Algiers sprouted grass and flowers. There was time to spend at his palace, with Aimée and Felicity and little Anthony. Harry took the boy down to the ships to let him get the feel of a deck beneath his feet, the scent of tar and cordage in his nostrils.

"You won't take him to sea as a babe," Felicity begged.

"As soon as he can use a sword," Harry told her.

That was a few years off, so she was happy. But then she was a happy girl by nature.

In the new year, a galley arrived from Constantinople, bearing a summons from the Sultan.

"Hawk Pasha," wrote the new Grand Vizier, Rustem Pasha, son-in-law of the Sultan, for he had married Roxelana's daughter. "The Padishah congratulates you upon your great victory over the Spaniards, and upon your many successes. He admires your prowess, and wishes you return to Constantinople so that you may stand at his right hand and contemplate a new campaign in Europe."

"What news from Constantinople?" Harry asked the captain.

"Why, there is little news. The Padishah goes from strength to strength."

"And he is in good health?"

"He has never been better, great Pasha."

Harry took the letter to Aimée.

"I am sure that were Roxelana dead or disgraced, there would be some rumour of it," he said.

"So you fear a trap," she said.

"I fear my latest triumphs may have proved too much for her to accept."

"Then temporise," she recommended.

Harry took her advice.

"The Padishah well knows," he wrote, "how desperate I am to be at his side. But the campaign in the Mediterranean is far from over. I may claim a victory over the Spanish fleet, but the Padishah knows that Tunis still stands in defiance of the Ottoman power, and until that city is again flying the crescent flag, I cannot consider my task completed. I therefore beg the Padishah's indulgence to permit me to remain in Algiers for another two years, so that I may complete my objective and raise the glory of your name still higher."

A month later he was at sea, before any reply could be received from Constantinople. His objective was to bring the Spanish and Genoese fleets to battle.

Felicity and Aimée watched him sail away. They no longer feared for him. Hawk Pasha and Dragut were establishing a reputation inferior only to that of the legendary Barbarossa. They had become used to Algiers, to the unchanging warmth of the climate. If they feared that one day the Spaniards would seek to destroy them, that remained a distant threat ... and no threat at all if Hawk Pasha was present. And the Spaniards never knew when he was there or not.

Meanwhile there was little Anthony to be enjoyed, as he grew into a three-year-old, toddled about on sturdy feet and waved his wooden sword.

"He will follow in his father's footsteps," Aimée said. "One of the best things that ever happened to the Ottomans was the day John Hawkwood was shipwrecked on the coast of Anatolia."

"But is it the best thing for the rest of the world?" Felicity wondered. She was seventeen now, and a most intelligent and thoughtful girl.

"Why, possibly not — at least for Europe," Aimée agreed. "But as we are tied to the fortunes of this family, we must make the best of it."

"I wonder," Felicity said. "Do you not suppose that the Emperor, or Genoa, or even King Hal himself, might not pay Hawk Pasha well to change sides and lead his ships to the destruction of the Porte?"

"For pity's sake, child, hush," Aimée begged. "That is treason, and could bring us all the bowstring."

"But do we not live under that fear all the time, anyway?" Felicity persisted.

"It is only because of that woman Roxelana," Aimée insisted. "Soon she will fall from favour or die. That is what your husband waits for. I beg of you, girl, remember always that only in the favour of the Sultan is there any hope for any of us."

Felicity did not pursue the subject.

In the autumn, the fleets came back, reporting another great victory, this time over the combined Spanish and Genoese fleets commanded by Andrea Doria himself, in the waters off Corsica. The crews were jubilant and so was Hawk Pasha.

"The Padishah will be pleased at this," he said, "for we all but destroyed their fleets. Next spring, before they have time to recover, we shall have retaken Tunis."

Work went on all winter fitting out the expedition, while word of the victory was sent to Constantinople.

"This time, Dragut," Harry said, "there will be no fleet to bottle us up."

By the spring Harry felt he had never commanded so fine a fleet or so enthusiastic an army. Everyone remembered how he had so cunningly extricated them from the trap that Tunis had become; and no one doubted that this time he would prove totally successful. His plans were to maintain a squadron of sixty ships at sea to hold off any Spanish or Genoese fleet, while his main force put to sea.

His only fear was that he would be leaving Algiers relatively exposed, but he was taking no risks with his family. Aimée, Felicity, Anthony and even Ayesha would be sailing in his own galley. Where he went, and how he prospered, they too would go and prosper.

"I shall be glad not to be separated from Harry," Felicity said.

She stood at the windows of Hawk Palace and watched the dromon — an unusually large galley — slipping into the harbour, her masthead a mass of identifying flags.

"A messenger from Constantinople."

"Another summons from the Sultan, I suppose," Aimée said. "I but hope he is not countermanding the assault on Tunis. Harry has his heart set on that."

She started down the stairs, and Felicity followed more slowly, glancing through the inner window to where Anthony was building castles in the sand of the centre courtyard, watched over by Ayesha.

She paused at the archway leading into the reception hall, where Harry was just emerging from his office. How splendid he looked, tall and strong and powerful, even if his beard was now streaked with grey.

She remembered her confused emotions when she had first beheld this man looming into her parents' cellar in England, drawn scimitar in hand. She had seized a pistol when the women had been ordered to safety, uncertain whether she meant to use it on the intruders or herself. When she had beheld that commanding figure in the doorway, she had fired at him instinctively. And when she had missed, her blood had turned cold with the anticipation of imminent death.

Granted that this strange man had then treated her like a sack of coal, he had nonetheless not ill-treated her. If she had been determined to hate him then, her heart had not been able to watch without pity the grief in his face after the destruction of his family.

How could she, little Felicity Martindale, pity a brutal corsair who had snatched her from the bosom of her family? Yet she had, the more so as he had not vented his bitter rage on her in any way. Instead he had brought her to the most fabulous of cities, and into the most fabulous of palaces, and introduced her to a beautiful and charming woman she was now proud to call friend as well as aunt.

She had sensed then that she was destined for his bed — and not as the playmate of an idle hour, to be discarded when sated. He was to be her husband. She had eventually sought nothing more than that, and had discovered the glories of being married to so noble a man. To bear his son had been the greatest privilege she could imagine.

She regretted, of course, that Harry served a man regarded by most of Europe as the anti-Christ. Yet she hoped she could one day persuade him to return to the Christian fold. And if she was ever to wean this family back to the paths of righteousness, it would have to be through the medium of that little boy out in the garden, who had more English blood in him than either Harry Hawkwood or the uncle he so revered.

Until that day she would have to be patient.

And that meant honouring her husband and his alien ways at all times. Enjoying his triumphs. Thus she stood at the foot of the steps, heart swelling with pride, as they waited for the messengers from Constantinople bearing the Sultan's greetings — and no doubt his congratulations.

There were four envoys. Dark-visaged men clad in splendid robes, they stalked into the reception hall and bowed low before Hawk Pasha.

"We bear greetings from the Padishah, my lord."

Harry Hawkwood bowed in return.

"And messages," the envoy added, his gaze difting over Aimée at the foot of the stairs, and then over Felicity.

Suddenly she felt chill.

"Messages to be delivered in private, great Pasha. They are of the utmost secrecy."

Harry Hawkwood nodded. "You'll come into the office," he said, and led them to the door.

Aimée took a step forward, as if about to speak.

Felicity discovered that she too had taken a step forward, and checked herself.

How could any mere female warn Hawk Pasha, so huge, so strong, so confident?

The door of the office remained open behind the men. From her position at the foot of the steps Felicity could not see into the room, nor could she clearly hear what was said.

Aimée moved closer to listen, and then turned, seeking her niece-in-law, as there came a peculiar sound from beyond the open door, half a protest and half a gasp.

"Felicity," she shrieked. "Run! Run for your life! Take the child and run! Only vengeance remains."

Felicity hesitated but a moment then darted across the hall towards the courtyard at the rear.

At the archway she paused to look over her shoulder. Three men had emerged from the office, bowstrings ready in their hands.

Not even Hawk Pasha had been able to resist the surprise grip of a bowstring round his neck. Now they sought her and Anthony. The Hawkwoods must be destroyed. But Aimée barred their way, hurling herself in front of them so that they tripped and fell to their knees on the marble floor. Cursing, they wrapped a bowstring round her neck.

Aimée, beautiful and dignified, who had suffered so much and waited so long to enjoy the love of William Hawkwood, was dying now so that she, Felicity, might live.

Tearing into the yard, she seized up the boy and kept on running — through the back of the house and out into the myriad streets of the Algiers kasbah.

Ayesha ran at her heels. Faithful Ayesha. Between them they would save Anthony's life.

For vengeance. For only vengeance was left.

BOOK THE FOURTH

The Full Circle

"'Tis all a Chequer-board of Nights and Days
Where Destiny with Men for Pieces plays:
Hither and thither moves, and mates, and slays,
And one by one back in the Closet lays."

OMAR KHAYYAM

17

THE CORSAIR

Ayesha hurried in from the front of the house.

"Lady!" she cried. "Lady! The fleet returns."

Felicity Hawkwood's head jerked, and she pricked her finger with her needle. But she ignored the spot of blood, laid down the sewing, and followed her servant on to the porch.

Not that Ayesha was a servant. The two women were the closest of friends. They had shared too much to be anything else.

Ayesha would know what emotions tumbled through Felicity's heart and mind every time the fleet returned; she shared those as well.

Felicity peered at the cluster of ships bearing down on the famous moles that had kept Algiers impregnable. Not so long in the past the Emperor Charles V had himself led an expedition to rid the Mediterranean — his Mediterranean — of the Barbary corsairs. A fleet had appeared off the city, an army had been landed. But that time it had been the turn of the Spaniards to suffer the vagaries of the weather. A sudden storm had shattered the fleet, the army had hastily to be withdrawn before it starved to death.

The Spaniards had not returned. And now even the Emperor had retired; he had abdicated his immense power and retreated to a monastery. His huge dominions had been divided: between his son Philip II, who ruled Spain and the Indies, and his brother Ferdinand, who had taken the title of Emperor and now ruled central Europe. The days when a single brain could determine whether or not to oppose the steady expansion of Ottoman arms were past.

It was possible to say that the corsairs had broken the Imperial power. Because it had been the Ottoman sea power which had defeated Charles. Where even Suleiman the Magnificent had failed time and again in his onslaughts on Vienna, the galleys had taken the fight into every Christian home in the Mediterranean within

443

twenty miles of the sea.

That tremendous project had been begun by Harry Hawkwood and Khair-ed-din Barbarossa. It had been carried to fruition by Khair-ed-din's now famous successor, Dragut.

And with Dragut there sailed Anthony Hawkwood.

The very last Hawkwood, Felicity thought. The very last.

"I see the Admiral's pennant," Ayesha cried. She was in a state of high excitement. "And Piale Pasha's."

The Hungarian renegade was Dragut's second-in-command.

"And Anthony's?"

Ayesha squinted into the morning; her eyes were better than Felicity's, although the two women were the same age: thirty-seven. For more than twenty years they had lived together, with their memories ... and the delight of watching Anthony growing from a babe into a boy, from a boy into a youth, and from a youth into the man he now was.

"There!" Ayesha screamed. "There! He is there, lady! He is there."

"Thank God!" Felicity whispered. "Thank God!"

She left the porch and returned to her chair, and to her sewing. She would remain there until he came to her.

Every time he went away, she thought she would die; she felt old, and afraid to look in the mirror. Because, at thirty-seven, her hair was streaked with grey. And there was sufficient cause for that.

But every time he came back, she felt like a young girl again.

It was not a cycle she had ever intended. When she and Ayesha had fled the Hawk Palace on that never-to-be-forgotten day sixteen years ago, dragging the four-year-old Anthony with them — bearing with them, too, the memory of Aimée Ferrand dying so gallantly that they might live — her only ambition had been to escape.

Aimée might have screamed for vengeance, but Aimée was of a different breed, and Aimée had lived her entire life in the midst of strife. For Felicity, it was all too new, and stark.

But escape, how? And where? Behind the city there lay only the desert.

She and Ayesha had cowered in a palm grove, uncertain what to do next — and there they had been found. They had gazed at the men with terrified eyes, seeking the bowstrings which would mean the end of their lives, and of Anthony's too.

But the men who had found them were not assassins. They had been sent by Dragut Pasha, to bring them to safety.

Dragut had been as shocked as anyone when he had learned of Hawk Pasha's death. That the assassins had carried the Sultan's warrant had merely bewildered him, for he knew that Suleiman had no more faithful servant than this English renegade.

It was not part of Dragut's nature to rebel, no more than it had been in Harry Hawkwood's nature. So, accepting the deed as the Sultan's will, he had feted the assassins and sent then on their way.

But, by then, he had already found Harry Hawkwood's wife and son. He had taken them into his own house, and raised the boy as his own. Aimée Ferrand had screamed for vengeance as she died. but that was not in Dragut's thinking. The Padishah had issued an instruction, that was sufficient ... The Padishah must have had reasons over and above any ordinary man's knowledge.

But that did not mean he, Dragut, could not love his dead friend's son, or raise him to be a naval commander — perhaps a successor to himself.

Felicity had been aghast at his pliancy but she had had no option. Dragut had welcomed her, and seen that she was neither molested nor sold, for all that she was about the most beautiful woman in Tunis, but he would not permit her to talk of leaving.

"The Hawks have always served the Padishah," he explained patiently. "There have been Hawks executed before, yet their sons became pashas. Somehow, I do not know how, your husband incurred the enmity of the Sultan Valideh."

For no one doubted that Roxelana was the true Sultan Valideh, even if Gulbehar still lived, and Prince Mustafa was still heir to the divan; it was well known that the Sultan spent more time with Prince Selim, his son by Roxelana, and that he valued her daughter just as highly.

"But the Sultan Valideh may well pass away," Dragut had insisted. "Or she may lose favour — who can tell? And when that happens, lady, your son will be restored to favour."

The whole idea had revolted Felicity, however much she had had to accept it. And it had grown more obnoxious as the years passed, and news from Constantinople told only of the Sultan Valideh's increasing power. In time Roxelana had married her daughter to a high official, Rustem, who was promptly made Grand Vizier. Then had come her crowning stroke; only three years ago, word had reached Algiers that Prince Mustafa had been executed for treason, by order of the Sultan. So Gulbehar had become no more than an elderly lady of the harem, and Roxelana was now Sultan Valideh in fact as well as by general acceptance. With her son as heir to the divan, and her son-in-law Grand Vizier, she all but ruled the Ottoman Empire.

And my son, Felicity thought, fights for her — she who killed his father!

But now, at least, he had once more returned alive.

She listened for his footsteps, and realised that he was not alone.

Since Harry's murder, she found any deviation from the norm alarming, and so she stood up, heart pounding, to watch the two men striding towards her.

Dragut Pasha was a tall man, with a hatchet face and a long black moustache which drooped to either side of his thin lips. He was, by repute, a harsh and cruel man to his enemies, or to any who would oppose him. He had never been either harsh or cruel to Harry Hawkwood's widow, save in his refusal to let her leave Algiers and take her son.

But Dragut was also a successful man. If he lacked the flamboyance of Khair-ed-din, he had yet more solid triumphs to his credit. And he enjoyed his success, and his fame. His clothes were finest silk, his sword hilt encrusted with gold and precious stones. He walked as should a man who had never been defeated in twenty years.

But Felicity had eyes only for the young man at his side. Tall as Dragut was, Anthony Hawkwood towered above him. Six feet four inches tall, with shoulders to match, glowing red hair and beard, sapphire-like eyes — and the immense confidence that only perfect health combined with a certainty of one's own abilities can bring.

Because she loved him to the point of jealousy, and feared to lose him to another woman, she had refused to allow him to marry, for all that he was now twenty years old. Instead he had been given two concubines, and these had so far been sufficient. Yet, of course he would have to marry, and soon. But a Turkish wife would strengthen the ties binding him to the Ottoman, and weaken those binding him to her. And Felicity was determined to put off that evil day to the last possible moment.

"Dragut Pasha!" She bowed her head to the elder man, then turned. "My son!"

"Mother!" Anthony embraced her. "We have the most tremendous news."

"You have had a successful voyage."

Dragut Pasha smiled. "Indeed, lady. Our holds are filled. But that is not what brings me to you. There is news from Istanbul."

For so had Suleiman decreed that the city of Constantinople should be renamed, the shorter name being a corruption of the longer, which did not come easily off a Turkish tongue.

Felicity caught her breath. "What news?" As far as she was concerned, Istanbul, Constantinople, call it what they wished, was the deepest pit of hell.

"You tell her, boy," Dragut prompted.

"It was a sea-captain we met, from Venice, Mother," Anthony explained. "He told us, Mother ... Roxelana is dead."

Felicity frowned at him. "A Venetian sea-captain told you this?"

"He was just out of Istanbul, lady," Dragut said. "It is all the news there."

"Well ..." Felicity slumped down. "If that is true, it is at least a cloud lifted from over our heads."

"It is more than that, lady," Dragut said.

Felicity raised her head to gaze at him.

"You will know that I have visited Istanbul regularly," Dragut continued, "and have had audiences with the Sultan and his viziers. The Padishah became aware some time ago of how the Russian woman had bedevilled him. He would not put her away, because she was the mother of Prince Selim, and, some say, because even to the end she retained some strange hold over him. Yet he does regret many deeds she inveigled him into. He now sorely regrets the execution of Ibrahim, and of his son Mustafa. And it is said, too, that he regrets the execution of Hawk Pasha."

"Rumours," Felicity said sadly.

"Things I have heard from the Porte itself, lady," Dragut insisted. "And it is at least true that he has sent away Rustem, and elevated Mahomet Sokullu to be Grand Vizier in his stead."

"How can those things concern us now?" Felicity asked. "Hawk Pasha is dead, and not even the Sultan can bring him back to life."

"But there can be another Hawk Pasha, lady," Dragut argued.

447

"For a hundred years there has been a Hawk Pasha. There should be one again."

Felicity looked at her son.

"The great Pasha is right, Mother," Anthony said. "You have told me of the riches our family once had, and the palace in Istanbul. Why should I not reclaim these things, now that the witch is dead?"

"Because you do not know if these rumours are true," Felicity cried. "To go to Istanbul, unbidden by the Sultan, would be to extend your neck for the string to be tied around it."

Anthony looked at Dragut for support.

"That is certainly possible, lady," Dragut agreed. "But the risk is no greater than that of being struck by a shot when we engage in battle. And the prize to be gained is far greater."

"The greatest prize of all, my lord Pasha, would be for my son and I to be allowed to leave this place, and find our way back to England and my family. Why will you not allow this?"

"Because it is the Hawk Pasha's place to fight for the Sultan," Dragut said patiently. "This is his destiny, revealed both by kismet and by his ancestors."

Felicity sighed. She and Dragut had debated this matter too often in the past.

"Besides," Dragut said, "have you ever asked your son if he wishes to return to England?"

Felicity gazed at Anthony. No, she thought. I have never asked my son, because you have bewitched him with the glory of fighting beneath your banner and with the tales of his father's prowess. You have turned him into a heathen pirate. And now you would send him to his death. But if he wishes to go, then is he lost to me whether he is executed or not. The favour of the Sultan would be the strongest of all bonds.

"Anthony, do you wish to return to Istanbul?" she asked.

"Yes, Mother. I wish to face the Padishah and know my fate."

Felicity looked at Dragut.

"Young Hawk's galley will leave tomorrow," he said. "I myself will accompany him."

"Then I also will return to Istanbul," Felicity sighed. If her son was going to die, she wished to be at his side. And this time she would not run away.

Anthony Hawkwood stood in the prow of his galley as it nosed its way from Marmara into the Bosphorus. He had stood there much of the previous night, eagerly awaiting his first glimpse of that city of which he had heard so much, for so long.

He had been conceived in this place, but had never seen it. Now he was returning to reclaim his destiny. His father had been executed by order of the Sultan, but this was a fate which overhung every pasha who might fall under suspicion. Thus equally Anthony did not doubt that he would be able to make his way with even greater success than Harry Hawkwood had ever done. Besides, he could conceive of no other way of life than captaining a galley in the service of the Sultan to make war upon his enemies. And one day he hoped to command a fleet.

Ayesha stood beside him. She was even more excited than he, because she too had never seen Istanbul. And, even more than he, perhaps, she knew that here was his destiny.

Which was also her destiny.

For she had nursed him ever since he could remember, and in many ways she was a second mother to him.

Now they gazed together at the great walls looming out of the morning mist, at the towers and domes beyond, and they gasped in wonder. To the already existing marvels of Constantinople, the mosque that had once been St Sophia, and the Blue Mosque, the Mosque of Mahomet II and the Mosque of Selim, had been added the Mosque of Suleiman, the greatest of them all.

"It is a creation of Sinan the architect," Dragut told them, joining them in the bow. "Much of the beauty that is Istanbul was created by that one man."

By now they could see the Golden Horn.

"When the infidels held this city," Dragut said, "they maintained a boom made of iron chain across the harbour, to keep their enemies out. Now there is no need of a boom."

For the Black Sea had become a Turkish lake.

The galley swept into the curving harbour, the oars were shipped, and the ship glided alongside one of the many quays. Dragut Pasha's pennant had been recognised, and a space hastily made for him, while the harbour captain himself hurried forward to greet the famous admiral.

Anthony gazed up the hill of Galata towards the Hawk Palace.

"Your great-grandfather built that house," Felicity told him. "I

449

have lived in it only briefly, but it was a wonderful place."

"You will live there again, Mother," Anthony promised. "And it will again be a wonderful place."

"We must make haste," Dragut told him. "Word of your return will be spreading. It were best we reached the Seraglio before rumour. Ayesha, do you escort the Lady Felicity to seek accommodation in Galata until our return."

"And if you do not return?" Felicity asked.

Dragut gave a snort of laughter, then handed her a bag of gold coins. "Then betake yourself to England, lady. Because we shall be dead."

Dragut hurried Anthony off before Felicity could protest further. They caught the ferry to the watergate on the city side of the Golden Horn, and pressed into the thronged streets. Men and women glanced at them, and then away again. Dragut was well known, but it was seldom he walked the streets virtually alone, and without the pomp surrounding his rank.

But was he alone? Or was that not a ghost striding beside him? It was not a question anyone was prepared to ask.

As Dragut and Hawkwood passed through the white gate into old Byzantium Anthony gazed in wonder at the marvellous architecture with which he was surrounded, at the space and air, so different to the crowded city behind them, and then at the Seraglio itself, the most splendid building he had ever seen.

"Follow me in all things," Dragut warned, as they approached the Porte.

Anthony nodded.

"Dragut Pasha, seeking an audience with the Padishah," Dragut told the captain of the guard. "You will inform the Grand Vizier of my presence."

He was one of the very few men in the entire Ottoman empire who could make that bold request, as opposed to merely taking his place outside in the yard and hoping to be noticed.

The captain saluted, and sent one of his men scurrying into the interior of the palace. He himself looked Anthony up and down.

"Your servant will wait here, great Pasha," he said.

"He is not a servant," Dragut told him. "And we will both speak with the Padishah."

This time the captain hesitated, then he turned and led them through the inner court, which was crowded with men speaking together. Everyone turned to stare at the admiral and his companion, then their chatter was renewed with increased excitement.

At the inner doorway a man waited. Though not very old, he was richly dressed, and wore the high square turban of the Grand Vizier. This was the man who had replaced Rustem when that scoundrel's peculations had become known after the death of Roxelana. Being the Sultan's son-in-law, Rustem had not been executed — but he had been exiled to his country estate, far from Istanbul.

Dragnut bowed, "My lord Sokullu."

"Dragut Pasha. Surely it is some great event that brings you so privily to Istanbul?" remarked the Grand Vizier.

"This is a private visit, my lord Vizier. I have a protégé to introduce to the Padishah."

Sokullu looked more closely at Anthony Hawkwood. "By the beard of the Prophet," he muttered, seizing his own beard.

As Anthony gazed at strong features, spoiled by a crafty expression in the eyes and the cynical twist of the lips, he recalled that Mahomet Sokullu, kidnapped as a child from Christian parents and raised in the Janissary school, had enjoyed a distinguished career which included the command of the Turkish eastern fleet. But since he had only recently been elevated to be second man in the empire, no doubt this Vizier did not yet feel his position secure. More certainly, he knew he would one day have to deal with Roxelana's son Selim, who was now heir to the divan.

Sokullu examined Hawkwood with no less interest, then said, "I knew your father, young Hawk."

Anthony bowed, wondering if Sokullu had had any part to play in the assassination. But he was not here for revenge.

"You shall have your audience," Sokullu went on. "I think the Padishah will be interested to speak with you."

Dragut and Hawkwood were ushered into the centre court, where there was yet another throng of men milling about and gossiping, many of them clutching rolls of parchment which they no doubt hoped to be able to present to the Sultan himself.

There were even men in the doublet and hose of Western Europe, speaking in a variety of tongues. But not in English, which Anthony had been taught by his mother.

Minutes after Sokullu had left them, a servant emerged from the

Porte and hurried into the throng towards them. All heads turned expectantly, and there were frowns of dismay and anger when the two newest arrivals were singled out and led towards the waiting Vizier.

Sokullu bowed. "The Padishah is pleased to receive you in audience, young Hawk."

Anthony glanced at Dragut, who gave him a grin.

"Be yourself, boy. That is all a man can ever be."

As they entered the Porte, they could see the legendary divan itself, but it was empty. Moving in front of them, Sokullu now took his seat nearby. To either side were seated other viziers — and other pashas, too, clad in steel cuirasses inlaid with gold and silver, around which their silk robes flowed in a variety of brilliant colours to match the jewels encrusting their helmets and sword hilts. For was not this the richest civilisation in the world?

"Welcome to Istanbul, my lord Admiral," Sokullu began formally. "And to you also, young Hawk."

Dragut bowed, and Anthony followed his example, all the while wondering where the Sultan himself was. Then he noticed the screen, set well back on the left of the room — and he knew. His heart pounded.

"I understand you have brought the young Hawk here to present him to the Padishah," Sokullu continued. "Tell me what you seek from our master, young Hawk."

Anthony gave Dragut another quick glance, and received another nod.

"I seek service worthy of my name and lineage, my lord Vizier," he said. "I am the son of Hawk Pasha."

"This is well known, and your sentiments do you credit." Sokullu glanced at the screen.

"I will speak with young Hawk," the voice of Suleiman was finally heard.

At the sound of the quiet voice, every head at once bowed. Then could be heard the rustle of silk and the soft closing of a door.

"Now is your future determined, should you please the Padishah, young Hawk," Sokullu whispered. "Go with this servant."

A eunuch had appeared at the side of the divan. Anthony glanced at his foster-father, and again Dragut nodded. Anthony followed the eunuch along a carpeted corridor, redolent with sweet scents, and into an inner chamber hung with the richest drapes he had ever seen. There the Sultan was seated upon a divan set against the wall, closely screened to either side.

The eunuch held out his hand, and Anthony hesitated, uncertain of the fellow's meaning. Then the eunuch pointed to his belt, and Anthony understood. He unbuckled the scimitar which hung at his side, and handed it over. Still the eunuch waited, until Anthony had also given him his poignard. The servant prostrated himself briefly before the divan, then rose to leave the room, carrying Hawkwood's weapons.

Anthony stared at the man whose subjects called him 'the Lawgiver', although his enemies called him 'the Magnificent' — the most powerful single human being on the face of the earth.

And he all but gasped with dismay. Though his mother had never laid eyes on the Sultan, Dragut often had, and had told his protégé sufficient tales of that greatness which had now for nearly thirty years astonished the world.

Anthony knew that Suleiman was sixty-two years old — and that seemed a great enough age to someone nearly forty years younger. But now he found himself staring at a shrunken, wizened figure, suggestive of one far older than that. The shoulders were hunched, the breath short and anxious, the cheeks covered in rouge to give them colour. The hands were tight-skinned, with every blue vein showing beneath the pale flesh.

Yet was the Sultan dressed in the richest of silk robes. Rings of incalculable value gleamed on his fingers, and more jewels studded his turban.

Finally Suleiman spoke. "Harry Hawkwood's son," he said. "Come closer, boy, that I may look upon you."

Anthony advanced towards the divan.

"Harry Hawkwood's son," the Sultan repeated. "Your father and I were once friends."

"This I have heard, O Padishah," Anthony ventured.

"We were more than friends." The Sultan appeared to brood. "I loved him like a brother."

"My father was a fortunate man, O Padishah."

"And have you also heard that I had your father murdered?" Suleiman asked.

Anthony could think of no reply to that one. How he wished Dragut was there to guide him.

"Yes." Suleiman understood his silence. "You have been told

that, young Hawk." He sighed. "Do you not suppose that a man, the older he grows, also grows to wish that with a snap of his fingers he might undo at least some of the past, and restore what has been lost? Perhaps he can. See ..." he snapped his fingers. "Am I not a magician? Harry Hawkwood once again stands before me. What matter that he has changed his name? He is still the giant with whom I once laughed, and played ... and campaigned." The Sultan stood up. "Come here, boy."

Anthony advanced, and to his amazement was embraced.

"If you knew how much I regret the death of your father," Suleiman said. "No matter ... the dead cannot be recalled. We can but make amends to the living."

Clutching Anthony's hand, he led him back down the corridor, to the stateroom where Dragut and Sokullu and the other pashas waited. The Sultan walked past them and into the Porte itself, and stood to look out at the crowd waiting there.

Everyone bowed at the sight of their master.

"I present to you Hawk Pasha," Suleiman announced in a loud, clear voice. "Hawk Pasha has returned."

Mahomet Sokullu hurried forward with a horsetail wand.

Anthony longed to hurry back to Galata and tell his mother his stupendous news, but first he and Dragut had to eat, seated one on either side of the great Sultan. With them sat Sokullu, and also Prince Selim. The Prince was a handsome man in his middle thirties, but Anthony could feel no rapport with him. Selim seldom looked anyone straight in the eye; he only played with his food, and from time to time was overtaken by violent twitching.

If Suleiman was aware of this behaviour, he gave no sign.

"Tell me of young Hawk's deeds, Admiral," he said.

Dragut did so. He spoke of raids on Spanish and French coastal towns, of ship-to-ship combat, and of the great battles in which he had been invariably victorious. He spoke of the capture of Tripoli, in 1551, and the flight of the Knights of St John to Malta; that had been Anthony's first campaign, as a fifteen-year-old. He spoke of the capture of Bastia in Corsica two years later, and of the Turkish expansion along the North African coast in the past three years, which had left the Spaniards in control only of Tunis.

"But Tunis will soon fall as well, O Padishah," he laughed. "This new King of Spain, this Philip, seems more interested in the

Atlantic Ocean than the Mediterranean. He mourns the death of his English wife ... some say he hopes to wed the dead Queen's half-sister and successor, Elizabeth."

And in all of these encounters, no matter how great or how small, Dragut boasted how Anthony Hawkwood had led in attacks, or, in retreat, had commanded the rearguard. Anthony himself could not but blush as the praise flowed.

"Verily did I fight with Harry Hawkwood often enough." Dragut said. "I had never supposed there could be another like him. But this boy is even greater than his father."

"It is well," the Sultan said finally. "My empire has suffered sorely these last twenty years ... You will not return to Algiers, young Hawk. You must remain here in Istanbul. I appoint you flag captain to Ali Monizindade Pasha. Prove your worth to him, and you will have a fleet of your own — this I promise. Dragut, you will have to find yourself a new hero."

Dragut merely bowed his head, but Anthony could hardly believe his ears.

You will return to live in the Hawk Palace," Suleiman instructed. "Now tell me of your wives and children."

"I have no wife, O Padishah."

Suleiman frowned at him. "No wife, and you a grown man?"

"It has been the decision of his mother, O Padishah," Dragut explained. "The Lady Felicity is English."

"Ah! Yes, I remember this. And she has brought her son up as an Englishman — the most tardy people in the world when it comes to marriage. But we must save you from this cruel dragon of a mother, Hawk Pasha." Suleiman smiled. "You fear your mother's wrath. That is good. A man should fear his mother. But I promise you that not even she will be angry with me. I will choose your wife carefully. Your mother has brought you up as an Englishman, and she has refused to let you couple with a Turk. Very well, I will make you a present of a Christian wife. Would that not please you?"

"That would please me, O Padishah."

"There is a young lady resident here in Istanbul, named Barbara Cornaro. I shall give her to you."

Anthony stared at him in amazement. "Just like that?"

"Sokullu," Suleiman said impatiently. "You will acquaint the Signora Cornaro of my determination regarding her daughter."

The Vizier inclined his head.

"The young lady is of very high birth — virtually a princess." Suleiman told Anthony. "Her great-aunt was Queen of Cyprus."

"Will such a personage consent to wed an unknown sailor, O Padishah?" Anthony was puzzled.

Suleiman's smile widened. "You are not an unknown sailor. You are Hawk Pasha, and, what is more important, you are in the favour of the Sultan. She has no choice, since she is here in Istanbul."

Sokullu later explained it to him.

"Caterina Cornaro was a Venetian of high birth, who was secured in marriage by James II de Lusignan, King of Cyprus, in 1472, in order to achieve a Venetian alliance. He died very shortly afterwards, leaving his wife pregnant. She duly gave birth to a son, James III, but the mother was required to act as regent until he came of age, and so she was accorded the title of Queen. She was but a girl of nineteen, and found the task of ruling such a turbulent community — especially one entirely surrounded by Ottoman territory — beyond her powers. Yet she maintained herself for sixteen years, but within that time her son had died, and thus she abdicated her throne and granted Cyprus to her native Venice. Returning home, she herself took up residence in Treviso, where she was granted an estate, retaining to the day of her death the title of Queen.

"This girl, Barbara, is the granddaughter of one of that Queen's brothers. Well, when, a few years ago, a new peace treaty was agreed between the Doge and the Padishah — the previous ones having all been broken when the Venetians thought it advantageous to resume the war — we demanded certain hostages. Drawn from the noblest of Venetian families, they came to live in Istanbul as a pledge for their country's honesty.

"A nephew of Barbara Cornaro was one of these. He came with his wife and infant daughter ... and has remained here ever since."

"A prisoner of the Padishah?" Anthony observed.

"That is true in fact, if not in form," Sokullu conceded. "Pietro Cornaro lives in his own palace and is treated with every mark of respect."

"Saving only that should the Sultan and Venice ever again go to war he will be strangled."

Sokullu inclined his head. "But is that not a fate which hangs over every man in the empire, Hawk Pasha — as you should well know? Believe me, I appreciate and respect the sharpness of your mind, but I would advise you to keep your thoughts and actions carefully controlled, at least when in Istanbul. As for the Lady Barbara, I am informed that she is a girl of wondrous beauty, and even more accomplishments. You will not find a better, even were she not commanded to your bed by the Padishah."

"These things I understand, my lord," Anthony said humbly. "I shall obey the Padishah in all things."

Yet was he uneasy. Well as his mother had tried to educate him, his accomplishments in learning were very limited — there had been few books in Algiers for him to read. And much as he felt he had pleased his concubines, he was aware that there had to be the world of difference between being sexually entertained by two young servants and attempting the same with a young woman who would undoubtedly regard herself as his superior.

Felicity was even less amused.

"A wife!" she declared. "Just like that!" She snapped her fingers. "A girl I have never even seen."

"It is commanded by the Padishah," explained Dragut, who had accompanied Anthony back to Galata.

"Ha!" Felicity commented.

"The lady is, by repute, very beautiful," Dragut continued. "And her family is known to be wealthy. She will bring with her a large dowry. And live in the Hawk Palace, which the Padishah has now restored to you, lady — for the use of you and your family for the rest of time."

Felicity could not but be mollified by that, especially when Dragut informed her that she possessed unlimited credit to restore the palace to its former glory. Yet she was not forgiving. "The Padishah assumes he can buy my forgiveness for the murder of my husband," she remarked.

"I doubt he even considers the matter in that light, lady," Dragut replied. "He but seeks to restore the Hawks to their former glory."

Felicity was even more pleased when Mahomet Sokullu himself called later at the palace. He surveyed the army of workmen who were busily restoring crumbled plaster and moth-eaten drapes.

"Indeed," he commented, "this will be a palace fit for a princess. And now Signor and Signorina Cornaro await you."

"My son is not here," she said. "He is in the harbour with his ships."

Sokullu smiled. "I know this, lady. That is why I have come. The Padishah has given instructions that this marriage is to be conducted in accordance with European custom. It is for you to approve her. Hawk Pasha will not see his bride until his wedding night."

Felicity caught her breath, suddenly nervous. "And for me to be approved by them?"

The Vizier continued to smile. "That approval is already certain. It is the will of the Padishah."

The door opened, and Beatrice Cornaro gazed at her daughter.

"The Englishwoman is here," she announced, "with the Vizier, no less."

Barbara rose from her chair. Her heart pounded and she could feel the heat in her cheeks.

"Sit down, girl," her mother commanded. "Before you fall down. We must keep them waiting, for a while at least. We may be their prisoners, but we are not yet their slaves."

Barbara sank back on to the cushion.

Her mother sat down beside her. "Are you afraid?" she asked gently.

"Yes, Mama."

"Well, so you should be." Beatrice Cornaro's strong features — she was a Mocenigo, and there was no older or greater Venetian family — softened. "We are the victims of a great crime. But if it must be your fate to suffer, you will remember at all times to carry yourself with the dignity and stoicism of the family name you bear."

"Yes, Mama," Barbara said.

"This lout, this pirate, is a favourite of the Sultan. Heaven knows why. But, then, heaven plays no part in anything Ottoman. It seems the Sultan murdered his father, as he has murdered so many, and now seeks to make amends to the son. It is probably as well that so few of his victims had sons to survive them, else would his conscience lead him to give away half his empire. Now listen to me, girl: he will seek to use your body in the most heathen of ways."

Barbara was having trouble with her breathing. "Yes, Mama."

"You will have no choice but to accept it, as the Doge himself has agreed to the match. Just as we have no choice but to accept your husband's decree — that you shall not be accompanied by your confessor. Can there be anything more barbaric? And he calls himself a Christian. But at least they have agreed to your maids being retained. You will not be entirely alone in that den of iniquity."

"Yes, Mama."

"Only remember that once you bear this villain a son, he is yours."

"Yes, Mama."

"Remember, too, that you are the most beautiful woman he can ever have seen."

"Am I, Mama?"

"There is the glass, girl. Look at yourself."

Barbara obeyed. Indeed, however much it was condemned by her confessor, looking at herself was now her principal recreation.

She looked first of all at her clothes. As she had been expecting this call, she wore her very best: her dark green velvet gown had a fur trimming, less because it was particularly cold this day than because Mama had elected to show off as much of their wealth as possible; her white underskirt — displayed from her waist to the floor as the gown was pulled back from her hips — was also of velvet, with a floral pattern; her partlet and sleeves were heavily embroidered; and she wore gauze ruffs at neck and wrists.

Both her girdle and her pomander were of gold studded with precious stones, and there was also jewelled gold on her wrist-bands and cap.

Her stand-up collar concealed the length of her hair, which was carefully tucked out of sight, and drawn back beneath her cap. This was fashionable — however regrettable in the case of someone like Barbara Cornaro, who counted her hair as one of her most attractive features. The colour of mahogany, it was thick and luxuriant with a slight wave, and when loose seemed to make the rest of her irrelevant. When drawn back from her face, however, it left the features exposed, though admirable. Her cheekbones were high, her jawline firm. She had a straight nose and a pointed chin, a wide mouth and wideset amber eyes. Save for the colouring, which was richly pink and white — she never went outside unless concealed by a veil — she might have been some Titian-inspired statue.

Her figure, already mature at sixteen, was no less eye-catching; her costume delineated the slender waist and hips, as well as the swell of her breasts; the positioning of her girdle indicated the unusual length of her legs.

She inhaled, as she stared at herself, and her nostrils flared.

Beatrice clapped her hands. "You are quite lovely, my dear," she said. "Come, shall we dazzle this Englishwoman with our splendour?"

Once upon a time, Beatrice Mocenigo had looked like that herself.

"She is delightful," Felicity told her son. "She will make you the happiest man on earth."

"If you are pleased with her, then I am already the happiest man on earth," Anthony replied.

He was not merely flattering her. These past few weeks, his life had bloomed in a manner he had never expected possible.

He was now Hawk Pasha. When he went abroad with his horse-tail wand, men stepped aside for him in the street, and those of sufficient standing in the community were anxious to be seen with him.

He had regained his destiny. Before leaving, Dragut had embraced him, then held him at arms' length. "Now is Hawk Pasha truly restored," the admiral had said. "I shall miss you, Anthony, but I know you will bring honour to both your name and mine. Remember always that it is your destiny to serve the Sultan, no matter where that path may lead."

Those were not words the young Hawkwood ever intended to forget.

Anthony encountered the Sultan or the Grand Vizier at least once a week, and was drawn into discussing the great affairs of state. This was a dazzling elevation in his social status, not least because of the suddenness with which he had virtually been adopted by the Padishah, but he was under no illusions. He was intelligent enough to understand that the Sultan was trying to recapture through him the energy, as well as the glories, of his youth — when, with men like Ibrahim and Harry Hawkwood as his commanders, he had

ridden constantly from success to success. Thus Anthony Hawkwood was less a man in his own right than a symbol of what had
been ... and what might be again.

For all his achievements, Suleiman regarded his inability to take
the imperial city of Vienna as the crowning failure of a failed life —
but one he was determined to rectify before he died. Plans were in
hand for yet another campaign.

It would become the responsibility of Ali Monizindade Pasha to
keep the eastern Mediterranean peaceful while the Sultan was at
war. And in particular to ensure that Venice kept the peace, and
did not — as the Republic had done more than once in the past —
go to war with them the moment the Doge felt the Ottomans were
fully occupied elsewhere.

For this purpose there was the eastern fleet: it mustered some
hundred and seventy galleys. Hawkwood had never served with
Ali Pasha before, but he quickly recognised him to be a capable
admiral, if not perhaps in the class of Dragut or Khair-ed-din
Barbarossa or Harry Hawkwood.

Ali Monizindade was also a young man, although several years
older. But he had a healthy regard both for Anthony Hawkwood's
reputation as a fighting seaman and the favour in which he stood
with the Sultan, and appeared to welcome him as his aide-de-
camp, even if he had also to regard him as a possible future rival.
The two men quickly became good friends.

In addition, there was the marriage of Barbara Cornaro to the
Sultan's new protégé. Suleiman had sent ambassadors to Venice
to inform the Doge of his intention to marry the heiress to his
favourite Christian commander. This was seen as a politic act, to
which the Venetian Council of Ten could hardly take exception,
and indeed, a reply was quickly received offering the happy couple
felicitations and a handsome present of gold plate.

Hawkwood conceived that he had fallen entirely on his feet. He
only wished his mother to be as happy as himself. That she was
enjoying herself in supervising the restoration and renovation of
the Hawk Palace was obvious. But that she had been nervous at
the thought of having to share it with another woman, who would
have at least equal rights with her own, had been equally obvious.
Now those fears were laid to rest.

"She is clean and quiet, very well bred ... well, what would you
expect in a lady of such lineage? And utterly charming. She is also

beautiful, Anthony. I could not have picked better myself."

"And is she also happy, dearest Mama?"

Felicity frowned. "Well, as to that I really cannot say. Her mother is something of a dragon, anxious to prove to me that she is a great lady — or was a great lady, at the least. I was equally anxious to convince her that her daughter could not possibly make a better marriage, at least in Istanbul. The girl seemed to understand this. But as to happiness — what business has a bride to be happy? At least until after the event."

"Well, girl, are you ready?"

Beatrice Cornaro's tone suggested that her daughter was about to ascend the scaffold.

But was she not? Barbara reflected. The Vizier had made much of the fact that Hawk Pasha, though an Englishman, was at least a Christian, but it could not be argued that Anthony Hawkwood was a Turkish pasha, the latest of a long line of Turkish pashas — a man renowned as a pirate and a renegade, as had been his forebears. He might pay lip-service to the Pope, but he could hardly be described as a Christian.

"He will seek to use you in heathen ways," Beatrice had warned. But she had not specified what those ways were.

Thus, however she had attempted to prepare herself during the days of waiting, Barbara needed all her strength, of mind as well as body, to accompany her father down the stairs and into the waiting carriage, with her pageboys anxiously gathering the long train of her white satin gown as she moved.

She was entirely veiled, and for this she was grateful. It was necessary for her to ride through the city streets to the Roman Catholic church which Suleiman — in pursuit of his belief in religious toleration — had allowed to be built, and the crowds which applauded her undoubtedly knew her purpose.

Strangely, there were crowds outside the church as well, although the congregation was relatively small — composed entirely of the Roman Catholic residents of Istanbul. No Orthodox believer would enter a church blessed by the Pope.

The Venetian ambassador was waiting to greet them, together with Barbara's confessor, officiating for the very last time — and looking like a condemned convict bound for the gallows. This duo proceeded up the aisle in front of her, and there, waiting at the altar, was her prospective husband.

Barbara quite lost her breath. Hawkwood was dressed as a Turkish pasha, and might have been going to fight a war. His tunic and breeches were blue silk, his boots a matching shagreen. His cuirass was inlaid with gold and silver, and sparkled in the sunlight drifting through the stained-glass windows above him. His head was bare, since this was a Christian ceremony; but his grooms-man, who was a Turk and clearly bewildered by the whole thing — in fact Admiral Ali Monizindade — still wore his steel helmet wrapped in a turban, and carried Anthony's in the crook of his arm.

A gold-hilted scimitar hung at Anthony's side; a matching dagger from his girdle.

But, though these were the outward trappings of his position and power, it was the man who mattered. Barbara had never seen a man so tall and broad; she was fairly tall herself, but her first reflection was that he could crush her to death.

But, then, she felt she had never seen a man so handsome — in his flowing red hair, his big strong features, his great blue eyes. As he took her hand she could feel the immense physical power flowing from his fingers into hers. She thought: if I am indeed being sacrificed to an anti-Christ, then I am at least being given to the best of them.

In later years she realised she had fallen in love with him at first sight.

To her surprise, Anthony made no effort to lift her veil and look at her face; perhaps he was even more of a Turk than she had feared. Yet he gazed into her eyes while making the responses, and she surmised at least anticipation in his face.

For the wedding breakfast the entire congregation returned to the Cornaro palace, and here they were joined by the Grand Vizier and several other pashas.

Here, too, at last she could raise her veil and allow her new husband to see what he had been granted.

He kissed her hand. "I must be the most fortunate man alive today," he remarked.

But he still had not kissed her mouth or shown any sign of passion ... while she was consumed with an anxious eagerness. Her fate was now decided for the rest of her life, and she wished it made certain by the consummation. Such a consummation, with some chosen man, had been her ordained fate since the age of puberty; now that it had at last arrived she felt strangely impatient to experience it.

But the speeches were tedious, and so were the toasts. She scarcely ate a morsel of food and did nothing more than wet her lips with the wine. She gazed in front of her, from time to time stealing a glance to left and right. Her husband scarcely looked at her, but her mother-in-law constantly smiled at her reassuringly.

At last the feast was over, and it was time for her to leave her parents' home for the last time. Her chosen maids had already hurried on to the ferry, and across to Galata and the Hawk Palace, to await her arrival.

Barbara was finally escorted upstairs for a last moment of privacy, of confession. "Keep the faith, my child, keep the faith even while incarcerated in the fiery furnace," said the priest. And then a last embrace from her mother.

"Be brave," Beatrice admonished.

"I shall, Mama," Barbara promised.

But I am going to happiness, she told herself. The faith will have to wait on that.

The entire congregation was now assembled in the courtyard, and if the ceremony had been a Roman Catholic one, Hawk Paska owed it to his rank and to his Sultan to take his bride home as a Turk.

The horse was richly caparisoned, and apparently docile, Barbara was glad to observe. To the applause of the onlookers, Anthony held her waist and swung her lightly into the side-saddle, himself inserting her right shoe into the raised stirrup, then doing the same for the other. It was the first time she had ever sat a horse in a gown rather than a habit, and wearing slippers rather than boots — the sensation was a strange one.

But, then, it was the first time her husband had touched any part of her body other than her hand, and that sensation was even stranger.

There were more cheers as Anthony led the horse from the courtyard, and Barbara was alarmed to discover that the street outside was packed with people, who also wished to cheer and offer advice. And, although her parents spoke only Italian within their house, she had learned enough Turkish from the servants to understand that a good deal of what was being shouted at her was obscene.

Once again she was grateful for her veil.

The journey down to the ferry was the longest of her life, for her husband never once turned his head to look at her, and she had to depend on his two attendants to keep the mob from approaching too close — even reaching out to touch her and trying to tear away pieces of her dress as souvenirs.

Then at last they were on the water, and she could relax a little — tensing again as she saw the lights of the Hawk Palace which rose above the hillside.

In Galata the streets were somewhat wider than in old centre of Constantinople, and there were fewer crowds. Now she could concentrate upon the coming minutes ... and hours ... the coming lifetime.

Anthony Hawkwood led his bride up the hill and into the court-yard of his palace, where his servants awaited him. He turned to her for the first time since they had left the Cornaro palace, and lifted her down. Instead of setting her down on the ground, however, he swept his left arm under her knees and carried her up the great steps to the high-roofed portico, while his people cheered.

She put her arms round his neck to assist him, and gazed into his face. As he looked down at her, she smiled at him, but there was no response in his tense features.

He is more nervous than I, she thought in amazement.

They climbed wide interior steps and entered a large, light, airy apartment. At the far end of the room, curtains had been drawn back from an inner room which was raised by a matter of two steps, and there waited the sleeping divan, wide and long, half concealed beneath a profusion of brightly embroidered cushions.

There waited her three maids, bowing low as their mistress was led into the room.

"You may go," Anthony told them abruptly.

They straightened in consternation, gazing at Barbara.

"Who will attend me, sir?" she asked in a low voice. It was the first time she had actually addressed him.

"We will manage between us," he said.

She felt her stomach muscles tighten with apprehension, but he was her lord, who now possessed powers of life and death over her.

465

"Go," she told the girls.

They hurried off, whispering amongst themselves.

Anthony waited for the door to close, then carried her across the room and up the steps to the divan. On this he laid her with considerable gentleness.

Then he straightened up, and looked down at her.

"I know nothing of the education of a Venetian lady," he said.

"I assure you that it is sufficient, sir, for all the eventualities she is likely to meet," Barbara replied timidly.

She could only hope she was telling the truth.

"What do you know of me?"

As he spoke, he reached behind him to unbuckle his cuirass. Barbara wondered if she also should begin to undress, but she preferred to lie on the soft cushions for the moment, and gaze at him, and wait for her nerves to settle.

He laid the cuirass on a chair, then returned to the bedside to look down at her. She sat up.

"Has your education prepared you for the embrace of a heathen?" he asked.

"I had not supposed you so, sir."

"Yet, do you understand that to be your fate?"

She wetted her lips with the tip of her tongue. "I understand that, my lord, and am prepared for it."

Their eyes held each other for several seconds, then suddenly he lent forward and kissed her, taking her face between his hands.

It was a violent, indeed a savage kiss. Her mouth parted and his tongue sought hers, while she felt his hands on her body. Uncertain how to respond, she fell back, and he was lying on her and then beside her, still kissing her. His hand stroked across her breast and then slid down her belly and across her groin.

Instinctively her legs came up, and were caught and held, his fingers sliding through the material to find her flesh. She gasped, and he moved his mouth, looking down, and using his other hand now, entirely to uncover her legs and then her thighs. He still held her legs in the air, and they gazed at her nakedness together, while she panted from a mixture of fear and excitement.

This was more violent than she had anticipated. More passionate, as well. And, yet, strangely gentle.

She was still exposed from the navel down, and reached for her skirt, but he caught her arm.

"I wish to look at you," he said.

She sucked air into her lungs, made herself lie still, as he stood up and discarded his clothing. She had no brothers, and thus little knowledge of the masculine body. Her mother had informed her of the concomitants of the marriage bed, but had recommended she pay as little attention to the male sexual function as possible, even to the extent of closing her eyes.

But how could she not stare at such a magnificent physique, or such a terrifying phallus.

She sat up, unable to lie still a moment longer.

"Do I frighten you?" he asked, returning to the bedside.

He was close enough to touch, only inches from her face.

"Yes," she whispered.

"Then I will be gentle — if I can. Take off your clothes."

Once again she found herself panting. She reached behind herself for the ties for her gown, while he took the cap from her head and released her hair, allowing it to tumble past her shoulders.

Then he held the shoulders of her gown and drew it forward, away from her neck. She stood up, and the gown slipped down to her thighs, and then the floor. She gazed at him as she did the same with the petticoats, one after the other, until the last. Now she hesitated. He was staring at the outline of her breasts, the upright nipples, clearly visible through the thin linen.

He reached for her again, gathered the garment up from her thighs and lifted it over her head, then threw it on the floor.

Eyes closed, she stood before him; naked, trembling slightly from shoulder to toes, quite the most beautiful object he had ever seen.

For a moment he was afraid to touch her, and her eyes slowly opened as she stared at him.

"Do I please you, my lord?" she whispered.

"Please me?" he asked. "Please me?"

He slowly extended his hand to touch her nipple and, as it responded, to circle the breast and hold it gently. Then his palm slipped up her shoulder, and round her back, and she was in his arms, held tightly against him as he sought her mouth.

She felt his hands sliding down her back to her buttocks, even as she felt him against her groin. Sensations she had never before experienced drifted through her mind, jostling against each other;

the sensuous awareness of being helpless, the excited desire somehow to participate, the breathless uncertainty of what was going to happen next, the swelling bud of eroticism which was threatening to burst within her, all merged to rob her of the ability to think, leaving her only able to feel.

She felt herself lifted from the floor and once more laid on the bed. She looked up at the man above her, his face serious and yet suffused with passion. She felt rather than saw him part her legs, gasped as he used his fingers tentatively, and yet still with that utter gentleness.

He held her buttocks to raise her from the bed for his entry, and her legs instinctively closed on his body, hugging him as tightly as she could, while she gave a start at the sudden pain, and twisted her head to and fro on the pillows, as he surged back and forth.

When he stopped, suddenly, she stopped too, gazed at him, panting, aware of great heat and damp.

To her relief, he was smiling at her.

"Yes," he told her. "You please me very much."

18
END OF AN ERA

"Come in and sit down," Felicity invited her new daughter-in-law.

Barbara felt hesitant. This was the first day since her marriage — a week ago — that Anthony had abandoned her. Today he had gone down to the harbour to resume his duties as flag-captain of the Ottoman eastern fleet.

Thus she was alone for the first time. She had scarcely noticed anyone else in the house during those seven days of rapture.

Even the maids who had bathed her in preparation for another bout of love-making — women she had known all her life — had seemed as nothing more than a dream. Reality was only to be found in Anthony's arms.

But now he was gone, and she was summoned to the apartment of her new mother — who had with her, as always, the Arab woman who was her shadow.

She bowed to Felicity, but would not do so to Ayesha.

"You have greatly pleased my son," Felicity told her.

"My lady is too kind," Barbara murmured.

"I am but repeating what he has told me, girl," Felicity said. "But that he is so happy with you makes me happy as well. So now I would ask you this: does he please you equally?"

Barbara had long determined her answer to this question. "How could any woman not be pleased by such a man, my lady?" she asked in turn.

Felicity studied her for several seconds, then patted the divan beside her. "Sit down."

Barbara obeyed, her hands in her lap.

"You are, perhaps the first Christian wife ever taken by a Hawk without violence," Felicity remarked.

Barbara frowned at her.

Felicity smiled. "Oh, indeed, I was plucked from my father's house at swordpoint by Harry Hawkwood. I even fired a pistol at

469

him. And yet I lived to love and honour him. So you see, my dear girl, you have an advantage over the rest of us."

"Yes," Barbara murmured thoughtfully.

Felicity continued to study her, then she said, "Ayesha, I need some more of this crimson thread. Would you fetch it for me?"

Ayesha rose and left the room.

"Are you equally pleased with the role your husband fulfils?" Felicity asked in a low voice.

"It is not my place to criticise my husband," Barbara answered primly, suspecting a trap.

"It behoves you to do so, Barbara," Felicity said. "He fights for a man who is also utterly ruthless. He may well please his master, but who can tell when that will change, and you may discover your beloved with a bowstring knotted round his neck?" She sighed. "As was my fate. Yes, he fights for a heathen who is ambitious of ruling the world. Who can tell when Suleiman's greedy eyes will again turn on Venice? Then would your husband lead his fleet into the Lagoon itself to bombard St Mark's. Can you regard that with equanimity? Will you sit by and watch your sons brought up as Turks, your daughters sent into a harem?"

Barbara found she was panting as this strange woman put into words all the nameless fears which haunted her midnight hours. But this woman? Her mother-in-law?

"What we have discussed here today must never be revealed." Felicity said. "Ayesha is a dear sweet woman, but to her Suleiman is almost a god, and she will hear nothing against him. Equally must we never reveal our private conversations to my son. He was educated to hold the same belief. Yet we must use our combined efforts to wean him away from this unholy purpose he now fulfils."

"To what end, my lady?"

"We must persuade him to flee Turkey — to take service with the Christians. Would not your Doge be pleased to have the aid of so famous a sailor?"

Barbara could think of nothing to reply to that. So far as she could guess, everyone in Venice regarded the name of Hawk with the same fear and loathing as that of Dragut or Khair-ed-din. Their most likely reaction to Anthony's arrival in their midst would be to garrotte him.

"I see you agree with me," Felicity said, and listened to the

470

sound of Ayesha's feet as the Arab woman returned. "We will speak of it again later, when we can be private."

The Turkish fleet spread wide across the Aegean Sea. It was the proudest sight Anthony had ever beheld, perhaps the proudest moment of his life.

The fleet formed three vast squadrons of eighty galleys each. The centre squadron was commanded by Ali Monizindade Pasha, the left wing by Uluch Ali Pasha — he was actually Dey of Algiers, but preferred to seek glory under the Sultan — the right by Pertau Pasha. As there was a light northerly breeze, the sails were set, but purely to provide auxiliary power. The oars dipped rhythmically into the sea, and the blades sparkled as they were recovered for the next stroke. Throughout the fleet, throughout the day, the steady beat of the drums reverberated, drowning even the hiss of water away from the huge, shining, gilded beaks.

On each foredeck two cannon were mounted, the gunners standing to attention beside them.

From each masthead floated the pennants of the commanders, and, from the flagships, the pennants of the admirals; Ali Pasha's masthead also flew the pennant of the Sultan himself.

It was a magnificent array of ships and men, the most powerful force on earth.

"If only we had someone to fight." Ali Monizindade smiled.

If was evening, and the ships were anchored in the vast bay on the south side of the island of Santorini. This same bay had been created by an earthquake many centuries before — indeed, there were scholars who said it was the Santorini earthquake that had put the legend of the lost city of Atlantis into the mind of Plato the Greek. Not that there was any evidence of a lost city beneath these crystal clear waters.

The admirals drank sherbet as they waited to dine with their commander-in-chief, and waited, too, to hear what he would say.

"The Spaniards will come again, one day," Uluch Ali commented casually.

"I doubt it," Ali Monizindade objected. "Their minds have been turning more and more to the Atlantic."

"Then perhaps we should seek them out in the ocean," Anthony Hawkwood suggested.

471

It had been a dream of his father, he knew: Dragut had told him so. Indeed, it had been on just such an expedition into the Atlantic that his father had found and seized his mother. But since Harry Hawkwood's death the Turks had seldom ventured through the Straits of Gibraltar.

"The Mediterranean is *our* sea," Dragut had declared.

"And if this new King of Spain was to launch an expedition, he would have to encounter our friend Dragut first," Ali Monizindade pointed out.

"Suppose he did send his galleons east towards us?" Pertau demanded.

"Bah. They would be a waste of time in these waters. They need strong winds to manoeuvre. We do not campaign in the storm season. In the settled season our galleys would move round them and shoot them to pieces without their being able to aim a shot in reply."

"What of these ships they call galleasses?" Hawkwood asked. "They have both sails and oars, and are massive floating fortresses."

"Have you ever seen one of these vessels, Hawk Pasha?"

Anthony nodded. "At a distance. But Dragut decided not to close with her on that occasion, and we rowed away."

"Did she not follow?"

"We were too fast for her."

Ali Monizindade gave a shout of laughter, and slapped his thigh. "There you have the answer. A ship like the galleass is neither galley nor galleon, neither fish nor fowl. She may well be a floating fortress ... but we do not have to engage a fortress unless we wish to. No, no, Hawk Pasha. As you well know, superiority at sea depends upon manoeuvrability. Here in the Mediterranean it is the galley which conveys that superiority, and we possess the largest fleet of galleys in the world." He winked. "As well as the best commanders."

"And suppose Philip of Spain builds a fleet of galleys greater than ours?" Uluch Ali inquired.

Ali Monizindade stroked his beard. "Are you suggesting that Philip is a greater sovereign than our Padishah?"

"By no means," Uluch Ali protested. "Yet is he a mighty monarch."

"If he builds galleys, why, so will we," Monizindade told him.

"We may possess the greatest galley fleet in the world," Hawkwood broke in, warming to the argument. "But suppose that the fleets of Spain, of the Pope, of Genoa, and of Venice were all to combine. Would they not outnumber us?"

Ali Monizindade gave another shout of laughter. "I doubt it. And in any event, suppose, Hawk Pasha that the sun and the moon were to collide, would not such an occurrence bring disaster to the earth? Spain and the Papacy combine? Did they ever combine against Khair-ed-din and your father? Or against Dragut and yourself? They hate each other too much for that. As for Genoa and Venice, they are far older enemies than Ottoman and infidel. What you suggest is an impossibility of human nature." Then he grew serious. "I may regret this as much as you. It is my dearest wish to lead the Padishah's fleet into battle against the Christians. That will never happen. But yet we will have to campaign before too long, my friends. And I will tell you against whom: our own kith and kin."

The vice-admirals tugged at their beards. They too had heard the rumours that Suleiman and his younger son, Prince Bayazid, had quarrelled, and that Bayazid had taken himself off to the mountains of Anatolia. He had not yet raised the standard of revolt, but it could not be doubted that the Sultan was displeased.

"Are not *both* the princes sons of the Russian woman?" Uluch Ali asked.

"Indeed," Ali Monizindade agreed. "More to the point, is not Bayazid a far better man than Selim?" He laid his finger on his lips. "I have spoken treason. Do not misunderstand me. Until the Padishah tells me otherwise, Selim is my future master, and I will serve him to the last breath in my body — even if he is called 'the Sot'. But I *can* regret that the better man must know the bow-string." He laid his hand on Anthony's shoulder — a gesture of great friendship, and indeed intimacy, from a Muslim. "A man can only do his duty and keep his thoughts to himself. Remember this."

It was a sobering thought, to find himself so suddenly in the very centre of the political intrigue that ever smouldered in the heart of the Ottoman world. Anthony had heard something of it, even in Algiers. His mother Felicity had always told him whatever she knew — and Dragut had told him anything the admiral had felt he

473

should know. His own father had fallen a victim to such intrigue, as had his great-grandfather. That William Hawkwood, the founder of the fortunes of the family, had survived was a tribute to his special qualities.

Anthony realised his own qualities must be no less. Do one's duty, and keep one's thoughts to oneself. Even if it entailed serving a drunkard. Because there could be no doubt that Prince Selim drank. Most of the Ottomans did. But, as wine was forbidden by the Koran, their drinking was confined to their private apartments, and practised in moderation. The Prince apparently could not get enough wine for his satisfaction. He often drank openly, and he frequently appeared in public the worse for alcohol.

That such a man would one day be Sultan was a worrying thought, yet it would happen unless Suleiman came to his senses in time.

That Bayazid, a man in whom many could see the martial virtues of his grandfather Selim, should perish because he was unable to tolerate the inadequacies of his elder brother was a tragedy.

But only duty counted. Where the Padishah pointed, Anthony knew he must go. Dragut had always insisted on that point.

Anthony Hawkwood loved the sea and the ships, he loved the feeling of power beneath his fleet, and above his head ... but at this moment, at least, he loved the thought of returning to Galata and the Hawk Palace even more. To the arms of his Venetian bride. He had never suspected that a woman could be so compelling, so demanding, and so satisfying all at once.

Almost, he could understand the hold that Roxelana had exerted over the Sultan. And Roxelana had surely lacked Barbara's beauty.

His heart pounded as he strode up the steps to the front portico, to be greeted by his bowing servants. Hawk Pasha, home from three months at sea.

He smiled at them, and then at his mother, waiting at the foot of the inner staircase, Ayesha as always at her side.

"Hawk Pasha!" She saluted him. "Welcome home."

He embraced her, and then Ayesha, but his eyes were roaming the stairs behind them.

"Barbara is well?"

"Never better. She awaits you in your apartment."

Felicity's eyes, which much of the time suggested a pool of shallow disinterest in life, could occasionally take on unfathomable depths. They were deeper than Hawkwood had ever before seen them.

But her secret, whatever it was, could wait. Anthony took the stairs three at a time. The Venetian maids bowed and simpered and scurried away before him. He opened the bedroom door, and gazed at his wife.

Barbara had been standing by the window, looking down the hill at the harbour. Undoubtedly she had overlooked his approach. But she turned at the sound of his footsteps, and now gave a shallow curtsy.

"My lord!"

He raised her up. "It is the duty of a wife to greet her husband before all others," he said, gently reminding her of her situation.

"I know, my lord, and I pray for your forgiveness. I but wished to see you alone."

"To tell me a secret, no doubt."

He kissed her nose and her eyes, then her mouth, taking her into his arms. She was quite irresistible.

Her breath rushed against his.

"A secret, my lord. Yes, I have a secret."

He held her away from him, began unlacing her bodice. Three months had been too long.

"Tell me this secret."

Barbara inhaled, deeply. "I am to have a child."

His hands fell away. "Are you certain?"

"Yes. So is your mother."

He held her shoulders, guided her to the divan, sat there beside her. The half-unlaced bodice flopped open to reveal her marvellous white breasts. She finished the unlacing herself.

"Can I bed you?" he asked.

She laughed. "Of course you may, if you wish to. It will harm neither me nor the babe."

"Oh, my darling girl!"

They rolled together on the cushions, shedding their clothing as it became necessary.

"Three months!" he shouted. "Three months."

Then, his passion spent, he lay still, and gazed at the richly decorated ceiling.

"A new Hawk," he said.

"Supposing he is a boy," Barbara murmured lazily from the crook of his shoulder. And then sat up. "Supposing he is a boy, what will you name him?"

"Why, I think John would be best. It is time we had another John in our family."

"Giovanni," she said. "Why, yes, I like that. And I am greatly relieved."

"Why?"

"I had supposed you would wish to give him a Turkish name."

"Why would I do that?"

"Well ..." She looked away from him. "Will he not be brought up as a Turk?"

Anthony held her arm and pulled her back down to him. "My mother has been speaking with you."

"Should we not speak with each other — since she is *my* mother now as well?"

"Indeed you should. But there are certain subjects which interest my mother more than others. Yes, our son will be brought up as a Turk, to serve the Padishah. He will be the sixth Hawk Pasha here. Will you not be proud of him?"

Barbara hesitated for some seconds, then she sat up again, and turned her knees to face him. He could tell her heart was pounding from the colour in her cheeks, and she was having trouble with her breathing.

"I would be prouder were he to serve a Christian monarch," she said. And then she caught her breath entirely, at her temerity.

Anthony grinned at her, and reached up to ruffle her magnificent hair. "Do not be afraid of me, Barbara. Never be afraid of me. I respect your opinions, and will always do so. But you must allow me to know what is best for our family. Our son will serve the greatest monarch on earth, as do I. No man can aspire higher than that."

"Then you care nothing for the hereafter?"

"It is our lives on earth that matter, my darling. There is a God. But the Muslims believe in Him equally with ourselves. He judges us by our deeds, not by our beliefs."

"That is heathen thinking," she protested. "It is faith that matters, not deeds."

He drew her down to be kissed. "Let us agree to differ," he said.

"At least, then, you may be as heathen as you choose in my arms, without fear of condemnation."

Her body was stiff.

"I had not suspected you to be a blasphemer."

"Barbara," he said quietly, "I will not discuss this matter further with you. We would lose our tempers. Do you wish that?"

She gazed at him for several seconds, then lay back beside him. "No," she said. "I do not wish that to happen."

But she had fired the opening shots in what she was determined would be her private war. That was sufficient for today.

To dine privately with the Sultan was the greatest honour that could befall an Ottoman subject.

Often they were a threesome, as the Sultan enjoyed entertaining his favourite poet, Baki — the nickname given to Mahmud Abdulbaki. Ten years older than Hawkwood, Baki was the son of a muezzin and had been trained for the church, but only the year before Anthony's return to Istanbul he had written a *qasidah* or ode, and submitted it to Suleiman. The ageing Sultan had been so delighted he had immediately given the young man a place at court — and in his intimate circle, it was his delight to surround himself with youth of talent and vigour.

But this night Suleiman and Anthony were alone.

"Your father and I often dined like this," Suleiman mused. "Many years ago. When we were young men." He was silent for a while as he brooded on what might have been — and what had been. Then he raised his head. "We would discuss great affairs. As I would discuss great affairs with you, Hawk Pasha."

Anthony swallowed a sweetmeat, and braced himself, for he knew not what. Previously throughout the meal the talk had been about light nothings, court gossip, campaigns by sea and land.

"But first," Suleiman said, "I am to congratulate you?"

"You have heard of my fortune, O Padishah?"

It never ceased to amaze Anthony how, although what went on in a man's harem was supposed to be private to him alone, it was invariably known to the entire city — if it was worth knowing. The eunuchs saw to that.

Suleiman gave one of his grim smiles. "I endeavour to hear everything of importance in my realm, Hawk Pasha. You are to

477

have a son to perpetuate your name and your fame."

Anthony bowed his head. "If it *is* a boy, O Padishah."

"If it is not, why then, you will seek another. And if your wife fails you, why, you will seek another there, too. Does the Venetian still please you?"

"In every way, O Padishah."

"Then are you blessed. I envy you. And yet ... you are about to father a son. Have you any concept of the difficulties that may lie ahead?"

"I have heard that some fathers quarrel with their sons, O Padishah," Anthony said cautiously.

"Ha," Suleiman commented, "I have had many sons. Most of them by concubines too lowly to be considered. Only three were by the women I called my wives. One proved false." Another brood. "Or he was proved false by others. I know now that he was innocent of any plots against me, but I cannot recall him. So now I have but two. And they are preparing to fight one another — in the expectation that I am about to die."

Anthony had no idea what to say as the Sultan paused again. Certainly Suleiman looked far older than the sixty-four years of his age.

"This cannot be," Suleiman said. "It would be a catastrophe even now. Were I to die and the empire to split into civil war, it would mean the end of the Ottomans. This I must prevent ... this I will prevent." He looked at Anthony. "The Prince Selim is my eldest surviving son. He is my heir. Will you serve him as loyally as you serve me?"

"I will, O Padishah," Anthony answered without hesitation — because he had known that at some stage such a question had to be asked. How he wished he could persuade the Sultan otherwise, but he dared not.

"Yes," Suleiman said. "I had no doubt of it. But this means that my younger son must be destroyed. Far better that I do it now, quickly and cleanly, than leave it for Selim after my death. It is a father's duty to preserve his eldest son. It is a Sultan's duty to preserve his people from the horrors of civil war. I am telling you these things, Hawk Pasha, because, like your father and your illustrious ancestors, you are loyal to the Sultanate and to nothing else. This I treasure. Ali Monizindade Pasha is a friend of Prince Bayazid's. I do not doubt his loyalty, yet I would prefer not to have

to put that to the test. You understand that I am speaking in the
closest confidence."

"I understand, O Padishah," Anthony said.

"Prince Bayazid has retired to Anatolia," Suleiman told him.
"There, I am informed he raises levies against me, declaring that he
seeks only to protect me from the intrigues of his brother. I am told
men are flocking to his standard. Next spring we will campaign
against him. The Grand Vizier will command the army, and you
will command a squadron of the fleet, independently. From this
moment I promote you rear-admiral. Ali will be pleased at this; his
reports to me on your prowess during the past months have been
very favourable.

"You will carry several divisions of troops, and you will sail
along the south coast of Anatolia, and put them ashore where
Sokullu will determine, behind Bayazid's army. Thus his people
will be caught between two forces: the Vizier's marching from the
Bosphorus, and yours behind them in Anatolia. Is this understood?"

"Yes, O Padishah."

"You will meet with little opposition at sea," Suleiman added. "It
is possible to raise an army, however poorly disciplined, fairly
quickly. But it is not possible to create a fleet quickly."

"That is true."

"This will be your first independent command, Hawk Pasha. Do
not fail me — or your ancestors."

"I will not fail you, O Padishah." Hawkwood drew a long breath.
"And after the Prince has been defeated?"

"I do not wish to look upon his face," Suleiman said sadly. "Or
those of his sons, whatever their ages. I wish only to know that the
brood is dead."

Was it really possible that the greatest of the Ottomans could be
afraid to look upon the face of the son he had just condemned to
death?

Hawkwood recalled what he had been told of the death of his
own father — or, indeed, of the death of Ibrahim Pasha, another
old boyhood friend of the Sultan's. That murder had at least been
carried out in Suleiman's presence; but the Sultan had looked
away, and had relied upon Harry Hawkwood and Khair-ed-din
Barbarossa to make sure there was no retaliation.

Yet was he the greatest of the sultans: this fact had to be accepted.

And it would be his own first independent command, Anthony brooded. *Do not fail me*, Suleiman had warned. I shall not fail you, Anthony thought. You are my sovereign lord.

But the campaign was not to begin until the spring, and until then the knowledge of it would be restricted to three men.

"I am, of course, in constant negotiation with Prince Bayazid," Mahomet Sokullu told Anthony, as they dined subsequently, also tête-à-tête. "I implore him to do nothing rash — only return to Istanbul and bow his head before his father."

"Will he do that?" Hawkwood asked.

"I am sure he has more sense."

"You mean he is still condemned to death, even if he now surrenders."

"That is so." Sokullu glanced at him. "If you have no stomach for this command, you had best say so now."

"I will command," Anthony assured him. "What of Prince Selim? Will he take part in the campaign?"

Sokullu paused. "The Prince has no stomach for campaigns." Another quick glance.

"Yet he will be our Padishah in the course of time."

"Indeed. But that will not necessarily prove a disaster. When the Sultan is weak, there are opportunities for greatness — perhaps more than where he is very strong. You should bear that in mind, Hawk Pasha, as I am sure you do seek greatness."

Anthony merely inclined his head.

Sokullu continued. "May I make a suggestion. There is a man named Joseph Nasi. Do you know of him?"

"He is a Spanish Jew who enjoys the favour of the Padishah?"

"Exactly. One who has been forced out of Spain, as have great numbers of his countrymen, by the fanatical Catholicism of the new King, Philip. Thus he came here, as our master's religious tolerance is well known, and Nasi has become a friend of Prince Selim's. I will not discuss whether he panders to the Prince's weaknesses, but his friendship is warmly reciprocated. This Nasi is a man of much loyalty to his people; in his own way, perhaps he is as fanatical as Philip. I have heard it said that he discusses with Selim the possibility of creating a national home for the Jewish people, where they can gather from all over Europe — from all over the world, in fact, after being dispersed for fifteen hundred years.

"Such a new state could only be forged within the Ottoman empire, owing to the antagonism to Jewry of the Christian nations. This idea has been suggested to the Padishah himself, and he has granted Nasi lands in Palestine, to see what he can achieve. I may tell you in private that the Padishah is not very interested in the project, but I'm informed that Selim inclines much towards it and considers that to have a Jewish state under the aegis of the Ottoman empire could be of incalculable value. Well, the Jews certainly have the knack of accumulating wealth, which can be lucratively taxed; and because they are scattered all over Europe, they certainly have the opportunity for collecting information which is useful, and sometimes valuable.

"I am telling you this so you may understand that our prospective master is by no means lacking in intelligence and shrewdness. I believe that you and I, together, may accomplish great things over the next few years. But throughout it all we must practise the utmost loyalty to our master, whoever he may be, because that is the only way for such as we."

Hawkwood again inclined his head.

Heady thoughts for a man not yet twenty-five, but rather terrifying ones as well. He had sought advancement certainly, but only as a sailor. He understood the wind and the weather, the currents and the dangers which might beset a ship at sea. Such political intrigue was new to him.

How he wished he had a confidant with whom to discuss the situation. But he had never had a male confidant, save for Dragut ... and he had an idea that to discuss Sokullu's words with Dragut might be dangerous — even had the admiral been available.

Far better to turn his back upon such thoughts for the winter, and instead enjoy his rapid promotion. As Suleiman had promised, this earned him only congratulations from Ali Monizindade, and from Uluch Ali — even if Petau Pasha stroked his beard and muttered about upstart renegades being given preference over experienced Muslim sailors.

None of these men was in the Sultan's confidence regarding his plans for Bayazid, and if Anthony's squadron therefore had to be prepared with extra care, this seemed part of the character he was already establishing as a young commander with an ambition to make his ships the finest afloat. Ali Monizindade Pasha looked on with benevolent disinterest. Despite Ali's gloomy prognostications, the empire was at peace. The Grand Admiral had no idea that those dark prognostications were in the process of being made true.

Just after the turn of the year Barbara gave birth, and to the boy they all wanted.

From Anthony's point of view there was an added relief. As the winter had deepened, and her stomach had grown, his wife had lost her sunny good temper and become fretful and querulous at the amount of time he spent away from her side. She suspected he was with his concubines, whereas he was always busy at the harbour — since his marriage he had no desire to sleep with any woman save his wife.

As Anthony had promised, the babe was named John, and he was properly christened by the Italian priest who had married his parents.

The pace of preparation for the campaign quickened, and could now no longer be concealed. As the troops summoned by Sokullu gathered outside the city and the Janissaries sharpened their swords, people whispered in the streets. But no one as yet knew which way the Sultan intended to point his army. When Suleiman required a secret to be kept, it was kept.

Yet questions continued to be asked.

"You are going to war," Barbara said. She sat on her divan, against piled cushions, surrounded by her Venetian maids. Her bodice was unfastened, and Baby John was sucking at her left nipple with great enjoyment.

"It is my profession," he reminded her gently.

She was silent for several seconds, then asked, "Will this be a long campaign?"

Once again he temporised. "It is always wisest to suppose a campaign will be long."

She sighed. "And you will be fighting against Christians?"

"No," he told her. "Not on this campaign."

She held his hands. "Then I will pray to God to protect you, and bring you back to me safe and sound."

He frowned. "Would you not have done so even had I been fighting Christians?"

"Indeed I would, my lord. But I do not know if He would have answered my prayers."

The fleet sailed in March: seventy galleys, each galley carrying a hundred Janissaries in addition to its normal crew. As the Janissaries fought on foot, there was no necessity to make space for horses, which was a great relief to Hawkwood and his captains.

Ali and Uluch, though not yet privy to the plan, were there to wish his squadron good fortune, even if he could tell that their former indulgent pleasure in his promotion was changing to some resentment at this secret command he had been given.

Even as Istanbul burst into gossip, Sokullu's corps was embarking to cross the Bosphorus. The Vizier's spies had informed him that Prince Bayazid had now established his court at Konia, the old Roman city of Iconium. Here, in the very heart of Anatolia, and sheltering beneath the immense peak of Bozkir Dag, existed a civilisation which according to legend extended back three millennia — where Perseus had used the head of Medusa the Gorgon to overawe the native population and established the ancient Greek city. More recently it had become the capital of the Seljuk Empire, after being wrested from the Byzantines in 1081. And here, at the invitation of the Seljuks, the famous Sufi, or mystic, Jalal ad-Din ar-Rumi had settled and founded his nest of Mawlawiyah, better known as the Dancing Dervishes. As the holy city of the Seljuks, it had long been a centre of opposition to Ottoman rule, and here the Prince was guaranteed of support so long as he opposed the Sultan.

Yet no one doubted that he would eventually be defeated and forced to seek refuge. Hawkwood had therefore been directed to make with his fleet for the Gulf of Alexandretta, where Anatolia adjoined Syria. For that was the direction in which both the Sultan and Sokullu were certain Bayazid would flee, following the loss of his army. There Hawkwood would land his Janissaries, and march inland to the city of Adana, which dominated the exits from the mountain passes.

Everything worked according to plan: indeed better than could have been hoped. For Hawkwood, a seaman by birth and upbringing, took his ships far out into the Aegean, certain of being able to find his landfall when he chose. Yet, by doing this, he was risking the weather — the early season being notorious for sudden storms.

And the fleet was beset by one of these within a week of leaving the shelter of the Dardanelles, but Anthony had trained his seamen so well that they rode the great waves without difficulty, even though the Janissaries were meanwhile chanting their last prayers to the Koran.

Once the storm was over, Hawkwood — having kept as careful a dead-reckoning of his position as possible — steered back towards the coast.

The Gulf of Alexandretta was an open roadstead, the city itself being some distance from the shore. But it provided shelter from all directions, and the arrival of the Sultan's fleet was totally unexpected. The beaches were secured, and Hawkwood had his Janissaries ashore before the local governor could make up his mind whether he was for the Prince or for the Padishah. Then he could only gape at the red-haired giant who accompanied the soldiers.

Anthony would have liked to do some exploring, for he knew that more than one of his ancestors had passed this way to wage campaigns in the mountains of the Taurus and Armenia. But this was the limit of his advance into Anatolia. His Janissaries quickly convinced the garrison that their best interest lay in maintaining loyalty to the Sultan, and although the weather remained fine, Hawkwood's main responsibility lay in ensuring that the fleet came to no harm. While he waited for news.

News was not long in coming; a messenger rode in from Prince Bayazid to inform the governor that the Vizier's army was marching upon him, and that he intended to give battle. He besought the governor to attend him with every man he could spare.

The governor, Makdil Pasha, immediately brought the letter to Hawkwood.

"You will ignore this," Anthony told him.

Makdil bowed, and went away.

Several weeks passed before there came another messenger. But this one needed no response. He was the first of a regiment of fleeing sipahis bringing news of the Prince's utter defeat at the hands of the Vizier. The Prince was certainly close behind, so Hawkwood gave orders that these sipahis were to be allowed through. He did not want to prompt Bayazid to turn back into the mountains of the central plateau. But how he hoped that the Prince would meanwhile be overtaken by Sokullu's Janissaries.

Three days later a party of horsemen made their way along the road from the mountains. Anthony had instructed his commanders to keep their men concealed as best possible, and the horsemen rode right through the loyalist ranks before being surrounded and forced to surrender.

Anthony was in the city of Adana when news was brought to him that Prince Bayazid and his two sons were now his prisoners.

Makdil Pasha was with him. "What will you do?" he asked.

"What I must do," Anthony told him.

Makdil pulled his beard. "The Sultan is an old man," he said at last. "And from what I have heard of Prince Selim, and what I know of this Prince Bayazid, there can be no doubt who would make the better successor. Now," he went on, "I have no doubt spoken treason, and you will have me impaled."

Anthony smiled, albeit sadly. "You have spoken the truth, old man. I would condemn no man for that. But, then, you would not condemn any man for doing his duty. And I must do mine."

The governor bowed his head.

Makdil himself brought the royal captives before Hawkwood. In view of his earlier temporising, he had clearly determined to prove his loyalty to the Sultan beyond contradiction, and had bound them tightly and obviously treated them with some contempt.

But the Prince's spirit seemed unbroken. Bayazid was taller than his brother, and handsome. He stood before Hawk Pasha with his head held high. His two sons, boys of ten and eleven, stood behind him. They were clearly very frightened.

"I am the son of the Sultan," Bayazid declared. "How can you dare to have me bound like a common malefactor?"

"I do what I must, my lord," Anthony replied. "Believe me, what I have to do grieves me, but my orders come from your father himself."

Bayazid stared at him, his brows drawing together in an imperious frown. "What orders?"

He would have made a splendid sultan, Anthony thought. And I am not cut out to be a murderer. But such is my fate.

He made a sign, and Makdil beckoned forward the two Janissaries, the bowstring ready in their hands.

Bayazid's frown deepened, though his cheeks paled. "What is my crime?"

"Rebellion in arms against the Sultan."

"The Sultan! You speak of the man who murdered your own father, Hawk Pasha. Will you now commit murder for him?"

"He is my Padishah," Anthony told him. "As he was yours — but you chose to forget this. Will you submit, my lord Prince, or must I summon more men?"

"Submit," Bayazid said. "What of my sons?"

Anthony sighed. "They, too, my lord Prince."

Bayazid's arms strained against his bonds for a moment, then relaxed. "Yes," he said, "I will submit. And may Allah have mercy on your soul."

A minute later all three were dead.

"Hawk Pasha!" Mahomet Sokullu embraced his admiral. "Was that not the easiest of campaigns?" The Vizier and the pursuing sipahis had soon reached Adana.

"My men scarce fired a shot in anger," Hawkwood acknowledged.

"And you have something for me, I understand."

Anthony indicated a square box which waited on the porch of the beylerbey's palace.

Sokullu raised the lid and looked inside.

"Most satisfactory," he said. "And I have already impaled all the rebel captains. The Padishah will be pleased." He gazed at Anthony. "But you do not look content, Hawk Pasha?"

"It is difficult to feel happy about murder," Anthony said.

Sokullu sighed. "I see we will never make a true Turk of you, Hawk Pasha. When a man's time comes, it comes. There is no use in attempting to postpone the event, or to bewail it."

"You mean if I drew my scimitar now and told you I was going to cut off your head, you would not defend yourself because your time had come?"

Sokullu smiled. "Of course I would defend myself. I do not *know* that my time has come."

"Well, then ..."

"But if you were to succeed, Hawk Pasha, then my time *would* have come."

"It is at least a comforting philosophy."

486

"Is that not the objective of every philosophy — to comfort? But you are determined to remain unhappy about carrying out this execution?"

"Bayazid was a far better man than his brother," Anthony said sadly.

"We have had this discussion before, my friend. Yet Selim will prove a far better sultan for us. Do not forget that." He clapped Anthony on the shoulder. "Come. The women we found in Bayazid's camp are superb. Let us go ashore and you can drown your sorrows in their arms."

"And the Prince's head?"

"That I will destroy."

"Do we not have to prove his death to the Padishah?"

Sokullu shook his head. "The Padishah will prefer to know nothing, save that his son is no more. This is the second of his sons he has destroyed."

He could not get the horror of it out of his mind. Even return to the Hawk Palace and the arms of Barbara could not exorcise the memory.

She gazed at him with sad eyes.

"They will make you commit worse crimes than that," she said at last.

"Woman, if you reproach me with your told-you-so's, I will cane you," Anthony warned.

"Then go and fetch your stick," she said, "for it needs to be said. They will make you commit worse crimes than that. And what will you do when the Sultan commands you to take your fleet against Venice?"

"That will never happen. Suleiman does not make war against his allies. It is up to Venice never to make war upon us."

"Anthony, my lord ..." she held his hands. "Can you swear to me that you will never war on my people?" She was clearly truly concerned.

"Except in justifiable defence of the Ottoman realm, I will willingly swear to that," he told her.

"You would defy the Sultan?"

He smiled, and kissed her. "I will not have to. Suleiman would never require such a thing of me. He is not merely a great king, but a great man. I may regret what had to be done to Prince Bayazid, but the Sultan was right — the death of the Prince saved the empire from civil war. And that was an act of greatness."

He kissed her again. "Yes, I swear to you, I will never take part in a war of aggression against Venice."

She seemed content with that.

Yet, as the man who had executed Prince Bayazid, his reward was not only the increased favour of Suleiman himself, but the friendship of Selim.

There was much to dislike in that young man. In his indolence, his voluptuousness — he kept a harem of young boys as well as his concubines — and above all his weakness for alcohol, he was a sorry descendant of Mahomet the Conqueror, Selim the Grim, and indeed Suleiman himself. Indeed, there were not lacking those who whispered that perhaps Roxelana had not been above cuckolding the Sultan, whatever the risk she ran of an unspeakable death.

Hawkwood could not agree with them. He knew no subject who had ever laid eyes on the famous Russian concubine, but all the rumours pointed to a woman who pursued her ambitions with singular determination, and her ambitions had been to manipulate the Sultan so that her own offspring would come to dominate the empire. She would never have risked adultery.

But there were other sure signs that Selim was most certainly an Ottoman. He was highly intelligent and highly educated; when sober he could be a delightful companion. He also, from time to time, revealed that streak of ruthless cruelty which had made this family the most feared in history.

And, as Mahomet Sokullu never tired of reminding Anthony, the Prince was their future master.

Selim's close friend, Joseph Nasi, was even more interesting, and to Anthony seemed far more dangerous for the future, either personal or public. Now in his early forties, Nasi came from a wealthy Spanish family, and had learned the intricacies of banking and international commerce and finance in Antwerp while working for his cousins, the Mendes.

At that time he had been a Marrano — that is, a Spanish Christianised Jew — and had been baptised under the name of Juan Miguez. His determination to alleviate the sufferings of the Spanish Jews, when Philip II began to persecute them, had led to his expulsion as well, whereupon he had reverted entirely to Jewry, married his cousin Reyna, and fled to Istanbul.

Here his ambition and his undoubted talent had quickly earned him Suleiman's favour. The Sultan had long wished to find a replacement for the financial expertise of Ibrahim which he had so carelessly cast away, and here to hand was the man he sought. Suleiman had more sense than to attempt to make a non-Muslim Grand Vizier, but Nasi had been placed at Sokullu's right hand, and been rewarded with those vast estates in the Tiberias region of Palestine where he was slowly accumulating a colony of Jewish refugees from various European persecutions.

In all of these achievements he was to be envied and admired, in fostering the continued prosperity of the Ottoman Empire. What was disturbing was his close friendship for Selim, which many saw as an act of politics rather than the result of any true regard. For Nasi's own strictly temperate personal life was such as to make him naturally contemptuous of such a man as the Prince.

Hawkwood had no doubt at all that, like Sokullu, Nasi was looking ahead to Selim's sultanate. That he would then use this friendship to forward his own plans seemed obvious even to Sokullu. What did not seem apparent to the Vizier, however, was that Nasi might already be planning to replace him. It was amazing how every Grand Vizier apparently considered himself essential, up to the moment the bowstring was wrapped round his neck. But that was Sokullu's problem.

What made Nasi especially interesting to Hawkwood was his profound knowledge of the West, and in particular of Spain.

"I think King Philip will wish to make war upon the Ottomans," he would contend. "But it will not happen until he has eliminated all religious dissension within his own domains: I am thinking of Holland in the main. Now, England sits on the sea-route from Spain to Holland, so much will depend on the attitude of the Queen of England. She is a determined Protestant, and has rejected all of Philip's overtures, thus far. But, of course, should Philip choose to destroy England, it will be a simple matter. The English have no army, and no navy." He glanced at Hawkwood. "Does that concern you?"

"I am a Turk, not an Englishman," Anthony reminded him.

"You have more English than Turkish blood in your veins," Nasi argued. "In fact, there is no Turkish blood in your veins at all, merely English, French, Italian and Greek."

"A man is what he is," Anthony insisted, "not what his ancestors were."

He believed what he said, because he could conceive of no other existence for himself which would allow him so much prosperity, and so much happiness.

Following Bayazid's execution, there were several years of peace within the Ottoman realm. The fleet regularly exercised in the Aegean and Ionian Seas, sometimes observed but never challenged by Papal or Genoese galleys. The admirals were able to spend much of their time at home, and for all her uncertainty at the role into which he had let himself be constrained, Barbara loved him too much to nag. William Hawkwood was born in 1562, and young Henry in 1563.

"Now you must practise contraception," Anthony advised her.

"Do you not wish for more sons?"

"Three is enough."

"Well, then ... a daughter? I should like to have a daughter."

"And I should not like to have you grow old before your time. You are twenty-one years old. I wish you to remain as you are for ever."

She smiled, and kissed him. "And your wish is my command, my lord. I shall see what can be done. Ayesha will know."

In these peaceful years, Anthony also found time to pursue another task. For, tucked away in an obscure inlet in the Golden Horn, timbers rotting and mast long decayed, he found the remains of a very unusual little ship which the locals told him had once belonged to his father.

Indeed, he had found the ship in which Harry Hawkwood had made his famous raid into the Atlantic ... and captured his mother, Felicity.

Anthony delightedly set his shipwrights to work, virtually dissecting the hull to find out everything about her design. Then he had a new ship built. Full-decked, single-masted, with a huge boom to control her lateen sail, she would carry a crew of six men besides himself, but he added a refinement Harry Hawkwood had never considered — a cabin aft, for it was his ambition to have Barbara share his pleasure with him.

He called the yacht the *Hawk*.

His wife was somewhat reluctant to take up sailing at first, but soon she began to enjoy it. So they ventured farther and farther into Marmara, often spending up to a week away from the city at a time. Anthony came to look upon these days the happiest of his life.

But he remained a vice-admiral of the Turkish fleet, and in the spring of 1564 Suleiman determined to crown his reign by making a third attempt on Vienna.

The campaign was elaborately planned. In May 1565 a fleet of transports sailed from Constantinople to join the western Mediterranean fleet now commanded by Piale Pasha — for Dragut had retired to spend his declining years in Algiers. Piale and Mustafa Pasha — who would command the troops — sailed for Malta, once again, to attempt to dislodge the Knights of St John.

Suleiman had convinced himself that the Western powers would have to send every ship and every man they possessed, to the relief of the Knights. Surprisingly, this did not happen. The Knights — under their remarkable general, Grand Master Jean de la Valette — were left to themselves, and quickly revealed themselves, as always, ready to fight to the death.

But yet was Christendom distracted. And at last Spain went to the aid of the hard-pressed Knights, sending a combined fleet and army commanded by Garcia de Toledo. In September the Turks would raise the siege, having lost more than twenty thousand of their men. But that same spring, while the siege still raged, Suleiman put the second half of his plan into operation.

The armies were marshalled, and the fleet. Anthony was given command of the flotilla which would ascend the Danube, repeating the manoeuvre William Hawkwood had carried out nearly forty years before.

The river ships were necessarily smaller than the sea-going galleys, and they had to be assembled in the estuary of the great river, which necessitated coasting them up the Black Sea. This took a great deal of time, nor was Anthony able to return to Istanbul for the winter, as there remained a great deal of refitting to do.

Throughout the following spring and summer, that of 1566, the flotilla laboriously made its way up the river. The Danube was by now entirely controlled by the Turks, yet there were vast stretches which were far removed from any sign of civilisation, and inhabited by ferocious mountain men who were not above attacking foraging parties.

Hawkwood was very happy, in July, to come into the shelter of Belgrade, where the army had wintered.

Here was Suleiman himself, but Anthony was shocked when he was ushered into the presence of the Sultan. Now in his seventy-second year, the most famous of the Ottomans was clearly too old for campaigning. Not even the liberal applications of rouge could hide the sunken pallor of his cheeks, and his breath came in great gasps.

"Oh, Padishah," Hawkwood said, "should you not be in the warmth of the Seraglio rather than in these damp and dismal climes? Your people need you even more than they desire a victory against the Austrians."

Suleiman smiled, a slow loosening of the facial muscles. "They will have to do without the former soon enough, Hawk Pasha. Would you have a Sultan who did not lead his armies into war?"

Anthony could not stop himself giving a quick glance left and right. Mahomet Solkullu waited, just out of earshot. But there was no sign of Prince Selim.

Suleiman knew what he was thinking. "The Prince commands in Istanbul," he said, "until my return."

"A wise move, O Padishah," Anthony said.

"Your father was never a sycophant," Suleiman admonished, mildly. "It will be your task, Hawk Pasha, to advise my son wisely, when I am gone. But it is my task," he said, with sudden fierceness, "to chastise these stubborn Hungarians who persist in revolting against my rule. This is our first intention, Hawk Pasha. The city of Szigetvar. I will raze it to the ground as a warning to the rest."

it was before the walls of Szigetvar, on the night of 5 September 1566, that Suleiman the Magnificent died.

19

THE TREACHERY

The news brought to the fleet — waiting to resume its advance up the Danube — conveyed nothing of what had happened. The messenger merely delivered a command from Grand Vizier Sokullu for Admiral Hawk Pasha to attend the Sultan's headquarters with the greatest possible haste.

Anthony knew immediately what had happened, but disclosed nothing of his fears to his aides. Accompanied only by his servant Kalil, he mounted for the ride to the beleaguered fortress.

Here he found the city a tumble of ruination, in which there must very recently have been a major catastrophe — smoke still hung above the shattered houses, and there was scarcely any sign of life. The whole area was, indeed, permeated with the stench of death. Yet the Turkish army was still encamped about the walls. Many of them binding their wounds, the Janissaries stared at Hawkwood as he galloped up, but there was no sense of concern or urgency in the Ottoman ranks.

Then I am mistaken, Anthony thought with considerable relief — throughout the ride from the river his mind had been filled with tumbling thought at how the Empire would take the news of the Sultan's death.

Something had happened, however. Suleiman's tent was surrounded by guards, every man of whom, as Hawkwood recognised, belonged to Sokullu's personal retinue. The Sultan's own men were nowhere to be seen.

My God, he thought, the fool has tried a coup d'état!

He was subjected to a stern scrutiny before being admitted to the gold and crimson tent — and there he found the Vizier waiting for him.

"Mahomet!" he cried. "What have you done?"

"Whatever was needed," Sokullu assured him. "Come."

Before Hawkwood could expostulate further, he was led into the inner chamber of the tent, where there waited only two deaf-mute eunuchs ... and the Sultan.

Suleiman sat cross-legged on his prayer mat, his back wedged against the cushions. His right hand rested on his knee, his left dangled between his thighs. He stared at Hawkwood with a peculiar intentness.

Anthony immediately bowed. "Padishah," he said, "I came at once."

There was no response, and Anthony slowly raised his head, to discover Sokullu now standing beside the Sultan and smiling at him.

"If I can fool you, Hawk Pasha, I can fool the world," he said.

Anthony stared at the seated figure. "My God!" he muttered.

"What I have done was by the Padishah's own command," the Vizier continued "We are several hundred miles from Istanbul, and from Prince Selim. It is a long journey. Were it to be undertaken with the body of a dead Sultan, who can say what might transpire before our new master could assume power? And at least we have gained the victory, even if it has been a barren one."

Hawkwood frowned at him. "What happened?"

"We had battered the walls of the city all but flat, and were preparing our final assault, when Count Zrinyi, who commanded the garrison, anticipated us. He led all his people, even his women, in an assault on our lines. It was the most remarkable thing I ever saw."

"He got through?"

Sokullu's smile was grim. "No, we killed them all. But the rascal had a surprise for us. My men promptly charged into the city, seeking loot and slaves. But Zrinyi had set a fuse to his powder magazine, and it exploded. Several hundred of my people were killed. Now, once we retreat, the Hungarians will shout a victory. But we will know better — and we will come again when we have settled matters at home."

Anthony continued to stare at the dead man.

"When did this happen?"

"Three nights ago. Before Zrinyi's suicide bid. The Padishah virtually died in his sleep. He woke briefly, and cried out, then died. His heart merely stopped. Well, he had lived a long time."

"And you think you can return to Istanbul with a dead man at the head of his army?"

Sokullu shrugged. "Why not? I had the embalmers inside the tent within an hour."

"And do you not suppose they will tell what has happened?"

Sokullu gave another grin. "Only to the devil, Hawk Pasha. Already they are on their way to his fiery portals."

Anthony licked his lips. "Yet you have sought to confide in me, unnecessarily."

"Oh, necessarily, Anthony. You have been as close to Suleiman as any man recently. If anyone could have told from a reasonable distance that he was dead, that man would be you. Besides, are we not partners? Have we not already considered that there is much to be accomplished, once Suleiman was dead?"

Anthony raised his head to gaze at him. "I will entertain no treason."

"And I have just spoken it. Do you then condemn me?"

Anthony shook his head. "No, Mahomet. The temptation is very great. I must assume that you have done right, and that for the good of the Empire it is best we seem to return to Istanbul with a living Padishah. But once we get there, we serve Prince Selim."

Sokullu regarded him for several seconds, then gave another shrug.

"As we are partners in life, Anthony, I must bow to your wishes. Permit me, however, to pray to Allah that neither of us lives to regret your loyalty."

It was always difficult to know, with Sokullu, just what he had in mind. Anthony supposed the Vizier was probably the most devious man he had ever known, particularly in contrast to the straightforwardness of his previous mentor, Dragut.

Dragut! he thought. The famous admiral should be informed immediately of what had happened — he might well be needed.

Sokullu played his part immaculately. "It is late in the year," he told the pashas. "Soon the winter rains will be upon us, and this plain will become a sea of mud. Perhaps you do not remember the retreat from Vienna in 1532. My father was there, and Hawk Pasha's grandfather commanded the army."

"My grandfather died before I was born," Anthony said. "But my father has told me of the horrors of that retreat."

Which was a lie: he had never been old enough to discuss campaigning with his father. But the lie was in a good cause, and

495

the pashas acquiesced in the Vizier's command, especially when told that it had been issued by the Sultan himself.

"The Padishah has developed a fever," he explained, "thus he cannot address you himself. And that is another reason for leaving this pestilential place."

The Janissaries grumbled, nevertheless. It was not their way to leave a battlefield after gaining a victory, except to advance further. But their senior officers, too, could remember the difficulties of withdrawing from in front of Vienna.

Thus the homeward march began. It would necessarily take several months.

"I must command the flotilla," Hawkwood said.

Sokullu shook his head. "Send them orders to withdraw to sea and make their way to Istanbul. It were best for you to remain here, on dry land. One of us must ride ahead of the army and tell the Sultan what has happened — in great secrecy, of course. That had best be me, I suppose."

They gazed at each other.

"That would place me in an invidious position, Mahomet," Hawkwood said. "I have neither the rank nor the military experience to command the whole army. What would I do if one of the pashas insisted on an interview with the Padishah?"

Sokullu stroked his beard. "And, besides, you do not trust me?" he remarked.

"I must trust you," Anthony said, "as we are now yoked together. I but seek the best for us both."

Sokullu gave a grin. "And I trust you, Hawk Pasha, so you will ride ahead and break the news to Selim. Remember that both of our lives, and fortunes, ride with you."

And not merely our lives and fortunes, Anthony thought as, with Kalil and a small escort, he rode ahead of the army: there was too much of value waiting for him at the Hawk Palace.

They crossed the Danube at Belgrade, where this famous admiral and known protégé of the old Sultan was warmly greeted by the beylerbey, anxious for news of the campaign.

"The Padishah seeks winter quarters for the army," Hawkwood told the governor. "Thus my haste."

"He is welcome to quarter the army in Belgrade," the beylerbey replied somewhat uneasily; he had to make the offer, but he knew that six months of feeding a hundred thousand hungry men would ruin his province.

"Be sure that your invitation will be conveyed to the Padishah," Hawkhood said. "But there are other matters I must attend to."

He hurried on, from Belgrade to Sofia, and from Sofia to Adrianople, always with the same story. Only a week after leaving Adrianople he was in Istanbul, and bowing before Prince Selim.

"I bring a message from the Sultan, for your ears alone, my lord Prince."

Selim glanced at Nasi who, as usual, stood beside his divan.

"For your ears alone, my lord Prince," Anthony repeated.

This was a dangerous part of his mission. As Suleiman was already dead, he was technically committing treason in addressing Selim as "Prince" instead of "Padishah". But he had no choice in front of others — for Selim had to be the first to know that his father was dead. A sensible man would understand these things, but he did not know how sensible Selim was. And sensible or not, he would always later have an excuse to execute the man who had so addressed him.

Selim waved his hand. "Withdraw," he said to those around him. "Remain within the chamber at a distance."

The guards and pashas surrounding the divan retreated against the walls. Nasi hesitated, then bowed and retired.

"One would almost suppose you feared me to be an assassin, O Padishah," Anthony said, in hardly more than a whisper.

Selim frowned. "What did you say, Hawk Pasha?"

Anthony bowed his head. "Suleiman the Lawgiver is dead, O Padishah."

Selim licked his lips, slowly and thoughtfully. But also fearfully, Hawkwood thought.

"Mahomet Sokullu determined that the news should be kept from the world until you were informed, O Padishah," Anthony said. "The Sultan has been embalmed, and rides at the head of his troops. They have been told he is suffering from a fever."

Another quick circle of the tongue. "How many know of this?"

Anthony drew a long breath. "Only the Vizier and myself, and the eunuchs who attend the corpse."

Selim considered. "How long will it be before the body of my father reaches Istanbul?"

"Another six weeks, at the least, O Padishah."

"Six weeks," Selim mused. "And will *you* keep this secret for six weeks, Hawk Pasha?"

"It must be my duty, O Padishah."

"Yes," Selim agreed. "The Vizier has done well in taking this decision. I am well pleased. Now go home to your wife ... and keep our secret."

Selim, in fact, seemed more dazed than elated by the news that he was now the supreme ruler of the Ottoman world; he was by nature a cautious man. Anthony suspected that he soon confided what had happened to Nasi, but the Jew also knew how to keep a secret; and nothing in Istanbul changed until the return of the army with the body of Suleiman.

His mother and Barbara were overjoyed to have Anthony back safe and sound — the boys were hardly old enough yet to appreciate his presence. But the women were naturally curious as to the reason for his unexpectedly early return, and were somewhat put out by his refusal to confide in them. Indeed Barbara became quite annoyed that he did not seem ready to trust her.

Thanks to Sokullu's prompt action, the transfer of authority from Suleiman to Selim was the most tranquil in Ottoman history. There was no trace of revolt or dissatisfaction in any part of the Empire, however the pashas might grieve the death of their great master. Even the Janissaries appeared to be happy to be commanded by the younger man.

"But they will still need to be commanded, O Padishah," Sokullu told his new master. "They mutter that the fall of Szigetvar opened all of Hungary to their arms. They wish to return and march before the walls of Vienna. The whole army and the navy wish to avenge the repulse from Malta."

"They will have to be patient," Selim replied. "But it is my intention to avenge our defeats as soon as possible. And you too, Hawk Pasha, will have ever greater opportunities for glory. For are you both not my most trusted pashas?"

Anthony wished he could be certain there was no trace of sarcasm in the Sultan's voice.

So the affairs of the Empire now ran smoothly, aided by the marriage of Mahomet Sokullu to one of Selim's daughters. As son-in-law to the Sultan, Sokullu clearly felt his position as Grand Vizier to be even more secure.

When they met again after the ceremony Sokullu was smiling his sly smile. "It was your decision that we give ourselves utterly to the Padishah," he reminded Hawkwood. "This I have done." He squeezed Anthony's arm. "But I shall not forget my friend. As I rise, so shall you."

Anthony could only marvel at the Vizier's prompt gathering of all power possible. He himself was employed at his favourite occupation, that of preparing his squadron for a naval campaign, even if he had no idea where he would be directed. The only thing to spoil this peaceful, contented period was news of the death of Dragut — of old age.

"A sad end for a famous warrior," Ali Monizindade commented. "But it means I am now the senior admiral of the Padishah's fleet."

He regarded Anthony speculatively as he spoke, for both he and Uluch Ali had been worried by the intimacy which had grown up between Suleiman and Hawk Pasha during the last years of the old Sultan's life, and which seemed to have been continued into the new reign.

The old proximity between the three admirals was gone.

"We could wish for no one better," Anthony said tactfully. But in fact he could think of no one more fitted to command the entire Ottoman fleet; Ali Monizindade had learned his seamanship under Khair-ed-din and Harry Hawkwood.

Hawkwood looked forward to fighting again when Selim at last decided to campaign; and was utterly taken aback when — four years after the Sultan's accession — he learned their chosen objective.

But then, so was everyone else.

All the commanders both on sea and land were assembled before the divan to hear the words of the Sultan. Grand Vizier Sokullu was also present, although confessing he had no idea what the Padishah had in mind. Most assumed that the assault on Europe and Malta would be resumed.

Not only Ali and Uluch and Pertau were present, but also Dragut's successor, Piale Pasha, called to Istanbul from the western Mediterranean. All the generals were present too, including Mustafa Pasha, who had failed at Malta. Disconcertingly, however, Joseph Nasi stood behind the Sultan's divan, as always — and this day he looked singularly confident as he gazed at the grizzled faces before him.

"The Ottomans have been at peace too long," Selim declared. "We are not men of peace. We are men of war."

The pashas pulled their beards and nodded their approval. It was at least a promising preamble.

"I have called you here today to give you my directives," Selim continued. "As to leading my people to war — and to victory," he added.

The pashas waited.

"But warfare must be undertaken with a worthwhile objective. You will know that I have long had in mind the foundation of a homeland for the Jews within the embrace of my empire. They are a hardworking and frugal race, who will greatly contribute to the prosperity of my realm. Alas, deciding upon the site of such a homeland has proved more difficult than expected."

"With respect, O Padishah," Sokullu ventured, "should they not be returned to Palestine, whence they originated?"

"Palestine is an arid country," Nasi objected. "I have investigated it thoroughly, my lord Vizier, and I have been unable to recommend it to the Padishah as a home for my people.'

'But you have recommended somewhere else?" Sokullu remarked.

"Indeed, and I have discovered the ideal place: the island of Cyprus."

There was total silence for several minutes.

Then Selim himself spoke, "What objections would you have to granting Cyprus to the Jewish people, Vizier? It is a large and prosperous island, where they will thrive."

"Padishah, the island of Cyprus is not yours to give. It belongs to Venice."

"Venice," Nasi sneered.

"Our oldest ally," Sokullu said. "Our only ally, O Padishah."

"An ally of little account," Selim said. "Venice has no army worthy of the name."

"But she has a formidable fleet, O Padishah," Hawkwood intervened, coming to the aid of his friend. "It is the knowledge of her alliance with Turkey which has so far restrained the Spaniards and Genoese from venturing east of the Adriatic."

"Is this fleet of theirs more powerful than mine, Hawk Pasha?"

"Indeed it is not, O Padishah, but —"

"Then it is of no account. Besides, the Venetians are getting ready to become our enemies. I have sent secret envoys to the Doge, asking for the cession of Cyprus in return for a substantial indemnity. And the Doge has refused to consider my proposal. Can I permit an upstart magistrate so to insult me? I have therefore determined on war with the Republic."

It did not seem to have occurred to Selim that he himself had insulted the Doge by making this proposal in the first place. Once again the pashas tugged at their beards.

"May I respectfully argue against this plan, O Padishah," Sokullu said. 'We have enemies enough: all Christendom save Venice herself, also Persia, and our Arab subjects grumble restlessly. Only Venice is our true and steadfast friend. To destroy that alliance in pursuit of . . ." he glanced at Nasi, "a vague and uncertain principle, would surely be a mistake."

"Will you pretend Turkey and Venice have never fought?" Nasi demanded.

"Indeed they have, Don José. But not for more than a generation now."

"Enough," Selim said. "I have made my decision. We will make war upon Venice." He glared at Sokullu.

"The Padishah's word is law," the Vizier acknowledged with a bow.

"But you have no stomach for the task?" Selim said. "Then it shall not be your task, Vizier. The army will be commanded by Mustafa Pasha."

Heads turned. There were many amongst the generals who felt that Mustafa had been fortunate to retain his head after his failure at Malta. Mustafa himself looked dumbfounded.

"The fleet will be commanded by . . ." Selim's eyes searched the admirals. He could read only disapproval in their countenances. "By Hawk Pasha."

Anthony's head came up in surprise and dismay. He counted as only the fourth amongst the Ottoman admirals. Besides, Cyprus was Venetian territory. "With respect, O Padishah," he said, "I am unfitted for such a task." Anthony drew a deep breath. "I am unfitted, O Padishah, because I am married to a Venetian."

Selim frowned at him. "Are you afraid of your wife? You will put her away, if need be. I will give you another wife."

501

"O Padishah, I honour my wife. I cannot fight against her people."

"Even at the risk of my displeasure?"

Anthony would not lower his eyes. The Hawkwoods had always dealt with fairly with the sultans, and been dealt fairly in return. But was this man a true Ottoman? Yet he had no alternative, now; he had given Barbara his word. "Even at that risk, O Padishah."

Selim stared at him for several seconds. "You are at least an honest man, Hawk Pasha. You are dismissed your commands, and will retire into private life. Piale Pasha, you will command the fleet, under the overall command of Ali Monizindade."

Piale Pasha bowed.

The Sultan continued, "Ali Pasha will establish the main fleet off the western coast of the Peloponnesus, there to block any attempt by the Western powers to attack us until after Cyprus has been reduced."

Ali Monizindade bowed his head. His eyes gleamed: this was the opportunity for which he had been waiting all his life.

"Those are my orders," Selim said.

The pashas bowed, and backed away from the presence. Nasi alone remained with the sovereign.

Out in the courtyard, the generals and admirals gathered in angry debate.

"To attack Cyprus will be to drive Venice into the arms of the Papacy and of Spain," Sokullu declared.

"The Papacy hates the Venetians more than us," Ali Monizindade objected.

"Hate is a relative term. Should Spain and the Papacy and Venice unite, with the fleet of Genoa in support, we will be faced with a most formidable coalition. Between them, the Christians could man the greatest fleet in the world."

Ali smiled. "Hardly greater than mine. And I shall defeat them. It will be the greatest feat of my career." He looked around his admirals. "Of all our careers." He gazed at Anthony. "You are a fool, Hawk Pasha," he said, "so to incur the Padishah's displeasure. How may a man put his domestic affairs before his duty to his master?"

"Perhaps we have a different concept of duty," Anthony replied.

The two men gazed at each other in silence for several seconds while the pashas waited.

Then Ali smiled again. "Perhaps. I am sorry to lose you, Hawk, just as it seems the battle for which we have waited so long may now be fought."

"No battle will be fought," Piale Pasha declared. "Cyprus is held by less than ten thousand men. It has only two fortresses, Nicosia and Famagusta. The island will be mine in a fortnight, and the Venetians will be happy to sue for peace."

Hawkwood could only pray that he was right. However he knew that Ali had been certainly right. The Ottoman ethic — to which he had been brought up so strictly by Dragut — was that service to the Sultan came before any other consideration. He had now broken that tradition which had been so important in his family. And all for the sake of a woman. That was something the pashas would never be able to understand.

It was also for the sake of his word.

It was not something his mother Felicity understood. Even if she had always dreamed of having her son abandon the Turks and return to the West, she had never been able to conceive of anything more than a stealthy departure in the middle of the night, with the Sultan's wrath close behind. For him to stand before the most powerful man on earth and refuse to do his bidding had not entered her thinking at all.

Ayesha was even more thunderstruck. "What will become of us?" she wailed.

"Why, nothing," Anthony told them, with more confidence than he actually felt. "The Padishah is displeased at the moment, but he will soon get over his anger. He knows that I am perhaps his best naval commander, and also a most loyal subject. We must just be patient." At least there were no financial problems; Anthony's earlier successes with Dragut had made him a rich man.

Barbara was overwhelmed when she learned the reason for his defiance of the Sultan.

"My lord," she said, "how can I thank you?"

"By not attempting to. My action will not save Cyprus."

It was galling to have to stand idly on the Galata shore and watch the fleet being prepared for sea. Equally it was distressing to learn that, following official declaration of war in January 1570, the elder

503

Cornaros had been imprisoned.

Anthony had to be concerned over the safety of Barbara herself. Sokullu assured him that his parents-in-law were in no danger and were being well treated. Barbara nonetheless remained very upset, the more so when she was refused permission to visit her mother and father.

However, it really did appear as if it would be a short war, albeit bloody. The Turkish fleet sailed at the beginning of July, and while a squadron masked the fortress seaport of Famagusta on the south-east side of the island, the main armament made for Morphou Bay on the north side. Here the army was put ashore, and Mustafa marched on Nicosia, the chief city in the island, situated on rising ground some distance from the sea.

There were some delays and the assault did not get under way until the beginning of September, but when it was begun it was irresistible. There were no Knights of St John, no Jean de la Valette, no Zrinyi to stiffen the backbones of the Venetian defenders and their Cypriot levies. Nicosia fell on 9 September, the entire garrison being put to the sword.

There was great rejoicing in Istanbul. Barbara put on the black clothes of mourning.

"It is a great relief to me, I can tell you," Sokullu confessed to Anthony. "The fleet has been immediately moved round to blockade Famagusta, while the army marches overland to assault that city. The sooner this whole business is out of the way, the better."

"Is there much reaction from the West?" Hawkwood inquired.

"Indeed there is — entirely as we expected. Venice has appealed to the Pope for aid, and he has agreed to an alliance. More, he has appealed to Philip of Spain, and has received a favourable response. Have you heard of Don Juan of Austria?"

Anthony frowned. "Is he not Philip's half-brother?"

"That is correct. He is the son of the Emperor Charles V and one of his mistresses, a German lady named Barbara Blomberg. Well, this Don Juan is to be put in command of an allied fleet, including squadrons from Spain, the Papacy, Genoa and Venice. Genoa and Venice fighting in harness! That is something that has never happened in history before. It has taken our Sultan to achieve the impossible."

"But this Don Juan can hardly be more than a boy," Anthony protested.

"He is twenty-three years old," Sokullu said.

"Then he can hardly have the experience to defeat Ali Monizin-dade, even with the greater fleet."

"You think so? Alexander the Great was no older when he defeated the Persians. Mahomet the Conqueror was younger when he took Constantinople. Do not be deceived by age, Hawk Pasha ... or lack of it. This Don Juan has a most formidable reputation as a soldier. Our best hope lies in the fact that this fleet is not yet assembled — and that there are still a great many mutual suspicions to be overcome on the Christian side. I can tell you that the Venetians have already sent an envoy secretly to Istanbul, seeking peace terms; they would pay a huge indemnity were they to be left in possession of Cyprus. The Padishah has turned them down, of course, but it shows the way their thinking is going. They would prefer to be rid of the war, which so interferes with their trade, than be avenged upon us. Should we be able to take Famagusta rapidly, and put an end to the campaign, I suspect the Venetians would accept the situation and make peace on any terms. Then this coalition will doubtless dissolve before it ever comes to a fight."

"Famagusta will be defended to the last man," Anthony told him, "both because Brigadino will know that a fleet is gathering for his succour, and because he will also know that the Nicosia garrison was massacred. He will never surrender."

"Then the place must fall to assault," Sokullu growled. "And soon."

But Marcantonio Brigadino, the Venetian commander, although he had only five and a half thousand men, was determined to fight to the last, as Hawkwood had prophesied.

In this he was helped by the weather, which soon deteriorated to the extent where any question of assault must clearly wait until the following spring. Mustafa Pasha therefore went into winter quarters, but the winds kept blowing the Turkish fleet off station, forcing it to shelter, and so allowing Venetian carracks to reach the port and replenish its supplies. Nor could it be doubted that Brigadino was sparing no efforts to improve his defences in preparation for the coming assault.

Now news drifted into Istanbul that an allied fleet was actually beginning to assemble in Messina. Sokullu began to pull at his beard.

"Oh, to see them smashed," Barbara whispered, staring down at the Golden Horn from the windows of her bedchamber. "Oh, to see the Christian fleet coming up the Bosphorus."

"That will never happen," Anthony told her. "And if it did, I should have to go out and fight them, and no doubt die while doing so. Besides, you are speaking treason."

Everyone in Istanbul pinned hopes on a quick and decisive victory in the spring. And as soon as the weather improved sufficiently, Mustafa Pasha launched his troops against the walls of Famagusta. He outnumbered the defenders by more than ten to one, and he possessed a great deal of artillery, yet he still could not batter his way through the walls and the ditches, and in Brigadino the Venetians at last had a commander worthy of the name.

Spring drifted into summer, and still the Venetians fought, and still news kept arriving of the increasing number of Christian warships assembling in the Straits of Messina and the harbours to the south.

It was early in July when Hawkwood received a summons to the Seraglio, where he was ushered into the presence of the Sultan, who was attended by Nasi and Sokullu,

"Well, Hawk Pasha," Selim said. This day he had already been drinking heavily; his eyes were bloodshot and his hands trembled. "Have you enjoyed your holiday?"

"I had far sooner serve you, O Padishah, if I can do so with honour."

"Ha," Selim commented. "Then you shall. This business in Cyprus must be ended quickly, and by whatever means can come to hand. Certainly before this Christian fleet can make a nuisance of itself. You will leave for Cyprus within the week."

"Padishah ..."

"I am well aware of your reluctance to break your word and fight against your wife's people," Selim said. "I am sending you to end this war, not to fight it. Mustafa Pasha informs me that he has appealed to this Brigadino to surrender with all the honours of war, and that the man has refused to entertain such a suggestion, claiming that he cannot trust a Turkish pasha to keep his word.

"Now, Hawk Pasha, Mahomet Sokullu has reminded me that your great-uncle negotiated the surrender of the fortress of Rhodes, by offering an honourable safe-conduct to the defenders."

"It is true, O Padishah." Hawkwood's heartbeat quickened.

"And if you were to go to Cyprus and offer the same terms to Brigadino, would he not accept?"

"He might, O Padishah. But he would have to be certain of my authority."

"He will be. I will grant you plenipotentiary powers to obtain the surrender of Famagusta. Use whatever means you wish. Mustafa Pasha and Piele Pasha will be informed that they are your subordinates until the place is ours. Is that sufficient?"

"It is sufficient," Anthony assured him. "I will leave within the week."

Sokullu accompanied him outside. "Are you sure you can accomplish this?" the Vizier inquired.

"I would think so."

"You must do more than think, Hawk Pasha. The Sultan remains displeased with you. I can tell you now that he has several times considered sending you a bowstring, for your defiance of him. I alone have protected you. It was my idea that your family's reputation for honour could be used in our present situation. Should you fail to obtain Brigadino's surrender, then it were best you never returned to Istanbul."

"As you are telling me this, you must still be my friend," Hawkwood remarked.

"I have always been your friend, Anthony. I will always be your friend."

"Then will you make it possible for me to take my wife and children, my mother and my old nurse, with me to Cyprus?"

Sokullu hesitated, then shook his head. "I cannot do that, Anthony, not even for you. It would mean my own ruin. It would be treason, as it would make it easy for you to desert the Padishah without making an attempt to bring Brigadino to terms."

"So my family is to be held hostage for my success."

Sokullu shrugged. "A man can always find another family."

"Not this man."

Sokullu clasped his arm. "Then succeed, Hawk Pasha. Succeed — and be restored to favour."

"Restored to favour," Felicity said. "Oh, happy day."

Barbara, predictably, was crushed. "You go to bring about the ruin of my country," she said sadly.

"I go to end the war," Anthony told her, "which, if it continues, will involve the deaths of a great many of your people. Can you reproach me for that?"

She sighed. "No, my lord. I must wish you success. And a safe and speedy return."

He kissed her, embraced his sons, and went down to the waiting galley.

It took four days to row south across the sparkling Aegean, round the island of Crete, and thence south-eastward to the mountains of Cyprus, so close to the coast of Turkey that it really was surprising no sultan had already claimed it. But great warriors like Mahomet and Selim the Grim and Suleiman had understood too much of diplomacy; not only was an ally in the West of intrinsic value, but it also kept Christendom in a state of turmoil and uncertainty, made the efforts of Pope or Emperor to unite against the Turks all come to naught. Cyprus was a small price to pay for that.

As Sokullu had truly said, it had taken the careless arrogance of Selim the Sot to unite all Christendom.

The five galleys of Hawkwood's little squadron rounded Cape Gata and in Akrotiri Bay, beneath the looming shadow of Mount Olympus, found a much larger squadron of Turkish ships guarding the seaward approaches to the besieged town.

These saluted the pennants flying from the mastheads of the arriving squadron, and their admiral entertained Anthony to supper.

"It is good to see you back in command, Hawk Pasha," he said. "Now perhaps, we will be able to bring these Venetians down."

Next day Larnaca Bay was crossed, and Cape Greco rounded. Now Famagusta Bay lay in front of them, almost the entire stretch of water to Cape Elea — nearly forty miles distant — being covered with the galleys of the Turkish fleet, most at anchor but with some smaller galliots plying back and forth.

Hawkwood's squadron brought up, and he was ferried across to Piale Pasha's flagship.

The Hungarian renegade did not look pleased to see him, for all that they had sailed together as boys with Dragut.

"I had supposed you had no stomach for this war, Hawk Pasha," he remarked.

"I have come to end it."

Piale Pasha merely snorted.

"There are despatches," Anthony said, and gave him the sealed envelope.

They sat together on the afterdeck while the admiral read. Anthony had no idea what Sokullu had written, at the behest of the Sultan, but Piale Pasha's brows drew together in a frown as he studied the words.

At last he raised his head. "You are in supreme command of the fleet," he said in wonderment.

Anthony smiled at him. "Briefly, I would hope. But I am also in supreme command of the army. Let us visit Lala Mustafa."

The general appeared even more astonished than the admiral to discover Hawkwood in his midst. Anthony was more interested in the scenes at which he had been gazing as he and Piale were rowed ashore and they had ridden up to the Turkish headquarters.

He could immediately understand the difficulties of this siege. Not only were the walls of the town among the most massive he had ever seen outside of Istanbul itself, but the approach was difficult because of the silting up of the river Pedieas just north of the town, which had turned the area outside the walls into a sandtrap — the very word *famagusta* meaning "buried in the sand".

Two hundred years before, this had been one of the richest cities in Christendom, situated on the trade route from Palestine to the West; and the island itself had been held by various crusading families ever since Richard the Lionheart had seized it on his way to the Third Crusade. Rules by the kings of House of Lusignan for many years, it had been the widow of the last Lusignan, Catherine Cornaro, who had sold it to the Venetians.

Barbara's great-aunt, Anthony reflected. How she would have been intrigued to accompany him here today.

But then again, perhaps not. Everywhere there was evidence of the siege and its repeated battles. Abandoned mineshafts left huge craters in the earth; parts of the city walls had crumbled and lay as huge mounds of stone; there had been fires inside the town itself, and in places these still smouldered, sending thin columns of smoke up into the still air.

And over all there hung the stench of death arising from the unburied corpses to be seen everywhere.

"It has been a grim business," Piale Pasha acknowledged.

Mustafa ushered them into his tent, then opened his despatch, reading it slowly and carefully. He too frowned at the beginning, but the frown faded as he read through to the end. He folded the parchment, and handed it to Pertau Pasha, his second-in-command. Pertau also read it, his face expressionless. But when he raised his head to look at Hawkwood, his eyes were gleaming strangely.

Anthony already knew that Pertau held him in contempt. Well, the feeling was mutual.

"You are here to negotiate, Hawk Pasha," Mustafa spoke at last. "I wish you joy of it."

"The siege must be ended within a month," Anthony confirmed. "That is the order of the Padishah."

"I wish you joy of it," Mustafa said again.

Next morning Anthony rode forward beneath a flag of truce. The Turkish guns were silent, and the Venetian guns also fell silent as they discerned his approach.

When a quarter of a mile from the gate, he commanded his escort to halt, then advanced with only his standard-bearer.

The main gate had been the centre of the fiercest assaults, and was no more than a heap of rubble, its drawbridge collapsed into the dry moat and the portcullis a twisted mess of iron. But it was still defended, and as Hawkwood approached many heads appeared amongst the stones.

"Halt there, Ottoman," someone called.

Anthony drew rein. "I seek General Brigadino. Tell him that Hawk Pasha wishes to speak with him."

His name had an effect. There was some movement behind the stones, and two men hurried off.

Anthony sat in his saddle and gazed at the walls. More and more men were gathering there, and it would take but a single hothead to lose control ... but they must know that he was their only hope of life.

He had waited fully half an hour when at last a man clambered on to the rubble and stood gazing at him. He was small and in early middle age, Anthony estimated, for he had removed his helmet and his dark hair fluttered in the gentle breeze rising from the sea as the land heated up.

"Has the Sultan sent a new commander for the *coup de grâce*?" he inquired.

510

"On the contrary, your excellency," Hawkwood replied. "The Sultan would end this war, with your compliance."

Brigadino stared at him, then past him at the Turkish encampment, the green and crimson banners, the masses of men; almost every soldier in the army was watching the negotiation. Mustafa Pasha and Pertau Pasha and their subordinate generals were mounted and waiting in a group before their troops.

Anthony used the pause to study Brigadino. The Venetian's face was haggard, his cheeks sunken. Clearly he was exhausted, and equally clearly half-starved.

"You serve the Ottomans," Brigadino said at last. "What man can put any faith in a treaty with the Ottomans? Are not we of Venice your oldest allies, yet you have made war upon us?"

"I know nothing of affairs of state," Anthony told him. "I am a sailor and a soldier. I refused to war upon you, as I am married to a Venetian myself. The Padishah accepted my decision, but now he has empowered me to offer you honourable terms of capitulation."

Brigadino snorted. "You mean he has heard that a great fleet is coming to our succour, and wishes to trick us into surrender before it arrives."

"It is true that a Christian fleet gathers, Your Excellency," Hawkwood acknowledged. "But it is far from ready to sail, and its headquarters are in Messina and a long way from Famagusta. Between Italy and Cyprus there waits the fleet of Ali Pasha, ready to do battle. There is no hope of succour for your people before next year. Meanwhile, do you not starve? Have you not fired off nearly all of your ammunition?"

This last was a shot in the dark, although a reasonable conjecture. How accurate he knew immediately from the twist of Brigadino's lips.

"The terms I offer are these," Hawkwood went on: "That your men lay down their arms, though your officers may keep their swords. Then you will march out of the city and be conveyed aboard our ships, to be removed to the nearest neutral territory."

"You say nothing of our women and children," Brigadino pointed out.

"You may take them with you," Anthony assured him.

"You are truly empowered to make such an offer?"

"I am plenipotentiary for the Sultan," Anthony said.

Brigadino stared at him. "You serve the Ottomans," he said once more, "and their watchword is treachery."

"My name is Hawkwood, as you know. Did my great-uncle betray the Knights of St John, at Rhodes?"

Brigadino stroked his beard.

"I pledge my word," Anthony declared. "The terms I have offered you will be honoured."

Brigadino looked past him at the Turkish ranks. "Can you so pledge the honour of your colleagues? Of Mustafa and Piale? Of Pertau? There is a dark and evil man. We have heard how he tortures his prisoners to death."

"I am plenipotentiary for the Sultan," Anthony repeated. "My word is law here."

Brigadino stared at him for several more seconds, then he climbed down from the rubble on to the sand. "Let me see your credentials."

Hawkwood dismounted and walked up to him. He handed over the Italian translation of the Sultan's command.

Brigadino studied it, then raised his head. "Then it seems I must trust you," he said.

Anthony made no reply.

"However, I must first confer with my commanders."

"You have one hour," Hawkwood told him. "In three-quarters of an hour I will fire a single cannon. Fifteen minutes after that we will resume hostilities."

Brigadino nodded. "I believe we will accept your offer, Hawk Pasha." He gazed into Anthony's eyes. "Had the Sultan sent any other commander but you, I would have continued to fight to the death."

As Brigadino returned inside his walls, Hawkwood rode back to the Turkish camp.

"Well?" Mustafa Pasha demanded.

"I have given him one hour to accept my terms," Anthony said. "He will do so. He has no alternative."

"Then you are to be congratulated, Hawk Pasha. The Padishah will be well pleased with you."

However the army remained ready for combat. "Should the Venetians decide to fight instead, we must end it now in one great assault," Mustafa explained.

Time passed quickly by. The sand clock had been started only on Anthony's return to the Turkish ranks, yet the grains seemed to flow out with remarkable speed. When three-quarters of it was gone, he commanded a gun to be fired. The explosion reverberated across the stillness.

Almost immediately there was a flurry of activity on the walls, and the Venetian flag came fluttering down the mast.

The Ottoman ranks erupted into cheers — while drums beat and bugles blew and cymbals clashed.

"Your men must maintain their positions, Mustafa Pasha," Hawkwood said.

Mustafa inclined his head.

"You will have transports brought into the harbour, Piale Pasha." Piale Pasha bowed in turn.

"But can we not first oversee the surrender?" Mustafa asked. His subservience was almost disturbing.

"Of course we must do that," Anthony agreed, and started forward, followed by the various generals and an escort of sipahis.

Out of the ruined gateway there came first a group of mounted officers whose horses could hardly stand. They were led by Brigadino himself, and he courteously introduced his commanding general, Astor Baglione, to the Ottoman pashas.

Then the remaining defenders slowly filed out, piling their arms as they did so. The Turks continued to cheer and play their triumphal music; the Venetians walked with downcast heads and bowed shoulders, their feet shambling through the sand. They were all clearly starving, and a good number of them were wounded.

Lastly came the women and children. These too looked starved and weak, and terrified now as they gazed at the fierce-visaged Turks to every side.

"Your people will encamp by the shore," Anthony told Brigadino. "My ships will be ready to begin transporting them tomorrow."

When the last of them had left, Anthony rode into the city — to find a charnel-house. Rotting bodies lay unburied in the streets, rats ran freely before his horse. Brigadino accompanied him, and showed him the arsenal, where there was hardly enough powder left for a single volley.

"You were brave men," Hawkwood told him. "I wish I had been sent sooner. Now, come, you will be my guest on board the flagship."

"I must stay with my people."

"That is not necessary. They are being fed, and they will not be harmed. You have my word but, come, let us be sure of it."

Together they rode to the beach where the Venetians waited, a huddle of exhausted and frightened men, women and children. Food and water from the Ottoman camp was being distributed.

"How hungrily your people stare at mine," Brigadino observed. "Like wolves surrounding a flock of sheep."

But nevertheless he was reassured and, with Baglione, accepted Anthony's invitation to dine on board the flagship.

"Ah, to breathe clean air again," Brigadino said. "What will you do with the city?"

"It will be rebuilt," Anthony told him. "Our master the Padishah has in mind the establishment of a Jewish colony on the island."

"Your master is a remarkable man," Brigadino acknowledged.

"When will the transports arrive?" Baglione inquired. He now wished only to be away from the scene of his defeat as rapidly as possible.

Anthony looked at Piale.

"The transports to remove the army will be here within a few days," Piale said. "The Ottoman army."

"What of the transports for the Venetians? I ordered them ready immediately."

Piale looked at Pertau.

"Mustafa Pasha has countermanded that order, Hawk Pasha," Pertau said.

"He has done what?"

"We are still at war with Venice," Pertau explained. "Merely to return two thousand fighting men once again to take up arms against us would seem a mistake. Mustafa Pasha has decided to retain a goodly number of hostages here, to make sure that the Republic agrees to make peace."

"Hostages?" Brigadino sat up very straight. "So this is Ottoman honesty. This is the value of your word, Hawk Pasha."

"I assure your excellency that Mustafa Pasha has made a mistake," Anthony said. "He has exceeded his authority, and these orders will immediately be rescinded."

"Mustafa Pasha has already given the orders," Pertau asserted.

As if he had intentionally timed his statement, a great wail arose from the shore.

Baglione was on his feet and running to the rail. "There is a massacre," he yelled.

Anthony was also on his feet. "By Allah, you will put a stop to this immediately, or I will have you hanged."

"You will have me hanged?" Pertau inquired mildly.

"You are as treacherous as any Turkish dog," Brigadino shouted.

"Seize him!" Pertau screamed, and instantly the two Venetians were surrounded by Turkish soldiers.

Baglione drew his sword but was cut down in an instant, sprawled across the deck in his blood.

Hawkwood stared at the scene before him in total consternation.

"Are you mad?" he shouted at Pertau. "Do you not suppose the Sultan will get to know of this?"

"The Sultan already knows of it," Pertau replied silkily.

Anthony frowned at him while an icy hand seemed to clutch his heart.

"I was given plenipotentiary powers," he yelled.

"Indeed you were, Hawk Pasha, up to the surrender of Famagusta. But the directive from the Padishah instructed Mustafa Pasha to resume command of both fleet and army the moment the surrender was accomplished. He also instructed Mustafa Pasha to make an example of the Venetians, so that the world may know that he is not to be trifled with. He has entrusted this task to me, as I am more experienced in these matters."

"Wretch!" Anthony shouted, and hurled himself at the general.

Pertau hastily skipped aside, and Hawkwood was seized by half a dozen soldiers. Struggling to reach his scimitar, he was then struck a blow on the back of the head. Before he could recover, his arms had been bound, his sword taken.

"Be thankful the Padishah also instructed that you were not to be harmed, Hawk Pasha," Pertau panted.

Anthony looked at Brigadino desperately. The governor had also been secured.

"I forgive you, Hawk," Brigadino said bitterly. "But may your people rot in hell." He turned his head to listen to the bestial sounds which were drifting towards them from the shore, then looked at Pertau. "Will you not strike off my head, and put me from my misery?"

Pertau grinned. "You are to be the example which will strike terror into the hearts of all Christendom, *monsignore*," he said. "Besides, it will be sport."

Brigadino's face paled and he looked at Hawkwood, who could still not believe that Selim had so betrayed him.

"Prepare him for the flaying," Pertau commanded.

Brigadino gasped in horror, but he was helpless. As the Turks stripped him of his clothing, Anthony wrestled unavailingly with his bonds.

"Piale," he appealed. "This man fought you honourably to a standstill. Can you now torture him to death?"

"It is the Sultan's will," Piale told him.

Pertau ordered, "Cut off his ears."

Brigadino had been forced naked into a chair, and now two knives flashed in the sun. The pieces of flesh fell to the deck, and blood tricked down the side of Brigadino's face. He uttered a moan.

Pertau sat opposite, smiling. "Now his nose."

'Pertau," Anthony begged. "Ask of me what you will. It will be yours, if you will but behead him swiftly."

"You have nothing that I wish, Hawk Pasha," Pertau pointed out. "And these are the orders of the Padishah."

Brigadino's nose was thrown to the deck beside the severed ears.

A single tear rolled down the Venetian's cheeks. He knew what would be next. Brigadino was stretched on the deck, his legs held firmly by several of the Turks, while others castrated him. His body heaved, and flecks of foam appeared on his lips as he bit them to prevent himself from crying out.

"Now flay him," Pertau told his people.

Anthony wished to look away, but could not. He knew what he was seeing would remain imprinted upon his mind for ever.

The grisly task was undertaken by two surgeons brought specially on board. They worked with great care, first opening the flesh with their razor-sharp blades, then peeling it away, slicing but always retaining the skin as a whole.

Now even Brigadino's courage could not stand the pain, and he screamed inarticulately, his voice high and terrifying in its intensity. From time to time he fainted, but the sailors were alert and emptied buckets of water over his head to revive him.

Anthony wished he could faint himself.

The flaying took some two hours to complete. Pertau called for sherbets, and he and Piale sucked the water ices while watching their captive's torment. They even offered one to Hawkwood, but he spat at them.

All the while, from the beach, the sounds of the bestial torment the other Venetians and their women were undergoing filled the afternoon air. But none of them suffered so much as their governor.

Hawkwood's brain was in turmoil as he watched and listened. He felt physically sick, but consumed with anger and self-hatred for having allowed himself to be associated with these evil people.

Allowed himself? – he had had little choice. That decision had been made more than a century earlier, by his illustrious forebears.

John Hawkwood the first, who had built the cannon to knock down the walls of Constantinople.

Anthony Hawkwood the first, who had been the intimate of the man they had called "Drinker of Blood".

William Hawkwood, who had ruthlessly carried out every order given him by Selim the Grim and Suleiman the Magnificent.

Harry Hawkwood, who had carried the Sultan's banner into the Atlantic ... and been assassinated for his loyalty.

And now himself, Anthony Hawkwood the younger, who had been able to dream of nothing better than serving these sultans as his ancestors had done. So could he honestly claim to be any better than these people before him? Yes, he thought fiercely: because I have never broken my word, nor tortured a man to death.

When at last the entire envelope of skin had been carefully removed, leaving only a bloody mess on the deck, Pertau clapped his hands. "That was well done," he said. "Wash it well, and cure it, and then stuff it with straw and stitch it back together. We will return to Istanbul with the Venetian flying from my yardarm."

"And the rest, my lord Pasha?" inquired one of the surgeons, looking down at the still moving mass of gory flesh, whence inarticulate sounds issued from the torn lips.

"Cut off the head and cure that as well. I shall mount it on a spear. As for the rest, throw it to the fish."

A scimitar flashed in the evening sun, and Brigadino's agony was at last ended. Four men picked up the unspeakable remains and tossed them over the side. Others hurried forward with buckets to wash away the blood.

Pertau smiled at Anthony. "Was that not sport? Now come, Hawk Pasha, forget your anger. It is done, and you have pleased the Padishah. And we have won a great victory. Will you not celebrate with us?"

Anthony stared at him. "May Allah have mercy upon your soul, Pertau Pasha," he said. "Because I will have none on your body."

20

THE ESCAPE

Pertau Pasha merely glowered at Hawkwood, then shrugged.

"You had best keep him bound until you regain Istanbul," he advised Piale Pasha. "There he can tell his troubles to the Sultan."

Anthony was forced into a chair on the afterdeck, and firmly tied to it. Two armed guards stood over him at all times, preventing any attempt to break free.

The sounds of the massacre on the shore were dying down as the Ottomans ran out of victims, but they were far from finished celebrating their victory. Anthony watched them go into the city, then listened to sounds of destruction drifting across the water.

Piale Pasha stood beside him. "They are digging up all the Christian graves in the church of St Nicholas," the admiral explained, "and scattering the bones. This is Mustafa's wish."

"Are you proud of your part in this, Piale?"

"I obey the wishes of our master the Sultan," the man replied. "You would do well to study this, Hawk Pasha."

I would do well to study this, Anthony brooded, as the galleys at last weighed anchor and the Ottoman fleet turned its prows for Istanbul.

Indeed he must. He did not know what reception he would receive at the Porte, but his own mind was all but made up. He could no longer serve such a man as Selim the Sot, unless Selim utterly disavowed the actions of Mustafa and punished his general. But there seemed little prospect of that.

That meant Anthony could no longer remain in Istanbul, because he now knew he had no friends there. Even Sokullu could no longer so be considered. Perhaps he had been a friend once, but the Vizier had certainly started to look to his own affairs — and had married into the Sultan's family to protect himself. Sokullu would certainly have penned the fatal order which had condemned

Brigadino to such a terrible death, but he had not thought fit to warn Anthony of the falseness of his position.

Brigadino! And, now, his own reputation. Anthony Hawkwood would become the most hated man in Christendom when news of the destruction of Famagusta was circulated.

Yet if he would bring a stop to this Ottoman curse, it was only to Christendom that he could turn.

He almost smiled in his impotent fury. Only fifteen years ago he had been a carefree youth. Then his only ambition had been to return to Istanbul and claim his heritage, establish his reputation, serve the Sultan as his ancestors had done. So much for ambition and glory. Now he must be twice a renegade.

Yet he still dreamed of a miracle. The Hawkwoods had served the Ottomans for too long lightly reject them now.

As the fleet finally steered up the Bosphorus, Piale had his bonds removed. "Shall we not return together as conquerors," he asked, "and share the glory?"

"I intend to denounce you to the Sultan," Anthony hissed at him.

"That is your privilege, Hawk Pasha. Be sure only that you do not denounce yourself, instead."

As the galleys turned into the Golden Horn, they were greeted by loud cheers from both banks. For a galliot had been sent on ahead to convey the news of the fall of Famagusta, and Istanbul was *en fête*. Not even the extreme August heat could lessen the enthusiasm of the crowds. Anthony looked up the hill outside Galata to the Hawk Palace. It, too, was decked in flags and pennants. Across the water drifted the shouts of "Hawk Pasha! Hawk Pasha!"

"You see that we have given you all the credit, Hawk," Piale said coaxingly.

Anthony merely glanced at him, then away. He was in no mood to be suborned by praise.

To his surprise, he found Ali Monizindade Pasha also within the Porte at the Seraglio. Ali embraced him warmly.

"Why so grim, Hawk Pasha?" he asked. "Are you not the victor of the hour? My own small successes are quite forgotten beneath the weight of your triumph."

"You have encountered the Papal fleet?"

Ali smiled. "I had no such fortune. They are still gathering at Messina. Whether they will continue to do so — since their purpose

520

was to relieve Famagusta — no man can say. But at least I have swept the Adriatic clear of Christian shipping. And I have taken my ships into the lagoon of Venice itself to burn their ships. Oh, they will not forget the name of Ali Pasha in a hurry."

"And where are your ships now?" Hawkwood inquired.

"I was tempted to remain off Venice, but then I realised I could be bottled up there, should a Christian fleet appear to my south. So I returned to the Ionian Sea, and have taken my fleet up the Gulf of Patras. The ships are anchored in security there, using Lepanto as their base. From there they can easily head out to give battle should the Christians approach; I keep a guard squadron of galliots always watching the heel of Italy. I doubt we will ever see them now. Although, if we do, it will please me greatly to have you amongst my admirals."

Sokullu joined them. "Hawk Pasha!" He too embraced the angry giant. "The Padishah awaits you." He turned to Piale. "Where is Mustafa?"

"He has remained in Cyprus, Vizier, to oversee our victory. I have a despatch from him."

Sokullu took the parchment. "I will study this. Come, Hawk. The Padishah is eager to speak with you."

They entered the palace together.

"Why did you not warn me I was to be betrayed?" Hawkwood murmured furiously. "You knew of the Padishah's secret orders, Mahomet. No doubt they were written under your seal."

"Ah. Yes," Sokullu said. "I regret that, Anthony, but I was acting under the command of the Padishah himself."

"Everyone shelters under the command of the Padishah," Anthony observed bitterly.

"Is it not our duty? As you once insisted to me?"

Hawkwood had no reply to make to that.

"I can only beg of you," Sokullu said, "to do nothing rash. It would be foolish again to disgrace yourself for the sake of a few Venetians."

"And my word? My honour?"

"A man's honour, like his life, is in the keeping of the Padishah. Had the Sultan commanded you to die, would you not have done so?"

"I would have done so sooner than surrender my honour, Mahomet."

"Then you would have been a fool." They had reached the door to the council chamber, and Sokullu rested his hand upon Hawkwood's arm. "Had I told you what was contained in those instructions to Mustafa, you might have refused to carry out your mission. Certainly you might have been unable to convince Brigadino of your honesty. Either would have been disastrous for you and yours. If I have offended you, I am deeply sorry. I did as I thought best. Now again I beg of you: look to yourself."

The doors were opening, and they were admitted to the presence of the Sultan.

Selim's divan was surrounded by his pashas and by armed guards. Nasi stood beside him.

The Sultan was smiling as he beheld Anthony's great frame.

"Hawk Pasha!" he said. "Come forward."

Anthony advanced to within six feet of the divan, and bowed.

"You have carried out my orders," Selim said. "I am pleased. As of now you are restored to all your commands — and I appoint you vice-admiral under Ali Monizindade Pasha."

Hawkwood straightened. "The Padishah is most generous. And what of Pertau Pasha?"

Selim frowned. "He will be amply rewarded as well, Hawk Pasha. All who took part in the reduction of Famagusta will be rewarded."

Anthony gazed at him. "I was inquiring, sire, as to the punishment you have in mind for a man who has besmirched not only my honour but that of all Turks."

Selim's frown deepened, and there was a nervous rustle amongst the viziers.

"I should be grateful," Anthony said, "if the Padishah would grant me a private audience."

"Are there things you are afraid to utter in public?" Nasi inquired.

"I will say my words wherever the Padishah chooses," Hawkwood retorted.

Sokullu gave a sign of despair.

"I have no wish to hear any complaints or squabbles between Pertau and yourself, Hawk Pasha," Selim said. "You have gained a great victory. I have rewarded you. Be satisfied with that."

"And the Venetians who were massacred after surrendering upon my promise of safe conduct? Their governor, who was brutally executed? I promised those people their lives, on my honour!" Anthony shouted.

Selim was on his feet. "Your honour!" he shouted back, arm outflung, finger pointing. "You have no honour, Hawk Pasha, save what I choose to give you. You have nothing save which I choose to give you. Now you have nothing! Get you from my sight. I shall not look upon your face again. Get you to your palace and remain there until the end of your days. Begone!" His voice rose to a shriek. "Begone!"

Hawkwood stared at him in amazement, never having seen a man so lose control of himself. Sokullu grasped his arm and hurried him from the chamber.

"Oh, what a fool you are, Anthony," the Vizier sighed. "What a fool. I doubt I can any longer protect you."

"Do I need protection?" Hawkwood shrugged himself free.

They were now in the Porte, and the men waiting there were shifting away from him — rumours of what had happened in the council chamber were already beginning to spread.

"Yes," Sokullu told him. "You need my protection. Our master may not have had the resolution to order in public the execution of so famous a pasha in the moment of his triumph. But he will certainly seek to have you killed clandestinely. Remember that you are married to a Venetian. Would you have your wife follow her parents to the grave?" He bit his lip, realising the enormity of what he had just said.

Hawkwood gazed at him almost in disbelief ... as if he could ever again disbelieve anything involving Turkish infidelity.

"You assured me they were safe and well?"

Sokullu sighed. "They were then — but our master had them executed the day you sailed for Famagusta."

Hawkwood's fingers curled into fists.

"Anthony," Sokullu begged. "We live in cruel times, under an uncertain master. The dead are dead. Only the living matter. I will do what I can for you, but ... farewell, Hawk Pasha."

He held out his hand. Anthony merely looked at it, then turned and walked away.

Hawkwood hurried from the palace, into the streets of Istanbul. Following his arrest at Famagusta, his staff and servants had been dismissed, and he had not seen them since. Thus he walked alone, though distinguished alike for his size and his colouring. The flags still flew, and to the people he was still the conqueror of Cyprus. They applauded him as he moved through them.

They would learn the truth, soon enough.

And then? The swirling resolutions which had been making him dizzy had at last hardened into determination. Sokullu had spoken the truth. In Istanbul he could do nothing more than wait to die. Whatever the risks involved, he must act immediately.

Besides, there was much to avenge.

He took the ferry to Galata, where the cheering crowds were even denser. They followed him up the hill to the Hawk Palace, and gathered in a great mass before the gates, shouting his name.

His mother stood in the portico to greet him.

"Anthony!" Felicity was in his arms. "Oh, but it is wonderful to see you. And with such news. They are saying the Sultan has restored you to favour."

"No doubt," Anthony said, and kissed Ayesha's hands. "I would have you join me in my apartment in ten minutes."

They frowned at him; his tone was hardly that of a happy man.

But he strode past them, to where Kalil waited.

"Welcome back, Chelebi."

"You too, Kalil," Anthony replied. "I wish to see you shortly. In my chamber."

Kalil looked thunderstruck. He would not oppose Hawk Pasha's wish to conduct his household in his own peculiar way — but to invite to his bedchamber a male servant who was also a whole man ... that was unheard of.

Hawkwood took the stairs, three at a time, and flung open the doors of his apartment. The boys were waiting there to greet him. John was now nine years old, and looked every inch the Ottoman. His brothers matched him in their garb, with play scimitars dangling from their belts.

"We offer you our felicitations, Father," John said, and bowed.

His brothers followed his example.

Anthony embraced them all, while looking past them at their mother.

"I am to congratulate you," Barbara said sadly. "All Istanbul rings with your praise."

"It is a temporary adulation, I assure you. Will you send the boys away."

She frowned at him.

"Only for a few minutes."

She clapped her hands. "Off with you now. Your father wishes to be alone."

Again the three of them bowed, and they slowly left the room.

"They are fine children," Barbara said. "They are young Hawks. You should be proud of them."

"I am proud of them." He took her in his arms, kissed her on the mouth. "I have committed a great crime."

Her frown returned. "I had not supposed you agreed with me on that."

His wife remained in his arms as he described the treacherous massacre. Now she stepped away from him. "You did that?"

"No. I wish you to believe me. But my plenipotentiary powers were ended as soon as the citadel surrendered."

"But did you not protest?"

"I did — and was bound prisoner for my pains."

Barbara stared at him. She had never thought of her husband other than as the strongest of men.

She collapsed on the divan.

"And now I have been sentenced to perpetual house arrest," he continued.

Barbara opened her mouth, and then closed it again.

"What will you do?"

"Leave this place — but you must come with me."

She hesitated. "Leave Constantinople? Leave my parents to suffer for me?"

"Your parents are dead. They were executed by command of the Sultan a fortnight ago."

She clasped her throat in horror.

"You never told me!"

"I never knew, until an hour ago. Now, will you come with me?"

Her eyes had filled with tears, even if it was several months since she had last seen Pietro and Beatrice Cornaro — since the day of their imprisonment — she had sent messages to their prison every day. But she did not weep. Instead she said, "I will come with you to the ends of the earth, my lord, if you will avenge the dead."

"That is my intention. But first it is necessary to risk the living."

She glanced at the door through which the boys had disappeared. "If you die, then do we all die. It were best we did so at your side."

He sat beside her, held her hands.

"Where will we go?" she asked.

"Venice."

"Anthony, they would chop off your head!"

"Then you will have to save me. Is not one of your uncles currently Doge?"

"Alvise Mocenigo? I know nothing of him, nor he of me."

"But he will remember, at least, your mother — his own sister. You will tell him that I now have much to offer Christendom, knowing as much as I do about the Turks and their intentions. And especially about the Turkish navy."

She demurred no longer. "Who will accompany us?"

"The fewer the better. The boys, of course, and my mother. Ayesha and Kalil, too ... it is a small boat."

Her jaw sagged. "You mean to sail in your yacht?"

"There is no Turk can match me for seamanship; many can match me on a horse, especially if we are encumbered by children."

"But they will follow you with galleys."

He smiled. "They are welcome to try. August is a windy month."

She gulped. "My maids ... I must take my maids."

"All of them?"

"They are only three. They are Venetians, Anthony. I cannot leave them here to be torn to pieces by the Janissaries."

He hesitated. "They will have to work their passages."

"They will do that willingly."

There came a knock on the door.

"Enter," Anthony said.

His mother and Ayesha came in, followed somewhat diffidently by Kalil.

"Close the door, Kalil, and guard it," Hawkwood said.

The servant obeyed.

Felicity looked at Barbara, and then around the room, seeking the children.

"What is happening, Anthony?" she asked.

"Sit down, Mother."

The two women sat beside Barbara.

"Now listen to me very carefully," Anthony said, and he

explained to them what had happened — and what was likely to happen in the future.

Felicity's face paled as she listened; Ayesha clasped her neck, in dismay.

"I have decided our only course is to leave Istanbul and flee to the West." Anthony gazed at them intently as he spoke. "Barbara is agreed with me on this."

"To the West," Felicity whispered. Here was her oldest dream threatening to come true. "Can we manage it?"

"I believe we can. If we fail, we die. But if we remain here, equally will we die."

Ayesha stood up. "You mean to desert the Sultan," she said in agitation. "The Sultan is lord of all. If you desert him, you will be outlaw and traitor. Every man's hand will be against you."

"That is a risk I must take."

"My lord," she begged, "you cannot do this."

"I must."

"Then you must leave me behind."

They stared at each other.

"I cannot do that. We need the advantage of as much time as possible."

"And you suppose I would betray you?"

"They would tear the knowledge from you with hot irons, Ayesha." He turned to the manservant. "Kalil, are you with me?"

"You are my master," Kalil replied simply.

"Then fetch silk cords to bind the lady Ayesha."

Kalil left the room.

"Will you permit this?" Ayesha implored Felicity.

"My son has no choice. We have no choice." Felicity turned to Anthony. "When will we leave?"

"At midnight," he told her. "Each of you may take only a single change of clothing. Barbara, you must alert your women and the boys an hour before we leave."

"But they will have settled for the night."

"Then they will have to be awakened. We cannot risk any of our discussion reaching the other servants."

She nodded, her face pale with determination.

Ayesha suddenly ran for the window. Anthony had no idea what she had in mind, to shout for help or commit suicide, but he swiftly seized her round the waist and hauled her back. She turned in his arms and struck at him, her breath hissing. Then she attempted to kick him, but he held her at arms' length so she could not reach him, and a few moments later she was exhausted.

The other women watched in amazement.

"What will become of her?" Barbara asked.

"She will become reconciled," Felicity assured her, "when it is done."

Kalil returned soon with the cords, and Ayesha was bound hand and foot, then gagged and placed on Anthony's divan. Her eyes were huge with anger and fear.

Anthony set about accumulating whatever he could take with him. Money, mainly, as much gold coin as could be carried in two leather bags. He did not anticipate charity from the Venetians, and his family would have to live on something until he secured new employment.

He knew the yacht would be partially stocked with food and water, but he ordered Kalil to gather what fresh food he could, without arousing suspicion from the other servants. The future, down to only a few months ago so settled and certain, now loomed as a dark path beset with dangers and uncertainties.

He was so busy deciding what to take and what to leave that the cry of the muezzin surprised him. Going to the window to look out, he wanted to shout for joy. It was a typical August evening. It had been very hot during the day, and there had been a strong sea breeze. Now the breeze had dropped with the approach of dusk, but to the north great banks of cloud had built up, and that there would be wind later on this night seemed certain, perhaps a great deal of wind.

They ate their evening meal as usual, and retired as usual; the servants made no comment on the absence of Ayesha.

Anthony joined Barbara on her divan, as Ayesha remained on his, and they lay anxiously in each other's arms.

"I used to dream of adventuring at your side," she said.

"Then your dream is coming true."

At eleven he roused her, and sent her to summon her Venetian maids, while he returned to his own apartment for his weapons and the money. Ayesha stared at him with hostile eyes.

It was a great temptation to take a few more of his male servants; they had a long and dangerous voyage ahead of them. But the yacht was only designed for a crew of six, and there would be six women in any event, not to mention the three children. Nor could he be certain of the loyalty of any other of his people, once they realised he was abandoning the Sultan. The women would just have to work.

But at least one of his prayers was answered. There was a wind, a strong one, whipping out of the Black Sea and howling around the minarets of Istanbul.

"Can we really put to sea in such weather?" Barbara asked.

"It is the safest, for us," he assured her.

Just before midnight he roused his mother Felicity, who, remarkably, was in a deep sleep. Kalil was already awake. They joined the women in his apartment, while Barbara roused her sons.

"What is happening, Mama?" John asked sleepily.

"There is a journey ahead of us," Barbara told him. "One we must undertake secretly."

"Will Father be coming?"

"Father will be leading us."

There was always one male servant stationed in the downstairs porch, to repel undesirables. Kalil and Anthony went ahead to deal with him. The man sprang to his feet at the sight of his master, but before he could utter a word Kalil had struck him on the head and laid him out — his turban saving his skull from serious damage.

"He were best killed, Chelebi," Kalil suggested. "He will recover in a few hours, and be able to give the alarm."

Anthony shook his head. "I will murder none of my own people."

They bound the watchman hand and foot, and placed him out in the yard. Then Hawkwood returned for the women.

He hefted Ayesha on to his shoulder, and the little boys stared at their father with enormous, puzzled eyes.

"Now come," Anthony said to them, "and remember, not a word."

The maidservants were clearly terrified, and he toyed with gagging them as well, but decided to rely on their understanding that if their escape failed, they would probably wind up in the slave market.

He led the way downstairs. His mother was at his shoulder, Barbara came behind with the three boys. The maids followed her, and Kalil brought up the rear. All were wrapped up in their haiks, and the women wore yashmaks as well.

They left the house and set off down the hill. Now the wind howled, and snatched at their clothes. At least the looming storm kept people off the streets. Those they did encounter cast sidelong glances at the hurrying party, but made no attempt to accost them.

At the harbour the wind was whipping the sheltered waters of the Golden Horn into wavelets, and the moored boats and ships rose and fell, warps and timbers creaking.

Above all it was utterly dark.

Hawk Pasha's yacht had a mooring of her own, alongside one of the many docks that thrust away from the Galata waterfront. As they hurried towards it, they saw an armed man, wearing a red and blue uniform with a white horsehair plume in his turban, sitting just in front of the gangway,

The Janissary rose as they approached.

"Identify yourselves," he said.

Anthony set Ayesha on her feet. "Hold her," he told Barbara, who threw both arms round the Arab woman, who could only utter a shrill squeak, instantly lost on the wind.

Anthony loosened his scimitar in its scabbard and stepped forward.

"I am Hawk Pasha," he said. "And that is my ship you guard."

"A thousand apologies, my lord," the man said, "but I have been told that no one can board this ship tonight."

"Then you must die," Anthony growled. His scimitar was already drawn, and before the soldier could defend himself, his head had been all but whipped from his shoulders, and his lifeless body fell into the water.

The women gasped. None of them had ever seen Hawkwood in violent action before.

He hastily led them on board. "Go below," he told them, "and stay there. Kalil and I will manage for now. When the wind drops, then you may help us."

The maids obeyed without question.

Barbara gazed out of the mouth of the harbour towards the Bosphorus, a mass of little whitecaps. Their holiday sailing had always been enjoyed in fine weather. "I am afraid," she confessed for the first time.

He put his arm round his wife and squeezed her against him. "There is no need to be."

"You say that because you have survived such desperate situations often before. There are so many aspects of your life in which I have had no share."

"For that you should be thankful," he told her. "Now, go to the boys, and reassure them."

Hawkwood and Kalil reefed the sail while still alongside the dock. Then they set it, causing the little ship to buck and heave. A few slashes of their scimitars cut the mooring warps, and the yacht fell away from the land, immediately gathering way.

Anthony grasped the tiller, while Kalil remained in the bow in an attempt to spot any unsuspected dangers which might lie between them and the Bosphorus. But Anthony knew the Golden Horn well enough to navigate it blindfold.

With the wind in the north, the yacht creamed to the east, lying well over on her starboard side. From the cabin there came stifled exclamations of alarm as the women huddled together in the confined space, holding on to each other in desperate fear. The three boys were crowded into the hatchway, whispering excitedly.

The *Hawk* shot out of the Golden Horn, and Anthony put the helm down. She swung away from the wind, and began to surge through the Bosphorus itself, surfing down the short seas.

Kalil came aft. "Is there not still too much sail, Chelebi?" he inquired.

"Perhaps. But we will not reduce it until Marmara. We cannot tell how much of a lead we have."

The speed was exhilarating, as was the motion of the yacht. Running free there was not even any great impression of wind or sea, although Anthony knew he would feel entirely different were he to be forced to come up into the gale. But things were different in Marmara, which they reached only half an hour after leaving the Golden Horn. As soon as they were away from the shelter of the land, the waves became larger, and the movement more considerable. Now it was a matter of slowing the yacht to prevent it from burying its bows in a wave and losing steerage way, and thus control; it was far safer to have the occasional wave break on the stern.

Kalil reefed some more of the sail, and they settled down to ride out the storm. They took turn and turn about on the helm; it was exhausting work, for the yacht had to be steered through the waves, veering from side to side to save the stern from being

531

picked up, but always being brought back before the wind to prevent any risk of yawing, which could leave them broadside to the seas with the consequent chance of being rolled over.

It was a battle between their brains and muscles and the elements, and was for that reason exciting. They looked at each other and laughed aloud as one particularly skilful piece of helming saw a larger than usual sea slip by without a drop of water coming on board.

Towards dawn Felicity came on deck to join them. "I think everyone is feeling better now," she said. "More confident." She gazed at the darkness, broken only by flashes of lightning and breaking crests. "Are we safe as yet?"

"We have got ourselves away from Istanbul, at any rate," Anthony said.

"Your father told me, once," Felicity said, "of how the first Hawkwoods tried to escape the city in just such a storm, and were cast away on the Anatolian shore. Indeed that was how your family came to serve the Ottomans in the first place. Has not history come full circle?"

"That will not happen again this time," he promised her.

"That was a hundred and twenty-one years ago," his mother mused. "Were they all wasted years?"

"Perhaps my ancestors were misguided in their loyalty. And I, too, down to a week ago — as you have always recognised."

She squeezed his hand. "I knew this day would come."

His smile was grim. "We have just to reach tomorrow."

Towards dawn the wind dropped, and though the seas remained lumpy, any real danger from the storm was past. To their great relief, Anthony was able to allow the women and boys on deck. The maidservants had been seasick, and the cabin was foetid. Barbara set the women to cleaning it up.

Now the storm was over, Hawkwood had to concentrate on the real dangers of their position. With the wind still in the north, they were scudding across the Sea of Marmara, making a good six knots, he estimated. By noon they were already well within sight of the island of Marmara itself, which they would have to pass in order to gain the Dardanelles.

There was regularly a squadron of galleys based on Marmara, and indeed one was out on patrol. Anthony hoisted his personal pennant. The *Hawk* was well known on the inland sea, and no news of what had happened the previous day in Istanbul would as yet have reached this far south. The war galley saluted as their yacht sailed by, and they gazed anxiously at the Turkish seamen watching the progress of the little ship.

Soon Marmara fell behind, and with the evening they came in sight of the hills to either side of the Dardanelles.

Here it was necessary to put in for water, but Anthony also sought to buy food, while he could. The hasty supplies Kalil had brought with them would hardly last much longer.

They entered the little harbour of Gallipoli late that evening. Anthony roused one of the local merchants on the plea of urgent business for the Sultan, and bade him open his doors. No one was ready to disobey Hawk Pasha, and supplies were quickly obtained, while Kalil filled the water casks.

They were away soon after midnight, and through the Dardanelles by dawn.

In the Aegean, the wind began to follow the normal summer pattern of relatively calm nights but quite strong daytime northerlies. The *Hawk* was able to make a hundred miles a day, thus within two days after leaving the Dardanelles they were passing between the island of Andros and the Euboea, and making south for Cape Malea at the southern extremity of the Peloponnesus. This they reached on the fourth morning from the Dardanelles, and the seventh day since leaving Istanbul.

They stopped round the headland for food and water, readily supplied by peasants in return for a piece of Hawkwood's gold.

By now everyone on board, save for Ayesha, was in high spirits. Sea-sickness had been entirely forgotten, and the escape, which had once appeared so terrifying, had now become an exciting holiday, with their safety apparently assured. Only Anthony knew better. So long as they were sailing south, or south-west, and the breeze remained fresh, their yacht could travel faster than any horseman or any oared ship. Thus even if galleys had been despatched after them, they would maintain their advantage.

But messengers would also have been sent to the west. It was not greatly more than five hundred miles from Istanbul to the Gulf of Corinth. Even making no more than seventy miles a day, a galloper would reach Lepanto and the Turkish fleet within a week.

That time had already elapsed, and the yacht had not yet even begun its journey northwards up the Adriatic.

Almost he was tempted to make straight for Italy and thence Messina, where the Christian fleet was reported to be gathering. But the risk was too great of his being seized and peremptorily hanged as a renegade — his name was far too well known to the Spaniards from his earlier exploits as one of Dragut's captains.

Only in Venice, and only by virtue of his wife's name and powerful connections, would he stand any chance at all of being received as a friend. Whether they would still regard him as a friend when they learnt about Famagusta was another matter. But he had no other course of action open to him.

It took two days from Melea to Zante. Hawkwood, of course, eschewed the passage inside the Ionian islands, more sheltered from the boras — or fierce north-easterlies — which came out of the Balkan mountains to scream down the Adriatic: inside the islands was where he was likely to encounter Turkish patrols out of Lepanto.

But Ali Pasha had also said there were patrols across the Strait of Otranto, separating the heel of Italy from Albania, and these would have to be negotiated.

To add to these hazards, the wind now became fitful; when it did blow with any force, it came from the north, the direction in which they wished to go, so their passage necessitated a succession of tacks, at once time-consuming and exhausting.

Fortunately, by now his odd crew had become a very able one. The boys had entirely taken over the deck duties, delighted to be "campaigning" with their illustrious father. The maids were prepared to haul on ropes, and his mother and Barbara, wearing the scantiest of clothing and with sun-reddened complexions, worked as hard as any.

Only Ayesha, released from her bonds now, sat in sad silence on the deck and refused to show any pleasure in their progress. Anthony could only hope that she would recover from her melancholia when she understood that they were finally beyond the reach of Turkish pursuit.

It was at dusk on the day they first sighted Zante, when the mountains of Cephalonia were still high on the eastern horizon, that they saw a galley coming out from the shelter of the island

and creeping across the calm water towards them. The breeze had dropped, and the little yacht was rolling gently, but making very little headway.

The vessel was still a long way away, but that it would close very rapidly could not be doubted.

Obviously there was no chance of bluffing their way through; the fleet at Lepanto would by now know all about the flight of Hawk Pasha, and would have the strictest orders to bring him back to face the wrath of the Sultan. Anthony broke out the sweeps. He took one, with Barbara and one of her maids; and Kalil took the other, with the other two maids. The huge oars went over the sides, through their rowlocks, and the slow and exhausting process began, of walking forward with the blade feathered, and then walking aft once it was dipped. This perambulation had to be done in exact unison with the other team, and caused some consternation at first, as each team in turn lost their rhythm and went stumbling to the deck.

But gradually they got into step, and the *Hawk* did move through the water, although nowhere as fast as the galley could.

"Will there be any wind?" Barbara asked in alarm. She did not have to inquire after their fate if they were overtaken.

Hawkwood looked up at the sky. There were little puffs of brown cloud drifting across from the Albanian coast.

"Yes," he said. "I think there may well be. Much will depend on how soon."

Darkness fell and, as they did not light their lantern, they soon hopefully disappeared from sight. But by dusk the galley had come very close, only some eight miles away, Hawkwood estimated. As she would be making six knots to their two, she would soon be upon them.

And still the wind blew at no more than a gentle breeze.

"What are we to do, Anthony?" his mother asked.

"Get down on your knees and pray to Allah for the Sultan's forgiveness," Ayesha said, speaking for the first time that day.

The rest of them endeavoured to ignore her.

"Only boldness will save us," Anthony assured them. "We are lost to sight for the moment, and the moon has not yet risen. Stop rowing and ship oars."

This the women were happy to do. They were all quite

exhausted, and collapsed on the deck.

Anthony took the steering oar. "Now bring her about, Kalil."

Kalil gazed at his master in consternation. Felicity raised her head, equally bemused.

"It is the one thing they will not anticipate," Hawkwood told them.

Kalil manhandled the long lateen boom across the yacht as Anthony put the helm down. The little ship came about almost in her own length; as the wind was northerly, she immediately gathered speed, sailing back to the south.

Now that they had shipped their sweeps, the night was utterly silent, the only noise the ripple of water away from their hull. But then they heard the sound of a distant drumbeat, and then the enormous splash of sixty oars entering the water together; a few minutes later the stench of the slaves drifted towards them ... *they* would have no rest this night.

Anthony heard the scratching of steel on tinder, and a spark flew. It was too dark to see who was endeavouring to light the lantern — but he did not have to guess.

He and Kalil acted together. Hawkwood dropped the helm and hurled himself at the cabin hatch, where Ayesha crouched. He knocked the lantern from her hand, just as it began to glow, and Kalil tossed it over the side. Anthony held Ayesha tight against him, his hand over her mouth.

"Did they see the light?" Barbara asked.

Hawkwood listened intently. The noise of the drum was growing louder, but it was also constantly changing direction; that meant the galley was crossing their stern — so it had not altered course towards them.

"No," he said at last. "They were looking to the west and north, not the south."

His mother came aft. "What is to be done with her?"

"You will have to take her below and bind her again."

The Venetian maids bundled Ayesha back into the cabin, none too gently. Felicity followed.

"I feel almost sorry for her," Anthony said.

Barbara did not reply to this. Instead she said, "When the galley does not overtake us, they will know we have altered course. Will they then not merely wait for daybreak, certain that we must eventually attempt to sail north?"

"Yes," he agreed.
"Then what have we gained?"
"Pray for wind," was all he could say.

He held his course until the drumbeat had entirely faded, which meant that the galley must have drawn away several miles to the north-west. Then he came about again. He knew that Barbara had been right, and were they to be sighted at daybreak, with the wind still light, they would then be lost — with some fourteen hours of daylight at her disposal, the galley could not help but overtake them, no matter where they headed.

But the wind did come — just before dawn. Kalil was on the helm, Anthony sleeping on the deck at his feet. But he was instantly awake as the yacht trembled and gathered speed. The wind was from the north, and it was necessary to tack, but, providing it pushed them along faster than the galley could row, Anthony was content — the warship's speed would drop in rough water, and her single square sail was only intended for running free, not making to windward.

By daybreak the seas were lumpy, and the wind strong. On the port tack, the *Hawk* raced towards the islands, crashing into the waves, sending sheets of spray over her entire length. From the cabin there came the inevitable cries of alarm. But Barbara and his sons came on deck to enjoy the excitement.

"There!"

Anthony pointed, and they saw the galley, etched sharply against the western horizon. She was again twenty-odd miles off, but it was clear that her lookouts had seen the yacht.

"Can she catch us?" Barbara asked.

"Not on a straight run. But we must tack in another few miles. That is her best chance." He looked from face to face. "It is one we must take."

He held on as long as he dared, until the north-eastern headland of Cephalonia seemed to hang above their heads; the risk here was that another galley would put out from the island to catch him between two fires. But, with the wind howling and the seas getting ever bigger, he felt fairly sure any craft would be reluctant to put to sea.

When he looked back at his pursuer, he could see that she was making very heavy weather of it, indeed. If water was breaking over the yacht's decks, it must equally be entering at the lower oar-ports of the warship. Soon she would have more on her mind than her quarry as she endeavoured to pump herself dry.

He put the helm up, and the *Hawk* came round very smartly, while Kalil carried the boom to port. Now the yacht travelled faster than ever, close-hauled on the starboard tack, making north-west.

The new course would carry her across the bows of the galley: at how great a distance depended on how fast the warship was able to move. That the Turks were aware that this was their best opportunity — and their last one — was evident from the bustle to be seen on her decks as the two ships closed. Hawkwood could make out men on the foredeck — constantly swept by driving spray — loading the cannon mounted there. Soon they would be within range. But the galley was rising and falling on the waves, and because of her huge gilded beak, now glowing in the morning sunlight, her guns could not fire straight ahead, which made the task of aiming them at a target so situated the more difficult — supposing they could keep their slow matches alight.

They would also take half an hour to reload. It was all a matter of timing.

The *Hawk* danced forward, and the gap between the two vessels narrowed. The galley was using its oars, as its sail was useless in these conditions, but the rowers were having a hard time of it as the ship lurched from crest to trough. Anthony could imagine the slaves falling about as their blades inadvertently bit air instead of water; the boatswains ranging up and down, using their whips; the officers in the stern shouting orders which could not be obeyed.

Yet it was going to be a close-run thing. The ships were now less than a mile apart, and the yacht had still to cross the galley's bows.

The first gun belched smoke, and the second. Hawkwood never saw where the balls went; they were certainly wide. And now, too, the yacht was directly ahead of the galley, at a distance of no more than half a mile; Anthony could clearly see the soldiers waiting to board him, if they could only close up.

Beside him, Barbara gasped and clutched his arm.

The port gun fired. At this range it was considerably more accurate, and the ball plunged into the sea only fifty yards away from the yacht's bow, bringing shrieks of fear from the Venetian women. One shot striking them would send them to the bottom.

But the last of the guns had been fired, and, although he could also see men reloading as fast as they could, the galley's chance was gone. The *Hawk* was across her bows and streaking to the north-west, and the warship remained floundering in the increasingly heavy seas.

"Saved!" Barbara cried, and embraced him.

He kissed her. "Tell your women to stop that yelling, and release Ayesha and allow her on deck. Surely even she will now realise we are going to escape."

There remained imponderables — for they had not yet reached the Straits of Otranto — but his confidence was growing every moment.

Ayesha came quietly on deck, wearing her haik, which she clutched close against the wind. She stared at the galley, now already a mile away, and falling behind every moment.

"There are our enemies, Ayesha," Anthony said. "We have outsailed them."

Ayesha stared at him, then back at the galley. Then she gathered her haik around her and leapt over the side.

Hawkwood was so taken aback that for a moment he was unable to move. Then he put the helm down, and the *Hawk* came smartly about.

He looked back to where the Arab woman had gone in, but she had already disappeared from sight in the now considerable waves. He knew she had never learned to swim.

"The sail!" he shouted at Kalil, who reacted quickly. The *Hawk* was now sailing south again, seeking the drowning woman.

"Anthony!" Barbara shouted in alarm.

The galley was now not all that far away.

Hawkwood stared at the dark waters, as the yacht retraced her course.

There was a boom from one of the galley's cannon. The shot was well short, but the gap was closing.

"Anthony," Felicity begged him. "Ayesha is dead. She wished it so. For God's sake think of the living."

Anthony looked down into the water, and saw the haik floating just beneath the surface. Of Ayesha there was no sign.

He sighed, and put the helm up again. Kalil adjusted the sail, and the galley fell astern.

"To her I betrayed a sacred trust," Anthony said.

"You have nothing to reproach yourself with, my lord."

"No," he agreed. "I have merely another death to avenge."

The crew of the *Hawk* was stunned by the unexpected tragedy. The boys lost much of their ebullience, for Ayesha had been their playmate. Anthony was more crushed than any of them. Ayesha's entire life had been devoted to him.

But there was little time for brooding. The weather would remain bad throughout the following week, but this was a benefit to the fugitives. The next day they passed through the Straits, and then made a series of long tacks, often as much as twelve hours at a time, up the Adriatic. The seas were big, and sometimes dangerous; more than once the cabin was swamped and all hands had to bail. Their food supply dwindled and they were soon down to half rations, with very little water to drink. But nothing the elements or their stomachs could do compared with having escaped the vengeance of Selim, and on the seventh day after Ayesha's suicide, they sighted the domes of St Mark's.

Their pennants had long since been blown away, and there was nothing to identify the yacht as she approached the islands which guarded the lagoon — save that the strangeness of her shape in this sea made it clear that she was not Venetian.

As they passed the outermost watchtowers, signals were flown, and at the entrance to the lagoon a small patrol galley was awaiting them. The Venetians were still clearly agitated by Ali Pasha's raid of a month earlier.

"Where are you from," the galley hailed, "and what is the name of your captain?"

Undoubtedly they could read the name on the bow. Anthony went forward, his head bare so that his red hair could the more easily be seen.

"I am Anthony Hawkwood," he shouted. "Known as Hawk Pasha. I am from Istanbul."

There was consternation on board the galley, officers conferred in great agitation, as if suspecting that their ancient enemy was but the advance guard of another Turkish fleet.

Signal flags fluttered to the galley's masthead.

"What is your purpose here?" the captain shouted eventually.

'I am on a mission to the Doge," Hawkwood replied.

There was more hurried conversation. By now the flags had been observed from the shore, and another galley was putting out.

"Then make for the main quay and go alongside," the captain instructed.

Anthony raised his hand to show that he understood, and returned aft to take the steering oar from Kalil.

'Perhaps you ladies would care to prepare yourselves," he suggested.

Hitherto the women had been rapt observers of the scene. Now there was almost as much commotion on board the yacht as they hurried below to wrap themselves in their haiks; Barbara's western-style clothes had long been discarded for the harem's pantaloons and bolero.

But Hawkwood was more interested in his surroundings, having never visited Venice before. The islands through which he was threading his way, before the light easterly breeze, were low-lying, and marked only by their several forts. In front of him, the city itself seemed to rise out of the sea, and as he drew nearer he could discern that the foundations of buildings were actually sunk into the waters of the Grand Canal. Even the square of St Mark's, which lay directly in front of him, and was dominated by the huge cathedral, was only a few feet above sea level, and was obviously liable to be inundated by any strong easterly breeze.

He felt a slight shudder of apprehension. But surely he would not have risked so much, and survived so much to bring his family to safety merely to meet the headman's axe?

The city was not very large, and the identity of this new arrival had clearly spread rapidly. All manner of small boats — quaintly shaped with raised bows and sterns, but entirely undecked, and propelled by means of a single oar — began to appear everywhere in the smaller canals and even in the harbour itself. The square soon became thronged with people, causing the pigeons to flutter skywards in great confusion.

But amongst the onlookers had appeared a company of soldiers, brightly clad in blue and black striped uniforms, armed with pikes as well as swords, and wearing steel helmets with ridged crowns and pronounced peaks.

Hawkwood judged his distance to perfection, and, at the command, Kalil swung the boom so that the wind was spilled from it. In almost the same moment he let the halliard go, and the sail came clouding down.

The *Hawk* retained just sufficient way to slide gently alongside the stone dock. John Hawkwood and his two brothers had already carried out fenders, large sausages of plaited ropes to keep the topsides of the yacht from being gashed, and now the boys also took the mooring warps ashore.

The soldiers moved forward to stand on the edge of the dock. Their captain addressed Anthony.

"Are you he known as Hawk Pasha?" he inquired.

"I am," Anthony said.

"You will come with us, if you please. I am to take you before the Doge."

Hawkwood nodded, and stepped ashore.

"Wait!" Barbara clambered after him. "I will come too. The Doge is my uncle."

"I am instructed as regards Hawk Pasha alone, lady," the captain insisted.

"You had best seek your family," Anthony advised her gently.

"Supposing I can reach them," Barbara muttered, gazing at the crowd which filled the square, pressing forward to the water's edge. No one could doubt what their mood would be when they learned of what had happened in Famagusta.

Hawkwood was aware of the danger in which they now lay — and he had to be the bearer of tidings which might set that crowd alight.

He was marched hurriedly through the muttering throng, and up the wide stairs which led to the portico of the Doge's palace. Here was a considerable number of notables gathered, amongst them a few familiar faces — either merchants who had done business in Istanbul, or past ambassadors to the Porte.

"It is Hawk Pasha," they whispered incredulously, as they recognised the red hair and beard.

At the top of the steps several elderly men were gathered, the one in the centre standing somewhat apart. He had a long white beard and wore a curious, tight-fitting black cap on his head, rather like the Jewish custom, only considerably more elaborate. His clothes were rich, and his manner one of total omnipotence.

Hawkwood anticipated his escort, and bowed. "My lord Doge," he said.

Alvise Mocenigo stared at him. "Hawk Pasha," he said. "You, dare to come here, in the middle of a war between our people? Should I not hang you higher than Hamann?"

"I have much advice to offer Your Excellency," Anthony said.

The Doge subjected his face to a close inspection. "Then speak," he said at last.

"What I have to say is for your ears alone."

Mocenigo considered for a moment. "My ears are those of the Council of Ten. You will speak to them, or not at all."

Hawkwood bowed. He had expected nothing better.

His arms were pinioned, and he was escorted inside the building and into the council chamber. Its members filed in and took their seats in high-backed chairs. The Doge sat down at the head of the table. Hawkwood stood at the front.

"Speak," the Doge commanded.

"First, my lords," Anthony said, "I must request a promise of safety for my family."

"You have no rights here, Turk," snarled one of the council.

"Unless their safety is guaranteed, I can only remain silent," Hawkwood replied sharply.

"Ha! We'll see how long you remain silent when you are stretched on the rack."

Anthony gazed at the Doge. "Your Excellency, my family are innocent of any crimes I may have committed. My wife is a Venetian herself, your very own niece ..."

"Whom you ravished against her will, no doubt," growled another of the council.

Hawkwood refused to lose his temper. "That, you will have to ask the lady herself, my lord. But you have just confirmed that she must be innocent. As are her three sons."

"Enough," Mocenigo said. "They will not be harmed. You have my word. They will be sent to the Cornaro palace."

'This fellow is too bold," someone objected.

"He is right to care for his family," Mocenigo said, considering, no doubt, that they were his own kin, too. He rang a golden bell, and a secretary presented himself in the doorway. Mocenigo gave the necessary instructions.

"Now we have done as you wish, Hawk Pasha," the Doge said. "It is your turn to satisfy us."

Anthony drew a deep breath, and looked around him at the

hostile faces. "The news is bad. Famagusta has fallen. Cyprus belongs to Selim."

There was an angry murmur around the chamber.

"When did this happen?" Mocenigo interrupted.

"Less than a fortnight ago, Your Excellency."

"We have had no word of it."

"The Sultan is content that you should find out in his own time."

They stared at him, and several whispered amongst themselves.

"And you are his envoy," Mocenigo said. "Hoping to call us to surrender."

"On the contrary, Your Excellency, I have abandoned his service. The Sultan now hates me even more than he hates Venice."

"There is some trickery here," someone said. "Speak plain, man. What happened at Famagusta? The citadel was impregnable."

"No citadel is impregnable, my lord. The garrison held out until they were destitute of food and ammunition. Then they surrendered on terms." He took another long breath. "I have to tell you that the terms were not honoured by the Turkish commanders, and your garrison has been massacred to the last child."

The room hissed to the sharp intakes of breath.

"The terms of surrender were negotiated by ... myself," Hawkwood told him.

A rustle went right round the table as men sat up straight.

"And you have the effrontery to stand here before us and admit this?" Mocenigo demanded.

"Yes. Because I myself did not break the terms. The moment the garrison had laid down its arms, I was superseded. That is why I have left the service of the Sultan. My honour has been besmirched."

"And yet you have come to us," Mocenigo brooded. "You must have some reason, since you know we will not forgive such perfidy."

Anthony looked straight ahead. "I have come to you because my heart cries out for vengeance, no less than yours. I have come to warn you that if the fleet now assembling at Messina should disband without firing a shot, it would be a disaster for all Christendom. By this time next year the Turks would again be encamped before the gates of Vienna, and Ali Pasha's galleys will be in your lagoon again, for certain. The Ottomans must be stopped *now* — and you will never have a greater opportunity. But give me a fleet, and I myself will tackle Ali Pasha. I know the man."

There was another rustle of muttered comment round the table.

"I can do this, my lords," Hawkwood insisted. "I have sailed with the Turks, I have commanded their fleets, I know how they can be defeated."

"You expect us to give you, Hawk Pasha, the command of our fleet?" someone demanded in outrage.

"I do not ask the command for Hawk Pasha," Anthony declared desperately. "I ask it for Anthony Hawkwood."

Mocenigo stared at him for several seconds, then said, "Withdraw, *monsignore*, while we discuss in private what you have told us."

The sergeant of the guard touched Anthony on the shoulder, and led him from the council room into a small antechamber. This had a window, to which Anthony immediately went. But it overlooked not the square, only the next small canal — and to his right he could make out the infamous Bridge of Sighs.

For at least half an hour he waited, watched impassively by the guards — until the door at last opened and a secretary entered.

"You will come with me, *signore*," he said.

Anthony followed the man back into the council chamber. He was not aware of fear, or even apprehension. Rather he felt suspended in time, until the judgement was given.

As he studied the faces of the men seated round the table, not one gave any indication of their inner feelings, or how they had voted.

"Anthony Hawkwood, known as Hawk Pasha," the Doge said, "you are well known as a lifelong enemy of Christendom. But there are records in this city of how your ancestor, William Hawkwood, visited our Republic as an ambassador from the Porte. He was welcomed by the Doge and given every assistance. For those were the days when Venice and the Porte had an understanding, an alliance. Now that alliance is ended, by the whim of your Sultan. Now we are at war, and you come to us as an enemy, and one, moreover, responsible for a hideous crime. We cannot absolve you of the burden of guilt which you, and every Turk, now wears for all time.

"That you ask for the command of a fleet is sheer effrontery. It is therefore the decision of this Council that you be taken from here across the bridge to the prison, and there executed. This will be our first act of reprisal against the Ottomans for their perfidy at Famagusta."

545

21

THE DON

"The sentence," the Doge continued, "is to be carried out at dawn on the day after tomorrow."

Heads turned in surprise, and Anthony gathered that it was the usual custom for death sentences to be carried out immediately.

But for the moment he was too shocked to consider what that might signify. He was not afraid of death: he had spent all his life in close proximity to it. But to die before he had had an opportunity to avenge the disgrace forced upon him by Selim and his commanders, before he had had an opportunity to remove the stain on his family name, for generations to come, seemed insufferable. At a time when the West so much needed him.

"Take the prisoner away," Mocenigo commanded abruptly.

Hawkwood was touched on the shoulder by the sergeant of the guard. He opened his mouth to speak, and then thought better of it. He would not stoop to beg these haughty, heedless oligarchs.

At least he was not to be exposed to the jeers of the mob, but instead was taken down a side corridor to that bridge he had regarded earlier, whose curving arch led him over the canal, and whose tightly latticed sides again prevented him from being seen or identified by any watcher.

He understood that this procedure was less for the sake of the prisoner's feelings than because, as the judgements of the Council of Ten were arbitrary and often designed to rid themselves of troublemakers and possible rivals rather than to forward the cause of justice, it was often necessary that a condemned man be spirited away and executed before his friends knew what was happening and could raise the mob in his support.

There was no chance of any mob coming to his aid, Hawkwood knew; rather would they cheer at his execution.

Once across the bridge, he found himself in another building, and was taken down several flights of stairs into the cell which was to be his last home on earth. He was relieved to think he would only spend twenty-four hours here. The dungeon was below the level of the canal; as well as smelling like the inside of a sewer, it was extremely damp, the only sound being the constant dripping of water — the floor was covered to a depth of two inches — and the scurrying of rats.

At least, in mid-August, it was not cold.

Inside the cell, his bonds were removed, but instead his ankles were chained to a heavy iron ball. This left his arms free to chase away the rats, but made movement a slow and painful business.

He had not been ill-treated in any way, and no sooner was he safely chained than his gaolers brought him some very palatable food, mainly pasta, as well as wine and water. Nor was there any indication that he was to be tortured — although it was difficult to think of any other reason for Mocenigo's decision to postpone his execution by an extra day. Hawkwood found himself wondering how he would react when faced with either the rack or the axe. He remembered Prince Bayazid: another crime to lay at his door, and carried out in the name of the Sultan.

There was no window in the cell, and he did not suppose the candle would last very much longer. He supposed his best choice would be to sit on the ball to which his chains were attached, and this he managed to push into the driest corner of the cell. There he was for the moment reasonably comfortable, with only his feet wet, while the rats regarded him from a distance. They would wait for him to fall asleep before attacking.

Leaning back against the wall, he thought of Barbara and his sons. He had to believe that Mocenigo would have kept his word, and sent them all in safe-keeping to the Cornaros ... and that Barbara would be welcomed by her family. If that could be so, then the three boys might yet grow up to be of some service both to Venice and to Christendom.

He was very tired after the tensions of the long voyage from Istanbul, and dosed off during the afternoon. As a result he slipped from his ball and landed in the water with a splash, which awoke him and frightened off the rats.

The candle had by now gone out. Thoroughly uncomfortable, he stood up for a while, hoping his clothes would dry faster. Then he heard the bolt being drawn on the door.

He certainly had not been in the cell twenty-four hours yet, so presumably he was, after all, to be put to the torture.

Aware of a quickening heartbeat, he faced the door as it swung inwards.

In came the same gaoler as earlier, carrying a torch, but now he was accompanied by another man, richly dressed and of considerable age; his features were gnarled and jowlly yet wind- and sun-burned.

Hawkwood realised he was in the presence of a seaman, like himself. And, further, who this man had to be.

"Hawk Pasha," the man said, "it is an honour to stand face to face with you. I am Sebastian Viniero."

"Then am I also privileged, *monsignore*," Anthony told him. He knew that Viniero was Admiral in command of all the Venetian fleets and, although he was seventy-five years old, was still a feared antagonist.

"You have abandoned the Sultan, and aim to fight against him?" Viniero said.

"I had hoped to do so, certainly." Hawkwood looked down at his chained ankles. "But it seems that I am prevented."

"Strike off those chains," Viniero instructed the gaoler. "Here is the warrant." He unrolled his piece of parchment.

The gaoler peered first at the seal, then took one of the keys from his belt and knelt to unlock the fetters.

"You have not been harmed?" Viniero inquired.

"No, *monsignore*."

"Good. Then come with me."

Anthony was led through another succession of corridors, to emerge into a courtyard. Here waited some more men, who provided him with a voluminous cloak to conceal his clothes, and a heavy-brimmed hat.

"Hold your cloak close," Viniero warned. "You must conceal your beard."

Thus wrapped up, Hawkwood was led from the courtyard and down some steps to the canal, where a gondola waited. He and Viniero got into it, and the boat was pushed away. For a few minutes Anthony enjoyed some warming sunshine piercing the range of houses to either side.

"You will understand," Viniero warned, "that to escape my custody would only lead to your death here in Venice."

Hawkwood nodded. He was in any event too interested in what

was about to happen.

The gondola had only a short distance to travel, obliquely across the canal, before bringing up at another short flight of steps rising out of the water. At the head of these was a barred door, which now swung open. Hawkwood found himself in another of the interminable dark corridors which composed this watery rabbit-warren.

Now he was led up stairs again, then passed through a hall in which there were windows and a trace of afternoon sunlight, to reach a small room whose walls were entirely lined with book-cases, and whose floorspace almost entirely occupied by a huge desk, littered with papers.

Behind the desk sat Alvise Mocenigo.

"You will excuse this charade, *signore*," the Doge said, "but it is necessary. Sit down."

There were two other chairs in the room. Hawkwood's clothes remained clammily damp, so he cautiously lowered himself on to one of these, while Viniero took the other.

"You were condemned to death by a majority of only two," Mocenigo advised him. "That is a narrow vote, although a decisive one. If I am to overturn a majority decision of the Council of Ten, I must be able to give irrefutable reasons. However, I happen to know that the hostile vote was less against you than in favour of our terminating the alliance we have made with the Papacy and Spain, so as to cut our losses and make peace with the Porte again.

"This is not mere pusillanimity. It is difficult to change the attitudes which men have assumed over generations. For many years we have been the allies of the Ottomans, and there are those amongst us who believe that it is our true fate to remain within the Ottoman orbit, that we should have ceded Cyprus when Selim demanded it, and that we should now seek peace as rapidly as possible.

"I am not one of those people, Hawk Pasha. These conciliators also hate and fear the Papacy. This is common to most Venetians, I fear, and is heartily reciprocated by the average Roman. The Christian kingdoms of the West mistrust us because we are a republic and our form of government is abhorrent to them. That we are a rich and successful republic makes us even more repugnant.

"I am well aware of these things, but it is now a matter of

determining which of these world powers today poses the greater threat to Venice: the Papacy or the Porte. In my mind it is the Porte, and, in Pius V, I have discovered a pope who thinks as I do."

He paused to take a sip of wine from the goblet on his desk. There was a decanter nearby, and Viniero filled another glass and offered it to Hawkwood. Anthony accepted it, but did no more than brush the rim with his lips.

"Now I believe," the Doge continued, "as do others, of whom Admiral Viniero here is one, that the only way we may ever strike decisively at the Ottoman power is by sea. I sense that you also realise this."

Hawkwood nodded instinctively.

"The West has sent countless armies against the Porte," the Doge continued, "and every one has been defeated. Over the past thirty years the Ottomans have had virtually unchallenged control of the sea, but that is due to our own incompetence and to our lack of co-ordination. And in that time they — and you — have created the greatest navy in the history of our world, far beyond the potential of any single Western state. Yet the beast *has* been defeated at sea in the past, has he not?"

"Yes," Anthony concurred.

"Thus he can surely be defeated again, so long as we put against him sufficient ships and men, and sufficiently able commanders. We have such an armament gathering now, at Messina. But it is gathering to relieve Famagusta. Once knowledge of the fall of Famagusta reaches it, I am afraid this alliance will collapse, and each admiral will lead his own squadron home. This would be a disaster of the first magnitude, and I doubt whether such a force could ever again be brought together. I am determined this will not happen, whatever the wishes of some of my colleagues. And I believe you may be of great value to our cause, *signore*, if you would be willing to go to Messina, and inspire the fleet commanders with some determination, so that they may overcome their mutual suspicions and put to sea before they hear of Famagusta."

"I am willing," Anthony said without hesitation.

"And I will be at your elbow," Viniero added.

Mocenigo nodded. "There is another reason why I wish to employ you, Hawk. I have said that we need not only ships, but admirals fully capable of defeating the Turks — and we do not have them."

Anthony glanced at Viniero in surprise.

Mocenigo smiled. "Our Admiral here knows the truth of what I say. Excellence in sea warfare is not gained by genius alone, however great that may be. It is the result of genius allied to experience, and experience not only of the enemy but of the seas and the winds. These things our commanders somewhat lack, since not one of them has ever fought a pitched battle against the Turks. And the designated Commander-in-Chief ... you have heard of him?"

"Don Juan of Austria."

"A mere boy, appointed because Philip of Spain would have it so." Mocenigo's mouth twisted. "The Spanish contingent is by far the largest in our fleet."

"The young man's reputation is highly regarded in Istanbul, Your Excellency."

"That may be — but as a soldier. He has won a few battles in his time, but he has never fought at sea." Mocenigo pointed. "He cannot of course be supplanted as Commander-in-Chief. You may, indeed, have some difficulty in persuading him to accept you at all. But if you can do that, and become his adviser, our cause will be greatly advanced."

"I will undertake this," Anthony said.

Mocenigo stared at him. "It is a mission of considerable danger, Hawk. There is at least a chance that the Spaniards may hang you on sight."

"I understand the risk."

"But you will have my recommendation, and that of Viniero here. And I will send you first of all to Rome. Persuade Pope Pius of your worth, and your battle is half won."

Anthony nodded.

"I should remind you that your mission is of considerable danger not only to yourself, but also to me, in that I will surely be pilloried for trusting a renegade — and can only justify myself through your success. It will be of even greater danger to your sons, should you fail — or, even more, should you have in mind any treachery. I would have you understand this, Monsignore Hawkwood. Your wife is a niece of mine, and her kinsmen were scandalised when we learned she was being forced into marriage with such a man as you.

"Monsignore Hawkwood, your family will remain here in Venice until you return in triumph. Should you help us defeat the Turks, you may ask of me what you will, and if it is in my power, you will have it.

"Should you not return here, because you died in battle, victorious or not, I will honour your wife and mother, and give protection to your sons.

"But should you be too easily defeated, or should you play the traitor and deliver our fleet to the Ottomans, I swear that, niece or no, you will hear the screams of your wife in hell as she is sent to join you — followed by your sons. Do you understand me?"

"Yes," Hawkwood replied grimly.

"It is well that you do. Now prepare yourself for your journey. Haste is all important."

Hawkwood was given a warm bath, and food and wine, in Viniero's own palazzo, and then clothes were produced for him to wear. They did not fit very well, but they at least transformed him from a Turkish pasha into a Venetian gentleman, and to make certain he was not easily recognised, Viniero's barber shaved off his beard.

Here was an odd experience; like any Ottoman, Anthony had worn hair on his chin since puberty. When the barber was done, he could hardly recognise himself.

"It has halved your age," Viniero observed, "whatever that may be."

"I am thirty-four years of age," Hawkwood told him.

"And without the beard you look ten years younger. I wonder what your wife will make of you."

Anthony wondered the same thing as he was taken from the Admiral's palazzo to that of the Cornaro family. It was late evening by now, and although the setting sun still drew brilliant reflections from the campanile of St Mark's, the air had cooled; the streets and squares and bridges of Venice were filled with promenading citizens, all seemingly in the best of humour. The Doge had not yet released the news of the massacre at Famagusta, and all they knew was that a famous Turkish admiral had been captured, and was no doubt being tortured to surrender his secrets.

So no one paid much attention to the tall, clean-shaven man who hurried past them accompanied by four retainers, his close-cropped hair concealed beneath a black velvet hat, his dark blue jerkin and matching trunk hose indicating that he was in every way an Italian, a man of fashion too.

But he breathed a sigh of anticipation when a postern gate was opened to allow him into a little garden, its latticework supporting a mass of vines which gave it a very real privacy.

His guards remained on the street, and he was left alone, gazing at the single door let into the side wall of the palazzo, which building rose several stories above his head.

After a few minutes the door opened, and his wife Barbara stepped through.

She also had been transformed — from a Turkish lady to a Venetian — and wore a dark red velvet gown with huge puffed shoulders; both her partlet and her underskirt were heavily embroidered velvet, and she had gauze ruffs at her neck and wrists, while her hair had been carefully dressed and pulled back from her face to leave it exposed. Beautiful as she had always been, he had never seen her looking so splendid.

While she stopped in consternation.

"I beg your pardon," she said.

"Is a wisp of beard that confounding, *signora*?" he asked.

Barbara frowned at him. "Anthony? My lord?"

He held out his hands, and a moment later she was in his arms.

"Oh, Anthony, I feel like an adulteress."

"I only wish we had the time to make you one, my sweet," he told her, "but I am allowed no more than a few minutes." He held her away from him. "Your great-uncle is sending me to Messina."

"Then you are going to war? Leaving us here?"

"Where you will be safe. I have the Doge's word. And for the future of our sons, should I not return."

She gripped him almost fiercely. "But you will return, Anthony. Swear that to me."

He kissed her. "I will return."

"And then?"

"Then, why, we shall seek nothing else but happiness."

He would not tell her of the penalties of failure, because there could be no failure. Should he not be able to gain the day, then he must die in the battle, as Mocenigo had recommended.

But Hawkwood had never lacked confidence in himself.

She summoned his mother Felicity and the three boys, and he said farewell to them, too.

"I wish I could come with you, Father," John pleaded. "Could I not be your page?"

"Your business is to care for your mother," Anthony told him. "Until my return at the least."

Felicity hugged him against her. "Will this really be the end?"

"For me, Mother," he promised her, and rejoined his guards.

Together with Kalil — delighted to be accompanying his master — Anthony rejoined Viniero and the Admiral's attendants and they left Venice by ferry before midnight; the Doge wanted Anthony well away from the city before the time ordained for his execution. Mocenigo was here steering as tortuous a political course as any Hawkwood had ever undertaken, and with equal danger to both — but his guiding aims were the destruction of Ottoman power and the recovery of the Republic, and he would use those twin ambitions to bludgeon down any opposition. Yet he could never wholly guarantee that Anthony would not be assassinated somewhere, somehow by an agent of the peace party.

Horses waited for them on the mainland, and they commenced their journey immediately. Yet Hawkwood was exhausted and it was necessary to sleep, so, once Viniero considered they were safely distant from the city, he called a halt and the party bivouacked under the warm August skies.

Next day they continued on their way, already into Papal territory. Anthony recalled his mother telling him of how his great-uncle William had fled along this same path, eighty years ago. But he suffered no inconvenience on this journey, for he travelled under the flag of the Papacy's new ally, Venice, and in the company of the Admiral.

Three weeks after leaving Venice, they arrived in Rome.

Viniero had warned Anthony of what to expect. In Istanbul the vagaries of the Protestant revolt against Rome had been little understood or heeded: Christendom was Christendom — another world. In the West, however, the religious upheaval, which had now been going on for more than a generation, was regarded as a far greater crisis than any incursions of Ottoman power.

Earlier popes confronted with this new ideology had been uncertain how to cope with it. But Pius V — once a shepherd boy named Antonio Ghislieri — had never any doubts.

In the five years since his elevation to the Papacy, he had launched the most vigorous attack ever known on what he considered moral laxity. He had banned all alcohol from the Vatican, confined the Roman prostitutes to a small section of the city marked off from the rest by red-painted lanterns, forbidden all recreation on Sunday, banned profanity, ordered all clerics to spend a certain proportion of their time in their own dioceses instead of gathering in Rome, and made the daily recital of the Catechism a matter of law. Any backsliders were handed over to the Inquisition.

Having thus cleaned up his own back yard, Pius had turned his attention to the international scene. He had begun by expelling the Jews from his Papal domains, except where they were essential for commercial purposes — and even there they were permitted only the status of slaves. He had encouraged Philip II of Spain to wage an unremittingly brutal war upon his Dutch Protestant subjects; and he had excommunicated Queen Elizabeth of England.

"As to what good will come of all these things, no man can say," Viniero told Hawkwood. "It is certain that he has made Europe a most uncomfortable continent in which to live. But he has one redeeming feature: he is determined to bring down the Turk. As this is your aim and mine, I would beg you to be careful when you meet him."

The Doge's letters were delivered to the Vatican, and within an hour Hawkwood and Viniero were summoned into the Papal presence.

Anthony found himself facing a little man with a fiercely hooked nose and pointed beard, who slumped rather than sat in his chair, as if he were not in the best of health. He was sixty-seven, but there was still fire in his eyes as he stared at the huge figure in front of him.

"Monsignore Mocenigo says you are a messenger with news of vital importance," he said. "Tell me it."

"First, my name, Your Holiness," Anthony said. "I am Hawkwood, known as Hawk Pasha. I used to serve the Turks."

The Pope sat up slowly.

As Anthony told him of Famagusta and its aftermath, the Pope stared at him. When he had finished speaking, there was silence for a while, then Pius said, "If you have served the infidel against us, can you give me one reason why I should not hand you over instantly to the Inquisition?"

"Monsignore Mocenigo felt the same way at first, until he reflected upon what I had to offer, Your Holiness."

Once again the Pope listened. At the end, he said, "Truly, Our Father moves in mysterious ways. I have sworn to bring down the anti-Christ before I die ... and are you the weapon I must use? Yet Mocenigo is right. I do not know how long the combined fleet can remain in being once news of Famagusta is received. And I am only too well aware of Don Juan's lack of experience. But you are of English descent, and they are a nation of vipers. What religion do you profess, *monsignore*?"

Anthony had prepared himself for this question. "I am of the True Faith, Your Holiness."

"Well, then, perhaps God is not so mysterious after all. I will give you a letter to take to the Spaniard."

"With the future of Christendom at stake, would he really have cast me aside had I declared Protestantism?" Hawkwood asked Viniero.

The Admiral gave a grim smile. "The latter, certainly. These Romans see in the disciples of Luther a direct challenge to their own authority, which, after all, exists only in men's minds."

But there was no time for metaphysical matters, for it was already September, a month since the fall of Famagusta. Not only would the weather soon begin to break for the winter — and there would be no hope of keeping the allied fleet together for several months without the tonic of a victory — but Anthony had no idea how much longer the news of that catastrophe could be kept secret.

From Rome they hurried to Civitavecchia, to join a Papal galley, and by that night they were at sea, making south for the Straits of Messina. Two mornings later they passed between the Rock of Scylla and the Whirlpool of Charybdis, and emerged into the broad stretch of water which, for a hundred miles, separated Italy from Sicily. And there came upon the allied fleet — combining ships of

556

Venice, the Papacy, Genoa and Spain.

"I should tell you," Viniero said, "that from here on you have to be even more careful how you go, Hawkwood. In the Venetian fleet, among my commanders, are two younger Brigadinos. They do not yet know of their brother's death — or how he died."

The fleet made a brave sight. A quick count convinced Hawkwood that there were some three hundred ships at anchor, covering a huge extent of water, and including everything from small galleys to ocean-going galleons.

Most interesting to him, however, were the six huge galleasses moored close to each other, true floating fortresses. He had only ever seen these mammoth vessels from a distance, and his practised eye could discern at once their weaknesses as well as their strengths. They needed several banks of oars, for when there was no wind, yet with the coming of too much wind, those oar-ports would need to be closed, after the oars had been shipped, and in a hurry.

Yet properly used, and in the right weather, he thought they might have a devastating effect on any battle.

The fleets were a mass of pennants and flags, and a mass of men, too. A tremendous hubbub rose into the still air, together with a tremendous effluvium. These ships had been here too long already.

No one paid much attention to the Papal galley — there were already quite a few ships flying the Roman colours — as it snaked through them and entered the harbour of Messina itself. There Don Juan of Austria had his headquarters in a palazzo in the city. Once again Hawkwood was kept waiting, while the letters from both the Pope and the Doge were sent in to the allied commander.

He was aware only of pleasant anticipation. Having seen the fleet, he had recognised at once that it was not so large as Ali Pasha's, and that the crews were undoubtedly stale from too long in port, yet he felt that they had a better than even chance, especially with the ideas he had in mind.

Supposing Don Juan would even listen to him.

As he watched, he found himself gazing at the young man who sat at the desk on the far side of the room. Clearly one of Don Juan's secretaries, for he was writing industriously, he every so often raised his head to look at the big man. His face was somewhat long and solemn, but he had lively eyes.

At last his curiosity grew too much for him.

"Excuse me, *monsignore*," he asked. "But I cannot convince myself that you are truly a Venetian."

"Nor am I," Anthony said. "I suppose you could say that I am English, although I have never set foot in that country."

"Then you are a wanderer, like myself."

"You, sir? I would have said you were Spanish, serving a Spanish commander, I observe."

"Indeed, *monsignore*. But yet am I a fugitive in Italy, sentenced to the loss of my right hand should I ever return to Spain" — there was a faint smile — "unless I can do so with sufficient patronage. Hence I have volunteered to serve the Prince. Can I cover myself with glory now, when we encounter the Turk I may hope for better things."

"A duel?"

"An affray. During which my opponent lost some blood. It sore beset me to leave my country, and my parents, and enter exile, but what would you, *monsignore*, without my right hand ..." He regarded it speculatively. "It is the hand I write with."

"Indeed," Anthony observed.

"*Monsignore*, I am a poet." He glanced at Hawkwood. "I have been published."

"My congratulations," Anthony said.

Messengers had been hurrying to and fro during the conversation, and richly dressed men had begun to arrive. Now Viniero himself appeared.

"We are summoned to a conference," the Venetian admiral confided. "It can only be about you."

He went into the inner room, and almost immediately Hawkwood was called. He turned to the young man. "I will wish you good fortune with your hands, and your talent."

"If you are volunteering for the fleet, *monsignore*, you will need little fortune. The commander will welcome you. But I will wish it for you none the less." He held out his hand. "My name is Miguel de Cervantes."

Anthony squeezed the offered fingers.

As he stepped through the doorway, he observed that there were several men present. But he had eyes only for the man standing behind the desk and gazing at him.

Don Juan was twenty-four years old, tall and slender, exquisitely but quietly dressed in doublet and trunk hose, both in black relieved by the gold chain round his neck and gold embroidery at the shoulders and cuffs. His head was bare, and his fair hair and beard indicated his German mother.

"Hawk Pasha," the young Habsburg said in Italian, his voice quiet. "I had never supposed to meet you, except in battle. But I would rather have you at my shoulder than before my face. Welcome to Messina."

He held out his hand, and Anthony grasped it, feeling his heart warming to this young man.

"I would have you meet my officers. From the Spanish navy, the Marquis of Santa Cruz, and Don Gil de Andrade."

Anthony bowed to the Spanish commanders; their gazes were hostile.

"From the Republic of Genoa, Admiral Giovanni Andrea Doria."

The two men stared at each other. Their fathers had fought against each other, and Anthony himself had followed Dragut in raids upon Genoese possessions fifteen years earlier.

Then Doria gave a brief smile. "Welcome, Hawk Pasha," he said.

"From the Papacy," Don Juan continued, "Admiral Marco Antonio Colonna."

Again a quick bow.

"Admiral Viniero you already know. His officers: Augustino Barbarigo, Marco Contarini, Federigo Nani, Marco Quirini, Ambrogio Brigadino, and Antonio Brigadino."

Anthony bowed. It took a considerable effort of will not to catch his breath as he gazed at the two young men who looked so like their dead brother.

"The general of my soldiers, Marshal Ascanio de la Corgnia," Don Juan continued. "And this is Cardinal de Granvelle, who represents His Holiness in our debates."

Like the Spaniards, the Cardinal's look was hostile, despite his master's letter of recommendation.

"His Holiness and His Excellency the Doge indicate that you have abandoned the service of the Sultan to return to the true faith," Don Juan said. "And, more important, that you have pressing news for us."

Hawkwood glanced at Viniero, who raised his eyebrows. Both Pope and Doge had clearly left it to their decision as to how soon to acquaint the fleet commanders with the news of Famagusta.

But now that decision had to be shared.

He looked Don Juan in the eye. "My news is for your ears alone, my lord."

Don Juan frowned, then glanced at his officers.

"We are a united force, sir," Cardinal de Granvelle snapped.

"Nonetheless, I must speak with your commander in private."

"To assassinate him?" inquired de Andrade.

"I am entrusted by His Holiness with my mission, *signore*. If you wish to distrust me, then send me back to Rome."

Anthony knew that only boldness would succeed with these men, each of whom in his heart must hate him ... but each of whom also hated every other.

"I will speak with you alone, Hawkwood," Don Juan decided. "If you will excuse us, *signori*."

The admirals hesitated, but Viniero urged them from the room.

"You had best be seated," Don Juan invited, when the door had closed, and he sat down himself. He gave a quiet smile. "The better to convince me of your purpose."

Hawkwood sat down. "First I need to be convinced of yours, my lord."

Don Juan's frown was back. "You are a singularly arrogant fellow."

"You mistake me, sire. The news I bring might shake the resolve of any but the most determined of men."

"You are about to tell me that Famagusta has fallen?" Don Juan looked shaken.

"I will tell you of it," Anthony said, and did so.

Don Juan listened in silence. Then he said, "You are also a singularly bold fellow, Hawkwood. But then, that is obvious. did His Holiness send you to me to be hanged?"

"To assist you in leading your fleets to victory, sire." It was his turn to smile. "If I do not, then you will have to take your turn in the queue to put the noose around my neck."

Don Juan slapped his desk. "I admire you, renegade Englishman — and I feel sorry for you. Your task is impossible. Once those men out there hear that the reason for our gathering here no longer exists, they will fly apart like the pieces of an exploding grenade. They threaten to do so anyway. As for when the Brigadinos learn what happened to their brother ..."

"I am perfectly willing to meet either of the Brigadinos, sword in hand, if they wish it so, my lord. But not until we have defeated the Turks."

Don Juan stroked his beard. "You have powerful reasons for wishing this campaign carried through, that is obvious. Can it be done? The Turkish fleet is very large, and strong."

"That is true. But tell me of yours."

Don Juan got up and went to a window which overlooked the harbour. "My half-brother, the King of Spain, has sent, under my command, a fleet of ninety galleys, twenty-four galleons, and fifty frigates and brigantines; this includes the Genoese squadron, but Doria will obey me. Viniero commands a fleet of one hundred and six galleys, six galleasses, two galleons and six frigates, but it is short of soldiers. The Papal fleet consists of twelve galleys and six frigates."

Hawkwood stood beside him. "Then you are gravely outnumbered. Ali Pasha will command not less than two hundred and fifty ships, and they will all be Turkish."

Don Juan's frown came back. "I do not understand you. We have more than three hundred."

"Of which only two hundred and eight are galleys, my lord. This will be a galley fight, because Ali Pasha will make it so. I believe the six Venetian galleasses will be invaluable ... but you can entirely discount your sailing ships. In the Adriatic, or in the Aegean, wherever we encounter the Turks, there will either be no wind at all, so that they will lie helplessly becalmed, or so much they will have all they can do to keep out of trouble, much less fight a battle."

"The devil!" Don Juan returned to his desk.

"But I believe we will still gain the day."

"You think so?" Don Juan's shoulders were hunched. "The problem seems to grow more and more insuperable every moment. As you have just remarked, all the enemy ships will be manned by men of a single nation. While ours ..."

"What is your total strength?"

The Prince shrugged. "I have approximately fifty thousand seamen, but that includes the galley slaves, and some thirty thousand soldiers. It is the difference in nationality that worries me. The Genoese hate the Venetians, the Venetians hate the Papal troops, my Spaniards hold the lot of them in contempt, and as for this de Granvelle fellow, I sometimes think he hates the world. The conditions he would continually impose upon me, as regards treatment of heretics ... or even suspected heretics! And you still say we can beat the Turks? I cannot be sure that, at the very moment battle is joined, my force will not commence fighting each other rather than the enemy. To be outnumbered as well ..."

Anthony now realised that the commander was too young to bear the mental burdens of the responsibility which had been placed upon his shoulders, not to mention the looming disapproval of his admirals, all older and more experienced than he — and all in turn overshadowed by the brooding personality of the Cardinal.

Yet Don Juan's charisma was evident. All he needed was the spur of action.

"I was sent here to help you, sire," Hawkwood said "therefore I will speak plainly, at the risk of giving offence. Every day your fleet sits here it rots, and the enmities within it grow. And the Turks grow stronger. You must put to sea immediately."

Don Juan sighed. "It is already September. My captains who regularly sail these waters say it is too late in the year, and that we must wait until the spring."

"By the spring your command will no longer exist. Put to sea, my lord. The weather does not break fully until the second half of October. We have a month. Put to sea. I know where the Turkish fleet is, and I will lead you to it."

Don Juan raised his head.

Anthony smiled at him. "And give you the victory ... if I may also give you some advice."

"Begin."

"I would like to begin by inspecting your ships, my lord."

Hawkwood already had his ideas fairly firmly fixed in his head; they were but strengthened by what he saw. The galleons were as powerful as he had always suspected, but as unwieldy except in a brisk sailing wind — from the right quarter. As he had told Don Juan their value in a Mediterranean battle could be written off. The same went for the frigates and brigantines, which were small, half-decked ships, very lightly armed, although he considered that the brigantines might be useful for scouting whenever there was a wind.

The galleasses, however, were even more powerful than he had anticipated. They carried no less than seventy guns each, varying from man-killers to ship-smashing cannon, and in addition, their rowers were protected by a deck above their heads. He reckoned one galleass, resolutely handled, should be able to take on half a dozen galleys with every hope of success.

But the battle would be won or lost by the galleys themselves.

The Christian galleys were on the average over a hundred and fifty feet in length, about the same as the Turkish, but he was interested to discover that their hull planking was some four inches thick, an inch more than the Turkish ships, and that here again their rowers were protected by wooden mantlets, something else the Turkish ships lacked.

They also carried an average of five guns on their foredeck, as opposed to the Turkish three. And each ship was armed with the great gilded ramming beak, which Anthony supposed had not changed an iota since the days of the Athenian triremes.

"What do you think?" Don Juan asked, when the tour of inspection was finally completed. It had taken several days — while the admirals stood around and pulled their beards and de Granvelle wrote letters to Rome.

"I think you have the makings of a fine fighting force here, sire," Anthony told him. "But you will be opposed by a fleet which has not known defeat this generation."

"And outnumbered," Don Juan said, again despondent.

"Thus we cannot rely upon normal tactics."

"What would you describe as normal tactics for a naval battle?"

"I am not qualified to speak of a battle in the Atlantic, my lord, where wind and weather plays as important a part as guns and marines. But here in the Mediterranean a normal galley battle is very like a land battle. The two sides array themselves in order, and then engage, the objective being to overwhelm a weak part of the enemy line, or turn his flank. For this reason most galley battles are fought close to land, so that one flank at the least cannot be turned. You may be sure that Ali Pasha will adopt this strategy."

"Can we not adopt something different?"

Hawkwood shook his head. "Not without danger. But we can, I think, adapt our tactics to our advantage."

"How?"

"Well, firstly, I would use your galleasses as prongs, to force the enemy into disarray. If you were to place them in pairs, one pair in front of each of the three divisions of your fleet, and send them ahead, boldly into the centre of the Turks, you would cause a mêlée of which your ordinary galleys may be able to take advantage. The Turks are apprehensive of the galleasses, as I know. They have none of their own and no experience in fighting against them."

Don Juan stroked his beard. "I stand the risk of losing the six great ships."

"It is a risk worth taking if it enables you to win the battle, my lord."

Don Juan stared at him. "Go on."

"Secondly, my lord, I would remove the beaks from the bows of every one of your galleys."

"Are you sure you are not demented, Hawkwood? How may a galley fight without its beak? Is not the main function of galley warfare to ram, or sheer off an opponent's oars?"

"That is true, sire. Or it would be more correct to say that it has always been true up to now. But to ram an enemy, or sheer away his oars, you must come into contact with him. You must have a mêlée. Once you lose your ships in a mêlée with the Turks, you will lose them indeed, because they will outnumber you both for ships and men. You must win this battle, or at least equalise your numbers, at long range — by the use of your cannon. You are more heavily armed than the Turks, but your guns are hampered, as are theirs, by being unable to fire straight ahead. Remove the beaks, my lord, and give your five pieces on each ship a clear field of fire. I believe you may gain the day without ever coming alongside an enemy."

"By all that is holy," Don Juan muttered. "You are either a genius or a fool, Hawkwood. But will my commanders accept such a radical approach? Will they fight, in any event?"

"You must be sure of it, by hanging the first man, of whatever rank, who dares to disobey you. As for their differences, why ... you must mix your people up."

"Eh?"

"You say the Venetians are short of soldiers. Put Spanish soldiers on board the Venetian galleys. Then take some Venetian sailors on board your own ships. Have a fully integrated fleet."

"Your concepts grow bolder by the moment. Tell me what else you have in mind."

"That is all that needs to be done at this moment, sire. Have the beaks stripped today, and let us put to sea as quickly as possible. Once we are at sea ... I have another suggestion."

"Tell me."

"We are outnumbered in fighting men as well as ships. This we must rectify."

"Do you not suppose I have sought additional recruits? They are simply not to be had."

"They exist on board your own ships."

"What do you mean?"

"How many of your galley slaves are Christians?"

"Why, two-thirds, I would estimate. But of those, more than half are Protestants, sentenced to the galleys by the Inquisition."

"They are still Christians, and we are going to fight the Turk. Just before we engage the enemy, unchain them, and arm them."

"Now I know you are mad!"

"And promise them their freedom after your victory, if they fight for you."

Don Juan leaned back on his chair. "Granvelle would absolutely forbid it."

"With respect, my lord, but may I ask who commands this fleet? Cardinal de Granvelle or Don Juan of Austria?"

The young man stared at him for several seconds, then slapped his desk. "Don Juan of Austria, by God."

The orders were given, and to the consternation of the admirals, the beaks were removed from each of the galleys. They were even more astounded when the Commander-in-Chief ordered Spanish marines on board the Venetian galleys, and Venetian seamen on to Spanish ships.

At least his actions stirred them up. Messina hummed with activity and comment, composed in equal parts of enthusiasm and dismay.

Then came the orders to put to sea and make for the Venetian-held island of Corfu.

"In September?" the Marquis of Santa Cruz expostulated. "It is too late, my lord, for the Adriatic. This English renegade is leading you astray."

"The fleet will sail, my lord Marquis," his commander replied, quietly but firmly. "The Turkish fleet is to be found up the Gulf of

Patras. We will make Corfu our advanced base."

The admirals had no choice but to obey. On 15 September 1571 the galleons put to sea behind a screen of frigates. With them went the galleasses.

The galleys left the next day. At Don Juan's insistence Hawkwood sailed with him in his flagship, the *Real*.

They spent their time discussing the actual tactics which would be required when the two fleets came to grips, hopefully after the Turks had been thrown into disarray by the gunfire of the galleasses and the unbeaked galleys. Anthony put at the Commander-in-Chief's disposal all of his long accumulated knowledge of galley fighting, reminding him of essentials like having soapy water ready to throw across his own decks to make them slippery should an enemy attempt to board, and having his boarding pikes greased for the last four feet of their length so that an opponent could not grasp them to wrestle them away. He also reminded the young leader that, because of the limited deck space on a galley, a squad of men must be detailed to throw dead bodies overboard the moment life was extinct ... or before that, in the case of an enemy.

"There are so many little points which need consideration," Don Juan conceded. "You must have been sailing galleys for a long time."

"All of my life," Anthony told him, simply.

"Then I thank God that He sent you to us. What else must we do?"

"You must order your line of battle, and acquaint your commanders with it."

"What would you recommend?"

"I would recommend three equal squadrons, and a reserve. Which of your commanders is the most capable of acting on his own?"

"Why, the Marquis of Santa Cruz. He is the most experienced seaman in the Spanish fleet."

"Then place him in command of the reserve. I would say twenty-eight ships, with orders to act upon his own initiative, and to support whichever part of the main battle most needs it."

Don Juan nodded. "Go on."

"Then divide the rest of your force, as I have said, into three squadrons, of sixty ships each. You will of course command the

centre. If, as I anticipate, Ali Pasha waits for you to come to him
..."

"Why should he do that, Hawkwood?"

"For two reasons. As I have said, he prefers to fight near a
headland, so that one wing is protected. But secondly, when he
learns the size of your fleet, as he will do, he will prefer to fight in
Turkish waters, so that if he is defeated he can safely retreat."

"While if we are defeated we lose everything." The commander
was again gloomy.

Anthony smiled. "But we are not going to be defeated, sire. I
was saying, if I am right, Ali will opt to fight within sight of the
land, probably in the mouth of the Gulf of Patras, and inclining to
the north shore, as it is upon that shore that his base of Lepanto is
situated. In that case, I would give command of your left wing to
the Venetians, who are most used to fighting in close waters. They
will be the ones nearest the shore."

"And my right wing?"

"Why, my lord, as I doubt you will yield it to me ..."

"I cannot, Hawk Pasha, much as I would like to. There is
sufficient concern at your being with us at all."

"I recognise that, sire. Well then ... give it to Doria."

Don Juan gazed at him. "He is your bitterest enemy."

"He is also an excellent fighting seaman."

"You have a broad spirit, Hawkwood. I will adopt your re-
commendations. Now tell me, what else must we do?"

"There is little else we can do ... save pray that the weather
holds."

For the moment the skies were clear.

The last stragglers reached Corfu on 25 September. By then Don
Juan and Hawkwood were in possession of some interesting
information. The island had been attacked by a Turkish force only
a week or two previously, the Turks withdrawing when they
learned through their scouts of the approach of the Christian fleet.

These small scouting galleys had been seen from time to time,
and Don Juan had only with difficulty prevented his captains from
setting off in pursuit. His only fear was that the Turks would
withdraw from Lepanto on the news of his coming, but Hawkwood
was able to reassure him on this: Selim would never permit it. Nor
would Ali Pasha wish to do so. This was the moment for which he

had been waiting all his life.

And indeed from prisoners taken by the Venetian garrison they learned that the entire Turkish fleet was concentrated in the Gulf, and that Ali Pasha had arrived to take command.

"Who has he with him?" Anthony asked the frightened men.

"There are many great commanders, Hawkwood. Ali Pasha has with him Hassan Pasha from Algiers ..." Barbarossa's son, Anthony thought sombrely, "Hamet Bey, Uluch Ali, and Mahomet Scirocco Pasha."

"Who commands the troops?" Hawkwood asked.

"Pertau Pasha, my lord."

"Pertau Pasha," Anthony repeated with venom.

"Is he more important than the rest?" Don Juan asked.

"To me he is, my lord," Anthony said, with grim satisfaction.

On 29 September the fleet, accompanied by the galleasses but less the galleons — for there was no wind — sailed across the narrow strait separating Corfu from Albania, and put into the port of Gomenizza on the mainland to pick up some more information. That evening Don Juan of Austria assembled his captains and revealed to them at last the news that Famagusta had been captured, and its garrison murdered. He also told them of Hawkwood's part in it, and of the fate of Marcantonio Brigadino, gazing at the victim's brothers as he spoke.

Ambrogio Brigadino was on his feet. "And that wretch," he said, pointing, "is now virtually second-in-command of our fleet? My lord, I demand he is hanged this instant."

Anthony also stood up. "*Monsignore*, I am perfectly willing to meet you, sword in hand, the moment this campaign is over. But we are here to serve a great cause, a cause to which I am prepared to sacrifice my life. Should we not avenge your elder brother, and all those doomed men he commanded, before we fight amongst ourselves?"

"Well said, Hawkwood," Don Juan broke in. "There will be no duelling until after the battle. After our victory."

Next day seventeen more galleys arrived. Eight were a squadron supplied by the Knights of St John in Malta, commanded by the Prior of Messina, whose name was Giustiniani — a direct descendant of the Genoese soldier who had so heroically defended

Constantinople against Mahomet the Conqueror. The other nine came from Venice; it seemed that Alvise Mocenigo had determined to put everything he had into the defeat of the Turks, and had stripped his defences bare.

The reinforcements delighted Don Juan, who was able to adjust his tactical dispositions; he increased each of his three divisions to sixty-three ships, and the reserve to thirty-five. With two hundred and twenty-four galleys together with the galleasses, he no longer felt quite so outnumbered. And if the galleons could by any chance be brought into action ...

Hawkwood was more concerned about the weather, as he observed wisps of cloud high in the sky. Once October dawned, a sudden storm was always possible, although unlikely before the second half of the month, as he had promised their leader. Still, he would have liked to get on in search of the Turks, but Don Juan still insisted that the galleons would be of use in the coming fight, and three precious days were lost waiting, in Gomenizza, waiting for the breeze which would enable the huge ships to put to sea.

There was another cause for concern, as sickness now appeared in the fleet, inevitable when men were cooped up for a long period; nor did the daily intake of fresh food from the Albanian country-side improve matters — rather it seemed to make things worse. Amongst those down with fever was the young secretary, Miguel de Cervantes.

These were days when tempers, already tense, began to fray. Meanwhile the clouds gathered.

"My lord," Anthony said at last in desperation, "you are likely to lose the whole game by waiting to make it safe. There is weather about."

"Where?" scoffed the Cardinal, who no longer bothered to hide his dislike for the Englishman. "There is not a breath of air."

"Which makes it more certain that there will be a great deal of air in a few days time." Hawkwood turned to address Don Juan: "Surely you can see for yourself how useless the great ships will be in such conditions as these?"

The young Habsburg gave in, and next morning, 4 October, the galley fleet stood out for the south, passing inside the islands and the harbour of Prevesa — the scene of the battle of Actium sixteen centuries before and of Khair-ed-din's victory over the Genoese fleet in 1538 — before anchoring for the night off Cape Ducato.

That night the wind which Anthony had feared finally arrived, screaming out of a clear sky just after midnight. The galleys rolled and began taking on water, signal lanterns bobbed, and men cried out in dismay.

"What must we do?" Don Juan hurried on deck to find Hawkwood already there.

"We must seek shelter, sire."

"But where?"

"Cephalonia. There is a harbour called Phiskardo, protected from the north. We will lie there in perfect safety."

"If we ever get there," the Cardinal muttered, and crossed himself.

Don Juan was already giving commands, and the fleet weighed anchor and battled its way to the south. The *Real* led the way, a mass of lanterns at its masthead so that if one was blown away there would yet be others to follow, and by dawn all the ships had come safely into Phiskardo.

Their crews were shaken, however, and in Phiskardo there occurred an incident which nearly wrecked the entire campaign. Hawkwood and Don Juan were dining on the afterdeck of the *Real* when there was a tremendous hubbub from the Venetian squadron.

Both men were on their feet in a moment, gazing through the forest of masts in an attempt to discover what was happening. The hubbub continued for some time, before a Spanish officer, white-faced with indignation, arrived at the flagship by boat, and spluttered out his story.

There had been an altercation between some Venetian seamen and some Spanish soldiers on board one of the Venetian galleys, swords had been drawn, and several of the Venetians killed. Whereupon Admiral Viniero, being informed of the incident, had had the Spaniards seized and hanged.

"They droop there yet, my lord," the officer cried. "Murdered by those republicans."

"Viniero must hang beside them," de Granvelle growled. "The insolent dog."

"By God!" Don Juan said, as angry as anyone. "He shall. Give orders to surround the Venetian squadron, and demand that their admiral present himself before me."

"My lord!" Anthony cried. "You cannot do this."

Don Juan turned towards him, brows gathering in an imperious frown. "Do you dare countermand my order?"

"I dare attempt to save you from ruining your enterprise, sire. Did you not say to me that your only fear was that your people might fall to fighting amongst themselves before they could come to grips with the enemy?"

Don Juan hesitated, biting his lip.

"My lord," Hawkwood went on, "we are merely fortunate that this is the first such incident that has occurred. The men are anxious to close with the enemy. *There* is the cure for all our ills — and we are close to them now. That must be our sole objective. To attempt to arrest Admiral Viniero would be to have the entire Venetian fleet sail for home. Then would you be utterly bereft, and at the mercy of the Turks."

Don Juan stared at him for several seconds. Then he said, "Countermand that order."

The waiting officers hesitated, then obeyed.

"But I will not speak with Viniero again," Don Juan said. "Mark this well. I will communicate only with Vice-Admiral Barbarigo."

Hawkwood bowed his head. He had at least averted a catastrophe. He could do nothing more than that.

The wind continued to howl all day Saturday, 6 October, and the fleet tossed at its anchorage. Don Juan still had some hopes that the galleons might now be able to join them, but Hawkwood knew this was a slim chance; big, unwieldy ships would be in great danger attempting to brave such uncertain weather in this maze of islands and rocks.

But that evening the wind dropped.

"Will it come again, Hawk?" Don Juan asked.

Anthony studied the sky. "Not for another twenty-four hours at the least, sire."

"And we know the Turks are in the Gulf. Will they not stay there, waiting for the weather finally to drive us away?"

"I doubt that, my lord. But ... we have not too much more time."

"Then we shall use that time." The young commander called his flag captain. "Have the fleet signalled," he said. "We put to sea tomorrow morning, for the Gulf of Patras."

The captain saluted, and hurried on his way.

"Am I being rash?" the Habsburg asked.

"You are taking the only possible course, my lord," Anthony assured him.

At two o'clock on the morning of Sunday 7 October, the Spanish-Genoese squadron, which was designated to form the right wing of the Christian fleet, set sail under the command of Giovanni Andrea Doria.

As soon as it was clear of the harbour, the *Real* set out, followed by the centre division, included in which was not only the flagship of Colonna, the Papal commander, but also Viniero, who had handed over the command of the left wing to Barbarigo, in accordance with Don Juan's orders; the old man was as distressed as anyone over the deaths on board one of his ships.

With the centre squadron there sailed the first two galleasses, commanded respectively by Captains Duodo and Guora. The second pair would sail with the Venetians. The third pair had been supposed to accompany Doria and the Genoese, but for some reason were late getting under way. No doubt they would catch up later.

The course set was between the island of Oxia and the mainland, to round Point Scropha into the Gulf of Patras.

"How slowly Doria moves," Don Juan grumbled, as the Genoese squadron seemed to lumber immediately ahead of them. "Increase the beat," he told his flag captain.

The captain hurried to the waist with the order, and the drum-beat was immediately quickened to one every second. The galleys began to surge through the water.

"May I counsel patience, my lord," Anthony suggested. "The enemy is there. He will not escape us now."

"I must lead, and be seen to lead," Don Juan declared. "Maintain the beat."

He was now in a fine fury of anticipation and elation. Abeam of Point Scropha the flagship was abreast of Doria's squadron, with the remainder of the fleet strung out behind. Ahead of them were the open waters of the Gulf of Patras, with the northern shore of the Peloponnesus lost in the morning mist, as the darkness faded to an uncertain light.

Hardly were the ships round the headland when Hawkwood observed signals flying from the masthead of Doria's flagship, the *Capitana*.

"Ships in sight," he said. "Where away masthead?" he bellowed.

"Two sail to the east," came the call.

Every officer immediately climbed into the port rigging, the better to see.

"Three, four, six, eight," called the masthead.

Anthony narrowed his eyes, staring into the sudden brilliance as the sun threatened to rise above the mountains surrounding the gulf. Eight, he thought. Ten. Fifty, a hundred, two hundred, three hundred ...

"There, my lord," he said. "There is Ali Pasha, and the Turkish fleet. This is the day we have waited for."

The day I have waited for, he thought — for ten years. But now I am on the wrong side.

Don Juan shouted, "Fire the cannon, captain. Signal, enemy in sight!"

22

THE BATTLE

Anthony climbed high into the rigging, the better to see the approaching fleet. As he had forecast would be the case, Ali Monizindade had divided his ships into three squadrons, and was keeping close to the northern shore of the Gulf to protect his flank.

From the pennants Anthony determined that the northern squadron, the smallest of the three although it still certainly numbered more than fifty ships, was commanded by Scirocco Pasha.

Ali Monizindade himself commanded the centre, which was very nearly double the number of the flank squadron. Close by the flagship, Anthony could make out the pennant of Pertau Pasha.

The left wing, a squadron as large as that of the centre, flew the pennant of Uluch Ali.

Meanwhile, Don Juan had ordered the pennant of the Christian League to be run to the masthead, at the same time signalling his various squadrons to take up their positions, and commanding the principal admirals to come on board the flagship for their final fighting instructions.

It was just dawn.

The fighting instructions were as determined earlier by Hawkwood and the Commander-in-Chief, with the exception that the command of the left wing, which would move inshore to combat Scirocco Pasha, was now entrusted to Barbarigo. Veniero remained in the centre squadron, on the left of the flagship. Colonna, in the Papal flagship, took station immediately upon the *Real*'s right.

While the admirals were conferring, the captains called their men to breakfast, and then stripped the ships for action. Immediately the conference was over, Don Juan had himself rowed right round the fleet, to be greeted by cheers from every ship as he stood on the quarterdeck, his armour glittering in the first rays of the rising sun.

The prospect of action had driven away all his doubts, Anthony was happy to see. And restored his humour. When he passed Viniero's ship, and saw the venerable old Admiral standing on his quarterdeck, he gave him a happy wave.

On the return of the flagship to station, the signal was given for prayer. By now all the Christians were in armour, and this huge accumulation of mail-clad men, thirty thousand of them, solemnly knelt on their decks to make their peace with God before placing their lives in His hands.

Anthony watched them in wonder. He had been equipped with a Spanish cuirass and morion, but had declined a rapier — the use of which he knew nothing — for a trusty broadsword, though he would far rather have retained his scimitar. He looked like any Spaniard or Venetian, but realised he was not really at one with these people.

Kalil, also wearing Spanish armour, gazed in awe at the Christians kneeling around him.

During the prayers both men kept their eyes on the Turks, who emerged into the body of the Gulf in a huge crescent. But this was slowly straightening as they approached their enemies. It was also easy to see that there was some confusion already in the Ottoman fleet, occasioned by the presence of the four huge galleasses moving slowly forward in front of the Christian squadrons. Unfortunately the other two galleasses were still far behind.

The Turks kept coming, and their shouting and yelling drifted down on the slight land breeze.

It was now nearly ten o'clock in the morning when, with an enormous clanking ripple, the Christian host rose from their knees. The sun, now high in the sky, reflected brilliantly from their armour — it was as if each galley had lit a hundred candles all at the same moment.

It was now time to estimate the tactical problems which were looming. On the Christian left, Barbarigo and his Venetians were maintaining a slightly faster striking rate than the rest of the fleet, and were slowly drawing ahead — without, however, closing the shore as much as Don Juan had wished. Obviously Barbarigo was afraid of getting caught in the shallows.

Now Scirocco Pasha, either ordered to do so or acting on his own initiative, also increased his striking rate, and advanced rapidly to meet the Venetians. Don Juan immediately commanded his own striking rate to be increased, to move up abreast of his left wing.

On the Turkish left, however, Uluch Ali had extended his already superior strength so as to threaten an enveloping movement round the Christian right. Doria had seen the movement, and now his squadron was steering away from its station in an attempt to keep pace with the Turks.

Anthony chewed his lip. Doria's action was opening a gap in the Christian line. But it was too early to call upon the Marquis of Santa Cruz to bring his ships up; no one could tell if they might not be more urgently needed elsewhere.

It was half past ten when Scirocco's squadron came within range of Barbarigo's galleasses, and the first shots of the battle were fired. Smoke swirled into the air, and the galleasses' aiming and their power were so destructive that several of the Turkish galleys were crippled within a few minutes, their oars shattered like matchsticks and, in some cases, their masts going by the board. The rest altered course to the right, away from the galleasses and towards the shore.

Their intention was obvious: to flank the Venetians. Don Juan pulled his beard anxiously as he watched them — the centre was not yet engaged.

"Barbarigo is a fine fighting seaman," Hawkwood told him reassuringly.

And sure enough, the Venetian admiral turned his own ships to meet the threat, reasoning correctly that as long as the Turkish galleys floated, his would also. A furious mêlée developed inshore, and Hawkwood pointed.

The entire Turkish squadron had been drawn into the fight, their line folding up. This had left the Venetian right wing, commanded by Marco Quirini, in the air, as it were. And Quirini, another able commander, had immediately sized up the situation and turned his ships also to the north, but inclining slightly to the east — so that he was in the process of entirely surrounding the Turkish squadron.

"There at least we should have the victory, my lord," Hawkwood told Don Juan.

But now it was time to look to themselves; the centre was within range.

Once again the galleasses did their work, the crews serving their guns so well that the Turks recoiled from attacking them. Instead they surged round them and rowed for the Christian fleet, setting up a tremendous hubbub. In their centre were the galleys of Ali Monizindade and Pertau ... and they were making straight for the *Real* and her consorts.

And suffering heavily as they did so. For while every gun in each fleet was blazing away as fast as it could be loaded and fired, the Christians were doing far more damage, thanks to being able to fire straight ahead, following the removal of their beaks.

But Ali kept coming, and that he had identified Don Juan's pennant was obvious.

"He means to board," Hawkwood said, watching the Turkish galley surging towards them at full speed, while the Christian ships were maintaining a slow and regular beat.

"Arquebusiers!" came the call, and the three hundred men armed with handguns assembled in the waist of the ship.

Screaming their fury, the Turks kept on. The galley seemed to rear out of the sea as it was urged forward. Anthony had only time to cast a quick glance to the right to find that Pertau had inclined away to attack Colonna, who was closing up on the *Real.*

But Pertau would have to wait. There was a tremendous jar which sent men tumbling in every direction, and Ali's galley had struck home, smashing into the starboard bow of the *Real,* scything away oars, and bringing screams of terror from the rowers.

Over the shattered bows of both vessels there swarmed a horde of mailed Turks.

The arquebusiers were back on their feet and reforming, their staves planted in front of them.

"Fire!" Don Juan bellowed, at the same time drawing his sword.

Anthony had already drawn his weapon, and now, to his surprise, discovered at his side the young poet-cum-secretary, Miguel de Cervantes.

"I had supposed you ill, *señor,*" he said.

Certainly the boy looked pale.

"Not ill enough to miss such an occasion," he replied.

Together they hurried forward, Kalil behind them.

The arquebuses rippled fire, and more smoke clogged the still air. The Turks, overrunning the foredeck, were checked by the flying lead.

"Now," Hawkwood shouted. "Swords and pikes. Follow me."

He ran through the ranks of arquebusiers, who hastily dropped their firepieces and drew their swords. He charged at the bow; and the few remaining Turks clinging to the shattered timbers — several of their number were dead and several more had fallen into the water — shrieked their terror.

"Hawk Pasha!" they yelled. "Hawk Pasha returned from the grave."

Anthony assumed that the galley-captain he had outwitted in the Adriatic must have reported him as lost.

The Turks fled back on to Ali's ship, but Anthony leapt behind them, fighting to keep his footing on the slippery deck. Someone thrust at him with a pike, and he cut the weapon aside before bringing his sword forward with a jar as it encountered bone. The man fell away, and Anthony watched the rest running back along the gangway between the rowers, still screaming his name.

"Bah!" shouted Ali Monizindade from the quarterdeck. "That is no ghost. That is the traitor, Hawk Pasha. Will you not cut him down?"

He drew his scimitar and himself led the counter-attack, pausing when within a few feet of Anthony.

"Well, Hawk," he said, "It is now to be my duty to take your head to the Sultan."

"Then take it," Anthony challenged him.

Their blades clashed, but before they could properly set to, there was another violent jar, which threw them off balance. Hawkwood actually fell amongst the rowers, but Kalil seized his arm and jerked him back out before he could be grasped by those hellish creatures soaked with sweat and blood from the deck above.

Another Turkish galley had driven into Ali's, so as to send their reinforcements on board the flagship; and the Spaniards were now retreating. Hawkwood had no option but to go with them — he was not yet ready to commit suicide.

"Stop!" he bawled. "Form ranks."

Don Juan was on the bow of the *Real*, attempting to rally his men, but the Spaniards were now outnumbered by more than two to one as the fresh Turks poured across the bow. And only a few of the arquebuses had been reloaded.

"By God, we are lost," Don Juan cried, as this time the volley failed to check the rampant Turks. The Spaniards had been driven on to the quarterdeck.

"The slaves," Anthony snapped, and ran down the ladder to the first row of benches. "Will you fight for God?" he shouted. "And your freedom!"

"Aye!" they roared back.

It was the work of seconds for him to uncouple the chains, assisted by the boatswain. A tub of pikes had been placed by the drum for just such an emergency, and each man armed himself before following Hawkwood back up on to the deck.

Just in time. The Spaniards were on the point of being overwhelmed — but the sudden appearance of a horde of naked men armed with pikes took the Turks by surprise, and again they fell back.

For the second time Hawkwood and Don Juan led the charge on to the Turkish flagship, and Anthony spotted Ali on the quarterdeck, screaming orders as he rallied his men and called for assistance. They were separated by too many heaving, cutting, yelling bodies, and although Hawkwood set out to fight his way to him, before he could get there two more Turkish galleys came alongside with shuddering, oar-smashing violence, and once again the Christians were driven back, while the Turks surged forward.

By now, however, Santa Cruz had observed the desperate conflict taking place in the centre of the Christian line, and sent forward half a dozen of his reserve squadron, crowded with men. These clambered over the stern of the *Real* to join in the fighting. But the Turks were still more numerous, and while blood ran in rivulets along the scuppers and discoloured the sea into which it poured, the men cursed and swore and hacked and jabbed and slipped and fell overboard or on to the half-empty rowing benches and screamed and choked, the Christians were still slowly forced back.

Hawkwood realised that only the death of Ali himself could save the day. By now he was exhausted, his helmet dented from an unexpected blow he had received, his left arm stinging to suggest that he had been wounded, his breath heaving in great gasps, his entire body a seethe of perspiration. But again he forced himself forward, his bulk no less than the power with which he swung his sword soon clearing a way for him, and suddenly he was face to face with his target, although at a distance of several feet.

Ali Monizindade grinned, showing his teeth. "Again, traitor," he said. "For the last time."

He dashed forward — then threw up his arms, and tumbled from the gangway down on to the rowing benches. Someone had shot him through the forehead.

Instantly Hawkwood leapt down beside him, knocked off his helmet, grasped his hair, and cut off his head.

Then he regained the gangway, holding the dripping head high in front of the appalled Turks.

"Ali Pasha is dead!" he shouted, his voice hoarse. "Ali Pasha is dead!"

With screams of dismay the Turks began to waver.

"Now," Don Juan bellowed, his voice as hoarse as Hawkwood's. "Now!"

For one last time the Christians surged forward. The sight of the Ottoman admiral's head had produced the effect Anthony had been aiming for, and the Turks had now lost their offensive spirit. They retreated, but this time there was to be no rally. There was no quarter either, as the mailed Spaniards, gasping for breath, relentlessly drove the Ottomans into the sea to drown or viciously cut them down, hacking at the wounded time and again to make sure of their deaths. Only a few minutes after Ali Pasha's death, his flagship was taken — as were the three galleys attached to it.

It was now time to consider what was happening elsewhere in the conflict.

A glance to the north assured Anthony that there complete victory had been achieved. Surrounded by the Venetians, thanks to Quirini's prompt action, Scirocco's squadron was in the grim process of being destroyed. Not one of the Turkish galleys would escape, and very few of their crews.

It was not an easy victory, as Hawkwood learned later, Barberigo had been mortally wounded, and his nephew, Marco Contarini, who had succeeded him in command, was killed outright. Federigo Nani had then assumed overall charge of the squadron, and it was he who achieved the final victory. Scirocco Pasha was dragged from the sea, also mortally wounded.

In the centre, Ali Pasha's squadron had also been virtually destroyed.

But on the right, things were not going well. Uluch Ali, having observed Doria's movement to the south to counter his threatened envelopment, had been presented with a choice of two tactical manoeuvres. One would have been to take his ninety-odd galleys directly against the Genoese squadron, and make use of an overwhelmingly superior force, which must have been very tempting — he would certainly have gained a local victory no matter what had happened in the rest of the conflict. But Uluch was as able a tactician as any of the Christian admirals, and rapidly observed that the right wing of the Turkish fleet was lost, and the centre in trouble. He therefore determined to do what he could to reverse the trend towards an overall Turkish defeat: he turned his ships and steered straight for the gap opened in the Christian line by Doria's manoeuvre, intending to fall upon the right of Don Juan's centre squadron, and hopefully roll it up.

To block him, Giustiniani turned the small Maltese contingent of galleys on the extreme right of the centre to meet this onslaught. But the Maltese were overwhelmed, their ships taken, and the crews put to the sword.

This catastrophe was discerned by Santa Cruz, who had promptly despatched eight galleys, under the command of Don Juan de Cardona, to assist the Maltese. Unfortunately they arrived too late to save them, and now found themselves in the middle of the fiercest mêlée of the entire battle, as each Christian ship was assailed by two Turkish vessels. It was at this scene that Hawkwood gazed first after Ali Monizindade's flagship was taken.

The Christians there were again overwhelmed, fighting almost to the last man. Cardona himself was mortally wounded, and of the five hundred soldiers on board his ship only fifty survived. On board the *Florence*, almost every man was killed, including the galley slaves; the captain, Tomasso de' Medici, severely wounded, found himself at the head of only seventeen Knights of St Stephen. In two other Papal galleys, the *San Giovanni* and the *Piamontesa*, there were no survivors at all, the galley slaves being killed in their rows as they sat chained to the oars.

This was the carnage observed by Hawkwood and by Santa Cruz. The Marquis was already hurrying up with the rest of his reserve ships, when Anthony clutched Don Juan's arm.

"My lord, our right is endangered."

Don Juan took in the situation at a glance, and also the fact that the Genoese squadron was now some miles away. Doria by now had realised that he had been outmanoeuvred, and had turned to come back, but it would be half an hour before he could make his presence felt.

"May God damn that man for a traitor," Don Juan growled.

"I do not think he is false, sire. He was merely outwitted. But whether true or false, we cannot wait upon him."

"You are right." Don Juan looked right and left, then gave orders for the captured Turkish galleys — in the process of being systematically looted before being set on fire — to be cast adrift and for all hands to return to their commands. Then he set out to work his way down to the rescue of the Papal squadron.

Once again there was a fierce mêlée, but Uluch Ali now realised that he was in danger of being overwhelmed by the entire enemy fleet, as more and more Christian ships abandoned their prizes to come to the support of their Commander-in-Chief, and as Doria approached from the south.

Uluch now, in turn, abandoned his prizes and took his thirty-odd remaining galleys back into the Gulf, showing his defiance to the last by flying at his masthead the banner of the Order of St John, taken from Giustiniani's flagship.

"We'll have them all," Don Juan shouted. "Signal general chase."

Anthony looked quickly from left to right. The Christian crews were in the main exhausted. Even Doria's people, though not actually engaged, had been rowing flat out for upwards of two hours, first one way and then the other.

Even more important, those telltale wisps of cloud were back, and low in the sky.

"My lord," he said, "if I may be so bold ... your people will not catch Uluch now. And have you not gained the most complete victory in the history of sea warfare? A fleet of three hundred ships destroyed, save for perhaps fifty."

"It is my duty to sink every Turkish ship afloat, Hawk," Don Juan insisted.

"But not at the risk of losing your own fleet, sire. It will be blowing a gale within twelve hours."

Don Juan looked at the sky. "What do you suggest?"

"That we seek shelter, my lord, as quickly as possible. There is a harbour close by, at Petala, where we may lie in safety until the storm blows itself out." He grinned. "Uluch Ali will still be bottled up in Lepanto when we put to sea again."

Don Juan hesitated, then nodded and gave the necessary orders. The entire Christian fleet went off to safety. When all were anchored by nightfall, the men could regale each other with their tales of derring-do and of tragedy.

Now it was time for patching up the injuries sustained in battle. As Anthony had his arm — pierced by a pikehead — attended to, he found Cervantes also amongst the wounded.

The secretary's left wrist was swathed in bandages; there was no longer a hand. "It was all but severed by a scimitar," he explained sadly. "The surgeon has done nothing more than complete the work." Anthony was aghast at such misfortune, but the boy was remarkably cheerful. "This incident has proved to me, *monsignore*," he said, "that no man may go against his fate. I was sentenced to lose my hand in Spain, and so I fled Spain, only to lose my hand in the service of Spain. But it has also proved to me that God is merciful, for where I was sentenced to lose my right hand, now I have lost my left. I can still write." Cervantes grinned. "And would you not say that I now have a great deal to write about, *monsignore*?"

Notwithstanding his own fatigue, Hawkwood took a small boat and had himself rowed across to Colonna's battered galley. He had a purpose in mind.

The scene here was the same as would be found on most other ships of the Christian fleet: exhausted men sitting around in groups, drinking wine as they ate their evening meal, or dressing each other's wounds, reminiscing and boasting.

"Hawk!" Colonna greeted and embraced him. Even Cardinal de Granvelle, who had not been visible during the battle, was smiling tonight. "A great victory!"

"Every man did his duty," Anthony told him.

"Save that perfidious Genoese," the Cardinal remarked. "He should be hanged from his own masthead."

"He made a mistake, good father. No man should be hanged for an honest mistake. But I am seeking information, *monsignore*." He addressed Colonna. "Your ship was attacked by the galley of Pertau Pasha?"

Colonna nodded. "We took it. It lies over there."

"What of the Pasha? Did he fall?"

"I cannot say — but there were survivors. Indeed, half a dozen are still alive. I will chain them to my own benches tomorrow."

"Will you permit me to speak with them tonight?"

"Certainly. Your men can take you there now."

Anthony clambered on to the captured ship, Kalil as ever at his shoulder.

Manacled at wrist and ankle, the Turkish prisoners huddled together, and their eyes rolled as they discovered Hawk Pasha looming above them.

"I seek news of Pertau Pasha," Anthony began. "Did any of you see him die?"

They shook their heads.

"The Pasha did not die," one of them said at last.

"What did you say?"

"We towed a galliot astern," the man said. "And when he saw that we were likely to be overwhelmed, the Pasha abandoned us. He took to the galliot and fled."

Anthony knelt beside him. "Are you certain of this?"

"I saw this with my own eyes, Hawk Pasha," the man said. "Our Pasha deserted us. I saw the galliot make for the narrows leading to the Gulf of Corinth. He abandoned us to seek the safety of his estates."

"How do you know this?" Anthony demanded.

"Because I was his servant, Hawk Pasha. And he abandoned me, together with all of his people."

Hawkwood stroked his beard. But he believed the man, who was clearly bitter at having been deserted by his master. And he knew that Pertau did have estates in the Peloponnesus, fairly close to the ruined city of Corinth. Pertau, being Pertau, would wish to make sure that his wealth and his wives were safe, in case the Christian fleet should ravage the coast.

Hawkwood returned to the flagship. The wind was already blowing twenty knots, from the east, but backing into the north, and the galleys rose and fell to their anchor lines — but in complete safety.

The Brigadino brothers were waiting patiently for him, and they embraced him warmly. "Now is Marcantonio avenged," they said. "We are honoured to have sailed with you, Hawk."

Don Juan frowned when he noticed that Anthony was hardly looking happy.

"What causes your anxiety?" he inquired.

"My lord," Anthony said, "I would crave the use of one of your brigantines for the night."

"To what purpose?"

"That I may take her up into the Gulf of Corinth."

"You would put out tonight? Into the storm?"

"I know these waters, and the weather, sire. And I have compelling reason for wishing to do this." He then described Pertau's escape.

"This is the man who murdered our brother?" Ambrogio Brigadino demanded.

"The same. I am sworn to kill him," Hawkwood replied.

"Then so are we," Antonio Brigadino broke in. "We will come with you."

"This is madness," Don Juan declared. "I cannot permit it."

"It would be to your advantage, my lord," Hawkwood told him. "For I can also reconnoitre for you the situation of Uluch Ali and what is left of the Ottoman fleet." He gave a grim smile. "At least you can be sure now I will not desert you."

"Have you any idea what they will do to you, if you are taken?"

"I can hardly be made to suffer more than Brigadino, my lord."

"And you hope to avenge his death." Don Juan sighed and clasped his hand. "Go and satisfy your honour, Hawk. But come back to me. I need you."

When Hawkwood called for volunteers, these were quickly forthcoming. Every man in the fleet now understood the part he had played in their astonishing victory and they would willingly have followed him anywhere. In addition the brigantine crews had played little part in the actual fight, so were anxious to prove their worth.

He took twenty men, including the Brigadino brothers, and put to sea. It was dark by now, and the wind was gusting above thirty knots. In the narrow waters of the Gulf the seas had not the fetch to become dangerous, but in such restricted waters seamanship of a high order was necessary, to prevent the little ship from being driven on to the rocks which abounded to either side.

Tacking into the northerly wind, and with the pumps active as sheets of spray clouded over the bows of the half-decked brigantine. Hawkwood made his way up the Gulf of Patras to the narrows, beyond which lay the deeper Gulf of Corinth.

Penetrating the narrows in bad weather was always a dangerous operation, but in addition it was immediately on the eastern
side of this passage that the town of Lepanto was situated, to
which the remnants of the Turkish fleet would certainly have fled,
and in which Uluch Ali would also certainly now be preparing to
withstand a siege.

Uluch's obvious course was to block the narrows themselves
with his ships, but he had not done so tonight. This was under-
standable, since his men were beaten and demoralised, and the
wind was increasing all the time. Uluch must have reasoned that
the Christians would also be sheltering from the storm.

There were not even guardships in the straits, and the brigantine
slipped through in utter darkness.

There were lights enough in Lepanto, however, and on the wind
was borne the clash of cymbals and the blowing of flutes as the
Turks mourned their numerous dead.

Hawkwood knew there was a chance that Pertau had also taken
refuge in the seaport, but he discounted this possibility. Pertau
would know that his defection had been witnessed by almost the
entire fleet; and he would have no wish to confront Uluch Ali until
he had prepared an acceptable excuse — if he could.

Hawkwood altered course to the south-east, now on a broad
reach under shortened canvas. The waves were on the beam, and
the brigantine lay well over, but she was scudding along at a fine
speed. The lights of Lepanto fell rapidly astern and were swallowed
in the darkness, and Anthony, no longer afraid of encountering a
stray Turkish cruiser, set his own masthead lantern to warn any
vessel that might be in their way, while Kalil took his place in the
bows and peered ahead.

They had proceeded for several hours before they sighted any
more lights, and those — still far distant — Hawkwood knew had to
be the village of Corinth, which had arisen a few miles away from
the site of the ancient city. But then Kalil called out that he could
discern another light, closer at hand to the south.

"It is moving, master," he shouted. "It is signalling."

Hawkwood altered course towards it, while now every man
stared into the gloom. By now the moon had risen, and through
scudding clouds there was enough visibility to make out the
darkness of the land only a few miles to the south — the whiteness

586

of cliffs and flurries of surf where the tumbling sea met outcrops of rocks.

"There, Hawk," said Antonio Brigadino, who had come aft to stand beside the helm. "It is a galliot, I am sure."

Anthony narrowed his eyes, and saw that the small galley was anchored in a bay on the Peloponnesian coast. She had obviously taken refuge when the wind first got up, and while it had blown from the east she had remained quite sheltered; but now that it had backed to the north she was totally exposed, and yet apparently unable, or afraid, to raise anchor and head out into the open waters of the Gulf. Or even to put her people ashore? She was certainly asking for help.

Kalil had also come aft, waiting for Hawkwood's decision.

"We'll stand in," Anthony decided. "He may have information about Pertau."

"There'll be rocks, master."

"So keep a sharp look-out."

He had sail shortened even further, and with no more than a scrap of canvas up, the brigantine's speed was further reduced. But the entrance to the bay was alarming, as the narrow stretch of water was covered in foaming whitecaps. As the brigantine crashed through them and into the violently disturbed waters beyond, Anthony's hands were tight on the tiller.

Now he could see the problems facing the galliot's captain in having chosen such an uncertain refuge. The bay was backed by cliffs rising sheer from the sea, not a hundred yards away, and the galliot had lost her boat. Her people would have to swim ashore — but there was no shore for them to swim to.

Hawkwood shouted his commands, put the helm down, and the brigantine swung round to come up into the wind.

The galliot was just two hundred yards away, her crew gathered aft and waving as they saw the brigantine come about. Anthony had to gain way again immediately to avoid being swept against the cliffs, and now the ship was on the starboard tack, steering to pass close behind the stern of the galliot.

As the two vessels closed rapidly, Anthony told Kalil to hail, in Turkish.

"What ship is that?" Kalil bellowed.

"We are the galliot of Pertau Pasha," came the reply. "We are making water. We need your assistance."

Kalil looked over his shoulder at his master.

Pertau! Delivered up by his own pusillanimity in seeking shelter long before the seas had become truly dangerous.

The brigantine was now past the galliot, and he brought her round again.

"Tell them we will come alongside to take them off."

Kalil shouted the message, and the men on the stricken vessel waved their acknowledgement. Its decks were now crowded.

Perhaps some of them were innocent, but Anthony could not take that into account. For the last time in his life, he must behave as an Ottoman above anything else.

"Load our guns," he called. "Depress them to aim at the water-line."

His men hurried to obey, while he brought the brigantine around again, and it surged up to the stricken galliot. Within fifty yards of her, Hawkwood could make out the figure of Pertau standing on the quarterdeck, waving as vigorously as any of his men at the unexpected prospect of being rescued.

But the matches were already glowing on board the brigantine, and as Hawkwood brought her broadside on to the galliot, he gave the order to fire.

The brigantine rocked beneath their recoils as the two cannon exploded. At point blank range the balls smashed into the hull of the galliot, just on the waterline, to screams of outrage from her crew.

Hawkwood then took the brigantine past the bow and brought her about again, turning her in her own length to pass down the starboard side of the galliot. The Turkish vessel was already listing to port, her starboard hull beginning to expose its weed-dripping surface.

"Fire!" Anthony shouted again, and the two port guns exploded. Once again the range was point blank and the iron balls smashed through the timbers.

Holed on both sides, the galliot sank like a stone; the tumbling water filled with drowning men.

Hawkwood steered into their midst, and some were hauled up to be confined below deck. But he was looking for one man only.

"Rescue!" Pertau was screaming. "Rescue!"

The Turk was clinging desperately to a length of broken rail. Hawkwood himself heaved the line, and Pertau grasped it — and was pulled into the side of the brigantine. Slowly he was lifted clear of the water, and dragged up to the gunwale. There, still clutching his rope, he gazed at Hawkwood and the drawn sword.

"Hawk Pasha!" he gasped, and then looked at the men standing to either side — and recognized from their facial features who they had to be.

"I give you a better death than you deserve," Ambrogio Brigadino told him, and swung his sword to slice off Pertau's head.

Both head and trunk fell separately into the sea.

"Now is our brother truly avenged," Ambrogio said.

In tactical terms, Lepanto was the greatest and most decisive naval battle ever fought. The Christians lost twelve galleys sunk, and one captured, with approximately fifteen thousand men killed, wounded or drowned. The Turks lost one hundred and thirteen galleys sunk, and a further one hundred and seventeen captured. A known thirty thousand men were killed, an entirely incalculable number drowned. In addition eight thousand Turks were taken prisoner and some fifteen thousand Christian galley slaves set free.

The wealth taken from the captured Turkish galleys was on no less a scale; on Ali Pasha's flagship alone were found one hundred and fifty thousand sequins. More importantly, Don Juan of Austria captured two hundred and seventy-four cannon.

The Commander-in-Chief magnanimously sent Hawkwood with the news of the victory, on board the *Angel* galley, to Venice. Anthony found the Republic in a state of tremendous anxiety, racked with rumour, at every moment expecting Ali Pasha and his vengeful fleet to appear off the lagoon.

As a result of the news the city was thrown into a hysterical reaction. Church bells rang, people danced in the streets and swam in the canals, the fountains gushed wine.

"I meant my promise," the Doge, Alvise Mocenigo, told Anthony. "Ask and, if it is in my power to grant your wish, you will have it. For you have helped deliver us from the hands of the Turks, and also you have avenged Famagusta."

"Our task will not be completed until we have taken Constantinople," Anthony told him, "so I must rejoin the fleet. I will seek my reward, Your Excellency, when the war is over."

But before he left he was able to spend several happy nights with his wife, and some no less happy time with his sons.

"You have achieved so much," Barbara whispered as she lay in his arms. "What next?"

He smiled into her ear. "I shall take you back to the Hawk Palace — as a conqueror."

In later years Hawkwood was to learn that his dream of that moment was entirely practicable. The news of the catastrophe of Lepanto had such a devastating effect in Istanbul — as an observer wrote — that had even fifty Christian galleys appeared in the Bosphorus, the city would have surrendered meekly.

Unfortunately, no Christian galleys ever appeared there.

Although Don Juan had every intention of continuing the campaign, it was too late to keep the fleets at sea that year, and so he left Viniero and Hawkwood and Jacopo Fascarini, the new Venetian vice-admiral, in command at Corfu, and himself returned to Messina, the various squadrons being sent to their home ports for the winter. Viniero was now too old to be considered as a fighting admiral, and so the command devolved upon Fascarini, with Hawkwood as his deputy and adviser.

Anthony remained buoyant. He sent scouting galleys ranging down to the Gulf whenever the weather was fine enough, but there was no sign of any Turkish activity; the Ionian Sea was empty.

"Undoubtedly Selim — or rather Sokullu — will be building another fleet just as rapidly as he can," he advised his colleagues. "But it will have to be composed of green timber and, more important, of green men. He has only one admiral left of any experience: Uluch Ali. So if he attempts to meet us this coming year, he will again be annihilated. And if we sail east as soon as possible, not later than June in any event, the Ottoman realm will just fall apart."

But on 1 May 1572, while the Venetians were expecting news of the reassembly of the Christian fleet, Pope Pius V died. Although many people felt relieved, this was in reality a catastrophe. The old man might have made himself intensely unpopular through his strict reforms and the harshness with which he had implemented them, but it was he who was the true driving spirit behind the Christian cause.

To make matters worse, Spain and France now again fell out, and Philip II of Spain found it necessary to retain part of his fleet to protect his North African possessions.

Nonetheless, the Christian fleet did reassemble in June. Uncertain that this would ever happen, Hawkwood persuaded Fascarini to put to sea with the Venetian fleet alone — and off Cape Malea the Turks were sighted. But, to Anthony's chagrin, Fascarini was so alarmed by the incredible sight of no less than three hundred Turkish galleys that he refused to attack. In vain did Anthony remind him that neither ships nor men were a match for the Venetians; the chance was lost. That Uluch did not pursue them was evidence that Hawkwood was right.

Later in the year Don Juan himself returned to the east and took command of the full allied fleet. Again the Turkish fleet was sighted, in October, this time off the Bay of Navarino; but this time it was Uluch Ali who declined battle, and escaped to the east.

"We must plan our next year's campaign more carefully," Hawkwood advised Don Juan. "We must force him to battle. Thus we must escort a fleet of transports with sufficient soldiers on board to be set ashore to ravage the coast of Anatolia. That will bring Uluch to action."

"Next year," Don Juan said despondently.

He was looking ill, his features drawn and pale, his shoulders hunched.

"Will there be a next year?"

There was not, for the allied fleet. The fatal divisions which had always endangered Christian unity now wrecked the great concept of bringing the Turks to their knees. When, during the winter, Philip of Spain decided not to send his fleet back to the eastern Mediterranean, but to concentrate upon the growing revolt in his Dutch provinces and his prospective naval war with England — both people being more hateful to him than the Turks because of their Protestant heresy — the Doge Alvise Mocenigo lost patience.

He recalled Viniero, and Fascarini, and Hawkwood from Corfu, with all the Venetian fleet, and sent an embassy to Istanbul to make peace.

"But that means abandoning Cyprus," Viniero protested.

"Cyprus is lost," the Doge told him. "Nothing we can do will bring it back. Thanks to the Spaniards, the war is lost. Now we must cut our losses — or we will find ourselves fighting the Ottomans on our own." He turned to Hawkwood. "You have not yet claimed your promised reward for your services before Lepanto, Hawk. As the war is now over, for us at least, will you not do so now?"

Anthony gazed at him.

He had dreamed of so many things. Perhaps even of tumbling Selim from his throne — the tyrant who had besmirched his honour.

As his mother had dreamed of so many things, too — especially of returning to England. But he had never known England, and the England which Felicity had known, the England of King Henry VIII, was vanished into history.

The fact was that life was not composed of dreams — although Barbara might have realised hers in returning at last to Venice, her home. Was not that simple dream the only one attainable? Here they were amongst friends, their best ally of all being this very Doge. Here he was all of a hero. And though he might now despair of ever bringing down the Turks in his lifetime, here was where his duty — as well as his instincts — commanded him to be.

And what of his ancestors? Had they all been renegades, as the world considered them? He did not believe that. The Hawkwoods had been forced by circumstances into the life and careers they had followed so successfully. Once adopted by the Ottoman sultans, they had served their masters with the utmost fidelity. It was the decline in the nature of these sultans that had eventually driven him out, and taken him to Lepanto — the first ever important Christian victory over the Turks.

Perhaps, therefore, that had been his allotted role in history: to help drive the first nail into the coffin of the Ottoman Turks.

"Well?" Mocenigo inquired.

"My reward, *monsignore*? Why, it is simply to be allowed to reside here in Venice, and fight for you. Even if we make peace now, there will yet be battles to be won before long, you may depend upon it."

Alvise Mocenigo grasped his hand.

POSTSCRIPT

Anthony Hawkwood was right, although his prophecy was not immediately apparent. The disunity into which Christendom fell during the next century — the wars of England against Spain, and the religious wars in Germany — seemed to leave Turkish power as great as ever before.

Don Juan of Austria, after pursuing schemes of romantic ambition — which included invading England to rescue and marry Mary Queen of Scots — died on 1 October 1578, just short of seven years after his great victory at Lepanto. He was thirty-one years old.

With his half-brother Philip II wholly committed to the Atlantic war with the Dutch and the English, Ottoman armies were able to besiege Vienna again and again, and the tread of the Janissaries was still heard from the Danube to the Euphrates.

Philip's dreams of conquering England were to lead to a naval battle inferior only to that of Lepanto. Fought in July 1588, in the English Channel, between the Spanish and English fleets.

Miguel de Cervantes, returning from Lepanto a hero, was taken prisoner by Barbary pirates, to remain a prisoner until 1580. On his return to Madrid, he did indeed continue to write.

The victory of Lepanto still ranks amongst the decisive battles of the world and was indeed the beginning of the end for the Ottoman dynasty. Although the sultans clung precariously to their heritage until 1918, there would never be another Mahomet the Conqueror, another Selim the Grim, or another Suleiman the Magnificent. Looking back from the perspective of time, it is now clear that the immense power which came to fruition when Constantinople fell in 1453, and dominated world history for a century, received its death blow on the waters of the Gulf of Patras on 7 October 1571 — a day still celebrated in Rome.

593